The Descent Series

Books 1-3: Death's Hand, The Darkest Gate, and Dark Union

SM Reine

Other Series by SM Reine

The Ascension Series

Seasons of the Moon

The Cain Chronicles

Copyright © SM Reine

Published by Red Iris Books

1180 Selmi Drive, Suite 102

Reno, NV 89512

The
Descent
Series

SM Reine

Death's Hand

An Urban Fantasy Mystery

The Descent Series - Book One

SM Reine

Part 1: Before

RUSSIA – FEBRUARY 1998

James spotted a splatter of blood through the tree boughs. It marked the snow like an ink stain on paper.

He pushed through the pine needles, and her bare feet appeared, blue-toed and limp. He saw the curve of a calf and a knobby, bruised knee. He saw the jut of ribs under her skin and an arm thrown over her face. And the next thing he saw was the twelve other bodies.

Nausea gripped James, but he covered his mouth and maintained composure. His guide was not so lucky. The other man dove behind a bush, gagged twice, and vomited across the frozen earth.

Elise was already dead. He was so certain of it that he almost walked away at that moment. But what would Isaac think of James abandoning his daughter's body? The indignity of leaving her naked on the ice for the birds to devour was too much, and he came so far to find her remains.

Yet he couldn't bring himself to step foot in the clearing. Elise looked peaceful, but the others were twisted in agony. Blood marked their fingernails. They had gone out fighting.

Each of the twelve other bodies could have been siblings. They had pale skin, slender forms draped in white linen, and white-blue eyes—he could tell, because they were frozen open. The snow around them looked fluffy, as though it were freshly fallen. Something about that struck him as wrong. It was cold, but it hadn't snowed in days, leaving the earth a solid sheet of ice.

Taking a closer look, James found it wasn't snow—the clearing was covered in feathers.

His guide had recovered and began babbling in Russian, but he spoke too fast for James to understand. He heard one recognizable word—*chort,* devil.

James hung back in the trees, fighting the urge to leave. He adjusted his balaclava, tuned out the guide's shouts, and stepped into the clearing.

The hair lifted on his arms. His skull began to buzz.

He tried not to look at the other corpses, but it was like they reached for him, pleading for escape. Their teeth were bared. Their tongues were purple and twisted.

That one had been stabbed in the chest.

The body by his feet was disemboweled.

Those two bodies had died clutching hands.

He couldn't look at them anymore. He focused on his feet and forced himself to take a step once, twice. Again and again. When he reached Elise, the buzzing grew so loud that he could no longer hear Maksim's protests.

James hovered a glove over her body. All the energy vanished. The clearing went silent.

He pushed the arm off her face to examine her. Dirty, frayed bandages were wrapped around her hands, so tattered that they looked like they might blow away.

Elise had her father's auburn hair and his strong nose, but her soft chin belonged entirely to Ariane. Her eyelashes were sealed by ice. How had she died? There wasn't a mark he could see.

He moved to unwrap one of her hands.

Her eyes fluttered.

"Maksim!" he shouted. Her broad lips parted to exhale silver fog. "Maksim! She's alive!" He forgot to speak in Russian, but his message didn't need translation.

His guide shouted and ran to the van. James shed his parka. The cold seeped through his undercoat as he wrapped her in his furs. *Alive*. It was impossible. Nobody could have survived an hour naked in the killing frosts of Siberian spring.

James watched the other bodies, waiting for them to jerk to life and creep forward, but they remained lifeless. Elise was the only survivor, even though it was impossible for one small girl to have survived an attack that killed a dozen others.

Unless she had been the one to do the killing.

He carried her out of the clearing without touching the other bodies. There was nothing he could do for them. He wasn't sure he would have anyway.

The guide opened the van, letting steam escape the back end. As soon

3

as James climbed inside, laying Elise between their extra gas tanks and a rattling space heater, he closed the doors again.

"Hurry!" James said, reverting to his limited Russian.

"She's a demon," repeated Maksim as he climbed to the driver's seat, and then he continued to speak so quickly that James couldn't understand if he tried. He picked up a word here and there—devils and hell, curses and fear—but he was too busy to translate.

He cracked heating packs open and pressed them to Elise's underarms, her groin, and the back of her neck.

James pulled a glove off with his teeth and touched his bare fingers to her throat. Her pulse was slow but steady. Color began to flush her cheeks.

A demon, Maksim said. Maybe. But she was also Isaac and Ariane's daughter, and James promised to bring her back safely. He kept all of his oaths, no matter how unpleasant.

His driver shouted and gestured. James interrupted him to say, "Town. Take us to town!"

The van bounced and groaned over the path. He had to brace his back against the fuel canisters to keep them from falling on Elise as he searched her body. He found no injuries. Aside from a few bruises, she was unharmed.

Surely a girl that young couldn't have killed so many people without injury. There must have been someone else in the wilds—someone he hadn't seen. It wasn't a comforting thought.

He peeled the bandages off and flipped her hands to look at the palms.

No.

James turned her hands over again, heart racing.

It was the first time James wished Elise had died on the tundra, but it was also far from the last.

Elise woke up five days after James found her in the forests near Oymyakon.

He knocked lightly and entered the room. There were no hotels in the small Russian village, so he had been staying in a house full of laborers under the guise of an ordinary traveler. Since bringing home the girl's body, their friendliness turned to uneasy whispers, and James seldom left Elise sleeping alone in what had once been a tiny closet.

4

James sympathized with their wariness. Even he had to steady himself when he found her crouched in the corner of her bed, staring at him with eyes rimmed by dark circles, and he was the one who had brought her there.

"The women told me you were awake," he said. "They say you're refusing to eat. Please lay down. You must conserve your strength."

She remained so still that she might have been a painting.

There were three bowls on the rickety table by her bed. It didn't look like she had touched any of them.

"The stew is safe to eat, I assure you. Babushka is an excellent chef. I've eaten a dozen of her meals since I arrived, and she has yet to poison me."

Her gaze flicked to the table and back to him.

James moved to sit on the stool next to her, but he caught a glimpse of something shining amongst the sheets. She had somehow stolen a knife from the kitchen. He froze at the sight of the blade.

Tension hung suspended between them. She didn't move to stab him, and he didn't show his fear.

"My name is James Faulkner," he went on after a long moment, speaking in the voice one might use to soothe an angry hawk. "The woman you were staying with, Pamela Faulkner, is my aunt. I found you three days ago. We're in Oymyakon now."

"Where's Pamela?" Her voice was throaty and hoarse.

He shut his eyes. He could see Pamela's body as he found it in her house: slumped against the wall as though she had decided to rest for a few minutes. Her body was mostly unmarked, but blood stained her ear canals. Her beautiful black hair, streaked with gray only at the temples, was in its perpetual bun with only a single hair astray.

James had been very close to his aunt as a child. She was the high priestess of their coven, and she revolutionized ritualistic magic when she invented paper spells. Pamela had arguably been one of the most powerful witches in the world.

Very little could have caught her off-guard. Even fewer things could have killed her.

"She's dead," he said.

This didn't seem to cause any emotional reaction in Elise. She got to her feet, letting the sheets tumble to the ground, and the sight of her skeletal frame made James's stomach flip. Even swathed in a simple dress borrowed from one of the village women, he could see every curve of every bone in her body.

5

She took a step toward the door, knife clutched to her side, and staggered. Her hand slipped on the dresser when she tried to catch herself.

James stood to help her back to bed, but the look she gave him burned with sheer loathing, so he hung back without touching her. That glare made her look just like Isaac.

"What are you doing?" he asked.

She carefully made her way toward the door, gripping the frame to lift herself to a standing position once more.

"Please, Elise, sit down and eat. I assure you, we'll leave as soon as you can walk. If He doesn't know where you are yet, then we're a step ahead of Him, and we don't want to lose this brief advantage."

Her nose wrinkled, like the idea of going anywhere with him revolted her. He was almost offended.

She fumbled for the doorknob.

"You're very weak and it's hundreds of miles to the nearest city. You won't survive alone."

Elise's only response was a silent glare. James was struck by the feeling that she was more of a feral animal than a teenage girl. He probably wanted to be trapped with her as little as she did, but neither of them had a choice in the matter.

She opened the door. James stepped in her path. She tried to shove him out of her way, but even though she was surprisingly strong for someone who looked like she should have been dead, he was stronger.

"Your parents asked my aunt to watch you until they came back. Since she died, the responsibility of your care falls upon me. I've sworn to keep you safe. I intend to keep that promise."

She transferred her grip from the doorway to a fistful of his shirt. He felt metal press against his stomach through his parka.

The knife. He tensed.

He breathed shallowly and forced himself to speak calmly. "I'm not safe now that I've found you, either. We need to stay together. It's the only way either of us will survive."

Elise radiated silent fury. He was struck by her resemblance to Ariane, although he didn't recall the sweet witch who had birthed her ever being so angry.

And then she released him and sat on the side of the bed, stubbornly ignoring his hand. With careful, measured movements, she lifted the stew to her mouth and drank its broth without dropping her gaze from his.

When the bowl was drained, she ate each piece of meat one by one

6

and set the bowl down again. She already moved without shaking. James doubted he would be able to keep her under control for long. It wouldn't be long before she was much, much stronger than him.

He wondered again if she had killed all those people in the clearing.

"I don't trust you," Elise said. "I will *never* trust you."

It was the last thing she said to him for a very long time.

December 1988

Isaac Kavanagh gave his daughter a pair of twin falchion swords for her seventh birthday. Wickedly sharp and too big for her hands, Elise accepted them with a grave nod before turning to kill her first demon.

She skewered it. The demon shrieked and wailed.

"Good," Isaac said with a proud smile. "Very good."

Later, they will say this day marked the beginning of the end of the world.

This is only half true.

Part 2: Retirement

Chapter 1

MAY 2009

STEAM drifted from the surface of Marisa Ramirez's coffee. She blew on it gently, cupping the mug between her hands to warm her chilly fingers.

Golden morning light rimmed the closed curtains over the sink. The thermometer outside the window read sixty-two, but the swamp cooler clicked on and blew chilled air into the kitchen anyway. Marisa shrank deeper into her sweater.

Augustin Ramirez sat across the table with his face in his hands. The ceiling rattled above their heads as distant screams and sobs peaked in time with fists pounding against the floor.

His left cheek muscle twitched. They exchanged glances, and he found his own haunted expression mirrored in her face.

Hands shaking, she lifted her coffee cup and took a sip.

The doorbell chimed. Their daughter shrieked in response.

"Are you going to get that?" Augustin asked. Marisa didn't respond. His jaw tightened. "I said, are you going to get that?" She ducked her head, lips trembling. The right side of her mouth was darkened with the shadow of a bruise. He made a disgusted noise, shoving his chair back as he stood. "Fine. I'll get the door."

She took another drink and set the mug down.

The living room blinds were shut and covered by heavy curtains, casting the room in twilight. Augustin navigated to the door by memory, unlocked the dead bolt, peeked through the door.

The woman on the other side pushed her sunglasses into her hair to study him with narrowed eyes. A single scar broke the line of her right eyebrow.

"Augustin Ramirez. Right?"

"Yes," he said. "I'm sorry…do I know you?"

She held out a hand. She wore black gloves with a button at the wrist. "Elise Kavanagh. James sent me."

He gave her hand a brief shake. Her grip made his knuckles ache. "James Faulkner?" Augustin asked. "He said he was going to send a—uh, an exorcist to look at our daughter."

Elise nodded. "Yes, right. I'm the exorcist."

"You're not what I…that is to say…"

"Yeah, I know. Can I come in?"

"Yes," Augustin said, stepping aside.

"I'm sorry I'm late. I was on my way to the office, and I wasn't expecting James to ask me to do a job. I haven't been an exorcist in a long time." She indicated her outfit with a sweep of her hand—a black skirt, white blouse, and black blazer. Augustin wasn't sure what he expected an exorcist to wear. Maybe leather and chains. Definitely not business casual.

She handed a business card to him. *Elise Kavanagh, Certified Public Accountant.* It was so absurd he had to laugh. "So you used to exorcise people a lot?"

"More often than I do now," Elise said. "I went into retirement five years ago. Anyway, I'm not going to exorcise your daughter. I'm going to determine if it's demonic possession."

"Demonic possession," he echoed. "You have me at a loss. Frankly, this all seems a little…absurd."

She gave a humorless, thin-lipped smile that might have been a grimace.

"You're here," Marisa said. She hovered in the doorway, arms wrapped around her shivering body. "I'm so glad you came."

Augustin frowned. "You know this woman?"

"She's always at the coven meetings," Marisa said. Her voice trembled slightly. "I think she does James's accounting. And he told me they're, uh, bound. Kopis and aspis."

"*What?*"

Her cheeks colored. "It's Latin."

"Greek, actually," Elise said. "Kopis means sword, and aspis means shield. It means I am—or used to be—a warrior against the forces of Hell,

9

and he's my partner." She wasn't laughing at all. She was completely serious.

Distaste twisted Augustin's mouth. "Coven nonsense. It's taken me awhile to get used to the idea of witchcraft in the first place, and I don't think—"

Elise held up a hand. "I have places to be. I don't have the time to let you get used to it, Mr. Ramirez."

His face grew hot. "I'm not—"

"Augustin," Marisa said softly.

He closed his eyes and took a breath. Their marriage counselor harped on him about counting to ten when he was getting to mad, but he gave it to twenty this time. Covens and "warriors against Hell." He could count to a thousand and still feel unsettled.

"Sorry," Augustin finally said. "We're stressed."

Elise accepted his apology by inclining her head. "Where's Lucinde?"

"She's upstairs. We'll go with you."

Marisa and Elise headed up the stairs. Augustin followed a couple steps behind, watching the legs of the supposed exorcist. She wasn't wearing nylons. Another scar marred her ankle, like a dog bite that had long since healed into a fleshy white mass, and his stomach turned. *Some accountant.*

Elise spoke to Marisa as they walked, oblivious to the reaction her scars evoked. "I need to ask you some questions. Have you summoned any demons or used a Ouija board?"

"Of course not."

"Any unusual noises or sightings? Animals with glowing eyes, objects flying across the room, strange noises on the telephone…"

Marisa shook her head. "Aside from Lucinde's illness, everything has been normal."

"What about nightmares? Have you experienced sexual dreams of a dark nature?"

"That's a personal question," Augustin interrupted.

Elise's lip curled, but she didn't respond.

"I haven't," Marisa said. Her voice was hardly louder than a whisper. "Augustin?" After a moment, he shook his head. "Lucinde was having nightmares before. Not…sexual. But she kept waking up screaming."

"Did she tell you what she was dreaming about?" Elise stopped to peer at a family camping photo beside an artful arrangement of silk flowers. In the picture, the Ramirezes were tan and smiling. Lucinde's low, croaking moans echoed through the house.

10

"She told me a monster was eating her heart," Marisa whispered. "I thought…I mean, what a strange thing for a little girl to dream about. She dreamed a monster ate her heart and sat in her chest."

Elise's eyebrows lifted. "Really."

"It's not weird for her to have bad dreams," Augustin interjected. "Especially not about her heart. She has a condition. The doctors don't think it should be fatal, but you know how kids are. Of course she's scared of bad things happening to her heart."

"What kind of heart condition?" They reached the top of the stairs, pausing down the hall from Lucinde's room. All the doors were open but hers.

"I don't think you need to know that to do your job," Augustin said.

"Just wondering. I assume you've already taken her to see a doctor and a psychologist?"

"Those were our first choices. They gave us the option of waiting to see if she would improve or sticking her in an institution. I wouldn't have let Marisa call you unless we didn't have any choices left."

"I see. I'm going to go in and look at her now."

"Be careful. She's gotten…violent," Marisa said.

"How violent can a five-year-old be?" Elise gave an unpleasant smile that didn't suit her angular face. "I'm sure I've handled worse."

"Just be careful. She's in here."

Elise approached the door Marisa indicated, and the Ramirezes hung back. The girl became quieter as she grew near. When she stood before the door, Lucinde became entirely silent.

Elise pushed the door open and went inside.

Lucinde's room was even colder than the rest of the house. Heavy curtains cast the room in near-complete darkness, and a portable swamp cooler made the air chill and muggy. A white canopy bed blocked the back half of the darkened room.

There were multiple obstacles strewn across the floor: an overstuffed comforter, rose-colored pillows in varying sizes, and a toy chest. Possible hiding places included the closet and the shadowed area behind a pink trunk with princess costumes draped over the sides. No girl in sight.

Elise didn't like the room's poor visibility. It felt confined. Dangerous. "I'm going to open the window, Marisa."

"She won't like it."

She moved toward the window, hugging the wall, and stepped over a toy unicorn with blood caking the mane to its neck. Ears perked for any hint of motion, she jerked aside the first layer of curtains, then the second.

11

Light filled the room. Someone squealed.

Elise rounded the bed in time to see bare feet disappearing under the bed. "Lucinde?"

She dropped to her hands and knees and leaned her cheek close to the carpet. A pair of luminous eyes stared back at her. The girl under the bed looked nothing like Marisa. Her skin was dark, like her father's, and her flat nose was offset by his same expressive lips.

"Cold," she hissed. "Cold!"

Elise's gaze traveled over her bared legs. Her knees were heavily bruised, purple and black and brown on the edges. The flesh on her shins looked like broiled strawberries. "Have you used force to restrain her?" Elise asked.

"She hurts herself," Marisa said. "We can't stop her."

"Colder!" Lucinde demanded again, sinking further into the corner as though she wanted to hide inside the wall. Elise glanced at the swamp cooler. *Colder.*

Lucinde tried to jerk away when she touched her foot, but Elise caught her ankle, pulling her foot into the light. A few remaining flakes of pink nail polish decorated her toenails under caked blood. One nail had been torn out. She released the child's ankle, and withdrew again.

"How are you doing?" Elise asked. "*Quomondo vales?*"

Lucinde froze. Her eyes widened fractionally.

"*Quomondo vales?*" she repeated. "*Loquerisne Latine?* No? ¿Hablas inglés?"

"She speaks English," Marisa said, offended.

"Of course."

Elise pulled the chains of her necklace over her head and picked a bronze pendant from amongst the other charms. It caught the sun and scattered gold light on Lucinde's forehead. The whites of her eyes were almost yellow, shot through with crimson veins, and a long, low hiss issued from between her lips.

"*Crux sacra sit mihi lux,*" Elise whispered. Lucinde recoiled, covering her face.

"What are you doing?" Augustin demanded.

Lucinde remained flat against the carpet, fingers spread through the dusty shag as though she feared being dragged away. She whimpered like a wounded dog.

She was so small. Elise was sure she had never been that small.

Elise leaned closer. "Can you speak?"

Marisa stepped forward. "Watch out—"

12

The girl's foot lashed out and the bedroom exploded into red stars. The pain struck a moment later like being struck in the jaw by a baseball bat.

She reeled, hand flying to her mouth. Lucinde scurried from beneath the mattress.

"Colder! *Colder!*" Her voice was shrill, piercing.

Lucinde's nails flashed. Elise raised her arm in defense—but the little girl stopped short, swiping the hand inches from Elise's face. Lucinde's wrist was roped to the corner of the bed.

Augustin hauled the exorcist to her feet, dragging her away from Lucinde. She shook her elbow free of his grip.

"We told you to be careful," he said, voice rough. "She's not normal anymore." Elise ignored him, meeting the girl's eyes.

"Cold," Elise echoed.

Marisa moved into the room, making soothing noises. Lucinde screamed a long note with the tenor of a beast. Augustin guided Elise out of the room and shut the door. Without windows, the hallway was darker than Lucinde's bedroom, but it felt much less oppressive.

"We won't be held liable for our daughter's—"

"I'm not going to sue you for my wound, if that's what you're getting at. I've had many injuries much worse than this."

"Good." His mouth twisted. "Good. What were you doing in there?"

"Testing her," she said. "This is the pendant of Saint Benedict. He's the patron saint of a lot of things—nettle rash, servants who have broken stuff that belongs to their masters. Spelunkers."

"Spelunkers?"

"He's also invoked during exorcisms. I wanted to see if she would react to Latin because a lot of Greater Demons don't speak any living languages."

"She's been speaking English," Augustin said. "She keeps saying 'cold.'"

"I saw that."

"So…what do you think?"

"I can't say if she's possessed," Elise said, touching the back of her hand to her mouth. It came away bloody. "She's definitely got an attitude problem."

"She was never like this before," Augustin said.

"I'm sure." She headed down the stairs, leaving Lucinde's screams behind her. "I'll do some research. I've seen my share of possessions and exorcisms, but never one as spontaneous as this. You're sure nothing has been flying around?"

"Completely sure. We're not *freaks*."

"You don't have to be a freak to be targeted by demons; just unlucky or stupid. Since you haven't summoned anything, you could be the former."

"We're not stupid," he said. Her eyes narrowed.

"Don't put words into my mouth."

Augustin puffed out his chest. "Can you exorcise Lucinde or not?"

"I could, if she's possessed," Elise said. "It definitely seems like a demon problem."

"Like in the Bible."

"Yes. 'Like in the Bible.' I'm going to confer with James, after which he'll be in contact with you. What would be the best number to reach you at?"

"Marisa's so-called high priest has it," Augustin said.

"Okay. Keep Lucinde in her room for now. Try to keep her eating and drinking water, because if she is possessed, she'll resist it on her own," Elise said. She touched her bleeding lip. "You already know to keep your distance."

"Yes."

He opened the front door to let in the hot summer air. The clouds had thickened since Elise's arrival, and it smelled like rain again. "You have my card. Call me when she gets worse," she said, stepping outside.

Augustin was already closing the door. He looked as inclined to give her a call as he was to offer a finger to his daughter's mouth. "Right, thanks," he said.

Elise paused by the Ramirezes' gate. She glanced up at Lucinde's window, half-covered in a heavy drape. As she watched, a hand came up to jerk it closed.

"You're welcome," she muttered. Elise turned on her car, cranked the radio, and pulled out of the cul-de-sac.

14

Chapter 2

ELISE'S OFFICE WAS conveniently located one mile from the airport and just across the street from the bad side of town. The toxic green carpet had been bought secondhand from a casino, but the loud pattern was downplayed by yellowing paint and fixtures that hadn't been replaced since the mid-seventies. Since most of her business was done online, Elise hadn't seen the point in spending much money on rent.

The mail room was empty except for a consultant who had moved in the week before. "Good morning!" Felicia sang.

Elise took the mail from her cubby and didn't respond.

Her box was labeled "Bruce Kent." Elise had been retired for years now, but demons had a long memory for revenge. Starting her business under a pseudonym had seemed like a good idea. It worked well enough. In the five years since their retirement, she'd only been attacked twice.

The first envelope on her mail stack proved to be yet another threatening letter from her former employer's lawyer. Elise moved it to the back of the pile. Her roommate would be happy to use the shredded paper in her compost. The rest of it was bills—lots of them.

"That coffee sure smells good," Felicia said hopefully. Elise walked away. "Say hi to Bruce for me!"

Her suite was just as dreary and green as the rest of the building. She didn't have any decorations to lessen the impact; the walls were bare aside from her diploma and proof of CPA certification.

Elise thought Augustin had been right to laugh at the absurdity of her career choice, but when she retired, she had no skills for a normal career. James had job experience from the time before he became a nomad, but she hadn't even completed kindergarten.

At the time, she toyed with the idea of becoming a police officer, but

15

she hated guns. Then Elise learned she had passion aside from the hunt: money. There was probably a joke to be made about going from killer to accountant, but a college education didn't bestow her with a sense of humor. She also didn't learn to be friendly to assholes, which was why her internship with an accounting firm was brief and ended up in court.

Elise settled her chain of charms next to throwing knives in the top drawer of her desk and prepared a fresh pot of coffee. Once she started working, she could go through two pots before lunch.

Her email was as pleasant to read as her normal mail. Elise filled a niche market: financial services for infernal and ethereal businesses. Most demons came to Earth to make trouble, but a few came to get rich. Their scruples—or lack thereof—gave them good business sense. But demons also had no morals, which meant they often didn't pay their accountant.

Elise paged through multiple emails full of excuses. Her frown deepened at each one.

"Fuck me," she muttered, drinking deep from her mug. It was going to be a three pot morning for sure.

The only highlight was an email from James. All it said was, "Dinner tonight?" Elise responded with, "Sure," and minimized her email program.

The rest of it could wait. Her daily allotment of patience for clients had been expended upon Augustin Ramirez, and the only company she wanted now was math: silent, unemotional red and black numbers.

She glanced at her knives in the desk drawer. Math, and maybe a sharpening stone. It *had* been a long time since she gave proper attention to her arsenal.

Leaning back in her chair, Elise balanced one of the slender knives across a finger. The blade glinted in the fluorescent overhead light. It was shiny enough to serve as a mirror, and the braid over Elise's shoulder was distorted across its surface like the promise of spilled blood.

If she had her clients' lack of scruples, she would bill the Ramirezes for services rendered. Why shouldn't she make money off her knowledge like any other consultant? The only problem was James. He would never approve of profiting off a five-year-old girl's life.

Elise tested the edge of the blade with her thumb. Maybe instead of billing families in need, she could start threatening her pre-existing clients with violence. Yeah. That could work.

She speared the stack of mail with her knife. It gave a satisfying *thunk* as the knife's point bit into the blotter.

The only warning her door was about to open was a single knock.

16

Elise jerked the blade out of her desk and dropped it in the drawer just in time for a blonde tornado to sweep in.

"Good morning, gorgeous!"

"Morning, Betty," Elise said. "How did you get here?"

Betty was the exception to Elise's steadfast refusal to develop a social life. Her roommate liked to describe herself as the sexiest research scientist in the West, and she played into that image with a dangerously low-cut blouse and what barely passed as a skirt.

"I'm just popping by. Cassandra and I are on our way to the university. I need a revision to my taxes!" Betty set her folder on Elise's desk with all the flourish of bestowing a gift upon her.

"No, you don't. I prepared your taxes three months ago. They were perfect."

"Yeah, but I think I found more deductions. Would you take a look? Please? I don't want to have to pay the IRS this year."

"You know every month you don't pay incurs a half-percent fine, right?" Elise asked. "And aren't you worried about splashing caustic chemicals on your cleavage?"

"I'm not doing work in the lab today. I have to see my mentor about my thesis," Betty said, giving Elise a knowing grin.

"I'll take another look at your taxes if you promise not to get kicked out of graduate school for sexual harassment. Nobody else is paying me anyway."

"Great! Well, except for the part where you're not getting paid. Are you going to make your half of rent this month?"

"Probably," Elise said. She silently added, *I hope.*

Betty wasn't fooled. She gave Elise's hand on the desk a comforting squeeze. "We're doing okay. Don't stress about it. But maybe it's time to hire some goons to have a talk with them, huh? Make them an offer they can't refuse?"

"Would you believe me if I said I'm seriously considering that as an option?"

"I'll believe anything with you, Elise. So what happened with your mail? Taking out your frustrations with a letter opener?" She wiggled a finger through a hole in one of the envelopes.

Elise shrugged. "They showed up like that."

"Yeah? I wonder if it was the postal service or the mailroom guy," Betty said. She lowered her voice to a whisper. "Ooh, you know, I bet it was that guy that does the credit counseling services. He's such a creeper. He always gives me looks when I go by his room."

"I think he's surprised anybody likes me enough to visit. It could also be your amazing disappearing wardrobe. I've seen strippers wear more than you."

Betty laughed. "Elise! Why are you seeing strippers in the first place?"

"I've got some weird clients." Understatement of the year. Betty didn't know that most of the people she worked for weren't people at all.

She swiped Elise's coffee, took a sip, and set it back down with a sigh. "Hate to demand deductions and run, but Cassandra's outside and my mentor is waiting." Betty wiggled her eyebrows. "You going to be home for dinner tonight?"

"No. I'm going to go see James."

"Oh *really*. So you're planning on *eating out*? Get it? You know, like—"

Elise didn't let her finish. "Not everyone lives in a porno like you do, Betty. It's not like that."

"I don't know why," Betty sighed. "If James was inviting me over for dinner, it would definitely be 'like that.'"

"Uh huh. I'll let you know about your taxes tomorrow."

"Thanks, love," Betty said. "By the way, you got some ketchup on your blouse." Elise glanced down, touching her injured lip. The smear of red on her collar wasn't ketchup. "See you later!"

"Bye, Betty."

She turned back to her computer, where the emails full of excuses were still waiting. Her smile slowly faded.

A lifetime of killing demons could never have prepared her for the ugly reality of being unable to pay her bills. It seemed cruel that she could be a skilled accountant creeping toward debt, but she didn't think many demons would be impressed by phone calls from debt collectors.

Elise's gaze wandered to the drawer with her knives again. Demons only responded to violence.

Screw discretion. Maybe it really was time to start speaking their language.

Click. The sign outside Motion and Dance Studio flickered and turned off. Rain tapped against the control box on its side, dripping onto the brown grass and running off into the gutter.

Elise locked the door on the control box and headed inside. Her footsteps echoed through the main hall as she moved from window to window to shut them. Elise's reflection on the mirrored wall behind her mimicked her actions, a dark silhouette of a long-haired young woman in an open blazer and low heels.

She peeked into the second, smaller dance hall. It wasn't quite as nice as the main one, since it had recently been converted from a garage. The studs were exposed on one side and boxes with branded t-shirts were stacked against the wall.

The windows were already locked, so Elise turned to leave again. Her own motion in the mirror caught her eye. She hesitated in the center of the dance hall.

A scar on her left breast peeked over the neck of her blouse, glowing pale white in the light from the street lamps. That injury had been delivered by a stone knife in the hands of a woman claiming to be a death goddess. She tortured Elise for hours by chaining her to a wall and drawing lines in her flesh. Most of them healed cleanly, but the one over her heart had been deep enough to scrape bone.

It was the last time Elise hunted a demon. She prevented apocalypse that day, but the costs had been too high.

She clicked off the flood lights before locking the front door, wiggling the handle to make sure it was secure. She hugged the side of the building to avoid the rain as she took the stairs to the second floor.

The door upstairs was ajar. She hung her coat on the hook beside James's jacket and shook out her hair.

"James?" she called, stepping into the kitchen.

All of the lights in the apartment were off. Elise flipped the switch to the stove's overhead light. Golden potatoes simmered under a glass lid, and two wine glasses were waiting nearby on the counter. The wine itself was still on the rack.

Her eyes scanned the arrangement of the furniture, the appliances. The table had been moved from the informal dining area to the living room. Half-melted candles marked with pentagrams and anointed with oil were arranged on low stands around the edges of the room. A large crystal had been set on a velvet cloth in the center of the table, and the last edition of the Sierra Witch's Almanac lay by its side.

It looked like James had been preparing for a ritual, but she heard no sounds in the house beyond the occasional hiss of steam and clicking as the stove's temperature shifted. He would never leave dinner unattended.

Where was he?

Elise slipped off her shoes, a thread of adrenaline thrilling through her stomach. She turned off the light again and approached the hallway. Lifting her skirt over her knees to free her legs, she lowered into a half-crouch.

"James?" she called again, softer this time.

Creak.

Danger.

Elise spun too late. The closet door slammed open, and a tall, dark form flew at her from its depths. Her hip hit the arm of the couch and sent the side table crashing to the ground. She let herself roll over the side, and the assailant flew past her.

She was on her feet again in a heartbeat, sweeping her leg high to strike his back. He cried out, stumbling forward, and Elise kicked again, lower this time. Her foot connected with a muffled *thump*.

He lost balance, barely catching himself on the half wall. He threw his arms up to block Elise's next kick, catching her ankle. She jerked and broke his grip.

Her attacker's fist flashed through the darkness. Elise twisted away. The blow landed on her right shoulder instead, and her arm numbed.

The blows between them were fast, smooth, like a choreographed dance. He swung at her, and she blocked him with her forearms to strike low, seeking a hole in his defense. Kick, kick, punch—Elise caught his arm and threw him against the opposite wall.

She grabbed him by the throat and pushed his head back. She tightened her fingers around his esophagus. It didn't take much force to hold him in place, even though he was nearly a foot taller than she was; one wrong move and his airway would collapse.

"Got you," she growled.

A frozen moment hung between them, his struggling breath hot on her face. He smelled of breath mints and aftershave, and a little bit like summer grass, and he all but radiated heat. He had been inside—waiting —for quite a while.

Her assailant gurgled. Elise relaxed her hands.

"Oh, sorry. Are you okay?"

He coughed once and cleared his throat. "Yes…I think so. You haven't lost your touch, have you?"

"There's no chance of that happening with your help." Elise backed off, allowing her aspis to step away from the wall. She flicked on the living room light, and James rubbed his neck.

"You could have pulled your punches," he said. "Didn't you recognize me?"

Elise smiled. She would have recognized him in total darkness. "It would be insulting to go gentle on you. What's that I smell in the oven?"

"Prime rib roast with red wine sauce."

She picked the side table back up. "Sounds great. What would I do without you?"

"Starve, I imagine," he said as he pulled an apron that said *Kiss the Crone* over his head.

James returned to his cooking while Elise fixed the mess she made in the living room.

The apartment was small, but he made good use of the space; James's sense of aesthetics was far superior to hers. All his furniture matched in a Pottery Barn kind of way, his walls were decorated with fine photography, and he even had some kind of fancy throw rug. Elise's idea of decorating was putting up movie posters with thumb tacks.

"It took you a long time to get up here," he remarked from the stove. "I hid for ages. What were you doing downstairs?"

"Locking up. Someone forgot to shut all the windows."

"I was busy making dinner." James turned on the oven light and peeked through the window. "Just a few more minutes, I think. Are you all right?"

"I'm fine."

He gave her the kind of look that said he knew she wasn't, but didn't feel like arguing it. "Did you see the Ramirezes today?"

"Yeah. *That* was fun. They're a mess."

James uncorked a bottle of wine and poured it into the waiting glasses. "Is it possession?"

"Maybe. Lucinde didn't like having St. Benedict flashed at her. She also kicked me in the face."

Elise picked up the Sierra Witch's Almanac and peered at the bookmarked page. James's coven published a new almanac every year with lunar correspondences and seasonal spells, and they always included an excerpt from their Book of Shadows in the back. The spell he was looking at seemed complicated.

He handed her one of the glasses. She dropped the book. "Your bruises look painful."

"She's got a nasty kick for a five-year-old. Nastier than yours, anyway," she said. He opened his mouth to protest, but she went on. "Marisa mentioned she was having nightmares. It's possible Lucinde was attacked by a mara or an incubus instead."

"But you don't think it's possession?" he asked, serving dinner using puffy blue pot holders.

"Probably not."

21

"Good. That will make it easier."

Elise shrugged. "It's not my problem. I'm not an exorcist anymore."

He turned on the radio on the windowsill.

"—other *spooky* news, a temp guard by the name of Richard Czynski disappeared from a cemetery in the north side of town," the DJ said in a voice far too perky to be discussing a missing persons case. "Curiouser and curiouser, he's not the only thing that's disappeared. The grave of notorious Amber Hackman, one of the only people to escape this black hole of a town, has also been raided. Obviously she didn't like having to spend her death here anymore than she did her life. Zombie attack? Your run-of-the-mill grave rob gone wrong? You ring in and let us know on *Spooky* News, your favorite—"

"What trash," he muttered, switching it over to a classic rock station.

She felt the motion before she saw it. James's hand whipped toward Elise.

Side-stepping his reach, she jerked his wrist forward and trapped his arm under hers. A twist, a hard shove, and she had him against the wall.

Elise grinned at him, and his returning smile was softer, but no less affectionate. It softened the coldness of his eyes. Ten years, and he hadn't won a fight against her once.

"Damn, you're fast," he said when she dropped him. He rubbed his elbow. "I'll get you someday."

"Sure you will," Elise said, mostly to be nice.

They sat down together at the table. James hesitated over a piece of potato, pushing it through the prime rib's juices with his fork. "I think you should keep working with the Ramirezes."

"Why? The coven can handle it, and I have too much work to do. Real work. The kind of stuff that pays the bills." Elise smiled over her wine glass. "Unless you think the Ramirezes would pay me a consultation fee?"

"You can't charge them money."

"And I can't pay the rent with gratitude." She tried to ignore his disapproving stare, but she could feel its weight as she picked at her salad. "I'll investigate. Maybe I'll find out something helpful."

"Thank you."

She grunted. "Do you still have my falchion?"

"It's in the locked case where you left it. Why? Did you want it back?"

"Not really. I was just thinking about it earlier."

"I've been thinking about it a lot lately, too," he murmured over his glass of wine. He didn't mean the sword.

The sounds of classic rock intermingled with the soft pattering of rain on glass, making for a peaceful meal. Elise made a good show of picking at her dinner to appease James, but as good as it tasted, she left her plate half-full. She cleaned up her place at the table, shoveling her barely-touched potatoes into a container.

James wasn't finished, but stood to help her anyway. "Eager to escape?"

"No, I just have to follow up on some clients that aren't paying."

He touched Elise's chin, his thumb hesitating over the gash. "Are you certain you're all right?"

Elise gazed up at him, momentarily breathless. James was a handsome man. He also had absolutely no interest in her romantically, which he had made *very* clear over the years.

"Yeah." She turned from him to put the leftovers in the refrigerator. "I'm fine."

He caught her elbow—a less violent gesture than their earlier fighting. "Let me take care of you," he said.

All she had to do was nod, and James ran his knuckles down her cheek, and his power flowed around them, gentle and warm. It breathed through Elise, and she felt as though she was sinking into the sky.

An instant later, it was over. Elise touched her lip. The wound was gone.

James held up a yellowed note card with a single, prominent rune inscribed on the blank side—an old healing spell.

"Found this in my fire safe yesterday. Might as well get some use out of my old paper spells. I don't plan on using them ever again. This, on the other hand…" He took a knife of the cabinet and handed it to Elise. It was as long as his forearm and intended to be worn in a spine sheath.

The corner of Elise's mouth twitched. "Hiding weapons in your kitchen? I'm visiting a client, not going on safari." She jabbed the dagger into an invisible enemy, and the muscles in her arm rippled.

"Yes, but between Lucinde's demon problem, and some of the other news I've been hearing…" He trailed off. "I would appreciate it if you humor me."

Elise led him to the entryway and showed him the throwing knives hidden in her blazer pocket. "I'm miles ahead of you."

James's smile was sad. "Be careful."

"Always," she promised.

23

Chapter 3

ELISE DIDN'T DEAL with many local clients, and of those nearby, only one would provide information as well as a paycheck: Craven's, a small demon-owned casino with six months of outstanding debt to their accountant.

Craven's wasn't one of those big hotel casinos that booked Cirque-style shows and courted high-rollers. It was a little dive a few blocks off downtown with boarded windows and no flashy lights. Elise only discovered it wasn't condemned when one of her oldest clients, a cambion that could barely stand, informed her that their racks of ribs were the best kept secret in the city. And they did have great ribs—but it wasn't always from the kind of animal Elise was willing to eat.

Her contacts worked in the basement nightclub beneath Craven's. It was the kind of place a kopis couldn't visit unless she wanted a fight, and it wasn't much safer for someone in a business suit, either. Instead, she went home to change into something club-appropriate. Elise didn't go anywhere except work and the gym, so all she had was a black halter top and Lycra pants left over from Halloween. The pants were skin-tight, with nowhere to hide a weapon, but she fit an ankle rig under her right boot and a small knife under her belt. It wasn't a fast draw, but it would have to do.

Elise was doing her makeup in the mirror when Betty got home.

"You look like you're ready for a hot date," she said, invading their shared bathroom without knocking. Betty was still in her barely-decent skirt, but her lip gloss was a pink stain at the corner of her mouth.

"How was dinner with your mentor? I take it your hunt was successful." Elise gestured at her own mouth. "You're messy."

Betty wiped what little lip gloss remained off on her finger and laughed. "Successful? Yeah, right. He only wanted to discuss biomedical sciences, and not the naked kind. You using the sink?" Elise stepped aside to give her room, and Betty bent to wash her hands. "You didn't answer when I asked about the hot date, I noticed."

"My mission for the night is far more innocent than yours. I'm going to drop in on a client."

"Really."

"Yes, really. Why?"

Betty folded her arms. "How often do you visit your clients wearing skin-tight Lycra?"

"Any time my client happens to work at a casino nightclub and it's a Friday night," Elise said, tossing her sponge in the trash. "I can't show up in business casual. I'd get laughed out of the place."

"That might happen if you try to seduce the money out of your client, too. I've seen the way you dance."

Elise pushed Betty away from the sink with her hip. "Out of my way. I'm an accountant on a mission."

"Uh huh. Sure. I'll keep my phone on me tonight, so give me a call when you're too drunk to drive yourself home."

"I appreciate the offer, but I'm taking the bus." She applied eye shadow with her fingers.

"Taking the bus and *not* planning on getting drunk? A likely story."

"The casino is downtown, Betty," Elise said. "There's no free parking."

Betty snorted. "Okay, have fun with your 'client.' I'm going to collect the withered scraps of my dignity and read research papers on the couch."

She left. Elise ran her fingers through her thick hair to detangle it and appraised her looks. The look wasn't "accountant," but she wasn't sure she would pass as an ordinary clubber, either. Elise didn't *feel* convincing.

Elise grabbed her jacket off the back of a chair. "See you in the morning," she called as she passed through the living room. Betty waved a hand over the couch.

She passed Betty's cousin on the way down the sidewalk. Anthony occupied the other half of their duplex, and he worked multiple jobs, so he was always coming and going at weird times. It looked like he had just left his job at the car shop. His jeans were covered in oil.

"Hey, Elise," Anthony greeted, pausing on the sidewalk. "How are you? Did you—"

"Have to catch the bus. See you later," she said, brushing past him without stopping.

She jogged down the street and around the corner. A breeze moist with distant rain washed into her face and down her shirt. The storm had passed, but the weight of the air promised more to come. A man in a bulky coat was slumped over the bus stop bench, holding the schedule over his head as though it was still pouring.

Right on time, the bus groaned up the street and paused at her curb. Elise took a seat near the back door. No amount of fresh, rainy wind could make the inside of the bus smell good—despite being cleaned frequently, it still smelled of sweat and the hundreds of people who rode it every day.

The lights turned off and the bus rumbled down the street again. It jerked and swayed with every bump in the road. The city quickly began to transition from small businesses into casinos, bars, and strip clubs. The change was abrupt—one second, Elise was staring at peaceful storefronts and the occasional tattoo parlor, and the next, she was surrounded by flashing neon lights and towering hotels.

The sign on an adult store displayed a woman wearing only a thong and a suggestive smile, its mannequins decked out in boas and corsets. The Wild Orchid's sign flaunted its topless dancers across the street from the city courthouse. The bus hung a right, and tall signs over what had once been a casino advertised an off-Broadway show and a car event, both of which had left over a year ago.

People crossed from sidewalk to sidewalk amongst slow traffic, ignoring the buses and cars as they lurched from a bar to a pawn shop to get money for one more pull on the slot machine. A woman with overdone curls and skin hanging limply from her bones almost got struck by the bus as it turned onto Center Street. She didn't notice. She wobbled on, disappearing into the maw of a casino and out of sight.

The bus stopped at the downtown transit center, tucked between a bowling stadium and yet another hotel-casino. Elise was the first to hop off.

The casino lights flashed in time with music piped over sidewalk speakers. A man by the front door played the saxophone. He hesitated when Elise passed. She gave him a quick once-over, taking in the translucency of his skin, his long, brittle fingers and strangely-proportioned face. Nightmare. Probably second class. Hardly a threat.

She nodded at him as she passed. He didn't look worried, so maybe he thought she was a demon, too. As far as the underworld here knew, there were no local kopides. What was there to worry about?

26

Elise plowed through the casino, ignoring the glittering machines and their inebriated patrons. She passed the poker tables, the blackjack, the rows of machines in front of huge plasma TVs, and the diner in the back. She exited through an unmarked door to an alley.

Wedged between the casino and its attached hotel, the dark passage appeared to have no purpose except for gathering trash. A chain link fence blocked one end of the alley, and the other side was a rotten brick wall that most people wouldn't realize belonged to the prettier side of Craven's. Elise never went through the front door—too many people watched it.

Elise ducked around a Dumpster, kicking a case of empty beer cans out of the way. A set of cement stairs led down into shadow.

Only a single word on a small, rusted sign hinted at the door's purpose—*Blood*, it said, the metal so pocked and rusted it was almost unreadable.

She pushed it open and went inside.

Elise was never sure how long it took to get from the surface to the club—time took on a strange quality in the descent, warping and fading. Maybe she only walked for a few seconds; maybe she walked for hours. The black walls narrowed as she moved down the passage, guided by the pulsing thump of bass.

In time, Elise came upon the end of the hall. A neon sign blazed a single electric word above the door: BLOOD.

She crossed the threshold and left the human world behind her.

Music thrummed around her, shaking inside her chest and against her eardrums. The back door was on the top level of Eloquent Blood. Humans sat amongst half-demons known as the Gray, doing business and swapping spit as though they weren't different species. Many of the humans probably didn't even know who they were associating with—a few idiots stumbled upon the bar thinking it was an underground Goth club, and nobody was in a hurry to tell them differently. Idiots were great incubus food.

Yellow sulfur formed a fine layer on the floor. The thick stench of sweat and whiskey almost overpowered the brimstone. They tried to keep it clean in the club, but Elise was all too familiar with the stink of demons. She could have recognized it if they drenched the entire building in formaldehyde.

She glanced at the dance floor two stories down. A DJ spun a dance beat and the bodies below pulsed in time to the rhythm. Hips rolled, arms twisted, and now and then Elise would see a flash of pale skin as another dancer stripped off her shirt. It was hot enough in Blood without dancing. Throw in a fast beat and a racing pulse, and it was nearly intolerable.

She moved through the tight press of bodies on the spiral staircase as she would have waded through an ocean tide. Speakers on either side of the bar pumped out music so loud it drowned out even the conversations hollered inches from her ears. Elise peered up at the bartender through fog from the smoke machines to determine if it was someone she knew.

The blonde girl on the bar swayed side to side, her hands trailing up her hips and stomach. Her fingers traced the swell of her bare breasts. Her nipples were erect despite the warmth, and her skin was dark olive. She was one of the Gray bartenders Elise didn't know. Probably part-basandere, judging by the heavy iron chain around her waist.

Someone waved at her from behind the bar. Neuma's hair was liquid midnight, like each individual strand had been dipped in an inkwell. As she moved toward Elise, she faded slightly into the shadows behind her until only her white skin and bathrobe were visible. The half-succubus Gray hadn't yet dressed for the night, and she earned a few strange looks for it.

"What you doing here?" Neuma asked, leaning on the bar. "Business or pleasure?"

Elise had to yell to hear herself over the music. "Business. Can we talk in back?"

The bartender's welcoming grin slipped off her face. "Sure." Elise jumped over the bar and followed Neuma down a hall. The volume of the music faded the further they went. "How you doing, doll?"

"You know me. You also probably know why I'm here."

Neuma grimaced. "Money?"

"Money," Elise confirmed.

An entire wall of the dressing room they entered was dedicated to shelves of alcohol. The other wall was a line of messy vanities. Black light illuminated the room, darkening everything but Neuma's skin, which glowed violet in the shadows.

She gestured to the alcohol. "What you want today?"

"Information and a paycheck," Elise said, dropping her jacket on the dressing table. "You can help me with the first one, but I'll need David Nicholas for the second. Where is he?"

"Shot of vodka it is." Neuma dragged a stool out of the closet and positioned it under the shelves. "I haven't seen you in a couple weeks— how's life being sugar and spice?"

"Not as profitable as I would like. I really need to talk to him,

Neuma."

She snorted. "Yeah, good luck. He left an hour ago to 'restock,' so the fucker's probably higher than the moon by now."

Neuma stepped onto the stool, lifting onto her toes to reach for one of the higher shelves. Elise watched her pale calves and ankles flex under the hem of her bathrobe. She made a triumphant noise and dropped to the floor again, alcohol in hand.

Elise forced herself to look away from Neuma's legs. "What's he taking?"

"I think he's gotten into lethe, but he ain't going to admit it." She took out two shot glasses and opened the vodka. "I can't imagine how a sexy girl like you got stuck accounting when you could be doing fun shit, like touring with me and the other Blood girls. We're leaving for St. Louis on the twenty-third. You can still come."

"I'm not an employee," Elise said.

"Could be by the twenty-third."

"Believe it or not, I like my job."

Neuma shrugged and handed her a shot. "The offer's out there."

"I'll keep that in mind." Elise tossed back the vodka. The alcohol burned hot all the way from her throat to the pit of her stomach. "When do you think David Nicholas will be back?"

"Could be a few minutes, could be a few days. Depends on how good the trip is."

A few days. She couldn't wait that long to pay rent. Elise dropped the shot glass amongst a pile of leather straps on the counter. "Where's the shift manager?"

Neuma's full lips split into a grin. "You're looking at her, beautiful!"

"Congrats. Where did our least favorite witch go?"

"Moved off to live with some aeshma." Neuma took a swig right out of the vodka bottle. "I hope she gets put into slavery by something with a lot of boils and a fetish for shit-play."

"Speaking of slavery, there's a lot of humans here tonight. What's going on? I thought you guys banned humans below the casino level."

"New policy from on high. We gotta play nice. Too many people wandered in and disappeared, so we're not letting humans into private rooms anymore, neither. We're gonna lose business like this."

"Demon business, but not the humans," Elise said. "And it will keep the police out of your hair."

"Cops are easy to pay off." Neuma sighed. "I kind of wish the Night Hag would come out of hibernation. Then we'd have someone to deal with public crap. You know?"

Elise grimaced to think of it. Demonic overlords were seldom thrilled to find kopides hiding in their territories—even retired ones. "Since you're the manager now, I need news. Anything you can tell me."

"There ain't much to say," Neuma said. She started changing into her costume for the night. "Like I said, I've heard tell the big boss is stirring, but you know, people say she's going to wake up every six months or so."

"Where did you hear it this time?"

"David Nicholas. I think he's just stirring shit up so nobody will kill him and take the casino, but..." Neuma dropped the bathrobe. "You know how he is. He's not even keeping hours down here anymore. He's got an office on the ninth floor like he thinks he's some fucking big shot."

"Is that all?"

"There have been some bodies going missing around town, too," Neuma said, grabbing a pile of leather straps off the counter. "Not just grave robberies. It's the hospital too, and it ain't some ambitious thief. When we gossip about it this much, you know one of us has gotta be involved." She donned her costume piece by piece, buckling the shorts on the side and holding one of the straps over her breasts. "Mind hooking me up?"

Elise pulled the strap tight and slipped it through the buckle, but her fingers wouldn't work the way she expected. The proximity to Neuma's skin was distracting. "Why would a demon stock up on bodies?"

"Food? Hell if I know."

Grave robbing didn't sound like a wholesome activity, but Elise doubted it had anything to do with Lucinde's problem. "Have you heard about anything big, bad, and incorporeal in the area? I'm looking for something that might be possessing people."

"Don't think so, babe. If there was something that nasty around, we'd already know."

"Yeah. You're probably right. Look, I'm going to go, but thanks for the shot. I'll try David Nicholas again tomorrow night."

Neuma pouted, sticking out her lower lip. It was ruby-black as though she had painted her skin with fresh blood. "I'd love to see you on the bar with me tonight. We could have a lot of fun."

Elise couldn't seem to tear her gaze from those lips. "No," she said unconvincingly, "I don't think we could."

The door to the dressing room swung open. A man with an angular chin and a too-large nose stuck his head in. "Why aren't you on the bar, bitch?" His gaze turned to Elise. It felt as though a wet rat slithered up the vertebra of her spine. "Oh. *You* again."

"David Nicholas," she greeted.

The club's manager was a full-blooded nightmare—hundreds of years old, but ages past his heyday. David Nicholas made people dream of rotting alive. He had been extremely powerful in the Middle Ages, when everyone feared leprosy, but now his specialty was being obnoxious.

"What do you want?"

"I'll give you three guesses," Elise said. "Let's have a talk in your office."

His lip curled. Smoke trailed from his thin lips to the caverns of his nostrils. David Nicholas stabbed a finger at Neuma. "Bar. Now."

She gave him an ironic salute, and Elise followed him out of the room. When she shut the door to the dressing room, Neuma's draw lost strength, and every step away made it easier to keep walking.

David Nicholas led her up the stairs behind the changing room, taking long drags on his cigarette. Elise could almost see the smoke billowing down his esophagus.

They emerged on the ground floor of Craven's. The lights were dim and the slot machines glowed like oases in the desert. A cocktail waitress that could have been Neuma's sister hurried by in little more than a leather leotard with a tray of drinks on her shoulder.

He led her up a couple levels of escalators, past a handful of imps that weren't pretending to be human, and through a locked door marked MANAGER.

David Nicholas's office overlooked the casino floor. Tinted glass dimmed the tables until Elise could barely make out the dealers, although monitors on the walls gave her a clear view of the cards. They were also the only source of light in the room, which Elise considered a mercy—it meant she could only imagine how bad the mess in his office was by the smell. It reeked like the dorms from Elise's college days.

She had to step over a pile of rags to get through the door. Piles of books and papers formed columns to her shoulder. Some had tipped over. And that was all what she could make out in the darkness—there were too many vague, shadowy shapes that could have been any number of horrible things.

David Nicolas twisted his lips and spat into a shallow metal bowl filled with cigarette butts and black smears of ash. "Let's make this fast, bitch, I don't have all night. What'd I do to earn a personal visit from the big boss's accountant? You got a problem with our taxes or some shit? I don't want to hear about it. It's *your* job to fix it."

31

"Everything is as good as can be expected with your finances, except for one thing."

"What?"

She leaned over him, arms folded across her chest. "I'm not getting paid."

"Bullshit. We paid you."

"You paid my retainer a year ago, and nothing since," Elise said. "That's six months of outstanding fines. I've sent you three notices."

He rolled the cigarette between two of his fingers, contemplating the glowing end. "Haven't seen anything. Maybe the Night Hag got them. Did you hear she's waking up?"

"She's not going to stir and you know it."

David Nicholas spread his hands wide in a helpless gesture. "Yeah, if that's what you want to think, but I can't pay anyone that much money without getting it approved. Rules are rules."

Elise set her jaw. "You want to do this fast? We can do it fast."

"Oh no. Don't hurt me," David Nicholas said in a tone of mock horror. "I'm so afraid of the accountant."

She drew her boot knife. "I need to get paid. I'm going to make that happen one way or another."

"You don't even know what to do with that."

She stabbed. It sank into David Nicholas's stomach as though he was made of putty rather than flesh, and she jerked the knife across his torso, tearing it out the side. Black smoke puffed from the wound.

He lurched out of his chair, spidery hands clutching the entry point. "Fuck! What the hell?"

"I can force you to insubstantiate, and I can make it hurt. Believe me, I know which buttons to push." She lifted the knife again, and he tripped over a pile of trash trying to backtrack. He hit the floor and pushed himself away from her with his heels. "Or you can pay."

"I don't need the Night Hag to wake up to ruin your fucking week," he hissed. "Some dark night, you're going to go to sleep, and I'll be waiting. And I'll be there the night after, and the night after, and every other night of your life until you die shitting yourself. You'll learn to fear sleep, and to fear me."

Elise gave a little laugh. "The first night I dream of you, David Nicholas, I'll tip off Aquiel. He'd be happy to know where you're lurking these days, and I'd enjoy watching you get ripped apart."

He stared at her. She stared back. A challenge.

"You'll fear your dreams yet," he whispered. He spoke so quietly that

Elise shouldn't have been able to hear him over the music, but she did. His voice was dead fingers scraping down her neck, and she couldn't help but shiver. She didn't show it.

"Money. Now. I take checks."

It looked like he had many colorful words trapped between the spikes of his teeth, but he swallowed them down.

Fifteen minutes later, she trotted down the stairs into Blood again, flicking the check against the fingers of her free hand. David Nicholas slunk behind her, his arms wrapped tight around his body. He wasn't going to fall apart yet—not if he could hold himself together long enough to feed. But Elise hadn't made it easy on him. His shirt was in tatters, and the flesh beneath it wasn't much better.

The amount on the check was more than what they owed her for six months of work. It would cover the next quarter, too—and two months of her office's rent. She tucked it down her belt along with her dagger.

"Pleasure doing business with you," Elise said over the thudding of music. David Nicholas's eyes flashed.

A scream.

Elise twisted, facing the direction from which the scream had come. *The dressing room.*

David Nicholas was already gone, jumping shadow to shadow to disappear from the stool and reappear at the end of the hall. He vanished around the corner in a swirl of tattered clothing.

Elise grabbed the doorknob to the dressing room and shook it. Locked.

Neuma screamed again, and the door rattled in its hinges as something heavy slammed against the other side.

She took a step back and unleashed a powerful kick next to the lock mechanism. The door shattered around the handle.

Elise kicked again. It slammed open.

Neuma was pressed against the counter, her back smashed into the now-shattered glass of the mirror. A gray creature with branded flesh crushed her, its stubby hands locked on her wrists as its slavering mouth lowered toward her chest.

"Hey!" Elise shouted.

The demon turned. Its bulging eyes were almost all black. Opens slashes across his face wept blood and pus, and saliva dripped from its mouth.

It focused on her, and its pupils dilated.

Elise drew back her fist and punched, throwing her whole body

33

behind the blow. The demon's head snapped to the side. It toppled with a keening scream.

The half-succubus cried out as she got off the counter. Several shards of glass stuck in her back, and blood poured down her perfect spine.

The little demon clambered to its feet. Elise pushed the bartender behind her.

"What do you want?" Elise demanded. The demon's thin gray tongue darted out of its mouth to lick where its lips should have been.

It lunged at Elise.

She moved into its attack and it slammed into her shoulder. They hit the ground, and she rolled with their momentum. Her entire body felt the impact. It was like getting hit by a raging bull.

The fiend recovered instantly. Elise wasn't quite so fast.

It came at her with a roar, and a flash of inspiration struck—the black lights, the vanity bulbs, the demon's huge pupils. Elise threw herself out of the demon's way, and it hit the wall behind her instead.

She launched across the room. Elise fumbled in the darkness behind the rack of costumes. She heard the sound of clawed feet against ground, and shut her eyes against the impact—then found the switch.

Click. The lights over the vanities blazed to life.

Her eyes watered from the sudden light, but it was nothing compared to the demon's reaction. It screamed and clawed at its eyes, stumbling toward Elise. A stray swipe of its claws slashed her arm. Pain flared, and she jerked back with a shout.

The demon plunged into the dark hallway.

"Wait here," Elise told Neuma.

She expected the demon to go make a break for the club—and the fresh meat the partiers could provide—but instead it went for a door she hadn't noticed before. Elise began to follow.

"No!" Neuma cried, grabbing Elise's arm. "Don't!"

"It's escaping—"

"You can't go in there!"

"Why? Where does that door lead?"

"It goes down to the Warrens," Neuma said. "You'd get eaten alive."

"Shit," Elise said.

"Shit," Neuma agreed, stepping back into the room. She twisted around to look at her back in the mirror. Some of the glass was still in her back, and the injuries streamed thin, watery blood.

Elise grabbed the bathrobe and moved to cover the wounds. "We need to get you to a witch right now."

"No. I'm fine. I have a charm to accelerate my healing to human speed. You know, for when I'm playing submissive." Neuma grabbed a shard of glass and jerked it out of her back with a sigh. "Jewelry box. Toe ring with a red stone."

Elise shifted through the gaudy bracelets and necklaces to find the ring. She passed it to Neuma, who leaned against the wall to slip it on her foot. The blood thickened and grew sluggish as she watched, slowing to an ooze.

"That's a new toy," Elise said.

"My girlfriend gave it to me. She likes playing rough." Neuma pulled another shard of glass out, and another, dropping them in the trash can.

"Why did that demon attack you?"

"I don't know. Don't even know what it was. Would you pick some of this out for me? I can't reach it all."

"I think that might have been a fiend," Elise said, ignoring the request. Neuma would have enjoyed it way too much. "They're lesser demons, but it takes a strong demon to control them."

"It looks like it dropped something," Neuma said, pointing at a crumpled scrap of paper on the floor. Elise smoothed it out on her thigh.

It was an Eloquent Blood staff photo printed off the internet, and the former manager was circled in pink highlighter. "You sure this was on the demon?" Neuma nodded, and Elise studied it more closely. Aside from the circle, there was nothing odd about it. "Maybe it wasn't after you. Maybe it was after that witch. Why would it have wanted the old manager?"

"I don't know. Dumb bitch could owe someone money. Where did you see one of those before, anyway? Those are hellborn, and I don't think you've been hanging out in Hell," Neuma asked.

No, she hadn't. Elise found herself recalling her fight against the death goddess again—the feel of her swords connecting with demon meat, watching the bodies hit the ground, the stink of their final, sulfurous breaths.

She had tried hard for so long to forget it that she wasn't sure if she was imagining it now, but she was almost certain that the demons had been fiends.

"Maybe I have," Elise muttered.

Part 3: The Clock

MEXICO – MAY 2004

Two demons were discussing the end of the world over crispy fish tacos. They sat in a shady corner of the patio to conceal their strange faces, and spoke Latin to prevent humans from overhearing.

"Hernandez says someone's taken over the pyramid in the undercity." The first speaker looked like a man whose eyes had been wrongly attached at the temples. His name was Vustaillo. He was a nana-huatzin, and he made his living trafficking slaves for the drug cartels.

"Who cares? Let them have it." The second speaker was a woman named Izel. Sharp teeth filled her mouth in rows like a shark. "Nobody wants that dump of a den anyway."

"But they said she's a goddess."

Izel dug into her fish and let the grease dribble down her chin. "Such a goddess must not have godly brains if she wants anything in the undercity. She's an idiot and a fool. May she enjoy her blessed ignorance."

Those kinds of insults made her companion uncomfortable. He toyed with his beer. "You heard the ninth bell ring," he whispered. "The clock's been wound again."

"More suicidal humans fascinated with death. They won't accomplish anything."

A shadow fell across their table, abruptly ending the conversation. A dark-haired human took a chair from an adjacent table and sat down. He wore a white button-up shirt and slacks, like a tourist on vacation, but he had a bandage on his cheekbone and not an ounce of body fat. Vustaillo could smell the magic pouring off of him.

"Good morning," said the newcomer. "I couldn't help but overhear your conversation."

He was speaking Latin fluently.

Izel's eyes narrowed to slits. "Who are you?"

"My name is James. Forgive me for intruding, but I heard you mention the clock, and I hoped you could tell me where it's located."

"*Bistak*," she spat.

James arched an eyebrow. "And you too."

What kind of human understood insults in the demon tongue and spoke Latin with such ease? Not the kind of human Vustaillo wanted sitting at his table. Definitely not the kind of human that should be anywhere near a doomsday clock, either.

"You should move on," Vustaillo said.

"Come, now. I'll buy your drinks."

Izel's hand lashed out, latching onto his forearm. Pinpricks of red sprung up where her nails dug into his skin. Even though she hadn't touched him, Vustaillo flinched. Izel's touch was murder. Sometimes literally.

"He said that you should—"

Izel froze. A figure had appeared behind her and pressed a knife against her throat. A thin line of blood dripped down the blade.

The woman at Izel's back was made of hard angles, from her Aquiline nose to the jut of her wrist. In the sunshine, her hair was like flame, and she looked furious.

"Get this blade off me," Izel whispered, barely daring to move her lips.

The woman spoke. "Let go of my aspis."

The color vanished from Izel's face, and Vustaillo felt dizzy.

Women did not have aspides. Only a kopis could have an aspis—but there were no female kopides.

Except one. And she was known as the greatest.

Demons whispered about her. They said she had no name and that she was as tall as a gibborim. She had become the "greatest" by slaying angels, which was something most mortals would not dare to do, even if they could. Obviously, the first two things were not true, but if the third was, then Vustaillo feared he and Izel did not have long.

"I don't want to die," Vustaillo said, and he wasn't ashamed to be on the verge of tears.

It was James who replied. "Then you might want to tell your friend to let go of me."

Vustaillo begged for her to comply with his eyes. One at a time, Izel's fingers uncurled. She slid her hand back across the table.

The kopis's blade did not budge.

"Release me," Izel said.

A single word from James: "Elise."

She sheathed the knife and took position at his back. He lifted his arm to show it to her. The demon's hand had left a red imprint burned on his skin, but he was not seriously injured.

Vustaillo pushed his plate away. The sight of food suddenly made him want to retch. "I'm sorry. For both of us. We didn't know."

"The clock," James said, voice mild.

"It's in the undercity—south of here, very far south. In Guatemala. The entrance is hidden. You would never find it."

"You might be surprised," he said, pushing aside the plates to clear space on the table. He spread a map in front of them. "Where should we go?"

The eyes of the demons met over the map. What would be more profitable—a truth or a lie?

Elise unfolded her arms and folded them again. Her biceps made Vustaillo suspect she could pop off his head with a pinky finger.

He pointed at the map. "There. I can't be more specific. I haven't seen the entrance myself."

"How close do you think that is?"

"I don't know." Vustaillo fidgeted under Elise's stare. She hadn't moved since almost slitting Izel's throat. "Within five miles."

"And how certain are you about that?" James asked.

"I said I've never been there, didn't I?"

He marked it with a pen, folded the map, and put it back in his pocket. "Are you going to eat that?"

Vustaillo couldn't think of a response. James ate the tacos, and he seemed to enjoy them despite the uncomfortable silence around the table. Music played at a restaurant down the road, the wind breezed through the trees, and the witch chewed loudly. He offered chips to Elise, and she shook her head.

"What else do you want?" Izel spat, fists clenched atop the table. She was trembling. "Our money? Our lives? You think you can threaten us without recourse because…what? You're *famous*?"

"If you're offering, we could use a guide to the undercity."

Izel barked out a laugh, but Vustaillo perked up a little. "For how much?"

James stood, wiped his mouth with a napkin, and dropped it on the empty plate. He was a full head and shoulders taller than Elise. Definitely not bigger than a gibborim. "From what we've heard, everyone dies if this clock strikes twelve. Humans. Demons. Anyone on Earth when Hell crashes into us. It's in your best interests to help."

"For how much?" Vustaillo pressed.

Elise turned to leave. The message was clear: They would not pay. He may not have been a demon of much prestige, but he didn't work for free. Even the cartels wouldn't be so insulting.

With a roar, Izel shoved the table. It exploded in front of Vustaillo. He flung himself to the ground and screamed as margarita glasses shattered around him.

Izel leaped over the table, lunging for James's throat with clawed hands.

She stopped short with a gasp.

Something crimson spattered on the back of Vustaillo's hand. He looked up to see a silver blade jutting from Izel's back. The exchange had taken a half a moment—no more. The only sound had been Izel's shout.

Vustaillo's heart shattered when she sagged against the kopis. Elise lowered her to the ground.

Nobody sitting outside the restaurant reacted. They continued eating and chatting, completely oblivious. Izel had picked the most discrete table, after all. Her body cooled beside him.

Elise stepped back and sheathed her dagger again. James put the table back in its place, picked up the plates they had spilled, and glanced uneasily at a waiter watching from the doorway.

"Get your friend out of here," James said. Disgust curled his upper lip. And then they were gone again, as silently as they arrived.

There is no currency more valuable than information. When it pertains to the location of the greatest kopis and her aspis, such information is priceless—and dangerous.

News of Izel's death reached the overlord of Cancun by nightfall, then passed to the overlord of Chetumal. Whispers traveled on shadows, crossed continents with the ocean breeze, and found waiting ears before dawn.

Vustaillo had been murdered by first light.

The tenth bell chimed two weeks later.

June 2004

Elise killed fourteen demons on the day that the clock struck ten. She knew this for a fact because she counted the skulls while piling the bodies.

Once they were stacked together, James tore a page out of his Book of Shadows, flicked it at the pyre, and whispered a word of power. They ignited in an instant bonfire, flushing Elise with heat and scorching her eyebrows. The fire didn't touch the foliage around them. The misty drizzle couldn't slow it.

"You've improved." Elise didn't sound complimentary so much as exhausted. Her hair was stuck to the back of her neck, and she wasn't sure if she was soaked in rain or sweat.

When the tenth hour chimed, the sky had split with fire and gateways opened, dumping demons on top of Elise and James. She killed anything that passed, but a lot of them had scattered. The villages were going to be a mess. And if the rest of the world was the same...

"Whomever is winding that clock isn't playing games." James took several large steps back before flicking another paper at the fire. The flames leaped fifty feet into the sky.

"At least we have this." Elise lifted a strip of skin between two fingers. She had skinned brands off one of the demons. If she could find the symbols in Hume's Almanac, they would be able to determine the demons' allegiance.

But it suddenly grew hot, and the skin blackened and crumpled around the edges. She gave a shout and dropped it. It was ash before it hit the ground.

"What did you do?" she asked, spinning on James.

His eyes were wide. "Nothing. That wasn't me." He clapped his hands, and the flames on the bodies vanished in a flash of smoke. There were no charred bodies where the fire had been—not even bone fragments.

"Shit," Elise said.

"Some greater demons clean up their minions to destroy evidence. This must be one of them." He groaned and rubbed a hand through his hair, leaving a streak of white ash. "Fantastic. At least that narrows it down to...oh, a few hundred demons."

Elise sheathed her swords, inspected herself for major injuries—nothing worse than a few bleeding claw marks—and started hiking back to the villages. James shadowed her. They had been combing the area Vustaillo noted on the map for days and hadn't found anything but mud, ants, and several rainstorms.

The village streets were empty of life when they arrived. There hadn't been many people in the first place, but the few who had stayed outdoors were dead now.

Elise and James turned a corner and startled a group of feasting demons. They were ugly things, like living grotesques hunched over half-eaten bodies with dirty fingernails and leathery skin. Elise had never seen the likes of them. She hoped she would never see them again.

She cut down the demons. They turned into ash a few minutes later.

"I got a couple of the symbols," James said. He had written down as many as he could before they ignited.

"Good. I have twenty seconds."

He looked at her. "Twenty seconds of what?"

"I timed the bells. There are twenty seconds between from the start of one to the start of the next."

"You timed them? While fighting?"

Elise shrugged.

"So that's four minutes," she said. "For twelve bells. Four minutes from the first chime until…" *The end of the world.* She didn't need to say it aloud. "I'll be back."

Elise headed to the post office, which was uninhabited by humans—living or dead. There was one package addressed to "Bruce Kent." She ripped open the box, took out the copy of Hume's Almanac sent by James's former coven, and threw the packaging in the trash.

She met up with James again, put Hume's Almanac in his backpack, and shouldered her own.

It was time to move on. There would be more victims, more demons, more battles to fight before they could find the clock.

"What happens with the eleventh bell?" Elise asked. "What happens with the *twelfth*?"

James shook his head.

"Let's get to the clock before we find out."

Elise went weeks without resting, but she couldn't keep moving forever. When she became so exhausted that she almost failed to avoid decapitation by a stray demon, James picked an abandoned condo in a

41

village on the ocean and insisted they stop to sleep.

At first, she refused. But fatigue won out. For a few blessed hours, she slept.

He studied as she rested, working his way through Hume's Almanac with the drawings of the demons' brands. There had been a letter from the high priestess tucked in the back, but no note from Hannah. She had never written to him, not in five years, and her rebuke almost didn't sting this time.

When he got through the second section of the book without finding anything useful, he dropped it on the chair with a sigh, leaned back, and massaged his sore eyes. He needed reading glasses, but every time he bought a pair, they got broken in a fistfight or dropped down a canyon or eaten by monstrous demon larvae.

James went to the bedroom door. Curled up in the stolen bed, Elise looked almost childlike, if he ignored the injuries. Her face was relaxed and unguarded. She didn't twitch when he sat on the edge of the bed. How long had it been since she slept?

His heart ached as he watched a curl in front of her nose sway with every breath. The urge to protect her was ridiculous. There was nothing he could fend off that she couldn't. But he knew, watching her sleep, that he would do anything to defend her. Anything.

James retrieved a page from his Book of Shadows. He touched it to her skin and whispered a word of power. The cuts closed. The bruises on her face yellowed. She sighed without waking up.

He went back to reading Hume's Almanac as darkness fell. He was beginning to doze in his chair when the sky blossomed with light and the eleventh bell chimed.

James jerked upright. Elise was already standing in the doorway, a falchion in each hand. Her hair stuck up in the back where she had been laying on it.

"Let's go," she said.

Demons poured through the streets. Pillars of flame flashed through the sky with each chime. The bells reverberated through the earth, and James clung to a tree, barely staying on his feet.

Elise slashed and stabbed, as light in her hiking boots as she could have been in toe shoes. She was locked in adagio with slavering grotesques. *Ballon, aplomb, allongé*—James's former students would have been envious to see it, if not for the splattering blood.

People shrieked and fled. James wanted to tell them to go inside, to lock themselves where it was safe, but the sky fire and ravenous horde had driven them to mindless fear.

Children fell under the jaws of the demons. Not ten feet away, a man's head was bashed against rocks. Elise danced to her silent andante, slicing through flesh and bone. Her swords glistened in the rain.

She climbed on top of a stall. Demons moved to follow, but James flung a page at them. Before the rain could soak it, he shouted.

A silent explosion rocked the air, knocking the demons off their feet as though the hand of God had swatted them aside. The ones still standing turned on James.

"Ayuda!"

An old man with his face covered in blood ran down the street. He was followed by two of the grotesques, and he reached desperately for Elise. She grabbed his forearm and hauled him onto the stall. Then she leaped down, lashing out with both feet. Skulls cracked.

Magic poured from James, swelling and crashing with the flick of paper. He was a shining light in the gloom, his Book of Shadows like a brilliant star. He set fires and brought wind upon the demons.

There were too many. Dozens. Hundreds. The jungle seethed.

He flipped through his Book of Shadows, searching for a spell that could stop everything, to save the people ripped open by blunt teeth. But then the earth rocked with the eleventh bell and he was slammed against a wall. The Book flew from his arms.

A demon crashed into him. He saw a flash of bloody tongue a heartbeat before its heavy foot mashed into the side of his knee.

James heard a wet crunch. He hit the ground. The pain struck him a few seconds later.

He roared, gripping his leg. The demon fell on him, pressing more than two hundred pounds of weight upon his chest like the crush of a boulder. Its breath stank of acid.

"James!"

Teeth ripped into his sleeve. He shoved the demon off of him, but another took its place.

And then it shrieked, blood sprayed out of its severed neck, and disappeared. Elise stood over him where its face had been. He couldn't draw enough of a breath to thank her.

She sheathed one sword before lifting. He tried to put weight on his leg and cried out. "Lean on me," she said, pulling his arm over her

43

shoulder.

"We can't go—those people—the Book—"

"I'll come back for it. Move!"

She dragged him from the village. Slowly, so slowly, they fought their way into the jungle, where the trees grew thick and the demons could not follow.

He slid to the ground with a groan.

"I think it's dislocated. My knee. I can't walk—can't feel my foot—"

Elise kneeled in front of him. His leg looked crooked through the slacks. She sliced open the pant leg, and her jaw tensed when she saw the unnatural twist of his knee cap. Seeing it made the pain worse.

"I'm going to relocate it," she said. "Try to relax."

"Maybe we should wait—"

But she had already put both hands on his leg and twisted.

When the sun rose, Elise sat in the common area of the village, wiping down her blades with a soft rag. It used to be someone's shirt, but they didn't need it anymore, and there was something immensely cathartic about cleaning blood off her falchions.

There were more bodies this time than after the tenth hour. Shopkeepers, farmers, laborers, friends and mothers and brothers. All dead. Losing so many lives was hardly a victory. It made her tense. Her neck felt like it might never unknot.

But cleaning her blades and gently oiling the metal—it was better than a professional massage, better than the comforting burn of whiskey, even better than her ex-boyfriend's ministrations. It made her feel a little less guilty to be sitting next to a child whose face had been torn off. Just a little.

Elise walked into an abandoned house. The doors had been left open, and rain made the carpet squish under her feet. She used the phone to call McIntyre.

"Fly to Guatemala. I need you here," she said.

His responding silence was long. "Elise…"

"Did you see what happened with the last bell?"

"How could I miss it? It was a massacre in the Warrens." He paused, and Elise thought she heard his girlfriend crying in the background. "You'd laugh if you saw how the news is trying to explain the deaths away. They're calling it a new outbreak of SARS. Those mundane bastards will make anything up to avoid seeing the truth."

"There won't be eyes to see if you don't help me," Elise said. "My aspis is out of commission. I need backup."

"And my aspis is pregnant."

Nausea flipped Elise's stomach. She gazed at the body on the couch. Flies were starting to cloud around it. "If you want Leticia to live to give birth, you need to help."

"Screw you," he said without real ire.

"You can be down here in twelve hours. We'll go get this together. It'll be the Grand Canyon all over again. Call some of your friends—I know you have a lot of them."

"And I'm the only one you have?"

That was probably meant to sting. "I have better things to do than make friends. Your priorities are fucked up."

This was an argument they had been through a dozen times. McIntyre switched tactics. "Would you leave James to save the world?"

Yes. That was the plan, after all.

"Just get down here," she said. She gave him the coordinates of the condominium. He said that he wrote them down. They hung up.

Elise found the Book of Shadows in a puddle of mud. Half of the pages were stuck together. She didn't need to be a witch to tell that they were ruined.

She stole a bottle of pills from an unoccupied pharmacy to soften the blow. James was covered in sweat and half-asleep when she returned to the condo on the beach. "Here," she said, folding two pills into his hand. "Sorry it took so long. Have you slept?"

"Barely."

He swallowed them while she looked at his knee. It had swollen to twice its normal size. She suspected there were torn ligaments and arterial damage—the kind of thing that would require surgery if he planned on walking again. "You'll get over this in no time," Elise lied.

He laughed. "Good thing I don't dance anymore."

She took an avocado from her jacket, sliced it lengthwise, and pried the pit out with her knife. He took half. "At least all the dead people mean we don't have to pay for food."

He stopped laughing.

By the time he ate the avocado and some plantains, James's color had improved, and he didn't look like he was in nearly as much pain. "We can't move you to a city for surgery," she said. "We don't have time."

"I know. But I think I can heal myself, with your help...and the Book

45

of Shadows."

She handed the Book to him. His face fell.

"Is it enough?" she asked.

He flipped through the pages and gave a hard swallow. "It will have to be. I can do a ritual."

"Why? You've written spells more powerful than this. You could fix yourself in a half second." She took the Book of Shadows, flipping through it to one of the pages in the very back. James jerked it out of her hands.

"All my benign healing spells were destroyed."

"So use one that isn't benign."

"Do you see this?" He turned it to show her a page. It was completely obscured with ink. "This is all I have left. It would 'fix me,' but requires a small sacrifice."

"How small?"

"If I used you as the subject, it would also render you unconscious for a week."

She couldn't afford to be useless any more than he could. She considered the page. "I could get someone else. A survivor from a nearby village."

"This spell might kill a normal person."

"That's dark magic, James. Your aunt would be ashamed."

He snapped the Book shut. "As I said, we'll use a ritual."

James made a list of supplies, and she collected everything from the village of the dead. The bodies were in the same places she had left them. Nobody was coming back to dig graves.

When she returned with the stones he needed—pried from cheap jewelry at a tourist shop—and some herbs, James had created a circle of power out of pillow feathers on the bed. "What next?" she asked, eyeing his circle dubiously. He was a powerful witch, but she wasn't sure he was powerful enough to work with such a weak circle.

"I'm weak. Let me piggyback for strength."

Elise didn't hesitate to offer him a hand.

He took it, and his magic washed through her. It sent warmth cascading from the top of her skull to her toes. Her awareness of James's senses came to her one at a time—first, the smell of rain grew stronger, and then she felt his knee (which hurt as bad as she imagined), and then she glimpsed her face as though peering through his eyes. Her cheeks and eyes were hollow. She looked skeletal.

His emotions came upon her last. He was tired. Worried. Relieved to have painkillers. Happy to see Elise. Angry at all the devastation. Once the power securely fastened around them, it faded, but Elise was left unsettled. James *felt* too much.

He leaned back against the wall with a low chuckle. "I didn't realize I looked that bad." Of course, he had seen through her eyes at the same time she saw through his.

She rubbed her own aching knee. "You're fine."

Elise followed his diagrams to apply the stones and herbs to his leg. James activated several spells from his Book and left them on the bedside as they worked.

"Careful now," he said when she pulled out the bandages.

She closed her eyes to process the information coming silently from James. He showed her the motions to make, and she did.

When she was done, he eased back against the wall with a groan. "How long?" she asked.

"I'll be dancing again by tomorrow."

Elise could tell he was lying through the bond. It would be days before he was in service again—and with a crippled Book of Shadows.

Her knee throbbed. James looked sympathetic. "I can lift the bond."

"No. You'll heal faster while piggybacked." She locked what was left of the Book in its case. "I called McIntyre again," she said, just to change the subject.

"Is he coming?"

"Yes."

"Good."

There was nothing else to say, after that.

Rain coursed down the eaves of the condo. Ocean rushed up the beach like it was going to devour them, and then receded after lapping at the wooden supports. It made the condo feel just this side of dangerous, even though James sat back on the bed. He kept Elise in the corner of his eye. She stood on the edge of the porch, and it made him nervous. He could easily imagine an errant wave rising to slap her off the balcony.

The spray blew back her hair as another crest swept toward their temporary condo. A thin layer of water sloshed over her feet. She reached out a hand so the rain drummed on her exposed fingertips, and a thrill raced through his stomach when he saw that her glove dangled from the other hand.

"Careful," James said.

She turned her hand over so the rain fell on her palm instead. "Who cares?" she muttered. "He can't get me if the world's going to end anyway."

"Let's not test the theory. Come in and close the door. Our room is getting wet."

She pretended not to hear him. She did that a lot.

James traced the outline of a symbol onto tissue paper. He could feel the power vibrating in his wrists as he wrote it. He had filled almost the entire notebook with spells before it was damaged, one at a time. He could do it again.

His aunt had been the inventor of paper magic, but he was the innovator. There were things she taught him that nobody else knew— ways to store immense, unthinkable amounts of power; methods of copying spells without performing them again; how to distort a spell after binding it to the page—and the knowledge was so dangerous that he seldom used it.

The only person he trusted to have in the room while he worked was Elise, and she wasn't paying any attention to him. She was staring at the ocean and getting soaked.

He wrote the final curl of the symbol. The page glowed with their shared power before fading.

James carefully stood, using a tall stick as a crutch to stagger to the patio. The wind gusted around him. He braced himself on the railing. "Come inside," he said.

She trailed a finger along her palm. "Do you think He can see when one of my gloves is off?"

He didn't even like discussing the subject. James grabbed her arm and slid the glove back on. "You only get this contemplative when you're exhausted. And don't forget, I can feel what you're thinking." He tapped his temple.

Elise tucked her hands against her sides. "It doesn't matter. The twelfth hour is coming soon. I should be searching."

"You can't do anything in this downpour."

Another wave sluiced over the patio. She finally went inside, helping James settle in bed again.

They sat in silence with nothing to entertain them but the thrum of magic as his knee knit itself together.

He tried to remember the last time they had sat together in comfortable silence for longer than a few minutes. James couldn't recall having ever done it before. They were always on the run. "This is nice," he said, surprising himself.

He was even more surprised when a smile spread across Elise's face. A real smile. "What if it was always like this?"

"What, if we were in a monsoon with a dislocated knee?"

"No," she said, gesturing between them. "Like…this. You and me. Not fighting. Not running."

James studied her for a long moment—damp hair stuck to her forehead, bruises on her jaw, bandages concealing her arm. "It can't ever be like this. We can't stop running."

"I know. But…what if we could?"

The question gave weight to the air between them. James was tired, and it wasn't just because of the healing. He was tired of having no home. He was tired of trying to stay a step ahead of the death that pursued them. In the past, he had imagined what would happen if he could stop, and it involved reconciling with Hannah and rejoining the coven, but James hadn't dwelled on those thoughts long. The fantasies hurt.

He tried to imagine stopping with Elise. Living a normal life. He couldn't fathom what that would be like.

"It would be nice to teach again," he said slowly. "I could start a dance company."

"I've always wanted to own a business."

"Really? I didn't know that."

She shrugged. It wasn't something they had ever discussed. "Maybe I could be in your company. I could be a professional with enough practice. I think it would be…fun."

Those were the probably most words she had ever strung together that didn't have anything to do with dying.

"You should sleep," she said, tipping a couple more pills out of the bottle on the bedside. He swallowed them. "You'll heal faster."

She was right. His eyes fell closed, and he let himself relax as the painkillers kicked in. His breathing grew deep and even, keeping time with the ocean, and he thought he could almost hear Elise's heartbeat. He could certainly feel the magic knitting his knee, even as he dozed.

The fatigue of healing and magic was powerful. It sucked him under.

He wasn't sure how long he floated in the gray haze before he felt lips on his forehead. "Take care of yourself," Elise whispered. It alarmed him on some distant level, but he couldn't rouse himself enough to figure out why.

When James woke up, the active bond had been closed, and Elise was gone.

Elise gave McIntyre sixteen hours before calling him back. He was still in Las Vegas when he answered.

"I've sent two of my friends down to help you," he said. "This guy, Bryce, and a kid called Diego—he's already close. They're going to meet you at the condo. They should only be four hours away, max."

"You're a goddamn bastard, Lucas McIntyre."

He blew air out of his lips. "Maybe you'll have a family someday. Maybe you'll understand then."

"Not a chance in hell," she said.

Bryce and Diego. Elise didn't know any kopides named Bryce and Diego, and she didn't *want* to know them. Whenever she ran across other hunters, like her, they were always a disappointment—too weak, too emotional, or too fixated on her gender. She had never met another kopis she couldn't hate, and that included her ex-boyfriend. She wouldn't go into a fight with anyone but James or McIntyre.

So Elise armed herself and went into the undercity.

The entrance was easy to locate. Demons left telltale marks to help each other find their dens: a stack of rocks, a symbol carved into a tree, a sign with demonic text written in graffiti on the back.

She found the trap door in the basement of a shop five miles away. It was dirty and smelled like a latrine, but the mark on the wall was unmistakable.

Elise descended the narrow steps. The air became still as the world above was blocked out, and soon, she only had her flashlight as a guide. When she finally reached the bottom, her legs were weak, her nerves were ragged, and one sword was drawn.

She took a deep breath and pushed through.

The undercity should have been a home away from home for the horrors that lived on Earth. It *should* have been teeming with life.

But it was motionless. The buildings were rotten from time and mildew, and faced the path with open doors. Empty.

Where were the demons?

Elise took a step forward and her foot connected with something soft.

She knew without having to look that it was a body, and once she recognized the first, she saw the rest—lumpy shapes spread across the uneven ground of the cavern.

She kneeled to examine the body at her feet. It had the same marks as the corpses of the humans on the surface. Bones gnawed by dull teeth, missing flesh, shattered skull. The tolling of the bells had struck underground, too.

Stomach acid soured the back of her mouth as she slipped through the undercity, stepping around bodies and avoiding sinkholes. Something smelled like brimstone.

She strode through the city, focusing on the path. Elise didn't want to see the racks where they hung slaves for sale. She didn't want to see the demons—many of which were indistinguishable from humans—that lay in bloody piles.

It looked so similar to Dis. There were even skulls over the doorways. They grinned at her with missing teeth and dusty eye sockets.

Many of the homes had pens in front of them, too. In Dis, it was where they kept their more docile slaves. In this undercity, there were strange, grotesque skeletons instead—unholy things that looked like a mix of pig and human. Chills rolled down her spine. She refocused on the street.

So many dead. The air was thick with it.

Elise ducked out of one cavern into the next, following a short tunnel that had been carved by a stream. It let out into a murky pool.

Something scraped on the shore. She lifted her swords, gripping the hilts so tightly that her arms trembled.

A dark form on the ground moved, then groaned. A survivor.

Elise made a wide circle around it, squinting through the dim red glow. It looked like a human, but no human had skin so papery-thin that the outlines of its bones were visible. Its eyes twitched open. They were completely black.

"*Tikest vo,*" it whispered in a quavering voice. That was the demon language. James spoke it, but Elise didn't.

"Don't move," she said.

It gave another groan, and spoke again, this time in Latin. "Help me."

Cautiously, she sheathed one of the swords and kneeled at its side. The young nightmare was dying. Its skin faded in and out of Elise's vision. For a few seconds it looked like a skeleton with a tangle of innards; then it faded back.

Nightmares couldn't be killed by physical means—it could suffer for

51

centuries without disappearing.

"I need to find the clock," she said.

A pale hand reached for her. She jerked back. "It hurts," said the nightmare. "Help me. Please."

Elise set her jaw. "Do you know where it is?" After a moment, it nodded. "I need to find it."

The skin faded. The nightmare shivered. "This path goes down," it said. "Down. Beyond the Temple of Yatam—a stair. Down, down, down."

"Is that where the chamber is?"

Its skeletal hand touched her arm. Elise's skin crawled. "The door is behind the statue." Its black eyes begged. "Please."

She didn't have her exorcism charms, but the blade of her sword was carved with some of the same symbols. She slid the falchion between two of its ribs. "*Crux sacra sit mihi lux. Non draco sit mihi dux. Vade retro, Satana, nunquam suade mihi vana. Sunt mala quae libas. Ispe venena bibas.*" The sword glowed briefly. The demon's eyes fell closed. "Return to the Hell in which you belong. Begone."

Its hand slipped off her arm, and a moment later, the body was gone. She stood over the place it had rested and stared at the empty ground. Killing demons was usually satisfying, but this time, she felt nothing.

"Be at peace," Elise said to the empty chamber, sheathing her sword. She was surprised to mean it.

There was only one other path leading down from the cavern. Elise took it. It sloped into darkness, away from the red glow of the undercity, and she followed it down, down, down.

It took her an hour to reach the Temple of Yatam. The path opened into a quiet chamber with smooth walls. A stream spilled down the rocks to her right in a frothy mist, illuminated by the flickering glow of blue flame.

The only thing that made the room look like a temple were nine columns surrounding a faceless statue. It stared at her without eyes. Elise edged around it. As the nightmare said, there was a stair behind the statue, spiraling deeper into the ground. The air grew warmer and warmer as she descended.

Distantly, through the earth, Elise could hear the clock. Every swing of its pendulum gently rocked everything around her. Rock groaned. Dust showered from the roof of the stairwell. The stairs felt like they swayed from side to side—the slightest motion that made the entire world vibrate.

Tick...tock... The clock echoed through the air.

52

At first, she didn't realize she heard it with her ears. But then she came upon a doorway and stumbled through, and she saw it.

The clock stood at the end of a very long chamber with sloping walls that rose high above her in the shape of four-sided pyramid. Elise wouldn't have been able to reach its face if she stood on James's shoulders. The mechanisms inside its body were made of glistening white stone.

The dagger-shaped pendulum rocked in time with every beat. It pulsed through her and made it hard to breathe. The hands on the face crept toward the place the twelve should have been—and all six were going to align simultaneously.

Dusty skeletons lay on platforms around the edges of the room. Scraps of red cloth hung from the bones, although time had eaten most of the robes away. They trembled with every *tick* and *tock* of the swinging pendulum.

Elise made her way through the room, stepping around metal grates that blasted hot air. She peered into one as she passed. It glowed red faintly, as though there were fires miles below.

She had to climb onto another platform to reach the body of the clock. It was almost too loud to approach. Elise drew her left-hand sword as she peered into the workings of the clock. Something throbbed in the depths of its cogs—a heart.

Why hadn't the hour struck yet?

She didn't wait to find out. There had to be attendants somewhere close.

Make it fast.

Bracing herself, Elise seized the handle on the cage of its body and swung it open.

A distant *thud* rocked the pyramid. The platform pitched beneath her feet. An invisible hand smashed into her chest, shoving her away from the clock.

She soared through the air and struck the opposite wall. The sword clattered out of her hand. Elise collapsed onto a grate and the metal seared her skin.

The *tick tock* was even louder than before. The beating heart thrummed. And when she rolled over, her face came up against a pair of bare feet. Her gaze traveled up bare legs.

The woman wore a necklace of skulls. Her dark hair was tangled with teeth, her dagger was carved of stone, and her hips were draped in folds of leather. The silhouettes of demons framed her—dozens of them. The

53

stink of brimstone was strong.

"What a surprise," said the goddess in perfect Latin.

Elise leaped for her sword.

Something connected with her head from behind. It cracked her skull and rattled her brain.

A flash of white light—and then darkness.

Elise could see the sky.

Her eyes opened to slivers. There was a window above her—an open square too small for a human to slip through. The sky was a churning mass of violet and crimson.

No, wait. That wasn't a sky at all. It was smoke from the fires beneath the clock.

Elise was still inside the pyramid. But she was in a separate room, with the same jagged gray stone and hazy air. Her eyes and throat burned with it.

She had been chained to the wall. Her hip burned, and she shifted her legs out from under her, stretching out to see a mess of blood smearing her shirt. When had she been injured?

"That came from my children. They wanted a taste."

Elise twisted around, trying to see the speaker, but the goddess stood beyond her field of vision. Her motion was limited by the shackles. "Who are you?"

The response came right behind her ear. "I am the cold kiss of death," she whispered, "and you can never defeat me."

Elise's stomach churned. "Let me go."

"No. You chose to come. Now you must live with that choice—and die for it."

"I'll kill you," she said. It wasn't a threat. Just a statement of fact.

"Maybe. Alive or dead, I will come back for you." The flames outside flared, turning the smoke from purple to orange before fading back to red. A blast of heat filled the room.

Somewhere in the pyramid, people were screaming. Human voices. Elise wasn't the only one trapped.

The goddess stepped in front of her, blocking her view of the window. In one hand, she held a staff of sharpened human bone; in the other, a stone knife carved with symbols. The whites of her eyes were consumed with the endless darkness of space.

"I didn't expect anyone to find me," she said, "much less the greatest kopis. I've heard of you."

Elise responded by twisting her wrists in the shackles. They rubbed against the skin of her right wrist, and she realized one of her gloves had been removed. She clenched her fist.

The goddess must have seen what was on her palm. She must have known what it meant. And she wouldn't have been there if she didn't need Elise alive.

"You're missing something for the clock—something that's keeping you from tearing apart Hell and Earth. It's a sacrifice, isn't it?"

"Astute," the goddess said.

Elise shifted, and her chains rattled. It wasn't hard to be astute when she was tied up like a pig waiting for the spit.

The woman kneeled in front of her. She smiled.

Then she buried the point of the knife in Elise's shoulder.

Pain flamed down her skin. She grit her teeth and took deep breaths, refusing to cry out. It only hurt worse when the goddess pulled the knife free.

"You can't think this will do any good," Elise said, her voice barely shaking. "You can't kill me yet. Not like this. Not without screwing up your apocalyptic plans."

Her laugh was deep and throaty. From anyone else, it would have been pleasant to hear.

"Who says I plan to use you?"

The goddess dragged the knife down her chest, drawing a line of pain along her skin in crimson ink. Elise's blood swelled and dripped in a line down her ribs.

I won't scream. I won't scream.

Her resolve lasted for almost an hour. The goddess lasted much longer.

Part 4: The Walking Dead

Chapter 4

RENO – MAY 2009

The afternoon arrived bright and sunny despite the steel-gray clouds lingering overhead. The sun should have warmed the air, but the light only succeeded in washing the colors out of the already-barren landscape. Beads of rain quivered underneath the letters on the street sign, *Westfield*.

Anthony Morales slowed his Jeep to a stop in front of Motion and Dance and glanced at the clock on his dashboard. Three-fifteen. Betty hadn't asked him to pick her up until four (or, as the text had said "get me or die!"), but Elise handled the finances for the coven, and she always went in on the esbats.

There was movement beyond the glass doors. It was probably Elise.

He examined his reflection in the visor mirror, trying to order his brown curls by running his fingers through his hair. Anthony only succeeded in messing it up further. He scrubbed at an oil mark on his cheek. It was the best he could do for his appearance—he couldn't make himself into Don Juan with a little spit and an attempt at a suave smirk.

He tried out the smile on himself, but it quickly faded. Smirk or not, Elise was way out of his league. She usually made him feel like nothing but Betty's kid cousin.

A man Anthony recognized as James, the high priest of Betty's coven, emerged from behind the building. He propped the open front door and went inside. All Anthony knew about the high priest came from his cousin, who liked to use adjectives like "dreamy" for him and said he was the most important person in the world to Elise.

"What kind of guy is a *witch*, anyway?" Anthony muttered to himself, climbing out of the Jeep.

Subsiding into half-coherent insults, he slammed the driver's side door and headed up the sidewalk to the front doors. He heard voices and hung back to listen, easing in sideways to see who was talking.

James and Elise were in the midst of an animated conversation. Her posture was straight, shoulders back, chin lifted, like she was ready to fight.

"You were the one who wanted me to investigate, and I did. You see this?"

"I'm sorry."

"This is serious, James, real serious, and I don't want to be involved. I don't want *you* involved."

"What will the Ramirezes do? Someone has to help them, and if—"

She cut him off. "I'm not going over this again."

All the tension drained from James's shoulders, and he leaned forward to press his lips to her forehead. She closed her eyes. He whispered something into her hair, but it was too quiet for Anthony to make out.

A swell of jealousy rose in his chest, and he bumped the door with his foot. The entrance bell jingled.

James's straightened. He glanced at Anthony without expression. "We'll talk more about this later."

Elise's mouth stretched into thin line. "Fine." James left, and she sighed, rolling her right shoulder to loosen it.

Anthony opened his mouth to speak, but words failed him—Elise always managed to render him nonverbal. Today, she wore a shirt that was swooped low in the front to reveal a lot of cleavage that he had to struggle not to look at. She was wearing gloves again—she always wore gloves—and cutoff shorts.

He cleared his throat and tried to find his voice. "Hi, Elise." He shouldn't stare at her legs, either. Really.

She sat down at the reception desk, dragging a squat filing cabinet to her side. "What are you doing here? Did you feel like taking up ballet all of a sudden?"

"No," he said. "I'm picking up Betty."

"The coven's not done for another half hour."

"I guess I lost track of the time."

The corner of Elise's mouth twitched. "That's fine. You can hang out with me while we wait for the witches to finish. They're boring when they're meditating."

"Awesome," Anthony said, and he tried not to sound *too* enthusiastic about it. He took the second chair and moved over.

The door between the entryway and the dance hall was open and James's voice echoed through the studio. "How did that meditation make you feel? Ann?"

"I felt in tune with the Earth," she responded. "It was relaxing. Finals have been crazy."

Others made assenting noises. Elise made a face at Anthony, and he grinned.

"You feel like working? There's a lot of paperwork to go through," she said. "I need to find where James stashed last year's registrations that came through the workforce education program. They have to be here. He's organized, but in the most obscure way possible."

"I would love to help," he said, and Elise turned the filing cabinet to face him.

Anthony absorbed himself in his search, trying to forget how tedious he found paperwork. She focused on her laptop, fingers ticking away at the keyboard, and Anthony shuffled through the folders. Elise's bare legs occupied the corner of his vision.

The seconds dragged. She hadn't been joking about James's bizarre methods of organization—everything was neatly tagged and labeled, but with indecipherable codes. He had no idea what "G-3B" had to do with receipts for cleaning supplies, or why the thick folder full of yellow-tabbed sheet music was marked "T6" (or why it was between the receipts and what looked like coven inventory lists), but it meant that Anthony had to read everything to figure out what it was.

He distracted himself from his chore by scooting his chair back enough to peek through the door to the next room. An assortment of women and men rested comfortably on cushions around a small altar. Smoke rose from a censer between them.

Anthony's cousin sat beside James, her blonde hair pulled into loose pigtails. She listened raptly to the high priest, nodding along with everything he said.

"As we discussed last week, Marisa's family is facing some troubles right now," James said. "An exorcist determined that Lucinde may be possessed. I believe we should partake in a cleansing ritual."

Elise began typing with renewed vigor. "Do you hear this?" he whispered.

58

"I don't listen to their crazy witch nonsense."

"Who's the exorcist?" Ann asked.

"She prefers to preserve her anonymity," James said.

"It would be so interesting to talk to her for my thesis. It's on the supernatural and old-world religion in modern times."

"I can pass along questions for you." His tone left no room for argument. "What do you all think of my proposal?"

"An exorcist," Anthony murmured. "It's like they think they're in a movie or something."

Elise typed harder.

"Do you mean actual demons, or the kind of demons we regard as goddesses, like Lilith?" asked a man whose voice Anthony didn't recognize.

"The two aren't mutually exclusive," James explained. "This one may be little more than an angry spirit, though. As such, it can be cleansed and cast out with ritual and positive energy."

"I don't think we should get into it," Ann said. "Demons are risky business."

Elise sighed and stretched in her chair, drawing Anthony's attention away from the conversations in the other room.

"It's hot in here," she said, slipping off her sweater.

He had to look. Her tanned skin was flecked with freckles, creating alluring trails that dipped down into the neckline of her shirt and out along her shoulders. He would happily explore those paths with his fingers and lips, if he could just get the balls to make a move.

And then the sweater dropped enough for him to see the gashes—three deep, parallel slices on her arm. That was what James had apologized for. Had he hurt her?

"What happened to your arm?" he asked.

"What? Oh. I got attacked by a bush when I was out running last night." She pulled her sweater back on. "It's nothing."

"I thought you said you felt hot."

"I changed my mind. I'm going to close this door, okay?" She shut it, and the coven's conversation became an inaudible mumble.

He struggled to think of something right to say. He had a hard time imagining James, who was a witch (of all the stupid things) and a dancer (even stupider) managing to injure Elise. But if he had, Anthony couldn't let it slide. He just wasn't sure he could take James in a fight.

Suppressing the wild and ridiculous urge to challenge James to a duel, Anthony held up a folder. "I think I found the registration forms."

She gave it a quick scan. "That's it. Great." Elise immediately turned her attention back to the computer. "Thanks for the help."

"Yeah, no problem," he said, and then he took a deep breath. "Maybe you'd like to hang out tonight. There's this band performing at the Knitting Factory. I know you listen to Black Death, and this band is supposed to be a lot like their early work."

"Yeah? What time?"

"Doors open at eight...but we could get dinner, if you like. Before the show."

Elise's eyes narrowed. "Are you asking me on a date?"

He gave her his attempt at a suave smile.

"Yes?"

The time until she responded dragged on. It couldn't have been longer than a moment or two, but the sudden racing of Anthony's heart made it feel like hours, and Elise's expression was unreadable.

She didn't smile at his suggestion, but she didn't laugh at him, either, which had to be a good sign.

"Yeah," Elise said. "That sounds good."

Relief washed through his body. The next second, it was replaced with nervousness. "Cool," Anthony said, jamming his fists in his pockets. "Cool. Since I'm just in the duplex next to yours, we could go together. That way, only one of us has to drive. With the price of gas and parking and stuff."

"Oh yeah. Gas is a huge concern from here to downtown," she said. "I have things to do tonight, so I don't have time for dinner, but I can meet you for the concert."

"Then it's a date," he said.

Elise nodded, turned back to her laptop, and started typing again.

Why did he feel even more nervous now than before he had asked her out?

The door between the rooms opened, and the coven emerged. James exited first, accompanied by a leggy strawberry-blond.

"We'll need more information on Lucinde before we decide to do a cleansing," the woman said. "I don't feel comfortable performing a ritual unless we've ruled out a health problem."

"What do you suggest?"

"Lucinde has had extended hospital stays, so her medical records should be there," Stephanie said. "I could look at them."

James cast a glance at Elise. "We should discuss this somewhere quieter. Come upstairs."

60

Ann trailed behind the last of the coven. Her ratty brown hair was pulled into a ponytail at the nape of her neck. She hauled a heavy backpack over her shoulder and wandered over, waving at Elise.

"Hi guys," she snuffled, digging through her pockets and coming up with a packet of tissues.

He gave a weak wave. Through Betty's chronic inability to dislike people, she had managed to collect some bizarre friends over the years—Elise included—but Ann might have been the weirdest. She was an undergraduate at the university where Betty worked on her thesis. They met at the library while researching obscure blood diseases, which led to Ann joining the coven, and now she was Betty's latest pet project.

"Weird stuff, huh?" Ann asked Elise.

She didn't look up. "Yes."

"What do you think about this whole thing with Marisa's daughter?"

"I don't think much about it at all."

"Just seems too bad, you know?" Ann stepped closer to allow Morrighan to pass, and Elise rolled her chair a few inches back. "Poor kid. Still going to the gym tonight?"

Anthony stole a look at Elise. She had finally given her attention to Ann. He had no idea what her expression meant, but if Elise ever looked at him like that, he would have run in the opposite direction. "Yes."

"Guess I'll see you there. Bye!" She lurched out of the studio. The heavy backpack on her shoulder gave her a lopsided walk.

A squealing golden blur struck Anthony in the side, and he staggered.

"You came!" Betty exclaimed, squeezing her cousin tight. Anthony made a gurgling noise.

Elise's cold look dissolved. "Did you leave any espresso at the Starbucks you violated?"

"I only had two triple fraps this morning," she said, and then she gave Anthony another squeeze. Betty was not a small girl—she was equal to Anthony in both height and weight, and he had to struggle to breathe.

"Why does Ann know we're going to the gym tonight?" Elise asked.

Betty released Anthony. "Ooh. I invited her to come along. That's okay, right?"

"The gym is a public place."

"Yeah, but I invited her to come, you know, work out with us. She looks like she could use some exercise, and I know she's got to be lonely going to college so far from her parents, so *please* tell me you were nice to her."

Elise chose not to respond, turning back to the computer instead.

61

"She was…polite," Anthony said. Betty rolled her eyes.

"Elise! Did you *have* to scare her?"

"I said she was polite," he protested.

"Yeah, but I know my roommate better than that. Look, if it's a problem, you can skip the gym tonight and I'll just hang out with Ann. Okay?"

"I don't mind," Elise said, although it sounded like she did mind very, very much. "I have to take these papers back to my office before we can work out. I'm going to go."

"Yeah, yeah. I should change clothes anyway. I'm not exactly exercise-appropriate right now." Betty pointed at her breasts, which were very prominently displayed in what was probably a continuing attempt to get James to look at them. "Ready, cuz?"

"Sure," Anthony said reluctantly. "Let's go."

"Cool," Betty said. "See you later, Elise!" She dragged him away by the elbow. "Come on, I want time to shower, too."

Anthony sighed. "I don't see why you want to shower *before* you go get sweaty."

"One day I'll explain the concept of 'looking sexy for hot guys at the gym' to you," she said, ruffling his hair affectionately. "I heard you making plans with my foxy best friend. What are you guys doing tonight?"

"What? Nothing," Anthony said, reaching in to unlock Betty's door.

She shot Anthony a sly look. "Don't give me that. I heard you flirting with Elise."

His cheeks heated. Oh God. Now Betty was never going to let him forget it. "I was helping her find some papers, and we talked a little. That's all. We were talking."

"Shopping amongst the cougars, huh? I thought I'd raised you better than that."

"You're sick, Betty."

"What were you talking about?"

She was staring at him, and Anthony had to say *something*. He thought of the gashes on Elise's arms, and her long legs, and James confronting Elise about her injuries. He thought of her smile and the Knitting Factory, and secretive high priests with exorcists on-call.

But he only shrugged.

"Just the usual stuff," Anthony said.

A half an hour later, Elise hadn't left for the office. She was still staring at the same cell on the spreadsheet with her fingers poised over the number pad.

Anthony had asked her on a date. It was…well, weird. Elise had only dated one guy before—another kopis, back when she was eighteen. He turned out to be a total waste of oxygen, but Elise's life had been too dangerous to share with anyone anyway. A normal guy like Anthony wouldn't have stood a chance.

Things had changed since then, but she still hadn't been on a date in years. Sex was nothing but a distant memory. Elise wasn't sure if she was excited, confused, terrified, or all of the above.

James wandered back inside the entryway, Stephanie at his side.

"Thank you for your help," he said.

"It's for Lucinde," the doctor said firmly, twisting a key off her key ring. Her fingers lingered on his when she passed it over.

"I'll return this to you tonight."

"I look forward to seeing you." She strode out of the room, three-inch heels ringing out against the wooden floor. Stephanie smelled like she bathed in Victoria's Secret perfume, and the scent mingled poorly with the odor of incense.

"The doctor has a great bedside manner," Elise remarked.

"We're going to retrieve Lucinde's hospital records tonight. Stephanie wants to be certain that there isn't some other problem we need to address before taking care of the metaphysical end of things, but she can't walk out with Lucinde's records for no reason."

"She's a better candidate for it than we are."

"She also has a meeting with the board scheduled. It's more convenient if we take them."

"That's called stealing, James," Elise said. "She could get a slap on the wrist for taking them. We'll get arrested."

James pinched the bridge of his nose and sighed. "We have the key to the records room, which is usually unattended at night, so we won't get caught if we're quick about it. You don't have to come."

She gathered the papers on the desk. "This is a bad idea."

"Fine, then I'll—"

"I'm not going to let you do it alone. I'll come along." Elise hugged the folder to her chest, taking a deep breath and letting it out slowly. "Look…you know I don't care about stealing, but we can't take long. I have plans."

"Plans?"

"Yeah. I'm about to go to the gym, and then I have a date."

James took a few seconds to respond.

"A date. I'm glad to hear it."

Elise's eyes narrowed. "You're not mad? You hated my last boyfriend."

"You were eighteen and he was an idiot. You should have fun." He checked his watch. "When do you want to go over to the hospital? I was thinking seven."

"That's fine."

James left to clean up the altar in the other room. "If he's so certain dating Anthony is okay, then why aren't I?" Elise asked the empty entryway. Unsurprisingly, it didn't respond.

She stopped by the bank to deposit David Nicholas's check before going to the gym. It made her feel warm to look on his signature and recall his expression as he slashed it underneath that large number, and Elise couldn't wait to turn those warm feelings into her half of rent for the month.

"This check is bad," the teller announced.

Elise had been drifting in a daydream of being able to pay off her credit card, but this announcement brought her back to reality as quickly as a blow from a hammer.

"What?"

"This check is bad," he repeated slowly, one word at a time. "There's a twelve dollar fine for attempting to cash a bad check. If you go down to the office of the—"

"How the hell is it *bad*?"

He typed at his terminal, looking bored. "This account number belongs to our bank, but it's been closed for a year. No money. Bad check. Twelve dollar fine. Understand?"

Elise made two mental notes: Firstly, that she should use a credit union instead of a bank apparently staffed by pure evil, and secondly, that David Nicholas was going to die.

The teller shredded the check as Elise watched, and her heart dropped into her stomach.

"Have a nice day," he said with a big smile.

Chapter 5

ELISE AND JAMES pulled into the parking lot in front of the hospital as the sun dropped behind the mountains, setting the sky aflame. A wet chill lowered the temperature several degrees. She shivered and shrunk into her coat.

"Nice summer we have coming along," she muttered.

James locked the car. "Let's get inside."

They passed through the hospital doors and all sound died. It felt as though the volume on life had been turned down low in the empty halls.

James glanced down at his watch. "Stephanie said the records room is empty during shift turnover. If we head down now, we should have enough time to get in and out before someone comes down."

"What happens if we get caught?"

He smiled mirthlessly. "We get arrested."

Her forehead throbbed with the first signs of a headache. She shut her eyes and pressed the heel of her palm against her temple. "That doctor of yours better help us out if we get in trouble. It's her fault we're here in the first place."

"But it isn't her fault Augustin Ramirez refused to cooperate with us," James said. A sharp pain lanced through Elise's skull, and she gave a small gasp. "Are you all right?"

"I don't know what's wrong. I feel strange. Almost as though..."

Almost as though there was something that didn't belong in a hospital.

She let out a slow breath and stretched out her senses, probing the strange presence.

"Elise?" James asked when she was silent for too long.

"It's a demon," she said. "Faint. Weak."

"An actual demon, or one of the Gray?"

She tilted her head to the side as if trying to catch the faint strains of a distant song. It made her ache from crown to jaw. "Hellborn."

"What's it doing in a Catholic hospital?"

"I would love to find out." Elise punched the down button.

The elevator began to lower, and Elise's sense of the hellborn grew stronger by every inch they dropped. She covered her eyes with the heels of her palms, pressing gently, as though she could squeeze the uncomfortable itch out of her skull.

The doors opened on the basement level, and James consulted a map Stephanie had scribbled on the dance studio's stationary.

"The medical records office is over here," James said, peering through a door with a window. "There should be a fax machine inside."

"Okay," Elise said. "Watch the hall."

She slipped into the records room. It was a long room filled with shelves, and at the far end stood a desk and plastic chair.

It clearly wasn't designed to be comfortable for human occupation: the walls were concrete and water-stained, and the carpet was hardly in better condition. The only lights were harsh and unsteady, flickering on when Elise flipped the light switch.

She went along the side of the room, searching for the records that began with R. She found them quickly, but locating Lucinde's records in particular was much more difficult. There were so many folders all over the place—she couldn't imagine how the hospital hadn't moved to digital records yet.

She thumbed through the names. Rand. Randall. Ramirez. *Success.*

Elise skimmed Lucinde's records as she began feeding them through. She continued to skim the second part of the stack, which contained duplicate records from Lucinde's general practitioner. Chicken pox, a case of the flu, referrals to several cardiologists over the years. Elise didn't see anything about psychoses.

Each sheet of paper seemed to take forever to feed through the machine, and slow inch by slow inch she grew more nervous. She strained to detect any noise from the hallway, half-certain she would hear James failing to ward off a nurse outside. With David Nicholas's bounced check, she definitely couldn't afford an attorney.

The fax kicked out the rest of the papers and beeped. She put them back in the folder.

A pulsing noise throbbed between Elise's ears. The pit of her stomach dropped, and a familiar nausea crept through Elise's body. She slid the folder into place and headed for the door, holding her stomach.

And then the pulse *burst*.

She staggered, slamming against the wall. Her dinnertime snack of yogurt and granola rose into her throat. She took slow, shallow breaths, trying to hold off the urge to vomit—and failed. The sour tang of bile flooded her mouth.

There was something in the hospital, and James was alone outside.

She spat into the trash can, wiped her mouth with the back of her hand, and threw open the door.

James was not waiting for Elise outside.

For a second, all she could do was stare at the naked man standing where her aspis should have been. He wasn't breathing. In fact, he didn't look like he was alive at all. A toe tag dragged on the ground beside him.

She would have been sure he was a corpse, except that he was standing, and staring, and drooling. Corpses couldn't drool.

Someone whispered behind Elise. *"Take care of her."*

She spun, but the hall behind her stretched empty. A light flickered several feet down.

A heavy weight slammed into Elise's side, and all the breath rushed out of her body. She struck the floor an instant later. Pain exploded in her shoulder.

Elise squirmed out from under his body, freeing her legs so that her foot could lash out. The kick landed in his face. He reeled, unable to get his balance. Another kick, and he collapsed.

His shoulders twitched, and a shudder ran through his body. His mouth flopped open, and his tongue rolled out, covered in thick green mucous.

"Elise," he said from the floor. His mouth didn't move to articulate the words, and the voice was garbled and echoing. He almost sounded… feminine. "I wish you hadn't become involved."

She stared. *"What?"*

The hallway lights flickered once, and went out completely.

Elise backtracked and hit the wall. She blinked rapidly, trying to make out shapes in the darkness, but the only light came from around the corner, and it wasn't enough.

Something moved, slipping across the floor, scraping on the linoleum.

She spun, trying to face the source of the noise. It moved behind her, and she raised her fists. "Who's there?" Elise said, trying to sound calm. Adrenaline sang through her veins.

More noises. Almost like…claws.

To her right.

She twisted, but not quickly enough. Pain flamed across her torso.

She cried out, clutching her stomach. Elise could almost see bulbous eyes sparkle in the darkness, but it darted away before she could focus.

She threw herself at the motion and barreled into something living.

They rolled. Elise punched blindly and was rewarded with the shriek of something inhuman, something terrible. Another fiend. She threw her body weight to roll it over, grabbing at what she hoped was its neck and pressing against the linoleum.

"Who do you work for?" she demanded.

It choked.

Something struck the back of Elise's head. A gong chimed in her skull, shooting pain down her spine, and she fell.

The fiend scrabbled away. It sounded like the footsteps moved all around her, up and down, inside her skull.

The noise faded. She floated in a sea of her own pulse, trying to feel her limbs. Her fingers twitched, and then her toes. *Thank God.*

Where had they gone?

"Elise?"

Lights flared on. Elise moaned, covering her eyes. The pressure in her head had suddenly disappeared, and despite the pain in every inch of her body, she felt better. The fiends—and the body—were gone.

"James," she groaned. "Help me up." He knelt by her side and lifted her into a sitting position.

"Are you okay?" he asked, touching her arms, her forehead, her shoulders, her neck. When his fingers brushed the back of her head, she flinched.

"Yeah," Elise groaned. "But...don't touch that again. Where did you go?"

"A nurse passed and I had to ask her where the bathroom was to allay suspicion," he said. "I doubled back as soon as I could. How bad are you hurt?"

"I could be a hell of a lot worse." She parted her jacket to check out her stomach. "Oh, damn. I liked this shirt." It was torn into bloody shreds.

"We need to get you upstairs. What happened?" he asked, helping Elise stand.

"That thing I was feeling earlier," she said. "It was a fiend. And something else, too."

"A fiend?"

68

She stumbled when she tried to stand. James caught her. "They're these little gargoyle-looking demon things." Elise touched her fingers to the back of her head. They came away clean. "I don't think they like me."

"At least we're in the right place for horrible injuries."

"I'm fine," she said. "All I need is a shot of whiskey and an aspirin."

"I want Stephanie to check you out," he said. Elise groaned. "Head injuries are dangerous things. We'll want that looked at." She didn't respond, so he went on. "You're saying a lesser hellborn was just wandering the hospital?"

"Not quite." They got into the elevator, and she leaned against the wall. Even that small motion made her ache. "The fiend was with someone. I don't know who. He was dead."

James stared. "...Dead."

"Yeah." The elevator chimed and began to move. "There was a toe tag on his foot and his skin was blue. He looked like he'd been dead for a couple days."

"So the fiend was dragging him."

"No."

"How was it moving him, then?"

"You're not getting what I'm saying," Elise said. "He attacked me. He was animate, but...unconscious."

"A zombie," James said.

"I guess. Damn, my head hurts."

"Hold still. We're nearly there."

They got off at the ground level, and James guided Elise toward the nurse's station. He interrupted a passing candy striper. "Excuse me, but do you know where Dr. Whyte is at the moment?"

"She just went that way." The girl pointed.

Just around the corner, Stephanie spoke to a pair of men in suits clutching attaché cases. She took one look at the blood on Elise's shirt and excused herself, ushering James and Elise into an empty room.

"What happened?" the doctor asked, snapping on a pair of blue latex gloves.

"I got in a fight. Something—someone—hit me in the back of the head."

Stephanie nodded. "Sit."

Elise perched herself on the bed, and Stephanie drew a chair up to her side. The doctor thumbed open Elise's eyelids. She had a second to register Stephanie's badge—Dr. Whyte, with so many degrees after her name they almost didn't fit—before a bright light blinded her.

69

"What year is it?"

"Two thousand nine."

"Hold still. What's your full name?"

"Elise Christine Kavanagh."

Stephanie shone the light in her other eye. "Good. Move your arms. Good. And your legs." She grabbed a blood pressure cuff off the wall and gestured for Elise to remove her coat. "Hold still for a minute."

"Is she okay?" James asked, hovering nearby as Stephanie worked.

After a handful of quiet seconds, the doctor took the stethoscope out of her ears again and removed the cuff. "If someone was trying to hurt you badly, they failed. Here, have a couple of these." Stephanie pulled a bottle of extra-strength headache medicine out of her pocket. "For the next few days, you need to watch out for headaches, sudden fatigue, difficulties with speech or sight. If you experience any of these symptoms, call an ambulance. What happened to your abdomen?"

"Fight with a rabid badger," she said curtly. "Do you have time to look at it or not?"

"I could be spending this time making friends with the directors." Stephanie pressed a thermometer to Elise's forehead. "You're surprisingly healthy for fighting badgers. Take off your shirt and lay back." She grit her teeth and lifted her shirt over her head. The skin below her strapless bra was torn and bloody. Purple bruises were rapidly rising on her torso. "When did you get in this fight?"

"Just a few minutes ago."

"Interesting. This looks hours old." Stephanie probed Elise's stomach with her fingers. "Did you two get what we need?"

"Yes," James said, slipping the key into her jacket pocket. "Thank you."

"How did it look?"

"You're the professional. You'll have to decide," Elise said. "Ouch. Is this necessary?"

"Does it hurt more when I press down or when I release?"

"When you press down."

"Lucky for you, all this blood isn't a sign of internal damage." She examined the scratches on Elise's arm from the night before. "Are you a frequent visitor to my emergency room?"

"No, I usually treat my own wounds," she said, pulling her arm away from Stephanie.

"Well, in *that* case..." She worked quickly—and not gently. Stephanie wrapped bandages around Elise's torso to hold the sterile pads in place.

"You two better get out of here. I'll review Lucinde's files later. Do you think you can get the coven together again tomorrow?"

"I'll do what I can," James said. "You have my phone number if you'd like to come over and look at the files, Stephanie."

"Come on," Elise interrupted, hopping off the table as she buttoned her jacket over the bandages, "let's get out of here. I have a concert to attend."

Chapter 6

ELISE WOKE UP tangled in blood-stained sheets.

Her first panicked thought was that she had been attacked overnight. She found the dagger under her pillow and gripped it like a teddy bear, staring around for signs of danger.

When nothing jumped out, she finally remembered her visit to the hospital. Dancing at the concert afterward must have been too much for her new wounds, and judging by the condition of her bed, she had been thrashing in her sleep, too.

She peeled back her bandages to examine the injuries. The bruises were already yellowing. Healing faster than the average person meant she would be back to normal by the end of the weekend as long as she took care of herself, but dancing had ripped open her scabs. Her skin was slick with blood.

"Shit," she muttered.

Elise showered in scalding-hot water, bracing her hands against the wall and letting her head hang between her shoulders. The water coursing down her skin stung her injuries.

Her nightmares were getting vivid again. She used to dream about the dead every night, and it was all returning because of James and his goddamn hero complex. Two fights with fiends were more than enough to get the memories flowing.

But she hadn't been dreaming of death last night. Instead, she had been remembering the day she woke up in the Russian wilderness with James standing over her like an angel.

She toweled off and rewrapped her injuries. Normally, she would have jogged to Motion and Dance for breakfast with James, but she needed to heal. Instead, she started a pot of coffee for Betty and hopped in her car to drive over.

There were already four other cars in the parking lot when she arrived. Elise's eyes narrowed. Motion and Dance didn't have any morning classes on the weekend.

James's apartment was filled with the smell of pancakes and an entire coven's worth of witches.

Elise stood in the doorway, staring at everyone intruding on their weekend breakfast. Ann and Morrighan chatted on the couch while Stephanie stared down a griddle covered in batter and sausages as though she had never cooked breakfast in her life.

The doctor was wearing the same clothes as the night before. She must have spent the night.

Elise felt numb as she shucked her jacket. So James and Stephanie were together. How long had that been happening?

"You made it!" Ann said brightly. She was eating a piece of toast smothered in jelly. A spot of butter dotted her chin.

"What are you all doing here?"

"We're going to visit the Ramirezes today to purify their house," Morrighan said. "We're getting ready. Are you coming?"

Elise fought to suppress her irritation. "No."

"Why not?" Stephanie asked.

She stared back in silent challenge.

James must have heard the door shut, because he peered out of his bedroom at the end of the hall. He had a phone pressed to his ear. "Elise," he called. "Could you please come here?"

She stepped into his bedroom. "You didn't tell me we were going to have company," Elise muttered. His private space was just as tidy as the rest of his house. He had even arranged Stephanie's shoes next to his own in the closet. "Who's on the phone?"

"It's McIntyre. He wants to speak to you."

Surprise melted away her anger in an instant. "McIntyre? Seriously?" She took the phone. "This is Elise."

"Hey there," he responded. Lucas McIntyre's voice flooded her with memories—mostly bad ones.

"What's do you need?" Elise asked. James hovered over her shoulder to listen to their conversation.

"The semi-centennial summit is coming," McIntyre said. "It's in our state. I thought you would want to know."

Every fifty years, the major world powers met to form treaties and settle disputes—the best of the kopides, the greatest demons, and the

73

most powerful angels. Her father had been on the planning board before he left.

"You're right. I do want to know. But I'm still retired."

"Still?"

"It's supposed to be permanent."

"I just never thought you, of all people, could lay down the sword for long." He chuckled. "I thought if you did give up those things, it would be to upgrade to guns."

"The summit is your problem, not mine."

"Sure, but they've taken over Silver Wells. There's also going be a lot of traffic through the state for the next few months. The travel licenses between Hell and Earth have been sold out and demons are starting to move in."

Elise and James exchanged glances. "Do you have a list of the summit participants?"

"My friend on the board gave me one. I can email it to you. Long story short, there might be some folk who recognize you. If you want to stay out of trouble, you better be careful."

Elise massaged her temple. "Great. Thanks."

"Leticia wants to talk to you. Here you go."

She talked with McIntyre's wife for a few minutes. Leticia chatted about Dana, their first child, and the names they were planning for the second one, due around Thanksgiving.

When she couldn't tolerate any more family gossip, Elise said, "I'm going to get going. Tell Lucas thanks."

"We're thrilled to help," Leticia said. "You haven't visited us in years. Promise you'll come down soon so we can catch up?"

"Of course. Talk to you later." Elise handed James the phone. "I'll visit them as soon as Hell throws us a pizza party. Did you call McIntyre, or did he call you?"

"He called me. He doesn't have your number anymore."

"That's not an accident. I don't want anything to do with this. And you should have told me you were going to have the witches over during breakfast." She barely refrained from remarking on Stephanie's shoes.

James frowned. "I hoped you would come with us today."

"Nobody else needs to know that I'm a kopis and exorcist. The Ramirezes are bad enough."

He sighed, running a hand through his hair. "Elise…"

"I'm going to the office to do some work."

"Are you angry about Stephanie?" he asked. She left the room without responding, but he followed. "Won't you at least eat something before you go?"

Elise grabbed a piece of bacon off a plate on the counter and bit off the end. The witches were all standing in the living room now, and they pretended not to notice that James and Elise were obviously arguing.

"Feel free to call me when you finish if you're not too busy fucking around," she said, tearing her sweater off the hook by the door.

She slammed the door shut behind her.

Chapter 7

EVEN THOUGH IT was drizzling again, Augustin Ramirez was waiting outside when James and arrived with the coven. The umbrella on his deck's dining set was folded down. Raindrops rippled in a tall glass of amber liquor.

He lifted his head from his hands when they approached. "What took you so long?" he asked.

Stephanie didn't bother hiding her severe frown. "We needed to confirm your daughter's health condition, since you wouldn't cooperate with us. Where is she now?"

Augustin waved vaguely at the front door of the house.

"Can we go in?" James asked.

The lawyer nodded and let his head drop on his folded arms. Ann was the first through the door, hurrying inside as though she was allergic to rain. Morrighan followed, holding her bag of supplies over her head as a makeshift umbrella.

James hesitated by Augustin. "Has anything changed?"

"Why can't you people just leave us alone?" Augustin asked without looking up. "We were fine two weeks ago. Lucinde had a ballet recital. She was fine."

It was hard to get angry when he looked so pathetic. "Hopefully we can leave you alone very soon, Mr. Ramirez," James said. "This shouldn't take long. Would you please come inside with us? The weather is only going to get worse."

Augustin didn't move.

James went inside to find the other three witches clustered near the front door, huddled together for support. He couldn't blame them—the house had been miserable when he first visited, but it had gotten worse.

The air was freezing. It smelled stale. Every window was closed and the lights were turned off.

And they could hear screaming.

All of them turned to look at the stairs. Something heavy was banged against the floor, and each thud made the wall photos bounce and rattle. One had already fallen off its nail and shattered on the steps.

That noise didn't sound like it came out of the lungs of a little girl. It didn't sound like it came from a human at all.

"I'm going to check on Lucinde," Stephanie said, but she didn't go for the stairs. Instead, she slid back until she could grab James's hand with clammy fingers.

A slip of paper on the mantle caught his eye. It was Elise's business card. James slipped it into his pocket, hoping nobody would notice, but Ann was watching.

"Where's Marisa?" she asked.

"She's most likely upstairs with her daughter." James took a deep breath and straightened his back. "Right. Let's get this done. Morrighan and Ann, bring out the smudges. I'll find somewhere to cast the circle."

His orders were enough to get everyone moving. They broke apart. Stephanie crept upstairs while Morrighan began removing things from her duffle bag. "Think we can open the windows and stuff?" she asked. "Everything in here now is doused with negative energy. It's horrible."

"Hold onto that thought. We should speak to Marisa first," he said.

Stephanie reappeared on the landing almost as soon as she left. "James?"

He joined her upstairs. The air felt heavier in the hallway, like James was moving through thick, murky water. He had to struggle to breathe.

"What's wrong?"

Stephanie pointed. He peered down the dark hall to see a shadowy form huddled against Lucinde's door. Marisa.

James knelt beside her. Her eyes were puffy and her nail polish had been chipped off until there were only a few flakes left. She hugged her knees to her chest. "It's getting worse," she whispered. He could barely hear her over the screaming and pounding.

"We're going to cleanse your house of all these negative energies and drive out whatever is hurting your daughter." He didn't speak with any conviction. He wished that Elise would have come.

When James moved to stand, she grabbed his arm, holding him in place. "You don't understand. It's not supposed to get worse. She's supposed to get better."

"Yes, I know, but—"

Marisa's chin quivered. "She's going to die."

"Nobody is going to die. We're going to open the curtains and windows. All right?"

"No! You can't do that! You'll hurt her, and she's already..." Her chest hitched. "She's already in so much pain. This isn't supposed to happen. She's supposed to get *better*."

James didn't realize Stephanie was standing behind him until she spoke. "I should check on your daughter."

Marisa shook her head. "She's out of control."

"I'm used to difficult patients."

He cut off Stephanie with a slash of his hand. "This isn't the time. Will you help us with the ritual, Marisa?"

She shook her head. A line of white rimmed her lips.

When they returned to Ann and Morrighan, they were parting the curtains and throwing open the windows. They had already positioned censers in every doorway. The smell of white sage drifted through the air. Lucinde screamed louder.

James did a quick search of the rooms downstairs and decided to cast the circle in the kitchen, where a ring of salt would be the easiest to clean up. It was also positioned directly beneath Lucinde's room.

He and Stephanie lit candles, laid out stones on each of the cardinal directions, and called the other witches into the kitchen without closing the circle. He handed each of them photocopies of the ritual. "You three should stay down here within the protection of the circle," he said. "Focus on the incantation."

"What are you going to do?" Stephanie asked.

"I'm going upstairs."

Ann paled. "Is that a good idea?"

He didn't think it was, but James smiled and nodded anyway. "Of course. You can begin the ritual as soon as I'm gone."

Stephanie sealed the circle behind him. The three women began chanting together. James could have spoken it along with them without glancing at the Book of Shadows—he had written the ritual himself, and they had used it before to great success.

Of course, they had never had to cleanse anything as horrible as Lucinde before, either.

With every step he took toward the locked bedroom, James became more and more certain that the ritual would be ineffective. The idea of using traditional magic against whatever had seized the house seemed

78

ridiculous. It was like waving a cardboard sword at a dragon.

Marisa had vanished from the hallway upstairs. A cold fist clenched in his chest.

And Lucinde suddenly fell silent.

He froze for a moment, heart pounding. He strained to hear something within her room—a hint of motion, or a whimper. But there was nothing.

Her door was unlocked. He pushed it open.

His eyes adjusted slowly to the darkness. The portable swamp cooler was on its side. Something dark was on the white bed sheets—something wet.

And the little girl was crouched in the center of it.

She grinned. Her teeth were stained red.

"Lucinde?" James asked. He wasn't speaking to Augustin Ramirez's daughter. He dropped his voice, hand tight on the doorknob. "What are you?"

"I am the cold kiss of Death," she rasped. "And you're next, James Faulkner."

She leaped off the bed with a shriek, hands extended.

He jumped back and slammed the door shut. Her body thumped into the other side. The wood groaned and the entire house shuddered from the impact.

Downstairs, the witches weren't chanting anymore.

"I told you, she's going to die," Marisa whispered. James spun to see her wavering in her doorway. He thought her hands looked bloody, too, but the vision cleared when he blinked. She was clean.

Lucinde was screaming again.

"What happened?" Stephanie asked when he came downstairs. All the candles had gone out, but there was no other indication anything had changed.

"Pack up. We can't do anything," James said grimly.

"What are you going to do?" Ann asked as Morrighan grabbed a broom and began to sweep up the salt. James didn't know how to respond.

Elise was wrong. Lucinde was definitely possessed.

Augustin didn't look up when they left the front door. Stephanie was dragging her feet, reluctant to leave without checking on Lucinde, but James kept a firm grip on her arm so she couldn't go back. He had seen possessions leap between people before.

"I'm going to return with reinforcements," James told Augustin while the other witches loaded the car. "I'm sorry."

The lawyer stood silently, went inside, and locked the door. By the time they pulled away, all the windows and curtains were shut again.

Chapter 8

THE PARKING LOT outside Elise's office was empty when she arrived, so she didn't have to hide the stack of unusual books she carried into her office: The Infernal Lexicon and Hume's Almanac, both of which were large, leather-bound texts that could hardly pass as light reading.

She shut her office door with a hip bump and settled in to reread the list McIntyre had sent her. Elise recognized many of the demons without looking them up; her father had drilled her on many of them as a child. The shedu had no interest in the dead, nor did Aquiel and his kin, and she marked them off. Those too weak to command fiends were also immediately crossed out. She halved the list in minutes.

Even after her eliminations, hundreds remained. It could take days to check them all.

Considering the alternative was following James around while he tried to relive his glorious youth of saving people, she decided she would much rather have the tedium. Elise started a pot of coffee, found a notebook, and began to work.

For hours, she searched. Elise immersed herself in the lore of Hell as shadows crept across her office floor, filling and refilling her mug. She covered an entire notebook page with writing. Then another. And another. Outside, the clouds moved in, and the sun inched toward the mountains. By the time she started on her third pot of coffee, her handwriting looked more like a series of tiny, angry slashes than language.

After a while, her attention wandered. Demons were boring. Elise had recently downloaded a book on ethereal lore, so she started researching the names of the angelic attendants instead. A single angel could match a thousand demons in power, but their snobbish attitudes meant they seldom lowered themselves to visiting the earthen planes.

Ethereal mythology was much more interesting than that of their infernal counterparts. A couple big names were going to the summit. Gabriel himself would make an appearance.

She read his section in her book, then scanned up to the Metaraon— the voice of God. There was an engraving of his face, unmerciful and cold. It gave her chills.

Elise had read his chapter before. He hired architects to construct seven angelic cities on Earth. There weren't any left—the angels abandoned them in centuries past. But there were supposed to be ruins left in some places.

In fact, they said angelic ruins were buried deep below the Sierra Nevada Mountains. Elise stared at the Metaraon's face and drummed a pen against her desk.

The ruins should have prevented most demons from possessing anyone nearby. It wouldn't be any minor lord stealing bodies and attacking Lucinde. Whatever it was had to be huge.

Her door opened, and Elise's hand dropped to a hidden dagger. The visitor came in back-first, but she recognized his broad shoulders and dirty shoes.

"Knock, knock," Anthony said. He cradled two large coffees and a brown bag to his chest, and he set them on the edge of her desk with a smile. "What are you doing?"

"Anthony," Elise said, flipping over her notebook and sliding it on top of the Infernal Lexicon. "Hey. I'm just doing some work."

A smile played at the corners of his lips. His hair was extra tousled, his t-shirt wrinkled, and there was an oily hand print on his jeans. "Secret work?"

"No." She didn't try to sound convincing, but he didn't seem to care.

"Betty told me you were working on the weekend," Anthony said, offering one of the coffees to her. "I thought you might need some energy...but I can see that's not really a problem." Dirty mugs were scattered around her office, and a new pot was percolating on her filing cabinet.

Elise took a deep sniff of the latte. "This is much better than what I've been having. Thanks."

"I got you a muffin, too," he said in a hopeful tone.

"Great," she said, sliding her books and notes into a desk drawer. Anthony leaned around to read the spines, but Elise shut it too fast. "What are you up to?"

"I just got off work and was on my way to meet Betty, but I thought I'd visit you first. Are you busy?"

Elise stood. Her back ached. The clock told her she had been hunched over her desk for over eight hours. Her injuries from the night before had stiffened.

She checked her cell phone, which had been on silent. Seven missed calls from James. Great.

"No, I'm not busy." She put her phone back in her pocket. "Don't let me get in the way of meeting Betty. I know she goes nuts if you're late at all."

"Let me walk you to your car."

"I'm right outside the door."

"Well...me too." Anthony ducked his head, peeking at her through his bangs. "Did you have fun last night?"

It took Elise a moment to realize what he was talking about. She had almost forgotten about their date. "Oh, yeah. The band was really good."

"I never saw you like that before."

"Like what?"

He flashed a grin. "You know...having fun."

"Did I embarrass myself?"

"No, of course not. It's nice." Elise arched an eyebrow at him, and he hurried to add, "I mean, you're always so serious. It's like some black cloud is following you around."

"A black cloud," she echoed—and then, surprisingly, she laughed. "I guess that's a fair description."

Elise locked the office door and headed down the hall. Anthony's hand stuck out at his side, and she got the impression he wanted her to take it. She pretended she didn't notice.

His Jeep was beside Elise's car just outside the building doors. "Thanks for walking me," she said. Elise moved to get into the driver's seat, but Anthony stopped her, grabbing onto the door.

"Maybe you want to hang out with me tonight?" he said. A pink flush had risen on his cheeks. "I mean, if you're done for the day, I just have to see Betty for a few minutes. We could go down for a walk by the river or something."

Elise studied him, head tilted to the side. Was she that intimidating, or was he just a nervous person? "You can just ask me on a date, you know."

"Oh. Okay. So, do you...?"

"Yes," Elise said. And then, to save him from the stuttering, she added, "Nine o'clock."

83

"Nine. Awesome."

She tried to get into the car, but he didn't let go of her door. He stepped in close, shadowing her from the sun, and she had to tilt her head back to look at him.

"Anthony, I don't—"

He bent down and kissed her. Elise stiffened. He tasted like coffee and chewing gum—totally benign—but she felt cornered, and a voice in the back of her mind screamed for escape.

Anthony straightened. "Are you okay?"

She touched her mouth. "Yeah." Her fingertips were tingling. Elise hadn't been kissed in years.

It wasn't that bad. Not really.

She leaned up to kiss him again.

His hand on her arm was heavy, and his breathing deepened as he leaned into her. She felt something stirring inside of her that she hadn't felt in a long time, and the foreign sensation made her knees shake.

The sound of the eaves dripping on the pavement and the cars rushing down the street suddenly seemed too loud, like a hundred eyes were watching and waiting for her to drop her guard.

Elise pushed on his chest—not hard, but enough to get his attention. He blinked at her like he was coming out of a sleepy haze. "What?"

She ducked into the driver's seat and slammed the door, leaving Anthony standing awkwardly next to it.

"I had a great time at the concert," she said, rolling down her window as her engine grumbled to life. Anthony looked bereft. His cheeks were flushed. "I'll see you again tonight, okay?"

She left before he could say another word.

Elise entered the studio to the sound of someone playing the piano. She set her folders on the reception desk and peeked around the corner.

James played piano in the blue light of the storm. The windows at the opposite end of the room were cracked, and a soft breeze smelling of wet sage drifted through. His brow was lowered over his eyes, and his mouth had taken on that distinct slant that said he was concentrating.

"'Marriage d'Amour.' Toussaint, right?" Elise said when his song trailed off, and he looked up, surprised.

"You haven't answered my calls."

"I've been busy." Sitting on the bench beside him, she spread her fingers over the keys. Elise pressed, and the piano responded with a warm *ting*. She struck another key, and another, in no particular order. "How was the visit with the Ramirezes?"

"It didn't do any good. Lucinde is getting worse." James selected a note an octave lower than the last one she hit, and his fingers followed hers up the piano. "You were wrong—she's definitely possessed. But you knew that, didn't you?" He struck the deepest note on the piano, and it vibrated through her hand. "Do you have any potential culprits?"

"I narrowed the list down." She dropped her hands, letting the last note ring through the silent air. "Do you think it's true?"

"Yes," James said, "I do think she's possessed, which is why you should have—"

"Not that. Do you think there are really ethereal ruins beneath the Warrens?"

He considered the question as he tapped out the beginning to "Für Elise." James loved to play that song for her, even more so because she found it irritatingly cute. "It's a distinct possibility." He pulled the cover over the keys. "We should see the Ramirezes as soon as possible. Lucinde must be exorcised."

"Fine. Call Father Night down from Washington. He can do it."

"I already tried to call him, and he's busy for the next week. You're the only person in the area who has ever performed a successful exorcism."

"I've got plans with Anthony later. I can't do it."

James folded his arms. "And that's more urgent than this family's problem? What happened to your priorities?"

"We retired," she reminded him. "We're in hiding. Doesn't *everyone* need help? There's probably a half dozen possessed people throughout the country who need exorcisms right now, and I'm not knocking on their doors, either. I said I'm done being a hero. I meant it."

She slid off of the end of the bench and moved to leave.

James spoke before she reached the door. "Does the phrase, 'I am the cold kiss of Death,' mean anything to you?"

Elise stopped and turned around slowly. "Where did you hear that?"

"Lucinde. Why? Is it familiar?"

"You remember...the last time we fought?" She didn't have to say, *the time we saved the world*.

"It would be impossible to forget."

"She said that to me while she was..." Elise trailed off. She touched the scar on her breast. James hadn't been there when the goddess said

85

that, nor had she told him anything about her long hours under the knife. "Are you sure that's what Lucinde said?"

"Positive." James frowned. "And then she told me I would be next. She knew my name."

"Next for what?" she asked.

"I don't know."

I am the cold kiss of Death…

"But we killed her," she whispered.

"Since that night, I've wondered if that woman was demon-possessed, rather than the deity she claimed to be. Killing a human might not have killed the responsible demon at all. Maybe it has returned."

They shared a long, silent look.

If the thing that tortured her really was back…now *that* might be something worth fighting about.

James opened his mouth to speak again, but Elise's phone interrupted him by ringing.

She answered it. "Hello?" The only response was a buzz and white noise. Elise moved closer to the windows. "Who is this?"

The call crackled. "—Ramirez, we need—help—"

"I can't understand you," she said, moving out into the entryway. James hung a few steps behind her. "Is this Marisa?"

"Lucinde—something's wrong—"

Static hissed, and then the line went dead.

"Hello?" Elise said. "Hello?" She sighed and snapped her phone shut. "Great. This place must have the worst reception in the city limits."

"Who was that?" James asked.

"It *sounded* like Marisa Ramirez," Elise said. "I think something's up with Lucinde." She tried to call the number again, but after several rings, nobody picked up.

Elise shut her phone again.

"No answer?" James asked.

"No answer," she confirmed. "I think we need to get over there sooner rather than later."

James rang the bell by the Ramirez house's front door. Rain drizzled off the drain pipe, splattering against the concrete porch behind them. A church tower rose beyond the roof of their house, the cross at its peak stretching toward the navy sky. Elise shifted uncomfortably at his side, cold and wet and extremely unhappy as minutes passed without answer.

He pressed the doorbell again, and the bells of the church tower tolled in response.

James peered at one of the windows by the door, but the curtains drawn to prevent even the faintest sliver of light from making it through. "Are you sure they're here?"

As if on cue, Augustin Ramirez opened the door. His face was haggard and gray.

"You came back. Thank God. Get in, quick." He locked the deadbolt as soon as they were inside, pushing the curtains aside to glance furtively at the street before closing it up again.

James's nose wrinkled. Something stunk of feces, urine, and blood, like a dirty litter box used by a dozen sick animals. But the Ramirezes didn't have cats. They didn't have any animals at all. It hadn't smelled earlier in the afternoon.

"You have to see her," Augustin said, trying to push Elise toward the kitchen door. "You have to exorcise her. You have to—you have to do that magic stuff again."

"What's wrong with Lucinde, Mr. Ramirez?" James asked. "Where is Marisa?"

"She's downstairs, in the basement," Augustin said. His hands were moving restlessly, as though he wanted to try to grab Elise again, or throw the door open and leave, or just do *something*.

"Take us to Lucinde," Elise said, outwardly unruffled despite Augustin's panic. But James could tell she was straining at the presence of a strong demon. Not for the first time, James was grateful that he couldn't feel what Elise could feel.

"The kitchen," Augustin said. "The door to the basement."

He pointed to the door and just stood there, the scion of a gateway he wouldn't enter. Elise pushed the kitchen door open and went inside, James following closely.

"What's his problem?" she muttered. "He's regressed to the behavior of a militant five-year-old."

"I don't know. I imagine we'll have to see for ourselves," he said, letting the door swing shut behind him. "Somehow, I don't think it will be pretty or pleasant."

Elise pressed the heel of her hand to her temple. "You've got that right."

The foul scent was more pungent in the kitchen, and it grew stronger as they approached the basement door beside the pantry. The basement door had a large panel of frosted glass, but they couldn't see beyond it—Augustin and Marisa had hung a black blanket over the back by stuffing the top into the small space between the door and its frame.

A woman screamed in the basement.

Elise flung open the door and ran into the darkness below. James hesitated in the doorway.

With the door open, the pressurizing air between the kitchen and the basement blew the stench of piss and blood into James's face. He gagged, covering his nose with his sleeve. The screaming had grown much clearer. He could almost make out words.

Even with the door open, the light did little to penetrate the darkness below. He made his way down the steep stairs, keeping a hand on the railing and the other over his face. The sounds of a scuffle echoed up the stairway.

The screams intensified, and then cut off. Something heavy struck the other side of the wall.

"Elise?" James called, quickening his pace. "Marisa?"

His eyes adjusted to the darkness, and he could make out a short hallway, a door set in the unfinished wall. The walls were only partially insulated, and James could hear the shrieks inside all too clearly.

Marisa stood on the other side of the door, sobbing over a stuffed rabbit. The stench was the worst down here, and he could instantly see why—feces were smeared on the unpainted wall, although it wasn't entirely excrement; some of it also appeared to be fresh blood, brownish black in the dim lighting provided by lone bulb.

Elise struggled with a growling blur. Claws lashed at her face, and she ducked, catching its wrist and twisting it behind its body. She put a foot on its bare back and pressed it to the ground, unwinding a rope she had coiled around her arm. It occurred to James that the beast was clothed, and he wondered why something like that would bother to dress itself.

It took James a full second to grasp that the beast with which Elise fought wasn't a demon—it was Lucinde.

She knelt on the girl's back, tangling the rope around Lucinde's body. Elise swiftly tied it off, securing it to a pipe jutting out of the wall. Lucinde kicked and thrashed. She looked more like a wildcat trying to escape than a human child.

Elise grabbed a piece of dirty cloth that had been laying nearby and stuck it in Lucinde's screaming mouth.

The little girl paused, as though to gather her strength, and then strained against the ropes anew. She shrieked and wailed, chewing at the gag and slipping a black tongue around the cloth. Elise backed off, letting the light fall on Lucinde's face. A symbol burned on Lucinde's forehead like her skull had been branded.

"How did this happen?" Elise demanded.

Marisa wept, smothering her face with her hands. "My baby...my little girl..."

As she sobbed louder, Lucinde screamed louder as well, throwing her head back. Her neck strained, and purple veins bulged from her throat. The gag did little to muffle the sound.

Elise grabbed Marisa's shoulders. "I can't help your daughter unless you talk to me. Did you see someone come in here? Did somebody, or something, come into your house?"

Marisa shook her head, and she kept shaking it, her entire body trembling. Her cheeks ran with tears and her chokehold tightened on the stuffed animal until it looked like it might burst at the seams.

"For the love of..." James swept out of the room, but Lucinde's screams followed him up the stairs and echoed against the walls of the basement.

Augustin stood at the door upstairs, leaning heavily on the counter. He had calmed in the minutes since James had gone downstairs, but not without help; he clutched a large glass of alcohol in one hand and a bottle in the other. It was cold inside the house, but Augustin was drenched in sweat. Damp patches stained his shirt at the chest and arm pits.

"When did she get like this?" James asked. "Your wife is incoherent."

Augustin gazed into the amber fluid in his glass, swirling the ice in circles. He was silent for a time, but his mouth moved as though he chewed the words he considered speaking.

"She had grown quieter. We thought she was improving after your ritual...*thing*. I even went into work for a couple hours. Marisa stayed home with...with Lucinde."

He took a long drink and wiped his mouth. His eyes were watery and red.

"She stopped moving. She stopped breathing. We thought she had fallen asleep, and we were glad. I mean, she hadn't slept in days. All she would do is crouch in her bedroom like some goddamn animal and scratch at the walls and eat flies. She was eating *flies*, for fuck's sake. She was catching them and smashing them and eating them and we were so happy when she fell asleep." He drew in a shuddering breath. "When we *thought* she fell asleep."

"What happened?"

89

"She wasn't asleep." Augustin laughed, and it turned into a sob. "She wasn't asleep. My God, she stopped breathing. Her skin had been hot for weeks and all of a sudden she was cold." His eyes met James's, and the pain in them was so harsh, so raw, that he had to fight not to look away.

"Are you saying she...?"

"My daughter *died*, Mr. Faulkner. I don't have to be a doctor to know that." He laughed again. "My daughter died. My little girl..." Augustin spun suddenly and hurled the glass into the sink. It shattered, shards of thunder crashing into stainless steel.

Augustin moved toward the sink, raising his arm as though he was going to smash the bottle too. He stopped short, breathing hard.

"God!" he cried, burying his face in his hand. He smacked the bottle against the counter, and the bottom cracked. Alcohol bled across the marble and dripped onto the floor. "But she didn't stay dead. She didn't stay. We were sitting by her, getting ready to call the hospital, resigning ourselves to what we had known was coming for—since—ever since she was born."

"But she wasn't dead," James prompted.

"Oh, she was dead, all right," Augustin said. "But she woke up, and all of a sudden she was worse than before. She got that shit on her forehead and she was screaming words I don't understand, and she ripped off her bed post trying to escape when we tied her down. We had to move her to the basement to keep her from getting outside. She's an animal. She's not human anymore."

Elise came up from the basement, a few shades paler than when she had gone down. She shut the door, and the screams became nearly inaudible again.

"James, we have to talk," she said.

He nodded. "You're right." He faced Augustin. "Elise and I need to discuss the...options."

"You won't leave," Augustin said. "You're not just going to disappear."

"We'll be right outside. We just need to talk."

"Okay," he said. "Okay."

He watched them go with frightened eyes, as though he didn't quite believe them. For being a powerful lawyer, he suddenly seemed very, very small. And that scared James more than Lucinde's screams ever could.

They stood under the shelter of the eaves, just beyond the light of the house. The neighborhood was completely silent and every house was dark. It was as though everybody had spontaneously gone out of town. Not a single car passed. The silence felt unnaturally heavy.

Elise glared at James. Her pale face glowed in the light that peeked through the curtains.

"I'm not going to do it."

"There's a little girl in there that will die if we don't help her," James said.

"I could die, too. Hell, so could you. Do you think the life of some kid is worth more than yours? We've seen possessions leap between bodies before."

"It only happened once. You can control it."

"Once was more than enough."

James stared at her. It was like he was speaking to a stranger.

It felt so long ago since they had traveled the world together to fight evil. The two of them against the world—that was how it had always been. They had rightfully earned a reputation for being amongst the best of the kopides and aspides.

A chasm had since opened between them since then—a chasm formed of people like Betty, Stephanie, and Anthony.

For some reason, James suddenly remembered the day he found her in the wilderness surrounded by bodies. Elise claimed she couldn't remember whether she killed them or not. He had only asked once, afraid she would tell him the truth. James didn't want to know anymore.

"You wouldn't have turned the Ramirezes away five years ago," he said.

"Five years is a long time." Elise stuffed her hands into her pockets. "I think the demon is after witches. Marisa's a strong witch, and Lucinde's showing signs of having a similar gift. Those fiends were also after a witch at Eloquent Blood. If what Lucinde said is right, you're next, and you're probably the most powerful witch in the entire country."

"Is that why you don't want to be involved? Because you're concerned I'll be hurt?"

Her eyes flashed. "Don't say that like it's some small thing. Of course I'm worried about you. What the hell do you expect?"

"I can take care of myself, Elise."

"Are you sure? I don't think they want the witch alive. Lucinde feels like the body at the hospital did." She touched her temples. "I think she died. That's what changed today."

James's fists clenched. He stared at the gray sky and the pouring rain. When he spoke, his voice was low and tense. "You have to do it. You can't leave them like this."

"But it's that death demon again. I know it."

"I know it, too." James reached out and took her hand. Elise's gloves were damp. "Please. If you won't do it for them, then do it for me."

She glared at him. "Sometimes you're a real bastard, James Faulkner. You know that?"

Elise went inside before he could think of a response.

They stood before Augustin and Marisa, dripping rainwater and mud onto the kitchen floor. Marisa had stopped crying. She stared at nothing, but Augustin focused on James and Elise, his eyes ringed with dark bruises.

"I'll do it," Elise said. "I'll exorcise her."

"And God help us all," James murmured.

Chapter 9

JAMES HALF EXPECTED Elise to vanish completely when she left. When she returned forty-five minutes later equipped with an MP3 recorder and her golden chain of charms, relief overwhelmed him.

A grimace stretched across her lips when she walked through the door, but by the time Augustin and Marisa turned to greet the woman they viewed as their last potential savior, she blanked her expression.

"I've got everything I need," she said.

"We're almost done as well," James said, gesturing to the paperwork he had been going over with Augustin. "We only need your signature."

"What's that?"

"A contract assuring that you're relieved of liability in the event of any ritual-related accidents," Augustin said. His face was purplish and dripping with sweat. He had discarded the pretenses of drinking from a glass and clutched a half-empty bottle of whiskey now, which Marisa had been sharing for the last fifteen minutes. "James insisted upon it. He seemed concerned the we would—we might press charges if Lucinde was accidentally hurt."

"We wouldn't," Marisa added quickly.

"Where do I sign?"

James scratched an X in the blank signature box and pushed the paper to her. She didn't read it before scrawling her signature across the bottom line. Elise dropped the pen and Augustin took the paper.

"Good," he said. "Good. So…what now?"

"We'll go downstairs and exorcise your daughter," Elise said. "You might prefer to stay up here."

Augustin nodded immediately. Just as immediately, Marisa shook her head. "I want to be with my daughter."

"It won't be easy," Elise said.

"I won't leave her. I won't."

"Suit yourself." She managed to make it sound like a death sentence.

They passed through the blanket-covered doorway. James caught a glimpse of Augustin staring at the contract on the table, the whiskey bottle pressed to his forehead, and then the door closed.

The darkness in the basement was palpable, as though they waded through warm water. James felt along the wall by the landing and found a light switch. He flicked it, but nothing happened, and he swallowed a lump in his throat. "I need to speak to Elise before we do this. Can you wait up here, Marisa?"

"Yes," she said, and she waited on the top landing as Elise and James went to the bottom.

Light shone from the cracks around the door to the room where Lucinde was held. James could barely make out the carpet underfoot, striped red and purple and stained with water or something worse. He could see that Elise's brow was pinched in the half-light.

"If you want to emotionally blackmail me again, so help me God, you better wait until—"

"No," he interrupted. "I was thinking—piggyback?"

She let out a breath, shoulders sagging. "Piggyback. Good idea. I haven't done an exorcism in a while, and…well, I'm not sure I'm strong enough anymore. I could hurt her."

"Or yourself."

"I'm not worried about that," she said.

"And that worries *me*."

Elise almost smiled. "Just do it."

He reached within himself, searching for the wellspring of power that flowed from the earth beneath his feet. He caught it and wove it within himself, tighter and tighter until it felt like it might burst out his skin.

James brushed his fingers down her cheek as he released his power. It cascaded through both of them, warming him from the inside out. At the same time, he could feel it warm Elise. He felt the churning sickness in her stomach from being so close to the demonic power of the possessed child, and the ache in her muscles from the earlier struggle.

And then the power coalesced around James's midsection, like a chain tying him to Elise. It was a secure, comforting feeling. Elise's sickness abated, and James's nerves settled.

For one instant, he shared in her emotions as clearly as though they were his own. She was angry, but some part of her did want to save the child—very badly, in fact. She regretted snapping at James. But her fear trumped all. She was terrified of fighting that thing again.

James's stomach dropped out, and it was as though they both free-fell from a great height. Her eyes shocked open, and she staggered backward, breaking the physical connection between them. But the chain didn't break. They were connected.

Neither of them was willing to look at the other. "I'm sorry," James said. "I don't want to fight that demon again, either."

"I'm sorry, too." And he knew she meant it, because he could feel it. "You can come down now," Elise called, her voice resonating with power. Marisa joined them.

"What now?" she asked.

"Now we perform an exorcism." Elise pushed the door open, and they filed in, one after another.

Lucinde huddled in the corner, her entire body trembling. Scratching echoed through the basement, and there were fingernail fragments lodged in the plaster. Marisa whimpered.

Elise turned on the MP3 recorder.

"My name is Elise Kavanagh. I am exorcising a demon from Lucinde Ramirez at the behest of her parents, Augustin and Marisa Ramirez. It's the ninth of May, two-thousand nine, at twenty-one hundred hours." Elise set the recorder by the door.

Lucinde glared at them over her shoulder, revealing a face that had only grown less human with the passing time. Swollen blood vessels rimmed the edges of her red-tinged eyes.

The girl's upper lip curled, baring even white teeth. Her gaze flicked from Elise to Marisa, resting briefly on James before focusing on the kopis once more.

Her pupils dilated, and her irises were completely devoured. A low, soft breath escaped her mouth, almost like a snake's hiss. The note carried demonic power and the stink of sulfur, and the mark on her forehead flared with power.

James felt Elise gather their joined strength around herself, and he fed into it. It built until the air trembled and her very skin seemed to be trying to shiver off her body, and still they kept gathering it, clashing against the energy of the demon. James felt their strength press against Lucinde, and she pushed back. Elise shuddered under the pressure.

Lucinde shifted forward, digging her bloody hands into the floor. Too late, he realized that the ropes Elise had used to bind the girl earlier were piled in the corner. She was free.

"Watch out!" he called.

Lucinde launched from the corner of the room. What was left of her fingernails slashed through the air.

Elise jumped to the side, throwing out an arm to block her. She brushed Elise aside and kept going, striking Marisa instead.

The mother screamed, and down they went.

Blood splattered to the floor. Lucinde growled. Her teeth sunk deep into the flesh of Marisa's arm, and she worried at it as a dog might gnaw on a bone. Marisa collapsed to her knees, trying to wrench her arm free of her daughter's mouth. "No, *bambina!*"

Elise clamped her hand around the girl's jaw and dug her fingernails into her skin, but Lucinde's bite only tightened. James leapt in, wrapping his arms around Marisa's waist. He tried to drag her away, but even with the strength of two sets of adult legs, they couldn't separate mother from daughter. Elise clutched a fistful of Lucinde's hair and yanked.

"Let go." Lucinde growled, and Elise jerked harder. "I said, let go!"

Lucinde released the arm. Marisa collapsed into James, cradling her bloody arm to her stomach.

The girl shot between Elise's legs. Elise turned, but Lucinde was too fast. She clambered up a half-complete shelf toward the narrow window at the ground level. She wiggled through the opening, bare feet kicking behind her.

Elise grabbed for an ankle, but missed.

"Shit!" she swore when the feet disappeared, jumping up to grab the ledge herself.

James was only just behind Marisa in running out the door, up the stairs, and into the kitchen. Augustin blinked wetly at them as they passed. "What...?"

Marisa hit the back door without opening it, stumbling over her own feet. She sagged, favoring her bleeding arm, and the skin began to boil. James caught her, lowering her slowly to the ground. Outside, Elise struggled with the girl in the muddy back yard.

James tried to block out the sensations Elise felt and concentrated on Marisa's bite, pressing his hand to the wound. "Does it sting?" he asked.

"It feels like acid!"

He reached into his pocket and withdrew a scrap of paper. His connection to Elise made summoning his magic easy, but all too quickly it began to draw off his partner. She wavered, and Lucinde took the opportunity to squirm out from under Elise and bolt for the fence.

James concentrated on healing Marisa's arm, flicking the healing magic into the air around her. She whimpered. The skin twitched and writhed, but it was no longer bubbling. It settled, red and raw but clean.

"Wait here!"

He joined Elise in the back yard as she tackled Lucinde, smashing both of them into the fence. It shuddered with the force of the impact.

Elise was completely covered in mud, from her knees to her gloves and jacket. Her hands slipped on Lucinde, and the girl darted for a pile of landscaping boulders at the opposite corner.

James moved to cut her off. She froze, then tried to dart in the other direction.

Elise was already there, uncoiling the extra rope in her fists. She was flushed, panting, and exhilarated, her excitement washing through James. Her chain of charms jingled at her belt, and the crosses seemed to glow. Lucinde glanced between Elise, and then to James again, and back. The rain struck her skin and sizzled, evaporating instantly. Her entire body steamed.

"We should get her inside before the neighbors call the police," he said, and Elise nodded.

Blood-caked fingernails flashed at Elise's face. She threw herself out of the way, grabbing the girl's wrist. Lucinde snatched the charms at Elise's belt. The belt loops popped, and she flung them aside. The charms sank into a puddle of mud.

James dove for Lucinde. She darted aside, but he managed to catch her arm. Her flesh was so hot it nearly burned his hand. He jerked her around, and she kicked him—hard—in the shin.

He growled, hefting Lucinde under his arm. She snapped at his arms with her teeth. He clamped a hand over her mouth.

Elise knelt in the mud, searching for her charms.

"I can't find them!"

"Forget it. Door," he grunted. Elise threw it open, and he rushed through.

Marisa and Augustin waited on the other side. The stuffed rabbit had reappeared, and she gave a ragged sob when she saw James and Elise come back inside with her daughter in tow.

"Out of the way!" she ordered. Lucinde kicked hard, nearly squirming out from under James's arms.

"Get her feet," he said.

Elise took her by the ankles, bracing them as James dragged her down the stairs.

Marisa squeezed around them and shut the basement window before they dropped Lucinde again. The girl scrabbled over to the corner, curled into a tight ball, and screeched pathetically at James.

Fumbling at the back of her neck, Elise took off her cross necklace and pressed it to Lucinde's cheek. Her voice hardened, deepening with power as she summoned up the memory of the oft-recited rituals from ancient books to do her first exorcism in years.

"I exorcise you, impious demon," she recited, and James could envision the same old pages Elise was remembering with perfect clarity. Lucinde's face screwed up with pain. "In vain do you boast of this deed. I command you to restore her as proof you no longer have any rule over her soul. I abjure—"

Lucinde swung. "Elise!" James yelled.

Her fist connected. Elise's back smacked into a wall, and Lucinde lunged.

Elise braced herself and took the impact, translating the momentum into a throw. Lucinde slid, but regained her footing immediately.

Elise scooped her rope from the floor, holding it in the joint of her elbow to keep her hands free. She grabbed the girl by her collar and slammed her into the wall. The drywall cracked.

"No—!" Marisa cried, throwing out a hand.

James caught her arm. "Stay out of it. Trust me. She isn't feeling any of this."

"I *abjure* you," Elise went on, voice rising as she shoved the cross into Lucinde's face again, "stripping you of the arms with which you fight. I revoke the powers by which—" the girl clawed at Elise's wrist, trying to pry her off, "—this creature became bound to your service."

Her back arched, even with Elise's hands holding her flat to the wall. Lucinde's nails dug into her sleeve.

Elise pushed the girl to the floor, pinning her arms to the dirty linoleum with her knees. She flung her head from side to side, but even with all the strength the demon provided, Elise had size on her side.

"This creature is restored, rejecting your influence, granted divine mercy for defense against your assaults!"

Lucinde began to scream, high and loud. Something pulsed underneath the surface of her skin where Elise held the cross.

She focused all the energy she possessed on that point, building it up between them. Heat rippled across James's skin. Elise seized upon the darkness within Lucinde.

"*Crux sacra sit mihi lux,*" Elise said, and the power poured out through her words. "*Non draco sit mihi dux. Vade retro, Satana—*"

The power of the demon boiled through the air like hot oil, simultaneously slimy and as dry as a desert wind. Her screaming reached a pitch, and Elise released the cross so she could cover her mouth with her gloved hand.

The girl bit down, but her teeth got nothing but glove. Even muffled against her hand, James could hear screaming. It didn't come from her throat.

"*Nunquam suade mihi vana,*" Elise continued. The stench of sulfur was almost choking. "*Sunt mala quae libas. Ipse venena bibas!*"

A silent clap of thunder roared inside Elise and James. Lucinde wrenched her head to the side, out from underneath Elise's hand. "Mother!" she shrieked in a hundred voices. "Sorrow!"

She roared once more, wordless and agonized, thrashing beneath Elise.

Lucinde gasped, and then slumped. Her eyes closed, her mouth hung open, and she stopped moving.

Elise released the child, and Lucinde didn't move. She lay limply between Elise's legs, unconscious but breathing. The black symbol rapidly faded. Her veins sank into her skin once more.

"*Madre de dios,*" Marisa whispered.

James followed her gaze. She was watching the same place as Elise—not at the girl, but at the ceiling. A dark shadow manifested above the room. A smell like burnt ozone and charred hair, traced faintly with the iron tang of blood, permeated the entire basement.

Elise dropped her necklace into the pocket of her jacket, staring into the depths of the demon's form.

"Servant," she said in a low, strong voice. "Return to the Hell in which you belong and never return. Be gone."

The demon dissolved. The pressure eased.

Elise pressed her fingers to Lucinde's throat. James could feel the pulsing of her heartbeat in his own fingertips, steady and strong.

She was alive.

"Lucinde," Marisa cried, pulling her arm free from James and scrambling over to her daughter. "Is she okay? What did you do to her?"

"She's fine, Marisa," Elise said. "You might both want to get checked out by a doctor, though. I'm sure Stephanie would be happy to pay a visit once she gets off her shift."

Marisa smoothed her hand over Lucinde's cheek. "Baby...baby, please wake up..."

The girl's eyes opened. The whites were no longer yellow and veined.

Lucinde had to swallow twice before she could speak. "Mama?"

"Oh, *bambina*." Marisa choked on a sob and collapsed over her daughter, raining kisses all over her face and arms and tummy. She spoke rapidly in Spanish, too quickly for James to understand, but he got the gist of it. "My baby, *querida, mi corazon...*"

James rested his hand on Elise's shoulder and lifted the magical binding between them. Her feelings disappeared from him in a rush. More than the physical sense of being tired, though, he felt drained spiritually—he couldn't have lit a candle if he wanted to, with or without paper magic.

He didn't need to read Elise's mind to see she felt the same. "I almost forgot what that was like," she said.

"Yes, but perhaps now we should..." he said, gesturing toward the door.

"Wait," Marisa interrupted, scooping Lucinde into her arms. Blood seeped through the makeshift bandage on her arm. "*Gracias*, thank you so much. She's okay again. You really did it. It wasn't..." Lucinde looked dazed, as though she wasn't quite sure what was going on. It was a pleasant departure from the screaming. "That was nothing like the movies."

"Life usually isn't," Elise said.

"How can we ever repay you?"

"Don't worry about it."

The temperature in the kitchen was much warmer than the basement. Augustin stood when they entered.

"Is she...?"

James pulled Elise aside from the doorway, letting Marisa enter the kitchen. He froze, going completely expressionless.

She blinked several times, squinting against the fluorescent lamps, and buried her face in her mother's shoulder. Marisa stroked Lucinde's hair, murmuring to her softly, but her eyes were all for Augustin. For the first time, James glimpsed real love between them.

And Augustin crumbled. He collapsed against the table as though he could no longer stand.

"Thank *God*."

Marisa brought Lucinde to him, and they cried, relieved and happy and still sort of drunk off the whiskey. The kitchen felt so much brighter without the weight of the possession heavy over the entire house.

"Call us if you need anything else," Elise said, but the Ramirezes weren't listening.

"Let's go," James said.

They left the kitchen, and even though all the lights inside were off and the curtains drawn, it felt nowhere near as dark as it had been when they had first arrived. James found his jacket, and Elise took a moment to go to the thermostat, flicking off the air conditioner before cutting around the side of the house to find her charms in the back yard. They met again in the front.

The rain hadn't let up. They got in the car, and James fished an old towel out of the backseat, drying off his hair. He offered it to her when he was done, but she gazed thoughtfully out the window and didn't see.

"How do you feel?" he asked.

"Good," Elise said. "I feel…good. Are you okay? I saw you healing Marisa, but you didn't take it from me."

"I'm fine, but I certainly won't be doing any more magic for a few days."

"What do you think about what Lucinde said?"

"'Sorrows,'" James repeated, and she nodded.

"What did it mean?"

"She said 'mother' as well, and I don't think she was calling Marisa. I believe it's a name." He removed a city map from the glove compartment and scanned it briefly. He pointed at a green oval on the north end of the paper. "See here—Our Mother of Sorrows, right by the university."

"Why would a demon yell the name of a cemetery?"

"A lesser demon, such as the one that possessed Lucinde, is merely an appendage of its master rather than an individual entity," he said. He started the car. "So as it is exorcised…"

"It goes back to its master and sees or thinks exactly what its master sees or thinks," Elise said. "I'm going to the cemetery."

He stopped at the red light. "*You're* going?"

"Listen, James…" She paused to collect her thoughts. When she spoke, her voice was soft. "You're right. I have to take care of this. This bitch—the death goddess—almost skinned me, and she owes me her blood. But I'd feel a lot better if you weren't around for it."

"You're completely unprepared."

"I don't have time for preparation. I have to get her now. Who knows where she'll be tomorrow?"

"You realize this is likely to be a trap," he said.

She nodded.

He gave a low, thoughtful hum, drumming his fingers on the steering wheel. The light turned green and James lurched into the intersection,

101

making a fast illegal left turn. Elise gripped the side of the door, staring at him. "James, Motion and Dance is the other way," she said.

"We're not going to the studio," he said. "We're going to Our Mother of Sorrows."

Chapter 10

ELISE AND JAMES sped toward the cemetery in silence. The windshield wipers whisked a quick rhythm back and forth, clearing sheets of water off the glass with every swipe. The air blowing through the vents was cool, like the air outside, smelling sweetly of petrichor and sage.

The white monolith of the cemetery's church rose out of the darkness. He parked in the circular driveway before the building, and Elise hit the radio button, silencing the oldies station in the middle of a Led Zeppelin song.

"It's really close to UNR," she remarked. A stone angel loomed in the dark distance.

"There are several graveyards around here," he said. "When old west towns such as this were founded, they always put the cemeteries at the tops of hills to keep the bodies—and their smell—out of the way."

She studied the faces of the apartment buildings on the ridge overlooking Our Mother of Sorrows. "Guess they didn't plan on people building homes out here. At least your neighbors would be quiet."

"Even your living ones, apparently," he said, taking the keys out of the ignition.

James was right: most of the apartments and houses surrounding the cemetery were dark. Even though it was almost the weekend, and there should have been parties in the college neighborhood, the blocks surrounding Our Mother of Sorrows were strangely silent.

"The dead aren't getting any deader," she said. "Let's go."

They climbed out of the car into the rainy night. She wandered toward the church, and James retrieved a flashlight from the trunk before joining her.

A small graveyard splayed in front of them. The newer headstones to

103

the front were in neat lines, arranged in narrow rows that left no room for walking without treading upon someone's final resting place. A single path led to a hill where the older graves stood. A lonely stone angel, illuminated by flood lights around its base, glowed like a star in the drizzly night.

James stepped on the grass. Energy swept over him, and he froze.

Elise caught his expression. "What's wrong?"

"Someone's been working magic here. The entire cemetery's inside a circle of power."

"That's not unusual. People cast spells in graveyards all the time." Elise kept walking. "Come on, hurry up. We don't want to get caught trespassing. Do cemeteries have security details?"

"Considering the gaping holes in their fence, I'm going to say no."

Elise and James moved between the graves, feet slurping in and out of the mud with each step. Grass was not native to the desert, so it didn't take root in the hard soil properly and melted into sludge at the slightest hint of rain.

James shone his flashlight on every marker they passed. "Mario Perez," Elise remarked. "I had that guy for class when I was a freshman."

"I remember that," he said, wiping rainwater off his face. "Stroke, wasn't it?"

"Yeah." She pulled out her cell phone, glanced at the screen, and pulled a face.

"What's the matter?"

"Forget it," Elise said, shoving it back in her pocket. "Let's find this demon bastard and get the job done."

They gave a quick search of the graves. In such a small cemetery, there wasn't much looking to do.

"You must have misinterpreted Lucinde," she said. "There's nothing here. It would be pretty obvious if a major demon was around."

He swept the flashlight side to side in fruitless searching. "It doesn't seem—"

"Wait. Is that an open grave by the statue?"

They weaved through the tombstones to the next row. The flashlight died when they stepped up to the very edge of the plot, and James bashed the flashlight repeatedly against his thigh.

"It's definitely open," she said. "Too bad we can't see it."

"I know," James said, looking down into the LEDs and jiggling the batteries. "From what I can tell, though, it almost looks new." The flashlight blared on, burning his retinas for an instant, and then turned off again. "Damn!"

"How can you tell that it's new?"

He gestured toward the sky, blinking green shapes out of his vision. "It's been raining for quite some time. The soil erodes rapidly. This grave, although messy, hasn't been washed out."

"Isn't that Amber Hackman's grave over there?" Elise said. "I heard something about her on the news recently. Her body went missing."

Their gazes met.

"You wouldn't remember when Amber Hackman died, but it was quite the event for the witch community worldwide," James said. "She's best known for her work as ambassador for the U.N., but she also fought to obtain asylum for witches in superstitious villages. Her work saved many lives."

"This grave is…" She squinted. "Grace Finch, beloved grandmother. I would bet anything she was a witch, too."

"How many bodies does this demon have?"

"At least three, probably more. All witches."

He let out a slow breath. "This isn't good."

"Is there something down there?"

She moved closer to the grave. The only warning James had when she fell was a surprised shriek, and suddenly, Elise wasn't standing in front of him anymore.

"Elise!" he yelled, stepping forward.

Loose earth crumbled under his feet, and he jumped back, landing on his backside. The light flashed once, and stayed dead.

James scrambled to his knees, moving carefully to the rim of the grave. "Elise?"

He could just make out her pale skin as she tilted her face up toward him. "My fault. Erosion. At least I had a soft landing. Can I get any light?"

"The flashlight won't work," he said, opening it to reseat the batteries and fiddle with the connectors.

"I think there's a pair of security guards down here," Elise said. A beat, and she added, "They're dead."

James closed the battery door and the bulb came back on. He beamed it down into the grave. Elise shielded her eyes, back pressed into the muddy wall.

The bodies looked like mud-covered sacks, half-concealed by a sheet flung over their legs. He could make out the *Securitas* logo on the breast pocket of the man on the right. His stomach pitched.

"Shine the light over that way," she said.

105

James obeyed, watching as Elise knelt in the space beside the bodies. She felt the throat of the closest guard and hovered her hand over his mouth. When she began wiping mud away from their throats to bare bloody gashes, James looked up at the sky.

Gray clouds, highlighted with shades of blue and purple, shifted slowly across the heavens. The moon wasn't even visible through the cover. Casino lights to the south turned the clouds green and orange and a dozen other unnatural shades of the rainbow.

"Someone slit their throats with a sharp knife. The wounds are pretty clean," she said from below. James took deep, shallow breaths, grateful that the rain kept the smell of death from reaching him.

"We should get you out of there. We need to...I don't know, report this or something."

"Report it? Are you crazy?" She dug her hands into the wall of mud, trying to haul herself up with the side of the grave. The soil slipped under her fingers. She lost her footing, stumbled back on the bodies, and one of the guards squelched deeper into the mud. "Uh, help?"

James offered a hand to her. She took his wrist, and he hauled her out of the hole. Elise crawled a few feet away from the grave before trying to wipe mud off her arms. "Are you all right?"

Elise cast a grimace at the grave. "Better than some people. We can't report this. Once the police are here, we'll never get the opportunity to find out what happened."

"But..."

"Business first. Then we tip off the law." She scooped the flashlight off the ground. "You never would have had a problem with this five years ago."

He glanced down into the shadowy depths of the grave and quickly averted his gaze once more. "You said it yourself. Five years is a long time."

Her head snapped up. "What was that?"

James scanned the cemetery with his eyes as Elise did the same at his back, but he heard it before he saw it—slow, shuffling, squelching. Footsteps.

"Perhaps it's the next shift," he muttered.

"Or maybe it's a zombie," Elise said.

She pointed, and James followed her finger to the street beyond the fence.

A figure slid into the light. His shoes were visible first, and then his shoulders illuminated. His hanging head shadowed his face and chest.

106

The man was clad in a poorly-fitting gray suit, torn and splattered with mud. There was no shirt under the jacket, baring a sunken chest covered in raised veins and swimming black marks that were darker than shadow.

His head lifted. Light spilled onto his nose and angular jaw, which were gripped with veins. A single sigil was emblazoned between his eyebrows. James didn't need to look closely to know it was the same mark Lucinde had borne not too long before.

"You again," Elise murmured.

The possessed corpse shambled forward. His eyes didn't quite focus on either of them.

Elise and James backed toward the gate.

A twig snapped.

James spun. A woman lurched toward them from the darkness at the other end of the cemetery, her straggly hair caked in dirt. She, too, was clad in clothes that didn't suit her—a plain frock and a pair of cheap sandals. The dress was several sizes too big, and it hung off her shoulder, exposing a sagging breast.

Black tears streaked her cheeks. The other possessed one was close enough for James to see the swollen blood vessels in his eyes as well, and he realized that the woman's eyes had burst.

James edged over until he was shoulder to shoulder with his kopis. "This is your area of expertise. What do we do?"

"Kill them." She held a long, curved knife in one hand. James hadn't seen her draw it.

The woman sped up, and the man angled to cut off their exit. It took him a moment to realize Elise wasn't following him toward the fence.

"If they're here, their master won't be far," she said.

"You're suggesting we fight."

Elise was never given a chance to respond.

The man pitched toward her. She ducked away from his clumsy hands, delivering a kick squarely in the middle of the back. He tumbled into the mud.

"James—look out!"

He spun, but it was too late. A pair of hands dug into his shoulders, and the earth rushed to meet his face.

There was a smack, a crack, and the female was suddenly on the ground with him. A small sound came from her throat, more instinctive than a protest of pain.

James gasped and tried to squirm away, but the mud sucked him down, making it hard to move. Elise's foot came down on the woman's face once. The possessed one caught her ankle. She stumbled out of the grip.

The possessed woman clawed at his ankles when James scrambled to his feet. Elise kicked her in the side of the head, even harder this time. It was accompanied by an even louder *crack,* and her skull caved in like a rotten egg that had been smashed against the asphalt.

The older man lurched forward, grabbing James's neck in both hands. He was slow, but too strong to stop.

James struggled to pry the hands away. "Elise," he groaned. "Help—please—"

The female grabbed Elise, dragging her to the ground. "I'm a little busy right now," she said.

He heaved with all his strength, peeling the arms away inch by inch. He could feel his pulse throbbing in his temple. The man, however, showed no signs of exertion. The possessed one pushed steadily on, its half-focused eyes fixed squarely on James's throat.

Out of the corner of his eye, he saw Elise grab a felled branch the size of his arm. She swung her makeshift club like a bat, and it hissed through the air, smashing into the woman's face.

James leaned back and pushed his knee between himself and the zombie, trying to kick him off.

The cold fingers tightened around his neck, the heels of his palms pressed into his esophagus, and the world grew darker—

Then a familiar blade came down on the servant's elbow, slicing across the inner joint. Blood gurgled sluggishly from the cut.

Elise cut again, and suddenly, all the pressure was gone from the right side of James's throat. The servant's hand fell limply to his side, and James wrenched away from him with a gasp. Fresh oxygen rushed into his lungs, and he coughed as the graveyard swam around him.

The man turned on Elise, groping for her with the arm that still worked. She flung him to the ground. "Hold him," she ordered, and James approached cautiously.

"Is he…?"

"I slapped him with the pendant of St. Benedict," Elise said, taking the necklace of charms from her pocket. It jingled in the night. "I stuffed it in his mouth. He won't be able to get orders from his master until he manages to spit it out."

James put his foot on the servant's chest just in case. "You still carry extra medallions?" he asked.

"I just started again. It seemed like a good idea."

"A very good idea," he agreed, watching as Elise hauled the dead woman to her feet. The rain made her bloody face run with red tears.

"Where is your master?" she demanded. The body twisted and writhed, fighting to break free with a whining shriek. "I know you can speak. One of your demonic friends spoke through a girl tonight, so talk!"

Motion caught James's eye. A small, leathery body emerged from behind a tombstone, perching on the top. Its bulbous eyeballs shone dimly in the light, yellow and bulging and focusing directly on him.

Another scaled the fence. He turned, and his gaze fell on another as it crept out from the shadows of the building adjacent to the cemetery.

"I told you to talk!" Elise said. She slapped the corpse across the face as James edged closer. Decomposing brain, like cottage cheese, crumbled out of the crack in her skull.

"Elise..."

Yet another gray demon crept out from behind the tree. This close, he could see the blood encrusting its nails and the droop of its lower lip as it salivated with hunger.

"What, James?" she asked without taking her focus off the struggling woman.

"I think we're about to have bigger problems."

Her face darkened in increments as she counted each demon. "Fiends. I *hate* those guys."

James swallowed. "We fight?"

"No. We don't stand a chance against three." The possessed woman suddenly stopped fighting and went limp in Elise's arms as though all her strings had been cut.

"What the hell...?" James wondered.

"The master must have realized the servants weren't doing anything," she said, dropping the body. "Run!"

She didn't need to tell him twice.

Elise leapt over the fallen body of the possessed woman, snatching at James's hand and dragging him along with her.

Their feet made sucking noises with every step, but James could hardly hear it over the pounding of his heart. He felt cold, awash with adrenaline. His gaze narrowed, focusing on the door to the cemetery's attached office, until all he could see was the door half-lit in the darkness of stormy night.

He hit the doors before Elise did, throwing them open. The lock was punched out—someone else had been there first.

"Get inside!" he bellowed.

109

They jumped in and slammed the double doors shut. Elise threw herself against it, bracing her back against the place in between the handles. The bodies crashed into the other side.

James dropped the flashlight to help, but she shook her head.

"Find something to hold the doors!"

He searched the room. There were potted plants, but none heavy enough to hold the door. He grabbed the edge of check-in desk and pulled experimentally, but it was bolted to the floor. James flung open the door labeled "janitor."

Another heavy *thud*, and Elise grunted.

"Soon would be good," she growled.

James snatched a steel-handled mop from the closet. "Push," he said, trying to fit the mop through the handles. "I can't wedge it in like this."

Elise lost her footing, and the door opened partway. A hand pushed through the opening.

She grabbed it and twisted. Something snapped. The fingers went slack.

Her weight still wasn't enough to close the door.

James threw himself into it. It smashed shut on inhuman fingers, and something on the other side gave a cry, jerking them out of the way.

The doors closed. He wedged the mop's pole through the door handles.

She stepped back. The corpses slammed into the doors, and the hinges groaned, but the mop held.

He sighed and leaned against the wall.

"Don't stop yet. Keep moving," she said, grabbing his collar. She burst through the hall to the office, shutting the sliding doors behind them.

James scanned the office. The stormy half-light of night outside filtered through slatted blinds, casting faint barred shadows across a cheap desk and filing cabinet. The brown shag carpet broke off at the head of a tiled hallway, and another door stood closed nearby with a sign that said "lab." A map of the building hung on the wall, with the fire exit routes marked in red.

The banging grew more distant, and more insistent. They jogged down the tiled hallway. Another set of doors stood at the very end.

"We might be able to get out and make a break for the car before they realize we've gone," Elise said.

"I'm not sure—"

Shuffling.

They turned, falling silent as they faced the source of the noise.

Fiends crouched at the end of the hall. It wasn't the small handful they had seen in the graveyard beyond the office walls—there were more, many more, perhaps a dozen. They shifted in the darkness, crawling over each other and halfway up the walls.

A pair scuttled forward and up, digging their claws into the stucco to scramble over James's head. He ducked, but they didn't stop. Instead, they dropped on the other side—between Elise and James and the exit.

On both sides, the demons waited, staring at them with luminescent eyes.

Elise gripped James's wrist. She didn't say what she was thinking, but he suspected it involved several expletives. He felt much the same. James shifted so his hand squeezed hers, and he hoped it was comforting.

The fiends growled softly. His heart raced, and adrenaline turned his blood to antifreeze.

Her body tensed. She was preparing to run.

The office door beside them slammed open.

James saw a flash of yellow claws and leathery skin. Small hands wrapped around his leg, and he jerked free, kicking it in the face. The little demon keened, reeling backward, but in its place came another.

Elise's knife flashed, glinting through the air like a blade of moonlight. She cut, ducking low and slicing along arms, across faces, pulling away from strikes. She moved smoothly, quickly, a dance of fist and blade. He fought to get free, trying to break from the increasing crowd of fiends as they clambered to grab him.

And then the demons from the end of the hall leapt into the fray, and James was swarmed. He elbowed a face, pushed another away. The tide of small bodies pulled him toward the conference room, and inexorably away from the slashing blade that was Elise.

She reached for James. "Elise!" he shouted, throwing his hand toward hers.

Their fingers brushed. The fiends yanked. James lost his footing, and he fell, caught by clawed hands a heartbeat before hitting the ground.

"James!"

He tried to grab the doorframe, but the fiends released him before he could orient himself. His face hit the stripping at the bottom of the door. Elise's sneakers moved—rising to strike a leathery body, pushing against the ground, fighting to get closer to James.

Then they jerked, dragging him down the floor. The carpet burned the side of his face.

111

"No!" Elise cried, struggling against the restraining arms of the fiends, pushing and hitting and scratching and doing no good whatsoever.

The door slammed shut.

The fiends wrenched James to his knees. He had an instant to see tiled floors, a drain, metal tables, and then the fiends pulled again. Nails dug into his arms. James didn't have to count the fiends to know there were too many to fight.

One of the demons clawed its way up his slacks until it stretched tall, almost up to his chest. Its fingers ran over his cheeks, his jaw, his nose.

The other demons jerked on his legs. James lost balance and his knees struck the carpet. The fiends made slurping, hungry noises deep in their throats, staring at him like a slab of meat.

Claws slid down his neck, catching on the hem of his shirt with a ripping sound. His chest was suddenly cold. His shirt had been torn open in one long line down the center, baring his chest and stomach.

He felt the sharp press of teeth against his hip and gave a shout.

"What are you doing?"

The other door opened. His heart leapt when he saw a feminine figure enter—but it wasn't Elise. The newcomer was swathed in a long jacket and a formless skirt. The fact he couldn't make out her face, or even her body type, didn't disturb James so much as the feeling of sheer *power* that poured off of her.

It wasn't the normal power that James got from other witches, like those in his coven. This feeling was unmistakably *evil*.

The witch drew a knife from behind her back.

"Oh," James said.

She touched the blade to his skin, and after that, all he could do was scream.

"No!"

Elise threw herself against the door. Locked.

Something scuffled behind her, and she spun, dagger raised for a blow. But the fiends had dispersed—gone from the hall as quickly as they had arrived in the first place. They had what they wanted, and it wasn't Elise.

The air shifted, and motion from a fiend she had killed caught her eye. Blood dribbled sluggishly out of the slit on its neck. And then... something changed.

112

In her biology for non-majors college class, Elise had watched a time lapse video of a decaying rabbit. Its skin had rippled and exploded with maggots, the flesh disappearing as tiny fragments were carried off by numerous insects. The decay of the fiend was similar—one moment, it was whole and complete, and the next, its skin crumpled and peeled and flaked off, baring bone that burned away as well.

She watched, stunned, as invisible flame spread from the brands down its back and devoured the entire body, leaving nothing but dust.

Only very strong master demons could destroy its minions after they died.

And it had her aspis.

He screamed on the other side of the wall.

"James!" she yelled. She shook the doorknob again, harder. "James!"

She took a step back and threw all her strength into a single kick. Her blow landed beside the doorknob. *Crack.*

His screaming grew strangled. She kicked again.

The door was made of heavy oak. It barely shook.

"Shit," she muttered. The room number, mounted on a gold placard beside the door, said *6B*. If there was a 6B, there must have been a 6A.

She left James's screams and scanned the map on the wall, trying to make sense of it in the dark. Finding the red dot marking her position, she traced the hall around the building.

6A. There was another door in the opposite hall.

Elise ran. Her feet pounded against linoleum, each step a clap of thunder.

James's screams suddenly silenced.

She skid around the corner and almost lost her balance, catching herself on a door. 6A. Elise tried the doorknob, and it turned smoothly.

She threw the door open, ready for a fight—but she was met by an empty room.

The embalming room was dark and windowless. Every surface was tiled or clean steel, from the table affixed to the wall to the sinks and ceiling. A sign read, "Danger: Formaldehyde Irritant and Potential Cancer Hazard. Authorized Personnel Only." A row of locked refrigerators for bodies lined the wall, and a pump sat on a desk next to the table with liters and gallons measured on the side of its barrel.

Elise picked her way through the shattered debris of the embalming fluids. The scent made her gag. She covered her mouth to keep from vomiting as she rounded the table.

Her breath caught in her throat. "James…"

113

He was slumped in the corner, limbs twisted like a ragdoll. James's shirt was torn open to reveal his torso. Elise didn't need much light to recognize the black smears staining his chest: blood.

She felt his neck for a pulse. His throat pulsed in a slow, weak rhythm under her fingers.

"Thank God," she murmured, pushing his shirt aside to examine the wounds.

Someone had begun to skin a patch of James's stomach over his solar plexus, but it wasn't a random, messy job. The looping lines were deliberate and strangely neat. The knife must have been incredibly sharp.

Elise recognized that knife work. She still had the scar on her chest. "Oh, James," she said, brushing his bangs out of his closed eyes.

Something moved.

Her gaze snapped over. A shape snuck out from behind the door Elise had left open.

Launching to her feet, she barreled into the intruder. The person screamed in a woman's voice. She gripped a short stone staff, dirty with blood and mud, and there was a pentacle charm on her bracelet.

It was a human—not a demon at all.

"Help!" she cried before Elise could smother her mouth.

She slammed the woman's hand into the wall until she cried out. Her fingers lost their grip, and the stone hit the floor.

Hands buried themselves in Elise's jacket and ripped her away.

She sprawled to the ground, catching a brief glimpse of a fiend as it pushed at the witch's legs. The jacket flared behind her as they ran from the room. Elise scrambled to the doorway in time to see the exit swing shut behind them.

Elise hesitated, casting a glance at James. She couldn't chase them without leaving her partner behind.

"Damn it!" she swore. James made a sound of pain, and Elise dropped to her knees at his side. "We need to get you out of here before someone shows up." His eyes half-opened at her voice, and she gave him a tight smile. "Come on. I'll help you up."

She lifted him carefully under the arms. He gave a weak attempt at getting his feet under him…and then went slack.

He was unconscious.

Chapter 11

THE DOOR TO James's bedroom banged open.

Elise rushed through the doorway with James draped over her shoulders. She tried to roll him onto the bed gently, but he slipped and hit the mattress hard. He made a small pain noise in his sleepy delirium.

"Sorry," she said. James didn't react to her apology.

She cut his shirt open along the sleeves and tugged it out from underneath him, chucking it in the trash. The bandages she had packed over his wound in the car had already soaked through with blood.

Elise searched through James's desk drawers for gauze and bandages, returning once she located them amongst a secret stash of Milk Duds. Blood welled up in the cuts as soon as they were bared to the air as though he had been sliced open anew.

She had suffered enough wounds to know that a little cutting shouldn't have knocked James out, nor should it have bled so much. Poison, or magic? Either was trouble.

Summoning first aid experience from the musty corners of her memory, Elise bandaged him carefully. Her gaze wandered to the phone on the bedside table as she worked. She couldn't call Stephanie. Even though the doctor would be all too happy to nurse James back to health, she would have questions Elise didn't want to answer.

But she couldn't give him the help he needed herself.

Muttering a terse prayer, she called Stephanie on James's cell phone. "James," the doctor breathed on the other end. "It's about time you called me."

"This is Elise."

"Oh. Really. What are you doing calling from his number at this time of night?"

"He's hurt. He might be poisoned."

"Poisoned?" Stephanie's voice sharpened. "Why are you wasting your time calling me? Hang up and call the poison control center, he needs—"

"We can't call anyone, go to the hospital, or attract any attention," Elise snapped. "He needs you. Are you going to come help him or what?"

"What are you doing, you stupid bitch? Call an ambulance! I'll meet you at the emergency room."

She counted slowly to ten, and then said, "Stephanie. I'm not messing around."

"What happened?"

Elise glanced at her prone partner. His face was ashen gray. "James is unconscious but breathing fine. He's bleeding from a shallow wound on his chest. I would guess that he's stable for the moment."

She cursed. "You did this to him, didn't you?"

"Now isn't the time for blame."

The doctor gave a disgusted sigh. "You're going to have to call someone else anyway. I was volunteered to take the directors to Sacramento International, so I'm still at least two hours away. If you care about him at all, you'll get proper medical attention."

"We have to wait for you." A grimace, and she added, "Please." She choked out the last word with no small amount of pain, but it made Stephanie pause. There was silence for a long moment. When the doctor spoke again, the venom had left her tone.

"If he dies…"

"I would care a hell of a lot more than you do. James needs to be looked at, and I can't do it myself."

"Make sure the wound is clean and well-wrapped. Two hours. Less if I rush."

"Then rush."

Elise hung up and sat back. She hoped she was right in trusting Stephanie. But…who would have known that Elise and James would exorcise Lucinde and get the "Sorrows" message?

The people in the coven might. They were the only ones who knew James was connected with an exorcist. But if Elise couldn't trust the other witches, she could be in even worse trouble than she suspected.

Elise studied James's room. What if Ann or Morrighan had left some kind of trap? She scanned the dark walls, watching closely for a telltale glimmer of eyes staring back.

James's bedroom was too small for anyone to hide in it. The walls

116

were lined with bookshelves, and not an inch of space was wasted. His bed rested atop several archivist boxes, each lovingly packed with texts that were too valuable to see the light of day. His headboard was stacked with shelving, too. The only free space was in front of the window where his altar stood. A statuette of the Goddess leaned against the right side of the window frame, mirrored by the Horned God to the left.

Elise sank into the worn chair at his desk and swiveled around so she could see James. A yawn caught in her throat.

Ignoring her body's demands for sleep, she withdrew the short stone staff from her jacket pocket. It felt heavier than it should have been at only twelve inches long, as though it was lead instead of rock. Elise rubbed her thumb on the surface, scrubbing away some of the dirt to reveal demonic runes.

The stone was cool under her hand, sucking her body heat deep into its core. The staff felt unmistakably alive.

And evil.

Elise cleared off space on James's desk, which was covered in notebooks with his precise handwriting and illustrations of sigils. Some of it was for the annual almanac his coven published, but some of it looked like fresh spellwork. Several were weighted down with crystals, collecting their energy for later use. She set the stone staff somewhere it didn't touch anything else.

James made a small noise again. His skin shone with sweat, and pain twisted his face into a grimace.

"Are you awake?" she whispered, sitting beside him.

He didn't move.

She let out a long, slow breath, letting her hand fall to his chest above the bandage. Sweat soaked through the material, and dots of blood were seeping through as well.

His eyes fluttered open. "Elise," he whispered. "Are you all right?"

"You're the one that got carved up by a big bad witch. Don't waste your strength worrying about me." He moved like he was going to sit up, but she held him down. It wasn't as much of a struggle as it should have been. "I'm here. Nothing will get you." He mumbled softly. "Nothing will get you," Elise said again, mostly as an affirmation to herself.

She sunk down lower on the bed beside him, rested her cheek against his upper arm, and laid her hand over his heart. The beat was slow. He sounded so...weak.

Elise could hear her own heart in her chest, beating strong. She wanted his heart to beat like hers. She wished so hard for a moment she

117

almost convinced herself she could keep him alive on willpower alone.

He stroked her hair weakly. "It's okay," he said, and it was such a lie that she had to smile.

"You're right," she said. "It's okay."

His hand slipped over hers when she sat up. "Stay."

"James…"

"Stay, Elise," he repeated, more strongly this time.

She didn't want to argue with him. The weight of her fatigue was too convincing. Whether or not Elise had time to take a nap, she was failing her battle against sleep. And why not? Stephanie was still two hours away.

Elise kicked her shoes off the side of the bed and rested beside James.

The air was heavy and still, but she didn't dare open a window to let it cool. His heart thumped its steady pace under her hand, and his shallow breaths marked out a rhythm like water rushing up the sand before sucking into the ocean again.

Or like wind blowing in the trees, sweeping through the branches.

Her muscles were leaden. Her eyes couldn't open.

The walls of the room collapsed slowly inward. Moss spread beneath her cheek as vines of ivy slithered up James's bookshelves. Leaves spread between the pages of the books.

Thunder rolled. Papers dripped onto the desk one by one and drizzled onto the floor.

Ivory fingers reached out to turn off the lamp, leaving the only light an occasional flash of lightning in the bellies of the red clouds. Rain began to tumble down the walls like a sticky-sweet waterfall.

Elise's parents stood beside the desk, waiting for her arrival as the second hands on the clock rushed toward twelve. She was running late. Somehow, she had gotten caught in the storm and lost her way.

She twisted and turned in search of a path. They were waiting. She couldn't keep them waiting.

A cool hand smoothed over her cheek, light as the kiss of the breeze. Forgiving. Her parents smiled down at her, calm but unseeing. Her mother's left eye socket was empty, and it rained within her skull.

The sky poured down, and Elise sat, her pale skin bared to the elements.

"*Crux sacra sit mihi lux, non draco sit mihi dux…*"

"Let the holy cross be my light, let the serpent not lead me astray."

"*Vade retro, Satana…*"

"Step back, Satan."

What do you think that means, Elise? A gentle smile. But who smiled? Where were the eyes belonging to those lips?

"*Nunquam suade mihi vana…*"

"What you offer me is evil…"

But what is evil?

The question wasn't part of the exorcism ritual. And neither was the second part—*what is goodness?* She had no answers for either. "*Sunt mala quae libas…*"

Such a sweet smile.

"*Ipse venena bibas…*"

"Drink the poison yourself…"

Fluid dripped from the corner of that mouth. There were hands, but they didn't wipe the poison away. It was dark burgundy, the crimson of wine…or blood.

One more time, Elise. From the top.

"*Crux sacra sit mihi lux, non draco sit mihi dux. Vade retro, Satana, nunquam suade mihi vana. Sunt mala quae libas, ipse venena bibas.*"

Very good. Again.

The branches scraped her vulnerable body.

"*Crux sacra sit mihi lux…*"

The ground disappeared. Elise fell, and fell…

The yawning blackness devoured her whole.

And fell…

Drink the poison yourself…

"I am the cold kiss of Death," the goddess whispered into her ear, "and you can never defeat me."

Elise's arms were bound to the stone wall behind her. Her face was bloody but set in a determined glare. Mud packed the open wound on her hip. A red cloak she didn't remember wearing pooled around her body. The death goddess—had she any other name?—stood high above her, swathed in shadow and holding a staff of sharpened human bone.

"Alive or dead, I will come back for you," the goddess murmured.

"You can't think this will do any good," Elise spat. The sky outside, visible through a small window near the ceiling, was black, blue, purple, and scarlet. Blood and pus bubbled from her wound. "You can't kill me yet. Not without screwing up your apocalyptic plans."

She laughed. Deep, throaty, bubbling like Elise's blood. "Who says I plan to use you?"

In her other hand, she clutched a stone dagger that sang with power. It was covered in symbols, some more familiar than others.

Her blood bulged in her veins. *Ipse venena bibas…*

The witch had clutched a stone, too.

James.

The sky faded to orange and back to red.

He ran through the jungle searching for Elise. The branches scraped at him, though the trees never moved, but still he searched. She watched him from her prison with the goddess, and she almost wished he wouldn't find her as much as she longed for him to save her.

The death goddess drew intricate designs in Elise's skin with vivid crimson ink.

Her breast rose and fell with breath. Her heartbeat fluttered.

The witch. The stone staff. Death.

Who says I plan to use you?

Her eyes flew open, and she *saw*.

Sleep ripped away from Elise. Consciousness slammed into her body. She gasped, flinching against the blow that never came—and then realized she heard the familiar sound of cars rushing by on the street outside.

Elise sat up. Nothing inside the room made noise but James's erratic breathing. He had pushed the sheets off to bare his body to the waist even though the room was only sixty degrees. She pressed her hand to his back. His temperature almost scorched her palm.

He made a small noise and moved into her touch, rolling over without waking up. His eyelids were dark, almost bruised.

"James," she said softly.

She searched for her cell phone in the darkness. Only an hour and a half had passed.

Elise slipped out of bed to search the closet for spare clothes. She located clean jeans and a shirt by touch, identifying it as her Black Death concert top by the hole near the hem.

When she finished changing, she returned to James. She checked his temperature with a hand to his forehead, and he was even hotter than he had been before. Sleep had done neither of them any good. James hadn't improved, and Elise had lost time.

Someone knocked at the door. She looked out the window to confirm that Stephanie's car was in the lot before meeting her at the door. The doctor's normally neat coif was frazzled.

"Thanks for coming," Elise said as Stephanie pushed past her into the house.

"Is he in bed?"

120

Elise nodded, and the doctor blew into his bedroom.

She sat beside him on the mattress and opened her bag. Elise waited in the doorway while Stephanie gave James a short and clinical examination. After a few minutes, the doctor took off her gloves.

"Can you take care of him here?" Elise asked.

"It doesn't look too bad," Stephanie said. "He doesn't seem to have lost enough blood to be struggling, and there hasn't been enough time for infection to set in." The doctor leveled a stern look at Elise. "He needs to be taken to a hospital."

"Will he die if he remains untreated for a few hours?"

"I can't be sure."

"I need you to stay and monitor him," Elise said. "I have to find the person that did this. Once they're out of the picture, you can send him to any hospital you want."

"Don't you think you should call the police?" Stephanie asked, following Elise out of the room. "Whoever attacked him is deranged."

"The police won't be able to help. You have to stay."

She folded her arms. "It goes against every good practice I know."

"Great," Elise said. "Now listen close. I'm going to lock all the doors and windows before I leave. Don't open any of them until I come back. James has set up wards around the apartment, so he'll be safe as long as they're shut. Don't let anyone in, don't call an ambulance, don't call the police. If you want James to make it to the hospital at all, you have to keep quiet."

Stephanie nodded reluctantly. "I'll take care of him."

"Thanks," Elise said. "Don't let him die."

She disappeared into the night.

The casino was full at three in the morning. Tricks of light and shadow made the room an endless plane of slot machines, where the drunk and down-on-their-luck hunched before digital screens. Listless, addicted gamblers fidgeted nearby as they watched for the next game to make them lucky.

Day, night. Neither mattered. Neither existed.

Money passed from player to casino attendant and became chips, and the chips went from hand to table, then to the dealer, and back to the attendants. The artificial clattering, jingling, singing sounds of slots and video poker paying out or begging to be played filled the air with discordant chorus.

The air was thick, and not with cigarette smoke. What it masked was impossible to ignore—an eternal depression, a feeling of being trapped. The feel of people imprisoning themselves in a place where the odds were low and wishing for a row of lucky sevens to change their ruined lives.

Elise moved quickly across the floor, watching each table as she passed. Cards whispered across the velvet—ten of spades, three of hearts, suicide king—and were taken into hands with nails yellow from tobacco.

She didn't enjoy the casinos here. She had been to Vegas and little back-alley stands in Eastern Europe where the dice were all hand-carved, and either was better. At least there was fun and good company to be had elsewhere.

It didn't take long for Elise to spot who she was looking for. David Nicholas never slept, and seldom worked, so he made up for decades of spare time with a platinum gambling card at every casino and a reserved spot at the Texas Hold-'Em table. He was a ghost beside two swarthy tourists with purple rings under their eyes. He cupped a stack of dwindling chips in one hand.

"Check," he said, tapping his cards on the table. He glanced up as Elise approached, his hand half-raised as though he expected a cocktail waitress. Then he realized who it actually was, and his face fell. "Shit."

Elise hauled him out of his chair and dragged him to the back door, flinging him into the alley behind the casino. The nightmare splashed into a puddle of rainwater and trash. He stared up at her with an expression like that of a rabbit spotting a hawk.

Jerking him up by the collar, she slammed him into the wall. "Tell me what you know," she snarled, pushing her dagger against the nightmare's stomach.

"Hang on, wait, whoa," David Nicholas said, holding his hands up. "All I know is I was winning a hand of hold-'em and you interrupted my streak. What do you think you're doing?"

"I've been inspired to take a break from accounting. If you cooperate, I can cut my vacation short. Understand?"

"I've got no idea what you're talking about."

"You're the one who told me something was coming when I visited Craven's," she said. "I'm starting to suspect you might have been onto something. I'm here to chat about it." Elise jerked on his collar again. He gurgled. "Chat, David Nicholas."

She dropped him back into the trash. Rats scurried away. "Don't think I got to chat about anything with you," he said. "It isn't profitable to play with humans…unless you want to try to make it that way, if you're catching my meaning."

She studied the blade of her knife, testing the edge against her thumb. "Tell you what. You tell me what you were talking about at the club, and I'll make it profitable by not stabbing you…again. I'm looking for a demon that can resurrect people."

He slipped a pack of cigarettes out of his sleeve and tapped one into his hand. He lit it, but didn't take a puff, contemplating the glowing end as he rolled it between his first finger and thumb.

"Demons can't resurrect people on their own."

"Yeah, but something is doing it anyway. Does the name *le Main de Morte* ring a bell?"

"The what *de* what?"

"The Hand of Death. That's what I said, the Hand of Death."

He sneered. "Death's Hand," David Nicholas murmured. "Old bastard."

"You know it, then."

"Know of it, yeah. It's hellborn. There was lots of talk about Death's Hand a few years ago. It was some big fad to talk about it, like, ooh, it's going to kill us dead, it's going to destroy Earth." David Nicholas took a drag. "Didn't happen, as you see. I wasn't worried about it. I never worry about that kind of thing."

"So it can resurrect people," Elise pressed.

"It can *reanimate*. Huge difference," he said, leaning one elbow on an orange crate. "Move corpses. You know, like a puppet."

"A little girl died," she said. "This Death's Hand thing possessed her. I performed an exorcism, and when he was gone, she was alive again."

"Treaty of Dis says demons can't perform resurrections. Only humans can do it, and not many of them at that. Just those special witches—you know, necromancers." He dropped his cigarette on the top of a nearby crate and ground it in with his fingers. His other hand was already moving to bring a second to his lips. "So can I go back to my game now?"

"No. What were you trying to warn me about?"

David Nicholas spread his hands wide. "What am I supposed to say? I got four hundred and sixty-three years of knowledge rattling around inside my skull. I could warn you about things that would give the Night Hag nightmares." His black eyes grew shadowed. "You got a necromancer on your hands, and you're in bigger trouble than anyone would be able to help you with."

"Tell me why."

"Death's Hand reanimates, right? Useful trick. You work your slaves to death, then bring 'em back and do it all over again." He shrugged, and it looked like his bony shoulders could almost pierce his jacket. "If it got a necromancer, though, it could resurrect, too. All Death's Hand's got to do is reanimate a freshly dead necromancer to create a bond with it, and—"

"I thought you said it couldn't come to Earth," Elise interrupted. "There are no necromancers in Hell. There aren't even any necromancers on Earth, come to think of it. Not in years."

"It can't actually come up. With a dark object, yeah, it can *appear* up here. But with the help of a necromancer, Death's Hand would have a heck of a lot easier time finding a witch to become a vessel."

Elise slipped her hand into her pocket, wrapping her hand around the stone she had taken from the witch. It vibrated ever so slightly as though it knew they were talking about it. "What do you mean, a vessel?"

"Someone to possess. A strong enough witch with the right power could become the body of Death's Hand. Like an ascension, you know, but without the centuries of building up its power first. 'Course, once Death's Hand has a body, it won't need a pet necromancer any more. It'll destroy him and keep the bits it wants, like everything else it reanimates."

"Destroy him," she echoed. "Do you mean…"

"Death's Hand destroys its legions once they're used up. Clean-up, you know. Real easy and nice. It won't need the necromancer to keep the power after awhile. Hypothetically, of course. That would violate the Treaty of Dis and bring down all kinds of hellfire, and nobody's stupid enough to do that."

"Good. Thanks." Elise turned to leave.

"*Vedae som matis,*" he said. He said the words with a strange accent, almost choking on them, as though they were spoken in the throat rather than the mouth.

"What?"

"*Vedae som matis.* It's the demon language, and that's what they call it down there. Thought you might be interested."

"What does *vedae som matis* mean?"

"Hand of Death."

Shocking. Elise stuck her knife back in her belt. "Thanks for the information."

"This is twice now you've made me had a bad day, cabbage," David Nicholas called after her as she headed down the alley. "First one was free. Second one's going to cost you."

"Send a bill to my office," she snapped. "The check bounced, by the way. I'm going to get that money from you in blood if I have to."

"Go ahead and try," he said. His eyes glowed.

Elise mulled over the information he had given her as she navigated the alleys behind the casino. *Vedae som matis*. Death's Hand. Reanimation, not resurrection. That would explain why it had possessed Lucinde. She must not have been strong enough to become the vessel of Death's Hand. James had enough power, but Death's Hand needed a dead witch.

She wrapped her hand around the stone in her pocket, as though it might give her answers. The sense of demonic energy had grown in intensity, ringing throughout Elise's senses.

Had the staff begun radiating more energy, or was it something... else?

Elise picked up the pace again and stretched out her senses. Yes, there were definitely demons around, and it wasn't hard to guess what would be tracking her.

Fiends. And they were close.

She gripped her knife. Elise hurried down the sidewalk toward the parking garage. Dancing casino lights lit her path, casting flickering shadows on the street before her, turning the night into a tired carnival of once-great businesses harping their unwanted wares.

A chill crept up her spine, and the demonic sensations intensified.

Motion blurred at the corner of Elise's vision.

She spun, cutting the dagger through the night air. A huge fist grabbed her before she could even see the attached face—the corpse from the hospital again—and slammed her hand into the wall. Concrete scraped her exposed fingers. Pain shocked up her arm. Her fingers lost their grip on the dagger, and it clattered to the concrete.

The possessed one twisted her around, jerking her into his body and wrapping a steel-clad arm around her. He threw himself backward into the shadow of a building, taking Elise with him.

She lost her footing, and the servant forced her against a wall. His hot hand clamped over her nose and mouth, cutting off her breath. The rag in his hand smelled faintly sweet, and slightly alcoholic. Elise had never smelled anything like it before, but she'd seen enough movies to recognize chloroform.

She held her breath, but her throat burned with the taste of chemicals, and it was too late.

125

Chapter 12

BETTY TOOK THE coffee pot out of the machine, grabbed a cozy, and set both on the table in front of Anthony. "Drink," she said.

Anthony slumped forward on her table and dropped his chin on his folded arms. He wore a button-down shirt and clean jeans, and there wasn't a spot of oil anywhere on his body. He was well-dressed for the crack of dawn. "I don't want it."

"Cheer up," she said. "Caffeine's a mood booster."

"I hate coffee."

She dropped into the chair beside him, moved the vase so it wasn't between them, and poured herself a cup. "Of course you like coffee. Everyone likes coffee. It's just a matter of how much sugar and creamer you need." She punctuated her statement by emptying the cream bottle into her half-full mug and sprinkling sugar atop it, stirring with a swizzle stick topped by a hula dancer. "Did you even change out of your clothes after last night?"

"No. I slept like this," he said. "I just don't get it. If she didn't want to go on another date with me, why would she agree to go out in the first place?"

"Isn't that just another delightful part of the enigma that is Elise?"

"It's fucked up, that's what it is." He glanced at the coffee pot. "What kind is that?"

"Komodo blend," she said, wafting the cup in the air. "Also known as percolated heaven. Sound good yet?"

"No."

Betty took a large slurp of the coffee and set it down again. "I'm going to give it to you straight, baby cousin of mine: Elise would not be afraid of refusing dates. If she thought your first date sucked, she would get that look that says in her not-so-sneaky way that if you speak to her again she'll break your nose. That's about as subtle as she gets. Agreeing to a date and then ditching you—that isn't her *modus operandi*."

He grunted. "I guess."

"Do you know how many boyfriends she's had in the time I've known her?"

"I don't think I want to know."

"None," Betty said. "Not one. And do you know how many guys have asked her out?" Anthony shook his head. "None. She scares everyone off. I think she was impressed that you asked her at all."

"Well, I'm not scared of some girl," Anthony said.

She smacked him. "Don't be an ass. Elise is terrifying."

"Fine, whatever, she's terrifying. I still really like her." He scoffed. "I *did* like her."

"Cut her some slack."

"She ditched me without a phone call. Her only text said that she got caught up doing something with James," Anthony said.

"Then that's probably true."

He leaned against the back of the chair, cupping his hands behind his neck. He rolled his thoughts around for a moment before speaking. "Do you think Elise and James…?"

She took a long, slow drink of her coffee, setting it down with a satisfied sigh. "No."

"But—"

"*No*. That dance studio is a monastery. I promise."

"Then she just doesn't like me," he concluded stubbornly. Betty ignored him. "I'm not going to wait around for her to notice me and I'm not going to give her another chance."

"Sure," she said. "Did I remember to mention that she joined that pole dance class at that rival studio? They're doing an exhibition next week and she's going to be dancing in a bikini. Gyrating. Sweaty."

His eyes lit up. "Really? When?"

"I'm lying, Elise didn't join the class. She doesn't even know where her hips are." Betty laughed. "'Giving up on her.' You're so full of shit."

He couldn't help but laugh too. "You're nuts, Betty. You know—" Anthony suddenly went rigid. His eyes widened. "Wait. Did you hear that?"

The window exploded.

Glass showered into the kitchen. Betty shrieked, throwing herself under the table, and Anthony followed, sliding to the floor for cover.

Something heavy—not large, but insanely *dense*—crashed through the broken window. It rolled on the glass shards, knocking the appliances from the counters to the floor, and hit the linoleum with the *thud* of a cannonball hitting concrete.

It stopped moving for an instant. Only an instant. It was gray, hulking, covered in twisted red scars. Eyes like soft balls stuck out on either side of its head.

And it was screaming.

Its eyelids flashed open and then shut again. It clawed at its own face, its screech the mix of a sob and a wail, and Betty slapped her hands over her ears to block out the noise. Blood trailed from the corners of its eyes and the gash of its mouth.

Icy terror smashed into Anthony's chest, and for an instant, he couldn't breathe.

His focus narrowed on the monster. *Fight.*

He knocked the table over, putting it between himself and the monster. It smashed into the tabletop. Wood squealed against the floor, and Betty cried out.

"Move," Anthony said, "move! Hide!"

It barreled into the table again and then fell back, still tearing at its eyes and screaming. Betty hurried to her feet, and he pushed her toward the hallway. She knocked over one of the chairs in her haste.

The monster rushed her, a blur of shrieking rage and agony.

Anthony threw himself into its side, knocking them both down. Its three-fingered hands clamped onto his arms like a steel vice.

He was airborne. The wall became huge in his vision.

Pain rang through his body, and his face hit the floor.

It went for Betty again. Anthony pushed himself to all fours and shook his head to clear his vision. His cousin threw herself into the closet and tried to pull it shut, but it had gotten a hand in the way and she was screaming and Anthony couldn't revel in his pain. He had to focus.

"Where's your dad's shotgun?" he yelled.

Betty's panicked eyes met his. "My bedroom closet—it's not loaded —"

He slid into the kitchen, scooping up the first sharp thing he saw. The monster tore open the closet door and reached for Betty.

"Hey," Anthony said, "hey! Over here!"

He flung the knife at the monster, missing by at least two feet. It turned its bulging eyes on him. Eyelids cracked, he could just make out a sliver of massive pupil staring at him. Betty jerked her foot into the closet

128

and shut the door.

Its jaw dropped wide and it roared, shrill and berserk. Sputum slapped against its chin.

Anthony made a break for the bedroom. The monster dodged into his path. He leapt over its head, dashing for the bedroom, and slammed the door. The lock clicked.

It crashed into the door with a wail.

Anthony paused for an instant, sucking in a hard breath of air, watching Betty's door. The monster hit again, but it held.

He went to the closet and began to search.

Tío Jacob didn't like the idea of his little girl living alone without protection, even with her cousin next door, so he had gifted her with a combat assault shotgun as a housewarming gift. At the time, Betty had teased her dad for being so paranoid, but it didn't seem nearly so paranoid now.

Anthony found the gun, unzipping the sleeve to withdraw it. The monster smashed into the other side of the door. It began to buckle.

He tore through Betty's shelves, knocking her collection of records to the floor and shuffling through a pile of stuffed animals to find where she kept the ammo. A stack of boxes were clustered in the back corner of her closet, dusty and unopened since the day Anthony had given them to her. He had bought her two kinds of rounds: one for target shooting, and double ought for making sure a live target would never get up again.

He grabbed the double ought.

Another hit. The door splintered.

Anthony slammed his shoulder into the crack to keep it from breaking entirely. His hands shook as he tried to get a round out of the box. He dropped it. Ammunition spilled across the carpet.

Swearing, he dropped to the floor and held the door shut with a foot, back pressed against the foot of Betty's bed. He slid open the loading port on the bottom of the shotgun.

Anthony counted out the shells he could reach as he loaded it—no time to panic—and pumped once. The chamber wasn't full, but if he needed more rounds to kill that thing, he probably wouldn't live to do it anyway. He kept the number of rounds hovering in his head—five—and let go of the door.

He had only an instant to get on one knee, shotgun braced against his shoulder, before the monster broke through. It rushed at him on all fours, its nails tearing into the carpet.

He angled down and squeezed the trigger.

BLAM.

The recoil knocked the butt of the shotgun into the pad of his shoulder and he rocked backward. The monster's arm disappeared in a spray of blood and pellets smacked into the floor.

He pumped the action and an empty casing went flying. *Four.*

It screamed a terrible scream that made his eardrums throb, rearing back on its stubby legs. Anthony braced properly this time and squeezed the trigger again.

BLAM.

Suddenly, the monster didn't have a face.

Three rounds.

With no flesh, Anthony could see all too well the pellets that had buried into its skull. There was blood everywhere, tassels of skin, the dribbling remnants of its left eyeball. Some of the pellets had implanted in the drywall behind its head and Anthony's ears were ringing.

It raised onto its remaining forearm and dragged its carcass toward him.

He stood, pointing the muzzle of the shotgun straight down at its head, and pulled the trigger once more.

BLAM.

The monster flattened without the back of its skull.

Two.

Was it dead? Anthony didn't care to find out. He pumped again.

BLAM. Pump. The casing hit the carpet. *BLAM.*

Empty.

Anthony lifted the shotgun and tapped the remnants of the monster with the toe of his shoe. Its mangled body didn't react. It occurred to him, distantly, that his only pair of nice jeans were soaked in blood and that he couldn't hear anymore.

But the monster was dead. *Very* dead.

"You can come out, Betty," he called. He wasn't sure if he actually yelled or not—he couldn't hear his own voice.

The closet door at the end of the hall opened and Betty crept out. Her mouth moved, and he knew she was speaking, but all he heard was a sound like a vibrating tuning fork.

She stood in the doorway, gaping at the body, and her mouth kept on moving. Judging by her expression, he was glad he didn't have to listen to her.

The quality of the air in the room changed, and the remnants of the monster dissolved into the carpet.

130

Anthony leapt forward and tried to grab what used to be a finger—for what, he wasn't sure—but it crumbled in his hand. Even the blood and chunks of intestine on his pants evaporated into puffs of smoke, leaving him as clean as he had been before the fight.

The entire thing was gone in seconds, and only the mess of shotgun damage proved there had ever been a fight.

Betty was agape. "Oh...my...god. What just happened?" It sounded as though she was whispering.

"I have no idea," Anthony said. Biggest understatement of his life.

"Dad is going to be pissed when I tell him what happened to his carpet." She stared at the floor—the empty shell casings, the chewed-up shag, and the pile of ash that had once been a body. Then she looked up at her cousin, the shotgun balanced between his hands, and a grin broke across her face. "That was *so* cool!" She punched his arm. "You're practically G.I.-fucking-Joe!"

He dropped the shotgun and collapsed on the end of her bed. Anthony's hands wouldn't stop shaking. "Fuck."

"Oh man, I think that might have been the most incredible experience of my life!"

Anthony worked his jaw around, trying to clear out his ears. His hearing had almost entirely returned, and the ringing was replaced by... silence.

"Why is it so quiet?"

Betty stopped quivering with delight to look at him. "Huh?"

"Where are the sirens?"

"There aren't any."

"That thing was loud. If someone had phoned in a disturbance, we'd have at least one car by now."

Betty peered through her window to the silent street beyond. "I don't know. There's nobody outside, so maybe no one's home—or the cops could be called away on something else."

"Or something big is going on," Anthony said. "I think someone just tried to kill us."

"Kill us? With a deformed monkey? Why?"

Anthony used Betty's bed post to haul himself into a standing position. "Something weird was happening with the coven. James said there were—I don't know, demons or something. He called in an exorcist to help him. Didn't he say that she was a friend?"

Betty nodded. "Yeah, but that was about Marisa's kid." A light clicked on behind her eyes. "Oh. *Oh.* But that's impossible, I would know if..."

"Elise is the exorcist," he finished. "She's been injured. She's not talking about why."

"Aren't priests the only ones who can do that stuff?" Betty asked, starting to pace. She didn't let Anthony respond before continuing. "Okay, let's say something is happening—maybe Elise is an exorcist or maybe she isn't. It already attacked Marisa's family. It attacked us. For all we know, it could have attacked Elise and James last night. Maybe that's why she ditched you." She gasped. "Maybe it's after our coven!"

"That's kind of a leap." He laughed. "This is ridiculous."

Betty rested her hands on his shoulders. "Anthony, not to sound patronizing, but you just killed a gargoyle on my carpet."

"Good point."

She left the room, searching through the rubble that had been her kitchen. "We need to find out if anyone else has been attacked. Help me find my cell phone?"

Anthony nodded. "Yeah, sure. Who's left?"

"Those two witches that live up at the lake," Betty said. "Windsong and her husband, Phoenix. Then there's Morrighan, but she left to visit her grandparents in Virginia this morning. Stephanie lives in the area, but I don't have her number. The only person in town is Ann."

He plucked Betty's pink phone from the spilled coffee pot. "Found it." Betty hurried to remove the battery, but it was too late—something inside the phone fizzled. She sighed.

"Okay, we'll just have to use the neighbor's house phone to call everyone."

"Ann lives just up the hill from the university. I'll go check on her. Want to come?"

She surveyed the damage around her. "No. I should patch the window and clean up all that glass."

"Call her and tell her I'm on my way. Whatever's going on...it's serious. Do you think you could get a hold of Elise too?"

"I'll make sure she's okay," Betty said. She grabbed the shotgun from the bedroom and gave it to him, as well as a new box of shells. "I'll make sure everyone's okay. Call me when you find Ann—we should get together and figure out what's going on. She's smart. She'll know."

"Okay," he said, dropping the ammo into his pocket. "Watch yourself."

He ran out to his Jeep and jumped in, stowing the gun behind his seat. Anthony suspected he was scared—probably even terrified—and he just couldn't feel it yet. He hadn't stopped shaking. It wasn't the time to

132

freak out. Later, the shock of what had just happened would probably sink in, and he could really freak out.

At the moment, though, he had a purpose, and that was enough to keep him moving.

Chapter 13

DRIP...DRIP DRIP...

Elise's head throbbed in time with a distant beat. Her shoulders and ankles ached. Her eyes felt sticky.

Drip drip...

Where was she?

"James?" she croaked. Her throat was too thick and dry to speak properly. She swallowed and smacked her lips, rolling her tongue around in her mouth. "James?"

Drip...drip...

Something was running down her arm. She tried to lift her head against gravity, which seemed to have tripled while she was unconscious. The plain gray ceiling had a drain in the middle. The floor was covered in exposed beams.

Wait. No. That wasn't right.

Elise was hanging upside down by her ankles.

She squinted at her arm in the dim light. Blood trickled out of the inner corner of her elbow, trailed down her hand, and dripped off her fingertip. That sound was her blood hitting the floor. Never a good sign.

She relaxed and shut her eyes to collect herself. It wasn't the first time Elise had been captured by a demon. This was like riding a bicycle. A hell bicycle made of damned skeletons and fire, but a bicycle nevertheless.

Counting silently to ten, she opened her eyes again to study the room around her.

It was empty. No furniture, which meant no obstructions to use as hiding places. She knew she must have been disarmed, but she double checked her waist anyway. Even her holsters had been taken away. She wasn't surprised to find that the stone staff was missing.

Flexing her abs to sit up, she held onto her ankles and examined the bindings. Silk ropes. What kind of demon used silk ropes? They were pulled tight against the iron hook by her weight, but nothing prevented her from untying them. She lifted herself on the hook with one hand while she picked at the knots with her fingernails.

The loss of blood made her weak. She had to rest twice before she could unravel the knots enough to get her first leg free. The second was short work after that, and she lowered herself carefully to the floor.

Changing orientation after being upside down for so long made her head rush. She braced a hand against the wall for a moment.

Deep breaths.

The only light came from the crack underneath the door. It looked like she was in an unfurnished, windowless basement, and her own blood was oozing toward the drain in the floor.

She finally got a good look at the wall she had been hanging on, and she jerked her hand back. The sigil from Lucinde's forehead had been painted in blood on the wall. It stretched from floor to ceiling. Elise had been hanging in the middle of it.

All that blood couldn't have come from her. She searched her body for injuries and only found a nick in the veins of each arm. It was already clotting.

She sniffed it. Definitely blood.

Someone moved on the other side of the door.

Elise crouched behind it, twisting the ropes around her fists and stretching them tight to form a garrote. Her heart wasn't even beating fast. A strange kind of calm settled over her—the calm before the killing.

It swung open. She prepared to jump.

And Ann stepped in.

Elise brought the ropes down in front of the witch, yanking them against her throat to pull her back against Elise's body.

She wrenched the ropes back. Ann choked.

"Elise—"

Turning her fists to tighten the ropes, Ann's words became incoherent gurgles. She slapped against Elise's hands as they sank to the floor together. The witch's feet kicked helplessly against the concrete.

Elise nudged the door open with a toe to look in the hall. Empty. Shouldn't there have been something guarding her?

Doubt crept in as Ann's struggles grew weaker. What if James had sent her?

Ann gave strained spluttering noise.

135

Elise released her. She collapsed.

"What are you doing here?" Elise asked, crouching over her body. She gave Ann's legs and sides a brief pat, searching for weapons, and didn't find anything.

The witch sucked in several hard breaths. Her ruddy face had broken out in sweat.

"They aren't kidding when they say you're like a human weapon, are they?" she gasped. "That *really* hurt. I thought you were going to kill me."

"I was," she said. There was no point dancing around the subject. "I thought you were working for Death's Hand. Did James send you? Is he okay?"

"James is fine for now." Ann sat up and smiled.

The situation felt completely wrong for a rescue. Elise wrapped the rope around her fists again. She recalled seeing those bright blue eyes under a ski mask at the cemetery—the same eyes that smiled at her now.

"James told me you're an herb witch," Elise said. "But you're the necromancer, aren't you?"

Ann shrugged. "Kitchen witchery is easy to fake." When Elise tensed, she held up a hand like it could stop an attack. "There are more than a dozen fiends in the house above us."

"Why?"

"I'm not a fighter. It makes sense to have guards."

"No. Why are you working with Death's Hand?"

She stood and dusted herself off. Ann's color was returning to normal. "*Vedae som matis* doesn't think I should tell you very much. She's usually right about things. Look, I like you a lot, Elise. I could have drained you dry to paint that sigil, but I used mostly pig's blood instead. We don't have to fight. There's enough room in the new world for both of us."

"New world?" Elise tried to make herself sound calm, even though she was watching the doorway and mentally calculating the odds of escaping twenty fiends unarmed.

"Sure. I know you're in Reno because of the Warrens, and you thought all the power from them would prevent your enemies from locating you remotely...right?" Ann didn't wait for a response before continuing. "But that protection doesn't come from the Warrens. There are angelic ruins below them."

She already knew that, but having her suspicions confirmed made a sick kind of chill settle over her.

"So this is a takeover."

"*Vedae som matis* is trapped in Hell, Elise. You know what it's like

136

down there? It's…well, it's Hell. All she needs to break through to this side is a corporeal body, and then we can build a kingdom together." She took the stone staff out of her pocket and gave it the kind of loving look most girls would reserve for a boyfriend.

Her opinion of Ann immediately shifted from "this girl is misguided" to "this girl is insane."

Ann stepped forward, holding out a hand. "We can still be friends. When *vedae som matis* takes over, she'll need a council, and I can suggest you and Betty if…"

"If what? If I agree to be a blood donor?"

"No," she said. "I've got all I needed from you. My house is done being anointed. *Vedae som matis* was right about that, too. Your blood is really potent."

"You can't use me as a vessel. I'm not a witch."

Her smile went painfully wide. "Who says I wanted you? I poisoned James for a reason, you know."

I am the cold kiss of Death…

Elise joined her fists together and swung, bringing both down on Ann's head.

The witch screamed as she fell, bringing up her arms to protect herself. It wasn't good enough. Elise kicked her in the face, and her nose snapped. Blood sprayed across the concrete.

A gray blur hurtled into the room, striking Elise in the stomach with all the power of an oncoming train. Her back slammed into the wall.

Over the fiend's head, Elise saw Ann try to push herself up, then collapse again.

Elise kneed the demon in the stomach, pushing it away from her. She ran for the door, but the fiend grabbed at her shirt with its clawed hands. She stuck her hip out and used its own momentum to throw it over her leg. It lost balance, and Elise jumped over Ann, pausing only to pick up the staff.

It made her hands burn, so she stuffed it in the back pocket of her jeans. She ran up the stairs and burst through the door to the first floor of the house.

The walls were lined with pictures. None of them featured Ann.

Something scuffled in the basement behind her.

Elise darted to the nearest room, throwing the door open. Empty bedroom. There was a bookshelf in front of the window. She opened another door—closet. Its shelves were covered in fragments of bone.

The fiend launched itself out of Ann's room, and she dodged. It hit the wall instead, and the drywall cracked.

"Get the kopis!" Ann shrieked from the other room. "Get her!"

Elise rushed into the darkened living room. It stank of brimstone and blood, and a trio of possessed corpses sat beside the battered couch. They didn't register Elise's appearance, even though she recognized two of them as the ones she had fought in the cemetery the night before.

But the pair of fiends huddled in the corner in the shadow of the television, eating a bloody scrap of meat, didn't fail to see Elise.

One of the fiends darted at her, and she backhanded it, sending it flying into the wall.

Fire burned a path down Elise's thigh. She cried out. The second fiend flung shreds of her jeans from its claws and slashed again, but she leapt away just in time. The backs of her legs bumped into something, and she stumbled. Her thigh gave out.

Elise hit the ground. The possessed ones animated and stood, staring at her with empty eyes.

She scrambled to her feet as they lunged, kicking a fiend squarely in the face. It flew backwards with a little squeal, striking the lone window through the curtains and sliding to the floor.

Elise flung open the front door, and light flooded into the living room. The remaining fiend recoiled, covering its bulbous eyeballs with tiny scarred hands.

She hurtled outside into fresh air and freedom. She ran to the end of the street and stopped short—Ann's house was on a hill overlooking the city, and below the hill stood Our Mother of Sorrows cemetery.

The other houses on the street were silent, seemingly unoccupied, but the sky was gray and growing darker by the minute. Black thunderheads rolled down the mountains toward the late afternoon sun. Once the sun disappeared, there would be nothing keeping the fiends from following her.

The possessed ones didn't care about sunlight. Something scraped behind her.

They were coming.

Elise's feet pounded against pavement. Her right twitched. The fiend's claws hurt like a son of a bitch, and the staff in her pocket hummed with furious energy.

The street behind her grew louder. More scraping, more motion. Elise's leg wouldn't go as fast as she needed it to—every time she set down her foot, her leg buckled and the best she could manage was a striding limp.

138

She glanced over her shoulder. Three possessed ones chased her, and they were picking up speed. Worse yet, Elise could feel the demonic presence of the fiends—they were vulnerable to bright lights, but that didn't mean they couldn't run blind. And Ann was furious enough to make them do it.

A Jeep passed the other end of the street and stopped at the corner.

"Elise!" The Jeep backed up, made a hard turn, and pulled up alongside her backward. Anthony stared at her from the driver's seat. "What's going on?"

"No time to explain," she said, grabbing the car's frame and hauling her body up. She didn't even wait to be fully inside the car before waving at him. "Go, Anthony!"

He adjusted his side mirror. "What are *those*?"

She clambered into the passenger's seat. The sense of the servants was almost overwhelming, and she didn't need to look to know they were coming up on the Jeep. "Drive, damn it! Drive!"

Anthony slammed his foot on the gas. The tires spun out, and the engine red-lined.

Then he found traction, and the car shot down the street. Elise was thrown back into the seat. She gripped the roll cage, twisting around to watch the street recede behind them.

He threw a hard left turn without slowing down. The Jeep felt like it was going to roll, but it barely kept its tires on the road.

The fiends couldn't keep up. Even better, there wasn't much traffic, so they didn't have to stop. Elise dropped back again and ripped her jeans open even wider to see the damage. Three parallel gashes marked the side of her thigh, hip to knee. Although they burned, the wound was shallow.

"Oh God," Anthony said, staring at her leg.

"Get to the studio, and take the back roads," Elise ordered, reaching into the back seat to search through his junk. She found an oil-stained polo with a university logo on the breast. "Are you attached to this shirt?"

He shook his head, and she dabbed at her wounds.

"Elise, what in the heck was—shit!"

Anthony slammed on the breaks. She hit the dashboard hands-first.

She looked up in time to see a hand swipe at her over the windshield, white eyes and a pale face dripping with blood pressed against the glass.

"Don't stop!" Elise yelled, pushing the hand aside when the servant reached for Anthony. He slouched low in his seat. "Faster!"

The engine roared. She pulled herself up on the windshield, hauled back, and punched the servant with all her strength. He didn't register any pain, but his one-handed grip on the roll cage weakened.

Anthony swerved, and Elise fell against the side of the Jeep. The possessed one tumbled off the hood.

Elise watched him roll down the asphalt. A truck several car lengths behind them swerved to avoid him as it turned the corner. The servant picked itself up, and then Anthony and Elise turned a corner as well. He disappeared.

"What the *fuck* was that?" Anthony asked as Elise plopped back down in the seat again. His chest was rising and falling rapidly as though he had been the one running. His face and knuckles were white. "That looked like—I mean—was that a *zombie*?"

"Not exactly. I have no idea why you were passing that street, Anthony, but thank God you were. I'm not sure I could have out-run them. I think they're getting stronger."

"Oh my God, they're still back there, aren't they? Ann lives up there! We have to go back, she might be—"

"Fuck Ann," Elise said. "She's fine."

"I'm going to take your word for it. I have seen the weirdest shit today," Anthony said. "Do you want to tell me what's the hell is going on?"

She studied the strong line of his nose and jaw in profile. He was focusing on the road, but the veins standing out on his neck belied how much of an effort it was for him not to stare at Elise.

"You know how you were saying you wanted to be a part of my life?" she asked. He nodded, knuckles white. "Wish granted. Now get me back to the studio."

Part 5: The Twelfth Hour

GUATEMALA – AUGUST 2004

When James woke up in the condo, he was partially healed, and totally alone. Elise's swords were gone.

He wasn't sure if it was instinct or Elise's history of getting into trouble that told him something was wrong, but he didn't bother waiting for her to return. He stuffed what was left of his Book of Shadows into a bag, slung it over his shoulder, and hobbled out the door with his makeshift crutch. He could barely feel his knee as magic knit the ligaments back together. Every time he took a step, it tried to buckle under him.

Worse yet, it was still raining, and as dark as night even though it was afternoon. The ground was slick and muddy. But slowly, deliberately, he made his way toward town.

He tensed when he saw two figures coming up the road toward him. When they drew close enough for him to realize they were human, he still didn't relax.

One of the men was built like a cinderblock, and the other was a boy with a shotgun strapped to his back and nervous eyes. "Where's Elise?" asked the first without prelude.

"Who are you?" James asked, raising his voice to be heard over the blasting wind.

"The name's Bryce." The cinderblock jerked his thumb at the other man. "This is Diego. McIntyre said Elise needs our help. Here we are."

So they were kopides. Both of them. "I thought McIntyre was coming himself."

"He couldn't make it," Diego said with an accent so thick that James barely understood him.

"Well, you're too late. She's already gone. She's gone into the undercity—looking for that clock."

"So she's dead," Bryce said.

James's fist clenched on his walking stick. "No. She's alive." He would know the instant she died. It hadn't happened. Not yet. "But that could change quickly. We have to find her."

Bryce looked excited at the prospect of going into the undercity. He grinned, and James saw that he was missing most of his teeth. His skin had the tough, scarred look of an old farmer even though he couldn't have been thirty yet.

"Fucking fantastic," he said. "Tell us what to do."

He opened his mouth to respond.

James!

Pain flared down his flesh. Burning silver spikes flayed his skin, baring his bones as the jungle blurred and darkened around him.

With a roar of pain, James staggered. A pair of hands kept him from falling.

"The hell—?" someone said.

But James was lost in a black pit of agony. Smoke burned his lungs. Hot stone dug into his spine, and metal bit his wrists, chafing until they went slick with blood.

No. Not *his* wrists.

A fist struck him across the face. His vision cleared in time to see Bryce rearing above him with his hand raised for another blow. "Stop," James said with a shudder. Elise's silent cried echoed through him. He hadn't even know she could scream.

Bryce lifted him and set him on his feet like he was a child. Diego gave James his dropped crutch.

"What's wrong with you?" Bryce asked warily. His hands flexed as he stared around at the trees, as though waiting to be attacked.

"It's Elise. Something is happening to her. She's—"

The pain blazed again.

James...James...

She was chained. Bleeding.

"What should we do? Tell us how to help," Diego said. His hands were trembling.

Help? They wanted to *help*?

He took a moment to size them up. Bryce looked as dumb as the mud beneath his feet, but he was pure muscle. Diego wouldn't be nearly so useful—he was too scared. He wouldn't last long in the undercity, and

142

James wouldn't make it far with his ruined knee, either. And he wanted that shotgun.

"Sorry about this," James said.

He dropped his walking stick, pulled a slip of paper from the Book of Shadows, and seized Diego's arm.

Electricity leaped between them. Diego's skin turned ashen gray, and he collapsed, dragging them both to the ground. Bryce shouted and drew his gun, but James held up his hands.

"He's fine," James said. "He'll be okay. He's unconscious."

Careful to stay out of arm's reach, Bryce checked Diego's pulse. "What did you do to him?"

"I borrowed his strength to heal myself." And to prove it, he stood up —slowly, no need to tempt the trigger finger—and stripped the bandages from his knee. It didn't hurt anymore.

James expected him to argue. There were so few living witches that rivaled his power that most people weren't aware such healing was even possible. But Bryce looked angry, not disbelieving. "Are you nuts?" he asked. "Now there's only two of us!"

"And I wouldn't have been able to go anywhere without healing first. Tell me: would you rather descend toward almost certain death with a scared boy, or the aspis who just defeated him with a single touch?"

Bryce couldn't seem to find a reason to argue.

Elise had no idea that she could hurt so much without passing out. Time made no sense anymore. Had it been minutes? Hours? Years?

Had the clock struck twelve yet?

Brilliant white pain burned through her bones. Blood raced down her skin from a thousand shallow cuts.

She was a roast pig on a spit. She was a rabbit being skinned. Pillars of fire raced along her spine, arced through the sky, scorched the earth.

When she thought it couldn't hurt worse, the knife dug in somewhere new, and it did.

"Amazing how well kopides heal," a voice said. "You may not even scar."

The words jangled in her ears. She screamed and screamed. Blood swirled past her head, filling the cracks in the stone, and flashes of black blurred her vision.

The tip of a stone knife scraped against her breastbone.

143

You may not even scar.

Her head swam. She had no blood. No skin.

The goddess of death held something over her, and it dripped warmth on her face, and Elise thought she recognized the strip of pink dotted by freckles and—*oh God.*

The world couldn't end soon enough.

James ran through the jungle. He didn't see with his eyes; he saw with Elise's. He saw a limp hand in front of her on the floor. He saw pooling blood. He saw iron chains and bare, dirty feet.

Pain. So much pain.

He muttered under his breath as he ran on his repaired knee, even though he wasn't sure she could hear. "I'm coming—hold on—stay awake—"

Bryce crashed gracelessly through the trees behind him, panting and swearing. Like many bulky, muscled men, he didn't seem to have focused on his cardio health. He couldn't keep up.

The rain poured around them, salty-sweet like the ocean. Trees swayed in the wind. James's shirt stuck to his back, and he hugged the shotgun to his chest to keep from catching on the foliage.

Where was she?

James tried to follow the feelings Elise radiated, but it was difficult. Her mind made no sense to him. Maybe if they had been piggybacked—maybe if she wasn't in so much pain—

A mark on a tree caught his eye. "Wait!" James called.

Bryce stopped and leaned on his knees, gasping for air. "What?"

A signpost was carved into the trunk of the tree. It was a marker from one demon to another, indicating the direction of the undercity.

His eyes tracked the signpost to the next tree, and the next. There were small marks all around him. They led back toward town. How could he have missed them?

"This way," James said.

He doubled back, climbing toward the road. Bryce followed as well as he could. "Hey!" he shouted. "We got company!"

James turned. It was hard to see through the motion of the trees in the wind, but something was moving higher on the mountain. Dark shapes.

"Demons?" James called back.

"A whole fucking century of 'em!"

144

He ran faster, the Book of Shadows bouncing on his back in its bag. He didn't like his odds against a centuria of demons—over eighty of them—not even with Bryce's help.

As he followed the marks closer to town, he began to hear yelps and howls. They were getting closer.

"It's in there," he shouted, pointing at a shop the markers indicated as the entrance. Bryce was hurrying to catch up, but he was still a hundred meters back. "I'm going down! Can you hold them off?"

The kopis responded by drawing his gun.

James dove into the shop and went into the basement. There was a trap door. It was open, but the stairs had collapsed.

James!

Elise was screaming again. She wasn't far. He could feel her through the earth, through the collapsed paths, just a couple miles away but completely unreachable.

Gunshots fired outside the shop. Bryce shouted.

Fear dragged on James's heart. What was he supposed to do? How could he get to Elise when the only entrance to the undercity was blocked?

He shut his eyes, trying to see through their bond again. *Where are you? How can I reach you?*

Through her pain, he glimpsed a bone scepter and a stone knife. James fought to push back the sounds of fighting above him and focus on her vision, trying to see beyond the bare knees of the goddess.

A wall. Smoke. Window. And beyond that, pyramid. It was tall. The chamber, and the clock inside of it, was huge.

James's eyes flew open. She wasn't at the end of a labyrinth of demonic undercity—she was just under the surface, in the jungle not far from him.

He quickly paged through his Book of Shadows, seeing how many battle spells he had left. There weren't many. The simple ones—casting fire, blasts of air—were almost gone. Everything else that remained were the powerful spells his aunt told him not to mess with. Horrible, deadly spells. He'd been carrying them around for years.

Whispering a short prayer, James ripped a handful of pages out of the Book and flew up the stairs to street level.

Bryce blocked the doorway with his body. Another one of the leathery gray demons had its teeth clamped down on the arm of his leather jacket. Dozens more demons rushed down the street.

James barely had time to register the sheer number of bodies before

145

they crashed upon them. He was lost in a rush of blood and drool and growls. He dropped the shotgun. "Get down!" he shouted to Bryce.

The kopis threw himself to the ground, and James threw a scrap of paper.

Power ripped from him. A dozen hearts stopped beating at once.

They fell like dominoes, but James didn't stop to watch it. He grabbed Bryce by the arm and hauled him to his feet. "Move," he said as the surviving demons clambered over their dead brethren. "Now. Hurry!"

The men sprinted across the road and into the jungle again. James could still hear Elise in the back of his mind, but it was faint. After another minute, he couldn't hear her at all.

"Why aren't we going down?" Bryce asked.

"We are going down," James said. "But we're not taking the stairs."

After an eternity of pain, Elise awoke. She tried to sit up, but her hands couldn't find traction. She slipped on something soft and slick. She looked down to see that it was a face with gaping eyes and no jaw.

Gasping, she jerked back. Something dug into her leg—an exposed rib.

There was nowhere safe to move. She slid to one side and rolled on top of a hairy chest with no head. When she slipped to the other side, her hand fell on a scapula.

The realization that she was in a pit of human meat came upon her slowly, and it was followed by emotional silence—a yawning void of feeling. Elise took one shuddering breath and stopped fighting to get away.

She settled back on the corpses and looked up at the steep walls around her. It was dark, but the occasional blast of flame revealed jagged rock. She could climb out. The clock was still rocking the earth with every beat of its human heart, and it sounded close.

She was still in the chamber. She was not dead.

But given all the pain she felt in her torso, she almost wished that were not true. No amount of emotional void could numb her cuts. Elise was slick with blood—both hers and that of the bodies—and she felt like she had gone through a cheese grater.

Her shirt was nothing but scraps, her weapons were missing, and there was a stab wound on her side. She flinched when she remembered the goddess burying the knife in her body. It was the last thing she

146

remembered before waking up.

She must have missed all Elise's important organs, but the goddess hadn't known that before leaving her for dead. Thrown her in a pit of bodies. Forgotten her.

Elise decided to consider herself lucky.

She counted to ten and crawled to the wall of the pit. The clock continued to tick.

Digging her fingernails into a jutting rock, Elise climbed to the top with her teeth grit. Stretching her arm to find another handhold hurt her stab wound. Putting her weight on one leg to push made the bites on her hip burn.

She rolled over the edge and scrambled to the shadows on all fours, finding a dark corner to crouch before examining the situation.

Elise could see the back of the clock. It was only a hundred feet away. Her side of the chamber was empty aside from the pit, sheltered by half-rotten columns, and the occasional blast of steam from the floor grates made enough smoke to conceal her.

She couldn't see many of those ugly gray demons around the clock, but she could feel them. There were hundreds. The goddess of death was talking to them, but Elise didn't stop to listen.

She made her way to the other side of the chamber, sticking to the shadows, and climbed unseen onto one of the platforms with the dead cultists.

A flash of silver caught her eye. The goddess had dropped her staff of bone and was carrying one of Elise's falchions as she paced across the dais.

There were four humans huddled beside her. It looked like a family. Their wrists were chained to the clock.

So that was the sacrifice. Elise wondered what it was about those people that made them a better sacrifice than her, the greatest kopis, who barely ranked as demon food. It would have wounded her pride if she had any.

She needed a plan, but she didn't have any idea of how to cross the room through a hundred demons, prevent the sacrifice of four humans, and stop the clock with numerous injuries and no time. She didn't even have her weapons.

Of course, that was fixable. If she could get one of her swords, she could bury it in the heart of the clock. It was the only thing she could imagine that might stop it.

Her time to plan ended. The death goddess stopped speaking and

147

whirled with the stone knife. It plunged into the neck of the man at her feet, and blood spurted from his throat.

Elise leaped off the dais, launching herself toward the sacrifices.

But it was too late. With a few swift strokes, all four lay dead in front of the clock. The minute hand groaned into the twelve position, and the first bell chimed.

James found a place in the jungle where the trees swayed and the ground vibrated beneath his feet. The clock was below him, and Elise with it. He was certain.

But he also had a hundred demons following him.

He and Bryce had evaded some of them in the jungle, but not enough. The kopis fired randomly into the horde behind him. Whether any of the bullets hit their targets didn't matter—there wasn't enough ammunition to kill them all.

Stopping where the vibrations were strongest, he tucked the shotgun under his arm. "I need a minute!" James yelled as he scrambled up a tree. "Hold them off!"

Bryce didn't respond. His fighting style completely lacked Elise's grace, but there was no denying the accuracy of his aim or the power of his swinging fists. He was a force of nature.

"Hurry up!" Bryce shouted.

James wedged himself between two high branches, selected a couple spells from his Book, and took out a pen. He muttered words of power under his breath as he drew new spells.

The rocking earth shifted. The tree shuddered, and the air grew thick.

A bell chimed.

The reverberations above the pyramid were so powerful that the entire ground tipped. Bryce lost his footing. The demons swarmed over him. He didn't get a chance to scream.

James tried not to watch as they overtook him. One demon leaped onto the trunk of his tree, then another, scaling it with their stubby claws.

He carefully folded three of the spells together. A hand swiped at his foot.

Then he threw the pages into the air.

The earth split with a dull thud, ripping open beneath the trees while the first bell continued to toll. Hot air gusted through the hole. Demons slid into the earth.

148

Holding his breath, James leaped off his branch.

Twelve bells. Four minutes. Elise was out of time.

One.

A dozen demons plowed into Elise like athletes piling onto a football. The back of her head cracked against the ground.

She jammed her elbow into a biting mouth and jabbed her fingers into an eye. The bell vibrated through the temple. It shook her blood, her bones.

Elise lashed out with a foot and felt it connect with something. It didn't do any good. There was no light under the pile of demons, no sense of gravity.

That was when the roof collapsed.

Two.

The rubble didn't crush Elise. But it did crush the demons on top of her.

She shoved her way out of the pile. Dirt and rain showered through the hole in the ceiling. Beyond it, the sky changed. Gray faded to crimson as Hell and Earth began to merge.

Elise gasped and coughed through the dust. Half of the centuria had been crushed at once. Nothing so much as touched the clock.

A hammer swung. The bell struck again.

Three.

The third chime was louder than the first two. Her skull ached, and even when she jammed her hands against her ears, her brain rattled.

Something moved on the dais. The goddess had survived.

More demons began climbing toward Elise over the rubble. She stumbled toward the clock, slipped, and almost fell.

Her hand caught the side of the dais. The vibrations traveled up her arm and down her spine as she dragged herself onto it.

The goddess was laughing.

Four.

"It's too late," said the death goddess. "Hell is come upon Earth."

That face. That laugh. Elise's wounds ached with the memory of the knife. "Shut up," she growled, raising her fist for a strike.

"Elise!"

She looked up. James climbed down from the surface, carefully making his way along a tipped column. The first thing that occurred to

149

her was that his leg was fixed. The second was that he had a shotgun. Where had James gotten a shotgun?

The goddess saw him. She stopped laughing.

"Catch!" he yelled, tossing the gun.

Elise caught it, balancing it awkwardly between her hands. She'd only held a shotgun once before. Her father had taught her to shoot, but she hated them.

Still, she was armed. It was better than the alternative.

She whipped the butt of the shotgun across the goddess's face. Her head snapped back.

Five.

The sky turned virulent red, and the world was falling. Elise's senses screamed—demons everywhere, all around her, like she had felt in Dis so long ago—and the air tensed like something was about to snap.

Demons were climbing toward James. She was helpless to join him.

The goddess regained her footing and came at Elise, falchion raised. She braced the shotgun against her shoulder, took aim, and fired.

The goddess's leg became a mess of red below the knee. She screamed in Latin. Elise smiled.

Six.

Elise tried to pump the shotgun so she could fire again, but the mechanism was stuck. Didn't matter. She preferred the personal touch anyway.

She tossed the gun aside and ripped her falchion out of the goddess's hand. The twin was next to the sacrifices. Elise grabbed it, too.

Holding both of her swords was like having her arms reattached. She was complete.

Seven.

Elise thought her skull might split in two.

The chime shook James off the pillar, dropping him in the crowd of waiting demons.

"James!" she shouted.

No response.

The dais rocked with the pendulum. She scrambled to keep her footing as the goddess lunged. Her stone knife slashed through the air and sliced into Elise's arm, deeper than before. She cut into muscle.

The air thickened, darkened, grew sour. Air gusted from the grates. It stunk of sulfur, like the planes of Hell.

A man screamed.

Eight.

150

The goddess was fast. Too fast for a woman with a ruined leg. She twisted and spun, meeting the blades of Elise's swords with her stone knife, swift and agile and skilled beyond imagining.

She deflected every swing, every strike. The ritual knife was a blur. Blades met, and Elise shoved her away. She couldn't take down a goddess.

The clock was her last chance—the only way she could stop the collapse of the wall between Heaven and Earth.

Nine.

The goddess flashed in front of her. The knife bit into Elise's injured side. She cried out, and her voice was silent under the bell's roar.

Pain seared through her body when the goddess shoved her against the clock. Elise's ears rang. Her vertebrae shook and scraped against each other.

The stone knife slashed open her brow. Blood cascaded down the side of her face.

Rain showered upon them. It tasted like acid.

Ten.

Her back was against the clock. She was *right there,* and she couldn't do anything to stop it. The goddess's stinking breath heated Elise's face as she smiled, baring bloody teeth.

If she couldn't reach the heart of the clock, there was another heart she could reach.

She kicked the goddess away. Just enough to have room to move.

A wave of demons crashed against the dais, clambering over the edge. Their mouths were bloody. Elise wondered if any of that belonged to James.

Eleven.

She plunged her sword into the goddess's chest.

The heart in the clock exploded blood, splattering against the inner workings. The hammer shattered.

The dais pitched and everyone fell.

The twelfth bell never rang.

When the eleventh bell died off, Elise was the only one left standing.

She clutched her sword in both hands as though it was her last line to life. Its blade dripped, her knuckles were white, and her gaze was empty. Her mind was a thousand miles away.

151

The pendulum no longer kept in time with the seconds. Its hand slowed with every swing.

Nearby, gray matter slipped out of a crack in a demon's skull, oozing across the tile. It trickled into one of the iron grates and dripped onto underground fires a hundred feet below. Brain hit flame. It gave a hiss and smelled like barbecue.

Barbecue. Her stomach lurched.

The sword slipped from Elise's fingers. Metal clattered against stone. The death goddess was sprawled at her feet, her necklace of skulls shattered, and her face had lost all its malice in death. She almost looked human.

The fires darkened and the heat faded.

Elise's eyes rolled up to the ceiling. Her fingers twined through the curls at her scalp as her mouth opened in a silent cry. She had screamed too much earlier in the night and no longer had a voice.

Her knees weakened. She collapsed.

The clock's pendulum continued to slow.

James pushed the bodies of demons off of him. Emptying every page of the Book—even the terrible ones he had sworn never to use—meant they had died in a thousand ugly ways. Ruptured organs. Suffocation. Burning from the inside.

His foot caught the pentagram-marked binder as he climbed free, but he didn't pick it up. He didn't want to look at it. He never wanted to cast a spell again.

The clock wasn't ticking with that terrible pulse anymore, and the sudden silence made his ears ring. Coughing, he slipped to the bottom of the pillar. "Elise?" he called, voice muffled in his ears.

He nudged a demon's body onto its back. The slash of its mouth gaped open, and the remaining air in its lungs sighed out with a whiff of sulfur. Covering his nose and mouth with his arm, he moved forward. James scrutinized each body he passed, half expecting to see Elise beneath them.

The room depressurized, and the demons began to rot.

Their skin dissolved to reveal bone. Their chests spread and tore. Organs twisted like worms within their guts as they vanished. One by one, they rotted away until the only body left was that of the goddess in the front of the room.

A glint of steel caught his eye. His gaze moved from the sword to the legs beside it, and he realized the goddess wasn't alone.

"Jesus Christ..." He scrambled onto the dais. Elise's skin was shredded and her chest was blackened with blood, and his stomach flipped when he realized it was all hers. "Elise—oh, Lord, Elise..."

Her eyes fluttered open. "James?"

"Are you all right?"

She sat up carefully, wincing. "I'm not the one with a sword through my chest." It wasn't funny, but he laughed. Even a hint of humor after that fight was enough to drive him toward hysteria. "Let's not do this again."

"I couldn't agree more." He helped her stand, and then picked up the sword she dropped. Elise turned to leave. "Don't you want the other one?"

She glanced at the falchion buried deep in the goddess's chest. Her lip curled. "No. Hell can keep it."

The bladed clock swung once more, and it stopped midway on the down stroke, forever frozen between *tick* and *tock*. The earth shook.

"We need to get out of here," James said.

Slowly, painfully, they climbed to the surface. Night had fallen, and the rain had stopped, leaving the air sticky and hot. They staggered almost a quarter mile before collapsing.

Elise shuddered like a tree in a hurricane. Her wounds looked agonizing.

"Can you heal me?" she asked. Her voice came out in a raw whisper.

"I'm sorry. I have nothing left."

She nodded without speaking. Her face was very pale.

They stared up at the vast black sky together. The clouds thinned, revealing stars and endless black sky. They waited until the sky faded to the deep navy of false dawn, and the sounds of night were replaced by birdsong.

When the sun broke the horizon, the light shone in Elise's hollow gaze.

They had won, but James couldn't help but feel they had lost something much worse than their lives. She sagged against his side. "Never again," he murmured into her hair. "Never again."

153

Part 6: Sacrifice

Chapter 14

"JAMES!"

ELISE BURST through the apartment door. The air inside was stale having the windows and doors closed all day. Nothing had changed since she left—paper spells were strewn across the kitchen table, and a rug was rolled neatly against the wall. There were even vacuum lines on the carpet from the last time James cleaned.

"I could use you at Motion and Dance, Betty," Anthony was saying into his cell phone, trailing behind Elise. "There's something going down. Elise is messed up and I'm confused and I need someone sane. Yes, you're sane. What? God, *shut up*. Just get over here, okay?"

Elise jiggled the handle on James's door, and it didn't open. She found the key on top of the molding for the bathroom door. The tumblers fell into place with an audible *click*.

James's bed was empty. She cut her gaze to the window—open—to the mess of papers and books on the floor. The sheets on his bed were a mess. Stephanie sat at his desk. She gazed blankly at the window.

Anthony came up beside Elise and peered over her shoulder. "Was there a fight?" he asked.

Elise gazed at the exposed mattress. Red drops blotted its surface. She ran her fingertips along one of the spots, and rubbed it between her finger and thumb. She didn't need a forensic expert to know whose blood it was.

"Stephanie," she said. The doctor didn't look at her. "Stephanie. Dr.

Whyte."

Slowly, so slowly, she looked over to Elise. "They took him," she said. Her voice was the kind of calm that came from having reached a point of such hysteria that she didn't have any emotion left. "Those...things. They came through the window. I cracked it to get some air."

Elise hauled Stephanie out of the chair and slammed her into the wall by the door. Anthony gave a startled cry and stepped forward, but she shot him a look that froze him mid-step.

"Are you working with her? Did you let Ann in? What the *fuck* did you do to him?"

Stephanie's face crumbled. "I didn't do anything. James was resting peacefully. I got a phone call and after I hung up, *they* came in. They knocked me out. I woke up and..." She wouldn't look at the bed.

"Who called you?" Elise demanded.

"Ann. She said she had a question for James."

"Did you tell her to come in? Did you tell her to take him?" She pulled back a fist, but Anthony caught it.

"Elise!"

He peeled her off Stephanie. Elise jerked her arm out of his grasp, but she didn't move to attack again.

The doctor adjusted her shirt, neatened her hair, and broke down into tears.

"I don't understand," she cried. "What *was* that?"

Stephanie sobbed for a good long minute, and Elise waited, drumming her fingers against her thigh. When the doctor showed no sign of letting up, she made a disgusted noise.

"This isn't helpful. Where did they take James?"

Stephanie sucked in a hard breath, straightening and grabbing a tissue to blow her nose. The tears stopped as suddenly as they began. Long breath in, long breath out. When she spoke, her tone was measured and even. She enunciated each word with great care. "I have no clue. I was unconscious."

"What were you doing all day?"

"I woke up a few hours ago and waited for you. I didn't know what to do," she said. "I think—I might go home."

"She's in shock," Anthony whispered.

"Fine. Get out of here. Have a drink and lay down or something. You're not doing any good," Elise said. Stephanie left without saying another word.

Elise stared at the spot of blood on the bed, her gaze narrowing until she saw nothing else.

James was gone. Ann had him, and Elise had been *right there* the whole time.

"I'm going to fucking kill her," she said.

Daylight waned. Clouds darkened what little sun remained. One moment, the air had grown still, and the next, rain poured out of the thunderheads. Lighting sparked over the mountains in the distance. Rain filled the streets and the people of the city took shelter inside.

Inside Motion and Dance, a storm also began to break within Elise.

"He's not here," she said.

"Who?" Betty asked. Her friend Cassandra had given her a ride as soon as Anthony called, but Elise's attitude made her wish she had taken a minute to put on full body armor first.

Her roommate paced the dance hall like a caged animal, limping on every other step. Her eyes were darkened pits of fury. She had become the spirit of vengeance itself, barely contained by human flesh.

Anthony cradled his forehead in his hands as he leaned against one of the mirrors in the main dance hall. He had stopped trying to talk when Elise almost punched him for it.

"Who's not here?" Betty repeated.

"James. She took him." She struck the palm of her hand with a fist. "I shouldn't have left so fast. I should have searched the house. I should have..."

"Hey, calm down," Betty said, touching Elise's shoulder. Her skin was hot. "Talk to me, girl. What's happened?"

"Ann has kidnapped my aspis for ritual sacrifice to a demon goddess of death."

Betty shook her head. "Yesterday, I would have said you were crazy. Today—well, you're still crazy, but it's contagious. What's an aspis? Demons? Is that what that gargoyle thing was?"

"That was a fiend." She flung herself into the chair, shredding her jeans along the hole to turn them into half-shorts. Betty leaned in to examine the gashes on Elise's legs. The blood had smeared, and the wounds were raw.

"I hate to state the obvious, but..."

"Yeah, it doesn't look good," Elise said. She pressed a towel emblazoned with the "Motion & Dance" logo against her injury. They were intended to be used by sweaty dancers. Elise's blood soaked through the cloth quickly, obscuring the logo of the ballet man wrapped around the ampersand.

"So what's this about zombies?" Betty asked.

"They're not zombies," Elise replied impatiently. "They're the dead, possessed by a demon called Death's Hand, and reanimated to do her evil bidding."

Betty began laughing again. When she saw that nobody joined her, she stopped. Elise's eyes were cold. She was serious. Deadly serious. Betty deflated. "Oh, jeeze," she said. "I can't believe Ann's evil. I mean, lazy Ann? 'Let's eat ice cream after working out' Ann?"

Elise dropped the towel in the trash can. "The one and only." She moved her leg experimentally, watching the gashes.

Betty spun on Anthony. "Why aren't you as shocked as I am?"

"We were attacked by some kind of mutant this morning, and then a dead body with bleeding eyes attack my windshield," he said dully. "My ability to get shocked has eloped with my sanity and run away to Africa."

"I think I need the Reader's Digest version of what's going on," Betty said.

"I don't have time for this. I need weapons and I need to bring all kinds of pain down on Ann." She snapped her fingers at Anthony. "You're taking me in the Jeep. Now."

"Fine."

Betty hurried after them as they went for the front doors. Elise spoke as she limped along.

"So here's what I told Anthony: I'm James's exorcist friend. When working with Lucinde, I stumbled across a demonic plot to ascend to Earth from Hell. Ann is a powerful necromancer and she's on his side. Now they're planning to sacrifice James. Good enough for you?"

"Wow. Uh. Okay. If Ann's got James, why can't we just walk in and take him? I mean, we've worked out with Ann. She's not exactly formidable."

"She has a small army. We can't 'just walk in' unless we deal with them first."

"Oh," Betty said.

Anthony opened the front door, letting in a wash of the moist air.

A small figure stood silhouetted against the rain. She wore a slicker too big for her tiny body, and she stepped inside without being invited. The girl pushed back her hood, revealing a face with white eyes and cheeks tracked by blood tears. Her skin was pale, almost papery.

Betty took a step back, covering her mouth with a hand. The little girl had a black symbol on her forehead, and her veins pulsed visibly beneath the skin.

Elise sucked in a hard breath. "Lucinde."

"It's like that zombie I saw earlier," Anthony muttered. "But...it's a kid."

The child's blank eyes focused on Elise. Her mouth dropped open.

"I have James," she said. Her mouth didn't move, and the woman's voice that came out sounded like a recording. "You have the artifact of *vedae som matis*. Let's be adults about this. I'll cure James of the poison, return him to you, and leave the area. You won't hear from us again. Just give back the staff."

Betty glanced at Elise. She was watching the girl with her lips set in a hard line.

She went on. "I'll take everything with me. You can return to living a normal life. I'm sorry we ever had to fight like this, Elise. I wouldn't have chosen it. I want to meet at Our Mother of Sorrows at ten o'clock tonight. Send your response with my servant." Her mouth clapped shut, and she stood, immobile, with her hand extended.

Anthony shuddered. "That's freaky."

"She looks like a demented doll," Betty agreed.

"Do you have that notepad in your purse?" Elise asked. She sounded calm, but tense.

Betty gave her a piece of Hello Kitty stationary and a green pen. Elise scrawled out a message and stuffed it into the girl's hand, which closed on the paper. She hid it inside her rain slicker.

Her mouth dropped open once more. "Thank you."

Lucinde walked out with a mechanical gait. Elise lingered in the doorway to watch her go. "Ann's actually willing to trade?" Anthony asked. "The way you were talking earlier, it seemed like James is too important for her to let go."

"He *is* too important," Elise said. "She's not going to let go of James now that she has him. I'm not going to return the artifact either."

"But you said..."

"I lied."

"Oh."

"I'm going to have to meet Ann, exorcise her servants, kill all the demons, and take James back," Elise said. She laughed harshly. "No big deal. I don't even think it's possible to perform a mass exorcism. It's never been done before."

Betty's eyes lit up. "We could do some exorcisms."

"You wouldn't have any idea what to do. There has to be another way."

"We could clone you," Anthony said in a "you're all crazy" tone of voice as he stalked away. "It's no more insane than everything else that's happening!"

Elise took something out of her pocket, and Betty recognized it as an MP3 recorder. "That's not a bad idea, Anthony," she said. "But first, I have some business with a lawyer and his wife."

When Elise reached the Ramirez house, Marisa was loading her car, sheltered from the rain by a blue poncho. Her face was red, but her eyes were dry now, and she carried two suitcases under each arm. She flung them into the back of her Hummer.

"Can I help you?" Elise asked.

Marisa jumped. "Oh—Elise. I didn't see you there."

She took a step toward the garage, but Elise moved in her way. "What's the rush?"

"I can't stay here," she said. "Augustin's...angry. Throwing things. I'm going to go live with my mother." Marisa took a deep breath. "We discussed divorce even before what happened to Lucinde. My bags have been packed in the garage for weeks now. But with what's happened recently..."

"Your daughter has gone missing," Elise asked. "Somehow, she got possessed again. I don't see how that could have happened unless someone surrendered Lucinde to the bad guy."

A look of panic shot across Marisa's face. "What?" Her hand fluttered at her breast, and it was only then that Elise noticed the bruise from her collarbone to her shoulder. "Are you—are you saying that Augustin let someone hurt our baby? *Madre de dios*...it makes sense. He's so angry!"

Elise frowned. "Has he been beating you?"

She jerked the poncho closed over her chest. "Yes." Marisa swallowed hard. "Yes, he has. He's gone crazy."

"Where is he?"

"Augustin is inside. Don't make me go back."

"Okay. Stay with your mom for now. I'll find Lucinde, and I promise she will be safe," Elise said.

Marisa gripped her arm. "I never meant for James to find out we were having problems with our daughter. Do you understand? I always meant to keep things private. Your involvement—his involvement—was an accident. I'm so sorry."

"Go. I'll take care of Augustin."

She bit her lip. Nodded again. "Thank you. My mother's phone number is on the refrigerator. When you have found Lucinde—if you have saved her—call me. Please." Marisa got into the driver's seat and slammed the door shut.

She pulled out of the driveway as church bells tolled.

Elise went inside without knocking. She held her breath to listen for sound—something like the pattering of feet or an accidental brush of leathery arm against the wall. The living room was empty and silent. She glanced into the kitchen, but there was nothing there, either.

Elise made her way up the stairs, fists raised in the anticipation of an ambush. One of the family photos on the wall was askew, and another was missing entirely, making a gap in the long row of family history leading to the second floor.

There had been a scuffle upstairs. A decorative pot that had once filled a wall cubby was now in shards on the floor. Lucinde's door was cracked open. Elise pressed her back to the wall beside it, easing her fingers around the frame to push it open another inch and peek inside.

There were no fiends inside, no possessed ones, and no Lucinde. Only Augustin—sitting on his daughter's tiny bed and staring at the photo missing from the wall. He looked up at Elise and his eyes were full of hope. "Did you find her?" he asked. "Our daughter…"

"No, Augustin," Elise said. Her knife emerged from beneath her jacket, and she held it at her side. "I know what you did. Did Ann offer you money? Power?"

"What? Who is Ann?"

"You sold your daughter out. Your *own blood.*"

He set the photo down on the bedside table. "Listen here. You may think you have some sort of—some *right* to come in and boss me around—but don't be mistaken. I'm still the man of the house, and—"

"I already got some of the story from your wife. Let me see if I can fill in the blanks." Elise shut the door behind her and stepped forward to stand over Augustin. "Ann gave you money. It wasn't a problem for you to betray your family; you don't like your daughter anyway. You couldn't even be bothered to be with her when I exorcised her. You get off on beating women, and—"

Augustin stood. He towered over her, and his face was dark. "What

160

did Marisa say?"

"She told me that she's leaving you. Marisa loves her daughter very much, which is more than *you've* shown."

"I love my daughter, just as I love Marisa. I could never hurt either of them," Augustin said. He laughed bitterly. "I'm surrounded by crazy women. I thought Marisa would be different from my first wife, but then she started throwing things at me, just like Louisa did. And now you!"

Elise opened her mouth to yell, but a thought stopped her. "Wait. Marisa's not your first wife?"

"Now I think I should have let Louisa have custody of Lucinde," he said. He sat back down again with a moan. "Marisa's leaving me. I should have known…"

"If you didn't beat her, then why is she bruised?"

"Our daughter was possessed by a demon! Where the hell do you think it came from?"

"You're going to have to make something clear for me," she said. "Is there any reason Marisa would sell your daughter out?"

"She wouldn't," he said dismissively.

"Your story doesn't match hers. She told me that you've been angry and beating her and that you gave Lucinde up to the demon. Now you're telling me neither of you did it?"

"There's no reason for you to think we've hurt Lucinde. Yes, Marisa and I have fought. This isn't even the first time she's left. But we do not abuse our daughter."

"If you're lying to me…"

Augustin took the picture off the bedside table again, cradling it in his hands. "Leave me alone." His eyes burned through Elise.

She stomped downstairs to the refrigerator to look for the phone number Marisa left.

A single magnetic clip held a folded up paper that said *Give to Elise Kavanagh*. She unfolded it. The handwriting was loose and messy, and she jumped to the bottom—signed by Marisa—before going back to read it more carefully.

I never meant for things to get so out of control. I love Lucinde. Ann told me this would cure her heart defect and make her powerful, but instead she died and now I've caused too much pain. This isn't how I meant to get away from Augustin.

Several lines were scribbled out and illegible. The next readable line said, *She keeps everything in the attic. Tell him I'm sorry.* Her name was scrawled hastily beneath that, and the pen had torn through the paper on the last letter.

Elise's fist tightened around the note. Her hand shook. "You should have asked for help," she muttered. Marisa would never make it to her mother's house—demons didn't appreciate people who betrayed them.

She dropped the note on the kitchen table and left.

Chapter 15

ELISE TOOK JAMES'S car back to the studio feeling like she was in someone else's nightmare. The only thing that warmed her was the thought of those six words—*she keeps everything in the attic*. She knew where James was. Now all she needed was a miracle so she could get into Ann's place again.

Betty and Anthony were still working on her miracle when she got back. She parked in the lot and watched them moving around the studio through the windows. They were almost done with the Jeep. It was parked outside, and there was so much extra metal on it that it looked like Frankenstein's monster.

She knew she needed to go inside and help them, but Elise felt like she was frozen to the spot. She didn't want to tell them what Marisa had done, and she didn't want to have to answer the millions of questions that must have been bursting inside Betty, either.

Shutting her eyes, she pressed her forehead to the steering wheel. Everything was so much simpler when it had been just Elise and James against the world.

She took a deep breath before getting out of the car. It took her a moment to realize she wasn't alone.

The three other people didn't make any noise as they slipped from the shadows of the building like oil oozing over water. As soon as Elise saw them, she stopped.

"How's it going, cabbage? Having a really dreadful evening, I hope."

David Nicholas.

Elise didn't respond. She recognized the woman on the left—it was the basandere from Eloquent Blood. Tattered pants revealed plump thighs and dirty knees, and a swooping neckline showed too many ribs between

163

her surgically altered breasts. She had strung her iron chain through the loops of her jeans like a belt.

The basandere was meaner than she looked. Elise was certain of it. She would be as great a threat as the dark-haired man on the right, who looked so high that he wouldn't have felt it if Elise knocked his skull off his shoulders.

And then there was David Nicholas.

"What do you want?" Elise asked, even though she could tell by the way they moved to circle around her that they weren't there for a polite chat.

"You think you can push people around and not pay for it? First you walk into my office and stab me—and maybe I put up with it because I owe you money, sure. But then you interrupt my card game? Threaten me for information? Who the *fuck* do you think you are? Don't put up with that shit in this town, do we?" He jerked his head the other demons. "Make it fast."

The basandere reached, and Elise knocked her hands aside, jabbing her elbow into her gut to send her stumbling.

She spun smoothly and snapped a kick at the junkie's face, but he ducked under it and grabbed her ankle. With a jerk, Elise's butt hit pavement. The shock of it jolted up her spine.

Before she could stand, a heavy boot smacked into her gut. Her ribs creaked. Her intestines mashed against her spine and her head bounced on the parking lot.

She rolled away from the next kick, gasping for breath, and got to her knees. A hand snatched her ponytail and jerked it back, nearly ripping the hair from her scalp.

David Nicholas drove the bony spike of his knee into her chin. Her teeth snapped shut on her tongue. The iron taste of blood flooded her mouth.

Elise lunged for him, but her hair was held tight. The junkie threw his arms around her. He could barely restrain one arm with his whole body. When he felt her shove against him, his face paled at her strength, but he held firm.

"You don't know what you're doing," Elise groaned as the basandere pulled her to her knees using her hair as a handle.

"You're a bully, bitch," David Nicholas said. "I'm taking out the trash."

He punched her. The ridges of his knuckles made fire blossom across her face as her head snapped from side to side. He didn't hit hard—she had been

164

beaten by worse. But it had been years. She almost forgot the sweet pain of it.

Her lip split. He hit her eye, and her vision blurred.

"She's not even fighting back!" the basandere said, shrieking with laughter.

David Nicholas stepped back, rubbing his knuckles. He looked disappointed at Elise's lack of reaction. She sucked on the blood in her mouth and spit it out.

"You done?" she asked. "I have shit to do tonight."

His face twitched. "I'm nowhere near done yet."

He brandished a knife with a blade like a straight razor. A cold calm settled over Elise, numbing her pain. She hated to lose a customer—but she hated to lose her life even more.

The junkie shifted to grab her other arm. She head butted him hard enough to snap his nose and send blood spraying down his lip. He sprawled out in a parking space.

Metal flashed. She ducked, tearing her ponytail out of the stripper's hand and leaving a fistful of hair behind.

David Nicholas's knife blew past her ear.

She twisted and yanked the chain out of the basandere's belt loops, popping two of them.

Everything slowed.

David Nicholas flashed through the shadows to Elise's other side, and she could almost track his progress through the darkness. Wisps of smoke followed him as he vanished and rematerialized.

She whirled, shoving the basandere out of the way, and whipped the chain toward David Nicholas as he reappeared.

It wrapped around his neck, catching him before he was completely corporeal.

She jerked.

His head disconnected from his body.

He flashed into black smoke again, knife clattering to the ground.

Elise snapped her arm to wrap the chain around her fist. The basandere screamed and ran at her, flashing blood-red fingernails. Elise backhanded her with the chain. Something cracked—something important—and the stripper went limp.

The junkie reached for the knife. His hand shook.

"Get the fuck out of here," Elise spat. Blood spattered on her chin.

He was gone before she could unwind the chain.

As soon as her levels of adrenaline dropped, the pain came roaring back. Elise didn't realize how much her body hurt until she fell to her knees beside the basandere. She thought the stripper was probably dead. She didn't care too much.

Elise evaluated her physical condition. Between the blood loss from Ann anointing her house and these new wounds, she might not return to full strength for days.

James didn't have days.

She got back to her feet with a groan. Pain radiated from the top of her head down to her ribs, like every bone was fractured.

"Hell of a time to collect on a debt," she muttered.

Elise threw the basandere in the trunk of James's car. She swallowed a handful of the ibuprofen he kept in the glove box and checked her face in the rearview mirror. Her face looked like hamburger.

Great. Just great.

She slammed the car door shut, turning.

David Nicholas stood in front of her.

He moved an instant before she did. His hands closed on her shoulders, shoving her back against the car. Elise's head thudded against the metal.

"You killed one of my girls," he said.

"It was self-defense. What are you going to do about it? Call the cops?"

Loathing twisted David Nicholas's features. "I should sell you into slavery, that's what I should do. You and that succubus bartender *bitch*."

Elise grabbed his wrists. Her fingernails dug into his wrists like they were sponges. Decapitation didn't do the nightmare any favors.

"Look," she said, carefully enunciating each consonant, "you and I can fight all night if we want, but it's a waste of time. You paid your debts with a bad check. You pounded on me, and I won this round. Let's call it even."

"Why should I do that?"

"Because I'll kill Death's Hand if you leave me alone for the night."

His expression dissolved into a grin so wide that the corners of his lips nearly touched his ears. "I just kicked the shit out of your skinny ass. You think you can take *vedae som matis*?" She nodded without returning his smile. He released her shoulders. "I like the idea of letting something else kill you."

"Only because you can't do it yourself."

David Nicholas swung, but she was faster. Before he could get a hand on her throat, she knocked his arms aside and pressed his own knife against his throat.

166

The nightmare froze.

"Try me," she whispered.

"Hey! What's going on?"

Anthony rushed out of the studio. David Nicholas's black eyes flicked to him, then back to Elise. He stepped away from her, lifting his hands.

"If Death's Hand doesn't kill you, we'll finish this conversation—and we'll do it under the eye of the Night Hag, you understand?"

Elise tossed his knife to him. "Won't that be fun?" she said flatly.

He vanished before Anthony could reach them.

So much for *that* customer.

"Jesus Christ! What happened to you?" he asked, grabbing Elise's shoulders to steady her.

"Don't touch me. I'm fine."

Anthony scanned her injuries, from the rapidly swelling black eye to her bruised cheeks and swollen lip. He ran his fingers through the hair that had come loose from her braid.

"Why didn't you call for help?" he asked.

She swatted his hand off. "I told you not to touch me. Is the Jeep done yet?"

"No, but—"

"Then you and Betty need to finish it. I'm going upstairs to get my sword. I'll be back down in ten minutes, and we're going to leave."

Her legs buckled under her when she hit the stairs. Anthony wrapped an arm around her waist.

"Whoa," he said. "Let me help you up."

Elise turned a cold gaze on him, letting all her pain and frustration show in her eyes. He jerked his hand back. "I told you not to touch me."

He followed a step behind her as she ascended to James's apartment. She managed to keep her hands steady when she unlocked the door.

She leaned against James's wall as she lifted the hem of her shirt to examine her stomach. Red welts had risen on her skin, and she probed the edges gently. Even a light touch made her wince.

"What can I get you?" Anthony asked.

"Bandages. They should be in the bathroom cabinet."

He disappeared, and Elise took a ritual mirror off the kitchen table to take another look at her face. In the minutes since she had last looked, her eye had nearly swollen shut. Her lip was bleeding.

She moistened a rag in the sink and washed off the blood. By the time Anthony returned with the bandages, her skin was clean, but there was no help for her shirt.

167

"Thanks," she said, pressing a fistful of ice to her swollen forehead. "I don't think I'll need it after all."

Anthony folded his arms as he studied her, and Elise studied him back out of her good eye. She didn't appreciate being scrutinized.

For the first time that day, she noticed he was wearing a nice button-up shirt and clean jeans, although working on the Jeep had gotten his hands dirty. His hair was even combed back. It showed off his full lips and dimpled chin. And he was muscular, too.

Elise wondered how long he had been so handsome. They had been neighbors for over two years, and she had known him as an acquaintance for four, and she had never seen him as anything but Betty's kid cousin before.

"Elise?"

She realized he had been speaking, and she shook her head to clear it. It made the bruises on her face throb. "Sorry. What?"

"You got pretty beaten. Are you sure you don't need bandages?"

"Yes."

She twisted to check her back in the mirror, and the movement sent pain lancing up her spine. She squeezed her eyes shut.

"Careful," he said.

"On second thought, I need you to look at my back and tell me how bad the injury is. Okay?"

He nodded. Elise turned her back on him and lifted her shirt over her head. She could feel him looking at her. Her cheeks got hot, and she was glad he couldn't see it.

Her heart was beating fast, but it was probably from the adrenaline of the fight. Probably.

She heard him step closer. "Hmm," Anthony said.

"Well? Do I need bandages?" she asked, keeping her tone level.

"You're scraped up, but it looks mostly like bruising."

"How about on this side? It hurts more." She turned and lifted her arm so he could check her ribs.

His fingers traced over the bruises on her side. Elise closed her eyes as chills prickled down her shoulders. "Same here. That looks painful." Warm breath blew over the back of her neck, tickling the hair behind her ear.

Elise hadn't been touched like that in years. Her body's reaction was almost violent—the way her stomach muscles jerked, the heat that flushed her face, the warmth between her legs. "That's not helping," she said, and her voice shook. It actually shook.

She turned to face him, and Anthony's cheeks had a warm flush. There was a certain intent darkness in his eyes as he focused on her. His gaze couldn't seem to make it above her lips, which was good, because her handful of ice had melted down her wrist and left her swollen eye exposed. "Huh?"

"You're not helping," Elise repeated. One of his fingers hooked under her bra strap.

"Oh," he said. His hand ran down her bicep as he lowered the bra strap. He dipped his head to trail his lips along the exposed skin. "I thought you said you didn't want help."

"Anthony..."

"Yes?" he murmured, pushing against her until her back bumped against the wall. She relaxed against him, letting the pressure of his body hold her suspended.

She half wanted to forget the danger pressing on them—and the danger James was in. But when her eyes opened, she saw the Ansel Adams photo over Anthony's shoulder, and the memory of the time her aspis bought it shattered the illusion of peace.

Anthony's hand slid over a bruised rib, and she flinched as pain stabbed through her side.

"Sorry," he said against her neck.

Elise took a deep breath and planted her hands on Anthony's shoulders. She could have thrown him across the room, but she made herself shove gently. "This isn't the time."

He caught her wrists. "We've got a few minutes."

"Anthony. Not now. I'm serious."

"But later?"

"The odds are pretty good." She smiled a little. "At least fifty-fifty."

He kissed her again, but this time, it was only a brief touch of his lips on hers. "I like my chances." He took her hand, giving it a gentle squeeze. "Can I ask one question?"

"You can ask."

"What's with the gloves you're always wearing? Is this some kind of weird demon hunter thing?"

Elise's mouth snapped shut. "Go see Betty. I still have to grab something, but I'll be right down."

"But you said I could—"

"You can't ask that," she said. "Go."

His tongue darted out to wet his lower lip. Elise was a lot more interested in the look of that than she liked to admit, but the heat building

169

inside of her dissipated at the thought of James.

"See you in a minute," he said, voice husky. He straightened his shirt and moved to go back downstairs.

"Anthony?"

He paused in the door. "Yeah?"

"You look really good." As an afterthought, she added, "I'm sorry I missed our date last night."

A brilliant smile illuminated his face. "Thanks, Elise."

Once Anthony had gone downstairs, Elise had trouble remembering where she dropped her shirt. She didn't have any other, cleaner clothing left at James's apartment, so she pulled it back on to cover her injuries.

The painkillers were starting to kick in. Lifting her arms over her head ached, but it was hardly debilitating.

She rolled out her shoulders, touched her toes, and reached for the ceiling. Full mobility. Painful, but workable. David Nicholas picked a bad time to take out his frustration on her.

If only Anthony had come a couple minutes sooner. She could have skipped a beating and saved her time. Elise pushed the thought aside. There was no point in regretting what she couldn't change.

Taking a set of keys out of James's desk, she went into the spare bedroom that used to be hers before she moved in with Betty. Now it was an extension of the library in his room, with a cozy chair for reading books…and a gun safe bolted to the wall.

James didn't own any guns.

She twisted a combination into the lock, whispering the numbers to herself. Two. Twenty-five. Nineteen. Nine. And eight.

Nothing happened when she twisted the key in the lock until she passed her hand over a charm James had welded to the side. The tumblers fell into place with a heavy, muffled *thud*.

Twisting the lever, Elise opened the safe.

Once upon a time, James and Elise hadn't had thousands of books. They hadn't had an apartment or a duplex or furniture. In fact, they hadn't even had a spare pair of pants between them. They'd had a handful of cash in various currencies, two tattered backpacks…and swords.

Elise's old chain of charms—which had since been replaced with newer, shimmering chains and tokens—was pooled at the bottom of the safe, and her sword was mounted against the back wall. Three feet long and gently curved like a waning sliver of moon, the falchion had a leather-wrapped hilt worn perfectly to the contours of Elise's hand. She

170

had rewrapped it a hundred times after a hundred battles in the twenty years since her father gave it and its twin to her.

"A falchion is meant to be wielded with a shield," Isaac had said as Elise studied her birthday presents with grave seven year old eyes.

"Then why two?" she asked.

"Because you don't need a shield if you kill everything that approaches you."

She still wondered if that meant Isaac never intended for her to have an aspis. Elise got the impression he would have disapproved of her partnership with James, and the lengths to which she would now go to recover him. She didn't care. Her father was a bastard anyway.

The magical engravings on the blade shimmered with more than the light when she took it in her hand. Elise swung the kopis through the air, slashing it at an invisible enemy. It felt strange to wield without its twin.

The back sheath was in a drawer at the bottom of the safe. Elise slung it on like a backpack and had to loosen the straps to make it fit.

Sheathed, the hilt of the sword protruded over her right shoulder. She flipped her hair back to hide it.

When she examined herself in the bathroom mirror, she couldn't see the sword, and the straps of the sheath looked innocuous enough. But her swollen, bruised face was all too familiar.

Elise didn't realize she had lashed out at the mirror until her reflection fractured. Glass sprinkled on the countertop.

"Damn it, James," she whispered as her knuckles bled through her gloves.

This was all his fault.

If she started hunting again, there would be no going back. No second retirement. Maybe she had been naïve to think she could have left it the first time.

She swept out of the apartment and didn't look back.

Chapter 16

ANN CLENCHED HER fist, and the city grew silent.

The matter of calming people was simple. Press magic against the right part of the mind, and a person would grow lethargic. Press again, and they became all but comatose. Another press...well, it would be a long time before someone woke up from that.

Ann had once been too weak with her akashic magic to calm a single person, but it had grown easier with time. Now, with the full force of *vedae som matis* behind her, she felt she could silence the world itself.

But the world was not her goal. Even the entire city was more than she needed for the time being. She envisioned only the surrounding neighborhoods and lulled them to silence. Normal people would panic if they saw Ann's demons and reanimated dead on the streets. With a calm laid over them, they felt nothing. She could operate in the day as easily as the night.

She was so *powerful* now. The universe's energy flowed through her veins, hot as molten lava.

Rain sluiced down the attic's lone window. The fading gray light was barely enough for Ann to make out her surroundings, but she knew her workspace well. She could have navigated it in absolute darkness. The only new addition was the pale form on her work table—a man so tall his feet dangled off the end.

Ann found her pen and nibs exactly where she had left them on the desk at the end of the attic. She paused to glance in her small ritual mirror —her nose was twisted, swollen, red, and her eyes were rimmed with dark purple bruises. Elise had mangled it with a few well-placed kicks, and Ann wasn't the right kind of witch to heal it.

She collected the special ink *vedae som matis* had instructed her to make and took it to the table. She studied the face of James, her high priest, in half-darkness. The poison worked so deep into his body that organs began to fail, and he looked very old. Deep lines furrowed his skin, accenting the faint hints of gray at his temples. His temperature was so high that Ann could feel it from inches away. The edges of his lips were blue.

The poison made it impossible for him to escape while Ann prepared, but once he housed *vedae som matis*, the demon would burn the illness from his blood. He would heal in moments, and James would be the perfect vessel. With maintenance, his body would last for centuries to come.

And Ann would be right there to witness it.

"I need my straight razor," Ann said as she shook the ink bottle, and her smallest helper, the girl once known as Lucinde, went to find it. "And a light, please."

The lamp on her desk clicked on. The room was filled with a pale pink glow. A huge sigil anointed the floor, drawn in the same mixture of blood that marked the basement.

James didn't stir when Ann touched the silver nib to his forehead. She drew intricate symbols on his face, repeatedly checking both to make sure she was drawing them correctly.

She cleaned a clumped fleck of red ink off James's brow and let her fingertips trace on his skin. Ann couldn't wait until her mistress had a body at long last. She was grateful that they had failed to prepare Lucinde properly. Ann could ignore a man's body as long as it was *vedae som matis* inside. She wouldn't have been able to deal with her mistress appearing as a five-year-old.

Ann moved down his body, writing the specific marks of transference on each critical point of his flesh. In order to preserve James for as long as they could, she had to inscribe over two dozen marks. She drew one carefully on his left shoulder atop a brilliant white scar he bore just over his chest.

Her smallest helper returned with the straight razor.

"Thank you," she said, brushing her hand across the top of the child-servant's head. "You can go sit in the corner again." Ann didn't watch to make sure she would obey. They always did.

Ann flipped open the straight razor and sliced it through the waist of his pants and down the legs. The cloth fell open as a snake shedding its skin.

A twinge of guilt clenched in Ann's gut as she cut away his trousers,

173

removing James's last semblance of dignity. Although she had never been close to her high priest, or even that fond of him, she knew he and Elise were close. It was obvious they adored one another. She would be devastated.

The kopis is the enemy, Death's Hand reminded Ann, brushing her mind. *She will not share in our vision. She will not accept your offer to join us.*

Ann didn't reply. Betty wouldn't share in her vision, either—or so *vedae som matis* insisted. Death's Hand had deployed a fiend to kill Betty without asking Ann, and now one of her creatures was dead. She was still angry, but she sensed the demon's jealousy—the worry that Ann would find she preferred human company. Ann tried not to feel too pleased with that. *Vedae som matis's* jealousy made her feel wanted, and it was hard not to preen a little.

Marisa has betrayed us. I must kill her.

"No," Ann said. "I don't want anyone else to die if they don't have to. You know I'm still mad you sent one of our babies to attack Anthony and Betty."

Her voice turned soothing. *It was necessary. I knew they would get in the way, and if you could see what they are doing now, you would agree. They are coming to kill me.*

"They can't," she said. "They wouldn't."

But the demon had already subsided from her mind, leaving her with a sense of the inevitable. Marisa wasn't a big deal anyway. She had served her purpose. *Vedae som matis* wouldn't kill anyone that didn't need to die —right?

She resumed preparing James, trimming the thatch of pubic hair over his genitalia so she could properly access the skin beneath. She carefully tried not to look at his naked body. Ann wasn't interested in the sexual sense, but it was so *distracting* trying to draw so close to a penis. She suppressed the insane urge to giggle.

He would be ready soon. She would only need the anointing oil, and perhaps a few herbs...

The clock chimed. Ten o'clock. Elise would be in the cemetery soon.

Ann smiled and continued to work.

"How's it looking?"

Betty leaned on the Jeep's roll cage to support her elbows, peering through a set of black binoculars. She hummed at Elise's question, lips pursed.

They were positioned in the driveway of a sports complex across the street from Our Mother of Sorrows. Even though they had been parked at the edge of a busy road for twenty minutes, not a single car had passed.

The view from their side of the five lane road wasn't good—the statue at the entrance of the cemetery was in the way, along with a few well-placed trees, and Elise could only barely see the illuminated angel statue in the back of the cemetery through the obstructions. "Hmm," Betty said, fidgeting with the focus. "Interesting."

"What?"

"It looks very black. Almost like it's nighttime and I can't see anything."

Elise grabbed the strap. "Hand them over. You don't know what you're doing."

"I'm not using them wrong and I can do reconnaissance all on my own, thank you very much!"

Anthony made an irritated noise and slouched in the driver's seat, folding his arms. His feet sloshed in the half inch of water that had collected at the bottom of his Jeep.

It was hard to maintain a good mood outdoors in the middle of a rainy night, and Elise felt like she had been here, doing the exact same thing with James, just hours ago.

Elise took the binoculars from Betty's eyes.

"Hey!" Betty protested.

"It's almost ten. We don't have time for this." She gazed through the eyepieces, searching for the street lights around the cemetery. At first, all she saw were tombstones, and then she began making out moving shadows behind them. The shapes were faint, but she could guess what she was looking at.

She lowered the binoculars. "The possessed ones are already here," she said, passing them to Anthony.

"What does that mean for us?" he asked.

"It bet it means Ann and James are there."

"Does that change the plan at all?" Betty asked, dropping into her seat.

"She's probably ordered her servants to take the artifact as soon as we show up. So no, this doesn't change anything. We stick to Plan A."

"I hate to be a party pooper, because you know I'm your girl whenever you want to be destructive, but don't you think Plan A is a little noisy for an ordinary neighborhood?" Betty asked. "*Somebody* is bound to wake up and call the cops."

"Ann lives nearby. I think she's been casting a calming on her neighbors in the surrounding streets. It's the only way I can figure she can get away with sending out her servants without drawing attention."

"A calming?"

"It's a kind of spell that compels people to go to sleep," she said. "James can do it to one or two people at a time. With her soul bound to a demon, it wouldn't be hard to do it on a broad scale."

"So I get to break things?" Anthony asked.

Elise nodded. "You get to break things."

"That's almost cool enough for me to stop being completely petrified," he said. "I do have to wonder, though—why did we bring that thing with us at all?"

"The demon is in it," Elise said, patting her pocket. "Part of it, anyway. It's watching. If we left it at Motion and Dance, we wouldn't have demons *or* Ann to fight here at all—they would be at the studio. We're not that important."

"They tried to kill me," Betty said, bracing herself against the additional bars they had welded to the roll cage. "I'm way important."

Elise sighed. "Do it, Anthony."

Chapter 17

JUST METERS AWAY, the possessed ones wandered through the cemetery. They moved aimlessly without acknowledging one another, vacant eye sockets glazed with mucus.

Occasionally, one of the servants would pass by the grave in which his body had lain, and he would pause, the faintest hint of recognition lighting up his face. Then the light would fade, and he would shuffle off once more.

The old grave markers were soaked and dark, and water puddled in the eroded faces of the more recent headstones. A breeze rustled through the trees, and fell again moments later. Our Mother of Sorrows was silent.

And then, distantly… "Woo hoo!"

Crash.

The fence smashed open and Anthony's Jeep exploded into the graveyard.

Elise's recorded voice roared out of the speakers bound to the front. The large crucifix forming the hood ornament blazed in the darkness. A length of fence stuck to the crude cowcatcher, and it clipped a shambling old woman, sending her flying.

"Crux sacra sit mihi lux, non draco sit mihi dux!"

Pain roared from the throats of the possessed ones. They twitched and flailed as though taken by a massive seizure, clawing at their own faces. Blood spilled underneath their nails, unable to feel anything but the pain of St. Benedict's prayer.

Anthony peeled through the paths of the cemetery at twenty miles an hour, skidding around tight corners intended for pedestrians.

"Vade retro, Satana, nunquam suade mihi vana!"

A shaking body—a teenager, only a boy—clawed at the side of the

177

Jeep. His hand caught, and he was dragged alongside them, fighting to climb on board even as his entire body shuddered with pain.

Elise drew her sword from underneath her hair in a single smooth motion. Her chain of charms was entwined between her fingers and the hilt.

The engraved symbols on the blade flashed as she swung. The blade sliced into the boy's wrist. He fell to the earth missing a hand.

"Oh, man!" Betty exclaimed, leaning back to kick at his still-twitching fingers. "Gross!"

Elise swept to her feet, bracing her legs against one of the seats. "There!" she called, pointing to a cluster of possessed ones near the center of the graveyard. "At your nine o'clock!"

Then her hand faltered, fell, as she realized what she was seeing.

"What?" Betty asked. She got to her feet, barely keeping her balance, and followed Elise's gaze. Her jaw dropped open. "Holy…"

There were so many possessed ones the ground seemed to seethe. Elise had grossly miscalculated how many servants Ann could have had —she'd clearly had several years to work up a collection. One dozen, three dozen. Maybe more.

The vessel of *vedae som matis* hung heavy in her pocket, growing so hot that it nearly burned her leg through her jeans. It snapped her out of her shocked reverie. "Be careful, Anthony," she said, climbing into the front seat. "Ann and James might be in there somewhere. Take out the edges first."

His response was to slide into line with the crowd and shift the old Jeep into a higher gear. He was grinning. Elise could only hope he would still be so thrilled when he was cleaning the blood off his car later.

Elise's voice continued to roar from the speakers. "*Ipse venena bibas! Crux sacra sit mihi lux, non draco sit mihi dux!*" The verse echoed amongst the tombstones and rattled the branches on the trees. They passed the ragged woman in the half-torn sundress, and as soon as the voice hit her ears, her spine went rigid. She fell to the ground, shaking, and Elise watched her pass with a critical eye.

"They're not getting exorcised," she said. "Damn."

"What?" Betty asked, leaning up on Anthony's seat.

She gestured to the servants. "The exorcism phrase isn't enough. It's hurting them, maybe even paralyzing a few, but on its own it can't actually free them."

"Hang on!" Anthony cried.

The Jeep shuddered as though it had struck a cement wall. Elise was

178

flung forward onto the roll cage, and a body hit the windshield.

The glass cracked, splintered. Betty screamed.

The body that struck their windshield slid off, but more rose out of the darkness, falling under the wheels and being flung to the sides. They were helpless to run. All they could do was get chewed by the wheels of the Jeep as Anthony fought to keep control and Elise searched for James.

The speakers crackled. *"Crux sacra—lux, non draco sit mihi—retro, Satana—"*

One of the possessed ones leaped at the car, clawing for Elise's jacket and the burning weight in her pocket. She threw herself out of its grasp, straddling the seat to keep her balance.

Her blade flashed. Blood sprayed.

The speakers made a static noise once more, and then died. *"Ipse venena..."*

Silence.

"The cable under the dashboard must have come loose!" Betty said.

A servant slammed into the hood of the Jeep, and it shuddered. This time, the man didn't slide away. He found grip near the windshield wipers, hauled himself higher, and pulled back his arm.

His fist punched through the glass.

Anthony cried out, falling to the side in his seat to avoid the groping hand. The car swerved, but Elise kept her balance. She brought her sword down, slicing into the possessed one's already-bleeding arm.

"We need the speakers!"

Betty crawled between the two front seats underneath Elise's legs. "I can reconnect it. I just need a second to find the break!"

The servant groped blindly and found the steering wheel. He wrenched it to the side as Anthony slammed on the brakes.

Betty squealed again. The three fell into one another, a jumble of legs and arms and confused bodies.

The Jeep lurched to a halt, and a man climbed over the side. His fist struck Elise in the face. Her injured cheekbone exploded in pain. Her vision blurred and darkened. She swung blindly and felt her sword connect.

Something warm splattered on her. It wasn't the rain.

Her vision cleared, and she saw her sword had sunk into the side of his neck. She pulled free and kicked, sending him over the side.

"Holy crap!" Betty exclaimed, untangling herself from Anthony.

"Fix the speakers," Elise said. She reached over the windshield and swung at the possessed one reaching through the cracks. Her sword connected with his back, but didn't cut. She took a deep breath, and began to shout. *"Crux sacra sit mihi lux, non draco sit mihi dux. Vade retro, Satana! Nunquam suade mihi vana. Sunt mala quae libas, ipse venena bibas!"*

The crucifix engraved in her sword blazed to life. The possessed one shrieked, jerking its arm out of the windshield and falling off the hood of the car.

More servants took his place, swarming the Jeep. Elise would kick one off, only for another to take its place climbing over the side. There were dozens. No matter how fast she swung, she couldn't keep up with them.

Anthony slammed the car into gear, but the wheels spun out in the mud.

"Betty…" Elise urged.

"I think I found it!" Betty announced from under the dashboard.

The Jeep's wheels found traction, and the car leapt forward, mowing down a pair of servants who had been coming up on their makeshift cow-catcher.

The speakers crackled, buzzed, and Elise's voice roared out of them once more.

"—dux. Vade retro, Satana! Nunquam suade mihi vana!"

Screams rose from the graveyard, as inhuman as the sounds that came from a slaughterhouse. "Success!" Betty cried, pumping her fist.

"Take this," Elise said, shoving the stone vessel into Betty's hands as she emerged from under the dashboard. "Ann can't perform the sacrifice without it, so it's safest with you. I trust you. Don't go far. I might need help transporting James."

Her friend nodded, cheeks flushed. "They won't get it without a fight!" Betty declared.

"Wait," Anthony said, power-sliding around the stone angel to a stop, "where are you going?"

"Ann's not here, so James isn't here," Elise said. "Ann lives across the street. I'm sure they're in there."

"You can't go alone."

"I'll be fine."

Elise prepared to leap down into the cemetery, but Anthony caught her hand. "Wait," he said, and he pulled her to him and kissed her. He was forceful, desperate, as though afraid it would be his last chance.

And then she jumped over the door before he could catch her again, disappearing into the night. She caught a glance of his face before she went—an expression of admiration, adoration, and fear.

Now that she no longer had the vessel, the servants ignored Elise.

They followed the Jeep, and Anthony gave them a good chase—he weaved in and out of the path, and the bigger spots in between the graves, driving over several of the shorter headstones as he made a line for the exit. The possessed ones couldn't keep up.

The storm overhead broke with slaps of thunder and lighting. Elise flipped her braid over her shoulder so she could sheathe the sword, and she ran toward Ann's house...and James.

The night grew darker.

One by one, the street lamps flickered and went out. A line of shadow crept up the street. The few people still struggling to stay awake began turning off their lights and going to their bedrooms, oblivious to the world around them. The heavy rain clouds that had briefly parted to reveal the moon's crescent covered it once more, and the shadow's hand gripped the Earth.

A single oil lamp illuminated Ann's room as the neighborhood's electricity turned off. Her outline was thrown against the wall in stark relief, a huge monster of a woman with massive shoulders and tiny legs.

The shadows beside her twisted and writhed. Ann's fiends covered every square foot of her house, silent and hungry. She passed the trap door, carrying the oil lamp to the altar, and peered down the ladder. The demons covered the floor below, and the floor beneath that as well. Elise wouldn't be able to get in without getting ripped apart.

Ann set the lamp beside James's leg and faced her altar, standing with her back to the open window.

The fiends touched her legs and stroked her arms and rested their heads on her feet. Some touched James, too, but he didn't stir. The high priest was unconscious.

She spread her arms wide. "Listen up, guys," Ann said. "Every beginning is the end of another. Tonight we leave behind the world we have come to know together for the past several years. Tonight we march to the ruins and transform everything. Tonight, you become the children of the new world."

Their lips quivered. They drooled.

"The city will be ours, and soon, this whole world will too. Why return to Hell under the law of another when we can have this Eden? You all deserve freedom. You deserve flesh. You deserve Earth."

Something clattered downstairs.

181

Ann cut off, frowning. She perked her ears, listening to the reports the fiends whispered into her mind when something happened. But there were no comforting voices from her demons—only a complete mental silence.

Elise.

"Take care of her, please," she said.

The fiends piled down the ladder, leaving the attic empty except for a handful of fiends and the two humans.

Ann rested her hand on his forehead. His pulse throbbed in his temples, rising and falling like the heart of the ocean. He was beautiful with symbols of transference and death painted upon his body. He was so lucky.

She took a step away from the table and began walking a slow circle, speaking quietly as she went. Ann drew runes in her mind and called upon spirits at the north, the west, the south, and the east—spirits few humans called in fear of their power. Her dominant hand pointed to the floor, and she felt rather than saw the energy burn an invisible path on the wood.

Ann clapped, and the circle of power erupted around them. James's eyes almost fluttering open.

"Did they get her?" Ann asked one of the fiends.

But before she could make out any reply, a dark shape darted out of the corner. She spun to see curtains flapping in the open window.

Nobody was there.

A fiend shrieked.

Elise stabbed again, driving her blade through the skull of the demon to silence it.

The weapon shocked Ann into silence. It wasn't just steel and leather —it coursed with magic, enchantments, prayers. It glowed in Ann's vision, both beautiful and terrible. She recognized it. Death's Hand had its twin.

Elise jerked her blade free, and a spray of blood spattered to the floor. The kopis decapitated the fiend's body with one smooth blow of her sword, and she kicked the head across the floor to Ann's feet.

Fresh blood flowed down the sharp edge of the sword. Elise's skin was flushed, her eyes blazing. *Vedae som matis* may have been the Goddess of Death, but Elise was the goddess of fury—and even with the power of a mighty demon at her back, Ann felt afraid.

And when Elise spoke, her voice burned. "Give me back my witch."

Chapter 18

"ELISE," ANN SAID. "Put the sword down."

Elise's eyes flicked between Ann and the nightmare of an altar with James as the centerpiece. His nakedness was a shock, but not nearly as horrifying as the black demon runes looping over his skin like the brands burned into the flesh of the fiends.

"Not until you let him go."

The necromancer scooped up the head at her feet. "Let him go?" she asked, cradling it in her arms as blood dribbled out the neck. "You killed my fiend."

"That will be nothing compared to what will happen if you don't give me James."

"I offered you a trade," Ann said.

"We both know you weren't serious." Elise took a deep breath. "We don't have to fight, Ann. This is between me and *vedae som matis*."

"I know," she whispered. "I know."

Ann straightened suddenly. Her head tilted, as though listening to some distant voice Elise couldn't hear. And then she began to smile.

"We have company."

The trap door banged open. Fiends jumped inside, dragging two larger shapes with them. For an instant, Elise half-hoped they were injured, struggling servants—but servants didn't fight and swear like these two.

The fiends threw Betty and Anthony to the floor. One of them ripped the pocket off her jacket, and the stone vessel thudded to the floor. Betty struggled, trying to take it back, but the fiends held her arms.

"Hey, get your hands off me! I'll punch you! Don't make me do it!"

Ann cradled the staff against her shoulder like a baby. "This night just got so much better."

Elise moved. Blood splattered on the walls.

The fiends holding Anthony fell. She sliced again, and the fiends holding Betty also fell. Intestines spilled onto the floor in a wash of red and yellow fluids, stinking of brimstone.

Anthony jumped to his feet. He punched another fiend in the eye. It keened, stumbling backward, and he hauled Betty to her feet before returning his attention to the little demons.

Elise twisted and jabbed, skewering a small demon on her sword. Something hit her wounded side. The breath rushed out of her lungs.

They hit the ground and rolled, and then it seemed like all the fiends were on top of Elise, clawing at her, grabbing and biting. The demons were nothing but shadows in the darkness of the room, blotting out all the light. She felt stubby teeth sink into her arm, and she threw the fiend off, struggling to stand. She was just a little too slow, a little too weak with the injuries David Nicholas inflicted.

Between the legs of an attacking fiend, she saw Betty fly at Ann like a manicured beast, her fingernails flying. Ann shrieked and Betty leapt onto her back, dragging them both to the ground.

Elise pushed away a fiend and swung blindly, feeling blade connect with body and hoping it was going to do damage.

Kicking off another demon, she flew to James's side at the altar. His closed eyes looked like they were bruised.

He stirred at her touch. "Elise?"

"Let's get you out of here, huh?" she said, throwing her jacket over his body. She felt around the ropes binding him to the table. "Hang on, it's going to take me a minute to figure out these knots."

"Finish the fight," James rasped.

She took a moment to plunge her sword into a fiend's stomach when it broke away from the others to attack. "I'm not leaving you behind."

"Ann will get away, Elise."

"She's not going anywhere. Betty's got her."

He gripped her wrist. His eyes had darkened, no longer that perfect shade of ice blue. A thunderstorm roiled in his gaze. Elise's fingers went still on the lock. "Trust me. I'll be fine. Get Ann."

"Okay." Elise pressed her boot knife into his hand. "If she gets close to you—kill her."

The room was in turmoil. Anthony thrashed in the grip of several fiends, but he wouldn't relinquish his position over the trap door, which he had locked. He bled from a gash near his hairline. The other fiends had turned their attention to the fight between Betty and Ann, which seemed to involve a lot of slapping and hair-pulling.

Elise smiled faintly. A slap fight. That was new.

And then a blade flashed from nowhere, and Elise's smile disappeared. Ann's hand cracked against Betty's skull with the flat end of the hilt.

"Betty!" Anthony roared.

Elise leapt forward, but the trap door suddenly exploded underneath Anthony. The force threw him forward into the waiting arms of the fiends, and the servants from the cemetery began to climb inside.

One by one, the attic filled with the possessed ones. The man from the hospital, his female partner. A burly, tattooed corpse Elise hadn't seen before. And then Lucinde.

Ann stomped to the front of the room again, standing beside the altar. "Restrain them!" she ordered, and three of the servants came forward, grabbing Elise's arms and dragging her to the end of the room.

A fiend ripped the sword from her hands and dropped it out of reach. Another dragged Betty's lifeless body to her side. It took two of them to restrain Anthony.

The rest had to hold Elise.

A knobby fist sank into her side, making pain explode through her body. She staggered and fell to her knees. Claws raked down her bruised face and smacked into her jaw.

Through blurry eyes, Elise saw James raise a free hand with the knife.

The motion drew Ann's attention. She slapped it out of his hand.

"This was going to be my night of glory. This is when I was going to show *vedae som matis* that I'm good enough for her. Don't you realize what you're ruining?" She slashed her dagger along the wound she had carved on his belly. Fresh blood began to trickle down his side.

Elise struggled, but the possessed ones held her in place. "You better not—"

Ann pointed the knife at her. "Shut up. I don't want to talk to you anymore."

"He doesn't deserve to die.!"

"Do you think he's a good man?" Ann asked as she sprinkled herbs over his head.

Elise swallowed. "The best I know."

"Then you don't know him as well as you think you do," Ann said. She traced her bloody finger down the bridge of his nose. "He's never told you the truth. You would let me kill him if he had."

185

Betty sat up, holding a hand to her head. "Ugh. What did I miss? Did we beat that—" Anthony threw a hand over her mouth.

Ann pulled an owl's skull from underneath the table. Sharp teeth that birds had never possessed on Earth filled its mouth. She laid it on James's chest.

"And now I can repay my debts to the Hand of Death," she said. Her voice was hushed, reverent.

She smashed the skull on James's chest. Pieces of bone flew everywhere, and blood seeped forth beneath it. She smeared it across James's solar plexus.

Elise's muscles were liquid. Every time she moved, little hands dug into her wounds, burying their nails into muscle.

If only David Nicholas hadn't attacked.

If only Elise hadn't provoked him.

If only she were a little stronger…a little faster…

Ann turned her back on them. She raised the dagger high, smoothing her hand over James's brow. Shadows rippled off her body.

Elise felt the press of Betty and Anthony's eyes on her. They were waiting to see what last-ditch trick she was going to pull out of her hat, like she was some hero from a movie with a plan always in place.

But she didn't have a plan. She couldn't think, or breathe, and she couldn't move with so many demons holding her down. She met Betty's gaze, and she saw her best friend's worried countenance dissolve into terror.

The stress of the last days built inside Elise, growing and swelling until she felt her ribs might burst. Exorcising Lucinde. Fighting the possessed ones in the cemetery. Losing James, and finding him again to realize he had been all but gutted like a pig and left poisoned. Her new life destroyed; her old life returning like an unyielding cancer.

I'm not ready for this.

Ann. Lucinde. James.

The witch shifted her grip on the dagger so its blade faced down.

Elise threw herself against the steely arms of her captors, but they were unyielding. "Ann! No!"

Her hand came down. The dagger buried into James's chest with a *crack*.

His mouth opened in a silent gasp, eyes blank.

For an instant, there was no reaction. The world was reduced to the space between Elise and James—so close, just inches away, and yet utterly impassable. Elise's breath caught in her lungs. Her pulse roared in her ears.

Betty let out a sob, deepening the silence rather than breaking it.

James's chest hitched, and blood spilled over his lip.

"James," Elise said. She was so cold.

His head lolled to the side, looking beyond the wall of servants to his partner. Their eyes met for a breathless instant, and his mouth formed a single word: *Elise*. No sound escaped his bloody mouth. His teeth were red.

The light behind his eyes faded, and that was all. His body sank into the table, muscles relaxing one by one until there was no sense of life in his face, his body.

And that was all.

"Berald, Beroald, Balbin, Gab, Gabor, Agaba," Ann was saying softly, her hands moving over James's body. A bracelet of bird bones dangled from her wrist, brushing against his bare stomach. "Berald, Beroald, Balbin, Gab, Gabor, Agaba..."

The world receded, slipping away from Elise. Her ears were ringing and her heart was thudding and she *knew* that James was dead. She could have been a thousand miles away, and she would still know with absolute certainty. It was as though, in his passing, a part of her had died, too.

The scar on her arm from the binding ritual that tied them together as kopis and aspis burned.

Dead.

Anthony was muttering under his breath. It sounded like prayer. The valley of the shadow of the death. She took another step back, and the fiends finally released her. Betty was on her knees. Anthony was beside her, holding his cousin's hands. They were pale and shocked and Elise barely even registered it.

James's eyes were empty.

"Balbin, Gab, Gabor, Agaba, Berald..."

She didn't feel pain anymore. She didn't feel anything at all. A glint of metal caught the corner of Elise's eye.

"...Beroald, Balbin, Gab..."

She dropped.

The hands of the possessed ones reached for Elise, but she rolled under their grasp and took her sword. She came up on her knee in one smooth motion, plunging it into a servant's stomach until the hilt slammed into flesh and the blade burst out its back.

She freed the sword with a jerk of her wrist and kicked the servant to the floor. It fell, lifeless and gaping.

Ann spun. Her jaw hung open. "That was mine," she said. "You little —"

Elise spun, burying her sword into the belly of a nearby fiend, tearing it out its side with a gush of blood and mucus. It dripped down the blade and onto her gloved hand.

"Plan B," Elise said. Her voice was dead.

The attic exploded in motion.

Fiends and servants alike dove for Elise. She dropped to her knees and slashed, slicing through hamstrings and driving her blade into torsos regardless of whether it belonged to a demon or had once been human. Her ribs ached and she thought something was broken and she didn't care.

Blood splattered on the walls. Someone screamed.

James's empty stare remained fixed on the wall.

Elise kicked, punched, and dodged entirely on instinct. She let her long-unused muscles twist her out of the way of blows just in time, feeling claws whistle past her cheek and slice into errant curls.

Something sharp sliced down her arm. She chopped off its hand.

Anthony fought behind her with less grace but no more regard for what he was fighting. His fists flew, making sledgehammer noises against flesh.

Elise threw herself around him, ducking low to stay out of the way of one of his blows even as she gutted another enemy. A body. It had once been the man from the hospital, but now he was mulch. He hit the floor in several pieces, and Elise's foot squelched on a piece of steaming intestine as she spun to attack another.

And she came face-to-face with Lucinde.

The little girl didn't look human anymore. The symbol on her forehead burned, and she reached for Elise with little hands that almost looked like the fiends' claws.

But her face registered in Elise's numbed mind. She froze mid-swing.

A fiend struck her in the side, sending them both bowling to the floor beneath the altar. Its slavering mouth flashed at her face, and she blocked it with her forearm. Its teeth buried into her flesh.

She used its own grip on her to slam its head into the underside of the table. She smashed its head twice, and it released her.

Betty had crawled between two bookshelves and covered her head with her arms. Elise couldn't hear her over the beat of her own heart, but she knew her friend was screaming, crying.

188

Another clawed hand came at Elise. A flash of her sword. Dismembered.

She rolled out from underneath the table, throwing a high kick into the face of a possessed one. Its head snapped back, and it stumbled into a set of shelves. Glass alembics and vials shattered against the ground, raining tinkling shards of glass across the wood floors.

"You idiot!" Ann stormed around the altar with demonic energies swimming in her wake. She burned with black fire. The tangled hairs on her head stuck straight out in every direction as though repelled by her flesh. "I've won! Can't you give up already?"

Elise's couldn't think of a response, so she didn't speak at all. She swung her fist, clenched around the hilt of the sword. It cracked against Ann's face and her head snapped back.

Ann slashed at her with the dagger stained by James's blood. Elise dodged it and kicked her in the head. Ann fell.

She rolled onto her belly, scrambling for the knife as Elise loomed over Ann's supine body.

"Get up," Elise said.

Ann's fingers brushed the hilt of her knife. Elise stomped on her hand, grinding with the heel of her shoe. Ann's bruised eyes were round and frightened.

Elise lifted her foot long enough to kick her in the ribcage. The witch cried out.

"You said this is your night of glory. Get up!"

Ann almost made it to her feet before Elise's knee connected with her temple. The bone made a sickening noise like a rotten tomato splattering against concrete. Her eyes were empty before she hit the floor.

This time, the witch didn't stand.

"Fight me," Elise said, but there was no response.

She faced the room. The trap door had been shut again, and all that remained in the room were a half a dozen bodies scattered across the floor. A handful of Ann's remaining servants had teamed up against Anthony, slamming him to the floor.

Elise began to move toward him—but a wall of demonic power struck her full force. Fire ripped through her body. Pain arched her back, and her sword fell from her fingers.

She clutched at her head as wave after wave of energy shattered her thoughts and twisted her brain, making her eyes explode with black lights.

Voices swam through her skull.

189

Crux sacra sit mihi lux...

I am the cold kiss of Death, and you can never defeat me.

Elise was on the floor, but she didn't know how she had gotten there. She stared up at the raftered ceiling, the bars of heavy oak casting dancing lines against the ceiling.

The breeze twisted through the window and extinguished the oil lamp with a pinch of its invisible fingers.

But the attic was not dark.

A man towered above her. Every inch of his bare, sweaty skin was bared to the attic, and his eyes welled with tears of blood. Thick veins bulged under his skin, crawling up his arms and neck onto his face. His muscles bulged as though they had been shot full of testosterone. His pulse visibly pounded in his throat, erection full and straining in a bed of trimmed black hair.

A symbol swam to life on his forehead and multiplied, spreading down his body. As it passed the painted marks, they flared with black shadows. The distant fires of Hell reflected on the marks.

The witch usually made a sound like chimes in Elise's skull when he was around, soft and powerful. Now he thrummed with the power of *vedae som matis*, and the air around him trembled.

"James," Elise whispered.

Chapter 19

DEATH'S HAND SURVEYED Elise with James's eyes. She tensed, expecting him to attack, but he stared at her without moving. His face twisted with a tangled mix of emotions.

Emotions? Could a powerful demon *feel*?

The silence of the attic around them was broken by shuffling feet. The possessed ones left Anthony's body to flank Death's Hand, heads bent in submission. Lucinde knelt with her small head resting against his knee.

The fiends crawled on their bellies to his feet. They laved their black tongues along his ankles, his calves, pawing his hips and stomach. Death's Hand didn't acknowledge any of them. His gaze remained steady on Elise, as though he was in no hurry to do anything but *look* at her.

Vedae som matis lifted a hand. She flinched.

Ann's body lifted from the corner of the room behind the altar, where Elise had left her. Her limbs lifted, and her legs twitched, but her head remained slack on her shoulders.

She came forward without taking a single step. Her toes dragged against the ground. Ann's face was blank and her mouth hung open. Her every motion was unnatural, as though she was a puppet with invisible strings. By the time she stopped moving just beside Death's Hand, Elise was certain she was dead.

Ann spoke. The language that spilled from her lips made no sense to Elise, foreign and guttural and inhuman. Foamy saliva dripped from her bottom lip as though she were an ancient Pythia controlled by a demonic Apollo.

Death's Hand gestured once more. Ann shivered, and when she spoke again, it was in English.

"Kopis," she said. It came from her throat, her vocal cords, but the words belonged to *vedae som matis*. "I have been eager to see you and your aspis, who thrived as I struggled to rebuild my withered soul from the brink of nothingness."

Another gesture. A fiend skittered from behind Death's Hand and opened one of Ann's drawers, withdrawing a long object wrapped in cloth. It supplicated itself at James's feet. He took the item from the fiend's hands, giving it time to scurry back before unwrapping it.

Steel glinted in the dim firelight.

"You recognize this, I'm sure," said Ann's body. Death's Hand turned the sword in his hands, hefting it by the hilt to examine the line of the blade. Someone had cleaned the falchion. It was in perfect condition. "Here we are again. Little has changed in the ensuing years, except you are fleshier. You have fattened upon the spoils of victory and comfort while I have floundered."

Elise finally found her voice. "You can't have James."

Death's Hand made his lips smile. "No?" Ann's chin quivered, and blood dripped from the corner of her mouth. "It is difficult to campaign on Earth. Things in Hell are much simpler. There are many complications. You and your aspis are a complication. What a coincidence that he would be a suitable vessel. It is fate."

"Fate," Elise echoed.

Blood pulsed in James's veins. "Or something like that."

"What about Ann?"

"She will survive in this form." The gesture *vedae som matis* made with the sword encompassed James's body, but not Ann's. "I have absorbed what I need."

"She was in love with you."

He rested the sword behind him on the table, out of Elise's reach. "She lives in me now. We are closer than ever before. She would prefer it this way." There was almost a hint of love in that voice.

Elise took a step away, inching closer to her sword where it lay next to a bookshelf. She could feel the bulge of the charm-draped chain in her pocket. "Anyone that's been possessed can be exorcised."

Vedae som matis nodded, acknowledging the challenge.

Ann's corpse fell, no longer necessary. Elise threw a hand toward her engraved sword.

The room exploded into black stars.

Elise was smashed chest-first into a wall. Hands gripped her wrists, pinning her in place.

His face buried in her shoulder, and pain erupted in her collarbone.

She screamed and tore free.

Elise put several feet between herself and Death's Hand before she touched the wound on her shoulder—and realized she had been bitten. Blood gushed from the raw flesh underneath her fingers. The inside of her body felt like the inside of fresh steak.

She turned. Blood dribbled down James's chin as a small chunk of her shoulder disappeared between his lips. His throat worked as he swallowed.

Elise lunged for her sword. She scooped it into her left hand and stood in the same smooth motion, twirling just in time to see James flying at her. She dodged and raised the sword. Her blade slashed across James's arm in a spray of blood that splashed across her chest.

Vedae som matis barreled into Elise and knocked them both to the floor.

She took their weight on her uninjured shoulder, trying to bring around the sword to slash at him again. Death's Hand didn't give her a chance. He grabbed her wrist and crushed it in his hand until Elise could feel something pop.

Her fingers went slack, and he ripped the sword out of her grasp, shifting his weight so his entire body pinned her to the wood. He stank of blood and decay and brimstone, and very faintly like Ivory soap.

Elise struck him with her right hand, but he grabbed her other wrist and pushed both of her arms to the ground. His body burned like a furnace.

She twisted her head away from his sulfuric breath. Death's Hand buried James's face into her shoulder, the same one he had bitten before. Elise fought harder, but it was like struggling against rock.

His teeth found her wound around the shoulder of her shirt. Something pinched, tore. She grit her teeth and refused to scream.

James's weight shifted just slightly, and something pressed into Elise's leg. Her charms. She squirmed around enough to see her jeans, and a glimmer of metal told her they were sticking just slightly out of her pocket.

"*Crux—crux sacra sit mihi lux,*" Elise panted. "*Non draco sit mihi dux. Vade retro, Satana, nunquam suade—*"

Death's Hand threw his head back, roaring. It tore through Elise's ears, and she screamed with him as her eardrums thrummed.

He ripped at her jeans, tearing away the pocket. The charms spilled out onto the floor.

James's teeth sunk into her shoulder again, and he worried at her flesh like a dog with a bone.

193

She beat her fist against his head, his shoulders, his hand where it pinned her other arm to the floor. He paid no attention, growling deep in his throat. She reached for the charms, but he shoved them out of reach.

Elise twisted and writhed, and all she could do was worsen the agony where he bit into her.

Vedae som matis pushed her shirt aside to get a better taste of her shoulder. The pain grew from agonizing to indescribable. His teeth scraped against bone.

I will not scream.

Her back arched, and he pulled his head away. A small strip of skin dangled from his teeth. The burning told Elise it was part of her neck.

Death's Hand began to lower to her shoulder again, and Elise felt faint. She wouldn't be able to remain conscious through another second of that horrible chewing, and if she passed out, the pain would be the last thing she ever knew.

Elise reached back. Her shoulder screamed.

Her hand flexed around a shelf on Ann's bookcase, and she *pulled*.

The shelves came down on Death's Hand, on Elise, and the books rained around them. The heavy wood of the shelf struck James's shoulders.

He roared his terrible roar once more, rearing to shove the shelves off of himself. The space between them was slight, but it was enough for Elise to throw all of her weight into him and push him off-balance. *Vedae som matis* tumbled away.

Elise scrambled to her hands and knees, closing the inches between herself and her sword. Her hand closed on the leather-wrapped hilt.

Relief washed through her. Adrenaline overrode the pain enough for her to lift it.

She turned as Death's Hand swung, but her head spun as she moved and dizziness swept over Elise. Blood loss slowed her. He knocked her blade aside and she felt the metal bury into his forearm.

Blood fountained from his arm and splattered against the floor. As Elise watched, the wound closed, healing without a trace.

She took a deep breath and pointed the sword at James. "*Crux sacra sit mihi lux,*" she gasped, pressing her hand harder over the wound on her shoulder. It grew more agonizing as it dried out and sent fire racing down her nerves.

Death's Hand smiled. It was James's smile, warm and friendly, as though he was beginning to assume her partner's habits.

She reached inside herself, searching for that wellspring of energy that James would always touch when they piggy-backed. It wasn't magic. It was older, primal—the force of a kopis and exorcist. "*Non draco sit mihi dux. Vade retro, Satana, nunquam suade mihi vana.*"

She took a mental hold of the power inside herself and tore it open.

Elise's senses exploded. It hit James, still in the clutches of *vedae som matis*, and kept going, sweeping through the servants and wrapping its invisible fingers around them. It poured through her sword, through her charm necklace, and she felt her energy curl around the demons with metaphysical fingers.

Vedae som matis screamed. The demon's voice ripped through James's throat, but Elise's power had taken a life of its own and it wasn't done.

Wind blasted through the open window, and papers around the room went flying, swimming in circles around and around Elise and James. Vials tipped and shattered, carpeting the wooden floors in shards of colorful glass and ceramic. James's hair stood straight up from his head, swaying as though he was submerged in the ocean.

His bleeding gaze cut through the chaos. He didn't speak—she wasn't sure he even could—but she could feel the fury of Death's Hand.

Elise kicked him in the face as hard as she could. He crashed to the floor, but his hand reached out and dragged her down with him.

He rolled on top of her and closed his hands around her throat.

She struggled, beating against his arms, but his muscles had turned into bands of iron. She shoved against him.

He didn't budge.

Blood thudded in her skull.

His bloody moth still grinned as the room grew dark. Her chest hitched with a desperate need for oxygen.

Elise had imagined dying before. She knew it could come in any number of ways. She never imagined it with James's hands on her neck.

Her legs might have been kicking, but she couldn't feel them anymore. Her brain was bulging against her forehead. Everything grew distant and dark, even her fingers, and she thought she might have gone limp.

James...

She wished she could tell him she was sorry.

"No!"

The pressure on her throat vanished.

Air stabbed into her chest, burning a path down her bruised esophagus.

Elise wheezed and coughed as color returned to the room, too vivid with the sudden intake of oxygen. James arched. His lips peeled back against his teeth and veins bulged at his throat. His muscles rippled, almost tearing. It was like his skull was trying to crack in half.

His nails dug into the sides of his head. "*Let go!*"

The voice belonged to James.

An internal battle wracked his body as he fought Death's Hand for control. Symbols swirled wildly over his skin. "James," she said, "James, look at me—"

But he didn't hear her. He twisted on the floor like he was burning in invisible flame.

Elise gathered both of her swords and stood over him, uncertain. She needed to help him, she needed to *save* him, but who was in control—James or the demon?

With another cry, he froze. His eyes fell on her.

"James?" she whispered.

His mouth was stained with her blood. "Elise, I—" James's expression twisted, and then stilled.

He was gone again.

Death's Hand thrust his fist toward the ceiling.

An explosion rocked the building. A huge roar filled Elise's ears, followed by a cracking like a glacier snapping off into the ocean. Fragments of plaster showered across the floor.

The entire roof ripped off the house and flung into the night with a blast of wind. There were no stars. Clouds boiled overhead as rain poured into the attic.

"James!"

His body lifted into the air. She leaped, clambering as high on the wall as she could to swipe at his feet. Elise wanted to catch him and drag him back. She couldn't exorcise him unless she could touch him. But an invisible wall had materialized around him, and her hand slammed into solid nothing inches short of his heel.

He dropped to the street outside, and Elise gazed hopelessly down at him, clinging to an exposed wall stud.

She dropped to the floor. The human servants had already gotten to their feet and disappeared down the trap door to follow Death's Hand. The fiends stirred again, like they were rousing from a long night of sleep.

Elise didn't want to give them the chance to move.

She took her swords—both of them—and plunged them into the heart of a fiend at her foot. She slashed and stabbed over and over again until blood coated her hand and spattered on her face and nothing stood in what used to be Ann's attic. There wasn't much left to kill. Almost everything had fled with Death's Hand.

Elise climbed onto what used to be a window, preparing herself to climb down the side of the building. Her shoulder burned, but she didn't care. She had to reach James. Maybe it wasn't too late, maybe she could—

"Elise—help—"

Anthony had come to consciousness pinned underneath one of the ceiling beams.

She hung suspended, her urge to follow James warring with Anthony's pleas for her attention. "Come on," he said, groaning as he shoved at the beam.

Elise sheathed one sword and dropped down. With their combined strength, it was easy to shift the weight of the rubble enough for him to slide out underneath. He was white with plaster dust.

Betty screamed on the other side of the attic. It was a single, constant shriek like the wail of an alarm.

Elise went to her, but when Betty saw her, she only shrieked louder and hugged her body tight into the corner. "Shut up," she said, kneeling in front of her. Betty tried to scramble back. Elise seized her wrist. "I told you to shut up!"

"Oh God, oh God, oh God—"

Elise slapped her.

Betty silenced instantly. Her free hand flew to her cheek. "Hey!" Anthony protested, but Elise turned her glare on him.

"You two need to listen to me. This is—"

A silent voice boomed through the air: *Sleep.*

"Did you hear that?" Anthony asked.

But before Elise could reply, she felt the command sucking her down into darkness, like she had a dose of narcotics injected straight to her heart.

Sleep...

Anthony and Betty's eyes went blank at the same time. She slipped to the side and went unconscious immediately. He managed to take a step toward Elise before his knees gave out and he, too, collapsed.

Elise shook her head, trying to clear the flies buzzing between her ears. "No," she said.

But it was like telling the sun not to set at the end of the day. Her eyes rolled up, and the world went dark.

Chapter 20

TIME PASSED, AND Elise awoke.

She rolled onto her side, groaning. Every muscle had stiffened. Her bloody shoulder felt like someone sawed into it every time she moved, and when she probed it with the tips of her fingers, she found blood caked over the injury.

With a jolt, she remembered James's flight from the attic. She sat upright.

Anthony and Betty were still unconscious. Elise over and shook him.

"Get up. We have to get Death's Hand."

He rolled onto his back without stirring. She pressed her fingers to his throat and found a pulse. Anthony wasn't dead, but he was equally useless.

Elise supported herself with what was left of one of Ann's walls, shutting her eyes against the waves of pain that rocked through her body. Everything felt torn, bruised, and broken, but there was no time for self-pity. She had no idea how long she had been unconscious. Death's Hand could have been miles away already.

She scooped her charms out of a puddle of fiend blood and lifted the trap door.

The house creaked and shuddered as she made her way down the stairs. A steady drizzle turned the pavement into a shining black lake in the night.

Elise ran down the hill and across the road to the cemetery, feet splashing in the puddles. Anthony and Betty had made it to the road outside before getting dragged from the Jeep.

The gas indicator was almost on empty. Her voice still crackled out of the speakers, quieter than before. "...*sit mihi dux. Vade retro, Satana...*"

She punched the power button to silence it. Elise had almost backed onto the street again before something strange caught her eye.

All the graves had been torn open.

Elise pulled herself up on the roll cage with her good arm to stare out at Our Mother of Sorrow's cemetery. Ann had raised several bodies from it over the last few weeks, but most of them had been untouched. Now every grave had sunk in on itself, pitting the grass and leaving piles of mud everywhere.

Her heart sank. Had Death's Hand resurrected *every* corpse as he passed? Elise didn't want to consider what that might mean. There were hospitals downtown, and more cemeteries.

And a lot of innocent lives.

Elise tore down the road, ignoring the speed limit. She approached tail lights and climbed the median to go around them.

The stoplight turned green. None of the cars moved.

She blew past the line and had to stomp on the brakes. A group of cars and trucks had stopped in the middle of the intersection, causing a minor accident. The drivers were all slumped over their steering wheels.

The calming must have spread far enough to stop everyone on this side of town. The streets were completely blocked. Elise pounded her steering wheel, biting back a curse.

She wove the Jeep carefully around the intersection. It looked like there had been parties celebrating finals at the university, because the sidewalks were covered in students sprawled out in skirts and heels. A few had even passed out in the middle of the street.

The Jeep's engine spluttered. The fuel indicator had dropped to the empty line. Elise made it another two blocks before it died, stopping in front of the school of art. The bar across the street had its lights on, and she could see everyone inside asleep on their tables.

"Shit," she muttered. "Shit, shit, *shit*."

She jumped out of the Jeep. The instant her feet hit the ground, she could feel the presence of Death's Hand.

Sleep…

Elise muffled a yawn. It weighed heavily on her, but it wasn't as strong as it was in the attic. Something about being a kopis—or maybe the particular kopis bound to James—seemed to make her resistant to the effects of the calming spell. The bite on her shoulder burned all the way down the scar on her arm. She wondered if James's scar burned, too.

Something flicked through the darkness up the street, and she reached her good arm up to one of the swords on her back. Giant eyes shone at her in the darkness, spotting her in the street.

Another pair of lights reflected behind it, and then another, as their heads turned to look at her.

She couldn't fight one fiend, much less three. Not with her muscles stiff and a ragged wound on her shoulder. Not with her aching ribs, which stabbed with pain every time she breathed.

With no other choice, Elise darted down the street and crouched behind a car and held her breath. The occupant inside had his cheek mashed against the damp window. Blood trickled from the corner of his nose, trailing down the glass like rivulets of rain.

The fiends yipped and growled as they scurried from the houses to the street.

Shutting her eyes, she rested her head against the side of the car and tuned out her pain to reach out and *feel* where the fiends were. She matched the noises—the scraping of claws, the brush of leathery flesh against branches—with the sensations in her gut that said they were behind her, just feet away. Something gave a heavy huff as it searched the air for her scent.

Elise eased around another car, trying to keep her feet from grinding against the grit of the pavement. Rain tapped out a rhythm on the sidewalk.

She peered around the tailgate of a truck, trying to see through the purple haze of night to the shadows she knew had to be there. Four fiends. There were four of them, even though she couldn't see them.

Creeping out another inch, Elise turned to look on the other side of the truck.

A slathering mouth opened in a wide, hungry grin.

Elise jerked back with a shout. She went for her sword instinctively— wrong arm—and pain flared down her back.

She fell with a splash. The fiend lunged.

Planting a foot in its gut, she snapped a second kick into its chin. It screamed. She kicked again and got an eyeball this time. It exploded like a pustule and splattered all over its cheek.

A dozen other fiends scurried to life at its scream.

Elise clambered to her feet and ran. Every pound of her feet jolted through her wounds. It burned through her body, like little strikes of lightning on her nerves.

Behind her, fiends dug their claws into the earth in pursuit.

Too many cars. Elise had to weave in and out, and the demons were climbing over them. They were gaining.

She cut across into the parking garage, which was mostly empty now that the semester had ended, and emerged on campus on the other side.

For a half second, she thought that people were still awake. Human figures moved down the paths toward the university buildings, slow on their feet and unperturbed by the rain.

But then Elise saw that many of them had only rotten scraps of clothing, and that some of them were rapidly healing—muscles wrapping around exposed, dusty bone before fat and skin rippled down their limbs.

She had to stop and stare at the power of Death's Hand. There were dozens of bodies—maybe hundreds—just where she could see. It was like they were being sculpted from flesh and blood as she watched.

And then the closest heard her running, heard the growls of the fiends echoing in the parking garage, and they turned to look at her.

Several hands reached for her at once.

Elise shoved them off. She elbowed a woman with no bottom jaw, kicked off a teenage girl with a gaping hole on the side of her head, and stumbled out into the open.

The healing corpses were sluggish, but their bodies made a great barrier between Elise and the fiends. She turned a corner around the building, leaving the demons struggling to get around the bodies.

There were more corpses further south. They were headed downtown. When Elise ran past them, they made half-hearted grabs for her, but she ducked out of their reach and was soon forgotten. They were too busy answering the same call she was—the call of Death's Hand.

She left campus and went for the casinos. The lights were still on, marching in lines down the sides of buildings and flashing titles taller than she was. They cast colorful, dancing shadows on the immobile cars and slumped pedestrians.

The closer she got to him, the louder his voice became: *Sleep.*

It was James's voice, but it was not James speaking. Anger knotted in her heart.

Elise didn't stop to look at the mangled cars down on the freeway as she ran over the bridge, shoving past the body of an old man. He pitched over the railing.

She had almost run past a casino with corpses clustered by the front door when she felt the presence of Death's Hand shift.

He was inside.

The servants of Death's Hand had all stopped on the street to stare at the casino as though they could see through the walls to their master. They were spread out several blocks south as though they expected Elvis

201

to burst through the front doors for an impromptu concert. None of them noticed her now. They were all absorbed by the silent call.

Elise tilted her head back to look at the glimmering sign over the door. Craven's. Somehow, she wasn't surprised. Beneath her feet, deep under the streets, Eloquent Blood would be blasting music. And miles below that twisted the Warrens. Death's Hand was marching for the ruins.

Elise stepped over the body of a security guard to get inside. There was a huge bite wound on his arm, much like the one on her shoulder. Blood shone on his shirt.

Inside, the air was thick with smoke and the molasses-thick sense of evil radiating from Death's Hand. Slot machines jangled and clanged and sang enticing songs. The keno boards on the wall were frozen halfway through a game. Cocktail waitresses were sprawled out with drinks spilled in their hair and on their skirts.

Elise saw motion in one of the mirrored walls, and she jumped behind the bar for cover. She stepped on a bartender and he groaned softly.

"Sorry," she muttered, crouch-walking to the end of the bar as quietly as she could manage.

When she made it to the end of the bar, she could see around the next row of slot machines, and the source of the motion became clear.

A broad, bare back was crouched over the body of an unconscious waitress. His shoulders twisted and jerked. The distortion of the mirror almost kept Elise from seeing what he was doing—almost.

Death's Hand dipped James's head again to rip into the waitress's side, digging in and pulling back to swallow. Blood coated his face and hands.

His power grew with every swallow. He was stronger now than he had been in the attic.

Much stronger.

He straightened with a fistful of ragged flesh in his hands, studying it with calm, black eyes as though evaluating a cut from a butcher. The symbols on his flesh were so thick now that she could see almost none of James's skin.

Death's Hand reached out his other arm. She hadn't noticed him take the stone staff when he fled from the attic. Maybe he hadn't—maybe it had followed him—but he clutched it now, and it had *grown*. It extended from his right arm, as tall as he was and twisted with demonic runes. They grew from it like branches. The stone oozed over his knuckles and wrist like lava, melding with his arm so they were one.

He aimed the stone staff at the floor, and the building rumbled. The bottles on the bar rattled. The earth shook beneath Elise's feet.

A mighty *crack* thudded through the air, and a giant slot machine with a colorful wheel shattered across the brightly-patterned carpet. The floor split. Death's Hand gestured, and a chunk of floor the size of a sedan lifted.

Elise slowly drew one of her swords with trembling fingers. The blade whispered in its sheath, so softly that she barely heard it beneath the tearing of the earth.

Death's Hand froze.

She tightened her hand on the hilt.

She saw him drop the chunk of flesh in the mirror. She watched him face the bar. She watched him move toward her one step at a time, his feet inches above the carpet. Her shoulder burned.

Elise couldn't struggle with him. She would lose.

She only had one chance to end it.

"*Crux sacra sit mihi lux,*" she whispered, and her charms began to glow at her hip.

Death's Hand stood on the other side of the bar.

Elise jumped to her feet, swinging her sword—and he caught the blade.

The force of his power slammed into her.

A cacophonous buzzing resonated through her skull. The sour tang of blood exploded in her mouth. Her teeth strained against her gums, trying to rip free of her jaw.

The muscles in her arms shook as she pressed against him. Her blade cut into his hands, sending blood dripping down his arm and onto the floor. It sizzled and evaporated.

Hatred filled James's eyes. She felt the floor crack beneath her feet.

The bar fragmented and tore away from them. She couldn't release her sword. Her muscles had locked up in the grip of the demon's power.

Her vision darkened at the edges. Slot machines began falling behind him, but all she could see was his furious gaze and his bloody mouth and feel his hand gripping her shoulder. His fingers dug into the wound. Elise tried to cry out and found she could barely move her mouth.

He challenged her silently. *Try to exorcise me. Just try.*

The energy between them swelled. Her intestines writhed within her like maggots. He pulled the blade forward, drawing her against his body, and his skin burned like fire. His sweat steamed.

"*Non—non draco—*" Her tongue was thick. She couldn't speak. It felt like hot oil dripped off his flesh, spattering against her.

The stone of the staff began creeping over his hand to her skin, locking down over her shoulder.

Death's Hand was going to take her. She could feel needles of stone piercing her skin. Ichor spread through her muscles.

The casino was suddenly gone behind him.

The edge of her blade bit into his stomach, and Death's Hand smiled.

"Non draco sit mihi dux—vade retro, Satana—"

Her power slid off of him. He was impenetrable.

Plaster showered around them, and rain began to drip through the holes. The stone locked into her bones.

The symbols on her kopis glowed, and then flickered.

You're out of time, Elise, Death's Hand said, and now he spoke directly into her mind. She could feel the weight of him oppressing her. He was going to kill her and fill her body and—

"—nunquam—suade mihi—vana—"

His fingernails scraped her wound beneath the stone.

"Sunt mala quae libas—"

Elise *couldn't* kill James, she couldn't do it, and Death's Hand knew it. Her blade cut him, but it hurt her far worse than it could ever hurt him.

But it's not James, not anymore, it's a demon—I can't do it—

His face spasmed.

For an instant—no more—Elise saw James in there. His eyes softened. His smile faded.

The power of Death's Hand lifted for an instant.

It was long enough.

"—ipse venena bibas!"

Bile rose in her throat. The power shut her throat and plugged her nose, roaring like drumbeats in her ears, snapping over her skin.

She tore the second sword from its hilt and plunged it into James's heart.

And everything became silent.

Death's Hand's eyes widened until she could see white at the very edges.

Elise," he said in James's voice, sounding stunned.

And then he threw his head back, and a soundless explosion rocked the ruins of the casino.

Waves of raw energy slammed into her, one after the other. Elise was flung against the wall as if swatted aside by a giant hand. Bottles of alcohol rained down on her, knocking into her elbows, her hips, and she threw her hands over her head to protect her head.

The mirrored walls fell. Glass exploded on the ground. The shelves slammed into her shoulder blades and pinned her to the floor.

A wind rose, knocking over the last of the slot machines. Dark energy blurred around James. A seizure shook his body. He clawed at his arms with fingernails as the black symbols cascaded off his flesh and vanished into the air.

James screamed wordlessly as the power of the exorcism rushed Death's Hand toward the passages between Earth and Hell.

His fists slammed into the ground and an invisible string drew him up by the solar plexus, arching his spine. His heels kicked helplessly against the ground. Her sword jutted toward the sky, lodged in his breastbone.

With a sick popping sound, Death's Hand was wrenched completely from James.

He stopped screaming.

Elise could feel the bodies animated by Death's Hand throughout the city. She could feel the demon in them, the little bits of *vedae som matis* left behind. She fought to push herself onto her elbows, gripping her first sword, but she couldn't support her own weight.

"Servants," she gasped, and the words were whipped into the tide of power. "Return to the Hell in which you belong. Be gone!"

The cord binding Elise to James snapped, whipping away from her body and lashing into the ether. Death's Hand faded away with a piercing scream. Every servant standing in the streets outside collapsed.

The wind died, leaving the casino in silence.

Elise fell to the floor.

And just like that, it was over.

Slowly, the city began to awake. Car engines came to life again. Pedestrians got to their feet and looked around in confusion.

Nobody moved in Craven's. Not the sleeping gamblers, who died when Death's Hand ripped the building apart. Not Elise, who was in too much pain.

What was left of the ground was cool beneath her cheek. Adrenaline drained slowly out of her in the space of many long minutes, leaving her muscles liquefied. The wall crushing her was heavy, and the shards of glass beneath her were little stars of pain in her stomach and thigh and arms.

She wasn't inside herself at all anymore. That pain belonged to someone else.

Elise never wanted to move again.

She half-dozed, somewhere between asleep and awake. Elise thought there was something she still needed to do, but she wasn't sure what. The casino was still.

Something dripped into her eyes. With a groan, Elise wiped it off, and then she planted that hand on the wall and pushed it off her body. One of her swords was near her leg. She picked it up as she stood. The blade was stained with blood—James's blood.

She worked her jaw around, trying to clear the ringing from her ears. She evaluated her injuries as she leaned on what was left of the bar for support. Blissfully, she seemed to have gone into shock. She couldn't feel her shoulder at all anymore. In fact, she couldn't feel anything else, either.

Lights on the surrounding casinos flickered. All the jangling slot machines were dead now. There were too many bodies to count. Elise couldn't seem to find it in herself to care.

She surveyed the bodies on the street, which she could see through what was left of the walls. One had been thrown to Elise's feet during the exorcism, and she could see that what Death's Hand had started earlier began to reverse.

The skin on the body's scalp shrank as it dried out. His lips drew back from their teeth in a shriveled grimace. Muscle melted away underneath his skin, and then that too dried, flaking and crumbling to white ash. His skull appeared in white patches, and then a burning odor filled the air, and his bones began to crack.

A fine webbing spread from his eye sockets and took over his entire skull like a window shattering in slow motion. Elise watched in distant bemusement as he became nothing but puffs of dust.

One by one, each body decayed and blew away, leaving the street empty.

Except for one body, laying in the middle of the sidewalk and surrounded by cratered concrete.

James.

She climbed over the rubble, almost slipping on a rebar as she made her way to his side. He looked like he had been thrown, too, but he had gone through a window. Her sword was still in his chest. She wrenched it free with a sick slurping sound.

Pressing her fingers into his throat, she held her breath. It was stupid, it was useless to hope, but she had to be sure.

There was no pulse, of course. Nobody could survive getting stabbed in the heart—not even the vessel of Death's Hand.

206

Elise bowed her head over his, pressing her mouth to the top of his head. His hair smelled like brimstone, plaster, and his shampoo. "I'm sorry," she murmured, eyes burning. "I'm so sorry."

Now she knew why she felt so hollow inside.

Was it supposed to hurt this bad? Was she supposed to feel like a fist had wrenched her heart from its chest, leaving a gaping void under her ribs? She had never felt such a thing. Not when her dog died as a child, nor when her parents left her with James's aunt because they moved faster without her. Not even when Pamela Faulkner died.

Her shoulders shook. She couldn't breathe. Elise tilted her head back, squeezing her eyes shut and gritting her teeth against the ache swelling inside of her gut.

A ragged wail tore from her, shattering the silence of the night.

Her fingers dug into James's chest, slippery with his blood. Becoming bound as kopis and aspis was an oath: to stand shoulder-to-shoulder in their battles, to protect one another, and when the time came—die together. She was supposed to guard him. She wasn't meant to kill him.

He gave up everything for her. Everything.

His skin cooled to the temperature of the air. Elise wanted to cover him in a blanket to give him the modesty in death Ann hadn't given him for the last few hours of his life. He shouldn't have to be naked and vulnerable when everything else had been stripped from them.

Elise's chest hitched. "James," she whispered.

And a voice whispered back.

Elise...

Her eyes fell on the stone staff. It was a few feet away in the crater, no longer alive even though it steamed slightly in the damp air.

All the mighty power of Death's Hand was gone, boiled down to a tiny flicker of demonic energy inside the cylinder. It gave a fraction of a roll onto its side, barely more than an inch.

Elise...

It was what was left of *vedae som matis,* but it sounded very much like James.

That tiny flicker of energy tugged at her.

Elise stepped away from James without thinking about it, sliding down one of the craters to reach for the stone cylinder. Her fingers hesitated just over its surface. She could feel the heat radiating from it.

It wasn't just demonic power. It was necromantic power, too—a little bit of the demon, a little bit of Ann, a little bit of James.

She glanced up at his body again, and the grief sliced through her anew.

He would never cast another spell. They would never have Sunday breakfast together again. She would never see him smile again, that special soft smile that she never saw him aim at Stephanie.

Unless…

She closed her hand on the stone cylinder even as every bit of her common sense screamed *no!* Elise had been tortured by the death goddess using the stone as a knife. She had felt it wrapping around her flesh as Death's Hand tried to possess her. It was the reason James was dead in the first place.

The flicker of light was fading fast.

She knelt over James, gripping the stone in both hands as she studied him. His skin was gray. There had to be some way to use what was left of its power, but she didn't know what to do with it.

How did James do magic? A circle of power. Incantations. Elise wasn't a witch. She couldn't do any of that.

She leaned over him. The stone vibrated, and she touched it very gently to the wound on his chest.

Light erupted from the stone.

Shocked, Elise tried to let go, but her fingers stayed welded to its surface. Heat rushed through her fingers, up her arms, and into her body.

The symbols tracing the stone doubled and split from its surface, one set rising from the vessel in burning white lines. They swirled over her body and ruffling the little hairs at the back of her neck. The golden light filled her vision until she couldn't see anything around herself.

It wasn't *vedae som matis* she felt in that moment. It was something more, so much more, like staring into eternity, and the only anchor keeping her from spilling out into nothingness was her grip on the vessel. Some great beast pulsed in the beyond, rubbing past Elise through the marks. It wasn't demonic, or even angelic. It was something greater still.

The golden fire shifted from Elise's arms to her palms, glowing through her gloves. The power beat in time with her heart.

God, the *power*.

She felt as though she had never lived before. Wouldn't anyone kill to feel this energy for any length of time—to gaze into forever and clutch it in her grasp?

Through the light, she could see James sprawled on the ground, but she could see the dead for miles and beyond. It wasn't the corpses themselves—those had all dissolved with the exorcism—but a vast, endless ocean of souls, animal and demon and otherwise. They formed the Earth beneath her, and Life roared above her as the sky.

She could resurrect anybody. Elise could put her hands upon someone laid to rest a millennia ago and bring them back at a whim. She could touch any number demons she had sent to Hell and reanimate them as her own. She might even be able to improve upon what Ann had done— she could make them as alive as she was. Their hearts would beat for Elise.

James brought Elise down from her high. The instant she thought of him, the souls around her came into focus, and she could feel him clearly. His soul glowed brighter than any other in the vast ocean.

The power began to slip from her grasp.

She gazed down at his face, and even through the light, she could see the triangle of his jaw, the day-old stubble, the well-defined cheekbones.

Elise didn't really want power. She just wanted James.

Her hands overflowed with the symbols needed to call a soul into a body, to make the heart beat and the brain function. The magic wanted to be used, so Elise didn't try to resist. She laid her hands upon James's temples. She opened to him like a flower's petals parting to the sun, and the symbols from the cylinder flowed from the sword into her shield.

James's soul, torn apart so violently by *vedae som matis*, began to mend as Elise watched.

His heart beat once. Twice.

The rhythm sped until its steady beat matched her own. Elise's lungs expanded, and his inflated as well, drawing air through his lips and into his chest. It was strained, difficult at first, and she labored to breathe for them both, but it became easier with every breath.

The blood began flowing. Color faded into his skin, and warmth spread into his muscles and tendons. Electrical impulses sparked in the air between them, and something seemed to click on in his brain.

Her heart beat with his, one muscle in two chests. Slowly, so slowly, Elise's heart became her own again, but even as she left, his continued to beat. It wasn't as clean a cut as she would have expected. Some of Elise remained in James, and some of him remained in her, but when he kept breathing it wasn't her life that made his lungs work.

Only when his body functioned did his soul return. It drifted into him, as softly as a feather fluttering into the ground. It settled into his body with a soft sigh that curled through the room, and she suddenly felt as though a hole inside of her had filled. She was complete again.

James…

Eternity shut down, withdrawing from Elise. The burning glow of her hands flickered, then disappeared. The power blew out of her again. The gold light emanating from the stone died, leaving nothing but rock in its place.

The world went dark.

Elise sagged, suddenly weak. Her eyes cleared and she could see the casino once more. Everything was still.

And James coughed.

He rolled onto his side. His legs drew up into his chest, curling around the sword wound. Every cough brought a fresh groan of pain, punctuated with another cough when he sucked in the dusty air. "James," Elise said, reaching out to roll him onto his back again. Her hands were shaking.

He frowned up at her, brow furrowed with pain, confusion. His eyes were clear now the poison was flushed out of his system, but the stab wound in his chest trickled blood. "Elise?" James's jaw chattered as he spoke, his skin clammy underneath her bare fingertips. "What happened? What's going on?"

"Oh, James," Elise said, her voice cracking. She rubbed at the blood on his cheeks, wiping it away with her gloves, and then gave up, throwing her arms around his neck.

Her relief was so strong that she couldn't hold it inside. A laugh bubbled from her throat. James stared at her as though she had gone crazy, his hands clenched over his wound.

He would have questions later, and so would others. His resurrection would be a beacon that called to demons and angels for thousands of miles around them through a thousand dimensions. There would be repercussions.

But for the moment, Elise didn't care—not one bit.

He was alive, and nothing else mattered.

Chapter 21

THE HOSPITAL RELEASED James the next morning. They were too busy to keep anyone longer than a couple of hours—the citywide coma had inflected tens of thousands of injuries, from car accidents to cigarette fires and people falling down stairs, and the hospital was swamped.

There was no accounting for the missing hours, but the news claimed that all the damage and dead were caused by an earthquake. It was a stupid excuse. Elise couldn't imagine anyone falling for it, even though the story was discussed worldwide as fact. She flicked through the channels on the hospital TV and saw it on every major news network.

"Can you believe this?" Elise asked, shutting off the television and dropping the remote onto James's bed. He was dressing behind a curtain while the nurses prepared his bed for the next patient. "Who comes up with this stuff?"

"Lord only knows," he muttered.

Stephanie stopped by to drop off a few forms and brush a kiss over his lips. "I'll visit you as soon as I can," she whispered, lingering in the door. "Maybe I should take you home."

"He already has a ride," Elise said.

"You're both on enough hydrocodone that I think—"

"It's fine, Stephanie," he said. "Thank you."

But it was true that Elise and James were both unsteady on their feet as they carefully made their way to the parking garage. Normally, Elise wouldn't have taken any of the painkillers they prescribed to her, but the injury on her shoulder was bad enough that she caved in. She was still better than James. He could barely walk.

He sighed as she settled him into the front seat of the car, shutting his eyes.

"Do you need help with the seat belt?"

"I was stabbed, not paralyzed," he said, but he couldn't work up the energy to sound annoyed.

He fell asleep again before Elise reached the street. Being possessed by a major demon, exorcised, killed, and brought back to life seemed to be pretty exhausting. James hadn't been awake longer than fifteen minutes since his resurrection.

Elise was hardly any better. She situated James in bed and passed out on his couch, waking up ten hours later to find he was still asleep, too. She staggered back to her car and slipped into the duplex without waking Betty.

Before the sun rose, she was awake and gone.

She stayed at the office over the next week while her injuries quickly knit themselves, avoiding Betty and Anthony and the long conversations they would need to have. Brushing her teeth in the sink and sleeping stretched out on her floor, Elise took her solitary time to mend—and seek out new clients online to replace David Nicholas and Craven's.

But Elise couldn't stay in her office forever. James called her phone at least three times a day, and although he never left a message, she was sure he must have been getting irate. Betty was—and she texted about a hundred times to make sure Elise knew it.

By the time the next weekend rolled around, her face and body completely healed other than her shoulder, and she finally gave in to the calls.

Elise found the Motion and Dance parking lot full. The main dance hall was occupied by a dance fitness class, so she found James in the back room supervising a "creative ballet" class for preschoolers, which wasn't a dance class as much as a play group filled with girls in tutus. He looked healthy but pale, slumped in a chair in the corner to watch the kids bounce around in pink leotards with a long-suffering expression.

She took a few minutes to observe him silently. She had missed him over the week, even as she hid out in solitude. There was a little color in his cheeks and a hint of beard growth at his jaw. He looked like he had on any other day. Normal.

Something tense inside of her eased. She hadn't *really* thought she would come to find him a revenant—or something worse—but he didn't look like he had been hurt by her little act of necromancy at all. Elise stood behind his chair and cleared her throat.

"Isn't this Candace's class?" Elise asked, standing over his shoulder.

James looked up, and his eyes widened. "Elise!" He tried to stand too quickly and winced, gripping his chest. She grabbed his arm.

"Hey," she said. "Relax. Sit down."

"Where have you been? I haven't seen you all week."

"I've been healing." She pointed at the last of the yellow bruises around her eye. Showing him her shoulder would have been a lot more impressive, but he didn't need to know he had eaten her flesh.

James eased back into the chair, studying her face. "It must have been terrible if *you're* not healed yet."

She ignored the implied question. "Where's Candace?"

"Her husband dropped a pot of boiling water on himself during the, uh, earthquake," he said. "First degree burns. She's taking care of him. Excuse me, just a moment." James clapped his hands and raised his voice. "You! Penny! I told you no running!"

Elise had to hide a smile behind her hand. James liked children about as much as he liked food poisoning.

"I can finish out the class," she suggested.

He sagged with relief. "Thank you. I'll be in the lobby."

Elise supervised the last twenty minutes of creative ballet. She didn't like kids any more than James did, but she had "taught" the class herself while she was still in college, so she didn't mind doing it one more time. Trying to convince a dozen four year olds to *plié* was a great exercise in patience.

When the class ended, James and Elise sat together in the lobby as the parents took their kids away. His friendly smile looked authentic until the door swung shut, and then he grimaced.

"Those people would do better with a daycare than a dance class," he muttered.

"They pay the bills. Your children's ballet classes are about half your income."

"I suppose. Would you like to explain why I've seen Betty more this last week than I've seen you? As you can tell, I really could have used your help around the studio. And not just with classes."

"I thought you would have Stephanie nursing you back to health."

"She's visited when she has time," he admitted, "but there's very little of that. Betty said you haven't been coming home while she's awake."

Elise shrugged, and then winced. Her bra strap rubbed against the bandages on her shoulder. "I have a lot of work to catch up on. I'm busy."

"Your work ethic couldn't have anything to do you're your roommate's incessant questions, could it?"

"That might have been a factor."

213

"She's been here every day. In fact, you missed her by a half hour," James said. "I've never realized anyone could be so damn inquisitive about demons. If you wanted to tell her the truth, you could have also had the decency to make yourself available for questioning."

"I'll keep that in mind for my next earth-shattering revelation," she said.

Something in her voice made him give her a sad smile. "What happened that night?"

"Didn't Betty tell you?"

"She didn't have all the details. I don't remember anything after our investigation at the cemetery myself, except bits and pieces of trying to sleep that evening."

That was a lot of empty ground to cover. Elise sighed and leaned her head on his shoulder. "It was Ann. She was working for Death's Hand. She tried to fight me, and they both lost. I don't want to talk about it."

"Betty told me as much, but that doesn't explain why I'm healing from several major injuries. Or what happened to almost two hours of everybody's life."

"Your wounds aren't that major. The doctors said they missed your major organs." Of course, Elise was confident that she had actually punctured one very significant organ, but resurrecting him had healed almost everything. "I have a question."

"Yes?"

"Ann said that you hadn't told me the truth yet. That there was something about you that would…" She trailed off, gazing at the smooth line of his nose and the curve of his chin. *Ann said I would want you to die.* "She said you hadn't told me something."

"Demons are liars," James said.

"She wasn't a demon. I'm not sure she was evil at all. I think she was…confused."

"Then she must have been confused on this point as well. I have no idea what she's talking about." He spoke forcefully, and his hand tightened on hers. "You know you can trust me, Elise. I would never lie to you."

"I know," she said. "I know."

They sat together in silence, watching the cars empty out of the parking lot. It would be at least an hour until the belly dance class, which was taught by an instructor named Kendall. They didn't need to wait. But Elise didn't feel like moving, and she doubted James did, either.

"I'm glad you came back, but you didn't need to avoid me. You can

214

tell me everything when you're ready."

"I wouldn't stay away for long." She took a deep breath. "What do you think?"

"About what?"

"Do we..." Elise picked at her thumbnail, avoiding James's gaze. She swallowed. "Are we going to have to run again? Should we go into hiding?"

She could feel him watching her. He gave a heavy sigh. "Do you *want* to run?"

It was a question that had been prying at her all week, no matter how hard she fought to distract herself.

Running would be the smart thing to do. Performing a huge exorcism —and having a city filled with the walking dead—ruined any chances they might have had of hiding.

But Elise had her job, and so did James. More importantly, it surprised her to find that avoiding Betty and Anthony all week made her a little lonely. Elise didn't want to leave them. For the first time in her life, she had friends. Real friends. People willing to go to battle with her. People she would die for, if she needed to.

"No," she said. "I don't want to go."

The corner of James's mouth twitched into a smile. "Good, because neither do I."

She thought that response would make her feel better. Instead, Elise felt they had just agreed to do something very unpleasant—something potentially deadly.

"Then we'll stay," she said with a tone of finality.

They sat together in silence, hands clasped, until the next class came in and life resumed its normal routine.

SOMEWHERE VERY FAR away—somewhere very dark—someone else listened to that conversation.

It had been a long time since He had seen Elise, or heard her speak. He had dwelled in darkness for some years, and although he could not tell if it had been ten or ten thousand, he longed for the succor of light—however momentary.

And then it came in a single burning, brilliant moment. He felt her power and saw her eyes blazing with fury. He saw her fist clutching the sword as she plunged it into the heart of a demon. From another time, another place, He saw her anguish.

He had found her.

He saw it was very good, and He smiled.

The Darkest Gate

An Urban Fantasy Mystery

The Descent Series - Book Two

SM Reine

Part 1: Before

HISTORY won't remember one of the most important meetings to ever occur. It was organized over secure phone lines by a third party, who selected a time and public location at random, and gave each attendant a day's notice to travel there—little enough time to ensure they could not prepare surprises in advance.

Nevertheless, James Faulkner was seated at the Pledger Bistro fifteen minutes early. He declined the offer of wine so the waiter wouldn't disturb him, then tipped his head back as though holding it up was too much effort. Even though he had washed and shaved in a train station bathroom, there was no hiding his gaunt cheeks and trembling hands.

The man who approached the table at three o'clock had the slim, dangerous appearance of a concealed pistol. He studied James from beyond arm's reach.

"My name is Alain Daladier. I've come to meet the greatest kopis."

James sat up. "A pleasure to meet you. I'm James Faulkner." The collar of his shirt was loosened to expose a white scar on his chest, and the sleeves were rolled back to show fresh pink skin at his wrist where he had been bitten.

Alain observed these details without changing expression. "Show me the sword."

He flicked back the collar of his shirt. Once Alain leaned forward to glimpse the leather-wrapped handle of a falchion strapped to his back, James concealed it again. "Satisfied?"

"I'm told you have two."

"Not today. Will you sit?"

Alain responded by stepping outside the restaurant. He was replaced

218

by a grizzled man with white hair and a designer watch. "Call me Mr. Black," he greeted, taking the seat beside James. They shook hands. His grip was surprisingly light for someone resembling an aged bodybuilder. "Alain says you're the greatest kopis."

"And I've heard you're not far from the greatest yourself. You went to quite a bit of effort to arrange our meeting today."

"Oh, yes. But it's worth it, to meet the greatest kopis…James Faulkner." Mr. Black covered a smirk with his hand. His brown eyes glowed with mirth. "Faulkner…hmm."

The waiter returned with menus and placed napkins in their laps. "Yes, that's my name," James said once they were alone again.

"What do you know about ethereal artifacts, Mr. Faulkner?"

"As much as anyone else. The information is limited. Angels had only a minimal presence on Earth before the Treaty of Dis was forged, and they're scarce now. Why do you ask?"

"Go on."

James sat back in his chair. "What's the meaning of this?"

"I wouldn't have spent this much time and money tracking you down for a private chat if our conversation wasn't important. Humor me. What else do you know?"

"Very well. Ethereal artifacts have three primary properties: They can be separated, but not broken; they are inviolable; and neither humans nor demons can use their power—which is immense." The scar on James's chest ached. He massaged it with two fingers as he spoke. "Angels don't make them anymore."

"Good, good. I'd bet a lot of cash that you know more about the subject than the average person. Would you recognize one if you saw it?"

"Most likely."

Mr. Black studied his menu. He was still smiling, as though he found James's answer amusing. "I bet you could. I've been searching for one particular ethereal artifact for some years now. It's in the shape of a bowl with notches around the edge. It looks like it's made of ivory, but it's not carved from the bone of any animal I've killed."

"I've never seen it."

"Didn't say you had, did I?"

"Then what are you expecting? If you need a lecture on the properties of ethereal craftsmanship, you could ask someone much easier to reach than I am." He fell silent when the waiter returned to the table with a basket of bread. Mr. Black ordered the duck. James's stomach was a gnawing hole beneath his ribs, but he said, "Nothing for me, thank you."

"Come on, now, you're practically a mummy. I'll pay for your dinner. You're my guest, aren't you?"

"No. Thank you."

"He'll have the fish," Mr. Black said, and the waiter left. "I know you're hurting for money, Mr. Faulkner. It's hard making ends meet sometimes, isn't it? But you don't need to starve." He took a piece of bread from the basket and smeared garlic butter across its surface. "What were we talking about?"

James watched his teeth sink into the baguette. "The bowl."

Mr. Black took his time chewing and swallowing. He wiped crumbs from his mouth with the napkin. "Right. I've discovered this bowl's location." He leaned forward and locked gazes with James. "I want it."

"Then you should go get it."

"Not many kopides survive to my age. I'm past my prime. I've left the pursuit of justice and saving humanity to younger men. I bought a nice piece of land down South, I've got a summer home, and I run a few businesses that employ a lot of folks. I'm doing pretty damn good, if I do say so myself."

James realized he was still rubbing his scar and forced himself to stop. Retired? Kopides and aspides never retired. The best anyone could hope for was dying in the service of mankind. The idea of being able to settle down was equally tempting and disappointing, since he knew it was something he couldn't have. He couldn't afford to eat on many days.

"What's your interest in this bowl if you've retired?"

"Call it…sentimentality. This bowl is difficult to reach, as you would expect. I need a young kopis—a great kopis—to retrieve it." Mr. Black's teeth were very white when he grinned. "I said I'm doing well, didn't I? I'll pay a good chunk of cash to have this piece added to my private collection."

"I'm not a mercenary. My services aren't for sale."

"That's fine. I don't want *your* services. You are powerful, Mr. Faulkner, I won't argue that. Alain felt you coming miles off. But you're not the greatest kopis."

James stiffened. "What—?"

"You're wasting my time. I hate having my time wasted." That smile had grown fixed on his face. Without making a single motion, Mr. Black suddenly appeared much more deadly. "Where is he?"

Trying not to glance over Mr. Black's shoulder was pointless. By the time James ducked his head, the motion had already given him away, and Mr. Black turned to point Alain across the street. As soon as he went

220

through the door, a young woman sitting at a table under a tree abandoned her espresso and entered the restaurant, invisible to Alain's searching gaze.

The waiter moved to intercept her, but she pushed past him and dropped into an empty chair at their table. The look of disbelief from Mr. Black as he took in her girlish face and brutally short curls almost made James laugh. She was hollow-cheeked, too young to be out of school, and wouldn't have blended in at a supermarket, much less a fancy restaurant. If James was a mummy, then Elise was barely more than a living skeleton.

"This is Elise Kavanagh," James said. "Elise, this is the man who has gone to so much trouble to find us."

"You can't be serious." Mr. Black wasn't smiling anymore.

The waiter was red-faced. "I tried to stop her, but—"

She kicked her feet up on another chair. Her hiking boots were covered in chunks of dried mud.

James waved the waiter away before he could go apoplectic. "She's with me."

"With all due respect, we do have a dress code, and she's—"

"We won't be long."

Mr. Black snapped out of his reverie. "It's all right." He waited to speak until they were alone again. "Miss... Kavanagh, was it? This must be a joke."

"I'm afraid not," James said.

"But this is a girl."

"Female kopides are uncommon, not nonexistent. I believe there are currently three. She is the strongest of them." James smiled behind a hand. "In fact, she's the strongest of all of you."

"How does a teenage girl become known as the greatest demon hunter above hundreds of men? No offense." Which meant, of course, he was absolutely trying to be offensive.

Elise arched an eyebrow split by a white scar. When she didn't reply, Mr. Black looked askance at James, as if they were old friends and she had intruded on their dinner.

In fact, two things had elevated Elise to that status three months prior: Defeating the previous title holder in a formal sparring match, and then outliving him. Those were publicly available facts. The Council of Dis, however, also credited her with the deaths of twelve angels, which no other human had done in recorded history. Nobody else knew this. James thought that was for the best.

"Her father serves on the Council as a touchstone." James shrugged.

221

"He must have recommended her."

Mr. Black gave no sign of hearing him. "All right. If the council thinks you're great, you've got to be pretty good. Are you mute? Dumb?"

James cleared his throat loudly to stop him. "Mr. Black wants to hire you to retrieve a dangerous ethereal artifact. I've explained that we're not mercenaries and not interested."

"We're not?" Elise asked.

"Lord in Heaven, it speaks." Mr. Black rubbed his hands together. "But let's be fair. I wouldn't describe this bowl as 'dangerous,' strictly speaking."

"Anything made by angels is dangerous by virtue of its very nature. Men aren't meant to possess these things, and if you think obtaining one for your 'personal collection' is benign, then you must be an idiot—or think I am. If you want to be fair, let's be fair. You have something planned. We won't have any part of it."

Elise wasn't listening to him. Even though she lounged between her two chairs, there was tension coiled in her muscles. "How much?"

Mr. Black faced her. It was as though James disappeared completely.

"You can walk away from this restaurant with ten thousand dollars. When you bring the bowl to me, I'll round that out to—say, twenty-five thousand? I want this bowl, and I'm willing to pay fairly for its safe deliverance."

"Fifty thousand. Cash."

James reached a hand toward her, but thought better of it. He liked having his limbs intact. "Elise—"

Mr. Black laughed. "Are you trying to negotiate with me, girl?"

She replied in French. James didn't understand the language, and he wasn't sure Mr. Black would, either. Yet the older man's fake smile vanished. When he responded, it was in also in French, and Elise's hands clenched into fists.

James was certain he had just missed something important.

She stood, gave Mr. Black a sharp nod, and left. Both men gaped after her.

"We won't do it," James said weakly.

Mr. Black finished his slice of bread and washed it down with wine. His fingers were shaking as he patted his mouth with a white napkin. "Can I give you some advice, Mr. Faulkner? As a friend."

"No."

"You better get the hell away from that girl. I think she might be the death of you."

And that was how one of the most important meetings in history concluded. James was never quite sure why that was true, but then again, he also never spoke French.

James found Elise waiting on the train platform with a hood pulled up and her hands shoved into her pockets. She could have been any other young traveler commuting home after a day out with friends.

He reached her at the same time the train arrived, and she got on without speaking to him. He took position at the yellow pole behind her.

The train leaped forward. He caught a glimpse inside her hood when she swayed. Elise was usually hyper-alert and watching her surroundings for an attack, but now she was drawn inward. She seemed troubled.

Together, they made several short transfers and walked erratic paths through the city's streets. James thought he saw Alain following them at first, but they lost him after a few blocks. This was nothing surprising. Unholy things often tried to follow Elise and James, so elusiveness was routine.

When they got on the final train, they had an entire car to themselves. James let a moment of dizziness overtake him and sagged against the window. He barely had the energy to lift his head.

His ribs itched, so he reached under his shirt to adjust the straps of the spine sheath. It barely fit. He had lost too much muscle from malnourishment in the last few weeks.

"Elise," he began.

She didn't look at him.

"I know that money must seem like a lot to you, and after all the troubles we've had, I'm not going to pretend I don't find it tempting. But believe me when I say that no sum of money is worth the trouble of Mr. Black's job. This bowl could get us killed...or worse."

His legs wobbled. He sat next to Elise and pretended it was to get her attention, which didn't work.

"Things will change soon," he whispered. "It's going to get better."

She finally lifted her head. The corners of her mouth were drawn into a frown. "Is it weird that I'm a girl? Mr. Black was surprised when he saw me."

James realized his mouth was hanging open, and he shut it. Two sentences. That must have been a record. "Yes. It's very unusual. Didn't your parents ever tell you?"

She bowed her head against her knees. He saw the hilt of the second falchion—the twin to the one he wore—bulging against the back of her sweater.

They rode on in silence.

Part 2: Gifts

Chapter 1

JULY 2009

THERE was blood on the stone.

The column loomed so far overhead that its apex disappeared into night. Looping lines marked its surface like ossified muscle on beams of towering bone. The once-bright sigils ringing the base were lifeless.

The gate was one of a dozen silent scions in a dead city. For endless millennia, they slept over the empty streets waiting for... What?

Elise...

Her bare toes hung over the tip of the world, hair swinging in her face as she craned forward to peer at the water miles below. Tiny stars sparkled in the water, like river stones reflecting moonlight.

The gate hummed at her back. She couldn't look at it. She wouldn't. She would prefer to fall into the abyss and shatter on the shore.

Elise...

There shouldn't have been anything on the other side of the arch. Nothing should have lived in the city.

Yet there was blood on the stone, and something called her name from the other side, beckoning for her to turn. Invisible fingers clamped on her chin and forced her back from the edge, away from blissful suicide and on toward damnation.

The dry air vibrated. Sinewy stone flushed to life, and a breeze stirred the dead air.

Elise...

She shut her eyes as she turned. She wouldn't look. She wouldn't watch the air darken until it devoured all light, wouldn't see Him reaching through with white hands...

But something peeled her eyelids back, forcing her to look upon the darkest gate.

And she *saw*.

"Elise!"

The tent collapsed on her head. An electric bolt of consciousness shocked through her.

Something heavy smashed into her face and chest, like a bear rolling over the tent. She couldn't inhale. Her neck strained as her head was crushed into the ground.

She felt a bare arm against hers—Anthony's—and elbowed him away.

For a disorienting moment, she was seventeen again, on the run and camping out in whatever bare patch of land she could find. Motels were too expensive and too easy to track. Elise couldn't remember why she was with Anthony instead of James.

A glistening black fang punctured the canvas by her head and brought cold reality with it. Venom gushed from the tip and splattered on her shoulder.

Knife. Where was her knife?

The body shifted enough for her hand to scrabble at the pillow, where she had tucked a blade before sleeping, but the attacker mashed against her again and she didn't have space to grab it.

The fang withdrew and punctured again. Elise twisted her face to the side.

"Anthony! Do something!" she shouted.

His hot skin moved away from hers. He fumbled with the tent. The zipper opened, and chilly night air rushed to fill her lungs.

The weight lifted, but before she could sit up, a foot the size of a trash can slammed into her gut.

Her intestines crushed against her spine. Canvas ripped.

Elise's hand closed on her knife, and she stabbed it into the foot. Something gave an inhuman shriek.

Its weight vanished.

She slashed and stabbed and tore until she could see the stars. Elise scrambled out of the tent's remains, bare skin flushed with goosebumps. It was dark in the desert, much darker than the city, and she could barely make out sagebrush and hills under the sliver of moon.

Her attacker was a hulking black shape perched on top of the Jeep.

226

Each of its eight legs was braced against the roll cage. Glossy black eyes reflected the starlight and shone with a faint red glow, as though fire burned within its furry carapace. It was a spider the size of a small pony.

Anthony brandished two halves of a snapped tent pole at the demon —like going after a tank with a twig.

The spider lunged. A half-second later, Elise jumped too.

She knocked into her boyfriend an instant before the spider would have. They rolled across the desert as the demon hit sagebrush.

Getting up again took too long. She whirled, bringing the knife to bear, but one of those huge legs struck her in the chest again.

Elise was airborne.

Her back hit the Jeep. Her lungs emptied. Her cheek hit dirt.

Anthony cried out. She got to her feet, gasping and wheezing and empty-handed. She had dropped her knife.

The spider darted at him. It moved at a ridiculous speed given its size, blurring through the night to slash with its fangs. He tried to roll out of the way, but a heavy leg pounded into the rock and blocked him. He kicked its face. The pincers caught his leg.

Elise sucked in a hard breath. "Don't let it bite you!"

"Thanks for the suggestion," Anthony grunted, snapping his free foot into its face.

It shrieked and reared. She dived onto its back.

The spider bucked beneath her, and Elise pressed her cheek into its furry carapace and clung tight to its abdomen. When it tried to bite Anthony again, she wrapped a hand around its pincer and yanked.

It ripped free with a wet crunch. Venom sprayed on the dirt.

"Find my knife!"

Anthony squirmed out from beneath them. The spider thrashed. Elise almost went flying again, but she wrapped her fists around its thick black hairs and hung on.

Each of the glistening black eyes rolled around to stare at her.

It flung itself sideways. She lost her grip and rolled across the dirt. The spider pounced, spraying venom and ichor from its open wound, and it stung like sparks of flame where it landed on her skin.

She punched her fist into its clacking mouth as hard as she could. It wasn't hard enough. The spider reared back to bite again, and Elise grabbed the first thing she could reach—the remains of the tent.

Elise flung the canvas in the spider's face. Its pincer tangled in the rope.

"I can't find it!" Anthony shouted.

Her hand fell on a broken piece of tent post.

Elise drove the splintered end into the spider's body. At first, she thought it wouldn't be able to pierce the exoskeleton, but then the metal slipped. It buried into the knife wound and kept going.

She silenced its scream by shoving with all her weight. The bar cracked through the other side.

Its legs flailed wildly, and she had to crawl away to avoid getting hit.

Elise picked up the other tent pole and plunged it into the spider's head. She pushed so hard that the tip sank into the earth and pinned the demon to the ground.

It finally stopped moving after that.

Elise let out a long breath. She was soaked in sweat even though it couldn't have been more than sixty degrees in the cool desert night, which quickly approached cool desert morning. A sliver of blue glowed over the hills.

"Hell of a wakeup call," she muttered. The spider's foreleg twitched once.

Anthony crashed through the sagebrush again and grabbed her arms. "Are you okay? I couldn't find your knife."

She gave her body a quick inspection. She was wearing underwear instead of pajamas, so she could see where bruises were developing, which was most of her body. The contact burns from the venom were worse, but none of them were too bad. She would recover quickly.

"I'm fine."

Anthony handed her a flashlight from the Jeep. "Is this the same as the other ones? It seems a lot bigger."

She located her knife by its glimmer in the bushes. He had been searching in the wrong place. "Yeah. It's a daimarachnid. Big fucking spider." Elise rolled the demon onto its back and knelt by its body, pushing the legs away to examine the branded underbelly.

Most demons were like animals with a temper problem: stupid and directionless. But powerful demons could mark them with brands and control their behavior to some degree. If she could find who "owned" those symbols, she would find out who was responsible, much like a rancher and his cattle.

Elise began slicing along the edge of the brands.

Anthony recoiled. "Jesus! What are you doing?"

She focused on trimming the leathery skin from the shell underneath. It was tough work. She sawed back and forth with the serrated edge of the knife until a strip of flesh two feet long and four inches wide came free.

"Get a plastic bag from the Jeep," Elise said, studying the strip with the flashlight. Someone had slashed crosses through each of the brands and made them hard to distinguish.

He handed a bag to her. Elise sealed the skin inside.

"What are you going to do with that?"

"I'm going to find out who's letting their minions loose and have a talk with them."

"And by 'talk,' you mean…"

"I'll kill them," Elise said. She put the skin in the cooler where they had kept their food all week. There was nothing left except melted ice and a couple cans of beer. "Still want to keep going hunting with me?"

To his credit, Anthony thought about it for a moment before answering. "Yeah. Camping has been fun." He grinned. "And, you know. The attack was kind of hot. Watching you fight in your underwear was…" He pushed her back against the Jeep and growled against her neck. She didn't react. "Aren't you kind of hot?"

"No."

He kissed down her collarbone and traced a finger along the tattoo on her hip. "Are you sure?"

"Getting attacked by demons doesn't excite me." She planted a hand in his chest to prevent his kisses from straying lower. "I'm not going to tell you again." She left the unspoken threat hovering over them.

"Would you stab me? Is that what you're saying?"

The corner of her mouth quirked up. "Would that turn you on, too?"

"You're sick," he murmured into her lips. Elise leaned against the car door with a sigh as he kissed her. His lips traveled to her earlobe. He nipped it lightly with his teeth.

"You think I'm sick?" She stretched her arm back to drop the knife in the Jeep's backseat, and he traced his hand down her exposed ribcage. His fingers found a path under her bra to graze the curve of her breast. "At least demon attacks don't get me horny."

Her cell phone alarmed. She peered over Anthony's shoulder to see it glowing blue underneath the tent canvas. He ignored it and pushed a knee between her legs. She stiffened, but he caught her wrist and pinned it to her side. "Ignore it."

Elise shoved him. He stumbled a few steps back. "It's time to leave," she said, turning off the alarm. Anthony groaned.

"But we were just—"

"I have a meeting with a potential client this morning and it's a four-hour drive from here."

He adjusted the waistband of his sweats. Elise gathered their broken tent and threw it in the back of the Jeep. "I think you like to torture me."

She planted a kiss on his chin as he passed. "It's an unintended bonus."

Anthony tried to glower, but Elise didn't acknowledge him as she finished packing. His mood lost steam without her attention.

After a week of camping, their clothes were crusty with sweat and dust. Elise gritted her teeth as she pulled on dirty jeans.

"What are we going to do with *that*?" Anthony asked when the only thing remaining in their camp was the body of the demon.

Elise kicked it in the side. It didn't move.

"We'll let the coyotes have it. I've got what I need."

They got in the Jeep and drove away, leaving the carcass of the demon to rot.

Elise stopped at home long enough to say goodbye to Anthony, take a shower, and slip into a clean skirt suit. Then she went into the office.

Since scraping together enough credits to graduate from college, Elise had done business as a certified public accountant. Cold, objective numbers were a comforting reprieve from life and death decisions, and there was decent money to be made in handling payroll for demon-owned businesses.

She rented a cheap suite in an old building by the airport, which was primarily occupied by failing businesses and nonprofit organizations that couldn't afford a nicer location. She had fewer neighbors as the months wore on. The economy was killing businesses faster than she killed daimarachnids, and the parking lot was never more than half-full.

Which was why she was confused when she arrived shortly before eight and had to park on the street. The parking lot was crammed with police cars, and a perimeter of emergency tape blocked the entrance. The employees who couldn't get inside were gathered on the sidewalk.

Elise approached a man she recognized as a therapist from the third floor. "What happened here?"

"I think it's a fire. They won't let us in." He dry-washed his hands and glared at the nearest police car. "I've already had to cancel my morning appointments!"

She checked her watch. The meeting with her client was ten minutes away, and she didn't have a number at which she could contact them. They had only emailed each other. She needed her computer.

Pushing through the crowd, Elise waved over a police officer. "Excuse me!"

"We can't let you in," he said, writing something on his clipboard. "It's going to be at least another half hour."

"All I need is my laptop. If one of you could …"

She trailed off. There was a shattered window on the south end of the first floor, where photographers and investigators were working.

It was her office.

Her stomach clenched with dread. The fire was in her room, and police were searching it. They would find the weapons in her desk. She ducked under the police tape and sidestepped the officer's grabbing hand.

"Hey! You can't go in there!"

"It's my office," she snapped as she stomped into the building.

The therapist was right. There had definitely been a fire, and it spread all the way down the back wall from the entryway to her suite. Smoke left brown-gray stains on the yellow wallpaper. The toxic green carpet squished under her heels as she hurried to her door.

Even though the fire had only consumed the left side of her office, her filing cabinet and ficus in the opposite corner were destroyed, too. Her desk had been pushed over. The base of her chair was snapped. The bookshelf was gutted, papers were spilled across the floor, and the nearest pile had something reddish-purple poured on it.

The police and firemen left no standing room inside, but shock rooted her to the doorway anyway.

It wasn't an accidental fire. Someone had ransacked her office.

She picked up a page and sniffed it. The stains were wine.

"Hey there," said a gruff voice from the hall. The officer had followed her into the building. "I have to ask you to step into the hallway. You'll interfere with the investigation."

"Okay," Elise said, letting the paper fall. "It's just—all of this belongs to me."

He studied her with a round, sympathetic face. The badge on his chest said Fred Turner. "You better sit down before you fall down."

"I'm fine."

Ignoring her protestations, he took her elbow, and Elise bit the inside of her cheek trying not to strike him. "Come on, take a seat. I've been robbed before. I was twitching for weeks. Let me get you a cup of coffee."

Robbed. No, it wasn't a robbery.

It was a message.

Elise sat on a chair in the lobby. She didn't want to be inside the building anymore. Hell, she didn't want to be in the state. Her nerves were ringing like a gong and everything was suddenly too loud, from her heartbeat to the footsteps down the hall.

Was it Him? Had they been found?

Her cell phone was in her hands before she realized what she was doing. She rubbed her thumb over the touchpad. James was number two on speed dial. He needed to know. They needed to pack, they needed to run—

She took a steadying breath. No. If James and Elise had been found, it was too late to run.

"Ma'am?"

It took her a moment to focus on the speaker. Officer Turner had returned with a cup of coffee. She took it. "Thanks."

"Could I see your identification?" he asked. She handed her driver's license to him. He scanned it with a confused furrow of his brow. "Your business is listed as being owned by 'Bruce Kent.'"

"I've filed the paperwork to operate under a pseudonym. It's completely legal. I could show you the documentation, but everything burned."

"Why use a fake name?"

She took her license back. "Do you think I set fire to my own office?"

"You're not a suspect. But considering what's happened, I don't think you'll be leaving town for a few weeks. Right? If we need to interview you later and you're gone, we'll be concerned."

"I'll be around," she said, her voice dead.

"Good."

Fred Turner left, and Elise took a slow sip of her coffee.

Her hand was trembling.

Chapter 2

THE BODY THUDDED to the floor. A hand whipped the hood off his head, and the man underneath blinked at the sudden light. His bare skin pebbled with cold.

A woman probed his torso for injury, pushing down the shorts that barely shielded his modesty, and then rolled him over to expose his arms. They were bound behind his back. His shoulder blades were red and irritated.

Portia Redmond sniffed as she returned to her seat at the table. "It's wearing an intake bracelet. You said it would be clean."

Mr. Black leaned forward. He was dressed to minimize the physical signs of age, such as a slight paunch to his belly and a sloped back. His hair was wolf-white with accents of gray, and his eyes were blue, very blue, with no hint of warmth.

"Is that an intake bracelet?" he asked, his voice a cool baritone.

Portia's spine straightened. "I think I would recognize the vehicle of my son's death."

A man shifted behind Mr. Black as though to remind Portia of his presence. He was slightly younger than Mr. Black, although he was wiry instead of stocky, and his rust-colored hair was barely touched with white.

There was a gun at his shoulder. He had removed the strap keeping it in the holster. Portia forced herself to relax.

"Your son was an addict?" Mr. Black asked. "Shame, shame. How old was he?"

"Old enough that I couldn't have another heir."

"What a shame. Miss Redmond—Portia—I don't lie to my customers, particularly those as loyal as you." He smoothed his wrinkled fingers

233

over hers. "You asked for spirited, so I brought the most spirited. That kind of fire doesn't come without cost. Controlling him can be...difficult."

"Lethe is a stimulant."

"For demons, yes. You'll find it has quite a different effect on his type. I'll supply enough to keep him under your gorgeous thumb for a year."

"How much?" she asked.

"Do you think I would nickel-and-dime an old friend? After we've known each other for so many long years?"

She pulled her hand back. "Yes."

"How predictable of me."

"What do you want?"

"I want use of your shipping fleet." Mr. Black waved his hand again, and Alain handed Portia a sheaf of papers. She unfolded them and began to read. Her expression darkened with every line. "I'm bringing in a few archaeological pieces from my personal collection, so I'll require unlimited use of your trucks."

"Unlimited use?" Portia slapped the contract on the table. "What about my needs? What about my suppliers?"

Mr. Black smoothed out the contract and flipped to the third page. "I have accounted for that: I will compensate you for the estimated loss of business. See here?"

She refused to look. "I don't know why you're bothering to ask. I know I have no choice."

"Of course you have a choice." He took a pen from his breast pocket and offered it to her. "Your son had a choice, too."

Her lips trembled.

"Let me inspect them closely. Both the contract and...*that*." Portia indicated the man shivering on her floor.

"He's yours. You can command him."

"The terms of our deal have changed. I won't take custody until I fully agree."

"This is why I love you, Portia. Just *adore* you. You don't tolerate nonsense in your business, and I have to say, I appreciate that." He snapped his fingers. "Nukha'il, stand up and turn around so she can see all of you."

The man picked himself up. Shimmering red-brown hair fell to his back in soft waves. His body was delicate, yet strong, and the top of his head was nearly level with the doorway. Nukha'il spun slowly. He was sheer perfection, despite the fact there might have been no muscles under his olive skin. The lines of his back were unearthly.

234

He looked a lot like Portia's son.

Her fist tightened, crumpling the contract.

"I'll take him," she said, her voice hoarse. Nukha'il raised his chin, giving her the kind of look that said he wouldn't go down easily.

The moment she signed the last curl on her surname, the papers were gone and the pen was whisked from her hand. Alain tucked the contract into his coat once more. Mr. Black smiled like the Cheshire Cat, his too-white teeth glowing in the lamplight. "It's always a pleasure doing business with you, my dear."

"Yes. Of course. You'll have to tell me your real name one day, Mr. Black."

He placed a kiss on her knuckles. The suit fit him even better when he was standing. Under other circumstances, she might have sought him out to become her third husband. He was wealthy and certainly attractive. But he was also a cold bastard, and he did dangerous business. She didn't want to be witness to the day it caught up with him.

"How do I contact you?" she asked.

"I'll be in town visiting some…shall we say, old friends. I'll be in touch. Don't worry about that."

Portia blinked rapidly, trying to process the information. "You understand if I don't walk you to the door."

"Of course."

She waited until they were gone before letting the shudders overtake her, but once they began, she couldn't stop.

Portia wouldn't look at Nukha'il. His presence nauseated her. She moved short locks of hair into place and dabbed at the sweat in the cleft of her breasts to give her hands something to do. Deep breaths in, slow breaths out.

"What should I do?" Nukha'il asked, making it sound as if he was offering to clean a toilet.

"Don't talk to me," she snapped. Raising her voice, she called, "They're gone."

The door behind her opened, and the Night Hag entered.

Portia had been assured that the overlord of the city was a demon, but she appeared to be a frail, ancient, and entirely human female. Her sagging face was a severe, bony mask that resembled the ancient mummies. Every breath rattled in her chest.

She was shadowed by a man so painfully beautiful that he could have been mistaken for one of Mr. Black's stock. His almond-shaped eyes were black, as though the pupils had overtaken the irises. He had been

235

introduced to Portia as "Thom."

"Mr. Black," the Night Hag muttered. "Bringing his 'collection.' I should have known! And now you've given him your fleet?"

"We can track his movements," Portia said, fighting to keep her voice steady. The Night Hag and her companion *looked* normal, but they terrified her in a deep, primal way. "And you instructed me to cooperate with him."

"We'll kill Mr. Black," the overlord said to herself, stroking claw-like nails down the side of her face. "Yes. We'll have to strike fast." She snapped her fingers. "Tell David Nicholas."

Thom gave a small bow. "Very well." His voice was deep and without accent. He turned to leave, but the Night Hag caught his arm.

"We'll need the kopis, too. Get to her before Mr. Black does."

"What about this...*thing*?" Portia interjected. "You asked for it, and I bought it, but I don't want it in my house."

"Nukha'il," the Night Hag whispered. "Yes. I have plans for you, my new angel."

Two years of client files. All the knives stored in her desk. A safe filled with important documents. Her laptop, her desk phone. Her favorite coffee pot.

Gone. All gone.

The police left after taking pictures, samples, and statements. It felt like her office had been violated a second time, and all that remained after the investigators were done was shattered furniture, smoke stains, and a lingering sense of grief.

She sank to her knees on a clear patch of floor by the window and let the silence engulf her. There was so much to be done. She needed to meet with the landlord, a cleaning company, her insurance agent—not to mention all her clients, whose private files had been stolen.

Elise rested her head in her hands. She had a headache. She never had headaches. It must have been caffeine withdrawal.

"They took my favorite coffee pot," she whispered. That part stung the worst.

She didn't bother locking the door on her way out.

Outside, the day was too hot and too bright. The lack of clouds felt like a personal insult. She jammed sunglasses onto her face, slammed the car door, and went home to start the recovery process. She blew through two stop signs on the way. Elise couldn't seem to focus on the road.

Her roommate greeted her at the door with a feather duster.

"Anthony's looking for you!" Betty announced, plucking a headphone out of one ear. She was a human hurricane of caffeinated enthusiasm, and all that energy was currently directed at cleaning their kitchen in tiny shorts that said "juicy" on the butt.

"Great," Elise said, dropping her satchel on the couch. "Thanks."

"He's probably on his side of the duplex. You can catch him before work if you hurry." Betty frowned. "You okay? You look tired."

It seemed like too much effort to rehash everything she had gone over with the police in exacting detail. "I'll tell you later."

She went into her bedroom and locked the door.

Anthony. He was exactly the person she didn't want to see. He would freak out and expect her to do the same, and then he would try to comfort her, and the thought of having to deal with that much emotion was exhausting.

The endless to-do list kept rolling through her mind: *Landlord. Cleaning company. Insurance agent. All her clients. The police.* Maybe the security company would have footage, maybe she should…

Elise threw herself on the bed without getting undressed and pressed the heel of her hand to her forehead.

She didn't even know where to begin. Backups? She could restore most of the data to the laptop in her bedroom. That would be the easiest place to start. But thinking of it reminded her that police expected copies of her files as part of the "evidence collection" process, and that got the torrent going again.

Landlord. Cleaning company. Insurance agent. Calling the clients.

"Fuck it," she told her ceiling.

Elise threw on jogging gear, tied her hair into a loose ponytail, and did a few twists in the living room to test her mobility. She felt like hell, emotionally speaking, but her body was in good condition after fighting demon spiders for a week.

"Leaving again?" Betty asked. She was listening to electronica so loudly that Elise could hear the bass through the headphones. "Don't you want to see Anthony first?"

"No."

She sighed. "So what should I tell him?"

Elise stretched a leg in front of her. "Nothing. I don't owe him any explanations."

Betty sighed again, as though that answer put her in physical pain.

She was still sighing when Elise rocketed out the door. Sometimes, Betty's antics were cute, but this was not one of those times.

Her feet pounded a rhythm on the pavement that kept time with the incessant thoughts.

Landlord. Cleaning company. Insurance agent. The police, the security company, offsite backups…

She put on her own headphones and blasted Black Death's latest album from the MP3 player on her arm. It couldn't go loud enough to muffle her thoughts.

Life was so much easier when Elise hadn't owned anything. There was a time she hadn't cared about coffee pots or the nice desk she bought as a treat for surviving her first year as an accountant. All she cared about was sticking close to James—and sometimes, she didn't care much about that, either.

James was the only person she could imagine talking to. He always knew the right things to say. Conveniently, she kept her monthly backups on flash drives in the safe at his dance studio, so that was where she was heading anyway.

He owned a studio called Motion and Dance, which had two classes in progress and a full parking lot when she arrived. Business had been good lately. Demand for his classes spiked when he was contracted to choreograph a casino show, and with another Christmas show in the works, it was only going to keep improving.

But he wasn't downstairs when Elise peeked into the dance hall. One of his employees, Candace, was guiding a group through hip-hop moves. The instructor waved at Elise. She didn't wave back. She jogged upstairs to the apartment over the studio and entered without knocking.

Elise took off her headphones.

"James?"

His apartment was a disaster. The couch was shoved against the wall. The kitchen chairs were stacked on the table. He had pulled everything out of the closets and turned the floor into a cluttered mess. Even the window-mounted air conditioner had been unplugged.

Spring cleaning? He was usually anal about tidiness. It was quiet other than the music downstairs, so he wasn't home to ask.

Disappointed, she went into the bedroom that used to be hers. Flat pack boxes were leaned against the wall, and everything else was separated into two piles. The belongings she left behind when she moved out had been dumped in a corner. "What are you doing, James?" she muttered, nudging the pile with her foot. She recognized her tattered

238

sweatpants and a bottle of shampoo.

The only thing untouched was the safe against the wall, which had been bolted in place. Elise entered the combination, twisted the key in the lock, and passed her hand over the magical sensor. The door swung open.

She kept a pair of falchions and a back sheath in the safe, as well as a chain of charms she used for exorcisms. The envelope of flash drives nestled next to an old Book of Shadows was laughably mundane amongst everything else.

Elise selected the one labeled with the most recent date and moved to close the door again.

But she hesitated. Her fingers trailed down the long gold chain of her charms, and they whispered to her in a dozen voices, hissing with magic and ancient words. Her finger stopped on a single stone between the ankh and pentacle. It was white and soapy-smooth, like polished bone.

Another voice whispered to her, a voice from her dreams: *Elise...*

A chill rippled down her spine. She locked the safe.

Elise pocketed the flash drive and sat on the laundry to check her cell phone. She had missed three calls while jogging. One was from Anthony, but the other two were from her insurance company and landlord.

Landlord. Cleaning company. Insurance agent. The police, the security company, off-site backups...

She called the remote voicemail service she used for her business.

There were twenty-six messages.

After a week of camping, she expected to find a few things on her answering service, but the majority of clients contacted her by email. She had to brace herself to play the first message. "This is Frederickson Lane. We need to talk about terminating our contract. Call me back at..."

Elise pushed the "next" button.

"I'm looking for Bruce Kent. I'm from Crimson Mark Incorporated, and we need to transfer our accounts from..."

Her heart sped. Transfer?

The next one began. They wanted to discuss ending their business with her, too. More than a dozen of the messages were from different accounts about the same issue.

Elise turned off her phone and set it carefully on the floor as though it had been possessed.

She only had a few clients. Since Elise served a niche market— supernatural creatures with Earth-based businesses—there was no competition, but there also weren't many accounts to take on. And it sounded like she had just lost half of them.

239

The numbers raced through her mind. Three percent from Crimson—that would mean thousands of dollars if they bailed. A half percent from Plymouth. Another few hundred dollars from Frederickson. She had already been on narrow margins after Craven's took their accounting in house...

Craven's.

Anger bubbled inside her. Who would have the nerve to call Elise's clients and tell them to find a new accountant? Who knew where her office was located, and had motive to vandalize it? The manager and owner of Craven's Casino, David Nicholas, was exactly the kind of bastard who would do both. And more, if given the chance to fuck with her.

Maybe it was time to pay him a visit.

Chapter 3

CRAVEN'S WAS A cesspool of a casino wedged in a dark corner downtown. Tourists didn't go there. They visited the big hotel casinos that hosted touring Broadway shows and served fancy buffets. The only people who visited Craven's were demons—and angry demon hunters.

Elise had contacts at Craven's that offered a steady stream of information, but she hadn't visited since David Nicholas fired her as their accountant and tried to beat her to death. To be fair, she had beaten him up first, and she ended up killing one of his cronies in his attack. She thought they were even. But apparently he didn't agree.

She still knew the way to his office, which was on the ninth level overlooking the poker tables. She navigated through the dimly-lit casino floor, where people gambled away their savings and drowned in alcohol, and headed up two sets of escalators.

A cocktail waitress spotted her. Her face might have gone pale if it hadn't been caked in so much makeup. She dropped her drink tray and ran in the other direction.

So much for surprising them.

She hurried up the stairs, found the door labeled MANAGER, and shoved it open. David Nicholas looked up from his desk.

"We need to talk," she said.

David Nicholas was a full-blooded, Earth-bound nightmare that hadn't been powerful since the Middle Ages and wasted the centuries since trying to recapture his old glory. He smoked like a factory and usually looked like a greasy scarecrow. But he had filled out in the weeks since Elise had last seen him, as though a layer of fat had developed beneath his papery skin. His yellow hair was cut to the chin and had been washed. His office wasn't even covered in garbage and tobacco ash

241

anymore.

In another time, his strong nose and chin might have been considered handsome. But that foul grin sickened Elise. She would never mistake him as anything but dangerous.

"Yeah, we do need to talk." He returned his attention to the schedule for the cocktail waitresses on his desk. "Heard what happened at your office. I knew you'd come crawling back for a job."

"Is that what you were trying to do? To get me to ask you for work?"

He stabbed the point of his cigarette into the ashtray and opened a desk drawer. Elise tensed, but he only took out another cigarette. "What are you talking about?" he asked out the corner of his mouth as he lit it.

"Someone's been calling my clients and telling them to leave. Likely the same person who started the fire."

"And you think that was me? That's precious."

She drew her knife. "Precious?"

He stood, shoving his sleeves above his elbows. His forearms had the illusion of being muscular now, but a nightmare's strength had nothing to do with its physical form. "You've been away too long, cabbage. The game's changed. You barely matched me last time—think you could take me now?"

"Yes."

He vanished with a swirl of smoke and reappeared inches in front of her, shoving his beak of a nose into hers. She held her ground.

"Want to try me?" His breath smelled like tobacco and rot.

She grabbed a fistful of his shirt. "You're in my space."

The stress of the morning built in her muscles and desperately wanted to be unleashed on his ugly face. *Give me an excuse. Just give me an excuse…*

His phone rang.

For the first two rings, David Nicholas didn't move. His eyes flicked to the desk and back to Elise.

She released his shirt.

He grabbed the receiver. "What?" he snapped. Whatever response he received wasn't good, because he pulled a face. "Okay." A pause, and then again, "Okay." David Nicholas hung up and held both hands out in a gesture of peace. "Game's up for the night. You've been summoned."

Elise laughed in disbelief. "Summoned? If you're trying to distract me —"

"I want nothing more than to see you broken on my floor, *accountant*." He bit out the last word like an insult. "The day you die is the day I'm a happy demon. I'll throw parties with hats and trumpets and streamers.

242

But today's not that day. *She* wants to see you."

"Who?"

"The Night Hag."

She scoffed. "This bullshit again?" David Nicholas bumped his shoulder into hers as he left the room.

Elise almost didn't follow him. He had been foretelling the return of the Night Hag for as long as she had been in town, but it had always been a lie. And that was a good thing. Part of the reason she had chosen to live in Reno was its lack of a demonic overlord. They didn't like having kopides in their territory.

But he walked with confidence, like he expected her to follow, and Elise sheathed her dagger. What did she have to lose?

They took a different path through Craven's than the one she used to find his office. They went down, down, down a set of stairs with walls painted black, and the thump of music began rising around them.

Eloquent Blood was a demon bar in the basement of Craven's, and during the afternoon, it was completely empty. The pit of a dance floor stood bare. All the neon was turned off, and the brimstone droppings were swept into a corner by a cleaning crew. Someone was cutting off the music and switching songs as they ran sound checks. A demon with horned shoulders wiped down the tables. It was...ordinary.

"Where's Neuma?" she asked. Being able to speak without yelling was strange. It felt like a cavern without partiers packing it to the brim.

David Nicholas shot her a sideways look. "You think we live here or something? The dumb bitch has an apartment. If she's not sleeping, she's shooting up."

Elise hadn't given the living situation of local demons much thought. In most cities, overlords kept their subjects close. They stayed in dens and rarely emerged.

The reminder of why they were going into Blood was sobering. She traced the edges of the leather sheath hidden at the small of her back. She had killed an overlord once in a surprise attack, but this time, she was the one taken off-guard. Elise wished she had worn her swords.

Tension built in her skull as they descended to the bottom floor of the club. It wasn't nerves. It was infernal power, and lots of it. "Believe me now?" David Nicholas asked with a sneer when he saw her expression.

She checked her knives for a third time. "Take me down."

They got into an elevator behind the DJ booth. It was an old mine lift, rickety and rusted, and a shaft extended endlessly beyond the grate under Elise's feet.

It rattled, squealed, and began to move.

Rough stone walls slid past them. Lights marked every few feet, but they were weak, and the shadow between them was immense. Every time they slipped into darkness, David Nicholas flickered out of view. But he always reappeared, yellow-haired and sweaty, with one hand on the lever.

The pressure in her skull grew too strong as they dropped, and when they reached the bottom and stepped onto solid ground, there was no ignoring the sensation of eyes on the back of her neck. A dark corridor stretched in front of them.

It looked empty, but they weren't alone. Elise could feel it.

David Nicholas strode ahead, shooting a nasty smile as he passed. She considered knocking the smug look off his face. But she wasn't in her own territory anymore. It was the Warrens—the place demons dwelled far below the city. Even she wasn't confident enough to think she could fight her way out alone.

He led her to a door, but paused before opening it. "Be nice. Or don't. Maybe today can be the day you die after all."

Elise stepped through.

The room beyond was like being inside a hollowed-out ribcage. Webbing as thick as her arms stretched from ceiling to walls to form a low canopy, and the black ground crunched with every step. It was too dark to see what she was walking on.

A man with shimmering brown hair sat on the floor by the door with his ankles chained to the wall. Pieces of white rock were scattered around him, and it looked like he was trying to piece together a puzzle the size of a small car. When he saw Elise, he dropped one of the stones. It rolled across the ground.

David Nicholas delivered a kick to his ribs. "Keep at it!"

He groaned and went back to work.

She moved deeper into the room. Tapestries hung from the supports that kept the sagging mineshaft open. Colorful threads glimmered in the darkness.

"Do you like them?"

Elise hadn't noticed an old hospital bed in the corner. Its sheets were stained, the bars were rusted, and the webs stretched toward it. She approached slowly. "Did you make the tapestries?"

"Yes." Something in the bed was moving. A light flicked on above them.

The Night Hag was illuminated in all her ghastly splendor. She was a skeleton with gray skin stretched over its joints, an IV in one arm, and webs wrapped around the other. Her skull of a face smiled at Elise, making the skin sag at her jowls. The expression was frightening, but not unfriendly.

Power radiated from her like a hand gripping Elise's throat. There was no mistaking that amount of infernal energy.

"I have to apologize for my state. I'm receiving a transfusion."

"Of what?"

Her eyes glinted. "Fluids."

Elise crossed her hands behind her back, resisting the urge to touch her knives again. "I should apologize for moving into the territory without your permission. I was led to believe you had died."

"David Nicholas tells me you had been informed I was merely sleeping."

"He's usually full of shit."

The Night Hag gave a soft, rasping laugh. "I've struggled toward consciousness for the past two months. The delicious scent of power lured me—your power, I hear. Someone's been getting into naughty things."

Elise kept her mouth shut. She had defeated a demon called Death's Hand in the spring, but only after it killed James and possessed his body. She harnessed its necromantic power to resurrect him. Things like that sent waves through all the dimensions, so it was no surprise that it woke up the overlord. But she wouldn't admit that.

When she stayed silent, the Night Hag lifted her chin regally. "I could kill you. You know that, don't you?"

"You could try."

"What an ugly fight that would be. A very ugly fight indeed. I know your reputation, and I'm sure you could kill many of my people before I killed you...and your aspis." The Night Hag paused as though waiting for a reaction. Elise kept her face blank. "My numbers are unfathomable and your loss is certain. But what a waste of time and talent."

"Opinions differ," David Nicholas muttered from the back of the room.

The Night Hag glared and snapped her frail fingers. He vanished in an instant, leaving a hole in Elise's senses where he had been a moment before.

The man by the door cried out.

Elise frowned. "Where—?"

"He has gone to a place of punishment. My men must show respect.

Isn't that true, Thom?"

It was only then that Elise realized someone else was in the room.

He sat in the darkness behind the hospital bed. He wore nothing but snug leather pants and a thin black collar. Thom could have been Neuma's human cousin. He was raven-haired and beautiful, but far more elegant than the stripper could dream of becoming. "Yes," he said simply.

"This is my witch. He takes care of things for me. Isn't he lovely?"

The hair rose on the back of Elise's neck. "Lovely" wasn't the word she would have chosen for him. Something about the witch struck her as wrong, like he didn't belong on Earth.

She forced herself to focus on the Night Hag.

"What do you want from me?"

"We share a common enemy. Unfortunately, as you can see, I'm not what I used to be. You are best equipped to kill him for me...with my help."

"Who?" Elise asked. She had a lot of enemies, but none had bothered her since she killed Death's Hand.

The Night Hag waved a hand. Thom stood and held out a photograph.

She didn't reach to take it.

"Look. Look!" the overlord said impatiently. "Before I decide to kill you and have done with it! Don't fear my witch. He's muzzled and harmless."

Harmless? She seriously doubted it.

Thom set the picture on the bedside table. Elise picked it up and turned it over. Cold, unfamiliar fear washed over her.

It had been taken at the house of someone rich. She could tell by the fancy windows, the furniture, the drapes. Judging by the odd angle and grainy quality, the subjects probably hadn't known they were being photographed. But she recognized the men in the picture. They had aged, changed, and grown harder, but there was no mistaking the Southern gentleman and his French bodyguard. The last time she had seen them, Mr. Black's home had been on fire. She had thought—had *hoped*—they died after that.

"Fuck," Elise muttered.

"I'm glad you see the issue."

"Where was this taken?"

"At a home on the southwest side of town. He was conducting a deal with a woman who has been on my payroll for years. I don't know what he wants to accomplish, but it can't be good for anyone."

Elise's legs couldn't seem to support her anymore. She sat down hard in the chair by the bed. But she kept her face blank and her hand steady as she set the photo on the table again.

So the vandalism of her office had been a message, but not from David Nicholas. She should have known he wasn't subtle enough for that anyway. It had been a kind of greeting from Mr. Black—one calculated to remind her of shared animosity and debts owed.

It took her a moment to realize the Night Hag was talking again.

"Worried Mr. Black will kill that handsome aspis of yours? You should be. From what I've learned of your past deals, I'm sure he's positioning his chess pieces to take your favorite pawn as we speak."

Elise clenched her fists. She wasn't a fan of that description. "We'll take care of ourselves."

"By hiding again, like you did for so many years? Where's the fun in that?" She cackled. "Oh yes. I'm familiar with your history. Here is my offer: You may continue to live in the city. I will assign a protective detail to your aspis. And we'll kill Mr. Black together."

"James would never go for that. He hates demons."

"He doesn't have to know, does he?"

Elise studied the overlord with a frown. "What's the catch?"

"During the duration of our agreement, you'll be my employee, and contractually bound to do errands for me—which may include things around Craven's and my other businesses, as needed—until such a time that Mr. Black is out of the picture and life returns to its usual equilibrium."

"What kind of errands?"

"I haven't decided."

"Can I refuse?"

"Certainly," said the Night Hag. Left unspoken was the condition of that refusal: the termination of their tenuous, momentary truce.

"I want to think about it."

The Night Hag waved a dismissive hand. "Fine. Go. Call me when you're ready to cooperate. But don't take long—we'll have to move fast to stop a man like Mr. Black." She smirked. "Hopefully he hasn't already killed all your friends, hmm? What a shame that would be."

She snapped her fingers again. David Nicholas reappeared, and he didn't look as fleshy and strong as he had earlier. His hair was thinner, his skin was papery, and he had to grab the wall to keep standing.

"You bitch!"

She was surprised to see his insult aimed at the Night Hag instead of her. The overlord wasn't impressed.

"Take the kopis back to the surface. Give her my direct number. We'll be seeing each other again soon—very soon."

Elise stood. "I wouldn't be sure of that."

But the Night Hag only smiled in response.

Chapter 4

"WHAT ARE YOU doing in here?"

Anthony jumped at the sound of Betty's voice, tripped on a pair of shoes, and almost fell over. "Betty!"

She grinned broadly at him. His cousin's hair was pulled into pigtails, which might have made her devilish grin disarming if Anthony hadn't known her too well for that. "You look awfully guilty," she said, propping her shoulder against the doorway. She wore a bikini and had a book tucked under her arm like she was ready for the beach. "What did I catch you doing?"

He snatched his shirt off Elise's dresser and hugged it protectively to his chest. "Nothing."

"You know, Elise is very private. She would hate to find out you were in here." Betty gave an exaggerated sigh. "Fortunately, she never has to know…if I don't tell her. But why would I want to do that?"

"I'm not the only one in her room while she's out of the house. What are *you* up to? I left the door shut, and there's no way you saw me come in."

"Don't try to change the subject. I could waterboard you." She jiggled the water bottle.

"I'm doing laundry, so I was picking up clothes I forgot here. Okay? Laundry is perfectly innocent."

"So there's nothing seditious going on? Too bad. I'm not up to anything innocent, for the record." Betty pushed past him. "In case you were worrying about that."

She set her things on the floor and got on all fours to peek under the bed. He gaped at her. "What…?"

Betty emerged with a shoebox, but she looked disappointed to find

249

nothing but knives in it. She pushed it back under the mattress. "You've spent lots of long, sweaty hours in here. Have you seen anything belonging to James?"

"What? What are you doing?"

She flung open Elise's closet and started digging. Only the professional outfits were hung neatly; all the casual clothes were piled on the floor. Betty dove into the piles first. "I'm looking for magic. Well, okay, I'm looking for spells. James won't let me see his secret stuff. He says I'm not a powerful enough witch to control that kind of magic." She huffed as she sat back on her heels. "Of *course* I'm not powerful enough yet! He won't let me practice!"

Anthony was torn. He didn't like to think of Elise's reaction if she found them riffling through her room, but he also didn't like James, and the idea of defying him was too appealing. "You don't want anything dangerous, do you?"

Betty's eyes became wide circles. "Dangerous? Me?"

She might as well have tattooed her forehead with "full of shit."

"All right," he said. She squealed.

He opened Elise's desk drawers. Her files were more organized than her closet, and a quick scan showed him she wasn't hiding anything there.

"What would it look like?"

"I don't think James would give her his Book of Shadows, so I'm thinking it would be a collection of loose pages with funny symbols. I know she keeps some for him as backup."

"Like this?" He pulled a spiral notebook out of Elise's underwear drawer.

"Ooh!"

He watched over Betty's shoulder as she flipped through it. It was nonsense to him. "What is it?"

"Paper magic. You know, that thing James does where he performs a ritual, and captures it on a page? He's got tons of these at his house. He showed it to the coven last month. But he won't share his secrets." She ran her hand down a page. "These ones aren't activated. This isn't enough. I need instructions or something."

Anthony edged toward the window and peeked at the street. "Maybe we should put it back. Elise will notice it's missing, and it wouldn't be hard to guess who took it."

She ripped out a few pages and tucked them in her paperback before restoring the notebook to the drawer. Then she plucked something red and stringy out of the dresser. "Hello there, sexy undies. I never would have pegged Elise as the lacy thong type."

He snatched it out of Betty's hand.

"I hope you're not going to get in trouble with the paper magic," he said, stuffing the underwear back where it belonged.

Her responding grin wasn't reassuring. But how much damage could she do with a few sheets torn from a notebook?

The doorbell rang.

Anthony jumped and slammed the dresser shut. Betty laughed. "Relax. Elise just walks in, you big dummy."

Cheeks red, he answered the door.

There was a basket on the step, and no signs of a delivery truck. "You've got something, Betty."

"Who's it from?"

He poked around the tissue paper. "No idea. I don't see a card."

Betty set it on the counter and removed everything. There was a bottle of wine, some cheese, and a jewelry box inside. She opened it.

Inside, a delicate silver crucifix pendant was nestled on a bed of cotton. It was plainer than anything she liked to wear, and too religious. "I don't think this is from one of my boyfriends. It must be something Elise ordered."

Anthony dug through the filling, but there was nothing left to find. "Huh. Whatever. I better start my laundry if I want to have something to wear at work." Betty was already searching the drawers for a bottle opener and didn't say goodbye. The pages from the notebook stuck out of her paperback.

He headed back to his apartment, feeling pretty certain he had just helped Betty get into a lot of trouble. But then again, what else was new?

By the time Elise got home from visiting the Night Hag, Betty was sunbathing in the front yard of their duplex. She had stretched out on a checkerboard blanket in an obscenely small bikini, waving a fan in one hand and cradling a paperback in the other.

"Take off your shirt and get down here, Elise! I've saved you some blanket space. And half of this wine." She lifted the bottle and jiggled it.

Elise couldn't find the energy to force a smile. "Maybe later."

All the blinds were closed inside their duplex to shade it from the harsh afternoon sunlight, but it was still nowhere near as dark as the mines below Craven's. Her mood was blackest of all.

She stood in the middle of her living room, looking around at all the things that made it home. Betty had hung a print of a scared cat done in the style of Andy Warhol's Marilyn Monroe portrait, eye shadow and all, over their dining room table. The coffee table was covered in research papers. Empty jugs of protein powder were repurposed as flower pots. And then she tried to imagine leaving it behind and running again.

No. She wouldn't do it.

There was a basket on the counter she didn't recognize. Betty had already ransacked it. Elise cracked the blinds for a little extra light, then picked through the remains.

All that was in it was a small wheel of cheese and a jewelry box, although there was enough room for a bottle of wine, too. Must have been from one of Betty's boyfriends. Elise could watch her sunbathing through the window like they were on a Florida beach, rather than a high-density downtown neighborhood.

She opened the jewelry box. Elise gasped and dropped it in the sink.

That was her necklace. It belonged to her mother, once upon a time. But the chain had snapped during a fight, and she lost it—at Mr. Black's house.

The wine.

She ran outside.

"Changed your mind?" Betty asked, using the book to shade her face from the harsh summer sunlight.

Elise took the bottle from the grass and sniffed its mouth. It was peppery, rich, and woody, with a smoky odor that wasn't typical of wine. She wiped a finger along the edge and tasted it.

Grapes took on the flavor of their environment. The air, the soil, and the amount of sun could have subtle effects on an entire year's harvest. It wasn't common for a vineyard to produce wine after most of it burned, but that one had, and the grapes had taken on the flavor of a fire.

She checked the year on the label. It was from 1999.

"Kind of a weird taste, huh?" Betty asked. "But I like it. Maybe we can go check out the vineyard later. I know you and James love wine tastings, you great big drunkards." Elise marched to the curb and dumped the wine in the gutter. "Wait—wait, what are you doing? Stop!"

She smashed the bottle on the street.

Betty ran over, all her bare parts jiggling in the bikini. She ripped off her sunglasses to gape at the wine mixing with runoff from a garden hose two units down.

"Have you gone nuts?"

Elise scanned the street, positioning herself between Betty and the rest of the world. "If you get any other packages, don't open them."

"That was perfectly good wine!"

She recognized all the cars. A neighbor washed his truck down the street with the help of his ten year old son. A pair of teenagers sat on the corner looking hot and bored. Everything seemed ordinary enough, but there were too many hiding places. Too many houses with closed curtains, too many bushes and trees.

"Get inside," Elise said.

The confusion drained from Betty's face. "What's wrong? Did something happen?"

"Don't argue."

Her roommate's mouth shut. She grabbed her blanket and fan and carried everything into the duplex.

The wine dribbled into the sewer. Bitter anger rose in Elise's throat. The gift of her mother's necklace could only mean one thing.

This was war.

Chapter 5

IF JAMES WERE to list "signs of impending apocalypse" from least worrisome to most, he would rank mundane things at the bottom—scrambled eggs, golden retriever puppies, a topiary in the shape of a dinosaur—and move up from there to slightly more worrying indicators. Earthquakes. Locusts. Raining blood. Dead cows.

Finding nine missed calls from Elise might not have been at the top of the list, but it was close. Perhaps directly below "death of all firstborn children in the nation."

He hadn't moved the power cord for his phone to Stephanie's house yet, so when his battery died, he couldn't recharge it. When he finally plugged it in his car to find a single terse text message from Elise ("Get back to the studio"), his stress levels shot through the roof. She had a way of doing that to him.

Twilight was falling when James arrived. Dry heat hung in the air, barely any cooler than it had been at midday. The pavement caught the heat and radiated it long after the sun disappeared behind the mountains. Leaving the air conditioned confines of his car was almost suffocating.

Hints of violet and orange touched the hills, painting the desolation in shades of sunset. Pink clouds faded to blue toward the east, where stars were already beginning to appear. The fading sun made the brick walls of Motion and Dance glow. His neighborhood was quiet that time of evening. The sprinklers kicked on at a dentist's office on the corner, a dog barked a few blocks away, and the illuminated sign for his studio buzzed faintly.

He parked beside Elise's car and jingled his keys in one hand as he headed for the stairs.

The back of his neck itched. He paused at the bottom of the stairs and glanced around the yard. "Elise?" he called. His hand slipped into his pocket where he kept a small notebook. "Is that you?"

A figure stepped from the darkness behind the sign. The light caught Elise's legs and left her a silhouette above the waist.

"I've been waiting for you all afternoon."

"Sorry. My battery died. What's wrong?"

She stepped onto the sidewalk to peer around the street. Elise was dressed for jogging in shorts and a tank top, but her posture made it look more like battle armor.

The street light flickered on and cast her in stark yellow light. She looked tired and grim and about five years older than the last time he saw her. "I've already checked your apartment. It's safe. Let's talk inside."

"Checked it for what?"

"I'll explain when we're off the street."

She tailed him up the stairs like a bodyguard waiting for attack, and watched the parking lot while he unlocked the door. Once they were inside, she put on the deadbolt, peered out the windows, and shut the curtains.

Elise hadn't been subtle about searching his apartment. The doors were open, every light was turned on, and his remaining belongings were more scattered than before. She didn't try to explain what was going on once everything was secured. Instead, she handed him a small blue box.

He tipped the lid open. The cross inside looked familiar, but it took him a few minutes to recognize it. "Isn't this Ariane's necklace? I thought you lost it years ago."

"It was returned to me today."

He tried to remember the last time he saw Elise wearing it. An image of her at a younger age came to mind, when she still had short hair and skeletal features.

And then everything fell into place, and the box slipped from his hand.

Neither of them moved to pick it up.

"Impossible," James said. "We killed them."

He sank onto the couch. Elise took the seat beside him. She didn't have to say anything else. The silence of the night felt heavier than before, and the shadows seemed too dark. He understood why she had turned on all the lights. James had warded every inch of the studio with spells, but it suddenly didn't feel like enough.

James's throat was too dry to swallow. "He'll want to play with us first. That's why we haven't been directly attacked."

She nodded. Lowered her eyes.

"We knew this would happen. When we fought Death's Hand. We knew that would draw attention to us."

Something bothered him about the jewelry box on the floor. He leaned over to pick it up again, and then he saw it: a faint blur of magic around the crucifix. Elise's mother had been a witch, but not the kind that enchanted jewelry. It was something new.

"There's a spell on this," James said.

Elise frowned. "What is it?"

He focused. It certainly felt like the kind of spell Alain would cast. There was no finesse to his magic. It was blunt and raw, almost jagged on the edges, like shattered glass. "It's a locator charm," he said, tracing his fingers in the air over the cross without touching it. "So they can tell where the necklace is at any time."

"That's pointless," she said. "They already know where I live and work. They don't need magic to track me if they have eyeballs."

"And it would do them no good to follow you here anyway. Alain could never get through my barrier spells." James shut the box and set it on the table. "Unless…"

"What?"

"They might have wanted to know when you left your house."

She sucked in a hard breath. "Betty."

They couldn't drive fast enough.

James and Elise raced through the back streets toward her duplex. They saw the plume of smoke before the fire—black, billowing clouds that blotted out the stars.

Sirens screamed. A fire truck blew past them and turned onto Elise's street.

Their building was engulfed in flame. A smoky column rose from the roof on the right side, exposing the building's skeleton. The dry lawn Betty had been sunning on earlier that day had caught fire, too, and was creeping up Anthony's side of the duplex. Even the front door was swallowed by live fire, leaving no way to get inside. Firefighters blasted their hoses at the neighboring houses, which smoldered, but didn't burn —yet.

Elise didn't wait for him to stop the car before leaping out. People had spilled onto the sidewalks to rubberneck, and James had to park at the end of the street. It was too full to get any closer.

James could feel the radiant heat when he jumped out of his car. It slapped him in the face and took his breath away. "Betty!" Elise shouted, shoving through the crowd. He hurried to catch up with her as she snagged a neighbor by the elbow. "Hey! Have you seen Betty?"

The man she had grabbed shook his head. "She was inside, I saw her cleaning—"

She didn't wait to hear anything more than that. Elise flew up the sidewalk.

A firefighter blocked her path. His gear was black with ash, and his face shield was tilted back to show his grizzled face. "You can't go in there."

"That's my house!"

"It's not safe to enter," he said. "Please step back so we can—"

"You don't understand! My roommate is in there!"

James stepped back while Elise had them distracted. Something was nagging at him—something similar to what he had felt from the necklace, but much more powerful.

Alain must have started the fire. And if that were true, nothing would stop it until the entire place burned.

"Let me go!" Elise yelled, waving her arms in an uncharacteristically panicked way. She caught James's eye over the shoulder of the firefighter and jerked her head toward the house. "I have to help her!"

The firefighter gave a long-suffering sigh as he tried to guide her away. Elise shoved him. It wasn't nearly as hard as she could have.

"Ma'am, I'm going to have to ask you to step away…"

James edged silently around them, slipped behind the neighbor's house, and climbed the fence into Elise's backyard.

The damage wasn't as bad on the other side. The vinyl siding had melted with residual heat in some spots, but there was no active fire. Elise's window was shattered, and smoke poured out of it as flames licked the walls. He felt a pang of fear. There was no recovering from that. She had probably already lost everything.

Alain's aura was so powerful that James knew he must have stood back there to cast the spell on Elise's room, but the witch himself was long gone. He hadn't waited to see the damage. And it hadn't traveled to Betty's room yet.

The other window was cracked. He ripped the screen off and tried to see inside, but even though the air was clear, the power had failed. It was too dark to see anything.

"Goddess help me," he muttered.

James hauled himself over the ledge and squirmed inside.

Her bed was empty. Smoke crept through the cracks around her door

257

and turned the carpet black. "Betty!" he yelled into the hazy air. Shouting made his throat burn. He coughed, hacked, and tried again. "Betty! Where are you?"

She didn't respond.

He felt her doorknob with the back of his hand. It was hot.

He wrapped a pink cotton sheet from her footstool around his face, then grabbed another blanket to open the door.

Smoke erupted into the room with a gust of heat. He staggered back, throwing an arm over his face. His eyes watered. He took a last gulp of clean air through Betty's window, and then pushed through.

Flames had devoured Elise's bedroom door, and he felt his arm hairs scorch as he jumped past it. It was like stepping into a pizza oven. He stepped over a burning patch of carpet to get into the living room—he couldn't see further than a few inches in front of his face—and kicked aside a table that had tipped over. One of Elise's protein powder plants was a shriveled crisp. Their couch smoldered. He glimpsed a burning wall through the smoke.

Hot. So hot.

"Betty!"

No response.

He could barely see or breathe. Their duplex wasn't large, but there was no sense of direction in the darkness. He had to escape.

James kicked open the bathroom door. Empty.

The change in air pressure sucked smoke toward him. He stumbled over a chair and landed on all fours in their dining nook. He didn't bother getting up. The air was too hot, too close. He could almost breathe on the floor.

He crawled into the kitchen and saw a bare leg.

Betty.

She had collapsed in front of the refrigerator and scattered food across the floor. There was a tub of cream cheese by her head. Her bleach blond hair was thick with ash. The counter next to her was burning—he grabbed her ankle and dragged her away from it.

He would have gasped at seeing her arm in the dim light of the fire if he could breathe better. The skin was raw and peeling from residual heat.

She didn't wake up when he lifted her into his arms and tried to stand.

A mighty crack split the air.

Elise's bedroom wall collapsed, and half the roof went with it. Burning wood exploded around him. The fire swept across the carpet,

258

and a gust of heat swept past him. He fell to his knees again, coughing and wheezing.

He had to set Betty down and lay beside her to keep breathing. "This was a terrible idea," he rasped.

Where were those firefighters?

It was all he could do to pull the notebook out of his pocket and squint at his symbols in the smoke. A spell to stop fever. A spell for broken bones. A spell that created flames—he didn't need more of *that*. And then he found what he was looking for: a spell that made wind.

"Hang on," he gasped to Betty.

He crumpled the page in his fist and spoke a word of power.

Magic ripped out of him. A blast rocked the building.

Metal screamed and windows shattered as a massive wind rushed around the room, like the hand of God punching through the walls. Everything on the counters was blasted aside. James threw himself over Betty to shelter her. Pain lanced through his back as a plate shattered against his shoulders.

A second gust followed the first, even more powerful than before. Fire funneled from the back of the duplex toward the front.

Something huge snapped. What remained of the roof crashed into the counters with a groan, and for an instant, the world was impossibly hot. His hair burned. His neck blistered. Coals showered around him, stinging his arms and back.

And then the third wind extinguished it all.

With a whisper of a breeze, the house went silent.

James looked up. The counters had taken the brunt of the collapse, leaving them framed with smoking wood and sheltering him from the worst of the debris. He couldn't get up without moving it, so he didn't try.

Groaning, he rolled onto his side and brushed plaster dust off his shirt. Chunks of wood crumbled at his touch. He could see stars through what was left of the walls, and the summer breeze felt cold on the places his skin had burned. Betty was still unconscious. He pressed fingers to her throat and found a pulse.

"Thank the Goddess," he whispered, and then he let himself go limp, too.

Every breath burned his lungs. The chill on his neck had to be bad. And he didn't care at all.

The voices of men approached as firefighters moved in. James slipped his notebook into his pocket before they grew close.

Then he heard a woman's voice. "James!"

He coughed. "Over here."

The debris on the counter shifted. Elise threw everything aside, forgetting to pretend she wasn't preternaturally strong. "Betty!" She dropped beside them. "Is she...?"

"She's alive."

Elise let out a sigh. "Good." And then she turned on him. "What did you think you were doing? Are you *suicidal*?"

He held out a hand, and Elise helped him sit up. The debris at the back of the house was still burning where Alain's spell had started it, and judging by the amount of smoke, Anthony's side of the duplex was on fire too. "Betty was inside. I had to do something."

"Like dive into a burning building? Why didn't you stop the fire from the outside?"

"Alain's magic—"

"Forget it," Elise interrupted. She threw her arms around him and almost knocked him into one of the smoldering beams. Her grip made his ribs creak and the burned skin on his back ache. "You are such an idiot, James."

"Ouch," he said helpfully.

"I'm thanking you for saving Betty. Shut up."

"Right. Sorry." He patted her on the back.

"Hey! Over here!"

A firefighter had found them, ending the conversation. Elise stood up. "We'll talk about this later. Let's get Betty to the hospital."

Chapter 6

THE CHECKER BEHIND the counter swiped Elise's debit card again. "I'm sorry. This one has been denied, too."

She pulled a credit card out of her wallet. "Try this one."

The hospital cafeteria was empty in the middle of the night. Several quiet hours had elapsed since loading Betty into an ambulance, and nothing had happened since the police finished asking questions. The sudden change of pace left her feeling restless, but with her office and home burned, there was nowhere else to go.

Now she was trying to buy a salad for a late dinner, and it was much harder than it should have been. Both her personal and business debit cards had already been denied twice. She could tell by the apologetic look that her credit card wasn't coming up any different.

"Sorry," he said, handing it back. "Maybe it's a problem with our system."

She gave him a ten dollar bill and took her salad back to the waiting room.

The lettuce tasted like tissue in her mouth, dry and flavorless. Maybe it was the dissatisfaction of having her cards denied, or the lingering taste of ash, but she dumped it in the trash after two bites.

She stretched out between two chairs, pillowed her head on her arms, and tried to focus on the television mounted in the corner. She had never been able to sleep in public before—in fact, she didn't even sleep when Anthony spent the night with her—but fading adrenaline and stress mingled to overtake her.

She could barely find the energy to fill her lungs. Every breath was slower and deeper than the last.

The news was reporting on the fire. Pundits discussed rising crime rates.

Elise's eyes drooped. The figures blurred.

She stretched with a yawn, trying to force her eyelids open. What if someone found her? What if she was attacked?

But she sank into her chair again as the news flickered in front of her, and her eyes fell closed. A dark and endlessly vast space settled around her. It sank into her skin and weighed upon her bones. Air ruffled the hair at the back of her neck.

Someone was calling her name.

Elise...

Fear thrilled through her stomach. She could still see the dim light of the news and hear them discuss investigations and arson. But the room wavered around her.

A pillar grew in front of her like a stone tree sprouting. It was wrapped with thick lines and glowing symbols at the base. It was soapy-white, unnaturally smooth. The pillar arced over her head, and she watched as the other end touched the earth and formed a gateway.

Not here. Not again.

She struggled to focus on the TV, but her eyelashes were glued shut.

"A home in downtown Reno burned last night in an incident the police suspect to be arson..." The newscaster's smile stretched and blurred. Her eyes sank into her skull, leaving black pits in their place. "You deserved it, didn't you? You're going to lose everything."

Her hand reached through the gateway, grin huge and looming. Pale fingers filled her vision.

"I see you, Elise."

Her voice echoed through the air.

I see you...

Elise's eyes flew open as her hand closed on a wrist. She wrenched her attacker off his feet. Her other hand went to the back of her shorts where she kept a knife.

"It's me, Elise, it's me!"

The haze lifted, and she realized the blurry face in front of her belonged to James.

Suddenly, she wasn't in that dark place anymore. She was in a quiet hospital with tan carpeting, bare walls, and murmuring nurses. She released him, sat up, and cradled her head in both palms. "Sorry," she said, blinking hard to clear her vision. Her heart thudded as though she had been running.

James sank to his knees next to the chair. He had ashy smudges on his

262

chin and a bandage across the back of his neck. "Are you okay?"

"Fine." She wiped sweat off her upper lip with the back of her glove. "I'm fine. What do the doctors say?"

"I'm all right, so I've been discharged, but Betty needs to stay the night. She inhaled a lot of smoke and has second-degree burns on ten percent of her body. Anthony will be here soon to stay with her." He offered Elise his hand. She ignored it and got up on her own.

"Will she be okay?"

"Yes, but she's in a lot of pain. They've sedated her so she can sleep." The careful way he spoke told Elise there was more to the story that he didn't want to say. They took the elevator to the first floor and went outside, and he continued once they were alone in the parking lot. "I think she was poisoned. Drugged."

Elise got into the car. "The wine."

"Most likely. That fire was meant to kill her."

"No, it was meant to kill *me*."

"He was surely tracking the cross and knew you weren't there. If Mr. Black wanted us dead, he would be more overt. I think he's trying to—well, punish us."

Her jaw clenched. "Fantastic. Where are we going?"

"The studio. You can't stay at the duplex anymore, and it's one of the only places with strong enough warding to stand up to Mr. Black."

That was optimistic of him. Elise wasn't sure an entire fortress would be strong enough. "Thanks. I'll find a hotel or something tomorrow. There isn't enough room for Betty and Anthony at the studio, and we're all homeless now."

"Actually..." He hesitated. Cleared his throat. "There are two bedrooms in my apartment, and I'm staying with Stephanie. That leaves plenty of room for all of you."

"You should stay with us. Stephanie's house isn't warded, either."

"Her old house wasn't," James agreed.

She shot a sideways look at him. He had always taken their lifestyle with grace. Even covered in soot, he didn't seem as beaten as she did. His black hair looked artfully tousled, while hers was a tangled mess of curls.

"But?"

"She's moved."

The terse response made her uneasy. But it wasn't until they got to the studio again that she realized exactly what it meant.

The last couple of times she had been there, she assumed the disarray meant he was cleaning. But now she saw that his most important belongings were gone. The photography prints, his kitchen utensils, his altar. She followed him into his bedroom and realized half of his bookshelves were empty. She didn't have to check the closet to know his clothes would be gone, too.

It didn't look like a place someone lived. It looked more like long-term storage.

Why hadn't she noticed earlier?

James gathered fresh blankets from the linen closet and tried to get a fitted sheet over the mattress. Elise took the other end and helped him pull it over the corner.

He changed pillowcases and folded the comforter at the foot of the bed. "There you go. Should be comfortable." When she didn't respond, James studied her face with deep furrows carved into his forehead. He misinterpreted her angry silence. "We'll figure this out. We defeated Mr. Black once, and we can do it again."

"I'm not worried about it," she said.

"You don't have to lie to me."

That almost made her laugh. Funny, coming from the man who had moved out of his apartment and hadn't bothered to tell her. "I should rest."

He nodded. "I'll sleep on the couch. I'm too tired to drive, and heaven knows where Mr. Black is right now."

"I can take the couch."

"You need the rest much more than I do." James reached out to tug on one of the curls in her ponytail. "You look terrible, Elise."

"Yeah. Thanks. We can talk more about Mr. Black when sunrise hits."

"A whole two hours of sleep," he said. "I can hardly wait."

Elise watched his retreating back before shutting the door. His room felt strangely vacant without him in it.

She wasn't sure if the tension in her shoulders was from James or Mr. Black. Either way, her urge to sleep had completely vanished. She changed into a spare t-shirt and sweat pants from her laundry pile and splashed water on her face in the bathroom, trying to cool her parched skin.

In the light from the vanity bulbs over the mirror, she really did look terrible. Hollow eyes stared back at her from a face that seemed gaunter than it had the day before. Her auburn hair was fraying from its ponytail. Her tan skin was gray. There was no color to her lips or cheeks. A droplet of water shivered from the hard point of her chin, and she brushed it off.

All those worries crept back in twofold. Insurance company. Landlord

—both for her office building and her duplex. The police would have even more questions. Her dwindling client list. All those unpaid bills.

Her gaze traveled to her wallet where she had dropped it on the back of the toilet. Denied credit cards.

A sense of foreboding filled her as she went back to the bedroom and turned on his laptop. She could hear James moving around downstairs, just as restless and unwilling to sleep as she was.

She logged onto her bank's website. Her heart skipped a beat at the account totals.

Two dollars and fifty-three cents.

Impossible.

She should have had hundreds in checking and thousands more in savings. But it was all gone. There were errors where her credit card statements should have shown.

Somehow, she knew if she called the bank, they would have her on record as having made the withdrawals.

"Burning my home wasn't enough?" she whispered.

Of course not. Mr. Black didn't do things halfway.

She stared blankly at a pair of loafers James had left behind. Without money or her home, all she had left was her car—and she could imagine waking up the next morning to find that stolen, too. The only clothes she had were exercise gear, which was now covered in dirt and debris, and some tattered sweats. Besides that, her total assets amounted to two dollars and fifty-three cents and a pair of falchions locked in a gun safe.

No money. No house. No job.

She dialed a number on her cell phone before she realized she made the decision.

"That didn't take long," purred the Night Hag. That hard, ancient voice gave Elise chills.

"I've changed my mind."

"And why is that?"

"It doesn't matter. But if I'm going to work for you, I need a salary. Money isn't a problem for you. I know, I've seen your books. You own all the demon businesses in the city."

A snort. "Greedy, hmm?"

"The bills don't pay themselves."

"And everybody has a price. Apparently I've found yours." The demand didn't seem to anger the Night Hag. If anything, she sounded appreciative. "Consider yourself salaried. But if I'm bleeding money for you, I'll expect you to earn it. And I need a commitment."

Elise braced herself. "I know."

"Excellent."

She heard a *snap* on the other side of the line.

Something whip-cracked through the air, something intangible that reeked of ozone, and Elise felt a hot sting on her shoulder. She pulled down the strap of her shirt and twisted around to peer at the shoulder blade. A brand the size of a penny had appeared, comprised of eight curling lines inside a circle. Blood trickled down her back.

She was marked—just like any demon in the service of a master.

"My witch will be visiting soon. Can't wait to get started."

The Night Hag chuckled as she hung up.

Part 3: Loyalty

MAY 1999

SHORTLY after meeting with Mr. Black at the Pledger Bistro, Elise told James she needed to see a doctor.

"Have you been injured?" he asked, propping his head up on an arm. James was stretched out on the floor, paralyzed by early summer heat in a hotel room that had no air conditioner.

Elise tossed a knife with a long, slender blade back and forth between her hands. She had just trimmed her hair to an inch short again, and reddish curls stuck to her gloves.

"No."

"It's not going to be easy to see a doctor. We don't have insurance. We don't have *money*."

"It's important," she said, and her strange tone of voice made him give her a second look. Elise was serious. "I need to see a—an obstetrician."

He almost choked. "Are you pregnant?"

"No. Mr. Black said girl kopides are unusual, and I was thinking…" Elise was so stiff that she might have acquired spontaneous rigor mortis. "I've never had a…" She stuttered. Stopped. Tried again. "I've never had a period."

A knot inside of him relaxed. "Ah. In that case, you want a—uh, a gynecologist. I've told you that I danced with a professional ballet company as a teenager, didn't I?"

The rapid change in subject made her blink.

"No."

"For three years. Between the stress of touring and low body fat, most of my female counterparts were like you. They didn't…you know. In any

267

case, they were healthy. It's nothing to worry about."

She folded her arms. "I'm going to see someone."

And that was that.

Finding "someone" was easier than expected. There were few doctors who knew anything about kopides, but a phone call to his former coven gave him the number of a nearby practice owned by witches. An appointment was arranged for the next week. The doctor was excited to see one of the only female kopides.

Which was how James ended up with the world's greatest demon hunter in a waiting room decorated with posters of babies.

Elise kept trying to draw her knife. He cleared his throat to remind her to stop. He wished he could have kept her from going to the gynecologist's office with concealed weapons, but he had no control over her—much less her decisions—and she arrived armed in the same way she might while facing a pack of werewolves.

After ten minutes of waiting, and several attempts at pulling a knife on the office staff, he whispered, "The pregnant women aren't going to attack you."

She glared at him. Her cheeks were red.

A nurse came into the waiting room. "Elise Kavanagh," she called.

Elise hesitated by the chair. "Come with me," she whispered to James. Her arms were locked at her sides.

"I don't think they'll let me. I'm not—"

She shifted on her feet, staring at the potted plant furiously as though she could set fire to it with her gaze. "Please." James could tell it pained her to ask. The tendons in her neck were rigid.

She was scared. Elise was *scared*.

Up until that moment, he had never seen her as anything but cold and detached—or, occasionally, furious and blood-thirsty. Yet being subjected to a physical examination petrified her. He couldn't see how his presence would help. She made it clear she didn't trust him. On most days, he thought she didn't even like him.

"Elise," the nurse called again.

Her cheeks burned red.

"Okay," he replied. What else could he say?

They walked into the back together.

The nurse, whose name tag said "Laura," took Elise's height, weight, and blood pressure, asked her to leave a urine sample in the bathroom, then led them into an exam room with a window overlooking the city.

Laura pulled sheets out of a drawer and began setting tools on a wheeled tray. Elise stood by the bed and glared at the room like she was awaiting execution.

"And you are?" the nurse prompted James.

Even though the doctors in the practice were witches, he wasn't sure what the rest of the staff knew, so he didn't try to explain the unusual relationship between a kopis and witch. "I'm her boyfriend."

Whatever Laura thought of a teenage girl dating an obviously older man, she kept it to herself. "I'm going to ask you some personal questions, Elise. Would you like your boyfriend to leave the room?"

She shook her head.

Laura asked about her health and her family's history. She asked about alcohol and drugs, too. When she asked if Elise was sexually active, she shook her head again, and the nurse gave her a skeptical look. She made a note on the clipboard.

"You'll need to strip down, but keep your socks on. It's chilly in here. This one is a vest," she told Elise, setting one folded sheet on the counter, "and this one is a blanket to cover your hips. Dr. Kingsley will be right in."

She shut the door behind her. Elise picked up the vest. It was made of flimsy blue paper.

James studied the city through the window while she changed. He waited to face her again until the paper on the bed crinkled and Elise said, "Okay." She had pulled extra sheets out of the drawer to protect herself and left her gloves on. She looked frail and childlike on the raised bed, and stared mistrustfully at the waiting stirrups.

"I can leave," he said.

She shook her head again.

They waited together without speaking. James shifted her clothes to the counter, careful to leave her knives concealed, and took the chair by the bed.

When the door opened again, a short man with a bushy beard entered with Elise's chart. He ignored James. "So you're the female kopis," said Dr. Kingsley. "Excellent! I'd say that I've wanted to examine one of your type, but that would sound odd, wouldn't it? The good news is that your pregnancy test came back negative. Can't imagine a pregnant demon hunter, eh?"

Elise looked horrified.

"Let's see what we can find. Lay back and slide to the end of the bed."

He positioned the stirrups and rolled his stool to sit between them. She moved stiffly, settling back against the bed with jerky motions. She

269

was shaking.

"James," she said.

Elise held out a hand. It took him a moment to realize what she was asking, but then he took it and squeezed her fingers.

She didn't let go for the entire examination.

Elise retrieved the bowl that evening.

She didn't want to stay at the hotel with James. It was too hard to face him. On the other hand, finding Mr. Black again was easy. She stood on a street corner until his slender, whip-like aspis appeared on the other side.

She walked to a bakery and looked in the window. His reflection appeared behind hers.

"I'll do it," she said, pretending to study green apple cupcakes. The sight of food made her stomach give a hard cramp, like it was trying to digest itself.

A thick roll of paper was pressed into her hand. By the time she turned around, Alain was gone.

He had given her a note wrapped around a roll of money. She didn't need to count the bills to know that she could buy all the cupcakes in the bakery if she wanted. Elise sat on a bench to read the note while savoring a flaky, buttery croissant.

So glad you came around to my way of thinking. Here's where you can find the bowl. See you tonight.

Numbers were written at the bottom. Coordinates.

She sneaked into the motel where James was showering, grabbed her hiking boots, and stuffed most of the money into the bottom of her backpack. The sound of water traveling through the pipes shut off. She left a handful of twenties on his pillow, tucked her spine sheath and swords under one arm, and slipped out the door.

Using a map from a corner gas station, she pinpointed the coordinates Mr. Black had given her. They were centered on grassy plains bisected by freeways, where great native civilizations had once occupied the land— civilizations that had since been destroyed—and left nothing behind but pottery fragments and earthen mounds.

Elise took a cab to the edge of town. There were no exits from the freeway directly to the mounds, so she climbed over a concrete barrier and walked along the rolling hills.

Cars whispered along the overpass. An occasional horn honked. She moved deeper into the hills without worrying anyone would see. The moon was nothing more than a yellow sliver glowing between wisps of clouds.

The grass grew long and lush as she moved into a valley between mounds. Dew misted on her bare legs. Mud slurped under her soles.

She had brought the map with her, but there wasn't enough light to make out the place she had marked. It didn't matter. A strange quiet settled over her as she approached the eastern mound. It pressed inside her skull like wool. She could tell she was getting close when she found signs of an archaeological dig: leveled ground, a few posted signs, strings stretched between stakes.

Elise hopped a low fence meant to keep tourists away from the excavation and beelined for bushes at the back that hadn't been cleared out yet. She pushed through the branches.

The hole she found was only a few inches narrower than her shoulders. It could have been mistaken for an animal's burrow that had been worn away by rain.

She grabbed fistfuls of mud and threw gobs of it over her shoulder. Once the hole was widened enough for her to fit in with the sheath on her back, she squirmed inside. Mud scraped against her shoulders, her hips. Elise dropped to the bottom of the hole just a few feet down and straightened.

Her vision adjusted to the darkness, but there was nothing to see. Roots dangled from the ceiling. Shards of rock pocked the uneven floor. It was small enough that she couldn't straighten fully. But the pressure inside her skull had worsened, and she knew she was in the right place.

Elise felt along the back wall. Her hand slipped into the damp soil, and her fingers met something hard.

Blowing her hair out of her face, she dug into the mud. There was smooth stone on the other side. She drew a sword and rapped the hilt against it. Hollow.

She drew back her arm and smashed it into the wall.

The stone crumbled. A few more strikes, and she made a hole. Light glowed on the other side, faint and gray, like early morning.

She returned the falchion to her spine and ripped clay bricks from their moorings. Once she removed enough of it, the wall fell apart on its own, and she soon had a hole as big as her last one. She squeezed inside.

That faint light didn't seem to come from any single source, but the chamber on the other end was obviously manmade. The walls and floor were chiseled, an old stone table stood in the corner, and there were engravings on the walls. A recession had been built into the stones at the opposite end of the room, just eight feet away. It was a different kind of

271

rock than everything else: white and smooth, rather than clay-colored. The platforms and etchings made it look like a monument or altar. And the bowl Mr. Black wanted was trapped inside of it by bars.

The bowl was smaller than she expected—barely any bigger than her fists. It looked mundane, dusty, and boring, but the way it vibrated in her veins told her it was ethereal, which meant it was none of those three things.

Elise tried to jiggle it free. It wouldn't budge.

She scanned the symbols surrounding it. A crucifix formed the center, surrounded by obscure symbols that most educated kopides would have realized were ethereal in origin. There was no other language like it, human or infernal. And no other kopis would have known the symbols were also a lock.

Elise looked at her hands. She wore thick leather gloves with a strap across the back, which she had recently shoplifted from a motorcycle shop.

James would tell her to leave. He would tell her to forget.

He would probably be right.

Her fingers shook as she ripped off the Velcro strap and removed the glove with her teeth, baring her hand to the dry air of the chamber.

Black lines marked her palm, like a freshly-inked tattoo that hadn't had time to heal. The skin was red and swollen around the edges. But Elise had never been under the needle of a tattoo artist, and she never would have chosen the design if she had. The marks didn't match the symbol on the altar, but it was close.

The stone vibrated to life when she stretched out her hand. Silver-blue light traced along the marks at the base.

Elise drew back. The vibrations slowed.

"God help me," she muttered. It was not a prayer. She never prayed.

She pressed her palm to the altar.

A strange singing filled her skull. The vibration vanished in an instant, and so did everything else—the room surrounding her, the stone under her hand, the darkness. A veil of heavy gray light pressed against her.

There was a face on the other side of the veil.

Elise...

That single word made her eardrums ache. The voice was great and terrible, tender and surprised.

She wrenched her hand free with a gasp.

And she was holding the bowl.

Elise blinked at her hands. She hadn't consciously moved the bars aside, but the bowl was no longer captive in the wall, and it was humming. It liked being held by her. There was no sign of breakage or shifting in the altar, so she shouldn't have been able to remove it.

She set the bowl on the ground and took a big step back to study the chamber. It didn't feel so empty anymore. Now the hollows looked like watching eyes, and spider webs swayed in the corner as if ruffled by a passing breeze.

She pulled her glove back on.

"I'm coming for you," she whispered, just to break the silence. "This is going to end."

Shucking her shirt, Elise wrapped the bowl so that none of the stone was exposed. Wearing nothing but a camisole was chilly, but it was better than feeling the ethereal artifact recognize her. It didn't hum so much when it was out of contact with her skin.

It was hard to climb the short, muddy slope to the surface again, but with enough grunting and wiggling, Elise emerged from the hill.

Three men were waiting for her at the top.

Two of them were standing. The other was kneeling with a gun aimed at the back of his skull. Elise probably shouldn't have been surprised to see the one on the ground was James. Alain Daladier's grip was steel on the pistol. Mr. Black stood in front of the others, smiling his most charming smile.

Her hands tensed on the bowl as she straightened. Elise was soaked in mud, and the slight breeze gave her chills. The odds weren't good. Not good at all. Mr. Black may have been old, but he would be fast. Elise didn't like her chances against him. It was an unpleasantly vulnerable position to be caught in.

"You made it," Mr. Black said in a warm voice, like a pleasant older uncle. He wore a fine white suit and leaned on a jeweled cane. "I'd be lying if I said I wasn't surprised, but you have impressed me mightily, young lady."

James was pale. "Elise—"

A nudge from the pistol cut him off.

"I'll take that now," Mr. Black said, stretching his hand out.

She didn't move. "The money."

"Surely you don't think I wouldn't make good on a deal?" He caught her glance toward James and feigned further shock, fluttering his hand at his breast. "Oh, my dear, I realize this must not look good. We spotted Mr. Faulkner trying to follow you underground. We were only concerned he

273

might have been trying to stop you. Don't you see? It was for your safety."

She considered the accusation. As persistent as James had been in following her around, he had never shown an inclination to hurt her. He was taking short, shallow breaths. Not injured. Just afraid. He didn't like having a gun aimed at him. Well, that was his fault for following her where he wasn't wanted.

"The money," Elise said again.

Mr. Black's smile widened with delight. "You don't find having your witch friend at gunpoint motivational? You surprise me again!"

"He's not my friend."

"Well, well. Then I suppose it doesn't matter if we shoot him. What do you think?"

"The money for the bowl."

"Cold, my dear. Very cold. I appreciate that."

Mr. Black gestured. Alain opened his jacket with his free hand, removed a piece of paper, and offered it to Elise. She hugged the bowl tight to her stomach as she stepped up to take it from him. James's features were drawn and grim.

The paper was another set of coordinates.

"I've hidden your money," Mr. Black said. "Couldn't risk having you take it from us without holding up your end of the deal, hmm? Now it appears that wouldn't have been necessary."

Elise thought back to the map. The coordinates weren't far.

"Goodbye," she said, more to James than the other men.

Then she tucked the bowl under her arm and started toward the lights of the freeway. When Mr. Black called after her, there was no good humor in his voice. "Where do you think you're going?"

"I don't see my money."

Alain moved in the corner of her eye. He was turning the gun on her. In a flash, she grabbed the pistol, slammed her hand into the joint of Alain's elbow, and kicked him to the ground. The bowl didn't even slip.

She aimed the gun at Mr. Black's face. Everyone froze.

He couldn't seem to work up a grin again. It flickered on his lips and was replaced by wary evaluation. Would she shoot him? "You want me to have the bowl as much as I do," he said in a low whisper that only she would be able to hear. "If you want me to kill Him."

"Yes. I also want my money."

He raised his voice. "Alain. Go get it."

The aspis got to his feet, glaring fire at Elise, but he obeyed without argument. He vanished down the hill.

James stood. His knees were wet and he was breathing hard. "You don't want to do that," he said, giving the bowl a look very much like the one he had given Alain's gun. He didn't seem much less nervous without a bullet aimed for his head. "You can still put it back."

Mr. Black wasn't sweating. "A deal's a deal, Mr. Faulkner. You know that better than anyone else."

"What do you know?" James asked, turning pale.

"I've done my research."

Before they could say anything else, Elise released the clip and offered the unloaded gun to Mr. Black. "When you do it, I want to be there," she said.

"Surprises again and again." He tucked the gun in his jacket with a scowl. It twisted his face into hard, frightening lines. "I don't think I like surprises."

Elise pocketed the clip. "I don't like being treated like I'm stupid."

Alain reappeared shortly holding a canvas bag that was almost as muddy as she was. At Elise's gesture, he handed it to James, who looked inside. "It seems to be more than enough," he said hesitantly, thumbing through a stack of money tied together with a rubber band. "But Elise, you shouldn't—"

She gave Alain the bowl. And just like that, Mr. Black was all smiles again. "Wonderful. We'll be in contact."

They walked away. James shook, as though fighting the urge to run after them. "Do you have any idea what they can do with that thing? Don't you realize what could happen?"

"Yes," she said simply.

He waited to speak again until both of the other men had gotten into their car, which was parked on the far end of the hill. The headlights receded into the distance. "I thought you were going to let him kill me."

She turned on him. "What's wrong with you? Why won't you leave me alone?"

"Excuse me?"

"You follow me everywhere. Always. Ever since Russia. There's no reason for it. Go home!" She flung out an arm, gesturing vaguely toward the horizon. "You're not the one who has to run and hide!"

"Your enemies are mine, Elise, and we're safer together than we are apart. You must realize this by now."

"Following me to get an ethereal artifact? That's safe?"

"Perhaps it wasn't the best-conceived plan," he muttered. "You can

275

hardly blame me. I was worried about you."

"Worried. About me."

"Is that so hard to believe?"

She opened her mouth. Closed it again. The breeze lifted, blowing the hair back from his face. James's expression was open and honest, as earnest as it had ever been, and she couldn't think of a response.

She turned to head back to the motel.

As always, he followed.

June 1999

Dr. Kingsley called several days later to say that he had the results of Elise's tests.

They met in his private office, which was decorated with hanging herbs and crystals. He shut the door and locked it behind them. "I don't want anyone to intrude. I haven't discussed your karyotype test with anyone else in the practice," the doctor explained as they sat. "I discovered something unusual."

"Is something wrong?" James asked.

"No, no. Nothing is technically 'wrong.' I had my theories about what could cause a female kopis, but... Well, the tests were informative."

"How so?"

"Some things are not surprising. First of all, you have a myostatin deficiency, which means you build muscle easily. That's an expected trait among kopides. What's more surprising is that you're completely androgen insensitive. Do you know what that means?" he asked. Elise shook her head. "Genetically, you have one X chromosome and one Y chromosome, like a man, but all the physical characteristics of a woman."

Elise's eyes widened. "I'm a man?"

"No. You're a woman with an intersex condition."

"I don't understand."

Neither did James. "Is that why she's never...?"

"You'll never menstruate because you don't have a uterus or ovaries, Miss Kavanagh. That means children aren't in your future, either. This explains so much about kopides." Dr. Kingsley rubbed his hands together, face bright with excitement. "We might want to consider surgically removing—"

Sudden motion cut him off. Elise shoved her chair back and stood, face red.

Her mouth opened, like she wanted to say something, but nothing came out. She gave James a helpless look before leaving the room without a word.

Dr. Kingsley blinked rapidly, as though trying to decide what might have upset his new favorite patient. "You couldn't have been more sensitive about that?" James asked.

"What do you mean?"

He had just told a teenage girl that she was not, strictly speaking, a teenage girl, and that she would never have children. And he didn't understand why that might be distressing.

James stood. "Thank you for your assistance. Forward the bill to my coven. I don't think we'll need further help."

"But there are other tests I want to run." The doctor moved in front of the door, preventing him from leaving. "Do you realize what this means? The impact this could have on our scientific understanding of supernatural phenomena? If we could just do exploratory surgery..."

Anger swelled in him. He grabbed the doctor's shirt in a fist and shoved their faces close together. James wasn't imposing, but he had a good six inches on the other man, and the temper to back it up. "We are done with your services."

James dropped him. Dr. Kingsley stumbled back, pale and shaking.

He followed Elise out of the office.

She wasn't waiting for him outside, so he decided not to search for her. Instead, he returned to their motel. Elise had used some of Mr. Black's money to buy food the night before, and there was actual fresh fruit on the table. He passed the time savoring an apple—the first produce he'd eaten in weeks that hadn't been half-rotten and dug from the trash.

Elise returned a few hours later. James didn't bother asking where she had been.

"Thank you. You aren't—I don't—" She bowed her head and cleared her throat. "I don't have anyone else. You didn't have to follow me to the mounds. And you didn't need to go to the doctor with me. So...thank you."

He felt a sudden, foreign burst of affection for her. "You're welcome. I'll always be here, you know. We're in this together now."

She leaned her head on his chest. He almost pushed her away until he realized she was hugging him rather than attacking him. James's hands hovered awkwardly over her shoulders. When several moments passed without Elise moving, he hugged her back.

James wondered what she thought of being unable to have children. It didn't seem right to ask.

A moment later, she stepped back. Her face was expressionless again.

"Well," Elise said. "Guess it's time to go kill Mr. Black."

Part 4: The New Job

Chapter 7

FIST connected with bag. Elise grunted. The chain rattled.

Her focus was narrowed on a worn square inch in the center of the punching bag. She struck again and again, feeling the shock all the way up to her shoulders as she rolled her entire body into each hit. The bag swung, and she darted to the side to keep from getting hit. Her chest rose and fell with heaving breaths. Her throat was still raw from breathing in smoke.

Elise had hung her old punching bag from a hook in the back room of Motion and Dance, where the coven usually held esbats. In a past life, it had been a garage, but it was also her personal gym in the year she lived with James. She hoped bringing it out for a beating would make her feel better. Now the bandages wrapped around her palms were soaked with sweat, her hair stuck to her neck, and her jogging bra was drenched. But it wasn't enough.

She leaned back and kicked. Even bare-footed, it was hard enough to make the chain groan and dust explode off the bag.

The door creaked. She spun, fists raised.

Anthony froze in the doorway.

"James said you were down here." He eased into the room and shut the door.

The sight of her boyfriend filled her with exhaustion. She had already spent hours being "interviewed" by the police, and hours more talking with James. She had no more energy for words.

She twisted and lashed out with a foot, hitting the bag again. When it swung back, she punched it once, twice, three times, loosing all her frustrated energy.

Anthony took position at the other side of the bag and held it for her. It was easier hitting it that way, but not as satisfying. She pounded it one more time before stopping. "What do you want?" she snapped. "You should be with Betty in the hospital."

"How can you ask me that? Our apartment burned, Elise. Almost everything is gone. I need answers."

She kicked the bag hard enough to make him take a step back. "I don't have anything for you."

"But you know who did it."

Elise nodded, rolling her shoulders out and digging her fingers into the muscle to try to release tension. She had healed from the bite wound delivered by James when he was possessed by Death's Hand, but it stiffened if she moved her arm too much. Anthony stepped forward like he was going to massage her. She stayed out of reach.

He dropped his hands. "Come on. I've been hunting with you. We killed giant spiders together. If you're trying to protect me—"

"I'm not."

"Then who is it? Let's get him. Let's *kill* him. He's jacked up our lives and we owe somebody serious pain!"

The thought of Anthony going after Mr. Black was laughable. Alain would shoot him on sight. "Go help James carry everything upstairs," Elise said, even though there was little to move. Not much had survived the fire.

"Let me help you. I'm almost as strong as you are. I have a shotgun. We can do this together."

"No. Drop it."

But he didn't relent. "Are you going after him today? Are you going to—?"

"Anthony," she interrupted. "Shut the hell up."

His mouth clapped shut. "You would take James along. Wouldn't you?"

She went back to abusing the punching bag.

Elise shut him out, shut the room out, shut out all her unpleasant thoughts of empty bank accounts and terminated contracts and burned buildings. All she felt was fury. Retribution. The impact of knuckles against leather.

280

After a minute of silent watching, Anthony left.

Her cell phone rang. It vibrated on the table by the mirrors hard enough to travel toward the edge. She patted the sweat from her chest with a towel as she picked it up. The phone didn't display a number, but she wasn't surprised when David Nicholas was on the other end.

"Your first job's tonight," he said.

She waited to catch her breath before responding. "Don't tell me I have to work with you."

"Ha. The Night Hag says I'm not allowed near you. She thinks one of us will die."

"She's sharp."

"As a fucking tack," David Nicholas said. "I'm on babysitting duty tonight anyway. Watching every step your witchy friend takes, keeping assassins away, you know how it is. His girlfriend is hot. Perfect tits. Bet you'd like to know what they were doing last night."

Elise didn't take the bait. "What's the plan?"

"Hell if I know. Thom's getting you from your *charming* new apartment at six."

David Nicholas knew she wasn't living at the old duplex anymore. It wasn't surprising, since they had to be watching closely to project James, but it was unsettling to realize she hadn't detected anyone watching them. Somehow, that still didn't unsettle her much as the thought of working with Thom.

"Tell me what you know about Thom," Elise said.

The nightmare snorted. "Sometimes it's better not to know things, and let me tell you, it's better not to know *anything* about that guy. Word of advice? Don't pull your spunky bullshit with him. He's the only person I know more unhinged than you are."

He hung up.

A black SUV pulled into the parking lot the instant Elise's cell phone clock turned to six. She met Thom downstairs.

If she thought the stuffy heat inside the apartment was bad, it was nothing compared to the scalding heat outside. The sun only touched the top of the mountains, but even approaching sunset didn't cool the desert. The pavement rippled.

Thom stepped out of the car, and she got her first good look at him in the sunlight. He was dressed elegantly in a black silk shirt and slacks with a snug leather choker. His skin was copper-brown—darker than she recalled—and his silken black hair was knotted in a ponytail that almost reached his hips.

The witch was so beautiful that she caught herself staring. She *never* stared at hot guys. That was Betty's job.

He ambled toward her, thumbs hooked in his belt loops. As he drew closer, she saw the slacks were made of leather. He didn't seem affected by the heat. "Where are we going?" Elise asked, moving for the SUV. He stepped in her way. She frowned. "What are you doing? Let's go."

"I want to see the studio." But he was looking at her, not the building.

She didn't waver. Elise was all too aware that her uncomfortable alliance with the Night Hag didn't change the fact they were inherently enemies—nor did she harbor the illusion that Thom was under anyone's control but his own.

"You can't get inside. Wards."

"I sense that." Thom circled her. His gaze was not sexual, but analytical. "That outfit will not suffice. Put on a dress." Elise arched an eyebrow. "We are visiting one of the overlord's contacts to gather intelligence about Mr. Black. She's having a formal event tonight. Your current clothing is insufficient."

"I don't fight in dresses," she said. "Or formal shoes, for that matter."

"Then you cannot go to this event."

"Fine. Intelligence won't help us against Mr. Black anyway. It would be much faster if the Night Hag gave me a small army and let me kill him."

Thom's folded his arms. "I'm sure it would, but this is what she has ordered us to do."

The fresh brand on her shoulder itched as though to remind her of the agreement. Scratching it only made the pain worse. She sighed. "Fine. We can do it her way."

"Then you must change your outfit."

The idea of playing by the Night Hag's rules grated at her, but she had already made her decision when she let herself be branded. "Two minutes," she finally said.

Thom nodded.

Even before the fire, Elise didn't have formal clothing (much to Betty's dismay). She never had a reason to wear the quintessential "little black dress." She did, however, have a new red sundress, which she had purchased from a drugstore with one of her last ten dollar bills. It was the only way to survive the summer heat in Nevada. She borrowed a few pieces of Betty's jewelry that had survived the fire and twisted her hair into a loose bun to make it fancier. There was nothing to be done about her plain black gloves, or her exposed scars.

The witch sneered at her feet when she came downstairs. "Sandals."

"My house was burned down. This is what I have."

He dropped the subject, which was as close to acceptance as she expected to get.

The interior of Thom's SUV was plush leather, and it scorched the back of her knees when she sat down. She turned on his air conditioning. He had been driving with the windows rolled up and the fan turned off.

Thom drove like traffic laws didn't exist. He sliced between lanes and blew past every car on the road. Elise studied his profile while his attention was on his driving. Something about the curve of his lips and chin reminded her of ancient statues.

"Where are you from?" she asked.

"Before this, I was in New York City."

"That's not what I meant. Where are you from originally?"

"Originally." Thom rolled the word over his tongue. "I was born in a place currently known as Myanmar."

He didn't look very Asian. In fact, she couldn't have pinned a single ethnicity upon him if she tried. Elise had been all over the world and never seen anyone with his strange mix of features: full lips, sloped nose, wide eyes, chiseled jaw. It was as though each part of his face had been deliberately selected to be as ambiguous as possible.

"Tell me why a witch from Myanmar is working for the Night Hag."

Thom gave an elegant shrug. "It's something to do."

The air grew thick with tension after his seemingly casual response. He watched her from the corner of his eye. It only grew worse as they drove further from the studio. He hadn't done anything to indicate aggression, but the way he looked at her without looking made her skin crawl. And he resonated in her skull like a cracked bell struck by a steel mallet.

She wished the Night Hag had sent David Nicholas instead.

"You are familiar with prophecies," he said, breaking the silence.

"I don't believe in them."

"Elaborate."

They entered the twisting roads in the foothills, and he accelerated instead of slowing down. Elise put on her seatbelt. "By the Treaty of Dis, only humans have the gift of prophecy. They also only see what happens on this earthen plane. That makes them uselessly incomplete."

"True. But you would believe if a prophet could see more."

"That's not possible."

"A man named Benjamin Flynn has foretold the end of the world," Thom said as mildly as though he was sharing a weather report with her.

"That's far from the first time that's been seen." She stared out the window at the passing trees. "A kopis will take care of it. One of us always does."

"So far."

Her fingers twitched at the knife. "Why are you telling me?"

"Benjamin Flynn's prophesies are being logged. There are three volumes to date. I have read them." She caught a glimpse of his gaze reflected in the mirror. His irises were almost black. "The end of the world will be willfully brought about by a kopis. A kopis with magic."

"He's lying."

"Perhaps."

His voice curled around her as though it had substance. She suppressed a shudder.

Elise waited for him to say more, but he didn't speak again until they reached a gated neighborhood at the base of the mountain. He stopped in front of a manor sheltered by so many pine trees that they cast twilight over the property.

She scanned the grounds as Thom rolled down his window. Dozens of cars were parked in front, and she thought she could see valets. There were any number of places armed guards could hide. The ridge would be perfect for snipers, too. But the people she feared wouldn't attack like that. She was much more concerned about magical traps. If only James had been there to sense them.

Thom pushed the intercom button. A woman's voice responded. "Yes?"

His expression didn't change, but his voice became lively and friendly. Almost flirtatious. "Hello! This is Thomas Norrel. I'm here for the party with Ms. Redmond."

"A moment, please."

It fell silent and he sat back.

"Multiple personality disorder?" Elise asked.

The gate opened. Thom pulled forward. "I behave as is prudent for the situation at hand."

She tensed as they rolled onto Portia Redmond's property. People could have been hiding anywhere, watching her unseen. She hated being unable to detect wards. She wished for James again—working without

284

him was like missing one of her hands.

"What do you feel, Thom?" she asked. He gave her a curious look. "This place. Are there any traps? Charms? Spells?"

"That's irrelevant."

Thom stopped at the end of the circular driveway. He got out, handed the keys to an attractive teenage boy with long hair, and then opened the door for Elise. He offered a pale hand to her. Revulsion knotted in her gut.

"Come," he said when she didn't move.

Elise got out on her own and straightened her dress so it fell naturally over the concealed knife. She studied the entrance to the house as they approached. Tiny markings were carved over the doorway. There were crystals in a ceramic bowl at the corner of her porch. A decorative arrangement of flowers was mixed with sprigs of herbs. Portia definitely had a witch on staff. Her skin tingled as she crossed the threshold.

The sounds of laughter drifted through the entryway. Everything was furnished with dark wood and gold, and offset by velvet drapes the color of pine. A haze hung over the room, like dinner had burned in the oven.

"This way, sweetheart," Thom said. He led her to the den.

A man in a black suit played an antique piano in the corner. A double staircase swept around either side of the room, plush red couches had been placed underneath, and hookahs were set on low tables surrounded by pillows so people could lounge on the floor while smoking. They passed what looked like sparkling sugar cubes between them.

She edged around the room, trying to watch everyone at once. The hookah didn't concern her, but the cubes did. Elise had seen lethe parties before. It was a powerful drug designed to give a high to creatures whose bodies ignored most intoxicants—a huge rush for demons, and often fatal for humans.

And everyone on the floor was human. Judging by their dress, they were businessmen and politicians. Older people. Beautiful people. People who might die if they dropped one too many lethe.

"Drink?"

Elise jerked away from the waitress she hadn't seen approach. She shook her head.

The waitress offered it to Thom instead, who plucked a glass off the tray. Each of them was filled with an unidentifiable green liquid. "Thank you. Tell me, where is the hostess?"

She pointed.

Portia Jericho sat stiffly on one of the red couches with a drink, a

285

polite smile, and a man with a half-unbuttoned shirt hanging off her shoulder. She saw Thom approach and blanched. "I didn't invite you."

"Let's go somewhere private, Portia," Thom said in a suave and husky voice. He winked. Elise's jaw clenched. "Let me assure you, I'll only steal this beautiful creature for a few moments."

"I suppose I don't have a choice," Portia said.

She disentangled herself from the couch and smoothed shaking hands down her blouse. Elise kept an eye on the other alcoves, but nobody was sober enough to move, much less attack.

Portia led them upstairs to an office with a claw-footed desk and turned on a single lamp.

Elise gave the room a quick sweep. There were more enchanted stones by the window, more engravings, and more herbs disguised as floral arrangements. Passive defenses. She positioned herself in the corner so she could watch the door and window simultaneously.

"What do you want this time?" Portia asked, lowering herself into the chair behind the desk. Her hands were in constant motion—adjusting her hair, tugging on the neck of her shirt to hide her considerable cleavage, smoothing down her slacks. "And who are you supposed to be?"

It took Elise a moment to realize Portia was speaking to her.

"This is Elise Kavanagh," Thom said. He wasn't flirty anymore. His changes in mood were fast enough to give her whiplash. "She was once the greatest kopis, but now she is a lapdog of the Night Hag like the rest of us."

She bristled. "Excuse me?"

"Greatest? What made you the greatest?" Portia asked.

Elise opened her mouth, but Thom spoke again before she could get anything out. "They say she's killed a dozen angels."

Portia's face went slack, and she sagged against the back of her chair as if all the strength had suddenly drained from her. "Oh thank *God*," she whispered. Elise flinched. "Then you must have been hired to kill Mr. Black, haven't you? You have to be fast. He's got an army, and he's moving as we speak."

"Indeed. We need your information to take action."

"But I'm the only one who knows anything. If you stop the shipment, he'll know who betrayed him."

"A shipment of what, exactly?" Thom asked.

She fidgeted. "How should I know? Guns? I've given him a truck and a man to drive it. That's it. I'm not privy to his plans."

"Where is this truck going?"

"Thom—the Night Hag—"

He loomed over the desk. He wasn't much taller than Elise, but he suddenly seemed to fill the room. "Tell me."

Portia's lips trembled as she opened a desk drawer, pulled out a map, and began drawing lines. "Here. They're coming from a port in Long Beach and going to a temporary depot. It's been set up in a lake bed… there." Her fingers clutched the map tight. "Giving this to you could mean my death."

"Life is a fleeting illusion. Regardless, Mr. Black is not your only danger."

She whispered a prayer as she let go of the map.

At a glance from Thom, Elise stepped forward to take it. She couldn't find any pity within herself. A woman who knowingly dealt with rogue kopides and demonic overlords was no victim.

"Be fast," Portia whispered. "Please. For everyone's sake."

Elise stepped back. Thom opened the door.

"Enjoy your party," he said.

Portia didn't follow them onto the balcony overlooking the lethe party. As soon as the door swung shut, Elise turned on him. "What was the point of that? You didn't need me to help collect information. She's scared shitless. You could have—"

"Silence. Tell me what you see."

She frowned. "Rich people on drugs."

"And?"

Elise gave the room a second look. It was hard to make anything out through the haze of tobacco and lethe beside the occasional flash of a glowing cube, like the flare of a firework. Then a glint of metal caught her eye, and she realized one of the men on the arm of a wealthy socialite was wearing a shackle. It was a bewitched shackle, with no visible chains, but a shackle nonetheless. There was a glimmer in the corner of her eye, a tugging at the back of her neck.

"Magic," she murmured. "That's magic, isn't it?"

Thom leaned over her shoulder, cheek brushing hers. His body was warm at her back. "Why would a kopis sense magic?"

She didn't think he expected an answer, so she didn't try to give one. Once Elise saw the magic around the shackle, she saw it elsewhere, too—twinkling on a woman's earring, haloed around the head of a gray-haired man, on several other wrists. They weren't all in the form of bracelets. Some were necklaces. One was an anklet.

The bound ones weren't smiling, as the others were. All of them had

287

pale blue eyes that were almost silver. And the resemblance didn't end there. Though none had hair or skin of quite the same shade, they all looked similar to the degree that cousins looked similar. Smooth-faced, androgynous, ageless.

None of them were human.

Elise gripped the railing. "Angels," she said, her voice so soft she thought Thom wouldn't hear.

Fingers grazed the back of her neck. "Look closer."

It was like a fog lifted from her mind. She could suddenly sense them the same way she sensed demons, and what was more, she could *see* them. Ghostly stubs glowed at their scapulas. Their wings had been severed, and someone was hiding it. They were enslaved.

"Now you know why I brought you to this party. You had to see— and be seen. Mr. Black will know the sword has come into play."

"He's not the only one who will know. Damn it, Thom, you never should have brought me here."

Even though she whispered, her voice caught the attention of an angel. Recognition sparked between them.

One by one, the slaves fell silent, and a dozen pairs of eyes fixed on her.

Their lips moved in unison to mouth a single word with three syllables. She didn't hear them, but she knew what word it was, and what it meant.

"This was a mistake," Elise said.

"A calculated risk." His hand curled around her wrist. "And now we must run."

Her eyes lifted to the opposite balcony. A gaunt man with shaggy brown hair stood on the other side, and hatred carved furrows into his sagging face. The years hadn't been kind to Alain Daladier. He looked like hell.

Elise retreated into the shadows, but it was too late to hide. He reached into his jacket.

Thom flashed down the stairs, and she ran after him.

A gunshot rang out above them. A bullet smacked into the railing. Wood shattered.

The angels didn't react, but the humans did. Bleary eyes stared around for the source of the gunshot. Someone cried out in surprise as Elise shoved through the room. Her knee bumped a table and sent the hookah crashing to the ground. A man tumbled off his pillow, and she jumped over him.

Still, the angels didn't move. Their eyes tracked her across the room.

Another gunshot cracked like thunder. It shattered a wall sconce as Elise passed it, raining glass into her hair.

Thom ran like the wind blew, shoving open the front door and disappearing into the night. Elise flung herself around the side of the door, drew her knife, and dropped into a crouch.

Her heart wasn't even beating hard. She felt calm, focused, like she was floating apart from her own body.

People screamed inside. She waited.

Footsteps pounded through the entryway. Her fist tightened on the dagger.

Alain took two steps out the door, and Elise jumped on his back, bringing her arm around his throat. His skeletal body buckled under hers. He gave a strangled grunt as they fell down the steps and hit the driveway face-first, tossing her off his back.

She rolled. Got to her feet. Pressed the knife to his belly.

Cold metal pressed into her temple before she could stab.

Alain bared his teeth in a vicious growl as he held the gun to her skull. "*Va te faire foutre,*" he spat, and she felt his arm tense as he squeezed the trigger.

Elise dropped.

The gunshot blasted over her head and shattered her hearing into a thousand shards of glass. The ringing almost muted Alain's shout.

Thom had appeared, shoving the wrist holding the gun so it aimed skyward. Another shot flashed and filled the air with the metallic tang of gunpowder. Thom twisted Alain's arm around, smashed it into his knee, and forced him to drop the gun.

Even while grappling, Thom looked peaceful. Almost amused.

He shoved Alain to the ground and planted a foot in his chest. Elise grabbed the gun and dropped the magazine.

Mr. Black's aspis looked so much older than he had ten years before. There were burn scars on his neck, purple spots on the backs of his hands, and scruffy white stubble on his jaw. But some things didn't change. His mouth twisted when Elise came to stand over him.

"You burned my office," she said, barely able to hear her own voice over the ringing in her skull. "You stole all my money!"

His mouth moved with a response. She was sure it would have been scathing if she could have heard it.

And then there was suddenly a second gun in his hand.

This time, Elise moved faster than Thom. She threw herself out of the way, instinctively shielding her face with her arms—though there was little that could do about a bullet aimed at her skull.

The bullet hit Thom. He fell to the lawn.

Alain scrambled to his feet and vanished into the trees.

Elise was a heartbeat behind him. She crashed into the edge of the forest.

His back darted between the tree trunks. Branches scraped against Elise's bare legs. Her strappy sandals caught on a bush, wrenched her ankle to the side, and sent her stumbling. "Shit!"

Her knees smashed against rocks. Pine needles stabbed into her gloves. She righted herself, staggering around a tree to pick up the knife she dropped. By the time she found it, it was too late—the night was dark and complete, and Alain Daladier had vanished.

Elise swore as she ripped the shoes off her feet and flung them into the night.

She limped back to the lawn after a few more minutes of searching, working her jaw around to clear her ringing skull. Kopides had improved healing in comparison to other humans, but the whine in her ears didn't make her optimistic about her ability to hear that pitch ever again.

Thom met her at the end of the driveway. His hair was still in a neat ponytail. There wasn't so much as a single grass stain or a drop of blood on his tidy clothes. "You're alive," Elise said, a little disappointed. "Where did he hit you?"

"You must be confused. I wasn't shot."

She frowned. "But you fell."

"Perhaps I was surprised," Thom said. He kept one eye on the house as though waiting for another attack. "Come. We must hurry to use our brief advantage. If Mr. Black and Alain realize what we've learned, their plans will surely change."

He set a swift pace to the SUV, which was parked with other cars at the side of the house. Elise lengthened her stride to keep up with him even though it made her ankle twinge. "The Night Hag should send someone to protect Portia. When Mr. Black finds out—"

"She's not your concern."

The fluttering of curtains caught her attention, and Elise faltered mid-step.

Angels watched through the windows. They had lined up along the bottom floor shoulder-to-shoulder, silent and calm, and every one of those pale blue eyes was fixed on her. Or, to be more specific, her gloved hands.

Waiting. Expectant.

"Yeah," she muttered. "Fuck you guys, too."

Chapter 8

BETTY DOZED IN a drugged haze. Pain kept her on the edge of consciousness. The saline drip was cool where they had taped it against the inside of her arm. The bed hissed and swelled as the mattress inflated, and then sighed as it deflated again. The machines by her head occasionally beeped.

She drifted through dreams of fire and smoke. Occasionally, a nurse would wake her up, but she never opened her eyes. It was too hard. It felt like all the moisture had been sucked from her eyeballs.

A dry cough made her chest hitch. Her fingers twitched for the nurse call button.

Morphine. Her bag had run empty, and she could feel it wearing off.

Metal rattled, and a sliver of light fell on her face. Betty finally peeled open her eyelids. Someone was moving around the foot of her bed, but she couldn't tell who had come to torment her with more diagnostics in the middle of night.

"What time is it?" she rasped.

Footsteps tracked past the sink. Cabinets opened and closed.

She let her eyelids slide shut again.

"Stephanie—Dr. Whyte—said no more tests until morning. I'm resting 'under sedation.' Supposedly," Betty said. Her irritated throat tickled. Another cough. She stretched a hand toward a glass of water, but couldn't reach. "I'm leaving in a few hours. All I want is sleep and more painkillers and no more shots in my ass."

Plastic crinkled, and then the door to the hallway closed, leaving the room in darkness.

Betty sighed in relief. It burned all the way down her chest.

But the visitor hadn't left. The curtain closed around her, and someone stepped up with a spare pillow from the wardrobe by the window.

Her fingers fell on the remote. She clicked on the overhead light.

The person at her bedside wasn't any of the nurses who paraded through in the last day, though she wore scrubs patterned with red geometric shapes. She was silken-haired with windblown features and delicate hands, which were wrapped around the pillow. Her pupils didn't dilate at the sudden light.

She was sober enough that the strange gaze struck a chord. "You're not here with morphine...are you?"

The nurse lifted her arms.

Betty realized what was about to happen an instant before the pillow mashed against her face and cut off her air supply. Her chest hitched as her lungs struggled to expand, but there was nothing to fill them.

She tried to scream. It came out as a muffled squeal.

The nurse pressed harder. Betty fumbled for the nurse call button and knocked the remote off the bed. Even though she had a full breath of air, sudden adrenaline killed all rationality.

She beat against the arms pinning her down. They felt doughy, boneless, but somehow as immobile as steel. Her hazy head grew thicker. Her pulse pounded in her temples. White noise roared through her ears.

The mattress inflated around her and deflated again.

Betty felt oblivion creeping up on her as her oxygen ran out. If it took her, she didn't think she would ever wake again.

She tried harder to fight, but her arms were heavy and weak. Betty's blood grew sluggish. Her limbs went limp. She screamed and screamed on the inside, but it didn't make a difference—and soon, even that grew faint.

This never would have happened to Elise.

"Hey—*hey*! What are you doing?"

And all that weight was suddenly gone.

Betty shoved the pillow off her face. Color rushed into her vision with a huge gasp of air. She gripped her chest in both hands, making the IV twist in her vein. *Oh God, that hurt.*

Black stars cleared from her vision. The nurse had plastered her back on the wall between two cabinets, and Betty realized with a jolt that her feet weren't on the ground. She was halfway to the ceiling like a bug on a window.

Anthony lunged for her. The nurse scrambled higher on the wall with jerky motions, then leaped and landed behind him.

He spun, swinging a hard right hook. His fist connected with the nurse's jaw.

Her head snapped off.

Betty shrieked, hands flying to her mouth. The nurse's body collapsed like an empty skin suit, and Anthony hollered as he jumped back. "What the *fuck*?"

The head rolled under the cabinet. Empty eyes glimmered at them.

A bulge shifted inside the body, like a balloon inflating inside what used to be the belly, and Anthony grabbed the chair from the bedside. He lifted it over his head and brought it crashing down on the pile of scrubs.

Something squealed and popped. Black fluid gushed out the neck hole.

"Oh, Jesus fucking Christ!" He smashed the chair on it again, and again. And then he slammed his booted foot into it for good measure.

Then he stepped back, shielding Betty with his body, and held the chair in front of him like a lion tamer. But the body didn't move again. He dropped the chair and fell into it, face pale.

"Are you okay?" Anthony asked. He was surprisingly calm, considering he had just decapitated an evil assassin nurse.

"Someone just tried to kill me," gasped Betty. The truth of it sank in, and tremors shuddered through her entire body. "Oh my *God* someone just tried to *kill me*! Why would someone want to kill *me*? I'm just a—I mean—"

"Hey, relax, it's okay."

Betty leaned forward to grab his shirt in both hands, dragging his face close to hers. "You don't get it! Somebody wants to *kill me*!"

"I heard you the first six times. Take a deep breath and lay back before you hurt yourself."

She shook him. "Don't you try to act like this isn't a big deal!"

Anthony gently disengaged her fingers from his shirt. "I *know* it's a big deal, but it *is* okay because they didn't succeed. You're alive. All right?"

"No! Not all right!"

The door opened. Anthony shifted his chair on top of the flesh pile on the floor as a man stepped into the room. Betty saw scrubs and shrieked.

"What's going on?" asked the nurse. He had brown eyes, three chins, and greasy skin. Just like a human should. Totally normal. The empty, rubbery arm of the body was still visible, so Anthony kicked it under the bed.

"Night terrors," he said.

"I thought I heard something fall."

"Nope," Anthony said, his voice an octave too high. "Just night terrors." He plastered a grin on his face. Betty followed suit.

The nurse obviously didn't believe them, but seemed too tired to push it. "Try to keep it down. People in the ward are sleeping."

"I want to check out," Betty said.

"It's after midnight."

"Yeah, but I'm ready to go now. I'm feeling much better!" She was certain her grin must have been manic and ridiculous. "This hospital sure is great!"

He looked dubious. "Let me go talk to the doctor."

The nurse left. Anthony and Betty both sagged.

"I'll call Elise," he said.

Betty snorted. It hurt her raw nasal passage. "Yeah. Obviously."

Anthony half-carried Betty up the stairs to the apartment above Motion and Dance. She was still too woozy from the leftover morphine to navigate the steps herself.

"I must be important," she said again. "They don't try to kill the unimportant people."

He rolled his eyes. "You are very important."

"Maybe I've scared someone. You know, I've been working on my magic." She wiggled her fingers at him, like she was pretending to shoot lightning from her fingertips. "Oh yeah. Bet someone caught wind that there's a powerful new player in town. Wicked witch of the west. Protégé to James Faulkner, the greatest aspis in the world."

"You're about as wicked as a ball of yarn," Anthony said. He knocked on the door and propped Betty against the railing to wait.

"A ball of yarn who can light a candle *with her brain*."

"I thought you inhaled too much smoke to speak."

Betty stuck her tongue out. "Sure, you're not afraid now, but just wait. Candles today. Whole cities tomorrow."

Elise opened the door. She took one look at them and went rigid. "Get in," she said, grabbing Betty's arm to pull her inside.

"I'll be right back," Anthony said.

He ran downstairs and grabbed the trash bag out of his trunk. Sneaking a boneless corpse out of a hospital had been easy at two in the morning. Getting Betty out had been harder. Finding someone to disconnect her from the IV had taken an hour, and Anthony kept expecting another creepy flesh-sack to attack in the meantime.

The body in the bag had begun to smell on the ride home, and now the entire Jeep reeked of sulfur and rot. His hands slipped on the plastic when he grabbed it.

"Oh man," he groaned. Some of the black fluids had eaten holes in the bag. His skin tingled on contact.

Elise met him at the top of the stairs. "Bathtub."

They dumped it in the bathroom without opening the bag. She turned the on the sink so hot it steamed the mirror and sprayed soap in Anthony's hand. The tingles were starting to become a painful itch. His skin was raw and red underneath.

"Did we wake you up?" he asked, shutting off the faucet with an elbow and drying off using embroidered hand towels cannibalized from the studio downstairs.

"No," Elise said.

He stepped back to take a look at her. She was beautiful with her red-brown curls piled on her head and a dress that hit just above the knees. "I guess we didn't. What were you doing this evening?"

"There's a dead body in the tub and you're interested in my night. I'm a bad influence."

Anthony plucked a piece of glass out of her hair and dropped it in the sink. "You look great."

"Uh huh."

Betty was half-asleep on the couch in the living room. "They tried to kill me. I must be important," she mumbled. Her injuries from the fire were covered in some kind of plastic, and the skin beneath it was completely raw.

Elise and Anthony went to a corner of the kitchen to talk without disturbing her. "Tell me what happened."

Anthony whispered a quick and dirty rundown, and by the time he finished, Elise was pacing. Her face was drawn into a grim mask. Her lips were white around the edges. "You'll have to stay here until I take care of this. Both of you. You can't leave the warded perimeter of the studio. It's not safe."

"But my job—" Anthony protested.

"They're watching me. They know who I'm spending time with. You can stay here or die."

"Why? Who is 'they'? What do 'they' want?"

She frowned. "That's not important right now. I have to do an autopsy before the acid destroys my evidence. We still have plastic sheeting from renovating the garage. I'll be right back."

Elise ran downstairs. "Why does she always do that?" Anthony asked the closed door.

Betty hugged a pillow to her chest as she sat up. Her face was still all puffy from the saline drip. "What, pretend you're too dumb to understand what's happening?"

"Yeah. That."

"Maybe because we're too dumb to understand what's happening."

"You're lucky you almost died or I'd kill you myself," Anthony muttered.

When Elise came back, she cut wide swaths of plastic sheeting off the roll and laid them across the kitchen floor. He would have helped, but Betty had become demanding again. She had a whole list of things she "needed," which included a glass of water, Tylenol, and a snack. Preferably cookie dough.

"What do you want now? Your teddy bear?" Anthony asked, exasperated.

"Do you think I'm twelve or something? I'll settle for a shot of tequila." She pressed a hand to her stomach. "Woo, those IV fluids aren't joking around. You could float me over a football stadium right now. I've got to pee like a pregnant woman. Help me up?" Betty stretched her hands toward Anthony. He obediently hauled her to her feet and watched to make sure she arrived safely at the bathroom.

"Two assassination attempts, and Betty's still Betty," Elise said, unrolling another yard of plastic and slicing it with a box cutter. She actually sounded affectionate.

"The entire world could catch fire and Betty would still be Betty."

"Don't tempt fate."

He helped her tape sheeting over the dining room table, which they had positioned in the middle of the kitchen. Once Betty surrendered the bathroom, Elise donned yellow rubber gloves and took the trash bag out of the tub.

The flesh suit spilled onto the table like a hunk of jelly. Anthony covered his nose.

"Jeez. Smells like locker room."

Elise peeled back the eyelids on the head. "Black irises," she muttered.

"What's that mean?"

"On its own, nothing. A lot of ugly things have black eyes." She set the head down. The neck was hollow and couldn't support its weight, so

297

it tipped onto its side. The mouth hung open.

"Turn that away from me," Betty said over the back of the couch. Anthony did as she asked.

"Go to sleep. You don't need to watch this."

"Are you kidding? And miss the show?"

Elise ignored them as she sorted out body parts to make it lay flat. She palpated the bulging abdomen, and fluid squirted from the neck hole. "Interesting," she said, separating the skin and peering inside.

He grimaced. "You're not going to—"

She reached inside. Anthony's stomach churned, but he couldn't seem to make himself turn away.

Elise's hand disappeared first, and then her elbow, and then her entire arm up to the elbow. It was like her arm vanished. The body didn't even bulge. "Interdimensional pouch," she explained when she saw his face. "It's an infernal power."

"Oh. Yeah. Of course."

She extracted something as thick as a tree branch and covered in wiry hair. Elise set it on the table and reached inside for more. She pulled out four of them before Anthony realized that he had seen something like them before. "Those look like spider legs. Like what we found in the desert."

"Mary Poppins would love this," Betty said.

Elise shoved the box cutter into the neck hole. Her face went slack with concentration as her back muscles worked.

A long minute later, she withdrew a strip of flesh covered in glistening black fluid—and demonic brands.

"Bring me the binder on the coffee table," she said.

Anthony flipped it open to the page marked by a sticky note. Elise had drawn a list of brands on the page and labeled them with "desert daimarachnid" and the date they had been camping. He held it up so she could see. Each brand matched, all the way down to the extra marks that obscured them.

"Does this mean the assassin was a giant spider in a human skin suit?"

"I'm saying it's a giant spider in a skin suit owned by the same master demon as the last one." She set down the skin, peeled off the rubber gloves, and scrubbed her arms in the sink. Her skin was red from the venom. "But it's impossible. Mr. Black has angels, not spiders."

Betty sat up. "Angels?"

"Long story." Elise rolled everything up in plastic and duct taped it

298

together so it wouldn't leak. The resulting mummy looked way too much like a small human body. "I'll dump this while I'm in the desert later today. I have to make our new favorite enemy have a very bad day."

Anthony brightened. "You're going to attack the guy who's been after us? This Mr. Black? Then I'm coming too."

"Fine. I can put your mechanic skills to use on this one. But that's not for a couple hours, so you should both sleep while we can."

Ignoring Betty's protests, Elise put her in James's bed, gave her a glass of water, and shut the door. Then she pulled extra sheets out of the linen closet and dropped them on the couch.

"Where are you sleeping?" he asked.

"I'm not."

He pulled his shirt off. Even though he had recovered a few things from his closet at home, including his trusty shotgun, pajamas hadn't been amongst them. "We could sleep on the floor together. There's plenty of room."

"I said I'm not sleeping." Elise's tone was curt, but she softened the delivery by dropping a kiss on his shoulder.

"What do you want to do if you're not sleeping?" he asked, lowering his voice so Betty wouldn't hear if she was still awake. He touched Elise's hip. Her eyebrows lifted.

"Seriously?"

"I don't think I told you how hot you look in that dress," he said, hooking a finger under one of the straps.

"What is it with you and giant spiders?" She spread her gloved hands across his broad chest and kissed his chin. "You've got serious issues."

"Coming from you, that means a lot."

She actually kind of giggled—or at least, what was a giggle for Elise, which was more of a growl. Anthony loved that he could make her do that.

He lifted her onto the back of the couch, pushed the dress up her thighs, and pressed himself between her legs. She was wearing a concealed knife, and she smelled like summer heat and sweat. Anthony wanted to devour her.

Having sex with Elise was never like "making love." Anthony had two girlfriends in high school that had been fun and affectionate and sometimes a little wild, but with Elise, it was more like fighting a forest fire. She didn't know how to surrender or be vulnerable. And she was never affectionate.

When he tried to bend her back for a kiss, she climbed his body and

299

dug her fingernails into his shoulders instead. When he tried to pull off her underwear, she locked her legs around him. He tried to grab her wrists and found himself pushed back against the kitchen table. The plastic sheeting crinkled under him.

It was an unpleasant reminder that they hadn't gotten rid of the body, and that someone was trying to kill Elise's friends. It should have been scary. But maybe she was right about him having issues. The adrenaline only made his blood run hotter.

He tugged the straps of her dress down her shoulders and found she wasn't wearing a bra.

"You did that on purpose," he groaned as he palmed one of breasts, which had a thick ridge of scar tissue down the side.

She ripped his belt out so hard that one of the loops popped.

"Hey!" Anthony protested.

Another little growl of laughter. "Deal with it."

He caught her lips with his and kissed her, long and hard. When he finally pulled back to take a breath, her eyes were lidded and her cheeks were flushed. She really could be so beautiful sometimes. Beautiful, and scary.

"Do you ever think about the future?" Anthony murmured into her neck, trailing his hand down her thigh. His fingers traced along the edge of the knife's sheath.

"No."

"But it can't be like this forever. Giant spiders and assassins." He kissed the soft hairs behind her ear and was rewarded with a shiver.

She still managed to sound stern when she responded, even though her voice had taken a husky edge. "You're optimistic."

Anthony leaned back. He searched her face and found no hint of joking in it. "You retired once. You could do it again."

"I don't think about the future. I'm too busy surviving today." Elise popped his fly open and snaked a hand into his boxers. "Why are you talking?"

Normally, he would have been happy to shut his mouth and enjoy himself. But her resistance to talking irked him. "What about...you know...marriage?" It was too hard to talk while she was stroking him. He caught her wrist. "Children? We're young, and there's lots of time..."

Her whole body went rigid. She pulled her hand out of his pants.

He realized belatedly that he had said something wrong, but he wasn't sure what offended her more: the idea of quitting again, or the idea of a family?

She stepped back and he didn't fight her. "You won't bring that subject up with me again."

Anthony laughed shakily. "We're dating, Elise. This isn't some taboo subject. I know you're not used to any of this stuff, but I can tell you it's normal for people like us to talk about things like that."

She pulled her dress over those gorgeous breasts again. It was like throwing a steel-clad door between them. "I will never have children," Elise said. "Kopides don't do that. And I'm never getting married, either."

It was hardly the coldest thing she had ever said to him, but it still felt a little like getting punched below the belt. "If we don't have a future, then what are we doing? What's the point?"

"We have sex. We spend time together. Isn't that good?"

"But what about a year from now? Five years?"

She fluffed the skirt out where it had become stuck in the thigh sheath. "I've told you what I think. You know what? I have things to do. You need to stay here and watch Betty."

"Yeah, but where—?"

Before he could finish the question, Elise threw the remaining pieces of the daimarachnid's body over her shoulder and went downstairs, leaving Anthony alone.

He tried to get comfortable on the couch, but it was strange being in James's apartment. Everything smelled like sage and jasmine and someone else's aftershave. It didn't help that his feet hung off the edge and that he still had half an erection that was quickly losing all hope.

Pulling the sheets up to his chin, he tried not to imagine the shadows on the ceiling were demons oozing with black pus.

After a few minutes, he heard the chain of the punching bag rattle downstairs.

Chapter 9

ELISE CALLED JAMES'S cell phone twice and hung up on the first ring both times. She glared at his name on her contact list.

He would want to know about Betty. He deserved to know what was going on. But every time she thought about his loafers at the side of the bed, lonely without the rest of his belongings, she found herself punching the off button again.

Before she could decide if she should try to call again, her phone rang. It was Stephanie on the other end.

"If you're trying to reach James, that's not the way to do it." She sounded exasperated. "He's at a rehearsal downtown and forgot his phone. All you're doing is preventing me from getting enough sleep for my shift tonight."

"Fine," Elise said.

"Why did Betty leave the hospital early?"

She didn't feel like explaining. The good doctor would have only taken it as another sign that she was a bad influence who shouldn't be allowed around normal people. Instead, she turned her phone off.

Hanging up had never been so satisfying.

It was almost eleven, but Anthony and Betty were still sleeping. Her boyfriend was sprawled across the couch with his arms and legs hanging off the side. She stood over him with her arms folded as he slept. Marriage. Kids. Three months together, and he had never once made the mistake of mentioning "the future." It left a foul taste in her mouth.

He didn't even twitch as Elise banged around in search of clothes. She ended up donning one of Anthony's shirts and the same jogging shorts she had been wearing the day before.

Her car smelled of brimstone, even though the body in the trunk was thoroughly wrapped in plastic. She yanked the air freshener off the mirror and tossed it in the back before parking in a garage downtown.

It wasn't hard to find out which theater was holding their dress rehearsals. The show James was choreographing was a major production, so there were signs plastered all over the casino to advertise it. Even so, it took Elise a few minutes to navigate the gloomy floors of the casino. Like all businesses of its type, it was designed to trap tourists among the slot machines with black walls, mirrored ceilings, and confusing signs.

She slipped in the side door behind the box office. It was propped open with an empty water bottle.

The theater smelled like fresh paint and turpentine. Pieces of the set were in place while others were assembled near the orchestra pit by stagehands. She picked a seat in the back of the theater and sat down.

"One more time, from the top," James said from the front row. He wore sweats and a shirt with the studio logo across the back.

When he gestured, a tech in the sound booth started the song again.

Elise watched the dancers, some of whom were in the bulkier pieces of their costumes, with mild bemusement. She had never been a big fan of casino shows. There was far too much glitter for her tastes.

"Having fun playing voyeur?"

David Nicholas had joined her. He draped himself over the chair at her side, reeking of cigarette smoke and filth.

"You're here," she said.

"Where else would I be? Unless you finished the Night Hag's to-do list and stuck that kopis six feet deep, I'm still on babysitting duty."

"You won't be much longer."

"Good. Want a smoke?"

Elise curled her lip at the proffered cigarette. David Nicholas was even fleshier than before. His shoulders were broader, his jaw was squarer, and he was starting to look like a thug instead of a dying addict. "Has anything come near James yet?"

"Nah. Too bad, huh? Sure would make this a hell of a lot more fun. I can only watch this guy bone his girlfriend so many times before it gets boring." At Elise's glare, he gave a helpless shrug. "Gotta keep my eye on him. What if the doctor tried to stab him or something? Sure would be a shame if I missed it."

"If anything happens to James, I will exorcise you to Hell. And then I'll come down, find what remains of your corporeal body, and remove your skin with a rusty potato peeler."

He clucked his tongue. "Naughty, naughty. Remember what the

303

Night Hag said about playing nice."

"Fuck playing nice. You and I both know we'll settle this the instant our truce is over anyway."

"Oh, yes." David Nicholas bared his yellow teeth in a grin that stretched back to flash every molar. It was a coyote grin, inhuman and hungry. "We definitely will."

"But your problem is with me. Don't touch James."

He laid a hand on his heart. "I wouldn't *dream* of it."

The music reached a crescendo. James walked onstage, clapping his hands to attract the attention of the dancers. He all but glided inches off the ground. Of all the things that brought him joy—magic and music and teaching his students—nothing made him radiate like being in his element.

Watching him gather the dancers made jealousy wash over Elise. There was a time he only smiled like that for her, like when they managed to save someone or won a vicious battle.

She realized she was staring and turned back to make a parting shot at David Nicholas, but there was only emptiness beside her. He wouldn't be far away. Nightmares never were. "I mean it," she whispered. "Don't touch him."

If the nightmare was listening, he didn't reply.

Elise found a program left on one of the seats and scrawled a note in the margin: *Anthony and I are making a move against Mr. Black. I'll call you when I'm done.* She didn't bother signing it.

When the music played again, James stayed upstage to watch the chorus line. She sneaked up to his pile of towels and tucked the program at the bottom.

She didn't stick around to watch anything else.

Anthony and Elise stopped at a taco truck to pick up dinner before getting gasoline at the corner station. He ate as she filled a half dozen red jugs and loaded them in the cargo area of the Jeep. They had moved the body of the daimarachnid nurse behind the seats, too, and covered it in sweaters and trash to make it look unremarkable.

Elise paid for their food and gas in cash. She grimaced at the last twenty in her wallet.

"I could pay for some of this," he suggested.

She snapped her wallet shut. "Don't worry about it."

They headed north out of the city, beyond the last housing development and into hills filled with wild horses. Evening fell fast in the valleys beyond civilization. The sky caught fire in a desert sunset, striping a violet sky with pink clouds and tinting the sagebrush blue.

Elise spoke on her cell phone for a long time as she drove. Actually, she didn't talk so much as listen, punctuating the conversation with an occasional, "Okay," or "Fine."

"Who was that?" Anthony asked when she hung up without saying goodbye.

"That was the people I'm working with on this raid. They were arranging to pick up the cargo."

"And who is 'they'?"

"A demonic overlord and her court of nightmares. Nobody important."

Anthony couldn't tell if she was joking.

She steered the Jeep off the road, navigating carefully around the largest of rocks. Night sank over them, and soon they could only see within the beam of the headlights.

When they reached the top of a hill overlooking a dry lake bed, she turned the Jeep off and double-checked her map.

"This is it," she said, peering through binoculars to the playa below.

There were lights at the other end of the valley. Wind rustled through the hills, carrying the sweet smell of sagebrush past them. The desert had probably gotten well over a hundred degrees earlier in the day, but the wind was already beginning to cool, and he found himself shivering. "See anything?" he asked.

"The odds aren't good," Elise said, lowering the binoculars. She tucked a dagger into her belt at the small of her back. "Probably a dozen guys out there. One per pickup. No sign of the semi yet."

"What's the plan?"

"I want you to disable the trucks so they can't get away with the shipment."

He held out a hand for the binoculars, and Elise passed them over.

They had assembled a loading bay in the middle of the desert and lit it with a generator-powered floodlight. He could make out the fleet of trucks, but he wasn't sure how Elise deduced the number of people.

"It's going to take a while to disable them all. I have to get into each glove box and pull the fuse for the fuel pump relay."

"My contact said the semi should be due in about…" She checked the map again. "Twenty minutes from now. We need to be in and out before they realize their trucks won't start."

"What if they see us?" Anthony asked.

She just looked at him. Shadows carved her face with deep crags and harsh lines. It was the face of someone who had gone against such odds before and come out alive. He felt immediately stupid for asking.

"We kill them," she said.

Anthony nodded and swallowed hard.

Elise took a moment to roll her shoulders and touch her toes, going through the motions of stretching while Anthony refilled the gas tank for a quick getaway. He dumped the plastic-wrapped body down a ditch, which felt like it had been almost entirely dissolved by venom, then fit his shotgun into his back scabbard and gave her a thumbs up.

She ran, and he hurried to follow.

The desert rushed past him. Elise dodged around the sagebrush and rocks and he followed. *It's just like our camping trip,* he told himself again, and he tried not think about their odds of coming back.

There was no subtlety in their run, no grace. The semi couldn't get to the bay before they did.

When they drew within a hundred meters of the ring of light, Elise stopped. He was breathing hard. He didn't do nearly enough cardio to keep up. "You good?" she asked, and he nodded as he wheezed. "We'll sneak around back." Another nod.

The men talked loudly by the loading bay—something about bitches and liquor—and didn't notice their approach. Elise and Anthony ran to the tall end of the loading bay.

She crouched behind it, pulled him down beside her, and peeked over the top of the wooden platform.

The pickups were parked in two neat rows. Most of the drivers talked and smoked in a cluster by the light, leaving the vehicles unattended. Why worry? They were hours from the city. "Fifteen guards," she whispered. "They're human. And armed."

He opened his mouth to speak, but she put a finger over his lips. Then she slid around the side of the loading bay, and he followed.

One man, a big guy with a tattoo of a kitten on his wrist, stood aloof from the others. Metal glinted under his untucked shirt. A gun. Great.

Elise pointed to the nearest truck. He crawled forward, keeping an eye on Kitten, and reached up to try the passenger door. It was unlocked. He reached in and opened the fuse box on the glove compartment. Removing the fuse for the fuel pump, he shut the door as quietly as possible and slipped back.

306

He showed her the number on the fuse. She moved for the next truck. Together, they worked their way up the lines. Each pickup drew them closer to Kitten and all the other men.

"My fucking wife just doesn't get it," one of the guards muttered. He offered a joint to the man next to him. "She's gotten fat, sure, but that doesn't mean I don't love her. I don't want anyone else."

"Even Candi?" chuckled a third man with a Disturbed concert t-shirt.

"Candi. Mm hmm. I'd like to stick it in that bitch," said the second, passing the joint back.

Anthony eased another door open and pulled the fuse. He took a quick count of how many he had in his pocket—five. Elise wasn't far behind in the other row.

"Fuck Candi, man. No way some slut makes steak as good as my woman. I'd never trade that in."

Only two vans between Anthony and Kitten. He searched for Elise amongst the other vehicles, but he couldn't see her. He did, however, see a pair of approaching headlights on the horizon.

The semi.

"What are *you*?"

He jerked up just in time to see Kitten looming over the van, an arm braced on the open door. His muscles bulged with veins.

"Uh," Anthony said in a stroke of brilliance.

Kitten clapped a hand on his shoulder and flung him into the crowd of drivers.

Shoulder met playa, and the breath rushed out of his body. Anthony groaned and rolled onto his knees. "What's this? We got a visitor!" crowed Disturbed.

Someone kicked him in the ribs. It was like getting slammed by a sledgehammer, and it shot spikes of pain into his groin.

He fell on his side again. Someone laughed a hyena laugh—a skinny man with a tattoo on his neck that said "Bad" in gothic letters—and he was echoed by others.

Kitten leaned over him. "What are you doing all the way out here? What is that you're wearing, a backpack?" He shoved Anthony's head to the side. "Kid's got a shotgun."

The tone immediately went from jovial to serious. Kitten eased a semi-automatic handgun out of his shoulder rig, and Anthony heard the telltale click of a safety turning off.

"On your knees," Kitten ordered.

He complied, moving slowly even as every nerve in his body begged him to run. He tried not to search for Elise, but he couldn't help but steal a few looks out of the corner of his eye as he got up. Anthony linked his hands behind his head and stared down Kitten's gun.

One of the men took the shotgun out of his scabbard, tossing it aside.

"I'm... I was just..." His mouth was dry, and he couldn't seem to think of the words he wanted to say.

"What are you doing out here?" Kitten asked again.

His mouth moved soundlessly. After a few monosyllabic attempts at speaking, Anthony finally said, "Camping. And...and hunting. Coyotes."

Kitten guffawed. "We look like coyotes to you?"

Following his cue, the other guards laughed as well. Anthony caught a flash of motion out of the corner of his eye. Elise ran from one truck to the next. She wasn't being as subtle now that he had everyone's attention.

"N-no," Anthony stammered. "I thought...uh..."

"Woo-ee! Little boy's going to shit his pants."

"What are we going to do?" another asked, glancing uneasily toward the approaching headlights at the end of the playa. "The boss will be pissed he finds out someone saw us."

"Take him out a half a mile and shoot him," Kitten said. He pointed at Disturbed. "You. Now. Make it fast."

The bright lights swirled around Anthony. *Shoot him*? He didn't feel like he was going to "shit his pants," but passing out wasn't off the menu, either.

Elise wouldn't let him get shot. She would save him. Wouldn't she?

Disturbed yanked Anthony to his feet by the back of his shirt and aimed a submachine gun at his midsection. "Walk," he ordered, aiming Anthony toward the nearest edge of the playa.

He briefly contemplated a struggle, but the logistics of an unarmed man against a dozen others wasn't pretty. But the pain was still radiating from his gut to his balls, his heart was about to splatter in his chest, and he thought he was going to lose his taco dinner in the dirt.

"I was just camping," he said.

The gun nudged him in the back.

So Anthony walked.

With every footstep, his head felt lighter. They left the ring of bright lights and Disturbed prodded him again. "Faster," he said, and he didn't sound too confident. Maybe he wasn't much of a killer. Maybe he didn't want to actually hurt Anthony. Maybe he would just let him go...

"Look, man," Anthony said, trying to talk around the cotton balls that seemed to have materialized in his mouth. "I was having fun. I didn't mean any harm, or...Jesus Christ, I won't tell anyone I saw you out here. I swear."

It was probably the most convincing lie he had ever told.

"Nothing should be coming out of your mouth but prayers right now, kid."

Anthony wasn't sure who he should pray to. God? Or his girlfriend, who was—he hoped—a hell of a lot more likely to save him?

The lights behind them faded. The edge of the playa surrendered to sage-filled desert.

Disturbed kicked him behind the knees. Dust ground into his palms as he hit. When he looked up, he stared straight down the barrel of the submachine gun.

"Oh shit," Anthony said.

There was something undignified about pleading. His uncle had a dozen war stories about facing death with stoic silence, and *Tío* Jacob would have chewed him out for being a pussy if he saw the way he was shaking. But at least he wasn't the only one.

"You can do this, dude," Disturbed muttered to himself. "It's not that hard. Just some guy. Come on, let's do this." He shook his shoulders out. The leather strap of the gun creaked. "Okay. You can do this."

Anthony raised his hands behind his head. *Come on, Elise...*

A nearby bush rustled.

He only had time to catch a flash of Elise's thick braid and her pale skin before she struck Disturbed in the side.

The submachine gun fired. They both hit the ground. Anthony flung himself behind the nearest rock.

There was the meaty sound of fist meeting flesh, and Disturbed grunted. Something big scraped against the ground. The submachine gun slid to a stop inches from Anthony's rock.

All his fear fled in a wash of clarity. He grabbed the gun, got to his knees, and spun to face the fight.

But it was already over. Elise crouched over Disturbed's body, one knee on his throat and the other pinning his arm to the ground. He flailed weakly. She shifted, and he went slack.

Disturbed didn't move when she stood.

Anthony joined her, holding the submachine gun awkwardly at his side. "Did you kill him?'

Elise wiped sweat off her upper lip with the back of her wrist. "No. And he's not going to be out for long. Give me your belt." Anthony hurried to strip it off, and she used the strap to bind the guard's wrists

309

and ankles.

The semi's headlights stopped beside the loading bay, and the men began to move.

"Oh man…"

"They can't leave," Elise said. "We have time. Relax."

"They're going to look for this guy when he doesn't come back."

She knotted the belt and stood. "And we'll be gone before they do."

"What's the plan from here, anyway? We have the fuses, but they have the shipment."

"Could you drive a semi?" Elise asked.

"Yeah, my uncle's a truck driver, he—"

She didn't let him finish. "Great. Let's go."

And then she was running again.

"God damn it," Anthony muttered before following her. Every thud of his feet against the dirt jolted through the bruise on his ribs.

They slipped behind the semi. He could hear shouting over the idling engine.

"Why the *fuck* aren't the vans starting?"

"You think I know? They worked on our way out here! Maybe the batteries died…"

"On all twelve of them?"

Anthony peeked around the back end of the truck. The door had been opened to reveal several huge crates stacked in the back, but nothing had been moved yet. Elise climbed onto the side of the cab.

"Fuck this shit," swore a guard on the other side of the semi. "The boss is going to shoot us!"

She eased the door open and gestured to Anthony. He slid across the bench seat to get behind the large wheel. The cab of the semi smelled like leather and fake pine. The radio was on a Christian station, and a young woman sang cheerily about her wonderful relationship with Jesus to a twanging Country background.

He gingerly set the submachine gun he had stolen from Disturbed atop a rosary.

Anthony had been telling the truth when he said he could drive a semi. But he hadn't done it in years, and not on a truck so new. He smoothed his hands over the wheel and checked the gearshift.

"Just like any other car," he muttered as Elise got in and shut the door softly. "Where am I supposed to go?"

"Forward. Preferably very quickly."

Quickly. No problem. He wasn't trying to pass any tests—just escape

310

a whole lot of armed guards.

Footsteps approached the side of the truck.

"Maybe we can jump the pickups or something…"

"Go," she urged. "Now."

Anthony put the semi into gear and hit the gas.

If anyone shouted at them to stop, he wouldn't have been able to hear it. They roared into motion, and seconds later, a spray of bullets ripped into the side of the trailer with a sound like hail.

"Jesus Christ!"

"Go, go, keep going—"

They tore across the desert, and the gunshots cut off fast. The truck shuddered on the rough playa.

"The doors are still open! Are we losing the cargo?" Anthony asked.

Elise rolled down the window and leaned outside. "No boxes behind us. And nobody's chasing. They wouldn't fire again anyway."

"Why?"

"They must not want to hit the cargo." She dropped back into her seat. "Keep going. We need to dump this by the hill for pickup, and we need to do it before they call reinforcements. Maybe a cliff. See any cliffs?"

Anthony laughed. The idea of going over the side of a mountain was hilariously terrifying.

The windshield suddenly exploded inward with a crash. Elise threw herself to the floor an instant before more pellets erupted through the driver's side window. He dropped low to the seat. Safety glass showered around him, catching in his hair and collar.

He gripped the wheel tight, struggling to keep the semi straight. There was nothing in front of him for miles—nothing but the occasional tree—and he could only pray they wouldn't find one on accident.

The sound of a van roared up beside them and pulled in front of the semi.

He peeked over the dash. The back doors popped open. Two men clung to the back, each holding submachine guns. The man in the passenger seat aimed with a shotgun. *Anthony's* shotgun.

Elise grabbed their gun and propped it on the dashboard without looking. Aiming wasn't too important where fully automatics were concerned.

She squeezed the trigger, and it exploded with gunfire. Someone screamed. The van swerved.

"Pull alongside them!" she yelled. "And give me room!"

311

He squeezed toward the side of the cab without letting go of the wheel. She climbed over him to brace herself against the door. Anthony flanked the van, and the orange needle on the semi's speedometer bounced at the seventy mark.

Elise suddenly ducked.

Shotgun pellets buzzed through the air over Anthony's head like a swarm of angry bees and buried into the roof of the cab.

She got up again, hanging halfway out the window, and Anthony swerved to the left. They hit the side of the van. The semi bucked around him, and Elise's whole body jerked. He grabbed her leg before she was wrenched out of the window.

"Give me that!" she shouted.

Another gunshot.

Elise dove back into the cab with Anthony's shotgun in her hands. Her elbow smacked into the side of his head, and he lost his grip on the wheel. The semi swerved. He scrambled to get a grip on the wheel again as his vision blurred.

She pumped the shotgun.

"I need a clear shot at the driver!"

No time for pain. He sat up enough to see the ground and swung around hard.

The change in direction made the trailer tip. For a breathless instant, it balanced on two wheels. Anthony braced himself for the trailer to unbalance and throw the cab on its side. But a moment later, all four wheels connected with the ground.

Elise rose, aimed at the van, and pulled the trigger.

It clicked. Out of ammo.

The driver of the van aimed a handgun at them.

Anthony hit the air brakes. The truck screamed. Elise gripped the dash to keep from getting tossed out the windshield. "He's coming around!"

He fumbled a couple of shells out of his pocket. Elise flipped the shotgun over to load it, but she dropped the first two. Her fingers weren't as confident on the gun as they were with a blade.

"Here he comes," Anthony warmed.

She managed to slip one in the chamber.

The van drew level with them. Elise propped herself up on the window and aimed down. The shotgun discharged with a bang.

The van wasn't next to them anymore.

"Did you shoot him?" Anthony asked, and he sounded shrill, even to his own ears. "Did you shoot the driver?"

"Don't stop. Get across the playa."

He made a loop around the sagebrush-filled shore. The bushes scraped and banged against the front of the truck and its bumpers.

"Did we make it?" he asked.

"That won't be the end of it," Elise said. "Too easy."

His pulse beat out a heavy cadence in his chest and throat. "*Easy*? We almost got shot a dozen times!"

She laughed. Elise *laughed*. She sounded as perturbed by the fight as she would have been on a shopping trip with Betty—maybe even less so. "Mr. Black could send an angel as soon as he finds out what happened. If it gets to us before we dump this, you might wish we were facing a whole firing squad."

He stopped in front of the hill with the Jeep on it and cut the engine. They jumped out to check the cargo.

The crates were strapped in, so they had stayed in place despite his stunt driving. He climbed into the truck bed to investigate the boxes. The moonlight was too dim for him to make out any detail.

"Hang on." Elise ran back to the Jeep for a flashlight.

"Let's just go," Anthony said. "We'll let your friends get rid of all this."

"I want to see what's inside first. Hold the light."

He turned on the flashlight and shone it over her head as she pried at the lid off one of the crate. "I don't know much about stuff with demons and angels," he said, "but I don't think those are weapons."

The box was filled by a column of stone. It was the color of ivory, and the end had a slight indent, like it was supposed to fit into another piece. Anthony reached out to caress it. The stone was smooth, almost warm to the touch. It sang against his fingertips.

"What *is* that?" he asked.

"Don't touch it!"

Her sharp tone made him freeze. "What? Why?"

She replaced the lid. Elise moved to another crate and ripped it open without responding. It also had a piece of stone, and Anthony went to open a third. All the same.

Something tickled at the back of his skull, like snakes writhing on his brain stem. He slapped the back of his neck and turned to see what had touched him.

But there wasn't anything there.

"Do you feel that?" he asked, scratching the nape of his neck.

313

A feather drifted past him. They both looked up.

Wings flared, and a man dropped from the sky.

He appeared young—hardly any older than a teenager—and he glowed like a star. His hair was as white as his flesh. It whipped around him like a cloak.

"Get to the Jeep," Elise snapped, drawing her blade.

"But the cargo—"

"Now!"

Anthony scrambled up the rocks, hurrying to reach the Jeep.

He was halfway up when Elise screamed.

A gust of wind blasted his bangs over his face. He flattened his body against the rock. Something hurtled past him, just inches away. The angel had thrown her. Elise's body struck the rocks beside him and bounced off with a crack.

Her fingers dug into a boulder. Anthony yelled, throwing out a hand to grab her by the wrist, but another gust of wind stopped him.

Hands fell on her shoulders. She kicked and shouted as the angel hauled her into the night sky, wheeling toward the stars.

"Elise!"

They ascended so quickly that Anthony soon couldn't see them. He hauled himself on top of the hill and searched the black sky for motion.

He spotted a black shape against the moon. They plummeted toward the earth, growing bigger rapidly.

They were falling right at him.

Anthony threw himself out of the way just in time. They struck the dirt like a meteor, angel on the bottom with his massive wings stretched wide.

Soil exploded into the air. He shielded his face with his arms.

One wing swept out as the angel struggled to right himself. Each one was almost as long as a school bus. It clipped Anthony's legs and knocked him onto his back.

Elise rolled off the angel. "Don't—stay back—" she gasped. The wind had been knocked out of her by the impact.

The angel stood, wings folded around him like a cloak. Feathers showered around him. Anthony couldn't breathe. The air had become thick and vibrated with sheer energy. It pinned him to the ground as surely as though one of the boulders had been dropped on his chest.

Elise got to her knees, ripped off a glove, and held out her hand. "Stay back," she said, blood trickling from her nose. "You see this? Don't fucking touch me!"

314

His wings flared out, catching the wind.

"You!" he hissed.

Air blasted around them as he swept into the sky again.

Elise grabbed Anthony's arm. "Run. Run!"

He leaped into the passenger's seat of the Jeep, but before he could slide over to the driver's side, she climbed behind the wheel. "Sit back!"

She punched the gas, and they tore across the desert. He twisted around to see if the angel would follow, but Anthony could barely make out its pale shape circling over the semi. "What did you do?" he asked. Elise held her bare hand out to him. There was a tattoo on her palm, and it was bleeding. "What is *that*?"

"A mark."

Anthony didn't get it. "Did you know that—that thing?"

"No. Never seen him before."

"Then why…?"

"Long story."

"It's a long drive back to town."

She shot a look at him from the corner of her eye. "Knowledge can be dangerous. You might change your mind if you knew."

Anthony laughed harshly. "More dangerous than what we just did? I think I can handle anything you throw at me."

So Elise told him.

By the time she was done, he wished she hadn't.

Chapter 10

STEPHANIE WAS FUMING.

"How in the world is Betty supposed to heal like this?" she hissed, cornering James in the kitchenette. The lights were dimmed in the apartment above Motion and Dance so Betty could sleep, but judging by the wheezing he heard from his bedroom, she wasn't going to get much rest.

"It's all right. I can help her. I have a ritual—"

She cut him off by stabbing a finger into his chest. "She wouldn't need rituals if she was sedated at the hospital the way she should have been!"

"They were attacked. Do you want fights in your hospital?" James asked, setting his glasses on the counter so he could pinch the bridge of his nose. It was a useless gesture. Nothing would stop the tension headache that had lodged between his temples when he found Elise's note at the rehearsal that morning.

Stephanie's voice sounded extra shrill. Every word was like hammering a fresh nail into his skull. "No! But that's another issue entirely. We wouldn't be having fights in my hospital if *that woman*—"

"Who happens to be my oldest and dearest friend."

"—would stop getting into so much trouble! This is why we should have relocated to the Bay Area."

James sighed. *That* discussion again.

In June, Stephanie had been offered a job in California. When James declined to leave Reno with her, she stayed, and insisted they buy a house together instead. He hadn't thought it was a big deal at the time. They spent most nights together anyway. But he was starting to suspect that the issue wasn't Stephanie wanting him to be closer to her. It was Stephanie wanting him to be further from Elise.

316

"Betty is here for a reason," James said, carefully enunciating each syllable. "She's safest between these walls. She'll be fine with some time and rest, which she can get here just as well as at a hospital. Probably better, actually."

"Magic is no substitute for modern medicine."

"Ordinarily, I would agree. But the magic I cast is not ordinary."

Betty gave a dry, hacking cough that turned into a full-blown fit. She barely had time to breathe between exhales. They both fell silent to listen.

"I should check on her," Stephanie said. She moved to leave the kitchen, but turned back with renewed anger before she made it three steps away. "Elise is dangerous."

He focused on a spot on the ceiling and took a deep breath before answering. James had the same thoughts himself, more than once. And he was angry at her, too, if in a completely different way than his girlfriend was. He had been on the verge of snapping with stress for hours.

But that was his business. Not hers. And he was about ready to slap Stephanie.

When he spoke again, it was in a careful, measured tone. "Yes, she's sometimes in dangerous situations…"

"She almost killed her friends," she interjected.

"You just don't—"

The front door opened.

James grabbed the notebook off the counter. He almost ripped one of the spell cards out before he saw who it was. Anthony entered first, dusty and hollow-eyed. Elise was a step behind him with a fist clenched to her chest.

She wasn't wearing a glove.

The sensation of falling filled his gut, like tripping off a cliff. James crossed the space within them in a flash to grab her wrist. He studied her bleeding knuckles, but she didn't relax her fingers. "What happened?"

Elise shrugged stiffly.

He looked at Anthony, but the younger man was too stunned to string together an entire sentence, much less respond coherently.

Stephanie shot a look at James. "I'll check on Betty."

At the sound of his cousin's renewed coughing, Anthony followed, leaving James and Elise alone. She finally pried her fingers open. There were deep indents where her fingernails had dug into the skin.

James didn't leave her palm exposed for long. He snagged a dish towel out of the drawer and pressed it against the mark.

"Where are your gloves?"

Elise sank onto the couch. "I don't have any other gloves left."

He found a box of cloth bandages over the washing machine and sat down to wrap her hand, but she gripped the dish towel like it was it was a grenade with a loose pin. "Let go," he said. She shook her head. "Please, Elise. We need to cover...that."

"Mr. Black is building a gate."

There was that falling feeling again. "How do you know?"

"He's shipping fragments of angelic ruin into the city. I saw them tonight. I tried to take them from him, but..." She lifted her hand. "He sent an angel to stop me. He has dozens of them."

"But he doesn't have the entire bowl anymore."

"What if he's found a way around that?"

They stared at each other, communicating silently in a way that only partners could after so many years. What if he *had* found a way around needing a complete keystone? Elise's hand clenched tighter on the towel. Her knuckles were white.

He squeezed her wrist gently until she opened her fingers.

James wiped the blood off her skin as quickly as possible and wound the bandages around her palm, careful not to touch the marks. He didn't let go of her when he was done. "Tell me what happened tonight."

Elise gave him the short version: a convoy, stealing the truck, and being stopped by an angel. "When I left, nobody else had arrived to pick up the semi. I don't know if Mr. Black got it or not. The angel was there, so I can only assume we lost tonight."

He frowned. "Who else would have picked up the semi?"

"Friends of mine."

She was a terrible liar. He knew for a fact the only people she considered friends were in the apartment.

"Elise..."

Her phone rang and cut him off. She paced to the kitchen window to answer it. "Hello?"

He returned the first aid kit to the closet and dropped the blood-stained towel in the washing machine. Even though he couldn't hear the other end of the conversation, Elise's terse replies were telling.

She hung up when he joined her in the kitchen. "I have to go. Stay here with Anthony and Betty."

"We can't hole up in the studio forever."

"It won't be forever. Just until I kill Mr. Black." She took a couple knives from James's kitchen and stuck them in her belt. He followed her to the door.

318

"What are you doing? Where are you going?"

"My contacts recovered the truck, but not all the pieces. I'm going to see what they found."

"You're joking," he said. When she reached for the doorknob, he leaned a hand against the door to keep her from opening it. She didn't fight him.

"Would I be walking around without a glove if I was making a fucking joke? I don't want to visit the Night Hag, but—"

"The *Night Hag*? But she's asleep!"

"Yeah. Funny story. She's not."

He could tell his raised voice carried through the apartment because the murmured conversation in the bedroom died off. James lowered his tone before continuing. "How?"

"Probably the same thing that let Mr. Black find us."

She didn't have to say any more than that. He suddenly understood. "It's because of that damned Death's Hand, isn't it? Every godforsaken creature on this Earth felt my resurrection. You aren't a necromancer, Elise, and by using that magic—"

"It wasn't—"

"By using that, we violated the Treaty of Dis, and everything knows it. If we survive this, Mr. Black could be the least of our worries!" He raked a hand through his hair. "We should have never done that. You should have left me dead."

"No."

That single word was so absolute that he turned on her, ready to argue, but her cold expression stopped his voice in his throat.

"No?" he asked.

"If Death's Hand killed you a thousand times over, I would do the same thing every time. I will always bring you back." Her throat worked as she swallowed. "Fuck magic. Fuck the Treaty. And fuck Mr. Black."

James faced away from her, bracing his hands on either side of the window and letting his head hang between his shoulders. The sidewalks outside were motionless. The street lamp at the corner flickered, but held steady. It was dark enough that there could have been anything outside— an entire army of angels waiting to strike against them—and he never would have seen it coming.

"You know what this means," he said. "The implications..."

Something touched the center of his back. He relaxed when he realized it was Elise's hand.

She slid her arms around him, hugged his ribcage, and rested her

319

cheek between his shoulder blades. He let out a long breath. She was very warm, even through his shirt. "I don't care," she said, softer than before. "I'll always choose you."

"Elise..."

James turned. She took a quick step back. Her face was blank again. "Don't leave. I mean it."

"Wait—Elise—"

She flicked the jacket over her shoulders to hide the daggers and pulled her hair out of the collar. Her cheeks were red. "Lock the deadbolt."

She left, and the apartment was very empty with her absence.

Demons unloaded the semi in the alley behind Craven's. David Nicholas supervised from atop a closed Dumpster lid, arms folded behind his head like he was on a beach chair by the lake.

The casino employed all kinds of local demons. The ones indistinguishable from humans were put to work as cashiers and waitresses—nightmares, incubi, the half-breeds. But the staff that worked in back were the uglier monsters. The ones that couldn't walk outside during the day.

A demon that looked like it was made of raw meat hurried past with a box three times its size when Elise entered the alley. It smelled like an outhouse.

Neuma took notes of the crates as demons lifted them out of the truck and carried them inside. She peeked into every one and wrote a short description before letting them move on. She wore snug jeans that had been attacked by a Bedazzler, a pushup bra that practically made her choke on her own cleavage, and a midriff jacket without a shirt. Considering her usual work uniform, it was downright decent.

Elise's usual revulsion at seeing David Nicholas was pushed aside by her total relief at finding the semi in the alley. She didn't even mind when Neuma greeted her with a hug that lingered a little too long.

"Why aren't you watching James?" Elise asked.

David Nicholas responded from his perch on the trash. "Thom's on babysitting duty today. Rest assured, he's well-supervised."

"And the angel?"

"Killed six brutes before it left. No big loss."

Neuma glowered. "We lost good guys. Manuel—he was just a kid.

Jerry has a family."

"Human servants?"

"No, they were Gray, like me," she said. That was what the mixed-blood children of humans and demons called themselves. "But they were good. That fucking angel is going to pay for it."

"Yes. It will."

Neuma leaned her head on Elise's shoulder and let out a sigh. It was such a sweet gesture from someone so aggressively sexual that it didn't occur to her to push Neuma away. Her skin tingled unpleasantly where the half-succubus's cheek rested against it.

"But we got the cargo," Elise said, talking over Neuma's head to David Nicholas.

"Sure. Most of it." He laughed at the alarm in her gaze. "Ooh, nosy little accountant is scared now, isn't she? The angel called in friends before we got there and flew off with a half dozen crates." He inspected his fingernails, which were painted with chipped black polish. "But we got enough to assemble the gate, I think."

Cold fear spiked through her. "You can't do that."

"Take it up with the boss. It's her game."

"Fine. Take me down there."

He sneered. "No."

Between having her boyfriend almost get executed in the desert and losing part of the shipment, Elise's patience was destroyed. She wrapped a hand around David Nicholas's ankle and hauled him off the Dumpster.

The demons scattered when she threw him to the ground. David Nicholas immediately scrambled to his feet.

"You goddamn bitch, I'll cut your—"

She fisted his shirt at the collar. "I wasn't asking," Elise said, breathing hard through her nose. It was all she could do not to throw him again.

"You're fucking unhinged," he spat.

"Take me. Now."

He shoved her off. "Suit yourself."

David Nicholas took the back paths through Craven's. The hallways were unlit. Elise had to keep a hand on the wall and follow the stink of his cigarettes to navigate down the stairs.

When they reached Eloquent Blood, there was no music, and nobody was left at the bar. Like last time, a cleaning crew moved through with mops and disinfectant to scrub off the worst of the encrusted brimstone.

She checked the time on her phone. It was almost sunrise.

"Losing your nerve?" David Nicholas asked, opening the elevator door.

Elise got in without answering.

They went a few levels deeper than the Night Hag's den this time. She watched the ground ascend around them as the elevator sank deeper and deeper into the earth, where noise could not touch them and the air grew motionless and cold.

When it finally came to a grinding halt and David Nicholas pushed open the cage, nothing greeted them on the other side but darkness.

He darted into the shadows without waiting for her.

"Hey!" Elise called.

His chuckle came from everywhere and nowhere at once. "Not afraid, are you?"

Elise turned on her cell phone's flashlight mode, which made the screen white. It wasn't powerful enough to break the tangible darkness, but it illuminated a small circle in front of her feet. Enough to see rough stone floor.

There was only one way to go—forward.

A powerful presence grew as she moved through the hall. It wasn't just David Nicholas as he flitted in and out of the shadows. There was something else. Something immense, and not demonic.

She came to a crossroads. She had to stop to let a line of demons pass, carrying crates between them on litters. They flinched at seeing her cell phone light. Their eyes were wide and bulging with huge black irises—perfect for seeing in dark mines. The demons were marching deeper into the earth, treading a dusty path split by footprints.

"What is this?" she asked, raising her cell phone to see the boarded-up walls. It looked like an old mine, but there wasn't stone beyond the boards.

"Top levels of the Warrens, of course," David Nicholas whispered. "Don't you want to see where the worst of us lurk? Like turning over a river stone and finding leeches and cockroaches and all sorts of slime."

"I just want to talk to the Night Hag."

"You will. Almost there."

The last of the demons walked on. Elise fell in step behind them.

"Almost there" was subjective. It felt like hours passed as she followed them through the twisting hall. Her breath fogged from her mouth and her skin rose in goose bumps. Then a dim light appeared at the end. A pair of tall doors stood open, leading into a dim cavern. The demons scurried off with eyes lowered.

Elise started to follow them—but she stopped when she stepped through the doors and emerged on a platform near the top of a cavern.

The room was so impossibly tall that the ceiling stretched up into shadows like an underground cathedral. Dim blue light emanated from stones in the walls, turning the shuffling line of demons into silhouettes as they stacked the crates. Several tapestries were hung in the back of the room, framing the room with images of alien forests and cemeteries.

Other demons unpacked the boxes beside a tall dais. And at the center stood a gate.

It was only halfway completed, but Elise already knew she had seen that gateway before. It wasn't quite like the ones in her dreams, but it was cast of the same soapy-white stone with brands around the base. It was thrice her height and wide enough to accommodate a train. She knew it because Mr. Black had built one just like it years before.

Someone moved through the demons to check their work—someone tall and beautiful and ageless. Even in the dim light, Elise recognized the man who had been chained in the Night Hag's cavern on her last visit. But now she recognized the glimmer of magic around his necklace and the silvery stumps at his back.

The Night Hag had one of Mr. Black's angels.

Elise moved down the ramp toward the gate. The angel caught her looking and stopped. The expression on his face was a mix of recognition and fear, just like the one the angel in the desert had looked when he saw her palm. How had she not known what he was before?

"Like it?" David Nicholas purred, reappearing from with a whiff of brimstone. "I'd be lying if I said your shock wasn't delicious."

"You people are making a huge mistake. You don't understand what that does."

"It's a gateway to a city."

Elise turned. The Night Hag had sneaked up behind her. She stood straight-backed and strong, arms folded and chin lifted regally. Her breasts and hips had become plump, with a tight-cinched waist, and her black hair was shot with gray. Instead of looking like a woman of ninety, she might have been James's age. But it was her. There was no mistaking the way the brand on Elise's shoulder burned when she saw her.

"I thought you were only trying to defend the Reno territory from Mr. Black," Elise said. "You have his gate. You have one of his angel slaves, which you need to operate the gate. You realize what this looks like to me?"

The Night Hag waved a dismissive hand. "Yes, yes. But we must be proactive. Mr. Black won't be the only one to come after the ruins."

"Do you know what can come through that?" Elise asked, stabbing the air with a finger.

The gate reacted to her motion. It hummed as the symbols glowed, then faded.

"Nothing. It's only a doorway to the real threat—the angelic city, which I suspect is buried deeper still beneath the Warrens. If we don't get there first, someone else will. Don't you see? The angelic city to which this gate opens is what makes Reno a powerful territory—and to keep control of the city above, we must control the city below."

"All of you will die if you go to that city," Elise said.

"It's a risk we've got to take. There are nine doors in the angelic city—nine. If we finish it and cross through before Mr. Black builds his, we can destroy all entrances to the city. Nobody will ever be able to seize it."

"You think you can control it—"

The Night Hag snapped her fingers. Bright pain flared in Elise's shoulder, and she cut off with a groan.

"Petulant worm," she said.

David Nicholas cackled.

"No. We can't control it. I am not suicidal, Elise Kavanagh, and I did not ascend to the position of overlord by foolishness. The only way I can keep my position is to destroy the gates at the source. This is my plan and you've agreed to work with me, so you'll deal with it."

Elise glared at the Night Hag, David Nicholas, and the gateway. Her fingers itched for her daggers. But she kept her hands at her sides. "Nothing good will come from the city."

"I've made my decision. Have you? Is our truce finished?"

"Please say yes." David Nicholas bared all those yellow teeth in a grin that literally stretched to his ears.

It took all of Elise's strength to say, "No."

"Good."

Elise was obviously dismissed. The Night Hag glided toward the angel, turning her back to the kopis as though she was no threat at all. But Elise called out to her.

"I stopped the convoy. I got the parts for your gateway. When are you paying me?"

"Payment. Money." The overlord snorted. "Petty things."

"If it's petty, then paying me isn't a problem."

"Fine. David Nicholas will take care of it. Now get out of my sight—I have work to do."

Chapter 11

THOM WAS WAITING outside the studio when Elise got back. He sat on the Motion and Dance sign, awake and bright-eyed, and he acknowledged her with a nod. "You will be pleased to know that someone attempted to cast a remote spell on the studio and failed."

She was too tired to care. "Great. Fine. Good job."

Elise started to march upstairs. Thom hopped off the sign.

"Quite a greeting for the person safeguarding your aspis. You appear displeased."

"It's four-thirty," she snapped. "The sun's coming up soon and I haven't slept. David Nicholas said he's going to pay me 'later' and I have nothing in my bank account in the meantime. Sorry if I'm not chipper enough for you."

Thom tilted his head to study her. "You saw the gate. Then you know the whole story. What will you do about it?"

She spread her hands wide. "What am I supposed to do? I'm branded by the overlord. My options are limited."

"Hmm."

"Save your pragmatic bullshit," Elise said. "Get out of here. Take a break. I'll keep an eye on my friends for a couple of hours."

"If you wish." He vanished, immediately and silently.

She stumbled upstairs, went to her old room, closed the curtains on the sunrise, and didn't sleep.

The air mattress she had dragged into the room for her and Anthony to use must have been leaking. It was almost flat to the floor. Her boyfriend snored without stirring when she climbed in with him. She never slept on the rare nights she allowed him to stay over, so she knew he was always terrible about that. It sounded like he was sawing wood.

Must have been nice to sleep so deeply.

Something scraped against the side of the building. At first, she thought it was a tree branch. But then it scraped again, and again, in a rhythm that sounded deliberate.

Elise stood and moved to the window.

She saw nothing in the street outside. The only motion came from shifting clouds a paler shade of gray than the dawning sky of morning.

Another scrape.

The dose of adrenaline put her body on high alert. Elise stretched out with her other sense—the one that would have let her track a demon blindfolded.

There was something downstairs.

Elise felt for the knife at her back on reflex, but there was, of course, nothing there. Nor were there any weapons in the bedroom. She had dropped her swords in the kitchen.

She slid into the hall silently. James's bedroom door was open, where Betty slept propped up by pillows. She wheezed in her sleep. Stephanie had dosed her with enough Vicodin to let her sleep through an attack from a horde of angels.

Elise sneaked around James—unconscious on the couch with an arm thrown over his face—and found her spine sheath on the kitchen table. She took one of the falchions. Its engraved blade gleamed dully.

She snagged James's keys off the coffee table before slipping out the front door.

Nerves singing, she crouch-walked down the stairs. The breeze made her sweat go cold. Grass crunched under her bare toes. She eased around the corner of the building, alert for signs of attack.

Nothing outside. Not even cars on the street.

She levered herself up to one of the windows in the main dance hall using her fingertips. The lights weren't on, so it was hard to see. Figures moved among the mirrors.

Nothing should have been able to get through the wards. Nothing.

She cupped the keys in her hand to keep them from jingling as she unlocked the front door and sneaked into the reception area. The footsteps were louder inside. It sounded like there were a dozen people stomping through the hall.

Elise set the keys on the table and peeked through the door.

One of the back windows was broken, but the magic seals James placed over the frames should have still been in place. Yet a trio of hulking forms moved between the mirrors. Their two-segmented bodies

326

were suspending above the ground by long legs.

Spiders. Giant, Malamute-sized spiders.

They weren't the same breed as the demons Elise had been fighting out in the desert. These were sleek and mean-looking, with boxing-glove mouth parts and shiny black flesh. One turned in her direction, and she had a glimpse of six glimmering eyes before she pulled back into the shadows.

She pressed her back against the wall to collect her thoughts. Elise wasn't scared of spiders, but these looked like dogfighters, fast and sleek, and three was two more than she wanted to fight at once.

A sense of calm settled over her. A challenge.

The spiders moved into the secondary hall, where Elise's punching bag waited.

She tried to follow, but her foot caught on something dry and clinging. Thick gray webbing tore free of a mass that stretched from wall to floor. She tried to wipe it off, but it only stuck to her fingers instead.

Spider webs. They had trapped the doorway.

The spider-demons stopped moving in the other room.

She crawled to the closet by the desk, trying not to make any noise or brush against the wall. Daimarachnids had poor eyesight and hunted by vibration. She was slower than usual, a little clumsier. Her foot was numb where it had been caked in webbing.

Their stomping steps picked up pace as they approached. She ducked into the closet.

Before she shut the door, a trap door in the ceiling caught her eye. An idea struck her. The crawl space between floors wasn't big, but it let out in the other room. She could get behind them.

Elise climbed on a box of records to push it open. There was a crawl space just tall enough for her to belly-crawl through on the other side.

She threw her falchion into the crawl space.

Something rubbed against the other side of the closet door. It sounded like a claw-footed bathtub come to life.

A demon struck the door and shoved it open. She came face to face with six glistening black eyes. Its mouthparts clacked.

She grabbed the sides of the trap door and hauled herself up just as the demon barreled into the box, knocking it over with a thunderous crash. Elise struggled to pull herself through the trapdoor.

It reached for her with its boxing-glove mouth. She pulled her legs inside. It knocked into the ceiling instead, and its thick, hairy forelegs scraped against the crawl space.

Elise pulled her elbows underneath her and wriggled forward as quickly as she could. Dust tickled her nose as she squeezed under the beams. Her falchion's blade was only two feet long, but it got in the way and made her crawl much too slowly.

Spider-demons scrabbled on the floor below. Spotting her had thrown them into a frenzy. But even if they were twice as smart as the spiders she fought in the desert, they would still be half too dumb to realize where she was going. She moved faster, dragging herself along with her free hand as wood scraped at her bare back and stomach. Elise was certain she had splinters in her arms. She could barely breathe.

Her hand slipped into an indentation.

Another trap door.

Elise shoved it open and maneuvered to exit feet-first. Her arm and back muscles flexed as she sank into a controlled drop, waiting in a chin-up position to gauge the distance to the floor.

The spiders had coated the room in webbing.

She froze, fingers trembling as she studied the mess they had left behind. It was stuck to the mirrors, the curtains over the garage door, and formed a net over the parquet flooring. The only bare spot was on the floor by the exit—a good ten feet to her right.

Okay. Maybe they weren't so stupid.

Elise aimed carefully and swung her legs in a wide arc. And then she let go.

She landed by the door, but her foot sank into a mass of web. The sticky strands held fast, refusing to relinquish her leg. It burned against her bare flesh. Vibrations spread through the web as she fought to pull free.

Hacking at the web with the falchion helped her rip away from the greater mass, but it stuck to her skin, forming a sticky gray stocking from foot to hip. It made her muscles prick and spasm.

Thudding in the dance hall.

They were coming.

Elise clambered over the webbing, her left leg immobilized at the knee, and carefully climbed under a thick strand that stretched from one side of the doorframe to the other.

A shadow rushed at her.

She dived and rolled, coming up with the sword above her head to bury the blade in the spider-demon's body.

Its legs thrashed. A meaty limb connected with her midsection. It was like getting struck by a baseball bat, and all the air rushed from her lungs as she fell to her knees.

Elise wrenched the sword free and drove it under the daimarachnid's mouth.

The point of the blade burst out of a liquid red eye. She stabbed again and again. The exoskeleton cracked. Fluid gushed from its body as the eight long legs curled inward.

With a final twitch, the spider died.

Elise took a moment to examine what remained of the spider in the moonlight: the red marks on its belly, the fine hairs on its legs, and the brands down its sides. Every mark had been scored to render them unreadable. "Damn," she whispered.

She heard motion in the lobby. There were still two others.

Need to move.

Elise climbed awkwardly out the open window, dragging her stiff leg behind her, and dropped to the grass. She couldn't get both feet under her. She sank to her knees in the yellow grass, and her useless leg barely bent. The web was hardening. "Shit," she muttered. Two more spiders. She couldn't be immobilized.

Crawling to the corner, she peeked around the wall. One spider dragged its spinneret along the lawn as it moved for the stairs on the side of the building. Gossamer stretched between its posterior and the wall, shiny and moist on the end closest to its body.

She slipped under the stairs and waited until it anchored the silken strand to the bottom step before moving. Elise stepped over the trip line it had created at the bottom and followed it silently up the stairs on her toes.

When it reached the landing, she struck.

The spider was too fast. It saw her and twisted. What she intended to be a death blow glanced off its side.

It smashed her into the railing and nearly threw them both off the side. She tangled her free hand in the hairs on its back and hung on. Unbalanced, her shoulders tipped over the rail. The world spun and flipped as she dangled. The ground was at least twelve feet down.

She hooked her ankle on the spider's leg, holding tight. Slimy pincers snapped over her face. She slammed her elbow into one of its eyes. It squealed.

Upside-down, she saw the third spider reach the bottom of the stairs.

Hauling herself upright, Elise threw her weight into the second spider and shoved them away from the edge. It crashed into the door. She slashed. Blood splattered on her face. It keened and fell.

And then the third one was there.

It slammed into her with its glossy body and knocked her onto her back. The hairs on its belly scraped against Elise. She drew her one good leg up to shield her stomach as fangs dropped out of its mouth. They came down on her knees instead of her ribs, and she twisted to the side before they could puncture.

Pincers rushed at her face. She flung her arm up. The sword caught in its mouth.

Red eyes bored into her from inches away as it pressed into her. Her arm trembled as she struggled to force it back. The angle was poor and it was too strong—a line of venom dripped onto her neck and slid into her hair.

She pulled her fist back, and for an instant, hairy feelers scraped against her face.

Then Elise shoved the blade straight into its mouth.

It screamed as it thrashed, twisting from side to side above her. The contortions seemed to only pull the blade deeper into its body. Her slippery fingers lost grip on the hilt.

One of its feet smashed into her leg, and another into her shoulder. Elise flung her arms over her head, trying to curl into a ball to protect her vital organs from its death throes, but its weight was too much.

With a final rasping sigh, the air left its lungs. It stopped moving.

The door opened.

"What—*Elise*?"

James stared at her through the tangle of legs.

"Help?"

He lifted the daimarachnid, and Elise wiggled free of the carcass. Venom and other, unidentifiable bodily fluids seeped out of its stab wounds. She looked down at herself. There was an imprint on her leg where it had almost managed to break the skin, at which point her blood would have been pumped full of all that poison.

"What happened?" he asked. His cheek was imprinted with the pattern of the couch fabric, but his eyes were alert as he took in the two bodies of the spiders.

"They were downstairs. I don't think they wanted to attack us. Hold this."

She picked at the web on her leg with her fingernails. It wouldn't come off, and she couldn't feel her skin beneath it.

"The wards," he said. "How—?"

"They're broken. I don't know how."

330

She shivered as she limped back into the apartment. Elise suddenly felt very, very vulnerable in her underwear and wanted nothing more than an actual pair of pants. "Impossible," James said, staring at the doorway where he had etched tiny marks of warding. "These are the strongest wards possible. Petty daimarachnids couldn't have broken them."

Anthony staggered into the hallway wearing nothing but his boxers. He had found a knife somewhere. "What's going on? Was it an angel?"

"Wake Betty up," Elise ordered, grabbing a clean pair of James's jeans from the laundry cubby. She pulled them over her stiff leg, threaded a belt through the loops, and pulled it tight. They were so long that they bunched over her feet. "We're not safe here anymore. We've got to move."

"I'll take them to my—" James stuttered. "To Stephanie's house. The wards aren't as strong, but nobody should know where it is."

Anger surged through Elise. Stephanie's house? She would have preferred to take everyone to the Night Hag's den. Biting back a nasty comment, she nodded sharply. "Fine. Let's get going."

Morrighan arrived at the studio exactly two hours later. Nobody in the coven approached James's skill with magic, but she was unusually good at protective charms—with the added bonus that Mr. Black wouldn't be out to kill her.

"Thanks for this," Elise said, stifling a yawn. "How long do you think it will take?"

The witch surveyed the studio with a binder hugged to her chest. "You want the entire perimeter redone? At least three hours. I'll have to do some measurements."

"Thanks."

Elise rolled her pant leg up to the knee and picked at the spider webbing stuck to her calf. Instead of sleeping, she had spent the last hour in a hot bath trying to separate the web from her flesh. She had peeled most of it off, along with half her skin, and was slowly regaining sensation above the knee. There was still a thick sock of slime over her ankle.

A car pulled up behind her. She prepared herself to turn away yet another dancer who hadn't gotten the message that classes were canceled for the day, and then realized it was Anthony's Jeep. And Betty was driving.

331

"Hey, what are you doing here?" Elise asked, offering her a hand out of the car. "You don't drive."

"I came to help redo the wards," Betty said. She still sounded like she had smoked an entire pack of cigarettes in one sitting, but the bandages on her shoulders were gone, and her skin was completely unmarked by burns. "I got coffee. Check the passenger seat."

"You should be somewhere safe. You can't be here until Morrighan finishes."

"There's nowhere safer than with you. Besides, Stephanie's house radiates bitch vibes. Didn't I tell you to grab the coffee?"

She found a cardboard container with four huge cups of plain coffee. "There's only three of us here."

"Those are all for you. I already drank mine, and Morr doesn't imbibe."

Elise had to smile. "Thanks. What happened to your burns? Did James take care of them?"

Betty grinned. "Something like that."

She took a sip to test the temperature. It was perfect. Elise tipping her head back and drank until nothing but dregs remained. She sighed and rolled her shoulders, enjoying the familiar warmth she had missed since losing her coffee pot. Betty's smile grew.

"Five hours," Morrighan announced, joining them at the Jeep. "Hi, Betty."

"Hey there."

"Whatever James did here originally is powerful. I'm going to have to cast three levels of charms to fix them. Do you have some touchstones so I can rebind the wards to him?"

"Sure," Elise said.

She went inside to gather some of James's remaining belongings. He kept a few broken things around for spell fodder—cracked coffee mugs, old bed sheets, jeans that had worn thin at the knees. Belongings James had used a lot but no longer needed. The wards would be tied to him and him alone.

Other than watching for attack, Elise could do little to help. She gave James's belongings to Morrighan, then finished cleaning up spider-demon corpses and the web they left behind. The bodies were easy—she skinned the brands off one, gathered as much of its venom as she could in a Tupperware for later, and then stuck their corpses in trash bags.

The webbing was much more difficult. Elise donned rubber gloves to remove it, but it was too tacky. It wouldn't come off.

She connected a hose to the tap in front of the house and power-washed the dance hall. It broke down most of the mess and left a blurry residue on the mirrors. James wouldn't be thrilled, but at least his workspace was clean. It was a start.

Elise paused to study herself in one of the wall of mirrors. She still didn't have any money to buy clean clothes and James's hand-me-downs were ridiculously baggy on her. She twisted around to look at her shoulder, bared by a wife beater that she had knotted at the waist. The Night Hag's brand was angry and red.

"What is that?" Betty came inside, sweaty and pink-cheeked from the summer heat.

"Nothing," she said, fluffing her hair over the mark to hide it. "How are you feeling?"

"I'm on so much Vicodin that I could be an amputee and I wouldn't know it. So I'm fine. When it wears off, though…" Betty's smile was wan. "The attempts on my life are not my favorite."

Elise clenched her jaw. "I know."

"You must have really pissed this guy off."

"Yeah."

"I'm sure he deserved it."

She nodded again, and Betty didn't ask any more questions. There was a reason they were such good friends.

They went outside and sat on the front step to watch Morrighan work. She was so focused on burying objects around the yard that she didn't seem to notice how hot it was becoming.

"I wouldn't blame you if you wanted to leave," Elise said suddenly.

Betty blinked. "Where would I go?"

"You could visit your family in Canada for a few weeks. At least until everything settles down."

"You're trying to protect me, right? It's sweet. But I'm a big girl. I understand the consequences."

"This isn't a game. You could die. The fact you haven't already is miraculous."

"Trust me. I'm getting to be a better witch." Betty glanced around the street, as though she expected someone to be listening, and then she pulled a notebook out of the back pocket of her jeans. "Check this out. I finally figured it out last night, when I couldn't sleep. James didn't heal me. I did, using copies of his spells."

Elise flipped through the pad of paper. Each page was labeled in Betty's looping, girly handwriting with a single word, like "candlelight" or "wind." The rest of each page was covered in huge black marks.

Paper magic. It was James's specialty, and he had never taught anyone how to do it.

"How did you make this?"

"I've been peeking at James's private Books of Shadows. They don't all work. I haven't figured out how to activate everything. But think about it! Imagine going into a fight with two witches who do battle magic!"

Elise's fist clenched on the notebook. "Betty..."

"I can make fires," she said, yanking the paper back. "See this one? It makes a big noise—sounds dumb, but I can think of some clever uses for it, and—"

"James can handle this magic because he's unusually powerful. It could kill you."

"I could be powerful. I just need practice. Maybe someday I could even bind to a kopis as aspis. Wouldn't that be awesome?"

Elise touched her friend's arm. "Promise me you won't use these. Not without James's guidance."

"Oh, come on."

"Promise. Or I'll take this from you right now."

Betty groaned. "Fine. I promise. Unless someone tries to burn me to death or smother me again—then all bets are off. I'm not going to be defenseless. Okay?"

"Fine."

She grinned. "Fabulous."

Elise didn't like the enthusiasm in her voice. Betty had always been too excited by life-and-death situations, but she thought if anything would put a damper on that enthusiasm, it would be assassination attempts. "Can I say anything to convince you to throw out that notebook?"

"Nope. You could tell me how amazing I am for healing myself, though."

"That is difficult magic," she conceded.

"Hell yeah it is. Say I'm amazing."

Elise shook her head and sighed. "You're amazing."

"That's what I thought." Betty leaped up to join Morrighan again, swaying on her feet as she ran over to help dig a hole for one of James's old sweaters.

"Damn it," Elise muttered.

There was a dark form beyond the witches. Someone stood under the trees near the fence. His back was turned, but something about the slant of the shoulders told Elise it was no stranger.

By the time she reached the trees, the man had climbed into the lowest branches with his feet dangling off the side. He lounged against the trunk, comfortable and casual as a cat. Thom was dressed in all black and a thick shirt that was almost woolen. He wasn't even sweating.

He plucked a petite apple from a branch and turned it in his fingers. "These will make a good pie soon," he remarked.

Elise didn't bake, and she definitely wasn't interested in casual conversation. "What do you want? You're supposed to be watching James."

"There are others watching him." He dropped the apple. "I have something for you." Thom swung his legs over the side of the branch and slipped to the ground in front of her. He held up what appeared to be a credit card.

"What is that?"

"This is a key to a penthouse in a downtown casino." Thom flicked it against his fingers. "A very fine penthouse. The kind of place where very rich men stay. You must have a key card to operate the elevator and reach that floor."

"Mr. Black is staying at a casino?"

The witch shrugged. "If you're not interested in getting the key..." Elise held out her hand. Thom didn't immediately give it to her. "The Night Hag does not know I am going to give this to you."

Her eyes narrowed. "How did you get it?"

"You would be amazed at what I can do." He waved it through the air to taunt her. "The Night Hag doesn't want you to confront Mr. Black directly. There is sense in that."

"Then maybe you shouldn't give me access to his penthouse."

"Hmm. Maybe." He held out the key. After a moment, Elise took it. The room number was written on the logo in permanent marker. "There's beauty in the spontaneity of chaos. Too few people appreciate it."

She stuck it in her back pocket. "Thanks."

"You were right when you told your friend she should leave, you know, but she is not the only one. You and all your friends would be wise to escape."

"And break my pact with the Night Hag? That would go over great."

Thom rested his hand on her shoulder. It was heavy, and her brand ached. The pain radiated through her arm, her chest, hot and cold all at once. It wasn't threatening, like when David Nicholas had done it. It was

335

almost...possessive.

His eyes bored into Elise. "Leave now and you may prolong your fleeting days on this Earth."

"Is that a threat?" she asked in a low voice.

His fingers flexed. The pain traveled through her body, heating her skin, quickening her pulse. Thom's face suddenly didn't make sense, as though it wasn't a human face—he was alien, unnatural, his eyes too large and his skin nearly transparent.

"I am not your enemy, Elise Kavanagh."

"You're not my ally."

The corner of his mouth lifted. A smile. Thom was actually smiling. His lips were a shade pinker than the rest of his skin, and Elise had the strange urge to reach up and touch them. "The world is permeable. Every day, it changes." His hand slid from her shoulder to collarbone, brushing up to her throat. "I am not your ally today."

A shudder rolled down Elise's spine. She took a quick step back.

"Don't touch me."

"Yes," he said. Thom hooked his thumbs in the waist of his pants, dragging them down an inch. Only an inch, baring a pale strip of skin and the lines of his hips. A fine brush of black hair disappeared behind his belt. "I suppose it is too late for you to leave. You will need help soon. When you do, you may summon me."

"Summon you? I thought you weren't my ally."

"Not today."

Elise glanced over at Betty and Morrighan. They were still working on the hole they had been digging minutes before. "Look, I'm not in the mood for—"

But when she turned back to face Thom, he was gone.

She turned in a circle, searching for him on the street, but there was nothing. Not even a hint of swaying grass to indicate a person's passage. Somehow, Elise wasn't surprised.

"Great," she muttered at nothing.

Betty was leaning on her shovel again when Elise returned. Her shirt was plastered to her chest and back by sweat. Morrighan wasn't much better, even though she hadn't been doing any of the physical labor herself.

"Do I even want to know what that guy wanted?" Betty asked, and Elise shook her head.

"No. You don't." She took the shovel from her friend. "Come on. I'll finish digging."

An hour later, Elise told Betty that she was going to run an errand and left for the penthouse.

She watched the hotel elevators from a bank of penny slot machines, where nobody would bother her as long as she continued feeding what little cash she still had into the slot. She lost five times as often as she won, but the free drinks helped make up for it.

There was no sign of Mr. Black as Elise emptied the change out of her wallet. But an hour and two Long Island Iced Teas later, Alain emerged from the elevator.

He wore sunglasses and a tan suit, and didn't look in her direction as he breezed toward the lobby. People gave him a wide berth even though he wasn't especially imposing. It must have been all the burn scars.

Elise stood once his back faced her and contemplated attacking. She had worn the red sundress again, since she had a habit of tripping over James's jeans, and there was no way to conceal her swords in it. She wasn't sure the daggers would be enough to take Alain down.

So she let him pass. He spoke on his cell phone in French with no mind for his volume—most likely confident that nobody else would understand him. But Elise did.

"I have a map of the mine shafts," he said. "I'll bring the car to you."

He disappeared into the lobby. She set her half-empty glass on top of the slots and ducked into an elevator.

There was no button for the top floors. Where the numbers for the five highest levels should have been, a card reader had been installed. It was obviously much newer than the rest of the sixties-era building. She swiped the penthouse key, the light flashed green, and the elevator doors closed.

Each of the walls was mirrored, so she could see her back and sides as she made a slow ascent. Even with her hair down, the Night Hag's brand was conspicuous on her back. Dim yellow light washed out her skin and made her curls the same color as the dress.

She double-checked the position of her knife.

The doors chimed and slid open.

A short hall terminated in the penthouse door, from which a "Do Not Disturb" sign hung. She pressed her ear to it. No sound.

She unlocked it and slid inside.

Mr. Black's penthouse was fashionable and impersonal. A spacious

337

entryway filled with a cubist's idea of furniture led into another sitting room. There were two bedrooms with sliding doors and a kitchenette. The tinted windows had a perfect view of the mountains and the city that stretched between them.

The air hummed. Elise didn't see anything to cause it and assumed it was the air conditioning.

With her ears perked, she moved to the papers stacked on the desk. Mr. Black had an old Royal Deluxe typewriter under a plastic cover and stacks of pages that he had annotated in red ink. She shuffled through them.

They were mostly business letters and invoices. The letters were stamped unevenly across the page, like the mechanisms on the type ball were out of alignment.

"Why a typewriter?" she muttered.

On a hunch, she tried to turn on the plasma TV. It wouldn't work. Electronics often failed around ethereal energy.

So the hum wasn't air conditioning.

She found a map that showed the route of the hijacked semi from Los Angeles to Reno. He had drawn a big red line through the segment that led away from the lakebed and circled the downtown area instead—not far from Craven's.

Elise pushed the map aside to find another one that indicated entrances to abandoned mines. Most of them were crossed out. One had been marked with more arrows than the others.

At the very bottom of the stack, she found a leather-bound journal. Elise opened it. It was new enough that he had only filled the first dozen pages, but she didn't have time to read it. She tucked it under an arm, put the papers back the way she found them, and went into the bedroom.

The bed was unmade, towels were piled on the floor, and the open walk-in closet was filled with Mr. Black and Alain's suits. A maid obviously hadn't been through since they began occupying the penthouse. But why? Elise would have expected it if they were storing fragments of angelic ruin, but there was nothing out of ordinary in the bedroom.

Long loops of ribbon on the bed caught her attention. Elise lifted one to inspect it. Someone—most likely Alain—had been drawing icons on them in black ink. They were similar to the symbols that had been marked around the gate at Mr. Black's vineyard. Symbols of warding and protection. They sparked silver-gray in the corner of her vision, like the magic around the angels' shackles.

338

It looked a lot like paper spells.

A door opened in the other room. Her pulse sped. Someone was home.

Elise drew her knife. Where could she hide? The bathroom? The closet?

Her eyes fell on the balcony.

Elise slid the glass door open and slipped out silently, closing it again behind her. It had high rails and was sheltered from the wind by the building's angle, but the floor-to-ceiling glass left her little space to hide. Far below, cars crept silently along the road, like bits of flotsam on a paved river. Above, there was nothing but an endless stretch of white-blue sky.

She pressed her back against the opaque wall panel between the bedroom and living room, clutching the journal to her chest. The beating sun made the concrete burn against her shoulder blades. Even in a cotton dress, she sweltered.

No noise made it through the windows. Someone could emerge onto the balcony at any moment and she would have no idea they were coming.

Was it Alain or Mr. Black inside? She could surprise them. Sneak up from behind, drive a dagger into his back, watch him bleed out on the carpet. It would be beautiful justice.

But a powerful urge to not get shot held her back. If it was Alain, he would have a gun. And if it was Mr. Black...even worse.

Elise peered around the corner into the bedroom.

Alain was staring through the window.

She hid again, heart pounding, but he hadn't seen her. He gazed at the mountains with his cell phone to his ear.

Elise opened the living room door.

Alain spoke loudly in the bedroom, discussing mine shafts and elevators. She crept toward the front door.

The handle turned. Someone else was coming.

Instead, she darted into the spare bedroom, careful not to make a sound. But the second room wasn't empty.

A dozen pairs of pale eyes stared at her. Angels stood shoulder-to-shoulder in rows and packed every square foot of the floor, from the wall to the bed and to the mirrors. All of them were shackled at the throat or wrist. None of them had wings.

Elise froze, hands raised to her shoulders. She recognized the angel from the desert, but they didn't attack her. They didn't move at all.

339

They just…stared.

Outside, she heard Alain speak again. This time, he was addressing Mr. Black, who responded in his Southern drawl. They were both just outside her door. She couldn't make out the specifics of their conversation through the wall, but she would have known that baritone anywhere.

A mix of anger and fear twisted in her. He was *right there*. She could kill him and end it all.

But if Elise wasn't certain she could take one of them with nothing but a knife, she was definitely sure she couldn't kill both. She stepped toward the angels. "I need to hide," she whispered.

They stepped apart without a sound.

Elise swallowed down her nausea and moved between them. They shifted their arms aside so she wouldn't accidentally brush them.

It had been years since Elise was so close to an angel outside of combat. They pulsed with energy so thick it was tangible, like trying to push through a steel curtain. Ants marched from her spine to her hairline. Her palms itched. Her mouth filled with the iron taste of blood.

Once she passed the first line, the second moved, and the third, and then she was at the back of the room.

The angels continued to face the door as she sank to a crouch behind them. Her muscles wouldn't support her for a moment longer.

The angel that was closest to her turned. It was a female-looking creature with thick brown hair, brown skin, and expressive lips. Her nose was almost flat to her face. "If you see Nukha'il, tell him that Itra'il lives. Please." She was so beautiful, but the idea of helping her made Elise's skin feel like it was trying to crawl off her bones.

Mr. Black's voice rose outside the door.

"Someone's been here."

Itra'il faced forward again. Elise's hand tightened on her dagger.

The men spoke in quieter voices that faded away. No words, no footsteps, no motion.

Then the door opened.

Through the legs of the angels, she could see gray slacks, leather loafers, and the base of a jeweled cane. The hand that gripped it wore a silver cuff bracelet that glimmered with magic similar to that of the angels' shackles. But this was far more powerful.

Mr. Black.

"Has someone been here?" he asked. His voice was so much harsher than Elise remembered. "You. Speak."

A feminine voice rose from the front of the room. "No."

340

"Then who touched my papers?" No response. "None of you are supposed to leave this room. You understand that, don't you?"

When they remained silent, he dropped his cane.

A cry rose from the front of the room. Elise saw one of them hit the floor, and a fist swung into view. The angel didn't make a noise when the blow landed on its jaw.

"Talk to me, you useless piece of shit. My journal didn't disappear on its own!"

"Mercy," whispered the angel.

Mr. Black fisted a clump of long blond hair and dragged it out of the bedroom. The other angels moved to the doorway, leaving Elise feeling exposed in her corner.

"Tell me where it is!"

She couldn't see what was happening, but even without a single noise of pain from the angel, she recognized the sounds of someone being beaten. The angels fanned out around Mr. Black to form a loose circle.

Alain was there, too. She could just see the top of his head. His back faced her. "Let me shoot this one. Perhaps that will help the others speak."

An angel glanced at her, then the door. A path to the exit was open.

"We can't kill any of them," Mr. Black said. "I need them all—for now."

Elise crept toward the door, keeping an eye on the kopis and aspis, but they didn't seem to notice her. They were too focused on beating the angel. It wasn't fighting back—she didn't think it could, with those shackles on—and the others weren't moving to help.

She held her breath as she opened the door a crack and crawled into the hall.

When she shut the door, the angel finally screamed.

Chapter 12

WHEN ELISE RETURNED to the studio, Betty greeted Elise with a shovel and a smudge of dirt on the bridge of her nose. "Mission successful?"

It took Elise a moment to realize she was being spoken to. "Yeah," she said, bumping the car door closed with a hip. She was carrying her dagger and Mr. Black's journal, which Betty eyeballed with way too much interest. "Are you finished?"

"I think so. Morrighan's taking a last look to make sure. Want to help?"

"It's probably fine. I'll take you back to Stephanie's house once you're done."

Betty frowned. "You're kind of pale."

"I'm fine. Check the wards."

Elise sat in the shade under the Motion and Dance sign as Morrighan and Betty made a last lap around the studio. She turned Mr. Black's journal over in her hands, considering the smooth leather and gold foil pages. It shouldn't have bothered her to see him beating his slaves; they were hardly her problem, and far from allies. But she couldn't seem to shake the sound of him punching the shit out of an angel on his carpet.

She shook her head and opened the journal. Much of it was handwritten, but he had inserted a few loose pages from the typewriter. Every entry was signed with the letter "P." She wondered what that name was supposed to indicate. A quick flip through the pages didn't give her any answers.

The first two entries were dull. He had written a short description of his initial deals with Portia, and outlined plans to assemble his gate in one of her warehouses.

The third entry was much more interesting.

Goddamn bitch, it said, as well as, *She stole my collection*. He could barely put together a complete sentence, and his anger turned into a rambling diatribe about legacy, failure, and dying. *What makes a kopis great? Or the greatest? What is my legacy? Nothing left behind...can't die...*

She skimmed the long, unbroken paragraphs of ranting until she reached something more coherent.

I have the artifacts. I have the angels to operate them. Why don't I have the power to summon Him?

"Looks good!" Betty chirped from across the yard. "Thanks so much, Morr!"

"No problem. I'll see you at the next esbat," said the other witch. She raised her voice. "Bye, Elise!"

She didn't look up from the journal. Elise turned to the very last entry, where a folded paper had been inserted between pages. She opened it. A single word was typed across the top in all caps: *GODSLAYER*.

A hot breeze ruffled the page. She smoothed it down with a shaking hand.

If I can't have the gate, I'll use the hag's. And I'll use that Godslayer bitch as God-bait. Maybe then it will work.

A shadow fell across the entry. "Why the sour puss?" Betty asked, flopping to the grass. When Elise didn't immediately respond, she lost her grin. "Okay, you can't fool me. What's wrong? What are you reading?"

Elise snapped the journal shut.

"Nothing. Are you ready to leave?"

Betty sighed. "Yeah. Sure."

Elise took her chain of charms and twin falchions from the safe before leaving. She didn't trust Morrighan's new wards to protect them.

Betty was smart enough not to ask any questions as they drove out to Stephanie's suburb. Elise brooded in silence, knuckles white on the steering wheel.

While waiting at a stoplight on Vista Boulevard, the brand on her shoulder flared with white-hot pain, startling her from her reverie.

An instant later, her cell phone rang. She answered it.

"Get to Eloquent Blood," David Nicholas said.

"Why the fuck should I? You still haven't paid me."

"Night Hag said it's my job to handle your payment. Yeah? You want money, you get down here now."

He hung up before she could ask anything else.

"Who was that?" Betty asked.

Elise set the cell phone on the dash of her car. "Nobody important."

Stephanie's house was exactly what Elise expected. She lived in an unfinished development bordered by golf courses, where the water traps doubled as duck ponds and biking trails wove in and out of each carefully-manicured garden.

James enjoyed the cooling air of sunset from the front step of a house at the end of a cul-de-sac, which had perfect green grass and a white picket fence. Elise felt something unpleasant clench in her throat, like being choked from the inside. It looked like the kind of place people raised kids. Big yard. Quiet street. And James fit in perfectly.

He stood when they pulled into the driveway, brow pinched with concern.

"Don't leave here until I get back. You hear me?" Elise told Betty. She didn't bother turning off the car. There was no way in hell she would go inside that house.

Betty climbed out. "Yeah, yeah. I get it."

She shifted into reverse, but James stepped into the drive before she could leave. He had a book tucked under one arm. The Book of Shadows didn't fit his cozy domestic image. "Are you making another move against Mr. Black?"

"No."

He leaned on her door. "I should come with you." There was a faint hint of scarring near his hairline. Where did he get that one? Elise couldn't remember. They had gotten too many scars together to distinguish them.

She snagged the journal out of the backseat. "Take this."

"What is it?"

"You'll see. Anyway, I'm just running an errand. I'll call you later." She waited, and he didn't move. "Let go of my door."

He stepped back. Elise turned the car around and gunned it.

She couldn't get out of suburbia fast enough.

Downtown Reno was dirty and cramped, as though every casino rejected by Las Vegas had banded together to struggle for survival on the banks of the Truckee River. Even at night, when the neon overwhelmed the stained faces of aging buildings, it didn't look like somewhere that fun things could happen. But whether it was the sticky heat or Elise's black mood, it looked even bleaker than usual.

She parked in a half-empty garage and walked down to Craven's. Elise left her swords in the car, but wore her charms like a necklace. They jingled as she passed through a casino and down the alley to Eloquent

344

Blood.

Blood's layout had been changed that night. Not only had the dance floor been cleared out and replaced with a huge iron cage, there were none of the usual humans hanging around seeking a quick thrill with an incubus. The patronage was distinctly infernal. The demons that hid in the Warrens had come out for a night of fun—the ones that looked like mutated sheep, the amorphous black masses of flesh, and even a Fury so tall that its head would have hit the top of the cage.

Inside, a succubus stripped to the waist took blows from a half-snake demon. It was an ugly, mundane fight. Knuckles connected with face. Blood spattered. They grunted, ducked, dodged, and struck again. Fist against flesh made a sound like pounding into a hunk of meat.

The snake flung the succubus against the bars. The cage rattled, and the crowd roared.

Moving through the crowd, which occupied every floor of Blood, Elise watched money exchange hands with envy. A nightmare threw a wad of cash at his companion when the succubus dropped to the floor with watery blood pouring from her nose. Waitresses hurried around to take formal bets. So much cash in one place.

For once, there was nobody at the bar except Neuma, who wore liquid latex smeared across her breasts. She hurried to fill drinks and drop them on the trays of passing waitresses. Her eyes lit up when she saw Elise.

"Hey, hot stuff! I have something for you! Jump on over."

Elise climbed over the bar. "What's going on?"

"It's our monthly cage fight night," Neuma said, blasting beer into a stein and passing it to one of her waitresses.

"How did I not know about this?"

"You're a human. No humans allowed." She pinched Elise's shoulder gently. "Now you've got the Night Hag's mark, it's an all-access pass to our events. Fun, huh? Here, pour a few drinks and I'll grab your paycheck."

Neuma passed a bottle of tequila to her, leaving Elise to quickly fill a few shots. She could see the edge of the stage from her position back against the wall, and another scream from the crowd cued her to look down and see David Nicholas throw the unconscious succubus over his shoulder. She was completely limp and bleeding freely from the face. Half-demon Gray were fragile creatures with virtually no ability to heal. That broken nose was probably a mortal wound.

The bartender bounced back with an envelope a minute later and

345

stuffed it down Elise's waistband. "Here you go. Gimme that back."

Elise handed her the alcohol, fished the envelope out of her shorts, and broke the seal.

The check was written out in David Nicholas's distinctively hideous handwriting. There was a cigarette burn on the corner. And the amount was for two hundred dollars—barely enough to fill Elise's car with gas all month.

David Nicholas strutted on stage with a microphone. "That useless cunt is down for the count!" he announced to renewed shouts as the snake demon pumped her fists in the air. "Anyone want to take the lamia? Can you beat this bitch?" A scuffle broke out on the bottom floor. Someone shoved a red-fleshed aatxegorri to the front of the line, and he scaled the steps to the cage with a cackle.

David Nicholas thumbed through a roll of cash before flinging it on the crowd. It showered like confetti.

"I'm going to kill him," Elise said.

Neuma's eyes widened. "What? No—no! Don't go down there!"

She ignored the bartender and vaulted over the bar, shoving her way downstairs as David Nicholas returned to his perch in the DJ booth.

He stepped in Elise's path. "The fuck are you doing in my club? You got your money. Get out of here."

"Where's the rest?"

"What you see is what you get. Not happy? Then you should have negotiated terms. No agreement about pay, you get what I give you."

Elise shoved her face into his. "I deserve more than this, and you know it."

David Nicholas gripped her shoulder, digging a bony finger into the brand. It felt like having a knife driven into the bone. "Challenging me? Again?"

She hauled back and knocked him across the booth with her fist.

He sprawled atop the sound board. David Nicholas scowled without getting up. "I'll tell the Night Hag," he hissed, upper lip curling to bare teeth yellowed by time and tobacco.

"Tell her what? That you're skimping out on my pay?"

"I'll tell her that you're violating the contract. The part that says you and me aren't allowed to kill each other."

"I got you those ruins, I made an appearance at that party, and if you don't pay me—"

He sneered. "Nobody ever said how much money you get. You deal with it, or you don't get paid at all. No complaints from me if you want to

346

call this truce off. I'll kill your aspis myself."

She grabbed his shirt in both fists and dragged him to his feet, then slammed his back against the panel. Elise shoved her face close to his. "Say that again."

"Whoa! Hang on there!" Neuma grabbed Elise's arm. "Let him go, doll." She lowered her voice. "People are watching. Calm down. Have a drink." She pried one of Elise's hands off of David Nicholas's shirt so she could shove a bottle of vodka into it.

Elise released him. She itched to turn his face into a pulpy mess, but it wasn't the time or the place. And he was right. She should have known better than to not declare the terms of her contract in the beginning. But two hundred dollars wasn't going to cut it.

She glanced at all the money exchanging hands below. The aatxegorri was completely destroying the lamia, and people were getting rich on it. The snake demon wasn't fast enough to withstand his bull-like strength, and he had already ripped open her tail with one of his horns. Elise had fought an aatxegorri before. They were hideous, but slow. She could outmaneuver them in her sleep.

She turned on David Nicholas. He raised his hands to defend himself, but she didn't attack. "Let me take the next fight. Hell, the next dozen fights."

He grinned. His split lip bled something black. "Why? Is it my birthday or something?"

"No, Elise, you don't know what you're volunteering for," Neuma said. "Drink. Drink!"

She took a swig. It burned hot all the way into her stomach. "I'll take the next few fights. You know I'll kick ass. Nobody expects a female kopis, so you guys can collect on all the bets against me—and I get a percentage."

"Deal!" David Nicholas said before Neuma could open her mouth again. "Here's the rules: You get in the pen and fight until one of you isn't standing. No killing." His mouth twisted. "Unfortunately. You keep at it for five rounds, or until you're kicked shitless and can't get up. I'll send you home alive with a cushy paycheck. A thousand bucks, if you win them all."

A thousand dollars. Her head buzzed, and she wasn't sure if it was alcohol or excitement.

"Neuma, get cloth bandages. Now," she said, taking another drink. "And I want to take you in the ring, David Nicholas."

Neuma ran off. He dragged on a cigarette she hadn't noticed him

347

lighting. "Fuck no. My life's worth more than that. You can have five percent of the bets."

"Fifty. I'm the one fighting."

"Employees got to get paid. Ten."

"Twenty-five, or I'll go to the Night Hag and let her pick an amount. I wonder what she would think of this."

His mouth twitched. He smashed the tip of his cigarette on the sound board. "Fine."

She stripped off her jacket. Neuma returned, and Elise took her gloves off one at a time, replacing them with bandages around her knuckles. In the cage, the lamia crumpled, and a waitress dragged her out by the tail.

The crowd started to cheer as soon as David Nicholas leaped onto the stage.

"Ladies and gentlemen, we have a fight!"

"No humans."

James squinted at the bouncer blocking the door to Eloquent Blood. It was almost twice his height and had to stoop to fit in the doorway. Thick tusks protruded from either side of its mouth. He thought it was a female, but it was hard to tell if sagging breasts were a sexual characteristic on demons or a racial feature.

"Pardon me?" he said, realizing he had been analyzing its exposed breasts for too long.

"No humans," it repeated, barely able to articulate English words. It crossed its massive arms over its chest. Each one was as thick as his waist.

"But this is the human entrance to Eloquent Blood. It even says 'humans.'"

"It's a cage fight night. No humans. Too dangerous."

James stepped back with a frown, tipping his glasses over his nose to study the alley entrance to Craven's again. If there were no humans allowed in Eloquent Blood on the night of a cage fight, then what was Elise doing?

He had left Stephanie's house five minutes after she did and followed her downtown. He didn't have to track her car to find her. James had a sixth sense for Elise in the same way she had a sixth sense for demons, and he could have found her anywhere on the planet. Her car was parked in a nearby garage, and he was certain he could feel her inside.

"I could pay you," he suggested.

348

The bouncer rolled its beady black eyes, backed into the hallway, and slammed the door. The rusted sign that said "humans" bounced and rattled.

He took a deep breath, tamping down on his frustration.

Knowing Elise, she was in mortal peril right that second, which was her idea of "running errands." He wouldn't have had to chase her down if she had just let him come along.

"Damn it, Elise," he muttered to the closed door.

He took the street entrance to Craven's. Since that was the door to the human entrance, there had to be one for demon patrons as well. And hopefully it wouldn't be guarded by some kind of troll.

Craven's was especially labyrinthine, even for a casino. Finding his way to the back was difficult, and it didn't do any favors for his mood.

He spotted a pale figure darting behind a row of slot machines with bare shoulders and a crate in her arms. She looked like some kind of waitress. James tailed her through the winding paths until she ducked in a back hallway. He made sure nobody was watching before following.

Now that he saw her unobstructed, he realized with dull shock that she wasn't just another cocktail waitress. She was a pale, voluptuous woman wearing nothing but liquid latex. Definitely one of the strippers from Blood. There was a black handprint on one of her otherwise bare ass cheeks. He caught her arm.

"Are you going down to the club?"

She didn't snap at him for grabbing her. Her eyes illuminated with delight, and she set the crate down as easily as though it was filled by feathers instead of jingling bottles of alcohol. Once her arms were free, she melted against his body, warm and soft and pliant.

"Well *hello*, handsome. What can I do for you?" she purred, rubbing a thigh against his. "I have a few ideas if you don't. My name is Neuma."

Bile crept up his throat. Demons. Mindless animal urges wrapped in something resembling flesh. Yet another thing he hadn't missed since retiring.

"I need to get to Blood—*without* the succubus charm, thank you. I'm looking for a kopis. Elise Kavanagh. About this height, kind of wavy hair..." He gestured at chest level.

"You're Elise's, huh? Ooh. She sure likes 'em tall. And mature." Neuma trailed her hand up the hem of James's shirt and stroked his hip bone. He caught her wrist to prevent her from dipping her fingers behind his belt. That didn't seem to actually discourage her. She circled around to plaster herself against his back. "Maybe she'll share if I ask nice."

She traced her fingernails over the white streaks at his temples and down the line of his jaw. He swatted at her.

"Stop that."

"I could be just as much fun as she is. Even more fun. Why d'you want her?"

Where a succubus was concerned, his mind was not in charge. It was hard to think when all the blood was being redirected from his skull to his pelvic region. "I'm her aspis," he said stiffly.

His arousal vanished in an instant, like a switch had been flipped.

Neuma took a big step back. "Oh." She heaved a big sigh. "Sorry. I didn't realize you're *James*. I never would have...heck." She glanced around as though she expected to see someone else in the hall, but they were alone. "I don't think I should take you down there."

"I'm asking politely. For now."

"All right, handsome. Don't blame me if you don't like what you see. But you get to carry the booze with those big ol' hands of yours."

Before he could protest, she shoved the crate into his arms and started down the hall again. He staggered under the weight of it as he hurried to follow her swaying hips.

"How do you know my name?"

She bat her eyelashes at him over her shoulder. "I read minds. You're having dirty thoughts about me, you bad boy."

"The hell you do."

"I like a temper on a man. Makes him tastier." She sighed, giving him a long look that said she was mentally undressing him. "Crying shame. Come on, keep up with me."

Neuma led him down several flights of stairs. When she pushed through a door marked "Employees Only," the sound of a roaring crowd spilled into the stairwell. She led him to a dressing room. There was an entire wall occupied by shelves of alcohol.

She started to unload the crate as he held it, but James dropped the box on one of the vanity counters.

"Where is she?" he asked.

Neuma jerked a thumb at the door. "Out there. You can't miss her, if she's still standing. Don't come complaining to me when you see what's what. You got it?"

James ducked out of the room. The end of the hall opened up behind the bar. It was mostly empty, but what was there almost made his eyes fall out of his head. He had only ever heard of Blood from Elise before, but she failed to mention that they didn't bother clothing their waitresses, all of whom appeared to be half-demon Gray. These ones wore nothing but panties, boots, and reflective electrical tape over their nipples.

The women gave him a few strange looks when he exited the bar, but nobody stopped him as he moved up to the rail to scan the crowd. He searched for Elise's auburn hair amongst all the motion. No humans. Most of them didn't even have hair.

And then he saw the cage.

"Oh hell," he muttered.

Elise faced off against two demons: an aatxegorri and a brand new nightmare, semi-transparent skin and all. She had a half-empty bottle of vodka and a swollen eye that dripped blood down her cheek. Her clear eye blazed. Her lips were peeled back in a grin. Every time her fist or foot connected, something like satisfaction surfaced in her expression before fading into the drunken haze again.

Intoxication hardly slowed her down. If anything, it kept her from holding back.

She *brutalized* her attackers.

Knuckles met face with a wet crunch. Her legs were a blur of kicks and lunges. She stopped only to throw back another swig of vodka, then twirled to backhand someone as they jumped at her.

The crowd loved it. They screamed, they cheered.

James was horrified.

He rushed down the steps and shoved through the crowd. It was hardly less violent in the audience. He took an elbow to the face and a hard shove on his way down, but he managed to fight his way to the front row and grip the bars of the cage.

"Elise!" he shouted. "Elise!"

She didn't hear him. The crowd was too noisy.

Elise snapped a high kick into the jaw of the nightmare. It cracked so loudly that the audience was shocked into a moment of silence, and then they cheered again with new vigor. The nightmare crumpled against the side of the cage. It didn't look like he was getting up again.

She pumped her arms into the air victoriously.

"Who's next? Who can take down this machine?" shouted an announcer.

The aatxegorri took the moment of distraction to jump at her again, but there was no surprising her. She whipped around, grabbed his neck, and smashed his face into the bars.

Clawed hands shoved wads of money through the cage. Elise grabbed a fistful and kissed it. "Oh dear Lord," James groaned. He couldn't even

351

hear himself over all the shouting.

A demon wrenched the door open, and only the succubus bartender leaping in the way prevented half the crowd from spilling inside. But when a Fury twice James's height stomped through the crowd, Neuma didn't even try to fight him. It stooped low and climbed into the cage.

Elise grinned when she saw what joined her. She shoved the money down her shirt, threw back another drink of vodka, and beckoned for the Fury to attack.

James's anger was forgotten in a wash of fear. Elise had killed a Fury before—and a multitude of other large and nasty creatures—but that was when she was armed, sober, and free to move around the landscape. Her remaining eye could barely focus on her attacker.

The Fury rushed her. Two pale, meaty fists seized her by the shoulders and slammed her into the bars in front of James.

The crowd roared and jostled him against the barrier.

"Elise!" he yelled again. She didn't see him. She kicked the Fury away.

The aatxegorri clambered to his hooves. With a snap of his wrist, a switchblade flashed in the stage lights. She was too busy with the Fury to notice.

"Watch out!"

She still couldn't hear him.

The aatxegorri inched to the side, waiting for an opening.

James leaped onto the steps, pushed Neuma away from the door, and got in. There were protesting shouts from the audience. He ran forward and punched the aatxegorri in the back of the head.

He hadn't thrown a good punch in years. The force of it radiated all the way up his arm and into his spine. One of his knuckles split open with a flaming shock of pain.

The demon whirled on him as he shook out his fist. He raised his hands to indicate no desire to fight. "I'm not—" he began to say, but it didn't wait for him to finish. It lowered its horned head and rushed him.

James knocked the knife out of its hands and took the full brunt of its body.

Getting hit by a bull-demon was a lot like getting struck by a car on the highway. James's back hit the bars, blinding him with pain so powerful that it took a good five seconds for him to really feel it.

What he *did* feel was the tip of a horn ripping his sleeve open and burying in his bicep. He seized the horns on instinct and wrenched them away, throwing the aatxegorri into the Fury.

They both dropped. The impact made the entire cage rock.

Elise's eye met his over the bodies. Her jaw dropped. *"James?"*

He jumped over the Fury and grabbed her elbow. He was about ready to give her a good shake, but she was so pummeled that he wasn't sure she would remain conscious through it. "What were you thinking? A *cage fight?*"

But it wasn't time for an argument. The Fury pushed itself onto all fours.

Elise shoved James out of the way. "Move it!"

She drove her knee into the Fury's face, and it fell again with a splatter of yellow blood.

Demons were yelling, the stage lights were blindingly bright, and James regretted jumping in. Neuma alone wasn't enough to hold the crowd back for long, and the entire bar was about to start fighting. The announcer seemed to love it. He shouted incoherently over the speakers.

The aatxegorri charged again. James dived for the knife. He clutched it in his fist and blindly jabbed.

It sank into flesh and jerked free of his hand.

An instant later, all the yelling outside the cage changed from excitement to panic.

The crowd shifted. Footsteps thudded. James ran to the bars to squint outside. The demons were feeling for the doors to the Warrens. Even the aatxegorri and the Fury shared in the panic—they both scrambled out the door and down the steps.

Elise chugged the last of the vodka and flung the bottle to the stage.

"Hey! David Nicholas!" she shouted, shielding her eyes from the spotlights. "What the hell's going on?"

It was Neuma who replied. She appeared in the open doorway again, breathless and wide-eyed. "There's a whole freaking army of cops. We gotta clear."

James's heart dropped.

Elise snatched his hand and dragged him off the stage with a pronounced limp. She scrubbed furiously at her blood-crusted eye. "Where are they?"

Neuma hung back on the steps, visibly torn between following Elise or the other demons. "The girls are trying to hold them off upstairs in Craven's, but I don't know—how would they know how to find the door to Blood anyway?"

"Mr. Black," Elise said, spitting his name like an insult. "Get out of here. Go!"

The bartender ran after the others. Where there had easily been two hundred bodies clustered around the stage moments before, there was nobody left a few moments later. David Nicholas was gone. One of the basandere waitresses darted up to the hall behind the bar and vanished.

Elise hauled James up the stairs to the human entrance. "Shouldn't we follow—?" he began.

"No. Can't go into the Warrens. We have to make a break for it." She stumbled over her own feet. He caught her.

"Jesus, Elise, you can't even run! How much did you drink?"

"Enough."

James propped her upright, but she sagged on him. "I think you and I need to have a talk."

"Lecture later. Move now."

She shoved him toward the door, and they broke into the long hallway back to the alley on the surface. The tusked bouncer was long gone. Nothing kept them from rushing out of blood and into the hot night air.

On the other side, someone had opened the gate blocking off the alley. Three police cruisers with flashing lights waited on the other side.

Elise tripped on a bag of trash and sprawled across the pavement.

"Don't move!" someone shouted. The spotlights mounted above the windshields blasted right at them, and James could only make out blurred shapes on the other side. He froze in mid-crouch with his hands on Elise's arm.

"A very serious talk," he muttered. Louder, he said, "I'll comply! We're not going to run, we're just—"

A man in uniform emerged from the light to take James's arm. Elise chose that moment to roll over and focus her bleary eye on them. Rage instantly filled her face at the sight of someone grabbing her aspis.

Elise lunged to her feet and swung one of her best punches.

The cop took it in the jaw. Out in a heartbeat.

"Don't fight, don't fight!" James cried, but it was much too late. Three of the others descended on her with pepper spray and batons.

He didn't get a chance to watch. The last officer was too busy shoving him against the police car and handcuffing him. He got into the enclosed backseat of the cruiser without arguing.

Elise put up a good fight, as always, but even she had her limits. Facing down four trained police officers after a long cage fight was apparently hers. They pinned her down, cuffed her, and tossed her in the cruiser with him. Her good eye was streaming from the pepper spray.

"What were you thinking?" he hissed when she drooped against him, coughing weakly. "Attacking a *police officer*?"

She responded by passing out drunk on his side.

Chapter 13

JAMES AND ELISE were fingerprinted, photographed, and thrown into jail.

He rested on his side to keep his swollen cheekbone against the concrete floor of his cell. The chill felt good against the heat of his bruises. His head throbbed and his arm ached, but the worst part was imagining what Stephanie would say when she realized that Elise had gotten him into a fight. Again.

"This is not one of my best days," he groaned.

Elise reclined against the wall in an adjacent cell, pinching her nose with her head tipped back. "I've had worse." Her voice came out tinny and nasal. She pulled the tissue off to examine what had come out of her nostrils, grimaced, and put it back.

"Do you want to tell me what that was?"

"That was a cage fight gone wrong. Or gone right. It's hard to tell."

He swore under his breath. "Yes. I saw that. The question is, *how* did you end up in a cage fight?"

"Long story. Not worth telling."

"We've been incarcerated for public intoxication and assaulting a police officer. You damn well better have a good reason for it. What is going on, Elise?"

"My office got trashed. Mr. Black has driven off my clientele, burned down my house, and destroyed my savings. I don't have clean clothes to wear. I can't buy anything new. I have no money."

He rolled over to glare at her. "And how was a cage fight supposed to help?"

"Percentage of bets. And..." She snorted into the tissue. Blood dribbled down her wrist. "I cut a deal with the Night Hag. I'm kind of working for her now."

"Good Lord, you couldn't have found something *safer* to do? Something less bloody?"

"I'm sure they would let me strip on the bar."

James's headache tripled in an instant. He mashed his bruised face against the concrete again to try to block out the mental image of Elise as a latex-clad bartender. "Why didn't you just ask me for help?" He managed to sound exhausted instead of angry. "I have plenty of money."

"Even though you just bought a house with Stephanie?"

The sharpness in her tone made him flinch, but he wasn't sure why. There was nothing to feel guilty about. "You know you've always been my first priority," he said in a measured voice.

"You didn't even tell me you were moving. I found out because all your stuff was gone." Elise's words were slurred. He wasn't sure if it was the bloody nose or the alcohol. "If that's first priority, I don't want to see second."

James gathered his willpower and sat up. All the blood rushed to his head. He groaned and pressed the heels of his palms to his temples. "This conversation isn't about me. This is about you becoming some kind of... I don't know what in the world you're becoming. A mercenary?"

"I did it for you."

She was quiet enough that he wasn't sure he heard her right. "What?"

"I said..." She snorted again. There was less blood this time, but pain furrowed her brow. "I did it for you. Jackass." Elise dropped the tissue and rubbed blood off her chin with a wrist. "Mr. Black is out to get us. Killing you would be the fastest way to get back at me. I can't go after him and protect you at the same time, and I needed money anyway, so I agreed to work with the Night Hag. She's had guys watching you."

"You've had demons following me? *Demons*?"

"You're welcome," she said, resting her head against the wall again. This time, it wasn't to keep blood from flowing out of her nose. She appeared to be on the verge of passing out. A fifteen-minute blackout had probably been the most sleep she'd gotten in days.

"I can't believe you've allied with an overlord."

"I ally with no one."

His fists gripped the bars. Now that she was beginning to sober, her chilly calm grated on him. "Then what do you call this?"

"Survival."

James laughed harshly. "Survival? Getting drunk and fighting for money is survival? Getting thrown in jail is survival?"

357

"Yeah, well." Elise gave a half-hearted shrug with one shoulder.

The only thing that calmed his temper—slightly—was when she moved her hand away so he could see that her face was practically hamburger. That damned sense of pity he always harbored for her had a habit of winning out over everything else.

She spoke again before he could find inner calm. "Did you read the journal?"

"No, I didn't have time. What's in it?"

"It belongs to Mr. Black. It says he wants to use me as bait for...for Him."

And in an instant, all the anger vanished from James.

"Jesus."

"Yeah. He seems to think it will give him power." She sounded calm, but he could see the fear in her expression. Even Elise wasn't good enough to hide that. "I won't let Mr. Black do it. There's no way in hell I'm going through one of those gates."

"Why don't I call Stephanie? She can post bail. We'll discuss Mr. Black and decide how to address him. There must be a better way than working with demons."

"Yeah, the good doctor's going to love this," Elise said. "Have fun with that."

He threw his hands in the air. "Do you think those new *friends* of yours are going to help us? I seriously doubt that!"

"Hmm. Such cynicism."

That wasn't Elise's voice.

James turned. There was a strange man outside his cell, with hair like night and darkly glimmering eyes. He set every one of James's instincts alarming, but it was hard to tell why. The un-tucked black shirt and slacks were hardly threatening. James found himself backing into the corner of his cell anyway.

"Who are you?"

The stranger gave James a languorous look from feet to face. Silver rings with heavy black stones glimmered at each of his fingers. "You may call me Thom. I am known as a witch in the service of the Night Hag. There's no need to introduce yourself; I am very familiar with you, James Faulkner."

"Did you come to laugh at me?" Elise asked, utterly unsurprised at his silent entrance.

"No. I am here to take you away. The overlord wishes to see you."

"I'm already going in front of a judge for assault. I don't need a jailbreak on my record, too. But tell the Night Hag thanks."

"You will have nothing on your record, and no officer will remember bringing you here," Thom said.

James squared his shoulders. "We won't go."

The other witch surveyed him expressionlessly. "You will owe us nothing, James Faulkner. The debt from this release falls solely on the shoulders of your kopis."

Even worse.

Elise tossed her tissues to the floor and climbed off the bench. "Fine. Let's go." She showed no sign of her earlier intoxication aside from flushed cheeks. James searched for something to say that might convince her, but words failed him.

"Don't," James said. Thom laid a hand on the lock to her door. It sizzled and filled the air with the smell of hot iron. Molten metal dripped to the concrete. "Elise—listen to me. Don't do this."

The cell sprung open with a whine. Thom offered his hand to her— the same hand that had just melted a lock.

Elise met James's eyes and laid her fingers in Thom's.

"This is your last chance," said the other witch.

"Go to hell," James said.

Thom grinned a disarming grin.

He took a step to the side, and without so much as a sound or a flash of light, they both vanished.

Instantaneous teleportation was not all it was cracked up to be. Elise's mind was unprepared to process the shift. She didn't black out and her vision didn't fade, so she had no frame of reference for a transition from the jail to Eloquent Blood. James's face watched her from the other side of the iron bars one moment, and then she was staring at a mirrored wall illuminated by blue neon the next. The air went from warm to cool. The smells shifted.

And then, too, did the contents of her stomach.

She doubled over. Her shoulders heaved, and with two short jerks of her abs, bile spattered at her feet. It tasted like vodka. Tears blurred her vision.

A smooth hand cupped her elbow, keeping her on her feet. "Don't worry. Your head will clear shortly."

Elise had to spit another mouthful of acid onto the floor before she could speak. Good thing she hadn't eaten anything in days. "That's impossible. How do you...?"

"Your aspis possesses magic of which other witches cannot dream. It is not inconceivable that there are greater and older magicks beyond that." Thom stood back and she righted herself with a hand on the bar.

All the house lights were on in Eloquent Blood. The paint was dull and boring without the mystery afforded by strobe and fog machines. Broken bottles and scraps of paper littered the floor by the empty cage.

It wasn't an illusion or a dream. She had really been transported.

"I believe this is yours."

Thom held up her chain of charms. They had been confiscated by the police before they put her in a cell to sober up.

She took them. "Don't touch these ever again."

"You're welcome. This is yours as well."

Where had he gotten her falchions and spine sheath? It seemed like a stupid question, considering he had magically whisked her out of jail. Of course he could get into the trunk of her car. She pulled the scabbard on like a backpack and pulled her hair out from under it. "Why am I back here?"

"You've been summoned to the Warrens. I prefer not to substantiate where demons will see me for now, and the walk will help you ground yourself. I thought you might also like to clean up."

He swept a hand toward the dressing rooms. Elise climbed over the bar and went inside—alone—to flick on the lights over the vanities.

Her reflection blazed in the mirror, and she grimaced to see herself. Blood caked her hair to her scalp. Her face was one big bruise from chin to forehead, and her left eye barely opened. There were lines on her brow she didn't think had been there before.

No wonder James had been so disgusted with her. She looked like she was dying.

Elise turned on the sink and stuck her head under the faucet, scrubbing her hair until the steaming water ran clear. Then she rinsed off her cracked knuckles, patted her face dry with a towel, and bound her hands in fresh bandages. The damage almost looked worse once she was clean.

Either Thom was too polite to remark on her appearance when she returned to the bar, or he genuinely didn't care. "Come." He strode off, ponytail floating behind him, and she realized belatedly that he wasn't wearing shoes.

Elise's head spun as she followed him, unsteady from the transition.

The floor tipped under her feet as she walked.

The long, slow elevator ride and journey through the mines left her nothing to think about but James's guilt trip. She couldn't push away the memory of his last plea: *Don't do this.*

Ungrateful bastard.

"He will come around," Thom said, stopping in front of the doors to the Night Hag's chambers.

"What, is mind reading another one of your super-witch skills?"

"I don't need to read your mind when I can read your hormones. The cortisol, the oxytocin—not to mention your heart rate. The flush in the cheeks. The longing stares." He sneered. The lines on either side of his mouth were strange on his blank, beautiful face. "Always the same, you people. So predictable."

Elise realized her jaw was hanging and clapped her teeth shut. "What are you talking about?"

He pushed the doors open.

"As you requested," Thom said, entering the room like a herald in front of royalty.

The Night Hag was in bed again, but she wasn't propped up by pillows anymore. Instead, she sat with a straight back and her arms resting on the bars like it was a throne.

Thom moved to attend to a bag of saline on her right, regarding the valve with the same impassive gaze he used on everything else. The rubber tubes on the overlord's other arm led to metal drums tucked behind the bed, where a whirring motor pumped something sludgy and black through the needle. There was no way her veins should have been able to accommodate so much fluid. Her skin was flushed with crimson.

She snapped her fingers. "You. Come here."

Heat stabbed through Elise's shoulder brand. Clenching her jaw, she limped to the chair at which the Night Hag pointed.

As she moved to the other side of the bed, a bloody pile writhing on the floor came into view. It looked like several thick, twisted worms draped in shreds of cloth.

A daimarachnid? She froze.

"Sit. Sit!"

Elise sank into the chair. "The payment…"

"Yes, I've heard what David Nicholas did, even though I explicitly told him not to fuck with you. I also heard about his little game with the cage. Funny. Very funny." Her lips peeled back in a grimace. "Unfortunately for his sake, I have no sense of humor."

She glanced at the pile of flesh when she spoke.

Oh no.

Elise's stomach flipped. She could see it now: the yellow hairs, the leather jacket, the shredded black jeans. It was as though David Nicholas had been turned inside out. Nightmares didn't have bones and organs and muscle the way humans did, so he was barely more than a rubbery mess of skin.

He moaned from a hole that might have once been his mouth. A ruined black tongue lashed between shattered fragments of teeth.

"Kill him," Elise said. "This is…"

"Lose the sentimentality. He knew the consequences of challenging me."

Sentimental? That was one adjective Elise had never heard used to describe her before. Was it sentimental to find the destroyed nightmare's agony nauseating? Was it sentimental to prefer quick, clean deaths to… *that*?

"You should know I volunteered for the cage fight."

The Night Hag's skin shivered. The flesh over her shoulders rippled as though something pressed against it from the inside. "And *you* should be thanking your beloved God that I need you more than David Nicholas, or I would do the same to you."

Elise gripped her chain of charms. "You're awfully confident you would win."

"Keep that mouth shut, kopis, or I'll rip it from your face. Remember who is branded by who! Now. We have two things to take care of. Firstly…" She lifted a hand. Elise tensed.

Thom stepped forward to offer Elise an envelope. Her skin crawled when she took it.

There was cash inside. She took the time to count it without caring if it was rude to do so. "Five hundred dollars? I brought you a semi full of angelic artifacts."

"No, you brought a semi *partly* filled with angelic artifacts. That's a failure in my book. Don't pull faces; you can earn more—much more. I'm not done with you yet."

Elise stuffed the money in her back pocket. At least it was more than David Nicholas had tried to pay her. "What else?"

A smile grew on the Night Hag's lips. It wasn't a happy smile, and it made her gut clench like she was going to throw up again. "The second thing, yes. Finish David Nicholas."

The pile on the floor groaned.

"Nightmares can't be killed," Elise said.

"Exorcise him. Send him back to Hell. Let him float in a mire of souls for a few hundred years."

Even though Thom didn't move or speak, Elise suddenly felt compelled to look at him. Indeed, his absolute stillness was what drew her attention. His eyes glimmered. They were completely black, from pupil to iris and consuming the whites.

She had exorcised nightmares before and would do it again. But she didn't want Thom to see her do it.

Elise thought of her empty checking account. The insurance company. Her landlords.

"Fine," she said, unspooling the charms from around her neck as she stood.

She considered David Nicholas at her feet. This was the creature that had irritated her like a fly she couldn't swat for months. He had refused to pay her. Treated her like shit. Abused his employees. Gathered his friends, jumped her in a parking lot, and tried to beat her to death.

He twisted, rolled over, and oozed a few inches to the right. His body left an imprint of blood and ichor. A fingerprint of misery. A single eyeball rolled in the mass that was his skull, and she thought it was glaring at her.

"Hurry up," snapped the Night Hag. "I have better things to do than watch this."

Elise wrapped the chains around her fist, then drew one of the falchions on her back and rested the flat of the blade against him. He thrashed weakly. "*Crux sacra sit mihi lux,*" she said, closing her eyes and focusing on her other sense. Those shattered yellow teeth were burned in her skull. "*Non draco sit mihi dux.*"

A light flared through her eyelids. The St. Benedict charm had illuminated.

She reached out with her mind to grasp the sense of the nightmare in front of her—a once-powerful demonic force that had begun fading like a dying heartbeat. He fought, of course. They always did.

Elise gripped him tighter. The mass on the floor grunted, bubbled, and fell silent.

"*Vade retro, Satana, nunquam suade mihi vana.*" A shriek. A twitch. "*Sunt mala quae libas. Ipse venena bibas.*" Elise envisioned the gates to the infernal planes, and all the pain that would be waiting for him there. "Return to the Hell in which you belong, David Nicholas. Begone."

It wasn't as much of a struggle as it should have been. The light flared brighter for an instant, blotting out the shadow David Nicholas cast upon her senses. But when she opened her eyes, all that remained in front of her was the ichor stain. Her charms were smoking.

He was gone.

"The flame of a thousand years quenched in an instant." The Night Hag grinned. "Fantastic."

Elise sheathed her sword and stood, trying not to look at Thom even though she could feel him watching. She shook the charms loose from her hand and hung them around her neck again. "Five hundred dollars won't last long."

"Yes, yes. David Nicholas's suffering has put me in a good mood, so I'll send along your winnings from the cage fight. Does that mollify your greedy soul?" She didn't wait for an answer before waving her hand again. "Get out of my sight."

Thom glided to the door, and Elise followed him. She felt odd without David Nicholas's taunts to follow her—odd, but satisfied.

The Night Hag called out. "Remember, kopis. If you piss me off, that will be you next time."

And with that friendly reminder, Thom closed the doors.

Elise strode briskly toward the elevator.

Thom stepped close, blocked her path, and stared at her with gleaming eyes. No, not at her—at her charms. "Interesting," he said.

"I want to go home." She took a quick step back when he reached for the chains. "I told you not to touch those again."

His hand dropped. "I suppose I would be defensive if I had a critical piece of angelic ruin around my neck as well."

Elise clenched her fists.

He knew.

The soapy white stone was the size of her thumbnail, suspended between an ankh and a Star of David, and completely innocuous. There was no way to tell that it was part of the bowl she had retrieved for Mr. Black a decade before. A kopis might have recognized it, if he knew what he was looking at, but a witch?

"Have you told her?" she asked.

"No. But she will seek it when her gate does not work."

"You know, when I was in Mr. Black's penthouse, there was a map of old mine shafts," Elise said. "He's found a way into the Warrens. The gate isn't safe here. She shouldn't assemble it."

"Interesting. But hardly my concern."

"Why did you send me there if you don't care?"

364

He bent down to whisper in her ear. "Because I wanted to see what you would do." His mild tone sent shivers down her spine.

She stepped around him and set a fast pace to the elevator. She hated having that witch behind her, but her urge to leave overruled everything else. He was so quiet at her back that she thought he had fallen behind, but when she turned to shut the elevator door, he side-stepped in before she could close it.

Thom pulled the lever. The elevator lurched into motion. He never stopped staring at her.

They ascended slowly, inch by inch, and the rock slid past them outside the cage. The lone bulb flickered. It cast strange shadows on Thom's face, making him look more like a statue than a human.

Her back hit the railing. She didn't realize she had moved away from him.

"Careful," he said in that mild voice.

"Stop looking at me like that."

"Like what?"

Elise's hand tightened on her mother's cross, where it dangled beside the charm of St. Benedict. "Like you're going to eat me."

He hooked his thumbs in the loops of his slacks. Jutted his hip to the side. Tilted his chin. It was a look of pure seduction, but those eyes—those black eyes—completely ruined it. "Would you prefer this?"

She drew her sword in response as the elevator shuddered. The light went out. Her heart pounded and her nerves rang like a cracked bell struck with a mallet. The darkness lasted only a second, maybe two.

When the light came back on, Thom had vanished.

Elise whirled, searching for him in the little six foot by six foot box. There was nowhere to hide. He had transported himself away again.

The lift stopped, and she kept her sword at the ready as she opened the door and moved into the hall behind the DJ booth. Someone had turned off the house lights in Blood again. Only a thin neon strip by the floor lit her path.

She couldn't see Thom, but he spoke. His voice came from the end of the hall. The only way out.

"Accelerated heartbeat. Vasoconstriction. Auditory exclusion. Loss of complex motor control." He gave a low chuckle. "I see how you move, hunter, I read your body signs. That is fear. Arousal."

Another step forward. There was nowhere else to go.

"Don't touch me," she said. "I said I'm leaving, and I'll go through you if I have to."

365

"It takes so little to disturb humans. Nothing more than a few tricks of light. After what I heard of you, I expected you to be different."

Elise reached the end of the hall. She eased around the corner, back to the wall, and faced the DJ booth.

Nothing.

"But you are what you are. There's no mistaking that." Thom's voice dropped, assuming that husky tone again. "I need you, and I will have you."

She didn't bother responding. Instead, she drew her other sword and stepped around the DJ booth.

Thom lounged by the cage, studying his fingernails. He didn't look the same as he had in the earth below. The shift was subtle, but distinct. A strange glow had come over his flesh, and his hair had turned to ink. It was as though he was airbrushed smooth, a dream walking on earth, and it was hard to look at him for very long.

"What the hell are you?" she whispered.

"That isn't relevant. What matters is that I know who you are." He pointed to her gloved hand without touching it, and his lips formed a single word: "*Godslayer.*"

Elise stiffened. "Where did you hear that?"

Thom pointed to the sky.

There was nothing above him but a roof painted black, smeared with sticky fluids that might have been cooking grease or blood or both. But she knew what he meant. And she felt cold, so horribly cold, like the chill that accompanied death had settled upon her.

Such knowledge was dangerous. Too dangerous.

Elise lunged.

The blade sliced through empty air. Thom darted to the side, and she spun and swung the sword again in a wide arc. But he was gone again, and again. Elise twisted and jabbed, sinking her falchion into nothing every time.

When she missed her third thrust, she unbalanced and staggered. Her left knee connected with the ground. The impact jolted up her hip.

Thom stood just out of reach, arms folded, completely composed. "You would kill someone for simply speaking that name."

"I have before."

"You could never kill me. You are weak."

Elise gritted her teeth. She threw her entire body into her dive, slashing and swinging. Thom stepped aside. The breeze ruffled his hair. Jerking her second sword free, she brought them both in a high arc. Elise cut across his body.

He was suddenly on the bar, and she hadn't seen him climb it. Elise leaped onto a chair, a stool, and onto his level.

Elise was a blur of motion as she moved on instinct. She had never been so fast in her life. But Thom was faster. She kicked glasses out of the way and they shattered on the floor. Another thrust. Another calm step back. Her swings were completely ineffective.

He landed on the floor again. She seized a bottle and jumped over him, knocked a table over, landed with a thud. She kicked the table toward him.

Thom moved just a tiny bit slower that time. It almost tripped him.

She rose to her knees and chucked the bottle at his head. It cracked into his shoulder, and he flinched—the barest reaction. Elise brought the glass bottle down like a club. She saw him duck out of the way. Another miss.

He spun and twisted behind her. He didn't trip on the fallen table. She reached for him, flinging her free hand out, and her fingertips brushed silk.

She knew a moment before he disappeared again that he would reappear on the other side of the table.

Her sword was there when he stepped back.

Thom looked down at her fist pressed tight against his side. The blade jutted from his back.

Blood rushed in Elise's ears, a roar of white noise that drowned out her breath. Satisfaction surged through her. She saw nothing but Thom's pale, surprised face, and the genuine shock in his black eyes.

"Good," he said, and her satisfaction vanished. Thom stepped away from her. The blade exited his body as smoothly as it had entered, and he didn't show any signs of pain. Her fingers went slack with shock. She almost dropped her falchion. "Clean your blade if you want to keep it."

When she didn't immediately move, he plucked it from her unresponsive hand and wiped it off on his shirt. He lifted the sword to study it in the bar lights.

Once he was satisfied it was clean, he returned it to her. She missed twice before sheathing it.

"What are you?" she whispered again.

"I am very many things. I have been sent to assist you."

"Sent by whom?"

He pointed to the ceiling again. "You are not the only one who wants Him gone," Thom said. "How do you kill something immortal? Truly

367

immortal? When man has no weapon that can touch it, when no wound can injure it, when it possesses no soul to exorcise…what do you do?"

"You stay the fuck away. That's what you do."

"But there is a solution. An ugly solution, no doubt, something intolerably wrong—but you are the key. You are the…"

"Don't say it again," she interrupted.

Thom inclined his head in acceptance. "You have been marked as different. You must be able to kill that which cannot be killed. You are the one who will end Him."

She shuddered, shutting her eyes to block out the sight of him. But that couldn't block her memories. "I've tried before. I don't know how."

"Not yet," he agreed, his voice heated. For the first time, she saw real emotion in him. It was uncomfortably similar to the desire in Anthony's eyes when she stretched naked in his bed. "But you will. When you do…"

He leaned toward her as if for a kiss.

She didn't wait to see what he had planned. Elise swung a hard right hook, and her fist landed on the wall. Thom was gone.

Part 5: Burn

MR. Black was not a good man, but he did have some honor—perverse as it may have been. Elise had told him she wanted to be there when he used the bowl, so he contacted her about it a few short weeks later.

The message arrived on her anonymous voicemail service, which she had just established using the money she earned for retrieving the bowl. She hadn't even shared the number with anyone yet.

"Hello again, my dear," said Mr. Black on the message. "I have put together a little something at my house using your kind donation to my private collection. Seeing as you expressed interest in it, I hope you'll join me for the activation next Saturday. I'll send a car. Don't be a stranger."

Elise played it again for James that night. He had sequestered himself in his room for three weeks to craft paper magic, and his Book of Shadows was bulging.

"Donation," he repeated with a scoff.

Thanks to the generous payment, they had moved from their stuffy motel to an upscale hotel. Their suite had two bedrooms, two bathrooms, and room service. Elise had never stayed somewhere so plush. She was actually bathed, well-fed, and had put on some muscle.

But she was not one to sit idle for long. Waiting for James to assemble his spells was killing her, especially when she knew Mr. Black would soon make his move.

"Will you come with me?" she asked when she finished dressing and emerged from the bathroom, fresh-skinned and smelling of peach soap. Elise latched her mother's cross necklace at the back of her neck.

James flipped through his Book of Shadows as if checking its

369

progress, but she thought he might have been hiding a smile. "Of course."

Their reservation was under a pseudonym, but a car was indeed waiting for them when Saturday morning arrived. James stayed in the lobby as Alain parked and got out to open the back door.

"I will check you for weapons," he said.

Elise took a big step back. "Don't touch me."

"You cannot see Mr. Black armed. It will only take a moment. Lift your elbows."

Reluctantly, she obeyed. He gave her a short pat down with the backs of his hands, missing the slender notebook in her back pocket, and then nodded. Elise didn't have any knives for him to find anyway. She didn't need blades to kill.

He waved her into the car.

"It is a long drive," he said in French as he took position behind the wheel again. "Make yourself comfortable."

She sat stiffly in the back and didn't put on her seatbelt.

They took a direct route out of the city and exited onto a rural road that wandered through lush green hills. Elise didn't try to see if James was following. He had tagged her with a tracking spell and would be miles behind them.

Alain had to go through two gates to get to Mr. Black's property, which was set in the very center of a huge field of grapevines. It felt strangely empty—there was no harvesting equipment or workers. The manor was huge and sprawling. It looked like a plantation taken directly from the South.

Mr. Black stepped onto the porch to greet them. "You made it!" he exclaimed, as though it was a surprise to see her.

Elise got out of the car, and he took her hand like he was escorting a debutante to a ball. She recoiled. He didn't seem to care. "Not comfortable with contact, are we? My sincerest apologies. I'm so thrilled you could join us. Just so thrilled."

"Where is it?" she asked.

"Straight to the point! Won't you let me give you a tour first? I don't get many visitors, and I love an opportunity to show off. You understand."

She nodded reluctantly. Each step she took toward the front door made pressure build in her skull, as though her brain was swelling. Her blood pulsed in her temples.

The gate was complete, and it was near.

She felt drawn toward the east wing of the house, but Mr. Black led her in the opposite direction. "This way!"

He had done well for himself indeed. Elise hadn't met many other kopides, but those she had lived in squalor. The life of a demon hunter wasn't one that lent well to being a productive member of society. But Mr. Black's choice to settle down and start his businesses had obviously borne fruit. His floors were polished wood, the architecture was spacious, and each of his rugs must have cost at least half of what he had paid her to retrieve the bowl.

She glimpsed more fields through the arched windows in a kitchen lush with marble fixtures.

"Is there a point to this?" she asked, rubbing the back of her neck to try to relieve the pressure.

Mr. Black beamed. That broad smile somehow made his handsome face a shade uglier. "Just showing what's possible when you put your mind to it, my dear. This has all been built with my hard-earned money, from foundation to rafters to those pretty pillars you see out back. Such good fortune is humbling."

That was a word for it. He made a big show of leading her into a wine cellar, picking out a bottle, and pouring two glasses for them. He held one under her nose. It smelled woody and peppery, more spicy than sweet. "Do you like it?" he asked, pushing it into her hand. "We grew it ourselves. Come, my dear, take a look."

He led her upstairs again to French doors at the back of the house, where a patio overlooked a field of terraced grapevines. The hill sloped steeply down, and the haze of the sun cast violet shadows on the vines. There were no more houses behind them—just rolling hills, golden brush, and a distant lake.

It was easier to breathe outside, but it had nothing to do with the fresh breeze that stirred against her legs. There was a palpable difference in tension when walking over the threshold. Alain must have cast wards all over the manor to retain the power of the gate.

Elise scanned the doorway. The marks were small enough to be unnoticeable to anyone who wasn't searching for them. A thin stripe crossed the patio, curved around the bushes, and vanished at the end of the wing.

"The equipment for producing the wine is in the shed out that way." He waved casually toward the east, drawing her attention back to him. Shading her eyes, she saw a sprawling building that could have passed for a small factory. "We're no major operation, but we make do. There

371

was a time I would have been able to work the fields myself, but…" He lifted his hands. The skin was rough over the knuckles from fighting. "I'm not as young as I used to be. Don't you think it's a shame we should only know such wealth when we're too old to enjoy it?"

Elise gave his broad shoulders a skeptical look. He may have been old for a kopis, but even in his fifties, he was in good condition.

"Sure," she said.

His smile grew fixed. "Of course you don't. You're young, and you're the 'greatest.' Your legacy is secure." A strange light filled his eyes for an instant, but the moment quickly passed. "There's plenty more to see. The main feature is yet to come."

Mr. Black ushered her inside. Elise dumped the wine in a potted plant when his back was turned.

He took her into his study. James would have been jealous. Every wall was covered in oak bookshelves, and there were statues in each corner that wouldn't have been out of place in a museum. A lockbox sat next to his desk. When he caught her looking at it, he nudged it under his desk with a foot.

"Let's be frank, Miss Kavanagh. You know why you're here."

"You said you were going to kill Him," Elise said. "I could help."

Mr. Black nodded and sat behind his desk, steepling his fingers. "Surely you must wonder why I would have such lofty aspirations. Killing a god. It's no small task. Have you heard the legends? The power that can be gained?"

"I have no interest in power."

"Charming. Really. Very charming. And humble—but that won't take you far." He leaned on his desk to give her an intent stare. "There's some way to harness that power. It involves the artifacts—including the bowl you retrieved—and ethereal beings. But I'm not sure how. Since you're so humble, I'm sure you don't care about eternal youth, immense strength, control over the domains of Heaven and Earth…?" He trailed off, waiting for a reply. Elise only glared. "No? You don't want to live forever?"

"I just want to stay away from Him. I don't care what it takes."

Mr. Black studied her for a long, silent moment. The smile faded. "Why you?" he murmured. "What makes a young girl so special?" He didn't give her a chance to respond. He pushed his chair back and stood. "I have a book that might interest you. See here, my dear."

He led her to a glass case at the back of the room. It held an ancient tome bound in leather and wood. Mr. Black lifted the glass and handled the pages tenderly, touching only the very edges as he flipped to a

372

bookmarked section.

"This is where I learned of what could be gained in His death. It's a record of prophecies. Look—this one is from the days of Apollo and Pythia. History says that he spoke the future through a mortal vessel for the benefit of farmers and kings, but some scholars believe it was truly about love. Isn't that touching?"

"No," Elise said.

"Imagine that. A god so enamored with a mortal woman that he needed to possess her body and mind. Think of the legacy that woman would leave behind."

She glanced at the exit to the room. He seemed pleased by her discomfort.

"There's a precedence for it, you know. See these prophecies? Hundreds of years old. They speak of Durga, a living weapon of Shiva, and Mahishasura—a demon god. She was so beautiful and desirable that he ripped apart the world to have her. And you know what she did?"

"She killed him."

"That's right. She killed him." Mr. Black turned a devilish grin on her. "Do you know much about Durga and Pythia?"

She stared at him blankly.

"The power of woman over man is an amazing thing. It's the stuff of legends."

"Where is the gate?" Elise asked.

He shut the book. "No curiosity. Shame. Very well; let's move on."

The east wing was populated by guest bedrooms, each of which was as mundane as the last. They weren't as well-maintained as the rest of the house. There was a layer of dust on the fixtures, and a faint, musty smell of places no human had been in months. Mr. Black didn't take long to pass through it.

But the further they moved down the hall, the heavier the pressure in Elise's skull grew. Something was humming. She took the notebook out of her back pocket and clenched it in her fist.

"I've converted the largest of the guest bedrooms to accommodate my...shall we say, unique art collection?" He chuckled. "Not that I need to deceive you, of course. You know what I have. Don't you?"

Elise nodded once, lips sealed tight.

Mr. Black stopped in front of the last room. The hallway felt darker at the end, even though the windows had been opened to the hot summer air.

"Here we are. The *piece de resistance*, in a manner of speaking." He

373

pushed the door open and stood back for Elise to go through first. She set the notebook on a table before entering.

Mr. Black hadn't just converted the room. He had knocked out the walls between several of the bedrooms, as well as the ceiling between the first and second floors. It created a cavernous space that took up almost the entire wing. They had somehow fit a mechanical crane inside. The flooring was removed, too, and poured concrete sat exposed.

And on top of that stood a finished gate.

It hummed when she walked into the room as though the stone recognized her. The graceful loop of the arch almost reached the top of the second floor. Sinewy lines banded it from bottom to top. The stone appeared to be braided together.

The bowl she had retrieved formed the capstone of the arch, and the air around it vibrated. Elise swallowed a swell of nausea.

"Beautiful, isn't it?" Mr. Black asked.

She had to take a long, deep breath before she could respond. "It's a monstrosity."

"Yes, I could see why you might think that. You've been through one of these before. Haven't you?" Elise gritted her teeth and didn't respond. "Does it surprise you that I know that? No? But I know a lot about you, my dear—even more than you would expect. I've done my studying."

She paced around the gate, scanning the symbols carved into the floor around it. Alain had been busy. There were twelve parallel lines of magic runes like the ones outside the house, most of which she didn't recognize.

"Will these kill Him when he passes through?"

Mr. Black gave her a wan smile. "No, I'm afraid not. Killing God isn't so easy. I've learned a few fascinating things about ethereal artifacts these past months, though—would you like me to share?"

"No."

He ignored her response. "All this isn't really made of rock. It's ossified bone. There are animals on the heavenly planes you can't even imagine—these mighty beasts that walk on air and exist beyond time. Truly amazing. And the angels slaughtered them to build with their bodies."

Alain was pacing, too, staying opposite Elise on the marks. She didn't cross the line. Every time she took a step, the gateway pulsed. Her palms itched.

When she passed by one of the windows, a shape flitted past the bushes. She only saw it for a half second, but she knew it was James. He had honed in on his notebook and found her. He flashed by a window further down, tagging it with a paper spell before moving on. He had prepared three dozen fire runes just for the cause. Once they were triggered, the entire home would be set aflame—including the east wing, judging by his trajectory.

Only Elise had seen him. Mr. Black went on, waving at the gate with a wine glass as he spoke.

"The truly terrible part is that these creatures would be eternal if not slaughtered, like all angels. Did you know that's one of the things the Treaty of Dis only gave to angels? Immortality? They're so very difficult to kill. And the greatest angel—the one you might call 'God'—can't be killed at all."

"You said you were going to kill Him," Elise said.

"I did, didn't I? But that's another one of the things I learned about angels. No human can kill God, but we can summon Him, and contain Him...and with the right gate, use His power." Mr. Black's eyes glowed with a hungry light. "Maybe even become immortal."

"So this has always been about immortality."

He drained the last of his wine and set the glass down. "You're still young. Powerful. The greatest, they say. You have no clue what it's like to feel your body dying."

Alain started to move for Elise. She quickened her step to stay on the opposite side of the gate. For a moment, she glimpsed him through the twin pillars of bone, and the air was distorted between them. The air vibrated with flashes of light.

"See that symbol on the top of the gate, my dear? That's a mark. You should recognize it. It takes three marks to open a gate and cross from one dimension to the next. It's somewhat of a safeguard against the wrong people using it. There's one mark on the gate, and one mark per angel. So it takes at least two angels to cross over with the help of a gate. Or..."

Alain darted around the circle, fast as a bullet. Elise didn't expect it.

He snatched at her, and she stepped aside fast enough that his swinging hand caught her necklace instead of her arm. The chain snapped. Her mother's cross vanished into a hole in the floor.

His second attempt to grab her succeeded. His fingers dug painfully into her bicep.

"Or one gate and one Godslayer with two marks," Mr. Black finished. The word shocked through her.

Elise twisted out of Alain's grip and made a break for the door, but the older kopis was in the way. Mr. Black blocked her with his body. She swung a punch, but he ducked.

She heard the click of a gun behind her.

Elise threw herself to the ground before Alain could fire, sweeping a leg out to hook it behind the witch's ankle. He dodged her, and Mr. Black was suddenly on top of her, pinning her to the ground with his hand at her throat.

There was no hint of the Southern gentleman in him when he struck her across the face hard enough to scatter her vision with black stars.

"The crane," he said.

Alain disappeared, and she heard the whirring of a machine a moment later.

She threw her weight into him, shoving Mr. Black onto his back. He grabbed her calf and forced her to the ground again when she tried to stand.

He fisted her shirt, lifted her head an inch off the ground, and punched her so hard her skull bounced. The world fuzzed around Elise.

Mr. Black sat up. Her limbs were too heavy to respond. He smoothed graying hair off his forehead. Gestured to Alain beyond the line of her foggy vision. Stood up, kicked her in the ribs. She folded around the blow as pain blossomed in her side.

"'Greatest,'" he said scornfully. "A travesty."

Blood pulsed through her veins, clearing her head with the speedy recovery of a kopis. But it wasn't speedy enough. A metal hook descended toward her face.

Elise took a deep breath, jumped to her feet, and made another dash for the door.

Her throbbing head made her too slow. Mr. Black caught her in a bear hug, and it turned out he was exactly as strong as he looked. Despite his age, he was easily Elise's match—except that he had a good fifty pounds on her, and in such close quarters, size would always win out.

She stomped on his instep and drove her elbow into his gut. He grunted, but didn't let go.

Alain forced her wrists together, pinning both of her arms under his while he wound rope around her hands. Then he peeled the glove off her right hand, and she spit in his face. Phlegm slapped in his eye.

"Get the other one," Mr. Black said.

She tried to twist her arms away, but there was nowhere to go. Alain removed the other glove.

"No!"

Elise clenched both fists shut. It was like trying to close her hands over crackling balls of electricity. Her skin tingled and burned from

376

fingertip to wrist.

The marks on her palms had minds of their own. They longed to be united with the symbol on the gate, and the harder she fought to keep them contained, the worse it burned.

"To the crane, please, Alain."

The aspis went to the control panel again and swung the crane six feet clockwise, within Mr. Black's reach. He let go of Elise long enough to grab the hook and loop it through her ropes.

Alain flipped a lever. The crane lifted with a squeal to drag her arms over her head. Gravity strung her body into one long line. And then her feet were off the ground, and she was swinging toward the gate.

She jerked to a halt an arm's length from the capstone. The stone vibrated, giving a low buzz that dug deep into her skull, and it was hard to breathe or think or move. Her spine and shoulders ached from the suspension.

"Wonderful," Mr. Black said, dusting off his hands as though he had just cleaned something filthy. "And now the wards, please."

Alain knelt by the curved lines of symbols and touched them, whispering words of power.

Light flamed to life around the gate. Heat flushed into the air, sweeping Elise in a torrent of flame and power. The marks on her hands were too strong to control. An electric shock of pain lanced down her arms.

Her left hand popped open and wouldn't close. Blood trailed down her wrist.

"No," she ground out through gritted teeth.

Where was James?

The fingers on her right hand trembled, and the gate glowed with life.

From her point of view near the top of the gate, Elise saw something stir beyond the line of light glowing from Alain's binding spells. Wisps of black smoke curled under the door to the hallway.

Mr. Black hadn't noticed. "This would go much faster if you relaxed," he called.

Alain crossed the other side of the power circle and touched it again. It pulsed with light. "It is ready. We can open the gate."

"Miss Kavanagh, would you be so kind?"

"Turn around," she yelled back.

He spun and saw the door. "What the—?" Mr. Black flung it open, and black smoke poured into the room. He coughed and threw an arm over his face. "Alain! Fire!"

The witch drew his gun and plunged into the hall.

Her right hand burned and her fingers twitched. The gate's hum had grown louder with the sense of her presence, and the air within rippled and swirled.

She could hear her name. Someone was calling to her.

Elise…

And then her right hand opened.

Her palms pressed together in a position of prayer. Blood spurted from the marks. Power erupted between Elise and the gate to form a thick cord of energy that shocked her deep into her bones.

Suddenly, there was no noise. No shadow. She floated in a white void with no arms, no dangling legs, no skin or body or marks.

A wistful, distant sigh pierced the emptiness.

Elise…is it really you?

Her eardrums rocked with the voice. Her skull split in half. She was falling apart, and it was all she could do to scream and keep breathing and stay within her mind. It could have been seconds or years or no time at all.

Oh, Elise…

Eternity stretched in front of her: the severe, frowning face of her father the last time she saw him; a cold expanse of Russian tundra; rain spattering against glass as a train rushed her through green pastures; pale white hands stretching toward her, stroking her cheek, touching her hands…

But just as suddenly, the void vanished.

Someone was screaming, and it wasn't Elise. She gasped and choked on smoke.

Fire consumed the east wing of Mr. Black's manor.

She blinked watering eyes, struggling to focus through the fire to the fight below her. The circle of power had failed. James straddled the lines with several paper spells clutched in each hand, and flames shot up the walls and devoured the exposed beams of the ceiling. Alain was unconscious at his feet.

"You idiot! Don't you realize what you've done?" Mr. Black shouted, but his voice was lost in the crackle of his burning home.

Elise recovered enough to swing her legs forward and then back, throwing her entire body in a wide arc. Then she flipped her feet up, kicked off the gate, and levered herself to crouch on top of the crane. Lowering her arms felt painfully good.

Where her foot had connected with the gate, the ethereal stone cracked. The bowl split.

Wrapping her knees tight on either side of the crane's arm, she reached over and clawed at the capstone with both hands. There was barely enough slack for her to reach. Even though it was old and crumbling, she only managed to wrench a small piece free—hardly bigger than a fingernail.

It was enough. The gate stopped humming and glowing.

With an almighty groan, it began to collapse.

One pillar separated from the second. Elise had half a second to realize that it was falling toward her before it crashed into the arm of the crane.

Her stomach flew into her throat as she tumbled toward flame.

The crane smashed into a wall, and she was flung off the top of it. Her arms were nearly wrenched from their sockets. She cried out. Her legs dangled a few feet off the ground.

The fire crawled toward her, consuming the remaining floorboards inch by inch. Plumes of smoke and burning air swept up her body as the second pillar collapsed into the opposite wall and shattered windows.

Wind blasted more heat toward her, and she kicked her legs up, trying not to get burned.

"James!" she shouted.

He glanced over his shoulder at her, mouth opening in surprise—and Mr. Black seized the opportunity to lunge.

Both men went rolling across the torn floor and vanished down a hole.

Elise groaned, twisting her wrists in the ropes again. They rubbed against her slick, bloody skin, but the loops were too tight to slip free. "Come on," she grunted, twisting her arms as hard as she could. The flames licked at her feet.

And then James staggered out of the smoke. He held a knife that looked like it belonged to Mr. Black.

He stretched on his toes to slice the ropes at her wrist. Elise collapsed, and he caught her. After having her wrists bound for so long, her arms tingled and burned with pinched nerves.

"Are you okay? Can you walk?" James asked.

She nodded. He set her on her feet.

"Mr. Black? Alain?" she said.

"Unconscious. Hurry!"

They found the door to the hall more through luck than by sight. James's spells had done the trick. Each of the external walls was

379

consumed in fire, and they had to crouch low to keep breathing.

When she moved for the entryway, he pushed her in the opposite direction.

"This way out!"

They found an open window in one of the bedrooms—likely the way James had entered—and climbed onto the lawn. Sucking in fresh air was a huge relief to Elise. But she didn't stop to enjoy it. She ran for the front door.

"Where are you going?" James asked, halfway down the path. "Elise, don't!"

She shoved into the building again and ran for the burning study, covering her nose and mouth with the crook of her elbow. Ash swept into her eyes, sending tears cascading down her cheeks.

Elise didn't need her eyesight to find the lockbox she had spotted on the earlier tour of the house. She remembered the position of the desk—kitty corner to the door, opposite the passage to the kitchen—and pushed blindly through the smoke to find it.

She heard James calling her from the entryway and ignored him, searching blindly under the desk with one bare hand while the other was still pressed to her side in a fist.

Her fingers touched metal. She closed them around the handle.

The lockbox was heavy and awkwardly large, but she hugged it to chest and barreled out the office again anyway. James looked relieved to see her, but he didn't waste time asking where she had been. He grabbed her arm and hauled her outside.

The roof of the entryway collapsed behind them, sending billowing clouds of dust exploding out the door.

All the smoke she inhaled caught up with her two steps later. Elise fell to her knees, lockbox cradled in her arms, and hacked something thick and black onto the grass.

"Are you okay?" James asked, kneeling beside her.

She nodded without speaking.

Elise turned to take a last look at Mr. Black's manor. The entire manor was consumed, as were half the trees and grass around it. The level of power required for such magic was staggering.

He gave a guilty smile. "I had to make sure," he said.

Elise recalled the gate and the voice and felt no shame. "Good. Help me up."

She shifted the weight of the lockbox under one arm, and James slung her other arm over his shoulder, bending over to lift her to her feet.

Together, they staggered down the path to the gate.

She was never sure if it was her imagination or not, but she thought she heard Mr. Black screaming behind them.

It took them three weeks to figure out how to open the lockbox.

First, James and Elise moved to another city—and another country, as a matter of fact. They ate good food, drank water until their throats no longer burned, and enjoyed the comforts of a nice hotel. And then they set their minds to the task of the box.

The combination dial wasn't the difficult part, nor were the double keys on the back. Spending months scrounging for survival and stealing to eat had taught them a few unsavory tricks for opening things that were meant to stay closed. Yet even when the tumblers were in place and the dial was broken, the lid still wouldn't open.

"Magic," James said, showing Elise a rune on the bottom of the box. "That damn Alain Daladier was a master of the binding spells. If anyone could contain a deity behind magic walls, it might have been him."

"Can you undo it?"

"Maybe. I'm not sure."

So for weeks, James worked. Elise bulked up on protein and bought lots of spare gloves.

And then, one Thursday morning, he gave an excited shout. Elise hurried inside from their balcony, where she had been staring at Vancouver and doing her best to think of blissful nothingness. She had finally grown comfortable enough with James to ignore him and relax, which was more than she could say about anyone else.

Elise stopped on the edge of his circle of power, which took up most of the hotel room. He was seated on a cushion with an array of crystals and a poultice that reeked of dragon's blood.

"Well?"

"I think I've done it," James said. "Watch."

He passed a pearl over the rune, and the lid swung open. He looked inside. His mouth dropped open.

Elise's heart beat a little faster.

"What is it?"

With one hand, he pulled out a stack of cash. With the other hand, he pulled out a diamond necklace. "I think everything is about to get a lot easier," James said.

381

She forgot that she wasn't supposed to break the circle and jumped on him.

They hugged, laughed, and counted their cash.

It was the first time they were genuinely happy together, and it was far from the last.

Part 6: He Comes

Chapter 14

JULY 2009

ELISE found herself walking by the river as morning dawned instead of returning to her car. She should have gone to bail James out of jail and check on Betty, but the idea of going to Stephanie's house was unbearable. That woman would blame her for everything. And she would be right.

She could still hear Thom's voice whisper from the recesses of her memory.

You are the one who can kill that which cannot die, he had said. *Godslayer...*

Elise stared at the river as it bubbled past, sloshing over rocks and forming eddies in the shallows at her feet. The pink light of clouds at sunrise painted the surface with shifting shades of crimson and violet. Further upstream, someone was already lounging in an inner tube and drinking a beer—getting an early start on summertime laziness. They bobbed toward her. She stuffed her hands in her pockets and headed downstream.

When she found a quiet spot under the bridge, she sat down on a rock and pressed her forehead to her knees. When was the last time she slept without dreaming of that damned gate? Days? Weeks? It felt like she might never sleep restfully again.

The weight of everything pressed against her. The spider-demons. Those staring angels. Thom's forbidden knowledge. All the things she tried to escape by retiring.

"There is no escape," she whispered to the water.

A homeless man stirred under the bushes nearby, poking his head up to give her a slit-eyed stare. When he saw her bruised face, he dropped back under his makeshift tent. Wonderful.

Her phone rang. She didn't check the number before answering. "What?"

"Is this Elise Kavanagh?"

"Who's asking?"

"I'm Portia Redmond. We met at my house party the other night." Her voice was so soft and quavering that it was hard to hear her over the rushing water. "I need your help."

It took Elise a moment to put a face to the name. "Portia. Right. What's wrong?"

"I have one of the missing pieces of the gate, but I don't want to see that man. That witch. He can't know about this. Thom and the Night Hag would only attempt to exploit it."

"I'm in a contract with them. Why would you trust me?"

"You're a kopis," Portia said in a soft, pleading voice. "Unlike Mr. Black, you're neutral. I know you can help me."

It was hard to argue with someone who sounded that pathetic.

"I can be there in an hour."

"Thank you," she said, and she hung up.

Elise climbed the riverbank to street level and retrieved her car from the parking garage. She sat behind the wheel for a few minutes without moving. She couldn't seem to work up the energy to put the keys in the ignition.

She had several hundred dollars of cash in her pocket and extra tanks of gas from the trip to the desert. She didn't have to go to Portia Redmond's house. Elise could head east at breakneck speed and lose herself a few states away. Or Mexico was only a long day's drive away. She hadn't been there since she retired with James.

Even though she had her fair share of enemies in Mexico, nobody had the power to destroy her life like Mr. Black. And best of all, nobody would have ever heard the word "Godslayer."

The brand on her shoulder itched.

She started the car. Her enemies wouldn't care if she was hundreds or thousands of miles away. Distance meant nothing to them. Someone would find her. They always did.

Elise made the drive to Portia's house and found the gate unlocked when she arrived. It was cracked open. Every light in the house was turned on, even though daylight had arrived. Another party? There were no cars outside.

She parked in front of the patio and got out, alert for movement in her peripheral vision as she knocked on the door.

It wasn't fully closed. It swung open.

Elise stepped into the entryway. The smoke from burning incense wafted around the hall, masking the scent of lethe that should have been hanging around after the party. That stench never came out of upholstery.

A small speaker mounted on the wall played "Für Elise" at top volume. The piano strains drifted through the entire house. James had thought it was funny to choreograph a student performance to that song when she still handled the grade school dance classes, so she knew it by heart. And she still hated it.

Unease crept over her. Elise stretched out her senses.

There was nothing infernal or ethereal in the area, but there were a lot of ugly human things that could be waiting, too.

"Portia Redmond?" she called, raising her voice to be heard over the music. "This is Elise Kavanagh."

No response.

The party room had been restored to what she assumed was its normal condition. Cushions and hookah pipes had been replaced with elegant couches and house plants. The curtains were parted, the windows were cracked, and a summer breeze ruffled a fern's leaves.

Something creaked on the second floor—a door opening from shifting air pressure.

Elise mounted the stairs. Beethoven grew louder until she couldn't hear herself over the pounding piano.

Light spread in front of a door at the end of the hall, broken only by the dappled shadows of a plant swaying in the breeze. The wind picked up and the door closed an inch again. Her hair was blown back from her face.

She stretched out a hand to push the door open, but something on the knob caught her eye. A smear of blood.

Elise drew her sword as the piano crescendoed.

She kicked the door in.

The room was motionless beyond the swaying of the trees outside Portia's windows. A thin trail of blood led to the bed. It was big enough to sleep five people, covered in plush pillows, and drenched in a sticky black puddle.

Elise felt nothing as she surveyed the body resting neatly atop the comforter. It belonged to a slender woman with her brittle hands folded neatly over her chest, and she thought she recognized Portia's jewelry, even though she had no head. Her wrists were slit, and if the staining on her dress was any indicator, they had pierced the femoral artery as well. The scent of iron and meat was rich in the air.

Anger crept in a few seconds later.

"Damn it," she muttered, sheathing her sword in the spine scabbard again. She couldn't even find it within herself to be disgusted now that she had seen the slimy mass that had once been David Nicholas. A decapitated corpse was downright cheerful in comparison—and definitely more the style of Mr. Black than the Night Hag.

So he had her phone tapped. Or maybe Portia's phone. Either way, he had been listening, and he had gotten there first to leave a message.

She searched the room for Portia's missing head. It had been set on top of a dresser next to a vase of roses and a half-empty bottle of wine. It was a tidy tableau: No blood splatters, or even an errant smear. All the blood was contained on the bed. Portia would have been drugged before they dismembered her. Her makeup was garish in the daylight.

A sealed manila envelope with Elise's name written on it in looping calligraphy was propped against the vase. Her wrist brushed against Portia's neatly-coiffed hair when she picked it up.

A letter and a few photos tipped out of the envelope when she opened it. The note had been typed with careful precision. Not a word was crossed out or rewritten. But the hammers had struck so hard in some places that they tore the page.

Good evening my dear:

So sorry to have missed you this afternoon. Given the state of the nearly-assembled gate, I hoped our long-awaited reunion would be imminent, but a complication arose. It seems one of my suppliers is trading with a competitor. Shame to lose an old friend to such disloyalty! Rest assured I've taken care of my supply chain issue. Everything is back on track. You and I will meet again soon.

In the meantime, I hear you've made a new friend; a certain fragile old businesswoman in direct competition with my interests. How well do you know your friends? Trust is so important in any relationship, don't you agree?

Find attached some pictures of interest. I'll spare you a narrative.

Dreaming of the time our paths will cross again,

Yours truly, Mr. Black.

She examined the glossy, eight-by-ten photographs underneath. The first one was of one the same daimarachnid breed she had hunted in the desert. The second was unmistakably of David Nicholas with the Night Hag surrounded by more of the spider-demons. They were deep in conversation and didn't seem to realize they were being photographed.

The question of how Mr. Black could have gotten pictures from inside the Warrens was not as pressing as the implications.

Clarity descended on Elise. Her pulse accelerated.

She examined the final picture. The almost-finished gate filled the right side of the frame. The image had obviously been taken by a digital camera, because the waves that came off the stone were powerful enough to distort and pixelate half the image. Nevertheless, a huge form lurked beyond it—something with eight thick telephone pole legs.

Elise crumpled Mr. Black's letter in her hands.

"It's a trap," she said to Portia's head. "He just wants me to kill the competition." The corpse didn't reply, but her silence was a compelling argument on its own.

The Night Hag knew Elise still had a piece of the gate. That was why she had sent the spiders into the studio, and it also explained how they had gotten in. James had bound the wards with Elise's blood. Now that she was marked with the overlord's brand, none of those wards would work against her.

It also meant she had tried to kill Betty. The reasons why didn't matter.

The Night Hag had to die.

Sudden footsteps pattered in the hall outside the door. She whirled.

A man stood in the doorway. He had bronze hair that brushed his shoulders and an elegant way of moving that brought to mind flags rippling in a breeze. An angel. But not just any angel—the one the Night Hag had building her gateway.

Elise waited for him to attack. But he didn't move.

"What do you want?"

He spread his fingers out to show he had no weapons. "My name is Nukha'il. The Night Hag sent me to watch you."

"That's not a job I would volunteer for," Elise said. "You know what I did to him?"

"Have mercy on me." He sank to his knees and bowed his head so sheets of shimmering hair fell over his shoulder. "I know who you are and what you can do. We whisper your name and carry it through light and shadow. You are—"

She raised a hand before he could say it.

"Shut up. Right now."

He crawled toward her, and she reacted on instinct. She drove her knee into his face with a crack. Angels didn't bleed like humans did, and he didn't cry out. His elbows hit the floor. His head hung between his shoulders.

"Why would you want mercy from me?" Elise demanded, voice cracking. "Don't you know that He's after me? Don't you know I've killed dozens of you to escape Him before?"

When Nukha'il looked up, she aimed the falchion at his face. But he didn't fight back, and his expression was not as subservient as his posture. The hands he stretched toward her were clenched into fists. "I know, and don't care. Mr. Black has clipped my wings and made me a demon's slave. The things the Hag does to me for amusement... I don't want to know this life anymore. I hate the earthen planes. I hate them! I need your blade to give me mercy."

Her blade wavered. "I won't kill you."

Surprise sparked in his gaze. "I'm not asking for my death. I'm asking for theirs. That demon, Mr. Black, his aspis—all of them dead at my feet."

Elise nodded and sheathed the falchion. "That's the plan. You don't have to beg."

"Restore my wings. You have her brand; you can release me. I can liberate the other angels and collect an army one hundred strong. We will kill them all together." He clawed at the necklace on his throat.

A hundred angels. That would be an incredible army. With that many ethereal creatures at her back, she could take down a lot more than the Night Hag. She could take down civilizations. And the whole time she marched, the angels would stare at her with those desperate eyes.

Her stomach twisted in on itself. "Sorry. I don't ally with angels."

"Then let me go, at least. Free me to exact revenge. *Please.*"

Elise hesitated. She didn't want to have anything to do with anything ethereal—not those ruins, not the things that lay beyond, and definitely not angels.

He gave her such a wretchedly hopeful look when she stood over him that she almost reconsidered her decision. But when she spoke, her voice was hard, and it didn't waver. "Don't follow me. Stay here until sundown, and don't tell the Night Hag I saw you."

Horror dawned in his eyes. If Elise could remove the collar, then she could also give him orders. The muscles in his back flexed as though he was going to stand, but he didn't budge. He couldn't.

"Mercy," he whispered.

"I'm all out of that for the day." She took a step away, but paused.

"You should know that Itra'il is alive."

He sucked in a hard breath, gripping his chest as though his heart hurt. "She's *alive*?"

"Yeah." Elise brushed past him. "Sorry."

The police allowed James a courtesy call when eight o'clock rolled around. He drummed his fingers on the desk by the phone for almost five minutes before deciding what number to dial.

It took Anthony two hours to show up with a stack of money fished out of James's safe at Motion and Dance. He stared around at the police station like he couldn't quite believe he was there.

"Thank you, Anthony," James said. "I can explain all of this."

"Yeah, I think you better," Anthony said. The beaten old Jeep waited outside in the parking lot. It was a welcome sight after a night trying to sleep on concrete. "Where should I take you?"

"The parking gallery, please. My car was left there overnight. You can go back to work afterward."

"It's fine. I should check on Betty anyway." He put the Jeep into gear and shook his head. "You know, I've seen some weird stuff since I started dating Elise. Zombies. Giant spiders. Exorcisms. But when I'm halfway through rebuilding the transmission on a VW and I get a call from you— *you*, of all people—asking me to bail you out of jail…that's got to rank at the top of my 'shit I never expected to deal with' list. You don't even *like* me. Why didn't you call Elise?"

"And that would be part of the story. I'll tell you everything. Later."

It was the longest, most awkward ride possible back to the parking garage, even though they were only a few blocks away. And true to his word, Anthony followed James all the way to the suburbs north of Reno.

"So?" Anthony demanded as soon as they met at the front door of his house.

James sighed. "Is now really the time?"

"I missed half my shift at the shop because of you. This is a *great* time."

His upper lip twitched. "Fine. Let's go inside, at the very least." It was a small mercy that Stephanie was nowhere to be found, and that Betty was still sleeping on the couch. James brewed a pot of coffee, uncomfortably aware of Anthony leaning against the opposite counter with his arms folded and an expectant look. "Do you take cream?"

"No, but—"

"You would take an explanation. Yes. I get it."

"I was going to say I take sugar, actually. But sure. How *did* you land in jail?"

"Elise. Elise got me arrested. Happy?" He poured two cups and sat down at the kitchen table, which was topped with rare Indonesian agarwood to match the paneling on the island, at Stephanie's insistence. James massaged a hand over his brow. "Of course it was Elise. That should go without saying, shouldn't it?"

"It's not like she's not a criminal," Anthony said, grabbing his mug. He didn't sit down.

"Your defensiveness is charming. It's lovely not having to be the one doing it, for once. I hope you get to enjoy many, many years making excuses for Elise."

"Do we have a problem?"

James barked a laughed. "No. Of course not."

"Good, because whatever you think, I just went through all the trouble of calling Milo into work to cover for me and opening a magical safe with one of Elise's gloves. I'm going to catch so much shit for leaving early. And you—you and me—" Anthony gestured between them with the mug, "—if we've got a problem, then I don't know why I would have bothered."

James pinched the bridge of his nose and shut his eyes. It was hard to open them again. He was going to pass out for a few years as soon as he got horizontal. "Then why did you bother coming to get me?" he asked dully.

"Because you're Elise's..." Anthony wiggled his fingers in what was probably supposed to be a rough approximation of casting a spell. "I thought she had to be dead or something, if you were in jail."

"She's not. Not until I get at her, anyway." James snorted at how offended the younger man looked. "That was a joke."

"If you're going to—"

The front door opened. Elise appeared in the space between the formal dining room and the kitchen like a ghost. Yellow, splotchy bruises covered the entire left side of her face. It wasn't as bad as her expression —that exhausted, miserable look of someone who hadn't slept or eaten in a week.

She looked so terrible that James forgot to be angry. He shoved his chair back and stood.

Anthony pushed past him. "Elise!" He wrapped her in a hug. Her arms stayed limp at her sides. "Jeez, are you okay? What happened?"

She handed him an envelope wordlessly. He removed a couple of pictures. James wanted to see them, but he remained frozen by the kitchen table instead. Elise's expression was telling enough. Whatever was in those photos would be very terrible, and very likely mean a fight.

Instead, he studied her as Anthony studied the photos. It was the first time she had set foot in James's new house, and she looked like a snake surrounded by mongooses. Her upper lip curled as she took in the nonporous countertops, the backyard, the framed photo of James and Stephanie waiting to be mounted in the hallway.

"Are these those spiders that we fought?" Anthony asked. Elise put a finger to her lips and shook her head. "What? Why are we being quiet?"

She pointed at James and Anthony, then at the floor. The message was clear: *Stay here.* And then she drew her sword and moved to the back door, peering into the yard. It hadn't been landscaped yet, although stakes with yellow flags marked where empty dirt was destined to become brick paths and grass.

"You don't need your sword. Stephanie isn't here," James whispered.

Even that couldn't make her laugh. She slipped into the living room, and he took the photos from Anthony.

James didn't recognize anyone in the pictures. The old woman had a distinctly inhuman appearance—the Night Hag?—and he was sure that the spiders were the same demons that Elise had been hunting in the desert. But that wasn't what gave him pause. The gate in the third picture made a chill wash over his body.

"What is that?" Anthony asked.

James dropped the envelope and followed Elise.

She was kneeling under one of the bay windows to glare at the neighborhood through a crack in the blinds. Betty was so buried under blankets and pillows that only the top of her blond head stuck out. She didn't stir when James crouched by Elise.

He tried to see what she was seeing through the window. Trees baked in the hot summer sun. His new neighbor gardened in a pair of purple Crocs.

And then—a flash of movement. Something darted past the back fence.

Elise hurried out the front door, which she had left cracked open. By the time James got to his feet, grabbed his notebook off the coffee table, and followed her onto the front step, she was wiggling onto the roof. All he saw were her feet kicking as she disappeared.

391

He swore under his breath and stuffed the notebook in his belt before leaping to grab the gutter.

The ceiling tile blazed under his hands. Stephanie had insisted on a white roof to reflect heat, so walking on it was like being trapped atop a range set to ten. He jerked his scalded fingers back.

Elise's hair was just visible over the slope of the roof. She was already crouched on the other side.

He squatted beside her. "What—?" he began, but she cut him off by pointing.

The house James and Stephanie bought was a recent addition to the neighborhood. The only thing at their back was empty hillside, which had been leveled into terraces and marked for future development. From their elevated position on the roof, they could see over the hill, and all the way to the highway. But Elise wasn't pointing that far.

His eyes fell on a hulking shape behind the fence. A daimarachnid.

"The Night Hag said she would have you guarded," Elise murmured. "I thought she meant by the Gray."

"Those photos—the old woman—"

"That's her. She's had the spiders this entire time. She's the one who tried to kill Betty."

The daimarachnid scuttled to the corner of the fence, and Elise pulled James behind a gabled section of roof. It was a half a degree cooler in the shade underneath. Sweat dripped from the back of his neck down his spine. "It's logical, in some sick fashion. How do you cement the allegiance of a reluctant warrior? Do you give them promises of safety and money, or do you take away the people to which they already hold allegiance?"

"Why not both?" Cold fury glowed in Elise's eyes. "We're killing her today. Right now. And I'm starting with that spider."

Without warning, she leaped to her feet, rushed around the gable, and launched from the roof.

James couldn't help it. He gave a little shout of shock and fear as she plummeted to the other side of the fence. It was barely a half second of warning, but it was enough—the spider attacked while she was still on her knees.

She brought up her sword. It connected with the mouthparts of the daimarachnid with a meaty thump.

Elise cried out.

The fence blocked his view, so his mind was immediately flooded with a thousand horrible thoughts of huge bite wounds and pulsing venom. James dropped to his belly—the roof burned even through his t-shirt—and slid down feet-first.

But when he got to the other side of the fence, the daimarachnid was already dead in the dirt. Elise stood over it, sweaty and panting with ichor caking her shirt to her chest. Relief swamped him. "I thought you got bitten. Those spiders—you know they're venomous."

"Yeah, I know. We have to move fast. The Night Hag is going to feel its death, and we have to get there before she realizes what that means."

She took a step toward him and staggered.

James tried to catch her. Elise's arms were so slick with the demon's juices that she dropped to the ground anyway.

"What—?"

"It's fine," she said, but then he saw the ragged flesh on her thigh, and he realized that she had been bitten after all.

He wiped some of the blood away with his fingers for a better look at the wound. From somewhere in the musty depths of James's memories of academia, he recalled the word "necrosis." It should have taken hours to develop, especially with Elise's robust immune system, but there was nothing normal about bites delivered by demons. The injury was already as big as his fist and blackening around the edges. It didn't bleed so much as ooze.

She grabbed his wrist when he pulled the Book of Shadows out of his belt. "Save it."

"We can't leave that," he said. "I have a spell—"

She pushed him back and shook out her leg. "I said I'm fine. It just burns. We've got to kill an overlord and shut an ethereal gate, so I can't let you drain your magic."

"How do you plan on fighting like that?"

"With this," she said, picking up her sword and sheathing it again. Her cheeks were pale. "Now help me push this body over the fence before someone sees it."

Chapter 15

ANTHONY WAS WAITING at the back door when they shoved the daimarachnid into the yard, and he hurried over to help them drag the body under the shelter of the house. Elise wished she could see how Stephanie reacted to finding a dead demon in her yard. That would have been a popcorn-worthy conversation.

She limped into the kitchen and took one of James's dish towels out of the drawer by the sink, where he always kept them. The spider bite burned like a cigarette jammed into her thigh.

"We have three major problems," Elise said, wetting down the towel and pressing it to the wound. "First: We just killed the spider guarding James, and Mr. Black is still out there, so he could jump on us at any moment. Second: We have to kill the Night Hag. And third: She's about a half mile under the city, so we have to get in and out without dying."

To Anthony's credit, he barely blinked. "Okay. We'll go together."

She lifted the rag to inspect her wound. The flesh was shiny red in the center where her skin sloughed away. She squeezed bloody water into Stephanie's stainless steel sink and wetted it down again.

"You can't fight like that," James said.

"I just need bandages. Anthony, wake Betty up. Tell her we're getting out of here."

He looked startled at the order. "Betty? Really?"

"We're not leaving her alone." Elise cast a disdainful glance around the kitchen. James might have organized it, but everything else was obviously Stephanie's doing. Betty was right. The house reeked of bitch. "Where's the bathroom?"

James pointed her down the hall. She limped through the formal dining room and helped herself into the guest bathroom. They had

394

seasonal towels and decorative soaps in the shape of frogs. She grimaced.

"Just let me heal you," James said from outside the door with exasperation. "This is ridiculous."

She hopped onto the edge of the countertop. There was no bathtub where she could rinse her leg off; they had opted for a glass block shower instead. "I would need an antivenin before you could heal it properly. Tylenol? Advil?"

He opened the medicine cabinet and tossed her a bottle. She turned it over to read the label. Percocet. Nice.

She chewed a couple of pills and palpated the edges of the wound with her fingertips. It felt like getting bitten anew. James watched her splash water onto the wound with a deep frown.

"If you say 'I told you so,' I'm morally obligated to slap you," Elise said.

He threw his hands in the air. "What's the point? You won't listen to me. You turned to demons for help and won't let me heal you, so obviously, you don't want anything to do with me these days!"

"You're the one who decided to move away from the studio we bought—together—without telling me. When you try to decide which one of us doesn't need the other anymore, you should think about that. Where are your bandages?"

"We don't have any."

"How can you not...? Never mind. Old t-shirt?"

James left and returned a moment later with a Motion and Dance polo shirt and a pair of scissors. Elise cut it into strips and bound them tight around her leg. The painkillers were starting to take the edge off.

"I want to say, for the record, I think—"

She held up a hand to cut him off. "Does Stephanie make you happy?"

"We just killed a daimarachnid behind my house and are about to attack a demonic overlord. Is this the time for such a conversation?"

"Yes."

Anger flashed across his face. "Well, believe it or not, I don't have to confer with you to make every decision. So tell me what you want to hear, Elise. Do you want me to say that she makes me miserable? Would that satisfy you? Because you seem to have this sadistic urge to make me suffer alone, and if telling you that will make you leave me to live my life, then so be it!"

The question that had been bothering her for weeks—months—leaped out before she could give it a second thought.

"Why aren't I enough?"

His face was inscrutable. "What?"

Elise shrugged and focused on cutting more strips. "You're all the companionship I've ever needed. Going to college, getting a job, trying to make other friends…it kept me busy when I wasn't hunting anymore. But I don't need Betty or Anthony. I don't need *any* of it."

Just you.

The last part was left unspoken, but it hung between them. He swallowed hard. "When you went missing over a decade ago—when the coven summoned me to find you—I had a life of my own. I had a home and plans to marry. Do you ever think about that?"

Anthony's open, imploring face came to mind. *Do you ever think about the future?*

"No," she said. "I don't."

"Well, I do. I'm almost forty. I can't get back all those years I've lost. You don't want a spouse? A home? Children? Fine. But most people don't find comfort in a splatter of blood and the company of demons. Some of us need other people. Intimacy. A real life." He waved a hand at the house surrounding them. "And while you're seeking satisfaction at the end of a sword, I…" He finally noticed her expression and trailed off. "I'm sorry. I forgot you can't—you know."

Her mouth twisted. "Anthony asked me about…" Elise mulled the words over. Just thinking about it made her sick again. "Marriage. Kids."

"After three months of dating? Ambitious." He made it sound like a joke, but he wasn't smiling. "Does he know?"

She washed her hands in the sink with soap and water, then swung her leg to test mobility. It wasn't pretty, but it worked. She couldn't expect anything better. She also couldn't seem to meet James's gaze.

He stepped forward, reaching out to touch her shoulder, but changed his mind. He sagged against the counter beside her instead.

"Death's Hand killed me, Elise. When I think back on that night—hell, on the thousands of nights like that one—I feel my age. You will not be able to save me every time. We were right to retire."

She tipped her head back to study him in the mirror. His reflection wasn't nearly as tired or aged as hers, even though she was twelve years younger. "You were the one who wanted to do it again."

"Once. Just once. Only because we needed to."

"Once for you, maybe. But that once was enough to ruin everything for me. I don't have any choice now. Everyone knows where I am, and Mr. Black has taken everything." She stuffed her hands under her arms,

396

hugging her ribs tight. Her feet dangled over the side of the counter. "I can't get out of this. Not anymore."

"He hasn't taken your friends. Or me."

"No. You did that yourself." James flinched as though she had punched him. A sick sense of satisfaction resonated through her. "So... does Stephanie make you happy? Really?"

"Yes." He almost sounded sure of himself. "Yes. She does." James brushed the braid over Elise's shoulder, and his fingers paused on her skin. It looked like he wanted to say something else, but the sentiment stuck in his gaze without making it to his lips.

"Fine," she said after a protracted silence. "Good. I'm happy for you." She didn't bother making it sound like she meant it.

"What is that, Elise?"

She had to twist around and look at her reflection to see what he meant. She had forgotten about the Night Hag's brand on her shoulder. It had mostly healed and left a fresh pink circle marked with eight radiating lines.

She didn't have time to answer. Someone knocked at the door, and James dropped his hand.

The door opened another few inches, and Anthony's reflection joined theirs. "Betty's awake," he said. "We can go."

Elise's leg buckled under her when she jumped off the counter, but she ignored James's attempt at giving her a hand. "Great. We'll take the Jeep."

"Family field trip," James muttered. "What joy."

Getting into the Warrens was the easy part.

Craven's was mostly empty in the afternoons other than the demon employees, who weren't surprised to see four heavily-armed humans march through on a mission. They did, however, give them a very wide berth. Nobody tried to stop them as they ascended to David Nicholas's former office.

His door placard was conspicuously missing, which left a blank beneath the "general manager" sign. Elise felt a faint twinge of guilt—but only a twinge. She made sure it was empty before letting everyone inside.

Where his office had once been filled with trash and bowls of masticated chewing tobacco, now it was nothing but a cavernous room overlooking the game floor. She found a light switch behind the desk. The overhead fluorescents cast the room in harsh blue light.

"What is this place?" Betty asked. Going on the offense had put a pink glow on her cheeks and a gleam in her eye.

"This is where the manager worked. There's a back path down to the club here."

Anthony cupped his hands around his eyes to peer at the tables on the floor. The dealers must have known David Nicholas was gone. They chatted and smoked around empty tables with their uniforms undone. "Where's the manager now?"

Elise glanced at James. He was flipping through his Book of Shadows and pretending not to listen.

"I killed him."

Betty's mouth opened in an "o" of surprise.

A quick search of David Nicholas's desk yielded a key ring and a dusty flashlight. She unlocked the door he used to get to Eloquent Blood, propped it open with her foot, and studied each of her friends as they passed through. They didn't look like much of a team. Anthony was greasy and exhausted. Betty wheezed when she walked. And James was still pretending to be absorbed in his Book of Shadows. She wasn't much better. She couldn't put any weight on her bitten leg.

They made it halfway down the stairs to Blood without seeing anyone. When they passed the ground level, Neuma rushed toward them.

Her shorts and pink tank top were so different from her normal clothes that Elise didn't recognize her until she smiled. She wasn't even wearing makeup. "Elise!" The half-succubus suddenly noticed everyone else, and her smile faded. "What's going on?"

In the corner of Elise's vision, Anthony had gone rigid. Even in her lazy day clothes, Neuma's sex appeal was enough to instantly decimate the brain cells of any red-blooded human in her vicinity. Fortunately, she didn't have the charm turned on.

There was no point in lying. "I'm going to kill the Night Hag."

Her face went slack with fear. "No—oh, no, you can't do that!"

"I've got two swords, two witches, and a shotgun. I'm not feeling bad about my odds," Elise said. Betty grinned at being included in the list of weapons.

"It's not like that!" Neuma grabbed Elise's hands and lowered her voice so the others wouldn't hear. "You're *branded*."

"It'll be fine."

"Even if she doesn't kill you on sight, which she totally can, the Night

Hag owns *everything* in the city. You know what happens if she dies? Have you seen what happens in a territory without an overlord?"

She freed her hands. "Consider this fair warning. It's about to get ugly. You can stick around to deal with the fallout, or you can run."

The bartender glanced nervously at the others again. "Been nice knowing you, hot stuff."

Anthony watched her ass as she fled up the stairs. Betty smacked him in the arm, and James coughed into his hand.

"Come on," Elise said.

It wasn't much further to the club. There were no waitresses in sight to distract Anthony, and the cleaning crew was absent from the floor as well. Their shuffling footsteps echoed. "Nobody here? This will be easy," Anthony said with a nervous chuckle.

Elise wasn't as optimistic. They would only get as far as the Night Hag wanted them to go. She had to have realized her daimarachnid guard was dead and connected it with Nukha'il's failure to return. If she was letting them pass unobstructed, it was because she wanted it that way. But she didn't need to scare everyone by saying it.

"Stay close."

The elevator into the Warrens stood open. The bulb had even been replaced. It didn't flicker anymore.

"So what's the plan?" Anthony asked as they approached it.

Elise blinked. "Plan?"

He gave that nervous laugh again. It was starting to get annoying. "It's not like we're going to walk into some demonic overlord's evil underground lair and expect to kill it without a plan...right?"

"Actually..."

"Just a moment, please," James said. He led Elise around the corner of the DJ booth. He glanced at the place the cage had stood the night before and pulled a face. "I know you didn't want me to say that I told you so —"

"And I still don't."

He folded his arms tight across his chest. "I know what that scar on your shoulder means." The brand ached as though it knew they were talking about it. "You can't confront the Night Hag like that. She can kill you with a thought."

"I know. That's why I thought we would piggyback."

"Are you certain that's a good idea?"

They hadn't joined in an active bond since the spring, when Elise used their shared power to exorcise a child. It made both of them

399

stronger, but only briefly. And sharing their powers always came with the risk of burnout.

"I'm not sure it will even work when I'm branded," she admitted. "But having an aspis is supposed to protect me from things like getting killed with a thought, so it's all I have. If it doesn't work, this could be a really short fight."

"We don't know if joining while you're branded will make you impervious to her, or make her impervious to us."

"I know."

He grimaced. "Then I won't do it."

She massaged her temples. Pressure was gathering in her forehead, and she wasn't sure if it was because they were so close to the Warrens or because James was stressing her out. "I know you're mad at me..."

"That's a word for it."

"But what other choice do we have?"

Elise glanced around the corner. Betty and Anthony were just a few feet away, pretending not to listen. When they realized she saw them, they turned away with nearly identical expressions.

"I'll do my best to shield you, but it's too dangerous to piggyback. I'm sorry, Elise." James marched toward the elevator. She had no choice but to follow him.

Fitting four adults into a small metal cage was cozier than Elise liked to get, but with awkward maneuvering, they managed to shut the door and flip the lever.

Something hard and intangible pushed against the back of her skull as they descended. Even the Percocet haze couldn't block it out. A sense of unease crept upon her. The pressure in her skull was growing stronger, and she thought she recognized it now.

It wasn't the feeling of a powerful infernal presence—it was ethereal.

The silence in the elevator was unnerving. Even Betty seemed to have run out of things to say. She gave an occasional cough that rang out in the too-quiet air, but she wasn't smiling anymore. Anthony gazed at the darkness above the cage. They could only see the walls a few feet above them before they were swallowed by shadow.

"So demons use mine shafts. Why am I not surprised?"

Nobody responded. He rubbed the back of his neck and stared at his feet.

When the elevator finally reached the bottom, Elise held up a hand to indicate that they should wait. A soft hum filled the hall. Betty shone the flashlight around the rock walls, but there was nothing to see.

"Maybe the Night Hag isn't down here. It's awfully empty," Betty said.

Elise shook her head. "She's here."

They walked down the long, empty hallway. Nothing was guarding the entrance into the chamber where the gate had been constructed.

Elise edged around the door. The gate had been finished, the empty crates had been carried away, and the working demons were nowhere in sight. Only a single figure stood in front of the door in a long black gown. It looked like the Night Hag was taking a solitary vigil.

"That's the overlord—the old woman by the gate," Elise said, pointing into the cavern. "I don't know where Thom is, but he has to be around. Watch for him. They say he's a witch, but he's much more powerful than that."

"What's he look like?"

"Like a supermodel. You'll recognize him if you see him."

She took another long moment to study the cavern and the gate. Instead of having the bowl fragments at the capstone, the Night Hag had redesigned it so that it was at the base instead. It wouldn't require wings to open the gate. Elise could walk down, touch the stone, and pass through to the ethereal ruins…if she wanted to. But she didn't plan on letting it get that far.

Elise gestured. They edged down the path with their backs against the wall.

She didn't make it six feet before the Night Hag looked up. Betty gasped.

The overlord wasn't alone after all.

Nukha'il knelt on the floor on the other side of the gate, hidden by its shadow. He glared at Elise with bitter fury. His face was swollen and bruised from a thorough beating, and chains at his wrists pinned him to the floor.

"This is a trap, isn't it?" Anthony asked.

An instant later, something massive dropped from the ceiling and pinned her to the ground.

Her injured leg couldn't take the impact. Her body struck dirt, and Anthony jumped back with a shout. A daimarachnid reared over her.

Elise drew her sword too slow. One of its legs crushed her arm to the dirt.

It didn't try to bite her. Instead, its mouth descended on her throat and snagged the chain of charms almost delicately.

The spider broke the chain and jumped off the ramp.

James grabbed for the charms and missed.

"No!" Elise shouted, scrambling on her knees to the edge, but it was already gone. It took the charms to the Night Hag like a dog fetching a bone.

"You have been very helpful!" called the overlord as she picked out the bowl fragment and threw the rest of the charms aside. "Shame that you should bite the hand that feeds. You are an incredible weapon. I would have loved to wield you."

She extended a pale, slender hand and inserted the pebble into the crack.

Elise felt like she had just jumped off a bridge. Her pulse thrilled. Her stomach leaped into her throat. Sudden wind whipped her hair around her face, battering her body, and all she could do was dig her fingers into the ground to keep from getting ripped off the side.

The gate was complete.

"Bring them down!" ordered the Night Hag.

A dozen more daimarachnids emerged from the other side of the cavern and scuttled toward the ramp.

Elise tried to get to her feet, but her leg completely gave out. She struck the ground on one knee. Pain arced from hip to shoulder, and spots of blood dotted the bandages.

"James!"

He was beside her in an instant. "We should run—"

The spider-demons were rushed toward them. Every rustling motion echoed off the high cave walls. She grabbed his arm, dragging his face down to her level.

"Piggyback," Elise said. "*Now.*"

"Elise—"

"Just do it!"

The blast of the shotgun roared above them. One of the daimarachnids had skipped the slope and climbed beside Anthony and Betty instead.

James swore and held Elise's face between both of his hands. A bolt of power shot through her. "Hang on," he said. She felt him open himself to her. Magic pulsed around them. He extended it to her, pale eyes glowing, and she opened herself to take it.

And then they both blacked out.

Chapter 16

ANTHONY THOUGHT HE coped pretty well with the whole demon thing. He didn't have a nervous breakdown after the zombie attack, which was pretty good considering he hadn't even believed in ghosts before that. When he went camping with Elise, he took a spider down on his own. Mostly. And he'd become pretty good with the shotgun. As far as "people who can't turn paper into fireballs" went, he would definitely say he was a useful team member.

But nothing could have prepared him for the moment Elise and James went limp on the ground and left him alone with his wheezing cousin, a demonic overlord, and a gateway into an angelic city.

He stared at their bodies.

"Oh no," Betty said.

They didn't have long to be shocked. A dozen daimarachnids reached the bottom of the ramp, which gave them about twenty seconds before getting overtaken. Anthony pumped his shotgun and stood over his cousin while she examined their friends.

"She's not responding!" Betty cried, jamming a knuckle into Elise's breastbone. The pain from that should have been enough to wake the dead.

He stepped around her, angled the shotgun down, and fired off a shot. The spider-demon in the front lost its eyes in a cloud of blood. It collapsed and tripped the spider right behind it.

Anthony didn't get a chance to fire again.

"Bring them down."

The spider-demons lifted James and Elise's bodies in their mouthparts. Their gentleness was surprising.

But the demons didn't try to be nearly so gentle with Anthony and

Betty. They drove into the back of his legs and shoved him down the path. "Hey!" he protested, twisting around to aim. They rewarded him with another, harder shove. He lost his balance and fell onto all fours.

The shotgun flew from his hands and dropped over the side of the path.

The spider-demon that had pushed Anthony seized him with its forelegs to lift him over its head. Its grip dug into his back and sides. When he was seventeen, he had body-surfed at a music festival after too much weed, and it felt a lot like that—except nobody in the mosh pit had pincers. He stared at its glistening eyeballs as it hauled him toward a woman he was pretty sure planned to kill him.

"It's okay, Betty, we'll be okay!" he yelled, trying to comfort his cousin. When she didn't respond, he twisted in the spider's legs to see what she was doing.

Betty was still at the door, kicking and punching and generally making herself impossible to grab. "Fuck you! Yeah! And fuck you, too! Ouch—hey!" Two of them finally jumped and pinned her to the ground. They dragged her down the slope. "Let go of me, you ugly bastards!"

At any other time, he would have laughed.

Each step of the spider beneath him was uneven and jolting, like riding a horse with too many legs. The demon holding Elise drew level with him. The hilt of the falchions jutted over each of her shoulders, and blood dripped from underneath the gloves. Her arms and legs dangled uselessly. So much for hoping she was only pretending to be asleep.

"Anthony? Anthony!" Betty wailed.

"Don't worry, it's going to be fine. We can—"

"Optimism. How sweet," said the Night Hag as the spiders dropped all four of them in front of the dais and stepped back to form a loose circle.

Anthony eyed Elise's swords. They were the only weapons left now, but he hadn't even touched them before. He played baseball in elementary school, though. How much harder could it be to swing a sword?

Before he could decide if he wanted to make a move, the Night Hag descended to examine him like he was a piece of dog shit on her kitchen floor. Her nose wrinkled.

She snapped her fingers, and a beautiful man appeared at her side. He had full lips, long black hair, and no shirt. Anthony found himself gaping and had to shake free of it. The new guy had to be Thom.

"What is this?" she demanded. "What are they doing here?"

404

"They are friends of Elise's."

"Idiots. Amateurs! You would think a kopis would know better than to bring children with her!"

"Hey!" Betty complained.

The overlord ignored her. "At least she came at all. Strip her gloves and open the gate."

"I'm afraid I can't do that," Thom said.

She spun on him. "Are you challenging me?"

"I have obeyed your every other order, but I will not expose her hands." He hooked his thumbs in the waist of his slacks. "Make of it what you will."

Several tense seconds passed.

Surprisingly, it was the Night Hag who looked away.

"Nukha'il!" she snapped. "Come here!" The chains fell away from the man on the other side of the gate. He stood slowly, as though he had been forced into a kneeling position for so long that he could barely move. He joined her on the dais. His wrists, rubbed raw by metal shackles, looked like they had delicate bird bones inside. "Grab the kopis. Remove her gloves. Open the gate. Do I have to spell it out for you?"

He glared, but he stepped down from the gate without arguing and knelt to grab Elise. Betty shielded her body.

"Don't touch her!"

He shoved Betty with one hand. It was the smallest of gestures, but she went flying as though he had thrown his whole body into the punch. She cried out. Anthony barely caught her before she hit the ground.

Nukha'il scooped Elise from the ground, propping her awkwardly against his shoulder so he could peel off one of her gloves. Crusty blood made the material stick to her hand, but when he ripped it free, Anthony saw that the black symbol wasn't black anymore. It glowed with the same faint, silvery light as the gate. Fresh blood dribbled from the center as if she had been stabbed.

"Hurry," the Night Hag said, gesturing impatiently. "Do it now." With an arm slung around Elise's waist, he lifted her hand to the gate.

Anthony had to do something. Before he could reach the first step onto the dais, he caught the beautiful witch watching him. Thom gave an almost imperceptible shake of his head. The intent was clear: *Don't do that.*

Nukha'il pressed the mark on Elise's hand to the mark on the stone with his fingers spread behind hers.

The glow went out of the stone.

405

He stepped back, leaving a bloody handprint where Elise's fingers had been.

Anthony was suddenly face down on the floor and had no idea how he had gotten there. He felt the pain an instant later—a splitting in his skull so much worse than having a wrench dropped on his head, worse than getting smacked in the nose with a baseball bat in Little League, worse than being tackled by spider-demons. It blinded him with white light.

He couldn't see. Couldn't think.

"Anthony!" Betty gasped, dropping at his side. "Oh my God, what —?"

The Night Hag was cackling, but Anthony couldn't focus on her. He could barely see past Betty's feet. "It works! Now, my angel, go through the gate. Make sure it's safe."

"No," said a soft voice that had to belong to Nukha'il.

A cry of pain.

"I am getting sick of all this defiance!" she spat. "Go through the gate! I will kill you if you don't. Make your decision."

Anthony squinted at the dais. There was so much light pouring from the stone arch that he could only make out the shadowy backs of the overlord and her minions. Why wasn't Betty screaming? It hurt so much.

Nukha'il dropped Elise. She tumbled down the steps and rolled to a stop beside Anthony.

"As you demand," said the angel in a low growl.

With an arm lifted in front of his eyes, he passed through the pillars and disappeared.

Everyone was focused on the gate. Anthony saw his moment. He took one of the falchions out of Elise's spine sheath, gritted his teeth against the pain, and got to his feet. Betty gaped at him as he ran onto the dais.

The overlord heard him coming and turned. He drove the falchion into her stomach.

Black blood spurted from the wound. The Night Hag cackled shrilly. "It stabbed me!" she said to Thom, turning to face him as though Anthony wasn't even there. "That little boy *stabbed* me!"

He shrugged. "That happens."

She shoved Anthony off the dais. The overlord was stronger than she looked, but not strong enough to throw him. He stumbled back to Betty as she jerked the falchion out of her stomach. "And to think I just finished improving this body. What a waste of time."

She wriggled her fingers into the stab wound and began to pull. Her flesh tore away like rubber. There was something underneath, something black and crimson and not quite blood.

Her body shuddered. She heaved. The skin on her face loosened. The mouth-hole stretched until all her teeth were visible in a skull's grin, and then they fell out one by one in sparkling shards of bone.

A huge, slippery limb pushed from the stab wound. It slid out like a tree branch birthed from her gut and felt around for the floor. When it touched down, the tip of a second limb joined it and ripped the hole wider. Her entire ribcage was bared as a third leg pushed through, and then a fourth. Each was as thick as Anthony's body.

The Night Hag's flesh sagged. Her arms and legs emptied into wiggling sacks.

A hulking spider rose from the remains of her human form—larger than the dais, larger than the gate itself, far larger than the semi Elise had hijacked. Anthony fell onto his back. The Night Hag loomed overhead.

Red eyes glistened on a brown and tan head. Brands blazed down her belly and legs. Her flesh was mottled with patterns meant to blend in with one of Hell's deserts.

Anthony had seen the picture of the giant spider next to the gate. But he hadn't imagined it would be quite so *big*.

"Uh," Betty said. She couldn't seem to process any bigger words than that.

They exchanged a glance. He didn't have to read her mind to hear the unspoken motto they usually shared in jest, but now with complete sincerity: *What would Elise do?*

There wasn't time to strategize. He let his mind return to their week in the desert—he killed his spider by running it over with the Jeep, but he would need a really big Jeep for this one—and thought of how Elise always went for the eyes, the joints, the comparatively soft underbelly.

The underbelly on this thing was about two feet over his head.

"This really sucks," Anthony said, and then he grabbed the second falchion.

"Kill the humans," said the Night Hag. Somehow, she sounded completely normal, like there should have been a woman standing in front of the dozen smaller daimarachnids.

Oh yeah. The other spiders.

Anthony swung the falchion into the mouth of a demon rushing Betty. She threw her hands over her head with a shriek. Ichor splattered on both of them.

It stumbled back, but a second spider took its place immediately. He

407

swung again, and again. There were so many of them. He couldn't tell which legs belonged to which body. The only way he knew he hit anything was that the blade would stop, something would shriek, and venom would splatter burning hot on his hands.

"Get out of the way!" Betty shouted.

"What?"

"I said, move it!"

Anthony sidestepped.

Something hot blasted past the side of his head and set fire to a spider-demon.

All those wiry hairs ignited simultaneously. The hard carapace shriveled as it screamed and flailed and kicked. All the other spiders stopped to stare, too—like time came to a complete halt as one demon burned to death. Something inside its shell popped as its innards cooked.

It flopped onto its side and stopped moving.

He whirled on Betty. She was clutching a notebook decorated by pink flowers and an ephemeral white unicorn.

"I told you I can cast magic missile!"

"Perhaps I spoke too soon about children," said the Night Hag.

Her leg swung over Anthony's head as she took a huge step. It only took one to reach them. The stink of rot and age overwhelmed him. Each one of her fangs was half as tall as he was. She hunched over, bringing that giant mouth toward their faces.

Anthony wrapped an arm around Betty's shoulders and launched into a run.

The pincers snapped shut where they had been standing a moment before.

"What else do you have?" he asked, swinging and hacking their way through the crowd of spiders. They all were trying so desperately to obey the Night Hag's orders that they stepped on each other, toppling and clumsy.

"Uh—just a second, I don't—"

"We don't have a second!"

She flipped through the pages and ripped one out from the back.

"Okay! Here!"

Betty ducked around him with a sheet of perfumed pink paper between her thumb and first finger. Her lips moved, but Anthony didn't hear anything.

The air popped.

A firestorm blasted around them and blew through the crowd of demons. The three daimarachnids closest to them caught fire like the first one had, shrieking and twitching and falling all at once.

Anthony had never been scared of Betty before. Never. Even when they were kids, and she was five years older, and her idea of babysitting was to literally sit on him. But watching the demons burn made fear thrill through his stomach.

"I traced that one straight out of James's Book of Shadows," she said. Her lips were pale. Her knees buckled.

Anthony had to let her fall. A particularly ambitious daimarachnid climbed over its burning friends, scuttling toward him like an attack dog. He dodged to the side and sliced, but missed. It twisted. Pain whipped through his calf as one of its pincers scraped him through his jeans, and then those fangs hooked on his shoe and jerked him to the ground.

He kicked it in the face and sent it flying. But another one took its place and knocked the falchion from his hand.

It was hard to throw a good punch from the ground, but he sure as hell tried. Hitting the daimarachnid in the face was like hitting a brick wall. His knuckles split open on contact. It reared back an inch—only an inch. It was enough. He lifted his knees, planted his feet on its hind segment, and threw it over his head with its own momentum.

Betty got to her knees and ripped another page out of her notebook.

Another word of power. Another silent explosion.

The spider that had been on top of him splattered.

The paper dissolved under the force of its own magic, and she wiped her hands clean on her shirt. "Oh my *God*. I didn't know—I don't—oh my God!"

"Freak out later!"

Anthony grabbed the falchion, getting to his feet again in time to take the impact from another daimarachnid. There were still almost a half a dozen—plus the big one over the gate, who seemed to be watching them with amused silence.

He stabbed the falchion through the top of a spider-demon's head with enough force for it to come out the other side. The tip of the sword buried in the dirt and pinned the demon down.

"I don't think I have anything else," Betty said, dissolving into a coughing fit.

"Help us!" he cried to Thom on the dais.

The witch was examining his fingernails, reclined against the gate as though it wasn't throbbing with immense, uncontrollable energy. Thom's eyes skimmed over Anthony's body, and something like approval flashed across his face.

"Oh, fine." Thom stepped down to Elise and brushed his fingers across her brow. He winked at Anthony. "You're welcome."

"What are you doing?" the Night Hag demanded.

He vanished. And Elise didn't move.

"Anthony!" Betty cried.

She was pinned by one of the smaller daimarachnids. He wrenched the falchion out of the ground, kicked the demon off Betty, and pulled her to her feet.

The Night Hag's leg swept over him with another step, and the lowest joint caught his attention. The armored shell was split so she could move.

He drove the sword up with all his strength. It buried into her flesh. Fluid sprayed from the Night Hag's leg. The giant spider jerked away with a screech, but Anthony followed her. He hacked at the joint like he was splitting firewood at his aunt's house—hairy, twitching firewood.

Elise's falchion got stuck in the exoskeleton and ripped from his hands.

She slammed him against the wall. "I am having a bad day," the Night Hag said in a low, cooing voice that came from nowhere. "And you are not helping anything." And then she bit.

Elise woke up feeling very strange.

Her skin didn't sit right on the muscle. Brilliant spikes of light filled the empty spaces in her skull. Her tongue tasted like ozone. And the air— so many new colors surrounded her. A not-quite-silver, a blue that wasn't blue, and so many shades of gray that she didn't see with her eyes.

It was the same thing she had seen on the chains binding Nukha'il, but it was magnified a thousand times and painted across the entire world. The light was brighter and the shadows were deeper.

Elise was seeing magic.

"James," she groaned as she sat up, clutching her forehead in both hands. Her leg didn't hurt anymore, and when she peeled off the bandages, she found blood staining unbroken skin. And one of her gloves was gone.

Her aspis was sprawled motionlessly beside her, and she grabbed his wrist to feel for a pulse. It beat steady and strong in his veins.

That was when she realized that Betty and Anthony were missing.

Elise riffled through James's shirt to find the Book of Shadows tucked

410

in his belt. "Sorry about this," she muttered, getting to her feet to look around.

The gate was open. Pale light flowed from its center, warping the air so she couldn't see through to the other side of the cavern. That explained why her glove was gone. But instead of the painful roar she experienced last time a gate was opened, this one chimed. It was a soft, musical note, like a chorus waiting in the white beyond.

It didn't hurt. In fact, nothing hurt. She felt...good. Maybe a little too good.

But there wasn't time to figure out what changed. An infernal presence was strong on the other side of the glowing dais, and Elise reached up to draw one of her swords.

Her hand met empty air.

She spun to search the floor. Her swords were nowhere in sight.

"Great," she muttered.

Elise stepped around the dais. There were more pillars near the wall, although they were black instead of white. Where had they come from?

Her gaze traveled up the long columns.

Her jaw fell open.

There was a huge spider in the room. It had Anthony pinned against the wall. And four or five smaller daimarachnids milled around them.

One of her swords was right in front of the gate. Elise dived for it. Getting so close to the gate made her entire body vibrate, but it wasn't nearly as agonizing as before.

The giant spider moved to bite Anthony. "Hey!" she yelled.

It looked at her. "Oh, wonderful. It's you." Elise recognized that voice. She was too giddy to be surprised that the Night Hag had turned into a spider.

"Yeah. Me." Elise lifted the Book of Shadows. "Betty!"

Her friend looked up. Elise threw the notebook, and Betty caught it. Her eyes lit up. "Should I—?"

"Make a miracle happen!"

The Night Hag rushed Elise, limping on an injured leg. As soon as it landed in front of her, she jumped onto it and scaled the spider's body, dragging herself atop the head. Elise nearly slid off the top when she thrashed, but her fingers caught a ridge near one of the angry eyes. It swiveled around to glare at her.

She levered herself onto her knees, lifted the sword over her head, and plunged it into the Night Hag's eye.

Betty spoke a word of power.

411

The air boomed as the symbols on the sword blazed. All eight eyes erupted at once.

The Night Hag roared. Elise lost traction. Her sword tore free.

It was a long way to the ground.

Anthony caught her. She had the presence of mind to drop her sword to keep from stabbing him, but his arms barely softened the blow. His elbow connected with her stomach. All the breath rushed out of her as they both hit the ground.

The spider stomped blindly toward them with a wailing shriek. Elise jumped out of the way of a crashing leg, pulling Anthony with her. She shoved him toward the wall.

She didn't even see the second leg coming at her.

It smashed her to the ground. Elise threw her arms over her head, trying to shelter herself from the thrashing limbs, and felt ichor shower onto her shoulders from the stab wound. Elise was an instant from getting crushed.

The light in the gate suddenly grew again. Nukha'il appeared at the top of the dais with a flash, looking winded and confused. "Nukha'il!" she shouted.

He glanced between Elise, under the stomping feet of the giant spider-demon, and the Night Hag herself.

A huge foot flew toward her.

Nukha'il darted in—a pale blur in the darkness. Cold hands grabbed Elise's. He dragged her out of the way.

"Get against the wall!" Betty yelled, standing over James's body.

Elise didn't ask why. She threw Nukha'il toward the side of the cavern and covered his body with hers.

Magic coalesced in a nimbus around Betty's head. Her hair stuck straight out in every direction as though she had been struck by lightning. There was paper clutched in both of her fists. Steel-blue light crackled around her. Elise had never seen James's magic before. It was so much darker than she expected.

Betty threw the paper at the Night Hag.

The spells hung, momentarily suspended, in midair. Then they rested against one of her telephone-pole legs.

She pointed.

The room filled with light and heat. All moisture vaporized from Elise's skin. Her clothing charred instantly as the tapestries behind the gate caught fire.

The Night Hag screamed.

412

Elise ducked her head so she wouldn't have to see. But there was no way to tune out the roars of pain and fury as she thrashed in her final death throes.

It felt like she screamed for hours. Days.

Eventually, they trailed into sobs, and then there was nothing but the echoes of crackling fire. The Night Hag had fallen by the dais. Her body was a black husk, and red embers glowed within her carcass. Entire tapestries had disappeared in a puff of smoke.

Both Anthony and Betty were covered in ash, but unharmed. Elise let Nukha'il sit up. He stared around with shock, as though he couldn't imagine a human causing such devastation.

"My Lord," he said.

Elise's mouth was too dry to speak. She worked her tongue around in her mouth to create saliva before saying, "Good miracle, Betty."

With a shaky laugh, Betty sank to the ground and pressed her face into her knees. Elise crawled over to her. "I'm okay," she mumbled without getting up, "I'm okay. Is James...?"

"He's still breathing. He's fine. What about you?"

"That *hurt*," Betty whispered. Her hands were closed so tightly around the remaining scraps of paper that her knuckles were white. Elise carefully opened her fingers.

"Relax. That's James's magic going through you. You'll be fine." Elise made herself sound confident, even though she wasn't sure that was true. What happened when a weak witch channeled power of James's caliber? She had never seen it before, but they were probably lucky Betty was still awake, much less alive.

Nukha'il dusted himself off and came to stand beside Elise. The magic on his necklace had faded, but not gone out.

"Free me," he said. There was no supplication in Nukha'il now—only defiance.

Elise stood. "Why?"

"I helped you. Free me."

She nodded. He turned around. Her fingers tingled as she pressed the latch open, and the metal fell to the floor with a clink.

A sudden swell of ethereal energy rose around him. Nukha'il sighed and rolled his shoulders. "Thank you," he said. "Finally."

"What will you do now?"

"Find Itra'il and move on. I have wasted too much time in servitude."

With a small bow, he turned to leave the cavern. Elise watched him go. The presence of an angel always left a sour taste in her mouth.

413

"Elise?" Anthony's call drew her attention back to him. He was gaping at the Night Hag's body. It seemed to have lost half its mass in death, but it was still terrifyingly huge. "Should we do something about the gate?"

"Sure. Why don't you stay here for a second, Betty?" Her best friend nodded against her knees. She was pale and trembling. Elise collected her swords, sheathed both of them, and joined Anthony by the fallen overlord. She was impressive, even in death. "She's dead, Anthony. We don't have to keep an eye on her."

"I just can't believe..." He blew a heavy breath out of his lips. "That was terrifying."

He probably was hoping for words of comfort. Elise didn't have any.

She turned to face the gate. The light inside whirled and swirled. She stretched a hand toward the broken fragment that had come from her necklace, but getting too close made her fingers burn.

"Here," Anthony said.

He plucked the stone out of the gate, and with a resounding clang like a heavy iron door shutting, the light went out. It sounded like the very gates of Hell swinging shut. But it was so much worse than Hell—and so much more satisfying.

A huge weight Elise hadn't realized she had been carrying lifted off her chest. She sagged against his arm.

His fist clenched around the rock, brown eyes burning bright. "What now?" he asked.

Now she would take that rock and throw it into the deepest reaches of Lake Tahoe. Now she wouldn't worry about anyone reaching those ruins again. Now the overlord and the brand on her shoulder were gone, and the city was hers. Now...

Relief thrilled through her chest, foreign and strange. She seized Anthony's shirt in both hands. "Now this," she said, pulling his head down to kiss her.

His empty hand pressed against the small of her back, crushing her body to his. It felt good. She could have done it forever, if they had the time. Forever turned out to be just a few short seconds, but when she broke free, Anthony pressed his forehead to hers.

"Wow," he murmured. "That good, huh?"

"Yeah. That good."

He laughed and swept her up in his arms, spinning her around. "Jesus, Elise! Thank *God* you woke up when you did. I was sure we were going to die!"

"You didn't do too badly on your own." She leaned on his chest when he set her on her feet again. "Remember when you asked if fighting was a little exciting in the desert?" she whispered, low enough that Betty wouldn't be able to hear. She didn't feel like being teased. Not when she was so relieved. He grinned.

But Betty wasn't even listening to them.

"Hey, lovebirds! I think James is waking up!"

Elise broke free of Anthony. "Of course he missed all the good—" she began, facing her friend, who had pillowed James's head in her lap.

Motion loomed in the darkness beyond Betty.

Alain entered from the hallway above, flanked by twin angels. They were statuesque and pale with the silvery ghost of wings sweeping from their shoulders. Both had swords that flamed with ethereal light.

And the witch's pistol was drawn and aimed at James.

"Watch out!" Anthony shouted.

Three things happened at once.

First, Betty saw Alain and lifted one of James's paper spells, bold challenge glowing in her eyes. Elise could see the confidence in her face. The surety that she could wield that kind of magic. But shifting to take the spell from his Book of Shadows put her directly between the gun and James.

Second, Elise shoved her boyfriend out of the way and drew her sword. The stone dropped from his fingers and clattered across the floor.

Third, Alain squeezed the trigger.

The explosion echoed in the great underground chamber, like two gunshots in quick succession. His muzzle flashed.

Betty fell.

Alain swung his arm and aimed at Anthony. He fired again.

Elise had moved fast to get him out of the way, but not fast enough. Her boyfriend shouted. Blood spurted on his leg.

She leaped over Betty's prone body, which had folded protectively over James, and buried her falchion hilt-deep in Alain's stomach.

He was still unbalanced from the second shot and couldn't protect himself. The impact of body against body brought her to a halt face-to-face with the witch, so close that she could smell the beer on his breath and see the hate deep in his eyes.

Her free hand bit down on his arm, digging her nails in until he dropped the pistol.

But he was smiling. Why was he smiling?

"Mr. Black sends his regards," he hissed. His tongue was stained with

415

his own blood.

The angels whirled with motion—not to attack Elise or defend Alain, but to snatch the stone from the ground and slam it back into position on the gate. The ringing of chimes roared through the chamber as the gate swept open once more. Wind lashed Elise's braid around her head.

She withdrew the falchion. Alain stumbled back, gripping his wound. Off-center. She may not have hit anything important, but it would slow him. Blood dribbled through his fingers.

Still he laughed, shrill and delighted, and when Elise turned she saw why.

Betty had been shot in the face.

She was slumped to the side on top of James. Her forehead was a ruined mess, though the injury was only as wide as a coin. From this side, the wound almost looked too neat to be fatal. But there was nothing in her eyes and her muscles were slack. Elise had seen the emptiness of death more than enough to recognize it without needing to check for a pulse or the rise and fall of breath.

One corner of Betty's lips was still spread in the tiniest smile.

Dead.

A ringing filled Elise's ears, drowning out the gate and the heavenly choir and even her own heart. She was frozen to the spot. Her fingers suddenly didn't have the strength to hold her falchion.

Translucent feathers swirled around her. An angel wrapped his arm around Alain's midsection. He mouthed words Elise couldn't hear: "Go! Now, go!" And both angels, with the witch in tow, leaped through the gate.

Her knees connected with the ground. She didn't realize she was scrambling over to Betty until she took the woman's shoulders and turned her gently onto her back. Something warm and sticky met her fingers. The exit wound at the back of Betty's skull was low, almost at her spine—Alain had shot from above and gone all the way through—and it dribbled down her neck.

Her blood was sprinkled on James's cheek like tears flicked on his skin.

"Betty," Elise whispered, taking her friend's hand. Her fingers were still closed around one of James's spells.

Someone was screaming.

Anthony limped over and collapsed. He was shot, too, but Alain had only hit him in the thigh. Shock turned him white and shaking.

"Betty—Betty—oh my God, Betty, you can't—"

His fingers clenched too hard on her shoulders. She was dead weight when he shook her.

"Stay with her," Elise said.

Anthony turned wide, helpless eyes on her as she stood. "Where are you going? You can't leave us! Betty needs help, she has to—"

"Betty is dead."

Her voice broke on the last word. Elise took up her sword with blood-sticky fingers and sheathed it. "Elise—"

"When James wakes up, tell him I've gone through," she said.

She felt calm. Composed. Total clarity descended upon her in a silent, crystal moment of realization: Alain and the angels had gone to the other side. She was going to follow him, and she would kill him.

Elise stood in front of the gate. It seemed so much bigger now that she knew she had to pass through it. The darkness beckoned to her with slender fingers.

Elise...

That voice. It had been calling to her for weeks.

Now she would answer its summons.

She glanced over her shoulder at Anthony, James, and Betty. So much blood. She clenched her jaw, tightened her fists, and took a deep breath.

Elise jumped through the gate.

Chapter 17

TIME AND SPACE had no meaning.

Elise floated through the void without a body, without sensation. There was…nothing.

She came back to herself in downtown Reno.

Much like when Thom transported her back to Craven's, her mind wasn't prepared to make sense of the shift in setting, and she initially rejected everything she saw. The light post standing over her. The bare branches of a bush. Traffic lights blinking red. A parking lot with no cars.

There was concrete under her fingers, and buildings to either side of her…but no sky.

Instead, she stared at a distant road a mile below her.

Her entire body revolted when she realized what she was seeing. Elise gasped and grabbed behind her for something to grab before she fell. She was hanging over the city. Nothing held her to the ground. She was going to fall and hit the road and—

No.

Her thudding heart skipped a beat.

Elise lifted her hands and didn't fall. Nothing was holding her up. Or rather, nothing was holding her down—except gravity. Slowly, carefully, she sat up to see where she had found herself.

She had somehow reappeared beside the El Cortez Hotel. It was an old brick building with an art deco sign on its roof. There were other motels to her right, and casinos just a few blocks down. She wasn't far from the river and the train trench. She had walked down that very street a hundred times on her way to Craven's and on her morning jogs. It was as familiar as her neighborhood.

There were no cars. Nobody walked their dogs. No bicycles. She had never seen the downtown area so empty.

A ghost town.

But...

Elise braced herself and lifted her eyes again.

Each building stretched toward a shimmering line in the sky, as though a sheet of water was somehow suspended in a bubble around her. The street she initially thought she would fall onto was actually a reflection of where she stood. The very top of the Eldorado's hotel tower brushed its mirrored roof. Silvery light radiated from everywhere and nowhere, even though there was no sun to cast it.

She was in the angelic city.

Elise got to her feet carefully and turned in a small circle, cupping her hands around her face to shield her eyes from the radiant light. It was like a hazy, fog-filled morning, unlike any the desert had ever seen.

She knew that angels didn't like to walk on Earth. She had never dreamed that they would build their city as a reflection of reality in a parallel dimension atop hers.

But the duplication was almost perfect. The buildings in the angel's city were nearly identical to their counterparts in reality above her. Everything around her looked a little more wind-worn and crumbling, the streets were paved with cobblestone instead of asphalt, and all the trees and grass were dead—but it was otherwise indistinguishable.

She had to brace herself to look up again, holding onto a fence so she wouldn't be overcome with vertigo. The streets above were filled with cars. People walked from building to building. That was reality.

Then she faced the casinos to the north, and a chill settled over her.

White stone arches rose above the center of the city with no reflection in the real world. Nine of them. One was taller than the rest, and it glowed with dark energy.

If she wanted to find Alain, she would want to start there. She was certain.

Her shock at finding herself in the angelic city was enough to make her forget, for a moment, why she had jumped to the other side in the first place. A wave of grief struck her as she remembered Alain's laughter, the gunshot, and Betty's blank face.

He needed to die.

Elise found her falchions a block away, as though they had been flung away from her when she jumped through the doorway. One was on top of a planter, and another was in the middle of the shimmering white cobblestones that made up the street. She moved to pick up the one

419

between the bushes, but hesitated.

The symbols she had carved into the blade were glowing. Her hand itched when she reached for it.

Elise turned over her bare palm. Most of the bleeding had stopped, but the mark underneath was raised and irritated. She didn't need to check the other hand to know it was the same. They were reacting to being in the angelic city.

She picked the falchion up with her gloved hand and sheathed it before retrieving the second.

Elise skirted around the downtown blocks with the gates, trying to find the city's boundary. She didn't have to go far. When she walked three blocks east, she found the new baseball stadium severed in half. The street ended in a white void with nothing but clouds beyond it. The break wasn't clean. The sidewalks were jagged and crumbling and a telephone pole's wires dangled uselessly into oblivion.

She could hear the river passing nearby. She approached the edge, hooked a hand around the light post, and peered over the edge.

The mirrored Truckee River roared as it emptied into a star-filled void, spraying foam in every direction. A sliver of moon danced in the sky. Her stomach flipped with vertigo. The wind gusted around her, almost blowing her off her feet, but she held tighter to the post.

"What the hell?" she whispered.

A chime split the air. She turned to see the darkest gate glowing.

Alain was opening it.

Elise swore and broke into a run.

As she sprinted toward the arches, she saw other figures moving toward it as well. It wasn't the two angels that had accompanied Alain—these were different ones. The angels she had seen in Mr. Black's penthouse. They seemed oblivious to her as they drifted toward the gates.

She turned the corner and skidded to a halt.

The base of the gate wasn't on ground level. Its two columns straddled a movie theater and a parking garage, leaving the space beneath it all the way to the street rippling.

The angels that came with Alain unspooled ribbons in a circle around the pillar. Even at a distance, she recognized the black icons inscribed on them. Those were the ribbons she had seen in the penthouse.

The witch stood between four crystals on the corner beside an inoperative stop light, muttering to himself as he spread salt. He was casting a circle of power—probably to activate the ribbons. "Alain!" she yelled.

He turned. From behind, she hadn't noticed that he was pale and hunched over his stab wound. He had pressed a poultice of herbs against it. Most witches didn't have the healing powers James did, and Alain was no exception, but he was doing his best to repair himself and finish the ritual.

His eyes darkened when he saw her. He reached into his jacket.

Elise threw herself behind the corner of the building. An instant later, the cement shattered with a gunshot inches from her head.

She shut her eyes to think back on what her father had taught her about guns years before. Pistols like that had twelve bullets in a magazine —thirteen, if he'd loaded one into the chamber before. One shot for Betty. One shot for Anthony's leg.

Three down. Maybe ten to go. Not good.

She took a deep breath and sprinted across the street.

Alain fired another two shots. One pinged off the cobblestone. Then she felt a bee sting on her shin and fell with a shout, tumbling behind an elevator into the parking garage.

"Come out!" he called in French.

Elise hissed as she inspected the wound. The bullet had grazed her leg, leaving a red stripe on her leg that trickled blood. It felt like getting snapped by a whip.

Why had he aimed so low? He had to know to shoot for the center mass.

She peeked around the wall. Alain staggered toward her, barely able to hold the gun straight. Elise drew her sword again and listened for his footfalls.

Just before he turned the corner, she threw herself around the other side and into his legs.

Elise knocked him to the ground. The gun fired as he fell.

She knelt over him, grabbing his arm and slamming the back of his hand into the street. He tried to twist it to aim at her. She gritted her teeth and struck his hand again.

It took three hits before his fingers loosed enough to release it. Elise threw the gun into the open door of an empty shop.

Alain shoved her off of him. She stepped between him and the door. Fury flashed through his eyes, but he didn't try to fight her again.

Instead, he ran for the elevators, trailing blood in his wake.

Elise was torn. Follow Alain, or stop the angels? The mental image of the exit wound at the back of Betty's skull was enough to make the decision for her.

She slammed into the elevator doors too late, unable to force her foot in the way. Elise cursed and launched herself up the stairs, taking them three at a time to beat him to the top of the garage.

The energy flowing from the gate was so thick that it was hard to run through it. It felt like she was swimming. The angels glanced at her when she rushed toward them, but didn't stop spreading the ribbons across the cement in long lines. The symbols glowed like the ones on her sword. Her hands bled anew as she forced herself through the thickened air to the lift.

She managed to reach the elevator just as it chimed. The doors slid open. Alain lurched out. Elise grabbed his jacket in both hands and smashed him against a window. He groaned and gripped his side.

"Help me!" he yelled, throwing a hand toward the angels.

They continued to unspool the ribbon, ignoring his cries.

Elise punched the elevator button. The doors opened again, and she shoved him inside.

"You're going to tell me what Mr. Black is planning," she said. "And you're going to tell me how I can deactivate the ribbons."

He snorted and spit a wad of bloody phlegm on her face.

She punched him in the stab wound. He cried out, but didn't fall.

When the doors opened on the bottom level again, he jumped at her. It was a pathetic escape attempt. He was so slow that he didn't get far. Elise caught up to him in three long strides and slammed the back of his head into the restaurant's wall.

"You're going to pay," she spat, tightening her hand on his esophagus. He gurgled. She pulled him toward her and slammed him back again for good measure, and was rewarded with a flash of pain in his eyes.

"The angels—" he squeezed out.

"You're on your own."

He shoved her arms off of him, but didn't make another break for it. Instead, he groaned and slid to the ground. He parted his jacket. The wound was bleeding worse.

Elise drew a sword.

"Wait!" Alain said, lifting his hands over his head. "Kopides protect humanity. I am human."

"Yeah? Well, your kopis is doing a good job of that."

"You can be better than him."

Elise raised the sword a fraction. Her skin was flushed and hot. It was hard to draw in a full breath of air with the pain stabbing in her chest.

She should kill him. She should do it.

The aspis's hands spread wide in a gesture of contrition, and his

422

fingers were sticky with his own blood. There was no color in his face. "What would James want you to do?" he asked. He flashed red-stained teeth when he spoke.

Do it. Just do it.

"Fuck you," Elise said, but the falchion drooped. She was light-headed and queasy. He was right—James would probably spare Alain. She might not have been better than Mr. Black, but he was.

Would it be better to kill him now, or make him bleed out on the street?

He opened his mouth to speak again, but his eyes focused on something over her shoulder and the words died on his tongue.

Before she could turn around, an explosion blasted behind Elise. Her ears rang.

Alain's face was blown off his skull. His body bounced against the wall with a spray of blood. She whirled to see Anthony just behind her, shotgun braced on his shoulder. His knuckles were white on the metal. Hatred filled his eyes as he pumped and shot again.

"Anthony," she said, voice muffled in her ears. He didn't acknowledge her except to shove her aside and stand directly over Alain's body.

Another pump. Another shot. Skull fragmented and brain splattered. The empty hull dropped to his feet.

He tried to fire again, but there was no ammunition left. The shotgun just clicked.

"You killed her," he said. "You fucking killed her!"

She grabbed his arm. He spun to aim at her, but Elise grabbed the muzzle and yanked it out of his hands. The metal scorched her fingers. She flung it aside.

Anthony swung a fist, and she ducked under it to sock him hard in the gut. He grunted. Doubled over.

"He killed her!"

"And now he's dead," Elise snapped, gripping his shoulders in her hands. "Look, Anthony!"

She forced him to face Alain's body. The witch wasn't recognizable anymore. Strands of hair stuck to the wall and the cavity that used to be his face. As they watched, the body slipped to the side inch by inch, and then landed on its shoulder. Fluid dribbled out of the neck.

The anger slowly drained from Anthony's face.

"Oh my God, Elise. She's..."

"Dead," she finished for him. It hurt to say it. "I know."

He dropped to his knees, and a scream ripped from his throat. Fury, grief, pain—it echoed off the high pillars and the reflection of the city below. His hands shook as they covered his face. His skin was flushed and red as tears coursed down his cheeks.

Elise stepped back. She thought there was probably something she was supposed to do. Comfort him? Hold him? Tell him it would be okay? "Hey," she said, crouching in front of him when he didn't stop screaming. "Anthony. Anthony!"

He didn't acknowledge at her. She hauled back and punched him again. His head snapped to the side, and it cut off his cries like a string snapping on a guitar.

He glared at her. Blood trickled from a split on his lip. "What the fuck is wrong with you?" he asked, voice ragged. "He killed Betty! How can you be so goddamn calm?"

"He's dead. You've got your justice. But we have a job to finish."

"Betty—"

"We can't do anything for her now." Elise swallowed hard. "Come on. We have to find Mr. Black."

The first thing James realized when he reached consciousness was that he was very cold and laying just a few feet away from the Night Hag's doorway—which was open. Light radiated from it in colors he had never seen before. It would have transfixed him if he had been alone.

But the second thing he realized was that Mr. Black was standing over him.

He groaned, trying to push himself away on instinct. But hands clapped down on his shoulders and hauled him to his feet before he could go anywhere.

The cool hands burned against his skin. He tried to pull away, but the angel was too strong for him to break free. Even if he could have, there were more angels waiting to stop him. James made a quick head count. Six of them. Where ethereal beings were concerned, it was virtually an army.

"So glad you could join us," Mr. Black said, drumming his fingers against a notebook tucked under one arm. The Book of Shadows. Fantastic. "I thought I'd have to throw you over my shoulder to jump through."

James tried to remember how he had ended up in the cavern and what happened. When had the gate opened? Why was there a dead spider the size of a small house on the other side? And where was Elise?

Then he looked down at where he had been laying. Someone was on the ground not far from him.

"Oh no," he whispered.

Betty had been laid out with her hands folded on her stomach and a shirt tucked under her head. She might have been sleeping, if not for the bullet wound.

He clapped a hand over his mouth and turned away. It seemed somehow obscene to gaze upon the body of Elise's best friend. Maybe if he didn't see her, it wouldn't be true. Maybe she would sit up and be fine again.

"Look at her," Mr. Black said. "Look."

James didn't want to obey, but he couldn't tear his eyes from the wound on her forehead and the bloody line running down her nose. He thought of all the times he had snapped at her for doing something absurd at the esbats, and her musical giggle, and he felt like he was going to vomit.

He turned on Mr. Black. "You're sick," he said, voice trembling with fury.

"Actually, that would be the mark of my friend Alain. Isn't he a good shot?" Mr. Black stepped close to James. The old kopis was three inches shorter than him. "I'll admit I was a tad offended when you burned my home and destroyed the gate. In fact, I've thought about very little else in the years that have passed."

"We didn't kill anyone."

"No, but you sure as God tried. Now, I hope you spend the rest of your life thinking about this…" He swept a hand toward Betty. "Like I've thought about you. However short that 'rest of your life' might be."

He tossed the Book of Shadows aside. It disappeared into the darkness, and James watched it go with longing.

"Elise is going to—"

"Shut up. I'll consider myself threatened and save you the effort." Mr. Black took out a pocket watch to study it. "Alain should have everything ready now." He pointed at the gate with his cane. A silver cuff glimmered at his wrist. "You first, Mr. Faulkner."

Elise would have argued. She probably would have fought him, and seen how many angels she could take out before they brought her down. But James was not nearly so brave. He couldn't stop staring at the neat little hole in Betty's skull.

"You've made a big mistake," he said.

He prodded James in the knee with his cane. "Walk faster, please.

We're on limited time."

There were only three wide steps to reach the dais on which the gate had been built, so there was little time to examine where he was going. James knew quite a bit about angels and their ruins, and this was not a gate to an ethereal dimension—that much he could tell. He suspected it would take him to the mysterious angelic city rumored to be under Reno. It was enough to get his academic heart racing.

He tilted his head back to gaze at all the shifting colors and shapes within the gate. He stretched a hand out and felt the vibrations in the air. He had never felt it like that before. Something had changed.

Mr. Black cleared his throat. When James didn't immediately move, he prodded him again.

Bracing himself, he stepped through the gateway.

When he reappeared a few seconds later, he was on all fours on a street corner. His glasses fell off the bridge of his nose. They cracked when they struck the cement sidewalk.

"Damn it," he muttered. His stomach wanted to reject everything he had eaten that day. He took shallow breaths and focused on holding it down.

He studied his surroundings through a fall of bangs. The angels had appeared around him on their feet. They were as calm and composed as though stepping through interdimensional gateways was an ordinary part of their day. For all he knew, it might have been.

Then he looked straight up.

He lost his battle against his own heaving stomach and vomited.

When he was done, he didn't dare look up again. One glance had been more than enough. The mirrored cities were too much for any mortal mind to process.

James trembled as he sat back, wiping his mouth clean. The angels watched him, showing no signs of concern. They looked so different to him now. His body reacted to them—a clenching of his gut, a tickle in his skull. It was like a whole new sense had opened for James.

And then he realized what had changed.

He could *feel* Elise.

To an extent, that was nothing new. He could always sense her. She was like his phantom limb, and sometimes he felt a little twitch that said Elise was thinking about him. But this was something new. He could hear her voice, like tuning into a fuzzy radio station.

Anthony shot him…going to regret that…damn it, Betty…

He glimpsed an image of a bloody skull and brain. James couldn't

426

make sense of it. He gripped his head in both hands as the images and voice grew stronger.

I can't do this…

James tried to see over the heads of the angels, but they were taller than him—a novel experience. He couldn't see anyone on the street. It didn't sound like he was hearing with his ears anyway. He was hearing her inside of his mind.

And being close to the angels made his palms itch.

"Elise?" he said aloud. She didn't respond.

He put his broken glasses back on his face. The left eye was fragmented into two, warping the buildings. It was not nearly as dizzying as the mirrored cities.

A moment later, Mr. Black appeared on the other side of his angelic guards.

The air warped, and he dropped a few inches to the cobblestone street. He lost his balance and fell with a cry. The cane flew from his hand.

James seized the moment.

He stumbled to a standing position and ran. He made it about three steps before his heaving stomach brought him to his knees again.

An angel swept in and took his arm. It was a beautiful woman, elegant and slender, and he tensed with the expectation of being dragged to his feet. But she only offered him a hand. "Be careful," she murmured. Coppery hair fell in soft waves around her shoulders.

After a moment of hesitation, he let her help him up. Something in her face was open and trustworthy. "Let me run," he whispered urgently.

She shook her head. "We have a plan. Wait."

By the time she guided him to their landing spot, Mr. Black had stood. Sweat drenched his brow as he clutched at his chest. "No," he gasped. "Where did he go?" He spun, staring wildly at the ghost city around them. "Where is he? Alain? Alain!"

James didn't see anybody on the street. "What are you on about?"

The kopis dropped his cane and seized James's shirt in both hands. "He's gone. Alain is gone. I can't feel him!"

"Perhaps he's not here," James said.

But he suddenly knew that wasn't true. He saw the bloody skull again, and could hear the faint blast of a shotgun. *Anthony shot him…*

Mr. Black shook his head. "No! He came ahead of me! That can only mean he's…"

His mind caught up to what he was about to say an instant before he said it. Horror dawned on his face.

427

Alain was dead. James couldn't find any satisfaction at the realization.

Why could he hear Elise's thoughts?

Mr. Black dragged James down the street. The angels drifted after them without being ordered to do so. "Impossible," the older man muttered. "He can't be dead."

Have to find Mr. Black…

The thought didn't belong to James.

The angels followed him with those beautiful, expressionless gazes. They flanked him to either side as if he might run from them. Where would he go? The only way out would be to go through one of those gateways.

He closed his eyes for a moment, letting Mr. Black's hand lead him on, and caught flashes of imagery in his mind's eye. Even though he couldn't see Elise, he felt like she should have been standing next to him.

An elevator. More angels. Parking garage.

She was close. He was certain of it. But he had no idea *why*.

He opened his eyes to search for her again. If she was that close, he was sure he would have been able to see her. He scanned the roofs of the nearby buildings as Mr. Black dragged him along.

Angels moved atop the nearest structures surrounding the dark gate. They were spreading long lines of cloth ribbon in rows. One strand had been laid across the street, and James took the opportunity to examine it when they passed. It was covered in magic symbols, like the pages in his Book of Shadows.

"Paper magic?" he said. "That's impossible—I've never shown anyone how to do it."

"Some of the spells you used to burn down my home never ignited." Mr. Black bit out every word, shooting a glare over his shoulder. "Alain studied them. Deconstructed them. His aren't quite the same, but they do the trick, and—my God!"

The exclamation made James look up. They had turned a corner to see a parking garage—the same parking garage he could see with his eyes closed, but from another angle. A ritual space had been established at the corner near a street light.

Alain's body was a few feet away with blood and brain drying on the wall behind him.

"*Mon ami,*" Mr. Black murmured.

Before James even realized the older man was moving, Mr. Black swung his cane. It cracked against James's skull.

His ears rang and his vision blurred. But he was ready for it when Mr.

Black swung again.

James caught the cane and tried to wrench it from his grip. They struggled. James was a good twenty years old and several inches taller—it shouldn't have been a fight at all. But even an older kopis was much stronger than the average human.

Mr. Black shoved him to the ground and seized a fistful of cloth ribbon.

"She killed him," he said, voice thick with tears. "My aspis—my companion—"

"Karmic justice," James said.

"Justice? *Justice*?"

He didn't even see the strike coming this time.

The force of the blow made James black out. It was only for a few moments, but that was enough time—when he roused again, he was dangling upside down over the shoulder of an angel as they ascended in an elevator. He watched the hazy mirror-world slide outside the window.

When the door opened, the angel carried him outside and threw him to the floor.

James stared up at the towering column of the gate. It was so much bigger than anything he had seen before. The very top almost brushed the real city, and light swirled between the pillars like a tear in existence. The symbols at the base were already glowing. It was almost open. All it needed were the matching marks.

Mr. Black knelt over James with a fistful of ribbons, blocking his view. "Activate it."

James's eyes traced the path of ribbon. The angels had completed the circles—all nine of them, each one slightly smaller than the last and nested within each other. It encompassed the entirety of the gate.

He could see the spells for entrapment in the line, which had been Alain's specialty. It was relatively harmless—if one considered trapping a god harmless.

"I won't do it," James said.

"Hold his arms!"

An angel pinned him down. There was no fighting against its grip.

Mr. Black threw the rope of ribbon around James's head and tightened it on his throat. Pressure crushed against his esophagus. He gagged and gurgled, tongue bulging from his mouth.

"Activate them!"

James would have said no again if he could speak. He fought against the restraints of the angel's hands to no avail.

429

And Mr. Black pulled harder.

His skull began to fill with white noise. The older man's face blurred in his vision. Elise's voice echoed in the back of his mind: *He's here... where is he? James?*

Such pain.

He stretched out a finger to touch the ribbon as Mr. Black tightened the ligature.

The symbols flared to life.

Magic flowed from him into the ribbons, stretching out over the city. James moved through his magic. He raced through every line and saw the angels with their hopeless stares as if he walked past them himself.

And he saw Elise running toward Mr. Black's back.

She jumped on the other kopis, knocking him off James. They bumped into the angel. The pressure vanished from his throat and arms.

Freed.

James ripped the ribbons off his throat, sucking in a blessed lungful of air. Anthony raced from the stairwell. "Stop the magic!" he cried, waving his arms.

But it was too late to take it back. The entire city was aglow with the symbols on the ribbons.

Elise and Mr. Black rolled across the roof, trading blows. They ended up on their feet on the other side of the pillar, just beyond the barrier of the ribbon.

She lunged toward him, but Mr. Black side-stepped her, moving out of the way as though she had telegraphed her move. She swung again. His arm struck hers, knocking it aside.

Mr. Black slapped her other hand when it rose to strike him. He twisted, capturing her arm, and bent her elbow the wrong way. She cried out.

He finally gave a hard shove, launching Elise over his head, and she stumbled over the line made by the ribbons. "Finally," he spat.

"Don't start celebrating yet," she said, striding toward him again.

But when she reached the ribbon line, it was like striking a wall. The shock of it resonated through James. She couldn't pass the magicked runes.

"I've envisioned this moment for years," Mr. Black laughed. "Years! And what a satisfying moment it is."

Anthony tried to rush the barrier of ribbons, but an angel snagged him in its arms, holding him back. "Elise!" he shouted.

She faced the gate.

Elise…

This time, it wasn't her voice that James heard, but another entirely—something great and terrible that rang through his entire being, vibrating down to the marrow of his bones.

She held up her ungloved hand. Blood streamed from the symbol again.

The marks *wanted* to open the gate.

Her legs moved of their own volition. She stepped toward the pillar, rooted deep in the concrete of the parking garage.

She fought it. She fought it hard. But there was no way to stop the inevitable march.

Before she even touched it, the gate began to open.

A gust of wind roared across the top of the parking garage, ripping through them and nearly blowing James off his feet. Electricity sparked and danced in the air around the pillars. A rumbling shook the entire structure, from the top of the gate to the very earth, and the angels backed away as white light erupted from the arch.

He flung up a hand to shield his eyes, but it did nothing for the painful brilliance that burned through Elise's skull.

Her hands were stretched toward the pillar, dragging her forward inch by inch.

James and Elise's eyes met through the light. He knew she could see and feel the way he did, sharing every thought and sense between them. Something had happened when they piggybacked. Something wrong. She shared his sore neck. He felt her grief at Betty's death, and the marks on her palms burned on both of their hands. He felt the pull as strongly as she did.

And he felt the moment she made a horrible decision.

"He can't have me," she said. "I'll never go back to Him."

"No," he whispered. He didn't have to raise his voice for her to hear it.

Elise drew one of the falchions. "Sorry, James."

She plunged it into her gut.

Pain ripped through him as though he had been stabbed, too. A scream tore from his throat. He fell to his knees. At the same time, Anthony yelled—but it was all so distant, so meaningless. James's palms burned and the gate throbbed and he could feel the blade scraping bone.

Mr. Black ran to the edge of the ribbon. "No!"

Elise hit her knees. Fell onto her side. Released the sword. The power rushing through the gate immediately faltered. Her vision dimmed, and

431

she felt *satisfied*.

He didn't stop to consider the ramifications. He shoved past Mr. Black, jumped over the ribbon line, and fell to his knees beside Elise. She swatted weakly at his arm, as if to push him back, but there was no strength in it. She was bleeding out too fast.

His Book of Shadows was still in the Night Hag's cavern. There was no time to cast a spell. James was one of the most powerful witches in the world, and yet his kopis was dying in front of him, and there wasn't anything he could do. "Goddamn it, Elise!"

She smiled to see him. "Hey," she said. Her vision snowed.

Elise's eyes unfocused. Her chest hitched.

He ripped the second glove off her hand, baring both bloody marks, and pressed them to the angelic stone.

Energy shocked through them. A mighty bell chimed.

The gate opened.

Chapter 18

DYING WAS A lot more painful than Elise expected.

She had given the subject a lot of thought over the years. Kopides seldom lived past thirty, so it wasn't a question of whether she would die a violent death or not—it was a question of *when*.

Since fights were seldom painful while she was in the midst of it—the adrenaline and endorphins took care of that—she expected the act of dying to be relatively painless, too. She thought she would go into shock. She might even be dead before she knew it was going to happen.

All of that was completely wrong.

The sword hurt as it was punched in, and it hurt just as much coming out the other side. Elise felt a twinge of sympathy for all the demons she had killed in that fashion.

But then she was falling, and she didn't really feel much of anything except the pain.

There was a commotion around her. People yelling. The towering bone pillars of the gate beginning to shake. She could see it all through James's eyes—including Mr. Black's horror as he rushed to the edge of the circle.

Good. Let him despair.

The blood loss caught up with her a few moments later, making the last vestiges of rational thought fade. A gray haze filled her vision.

Scraps of random thought flitted through her mind. She wasn't in the angelic city—she was buying the studio with James, bumping her shoulder against his and enjoying the glow of companionship. She was meeting an incubus in her new office, hoping to acquire her first client. She was taking a test with Betty in a lecture hall at the university. She was sinking deep into the snow...

433

Cold.

She was so cold.

Elise remembered running.

Her bare feet slapped against white cobblestone as a pale dress streamed behind her. Angels flanked her to either side. "Help me!" she had cried, and they rushed in to take her hands. She was a little smaller, in those days. Thinner and less muscular. Younger. But not weak.

"He will be so angry when He realizes you've gone," one of the angels told her. "He will tear apart the world to find you. He will destroy *everything* to bring you back."

"Let him," she said.

So they ran—Elise and twelve angels.

She had only been sixteen years old. She hadn't deserved what He did to her. She didn't deserve to be trapped in a black garden where light and hope did not exist.

There was a gate then, too. The angels took her there.

She had put her bandaged hands upon it. Her palms bled, the gate opened, and she jumped through to the other side.

Those were the facts. She understood that was what happened. But she didn't remember anymore.

Hazy memories. Scraps of time drifting on the wind.

She could see the pale hands reaching for her and hear His voice as He shouted for her.

Elise!

And when she awoke again—only for a moment—it was in the depths of snowy winter with James kneeling over her.

At the time, she thought he was another angel who had come to rescue her from His grip. She had been trapped for months—month upon month of torture, insanity, and pain under the guise of loving care. It only ended when James took her away.

She tried to forget. It was better to forget.

The concerned face of her aspis loomed overhead. "Goddammit, Elise," he muttered from a million miles away. He was turning her over, helping her face a sky filled with white light.

She wished he wouldn't look so sad. She reached up to touch his cheek, but her hand was too heavy.

"Hey," she said. She wanted to add, *It's okay.*

434

Feathers drifted through space.

It was so very cold.

James saw the instant that Elise lost consciousness. Her eyes went empty. The lids fell shut.

A moment later, the world flipped upside down.

For a horrifying moment, he dangled from the roof of the parking garage and stared at the real city beneath him. His stomach rose into his throat. His feet lifted from the cement, and he clutched Elise's limp body to his chest as if he could save her from the fall. But then pressure built within the barrier of the ribbons that pinned him in place.

A fissure appeared in the air between the gate's columns like a lightning bolt suspended in midair.

It split open.

Black, yawning darkness waited on the other side of the gate. It was pure nothingness, colder and emptier than the void of space. Like staring into the nonexistence of death.

He is coming.

Although He was pure energy—and inconceivable to the human mind—James knew the instant that He stepped through the door. Everything within the ribbons turned to white fire. The air scorched his flesh. He folded himself over Elise to protect her, but she was burning, too. All the oxygen vanished. James tried to suck in a breath—and failed.

The magic on the ribbons flared with power, straining to contain Him.

Beyond the ribbons, Mr. Black had fallen to his knees. He mouthed words that James could not hear.

James gathered Elise in his arms and struggled to stand. She should have been light. He always thought of her as hollow-boned, like a bird, and through a thousand rehearsals and a hundred thousand dance lifts, he never had to fight to lift her. But now he couldn't breathe. Couldn't think.

Ridiculous thoughts to have in the face of their greatest enemy.

His muscles trembled. "I have Elise," he gasped. He felt the voice in his throat, and the spasm of his lungs as they struggled to breathe, but his words were sucked into the abyss. "Now heal her!"

The light faded as he rushed toward unconsciousness. James fell, unable to support Elise's weight.

Heal her…save her life…

435

He wasn't sure if it was his thought, or if it belonged to the vast entity surrounding him. The light faded as He realized he was trapped. He wouldn't cross the gateway into a cage.

"You can't go until you heal her," James croaked, doubling over. "You can't..."

Another figure moved behind Mr. Black's shoulders. It wasn't one of the enslaved angels. It was a man that burned with inner light, despite the overbearing light of God, with broad silver wings stretching behind him.

He landed at Mr. Black's side and seized his arm.

James didn't need to hear him to read his lips: *Burn in Hell.*

The angel smashed Mr. Black's silver cuff.

The outermost ribbon ignited, flashing with flame and turning to ash. The pressure eased off James. Oxygen rushed into his lungs. All sound resumed.

Mr. Black's influence lifted from the angels on the rooftop. A couple of them looked around as though they had just woken up. The one who had been holding Anthony sank to his knees and began crying.

The rest went insane.

The angels attacked each other. From the other side of the ribbon barrier, they were an indistinguishable mass of seething bodies. James couldn't see any detail through the brilliant light, for which he was grateful—but there was no way to drown out the sounds. Screams tore the air. Slick crunches and thick splats punctuated every cry.

"Anthony—run!" James yelled.

He rushed for the stairs at top speed, fists pumping and feet pounding against the cement. He jumped over the rail to the level below. Mr. Black followed suit and bolted—but much slower.

His motion caught the attention of the angels that had gone mad.

They flew at him with wings that were beginning to blossom again and fell upon him before he could take three steps. They dragged him to the ground just a few feet away from James. He saw everything.

Teeth sank into Mr. Black's shoulders. Clawed fingers dug into his belly. The suit was stripped from his body, and then the flesh from his bones in a spray of blood.

An angel tore the jaw free of his face. Hands pressed against the sides of his face and crushed his cheekbones. One eyeball bulged, then exploded. White matter splattered against the invisible barrier over the ribbon. The attackers dug elbow-deep in his body to yank viscera free.

James saw the copper-haired angel descend and remove a female from the fray. Her lips were stained with Mr. Black's blood.

"Itra'il!" he cried.

She struggled against him, but he lifted her into the air as though her kicks and punches meant nothing. Another angel took her place over Mr. Black's body as both disappeared into the glowing sky.

The rest of the ribbons caught fire and disappeared. A line of blood spilled across the place the barrier had been a moment before.

James wasn't going to wait for the angels to notice.

He threw Elise over his shoulder and ran for the stairs. Nothing stopped him. Every ribbon was broken and his path was clear. Carrying her body made him even slower than Mr. Black had been, but the angels were so preoccupied that it gave him a few seconds' head start.

They reached the top of the stairwell before the angels began alighting on the wind. Massive wings whipped behind them, only a shade darker than the light from the gate.

James didn't watch.

There was no sign of Anthony as he rushed through the streets with Elise hanging over his back, and he didn't dare search for him. Angels swooped overhead with wailing screams.

The windows on every shop had shattered when the gate opened, leaving shards of glass scattered on the sidewalk. His every footstep crunched. There was nowhere safe he could hide from the angels with the shops open—and he didn't dare pass through one of the gates.

But the river wasn't far. He could hear it roaring less than a block away.

James rushed around the corner, across a brick plaza, and down white stone steps toward the water. Angels wheeled around the buildings. One passed so low that it ruffled his hair. Feathers snowed around him, loosening from ethereal wings that had sprouted anew, but he didn't look up to see if they were coming for him.

The Truckee had risen on its banks to swallow the walkways that surrounded it. James's foot slipped and he sank knee-deep in water. It was so cold that it burned.

He sloshed through the shallows to shelter under the bridge as another angel shrieked past. James set Elise's body on a narrow strip of rocks and climbed beside her, crouching under the low shelter of stone. She stayed dry, but he was wet to the hips.

James peered out at the blazing white sky. He couldn't see the gate from their hiding place. Was it still open? Had He gone back, or was He in the city?

437

There was no way to tell. He turned his attention to Elise.

Her skin was colorless. James pressed his hand to her throat and found her pulse sluggish—and slowing.

Something splattered on the opposite bank.

James moved to shield Elise, but it wasn't an angel, and it didn't move to attack. It was a lumpy red mass—what remained of Mr. Black's body. The angels had dropped it on them. His blood clouded the water.

He scanned the sky. The angels spiraled overhead with no indication of dropping. Everything was bright and colorless, as though He should have been close. James had been so certain that He wouldn't be able to resist Elise. It was the only way to heal her. "Come on, where are you?" he shouted to the sky. "Why won't you heal her? She's going to die!"

Something shifted behind him. James turned, expecting to see Him. Instead, he saw the shattered husk of Mr. Black getting to his feet.

It should have been impossible to move. The muscles had been ripped from his right leg, leaving the bones exposed from hip to ankle. There were deep teeth marks in his femur. The cavity of his skull dripped onto his shoulder. Parts of his spine were missing.

But still, he stood. And what remained of his face was trying to smile.

"Hello," he rasped through a flapping esophagus.

Another voice echoed behind Mr. Black's—one greater and far more terrible.

Hello.

That single word felt like having a stiletto driven through his ears. It resonated in James's chest. For an instant, his heart did not beat.

Mr. Black's arms stretched out.

"You've brought her to me. Thank you."

Thank you.

James's teeth vibrated in his skull. A sharp pop against his cheek told him that a filling had exploded. The scar on his shoulder blazed with white-hot pain, and it took all of his strength to respond. "She's dying. You have to heal her—I know you can do it, you can do anything—"

Mr. Black splashed forward, and his bleeding fingers stroked Elise's shoulders. Shredded skin hung from his wrist. A fingernail was missing. "Yes. I will take care of her."

She's mine, mortal.

This time, the voice did not just hurt James. It stirred Elise.

Her eyes opened to slits. She looked up and saw Mr. Black. Their bond was so strong that James could see through her eyes as though they were his own, and she did not see a corpse. Instead, He looked like a

438

glowing man, taller and brighter than the sun, with endless voids where His eyes should have been. He smiled for her.

She knew Him.

And she mumbled a single word: "Thom."

A shadow moved over them. The light was eclipsed by a mighty darkness—a black fog that oozed from the empty windows and doors of the angelic city.

"No!"

The responding echo was weaker than it should have been.

No…

A new man stepped from behind the bridge.

Thom had changed since they met at the police station. His hair extended into shadow, vast and infinite. Fire burned in his eyes. He was as beautiful as Mr. Black's body was hideous, and when he turned to appraise the situation, James saw a sweep of translucent black wings at his shoulders.

"I've been summoned. What is this?" he asked, his tone far too mild for the situation.

"Get away," said Mr. Black's body.

She's mine.

"Is that so? I don't believe that's true—yet." Thom tapped his chin with a finger. "You were already barely in this dimension, and now you've taken a tangible body. What a terrible idea. You didn't give that decision much consideration at all."

You know who I am.

"Yes."

You are not my match.

"No, of course not. Not when you're in your true form. But this…" Thom waved his hand at the body. "As I said—terrible idea."

He rushed toward Mr. Black.

Shadow clashed with light, and James's mind completely refused to process what he saw. It couldn't handle the information. His vision blanked, and his ears filled with a dull buzz.

When his senses cleared a few seconds later, he saw Thom seizing Mr. Black's shoulders and lifting Him into the air.

They blasted through the sky, receding into a pinpoint between the parking garage and its mirror. Both Thom and Mr. Black's body vanished through the dark gate.

The air was rent by the sound of a door slamming shut. It resonated through the entire city, sending a wind sweeping along the streets that kicked up glass shards and blasted away the light.

All the pressure vanished. The distant chimes went silent.

It was over, and He was gone.

Elise was still pale and unmoving, and the wound on her stomach wasn't bleeding anymore. He didn't have to check for a heartbeat to know she didn't have one. He felt it in the way his own heart shattered. "No," he said, smoothing a hand over her forehead. "Please, Elise…"

He searched inside himself for something from her. A hint of thought, a memory, a single neuron firing… *Anything*. But he had nothing. His mind was empty where Elise's presence should have been.

The angels were gone, and the air was still. A twilit fog settled where the light had been. The riverbank felt very lonely.

Anthony must have still been somewhere in the city. He would want to say goodbye to Elise, too. But there was no time for that, and it was probably better that way. It had always been the two of them—Elise and James versus the forces of Hell and Heaven. It seemed fitting that it should end that way, too.

He pressed his forehead against hers. It was cool and clammy. "You're always so damn difficult," he whispered.

"This is touching. Shall I give you a few minutes?"

Thom stood knee-deep in the river with his thumbs hooked in the waistband of his slacks. It was a bizarrely casual position for someone who had just flung a god into another dimension. His skin steamed.

Anger choked James. "You let her die!"

"Such melodrama. All that activity in your lateral orbitofrontal cortex must be exhausting."

"*What?*"

Thom pushed James aside and took Elise in his arms. He gazed at her with an expression that could only be called adoring. "So it is true," he murmured. "She is the Godslayer. Such a thing exists."

"She *was* the Godslayer."

Thom snorted. "Elise isn't dead yet. Her brain has oxygen, and a heart is an easy thing to restart. I won't permit her to die. Would you like to go back to Earth?"

"How? The gates are all closed."

"That's not a problem."

James started to agree, and then remembered that Elise hadn't come into the city alone. "There's another man. Anthony…"

Thom shifted Elise in his arms so he could touch the red choker at his throat. "I will bring him, too. Do not concern yourself."

He snapped his fingers.

Chapter 19

PASSING BETWEEN DIMENSIONS a second time was just as difficult as the first. The instant James reappeared, he vomited across the dusty stone floor of the Night Hag's cavern. There wasn't much left in his stomach. Two short heaves, and he was done.

The underground chamber was too dark after the brilliance of the angelic city. He blinked green shapes out of his eyes as he tried to make sense of his surroundings. Anthony was sprawled a few feet away, unconscious but breathing. Beyond him, Betty's body was still resting—paler than the last time he saw her, but untouched.

Where was Elise?

He stood and spun, searching for any sign of her between the silent gate and the spider's body, but all he found were pages from his Book of Shadows scattered across the floor.

A sigh whispered through the room. James looked up.

Thom drifted from the top of the cavern, black wings spread wide. The span was so great that they brushed the distant walls. Elise was curled in his arms with her head tucked under his chin. She was still unconscious. It was the only time she could look so unguarded and innocent. James felt nothing from her—no dreams or emotions—but as Thom grew closer, he saw the rise and fall of Elise's chest.

His bare feet touched the dais. He settled to the earth, and his wings folded behind him. They vanished. The glow of his skin faded. "I see your apprehension," Thom said to James. "Don't worry. She only sleeps."

James took an unsteady step toward the dais, stretching out his arms. "Give her to me."

"You want her now? You, who was so eager to hand her to her greatest enemy just moments ago?"

"She was dying."

"And now she is healed without a mark of blood on her body. You are welcome for the favor, and to make it better, I will do another—I will retrieve her falchions and return them. But later. Even I must rest when traveling between dimensions." Thom quirked an eyebrow. "So. You attempted to surrender your kopis to a mad god. I don't know her as well as you do, so perhaps I am wrong, but tell me what she would choose if she were conscious: life in His garden, driven to madness, or the peaceful void of death?"

"Elise doesn't always know what's best for her."

"How fortunate that you do."

He hesitated. "When she wakes up…will she remember…?"

"Nothing. She will have no clue you tried to surrender her unless you share that fact, which I don't recommend if you treasure your relationship with her."

James tried not to look relieved. "Give her to me now."

Thom stroked the hair back from Elise's face. "There are many great mysteries in this world, James Faulkner, but few of them puzzle me after thousands of years. Yet when a deity chooses to elevate one of mankind above the rest, I can only marvel at such a decision. What makes this one special? Why should any of you be special when your lives are as short as a beat of my black heart?"

Thousands of years? He struggled to think of a response. "Elise is certainly unique," he said cautiously.

"'Unique' is inadequate. She has been touched by God and bears two marks. Why?"

"Do you expect me to have an answer for that?"

"Perhaps not. You are only human." Thom knelt and rested Elise on top of the dais. James crouched over her in some semblance of protection, though he was very sure that anything that could drive a god back to his kingdom would not be impressed by the mightiest of his spells.

"Are we safe? Is He gone?"

"He's not on Earth, if that's what you're asking," Thom said. "The angels whose minds have been destroyed by Mr. Black are contained as well, but they live. Safety is subjective."

He sat beside James, completely human in appearance once more. His brown skin had pores, the light touched his hair, and the hand reaching for Elise's cheek had manicured fingernails. "Don't touch her," James said.

Thom ignored his protestation and stroked her hair. "No matter the

443

why, she is the Godslayer. Watch her well, James Faulkner, because she is mine. I will be back for her."

"What the hell are you?" he whispered. "Some kind of fallen angel?"

"Oh no." Thom smirked. "I'm something much worse."

He vanished without another word.

When Elise and Anthony woke up an hour later, night had fallen. She carried Betty's body out of the Warrens to the hospital. It was only a few blocks away. She refused to let anyone help her.

What happened after that was a blur. They didn't admit Betty because there was no treatment to be done for a dead body. Stephanie cried when she saw the wound, and James comforted her. Elise didn't stick around to watch.

Time passed. Things happened. Elise watched as if from a very long distance, going through the motions of filling out paperwork and giving them the phone number of Betty's parents and sitting in a waiting room.

Somehow, she found herself sitting with Betty's body. They had put her somewhere quiet and dark with only a single light to illuminate the bed. Her skin was the same color as the white sheet tucked under her arms. Elise stared at her, disconnected from herself, and thought that Betty would probably want to put on some kind of makeup before anybody else saw her. She hated to be seen without makeup. The pale lips and mascara-free lashes looked unnatural.

Anthony knelt at her bedside as tears cascaded down his cheeks. He had started screaming again, after Stephanie told them they could take their time saying goodbye before she was transported to the morgue, but he had been quiet for almost fifteen minutes.

"Do you want to say something?" he asked.

Elise folded her arms tight across her chest. Say what? Goodbye? "Sorry my enemy shot you?" No good words came to mind, so she just shook her head.

He reached out to touch her hand. "I killed him," he said thickly. "That guy is dead, and it's not good enough. She's still..." Anthony dropped his forehead to the bed. His fingers tightened on her wrist. "I don't blame you."

"What?"

"I know this isn't your fault. Betty was too eager. She didn't..." He sucked in a shuddering breath. "She knew this could happen. So I don't blame you. I thought you should know."

The idea of it hadn't even occurred to her.

Elise got up and stood by Betty's head. She gazed down at her friend, knowing it would be the last time, and tried to see past the bullet wound. That wasn't how Betty would want to be remembered. Elise's eyes roved over her plump cheeks, her freckled shoulders, the curve of her body under the blanket. She wanted so desperately to feel a connection between herself and Betty, something that would give her what Stephanie called "closure," but she didn't feel anything at all.

That wasn't her friend. It was a body. The chance for goodbyes had long passed.

"I'll be outside," Elise said.

She went into the hall and leaned back, gently bumping her head against the wall. The curtain wasn't enough to separate her from Anthony's grief. His renewed sobs echoed through the hallway.

Once she was away from the body, she couldn't tune out James's thoughts anymore. With nothing to look at but a blank wall, her mind filled in with what he saw instead. He was in the lobby. There was an older woman with him, and although Elise had never seen a picture of Betty's mother, she had been told about all the bangles she liked to wear and the horrible perm. The woman was sobbing. James held her hand.

Shock had wiped his mind almost as blank as Elise's. Small mercy. She didn't want to have to hear her own thoughts, much less his.

A figure moved at the end of the hallway. Wearing a plain t-shirt and jeans, Nukha'il looked nothing like the angel that had attacked Mr. Black in the city. It seemed he had gone shopping at a thrift store. His wings weren't substantiated, but there was no hiding the subtle, shifting light that followed him.

Elise welcomed the distraction of his presence. "I didn't think I would see you again."

"Itra'il has gone mad," he said. "She is not the woman I knew. But with time..." He trailed off. "She won't be a danger to anyone. I'll keep a tight hold on her."

"Good. I don't want to kill anything else."

The angel didn't react to her threat. He stood beside her and faced the window into the room. The mini-blinds were mostly closed, but Elise could see Betty through the slits. Anthony had his hands folded at the side of the bed. His entire body shook with sobs.

"You lost your friend in this fight. Didn't you?" Nukha'il asked.

Elise nodded, lips sealed tight.

He crossed himself, bowed his head, and whispered a prayer. When he lifted his head, tears gleamed on his cheeks.

"I will carry the pain of your grief in my heart. For your friend, and for everyone else who lost their lives to this fight. But she is in a place without suffering now. You should take comfort in that."

His words didn't warm her. Betty might have been in a place with no pain, but she was also in a place where she wouldn't get to sunbathe, either. She would never sexually harass another colleague in good humor, or finish her research at the university. She would never feel the sun on her face again.

"It's a black place," Elise said dully. "A place with no light."

"Don't you believe in Heaven?"

"I've been to the ethereal and infernal planes, and there are no human souls there. When we die…that's it."

Nukha'il gave her a sad look. "Nobody knows what waits for mortals on the other side. Not even we do." He watched Anthony for a moment without speaking. Elise turned away. "I hope you and your loved ones find peace. I'll pray for you."

She shook her head. "Don't do that."

He briefly laid his hand on her shoulder before leaving. It didn't sting to be touched on her shoulder blade anymore. The Night Hag's mark had faded with her death.

Elise felt a presence at the opposite end of the hall and realized that James was approaching with Betty's mother. There would be more tears. More questions. The same lies she had written on the police reports about gang violence. More grief.

She left before they came around the corner.

James didn't think he would ever sleep again. Yet when he climbed into the bed he shared with Stephanie, he passed out immediately and didn't wake up for a long time.

The sleep wasn't restful. He awoke feeling like he hadn't slept at all.

He waited a day before seeking out Elise. He could tell by the tumult of emotions through their bond that he wasn't welcome. But when night fell again, and a new morning dawned, he couldn't stay away any longer. He didn't have to search. He only needed to close his eyes to see familiar couches, the late-afternoon haze glimmering on dust motes, and the window-mounted air conditioner.

446

He knocked lightly before entering the apartment above the dance studio.

Elise knelt between two boxes on the living room floor. She didn't look up when he came to stand beside her.

She had a white photo album spread across her legs and stared at the pictures with no expression. Her gaze was unusually opaque, even for her, but the bond had opened an entire new dimension to him. What he felt staggered him. Grief and rage and regret roiled through her like an angry wound.

He had to brace himself with a hand on the back of the couch. "Elise," James said, voice ragged.

"Betty had her wedding album in the fire safe. She didn't have her social security card there, or her passport, but she had her photos."

"Whose wedding photos?"

"Betty's. She got married at eighteen. When we met at college, she was going through a divorce." Elise ran a hand down the page and rested a fingertip on one of the pictures. "I met her ex-husband once. He wasn't a bad guy. They just…grew up. Grew apart. People change. He wanted kids and she wasn't ready."

James swallowed a lump in his throat. "I had no idea."

"There's a lot people don't know about Betty. Even Anthony doesn't know…" She pulled a photo out of the plastic sheet. "Well. It doesn't matter now."

Elise handed the picture to him. It was a solo shot of Betty in front of a trellis of roses with her train stretched across the grass and flowers in her hair. She beamed with none of her usual mischief.

"She looks so young."

"Betty would have been twenty-eight next month. She *was* young. What was I thinking? I never should have let her come."

"Elise…"

She put the picture back and snapped the album shut. Her face was red when she finally looked at him. "I wish I had died."

"Don't say that."

"I killed Betty. There are insane angels running loose in a parallel dimension that could break out at any time. And He knows where I am now, so sooner or later, He will come for me. You should have left me there to die!"

He refused to match her fury. He knelt at her side and stroked a hand down her healed shoulder, brushing the hair behind her neck. "I will always bring you back, Elise," he said, echoing what she had told him

447

just days before. He traced his thumb along her jaw. It made her grow still like a hawk that had been masked. "Always."

She pushed his arm away. "Don't use that on me, not when—"

"I'm sorry."

"You're sorry? For what?"

He rested back on his heels with a sigh. There were so many things he wanted to tell her. Things that a thousand apologies couldn't amend. "For everything."

"It's too late for that." She stuffed the album back in the box and closed it. "Anthony wants to go through what's left of Betty's belongings. I should get her purse from Stephanie's house." Barely-restrained tears made her voice thick.

"Betty was your best friend. You can cry for your friends."

"No. I can't." He tried to wrap his arms around her, but she shoved him away. "Don't touch me." Her chin trembled. She took a deep breath and furrowed her brow as she concentrated on the wall. He could feel her fighting to hold onto her composure.

"It's okay."

James embraced her again. Her attempts to fend him off were much feebler the second time. She finally buried her face in his neck.

The pain poured out of her. The fear of being found. The horror of what Mr. Black had done. The loss of Betty.

Her thoughts faded and out of his mind.

Why Betty? Alain didn't feel enough pain when he died... I hate this...hate everything...

He thought Elise would feel better once she cried, but he was wrong. Instead, her sorrow reached new depths to fill every crevice of her heart and mind. It was almost too much for him to take.

He pressed his lips to her brow. "It will be okay," he murmured against her forehead.

Elise thought that his breath was too warm in the summer air. The angry murmur of her thoughts latched onto it, seeking something she could control. He heard it, and she knew he heard it. James also knew the question she would ask a moment before she said it.

"What *is* this? What happened to us?"

He had been wondering the same thing since they returned from the city. None of his books talked about such a phenomenon, but he had a theory.

"When I died and you resurrected me, I think it...changed us. We're somehow trapped in an active bond—a permanent piggyback. I've tried

448

to end it several times, but it's like we're stuck."

"Great. Just fucking great. Betty's death is my fault. Your death was my fault. This...*thing*...is my fault." Her mind had gone distant, retreating into a dark recess of memory. "I pushed Anthony away when I saw the gun. Alain wasn't even aiming at him, but I moved to save my boyfriend instead of Betty. If I had gone for her..."

"Then Anthony might be the one who died."

"I should get away from him. I'll kill him next."

"You didn't kill Betty," James said, smoothing a hand down the back of her neck. Her skin was feverish from crying. "Listen to me. You didn't kill Betty."

Her chin trembled. "I might as well have." She drew her knees to her chest and wrapped her arms around them. "God, it hurts. How do you feel like this all the time? How do you handle so much emotion?"

"What?"

"This is yours," she said with a hard sniffle. "This...crying thing. All this grief. This is your weakness, not mine."

He took her hand, and he could feel it from her perspective as well as his own. James didn't just feel the supple leather of Elise's gloves. He felt the roughness of his skin, too. "Have you considered that you might not be getting it from me? You loved Betty. It's natural—not weak—to grieve for those we love."

Elise dropped his hand. "This isn't me. It's not." She swiped the tears off her face and straightened her back. "I'm going to help Anthony make arrangements. Betty wanted to be cremated, so there's..." She swallowed. "And I'm going to Craven's. They need help, now that the owner is gone."

"What's going to happen to the city without the Night Hag?"

"Reno survived without an overlord's help for years. But the threat of her presence kept challengers out, and I killed the only person who might have taken the line of succession. Now it's going to get messy. There will be territory battles."

"You can take time to grieve," he said.

Elise stood and hugged the box to her chest. There was one other box, too. That was all that remained of Betty's life—two banker's boxes in a half-empty apartment.

He followed her to the front door.

"I don't need time," she said. Her voice was dead again. The tears were gone. "What would I do with time? Wait for Him to find me? Throw myself on the floor and cry? Waste my time wishing that Betty hadn't..."

Her lips sealed shut before the last word could emerge.

James reached for her again, but she pushed away from him, opened the front door, and stepped onto the stairs.

She glared at the horizon. The tops of the casinos downtown were visible just over the trees. There was no sign of the city mirrored above— not so much as a waver in the air.

"Let me help you," James said. "Please."

Elise shook her head. "I can't handle this. Any of it."

She walked down the stairs, and James watched her disappear into the blazing sunlight.

DEAR READER,

I hope you've enjoyed The Darkest Gate. The story continues in book 3 of the series (Dark Union), which is available now!

If you'd like to know when my next book comes out, visit my website to sign up for my new release email alerts. I hope you'll also leave a review with your thoughts on the site where you bought this book—I can't wait to hear what you think of it!

Happy reading!
Sara (SM Reine)
http://authorsmreine.com/
http://facebook.com/authorsmreine

Dark Union

An Urban Fantasy Mystery

The Descent Series - Book Three

SM Reine

Part 1: The Murder

MICHELE Newcomb's body was still dying, but her mind was long gone.

She was convinced the desert hated her bright yellow SUV, and the oil it dribbled onto bare rock six miles away. It hated the fingers that ripped roots from the earth as she crawled through sparse foliage. It hated the trail of browning blood she left in her wake.

Michele believed that the harsh, hostile world hated everything about her, and it was glad that she was about to die alone.

Her throat was raw and dry. She tried to suck in air to soothe her burning lungs, but the motion made her chest jerk. Her abs ached from the force of it. Blood rose in her throat like bile, and it spattered over her lip.

Michele took another hard breath—coughed blood again—and squinted, trying to focus on the world above the sagebrush. The cruel sun bore upon her back like an iron pressed to her flesh. The world was white. Her eyes burned.

Something dark loomed at the edge of her vision. Silvery mirages danced with the promise of water.

Her bloody fingertips dug into the soil. She crawled forward two inches. Pain ripped through her as the injury tore wider.

The gunshot wound didn't even hurt anymore. That had faded quickly, relatively speaking. The real pain was the knife wound—and the knowledge that the one who delivered it was walking free.

She had to tell Gary what happened. He had to know the truth, had to finish the job before it was too late.

Michele groaned and dragged herself forward another two inches.

453

She coughed up blood again, but not as much as before. She quickly began to miss the moisture of blood in her mouth. Her dry, swollen tongue hung uselessly over her cracked lip.

Another two inches. The shimmering mirage receded, but the shadow didn't.

It was a building. A real building.

Still a hundred feet away.

Her hand sought something to grip. She found a rock and clenched it. Something scrambled over her fingers—probably something venomous. It didn't bother biting her.

Two inches.

Michele pressed her face to the scalding earth, and if she had possessed any remaining moisture in her body, she would have wept. A gasping sob jerked out of her mouth.

She reached for a handhold and found nothing.

"Help," she croaked out. Her voice was tiny.

Her other hand touched a bush.

Two more inches.

She tried to focus on the building instead of the pain. It had to be there, but she couldn't see that far anymore. The bright desert was growing murky and dim. How could it still be so hot if it was becoming dark?

Michele couldn't blink anymore. Her eyelids were sandpaper.

Two inches. And another. And another.

She ran out of strength for two inches, so it became one, and then a half inch, and then just millimeters.

But eventually, after an eternity, Michele's fingers touched something cool.

A blurry line of shadow crossed the hot ground in front of her.

She looked up and saw a window. The rusted tin sign said that the gas station was closed. If there was a gas station—even one that wasn't open—a road had to be on the other side. She didn't see the wind-torn curtains, or the shattered posts that marked its anterior boundary. She didn't see the broken pumps that had been dry of gasoline for fifty years. She also didn't see that the road on the other side was empty—and had been for months.

All Michele saw was a building, and the "closed" sign that would say "open" if someone flipped it over, and decided her crawling was done.

With a final burst of strength, she flopped onto her back. The heat pounded into her bare wound. Dirt stung the open blisters.

"Thank you, God," she whispered to a burning sky.

Gary was going to find her. It wasn't too late after all. She could still tell him the truth.

But it was all so distant.

Michele just had to wait for the owner to open the store. Then she would get a soda—diet, of course. Maybe she could have a scoop of ice cream after she washed her face in the bathroom, which would be cool and air conditioned. The owner could loan her a quarter to call Grandma —but Grandma was dead—and then the team would pick her up.

Everything would be okay.

Sunshine. Grandma smelled like sunshine.

Michele's hand rested in the cool shadow, and she managed to shut her eyes. Her lips bled as they spread into a small smile.

She died at peace with a belly full of flies.

For the first time since January, a car approached the gas station. It was a shiny black monster with nearly-opaque windows, and it had cost more to purchase than the land on which the gas station stood.

The car stopped beside the pumps. Three forms clad in black stepped out.

"Over here," said one, leading the others to the side of the building. He was young and stringy, and his hair was densely curled in kinky ropes.

A man pushed past him. His hand rested on the gun at his belt as though it was another appendage. The butt was engraved with his name: ZETTEL.

He kneeled beside the body of Michele Newcomb. She was barely recognizable as a woman, or even a human. She resembled meatloaf. The swarming flies seemed to agree. Zettel rubbed a finger on her cheek and found the blood was fresh. "We were only a minute too late," he growled.

The third person huffed. She was almost as muscular as Zettel, and equally undisturbed by the body. "Just fucking great. Should we bring her back?"

"No." He scowled at the younger man. "This is your fault, Flynn. We're not bringing her back. You got that?"

Flynn stared at his feet, trying not to blink so his tears wouldn't fall.

A fourth man jumped out of the SUV with trash bags and a saw. "I've got the corpse! Who wants to be on scrubbing duty?" Boyd asked, far too

455

cheerful for such a hot day.

"We're not cleaning this one up. The coyotes can have her." Zettel fisted the boy's collar and jerked his face down. "Hear me, Flynn? She's going to the animals. They're going to eat her."

"It would have been too late days ago," he said, voice trembling.

The woman got in the driver's seat again. "Come on. Let's get out of here before the animals get us, too."

Their SUV kicked up a trail of dust in their wake.

The coyotes didn't settle in to eat Michele until nightfall.

Part 2: Debt Owed

Chapter 1

IT WAS A miserable day. The temperature had reached one hundred degrees Fahrenheit, there was no wind, and Anthony Morales had been trying to sell his Jeep to random assholes from Craigslist all afternoon.

"What the hell have you done to this thing?" asked potential buyer number three, who claimed his name was "Buddy," and was as thick in the waist as a baby elephant.

They stood in the shade of a high-rise apartment building, which funneled heat directly toward them over rippling asphalt. Anthony hoped that parking his Jeep in an alley stained with oil, covered in trash, and overlooked by barred windows might make his car look a little less offensive in comparison. Instead, the Jeep looked like it belonged in one of the big green dumpsters.

Anthony rubbed a hand down his face and left behind a greasy smear. "There were pictures in the ad."

"Is that what I asked? No. I asked what you did to it."

"I told you. I'm a mechanic. This was my hobby vehicle."

Buddy snorted. "Is your hobby beating it with a goddamn crowbar?"

Anthony tried not to feel wounded. The Jeep was his first car, and it had been through a lot with him in the ensuing years. Sure, the bumper was missing, the upholstery was ripped, and the body was thoroughly dented. That was what happened when you drove through a cemetery full of zombies. But the engine was great and the tires were new. He had put a lot of love into it.

"Do you want it or not?" he asked in a dull voice.

The buyer walked around the Jeep again, his considerable girth swaying with every step. "I'll give you three hundred for it."

"I'll only take twelve hundred."

"You kidding? Three hundred is a good deal for this piece of shit."

Anthony's patience was gone. "Okay. Fine. Sorry to waste your time."

He climbed into the Jeep, but Buddy leaned on the hood to prevent him from moving to a shadier spot. "Five hundred."

"Now you're wasting *my* time."

"Come on. You can't seriously think it's worth twelve," Buddy said.

Anthony's girlfriend came around the end of the alley at that moment, sparing him from having to think of a response that didn't use words like "insulted" and "asshole." Elise's curls were pulled out of her face in a thick braid, and she wore faded shorts, a tank top, and sneakers, yet still managed to look like a Greek Fury as she stalked down the alley.

She was followed by a teenage boy and his mother—potential buyer number four.

Elise glanced at Anthony. "Is he buying it?" she asked, jerking a thumb at the fat man, who smoothed a hand over his sweaty pate as he took a long look at Elise's legs.

"He's trying to get it for five hundred."

"Get out of here," she told Buddy. "We're done with you." He opened his mouth, and she didn't seem interested in discovering if it was to argue or make a counter offer. She turned the full force of her stare on him and said again, "Get out."

Buddy waddled his elephantine mass toward the street with a flip of the bird.

Why didn't Anthony have that kind of gravitas? Someone was always screwing with him, whether it was over the sale of his Jeep, the cost of labor at the shop, or the grades he got on his college papers. Nobody screwed with Elise.

Of course, she also wasn't much of a salesman.

"This is it," she said to potential buyer number four, who was watching the alley like she expected muggers to jump out at any second.

Anthony jumped down to join them. The mother had contacted him by email that morning to see if she thought the Jeep would be good as her teenage son's first car. "Hi," he said, wiping his palms dry on his jeans and holding out a hand. "Thanks for coming all the way downtown. I'm —"

"Twelve hundred," Elise interrupted. "Firm."

458

The mother looked doubtful. "I don't know…"

"What happened to that thing?" the boy asked. He had braces and a Grateful Dead t-shirt.

Anthony's heart sank. *That question again.* He prepared to give his response about it being a project car, but Elise spoke first. "We drove it through a cemetery of zombies. There used to be a cowcatcher on front, but it crumpled after hitting the first dozen bodies."

"Seriously?"

"Yes."

The mother shot Elise a long-suffering look. "Does it run?" she asked, sounding exhausted.

"Perfectly. And insurance is cheap," Anthony said.

"Great. I'm sold."

She pulled out her wallet as her son pumped his fist in the air. He jumped in the driver's seat and ran his fingers reverently over the wheel, like he had just gotten his first Porsche. Anthony resisted the wild impulse to push the boy away from his car. Twelve hundred dollars was more money than he and Elise had possessed for weeks.

"You can bring it to my shop if anything goes bad in the next month or two, but it shouldn't be a problem," he said, exchanging a business card for a small stack of twenties. "I just replaced the tires and transmission. Everything is in perfect condition."

"I don't really care," said the mother. He spread the paperwork out on the hot metal of the hood, and they each signed it. "Anything to get him to leave the house for once. Maybe he'll even get a few friends."

"This sound system is totally sick!" her son enthused.

"We installed it for use in a mass exorcism," Elise told him, leaning her elbows on the door. Anthony groaned. It was the truth, but nobody would ever believe her. The miniature zombie apocalypse in May had been treated like a natural disaster in the mainstream media. But Elise didn't seem to care. She smiled a little as the kid swung the wheel around.

"What were you exorcising?" he asked.

"Demons. Really nasty ones."

"That is *so* cool."

"Don't encourage him. He already plays too many video games," the mother said. "And move over, Travis. I'm driving it home."

"Mom!"

She climbed in, and Elise stepped back beside Anthony.

A few seconds later, the tail lights disappeared around the corner. His

459

heart twisted painfully.

It only lasted for a second. He had lost everything in the last few months: his Millennium Scholarship (because fighting demons did zero favors for his grades), his cousin Betty, and now his beloved Jeep. It was getting to the point where the pain was a constant stabbing in his chest. He couldn't work up additional grief over his car for longer than a few seconds.

"Let me see that," Elise said, holding out a hand. He gave her the cash. She counted it out. "Great. This is rent for two months, at least." She pocketed a few bills and returned the rest.

"Hey," Anthony complained.

"Do you want groceries or not?"

He didn't really care. The Jeep didn't belong to Elise, and she had no right to the money. But what was the point in arguing? They had gotten an apartment together downtown—a furnished one bedroom for five hundred a month, which smelled like tobacco even though neither of them smoked—and all their money was getting poured into bills and debt and Top Ramen anyway.

"What now?" he asked dully.

"Now I'm going to run errands." Elise stretched up to kiss his chin. "I'll be home late. Don't wait for me."

She left before he could try to kiss her properly.

Anthony thought about going back to their apartment, which was just around the corner, but he found himself staring at the spot his Jeep had stood only minutes earlier.

That twinge was back.

He sank to a crouch, covered his face with his hands, and didn't move for a long time.

Chapter 2

ELOQUENT BLOOD WAS dark, and the sign on the alley door said CLOSED, but Elise walked in anyway. Its usual patrons weren't bothered by heat, so they didn't bother air conditioning the bar, but being positioned in the cavernous basement kept it temperate. The sweat on Elise's skin cooled and made her shiver.

"Neuma?" she called, pausing by the railing to peer at the bottom several levels down. The DJ booth was empty. Three walls of a cage stood where the dance floor should have been, but it would be hours until the fights started. A demon with three eyes mopped the stage. "Hey! Is Neuma in yet?"

It nodded without looking up.

The fluorescent blue lights behind the bar were turned off. The stripper pole hadn't been cleaned yet, so it was covered in fingerprints, sweat, and flecks of brimstone. But there was no sign of the bartender.

Elise hopped over the bar, snagging a bottle of tequila on the way. She was more than just a frequent patron of Eloquent Blood—she used to be the accountant, before getting in a fight with the owner. She had since killed David Nicholas and any chance of being gainfully employed with them again, but she still made frequent visits to enjoy Neuma's generosity with the liquor.

She headed down the back hall. "Neuma, it's me. Where are you?" Something bumped against the wall. Elise jiggled the handle to the dressing room. Locked. "Hey. Open up. I can hear you in there."

"Go away," Neuma said from the other side.

Elise's senses sharpened. "Are you okay?"

"I'm peachy."

"Bullshit. Open the door or I'll kick it in." She had done it once before,

461

and she had no qualms about breaking the handle again.

"No, don't do that," Neuma said. "Hang on."

A pause, and the lock clicked. Elise pushed inside.

The dressing room was even more of a mess than usual. Costumes were spread across the floor like a rug of latex and silver chains. One of the vanity mirrors was shattered, leaving shards of glass sprinkled over the strippers' outfits, and half of the bottles on the shelves had been broken. It reeked of sulfur and booze.

Neuma was slumped in a chair by the door. Her skin and white bathrobe glowed in the black light, but her ink-dark hair was a shadow puddled on her shoulders. She had a hand over the left side of her face.

"What happened in here?" Elise asked.

"Nothing. Just haven't cleaned in a long time." Neuma's voice was about an octave too high.

Elise sniffed the air. As if the wreckage wasn't evidence enough, every sense told her that a powerful demon had been on the premises—from the uncomfortable pressure at the back of her skull, to the sour bite of brimstone in her nose. It was too strong to belong to Neuma, who was only a half-succubus Gray. She was mostly harmless. Her greatest threat was being a little too sexy.

The sight of the destruction was enough to trigger Elise's protective instinct. Setting the tequila on the counter, she picked up a costume, shook out the glass, and threw it in the closet. "Your parties are getting too wild," she said, working quickly to unclutter the floor and sweep the glass into a corner.

Neuma smiled weakly.

When Elise finished, she turned on the overhead lights without waiting for permission. The bartender flinched. She pulled her hand away from her face for an instant, but it was enough for Elise to see a massive gash running down the side of her face. Thin, watery blood poured into the collar of her robe.

"Jesus, Neuma."

"I think I need a witch," she whispered. Half-demons were fragile creatures. They couldn't heal on their own—given a few hours, they could bleed to death from a paper cut. "Treeny, up in Craven's—cocktail waitress for the sport's bar—she can do a little hocus pocus."

Elise pulled Neuma's arm over her shoulder and supported her as they limped into the hallway. The facial injury wasn't the worst of it. The robe gapped to show a missing chunk of flesh in her thigh.

They took the stairs to the manager's office, slowly and carefully.

"Tell me who attacked you," Elise said.

"Name's Zohak. This thing, this demon—he took all our money, and I couldn't do shit about it. He bit my leg and fucking *laughed* at me."

"You couldn't have fought?"

"I did," Neuma said. "But half the bouncers left when David Nicholas died. There's nobody left to help during the day anymore."

They reached the office, and Elise helped her sit on the executive chair. The room was empty aside from a single filing cabinet and paperwork scattered on the desk. Neuma had been trying to keep up on bills and taxes, but she didn't have the organizational skills.

"Wait here," Elise said. "I'll find Treeny."

It wasn't hard to locate the cocktail waitress. Most of the employees had worked for Craven's when Elise and Death's Hand destroyed half of the casino, and they were properly intimidated by her. She ordered the first demon she spotted to send Treeny to the office, and they scurried off to make it happen.

The waitress met them upstairs a few minutes later. She wore a tiny dress that barely covered her butt, hugged an empty drink tray to her chest, and trembled under Elise's scrutiny.

"What's up?" Treeny asked. To her credit, her voice didn't shake nearly as much as her knees. A pentacle ring sparkled on her thumb. It danced with silver light in the corner of Elise's vision, which meant it was enchanted.

"I'm told you can heal," she said, wiping her hands off with a tissue. She had patched up the wound on Neuma's thigh to slow the bleeding, but the bartender's skin was ashen, and she could barely lift her head.

Treeny's face lit up. "Oh. Yeah. A little, if I have time for a ritual. But I'll need supplies."

"You've got fifteen minutes to get them. Go fast." The witch ran off, and Elise helped Neuma to the bathroom attached to the office, and the bartender washed the blood off her bruised face. "I don't think you're stripping tonight."

"No kidding. That's not sexy at all, huh?" Neuma tilted her head to study the damage in the mirror. "Forget it. I'll have to call someone in, if I don't die first." She heaved a sigh. "Thanks for helping, doll. Is there a reason you came to see me? Are you covering my shift tonight?"

In the aftermath of the attack, Elise had completely forgotten that she visited Craven's for a reason. "I got some cash, so I wanted to pay my bar tab. What am I up to this week—eighty bucks?"

"Nothing. It's on the house." Neuma tried to smile, and failed. Her skin had completely lost its usual glow. "It could be on the house forever if you would help me."

Elise's mouth twisted. Neuma had been trying to talk her into taking over Eloquent Blood and Craven's casino—which continued to operate only by habit and the force of Neuma's will since the overlord died—for the last several weeks. Every time she showed up for a drink, it was the same thing again. *Help me,* and, *I need you.*

It was getting on her nerves. Elise couldn't help them—she couldn't help anyone.

But the half-succubus's eyes were wide and pathetic. It was getting harder to resist her pleas. "I just can't handle this alone anymore," Neuma whispered when Elise didn't respond. "I thought it would be better if we could get rid of David Nicholas. I thought I could keep up on it myself. But I can't, and everything's falling apart. With the Night Hag gone..."

"How many times do I have to tell you no?"

"*Please.* You could protect us, at least. This isn't the first time someone's rolled in to screw with us. If we could stop getting attacked for a few weeks, maybe we could find someone good to take charge. Maybe —"

Elise slapped two fifty dollar bills on the desk. It only left twenty for groceries, but she had been living off dried beans and rice for weeks anyway. "That's for my tab."

"Don't go! Zohak will be back—he said he would."

"I have stuff to do. Try not to die. I'll see you later."

"Elise!"

She left the office without looking back, and bumped into Treeny on the stairs. Elise didn't need to see Neuma—that pathetic stare was stamped permanently on the inside of her skull.

It was hard being asked for help. It was even harder to deny it.

The walk to her new apartment was short—just two blocks from Craven's. But even that distance was miserable in the afternoon sun. It was the kind of heat that melted the rubber on shoes and turned metal into a searing brand. Elise bumped the crosswalk button with her hip.

Her phone buzzed in her pocket as she crossed the street. She ducked under an awning's shade to check the screen.

When she saw the number, her heart stopped. It took her two tries to speak. "Hello?"

"Hey, Kavanagh," responded a masculine voice. "It's McIntyre."

Elise knew immediately that he was calling for help—and this time, she wouldn't be able to say no.

Chapter 3

LUCAS MCINTYRE WASN'T a patient man. He didn't have to be. He lived life on his own schedule, and he liked to be in constant motion—jogging in the desert behind his mobile home, or lifting weights, or doing whatever chores his wife assigned that day. It was how he lived since he gave up on high school at the ripe age of fifteen and moved to his grandma's trailer outside Las Vegas.

He wasn't the most educated man, either, but he took care of his family. Always working, always surviving. Waiting was foreign to him.

Yet he found himself in the parking garage outside McCarran International Airport at eleven fifty-five at night, sitting on the hood of his 1983 Ranger, and trying not to go crazy while he waited for help to arrive.

McIntyre dug under his fingernails with a flip knife. The blade was damaged—etched by the ichor spilled by spider-demons the size of his truck.

They had wandered out of the north and tried to kill him. All the bad stuff came from the north.

He flicked dirt, dried blood, and dead skin onto the pavement and checked his watch again. The scratched face said only a minute had passed. He flipped the knife shut, then open again. He put it in his pocket. Took it out. Checked the time.

Still eleven fifty-six.

Finally, he caught a glance of the person he was waiting for on the other side of the walkway. He raised an arm to catch her attention. She strode over with some guy he didn't recognize.

Elise Kavanagh had aged and softened since the last time McIntyre saw her. She used to be a hard motherfucker—all hard lines and scars and barely-bridled fury. Years later, she looked like any other woman. Lots of brownish hair. A few more scars that she tried to cover with a long-sleeved blouse, fingerless gloves, and knee-length shorts.

She didn't look anything like the person who helped him take down a centuria of demons in the Grand Canyon eight years back.

They gripped each other's wrists in greeting. There was something hard under her sleeve—knife sheaths. So she hadn't changed that much after all.

"Security fucked up on that," he said by way of hello.

"Checked baggage. I put them on after I got off the plane." Her speech was more precise than it used to be. Elise had gotten educated.

He jerked his chin at the man behind her. "The hell is this? Where's James?"

Elise swayed on her feet and put a hand to her forehead. She took a deep breath. After a beat, she straightened again, and gave no sign of her momentary weakness. "Lucas McIntyre, meet Anthony Morales. He hunts with me."

Anthony set his suitcase on the ground and shook hands with McIntyre. "I'm her boyfriend, actually." His skin was creamy brown, and a cowlick made his hair stick up in front. There wasn't a visible scar on his body.

McIntyre chewed on the corner of his mouth as he studied both of them. By the way Elise stood two feet away and barely acknowledged Anthony's existence, they looked about as intimate as a lion and the gazelle she would have for dinner. Leticia was going to have a field day with them. "All right," he finally said. "Put everything in back."

He opened the camper shell. They had only brought a suitcase and a backpack. Anthony threw the first one in, but Elise hung onto the second as they climbed into his truck.

"How's Leticia?" she asked. He could tell she was just trying to be polite. That was new for her, too.

"She's in a good mood," McIntyre said. He threw the truck into gear.

Elise arched an eyebrow. "At least that's one of you."

He hadn't been in a good mood since the doctor told him that fluid levels were low in his wife's womb—whatever the hell that meant—and that her cervix was opening. Those two things were bad, apparently. She'd been on bed rest for weeks, and they had an induction scheduled if she didn't "stabilize," even though she wasn't due for another month.

She hadn't stabilized. Her induction was in five hours.

It was silence in the truck as they got on the highway. Elise's supposed boyfriend was staring out the window with puffy red eyes. She

467

hugged the backpack to her chest and picked at her thumbnail.

The road out of Vegas was long, and they had to go through a lot of suburbs to get there, but traffic was pretty much dead. It wasn't long before the downtown lights receded.

"Thanks for coming," McIntyre said after a few dozen miles of listening to static-filled country on the radio.

Elise gave a slight shake, like she was clearing her head. "You called in a really big favor to drag me down here. I had to borrow three hundred bucks off James to even make the flight. So let's get to it—what do you need?"

"I emailed all the info I have to you."

"Anthony and I got on the plane an hour after you called. I didn't have time to read your six attachments," she said. "Give a recap and save me a few minutes."

McIntyre blew a breath out of his lips. "Okay. The summit runs tomorrow through Sunday afternoon. You sign in at—"

"What summit?" Anthony interrupted. He sounded more annoyed than interested.

"It's this thing they hold every fifty years," Elise said. "Angels and demons hash out their issues while kopides make sure nobody dies. It's between the Reno and Vegas territories this year, but I wasn't invited. I didn't plan on going."

"That's because everyone thinks you're dead," McIntyre said. "Anyway, they only invite the best of the demon hunters." He shrugged one shoulder. "I'm think I was invited because I know most of the kopides alive right now. But Tish is going into the hospital in the morning."

Out of the corner of his vision, he saw Elise watching him. Her skin glowed in the street lights as they soared past. "So what? You want me to go to the hospital and hold your wife's hand?"

"I want you to go to the summit and pretend to be me."

She laughed. He didn't think he'd ever heard her laugh before, and it turned out that it wasn't a particularly nice or happy sound. "Are you serious?"

"You've got to do it. There's these guys at the summit called The Union of Kopides and Aspides—'The Union' for short. They've taken over the whole thing."

"Great. If the Union's got things covered, you don't need to attend."

"These guys are trying to become a big player. They got half of the European territories under control in the last couple of years, and now they're taking over of all of goddamn North America. They're turning kopides into soldiers. You surrender your territory, get enlisted, get trained, and get reassigned to somewhere new. And they're matching every kopis who doesn't have an aspis to a witch."

She frowned. "That's impossible. I would have heard about that happening."

McIntyre took the exit off the freeway. The road noises grew softer as he slowed, and it filled the car with ominous quiet. "You've been out of it too long. They've got Mexico. French Canada, too. The US is a big nut to crack, so they're starting with this summit. If I can't make a good show and get them to back off, they'll take Vegas."

"Can they make you enlist?" Elise asked.

"I hear they're pretty convincing." McIntyre stopped at a four way intersection. It was completely dead, but he didn't go through. He took his hands off the wheel. "They could take everything I've got. You're the only one who can help me."

"They'll know I'm not you."

"Sure, they would. But this guy can pretend to be me, and he's nobody. He won't be recognized," he said, waving at Elise's boyfriend. "I get around with the local demons, but I've never met the Union; as far as I know, they don't have any pictures on file. So your boyfriend is me, and then you say you're Leticia."

Elise's mouth twisted like she tasted something sour. "It's a bad idea."

"It's all I've got."

Anthony didn't seem concerned about Elise's decision. He went back to staring out the window, even though there was nothing to see—they were beyond the last of the manicured suburbs, and there were trailers on one side and empty desert on the other.

The Elise he used to know would have refused. She wasn't one for sympathy. He could only hope that saving her ass a half dozen times would be enough to coerce her.

But she didn't need to be coerced. "Fine," she said. "I'm already here anyway."

He didn't thank her. He knew she wouldn't like that. But he nodded, and she nodded back, and that was more than enough. McIntyre stepped on the gas and everyone in the truck went back to ignoring each other.

McIntyre's plot of land was in the hills at the end of a long, narrow dirt road flanked by the silhouettes of Joshua trees. When they pulled up in his truck, a cat darted out of the space under the stairs and disappeared beyond the pool of light from the spotlight over the door. Even at night, Elise could tell that their mobile home had been through a lot of battles since her last visit. The side panels had been replaced and patched several times. The lattice skirting was broken in a few places. One of the windows had plastic over it.

Leticia waited for them on the front steps. She had to grip the rail to haul herself to her feet. Her hair was a faded shade of pink that had grown out to show natural dirty blond at the roots, and her belly was so big that it stuck out of the bottom of her tank top.

"Hey!" She waddled over to hug Elise, but faltered mid-step when she saw Anthony. "That's not James."

The very mention of his name made Elise's forehead ache, and for a confusing moment, she was no longer in the Nevada desert. Instead, she saw the vaulted ceiling of a moonlit condo in California, and a pair of hands much larger than hers cupping the leather spine of a book as gently as an infant. James was on vacation to meet his girlfriend's family, and he wasn't sleeping.

She had gotten used to the disorientation of having her mind split by her aspis's consciousness. She recovered faster every time. "James is busy," Elise said with a small shake to clear her vision. "This is Anthony. Anthony, this is Leticia McIntyre."

He grunted as he grabbed the suitcase out of the truck.

"Nice guy," Leticia said dryly. She stretched up on her toes to peck McIntyre's cheek. "Dana's sleeping in our bed. We can put them up in her room."

Sleep in a child's room? It sounded about as much fun as trying to have a decent conversation with Anthony. "I don't need to sleep," Elise said.

Leticia rolled her eyes. "Don't pull that kopis 'constant vigilance' bullshit on me. I don't think it's as cool as you do. Come on, get inside. Walk quiet. If we wake Dana, she'll be up all night."

Although the mobile home was small and old, Leticia kept the inside tidy. Their sixty-inch flat screen took up one entire wall and played a superhero movie on mute. It smelled like new paint inside the trailer, and the paneling was a cheerful shade of gold.

Leticia leaned her massive girth against the arm of a white leather couch backed by ram horns. It looked recent, too—there were imprints in the carpet where an older, smaller couch used to sit.

470

"You're doing well," Elise said.

McIntyre almost looked embarrassed. "We get pretty good tithes."

"You're tithing from the local demons now?"

He shrugged by way of response. "Put your stuff in there. That's where you're sleeping," he said, pointing at a door as Anthony entered.

Anthony took the suitcase into waiting bedroom, shut the door, and didn't come out again.

Both of the McIntyres looked at Elise. She didn't feel like trying to excuse him—he had been like that for weeks—and remained silent.

She moved to sit on the couch, but changed her mind when she noticed there wasn't any room. Leticia had taken over half of it with a nest of pillows and boxes of leftover Mexican food.

"How much are the tithes?" Elise pressed.

McIntyre just shrugged again and got two beers out of the fridge. He opened both of them with his pocketknife.

"Two and a half percent," Leticia said. "Those demons were always harping on us for mediation. I figured we might as well get paid for it, so we set up a contract. Now when we broker a deal with a demon that wants to build a new casino or something, we get paid, too—and then some off the top of their profits. Protection money sounds mercenary, but we earn it."

Elise took one of McIntyre's beers and cupped it between her gloved hands. "That's a good idea."

"Good idea? James talked shit about kopides that tithe last time you were down," McIntyre said, flopping into one of the kitchen chairs. "'Unethical,' James said. Something about organized crime, too."

Elise could see that James had set down his book, and was no longer pretending to ignore them. He stared at the moon through the window as he listened to their conversation.

"James and I don't agree on a lot of things," she said, knowing he would hear it.

Leticia chuckled. "Ain't that the truth. So where is your witch? He never lets you out of his sight. I can't believe he wouldn't have come along."

"He's alive, if that's what you're asking."

The McIntyres exchanged glances. After a moment, Leticia sniffed. "Then you tell him he's in trouble for avoiding us."

"Yeah. Sure. I'll do that."

In California, James picked up his book again.

Leticia glanced at the clock and turned off the TV. It took her two tries

471

to lower her bulk enough to set the remote on the coffee table. "I guess I better sleep if I'm having a baby today."

Elise helped her stand upright again and hovered as she shuffled into the bedroom. The witch's waddling motions and giant belly were worrying.

The blond head of a five year old girl poked out of all the sheets in the McIntyre's bed. "Night," Leticia whispered, careful not to make a noise when she shut the door again.

With nobody left to entertain, Elise joined McIntyre at the table. "Aren't you going to sleep?" he asked, and she shook her head. "Of course. I remember that." He waved his knife at Dana's bedroom. "What's up with your boyfriend?"

She ran a finger around the moisture on the rim of the bottle. "His cousin died recently."

"Was his cousin a friend of yours?" he asked. She nodded stiffly. "Sorry."

"Yeah." She threw back a long swig of beer and banged the empty bottle on the table. "Is there more?"

He leaned back on two chair legs, grabbed another beer out of the fridge, and opened it with his knife. McIntyre slid the bottle across to Elise. She caught it and drained the bottle in three long swallows.

"Did the demonic overlord kill her?"

"So you heard about that," Elise said. Her head was getting warm.

"Everybody heard about it."

She snorted out a short, mirthless laugh. "Great. No, it wasn't the overlord who killed her." She didn't want to talk about Betty anymore. Preferably not ever again. She changed subjects. "What are the issues at the summit this year?"

"There was all this stuff when they sent out the first papers—territory disputes in New Zealand, something about undercities getting eaten by sentient shadows, accusations of demons trying to break into the lowest level of Heaven. You remember how that goes. But they wiped that off the schedule a few weeks ago. There's only one item now."

She arched an eyebrow. "More important than an attempted assault on Heaven?"

"Check this out."

He grabbed a packet of information and pulled out the agenda, which was marked with a Union logo at the top. There were only two lines on the page.

Priority Item: Violation of Quarantined Dimension

Access to quarantined supra-ethereal dimension violated via gate rifts. Coordinated intervention requested. Negotiation supervised by Union kopides in all slots.

Elise realized she was about to tear the paper in half and forced her hand to relax. "Violation? When did this happen?"

"A few weeks ago, I guess."

"Which dimension?"

"I don't know. They'll talk about it at the summit," McIntyre said with a shrug. He noticed her expression and set his beer on the table. "What's wrong?"

She stared at the words on the page. *Quarantined supra-ethereal dimension.* There were a few quarantined levels of Hell—mostly because the atmosphere was deadly to non-natives—but she only knew of one quarantined level of Heaven. It was supposed to be completely blocked to all traffic.

Elise had been there before. It was quarantined for a reason.

Her response took too long, so McIntyre asked again, "What's wrong, Kavanagh?"

"Nothing," she said, trying to blank her mind before her stress drew James's attention again. Elise also wasn't going to discuss the quarantine with McIntyre. Not with anyone. She changed subjects. "So you still talk to half the kopides in the hemisphere, right? What does everyone know about me? Do they know I'm back?"

"The word is that some new kopis has taken over in Reno, but nobody knows who it is. Nobody except me. So it's not like anybody's going to expect to see you at the summit."

"What if someone does recognize me?" she asked.

"Then we're fucked, and we deal with it." McIntyre finished his beer and sighed. "I should curl up with the wife for a couple hours. She gets pissy if I stay up long. I've got all the stuff I emailed stuck in this binder, if you want to catch up."

"I'll read it."

"Summit check-in starts at eight, and it's three hours out of here, so you guys should probably be out of here by five. You can take Tish's car. Keys are on the hook." He stood and stretched. "Good to have you back, Kavanagh."

McIntyre disappeared into the bedroom.

Instead of reading the binder, she checked his refrigerator. They were short on food, but there was another six pack of beer on the shelf. She grabbed a bottle and sat on the front step with the agenda clutched in one hand.

She kept reading the first line over and over. Each time she did, she felt queasier.

But she wasn't sure if it was nerves, or something else. The mobile home buzzed around her with the residue of powerful magic. That was no surprise—Leticia was a witch, after all, and her pregnancy had probably limited her to casting all her spells at home. Elise wasn't used to being able to feel that much magic.

In the silent darkness, Elise had nothing to distract her from James's thoughts, so she tentatively prodded him. He would have been able to interpret the magic she was feeling. But he had somehow managed to fall asleep, and was dreaming of cabins in Colorado. She was alone.

She got through the entire six pack before sunrise.

Chapter 4

MORNING CAME TOO soon. Elise loaded Leticia's car before Anthony woke up, and they left with the sunrise. He read the notes on the summit as they headed north toward Silver Wells. They couldn't pick up any radio stations in the middle of the state, and the tape deck didn't work, so there was nothing else to do on the long drive.

After a couple hours of driving, the sun rose, the inside of the car grew hot, and the air conditioner started to give up. Anthony's forehead shone with sweat when he finally set down the binder. "This isn't going to work. I'm not a kopis. You're not a witch."

"Nobody needs to know that," Elise said. Her head ached from too much beer and not enough breakfast.

"What if they want you to cast a spell?"

"Most witches don't have James's ability to do magic in a heartbeat—Leticia can't cast spells without crystals and chanting and hours of preparation. If I need to do a spell, I'll wave my hands and speak Latin. It'll be fine."

Anthony shook the page with the schedule on it. "I have to go to meetings. I have to *mediate*."

"It's easy," Elise said. "You're just there to break up fights."

"Fights between the most powerful angels and demons on Earth? Yeah, no way that's going to go wrong."

Her response was interrupted by the car's sputtering as they mounted a hill.

The dashboard lights turned off. The engine died.

Elise swore as she steered the gliding car onto the side of the road. Gravel pinged off the windshield.

Once they stopped, she popped the hood, and Anthony got out to

475

check the engine.

"Nice of the McIntyre's to send us with a lemon," she said, leaning against the bumper beside him. The heat radiated through her jeans.

After a moment, Anthony straightened, wiping oil onto his jeans. "I don't know what's wrong with it."

"Is it the heat?"

"No. I mean, I don't know. Maybe. But they take care of their car; everything is in good condition. I don't see any problems."

Elise tried to turn on her cell phone, but the screen stayed black. The battery was dead.

"Your phone working?" she asked. He checked and shook his head. "Then it's not a car problem." She opened the trunk and put on her backpack.

"What is it?"

"Angels," Elise said. Electronics didn't work right around strong ethereal presences.

"What are we going to do?" he asked.

"We're walking."

"In this heat? Are you serious?"

"What else would we do? Do you have a horse in your suitcase?"

Elise threw the backpack over her shoulder and got moving. Anthony kicked the bumper of the car before following.

Silver Wells was just over the hill—which, as far as the desert was concerned, was impossibly distant. It was just like every other ghost town they had blown through at forty-five miles per hour. There was no indication of what was going to happen there aside from a collection of RVs and modular buildings to the north, which resembled a small military installation.

There was no heat like Nevada heat. Standing on the pavement felt like being in a broiler. The world was made of rippling lines and silver mirages, and Elise could feel her neck and nose burning.

Two miles was a long walk in that heat.

The first buildings they came across were empty tin shacks, which were worn by wind and pocked by rust. An ugly, abandoned bar with peeling yellow paint came next, and then a trailer park without any trees or grass. A dog tethered to a fence post growled at them.

There was no other sign of life in Silver Wells, but McIntyre's report said the town had a population of two hundred. All of them seemed to have gone into hiding at the sight of visitors. Given the quality of the visitors incoming, it was probably a smart move.

476

A convoy of black SUVs passed them. Elise and Anthony had to get off the road to keep from getting hit.

"The Union?" he asked the bumpers receded into the distance.

"Probably."

He glared. "Good drivers."

The SUVs stopped outside a small elementary school. Someone had mounted a sign that said REGISTRATION in the dirt pit that was supposed to be a parking lot, and the doors to the gymnasium were propped open by a sputtering box fan caked in gray dust.

Elise and Anthony went inside. It was no cooler than outside, but a break from the sun was a relief. The faint breeze from the fan was almost chilly on her sweaty back.

Warped boards formed the floor of the basketball court, bordered on one side by metal stands. A pair of folding tables had been set up at the end of the room, and a handful of men, none older than thirty, were lined up in front of them. They were unmistakably kopides: they refused to stand with anybody at their backs. A few women sat on the benches—probably aspides. Magic glimmered on their necklaces and hair clips.

The line in front of the table dissipated shortly. The men peeled off one by one, taking their witches with them.

"Go sign in, McIntyre," Elise said.

Anthony approached the table.

"Name?" asked a cocoa-skinned woman with hair cropped short to her scalp. Her shirt was stamped with "Unit B26" over the breast.

"McIntyre," Elise said from behind Anthony's shoulder. "Lucas and Leticia."

The woman looked up at them. She had a hard face, like she was constantly seconds away from a stern reproach. "McIntyre?"

"Yeah," Anthony said. He had grown still with tension.

"We've been waiting for you." She shuffled through folders in a plastic bin and came up with one tagged by a red sticker. She handed it to them. "Keep your ID on you all weekend. Checking in at the motel is your responsibility."

He stepped back. "Thanks."

Everyone in a black Union polo watched as they headed back out into the summer heat. A sense of unease crept over her.

"Let's get out of here," she said.

Inside a motel room labeled by a tin zero hanging from one nail, the Union of Kopides and Aspides was preparing to move.

The motel was enduring renovations, and the wall between rooms zero and eleven had been knocked down to make it one large chamber. Unit B13 used the four beds to house their computers, guns, and other equipment; the actual team members slept on the softest spot on the floor they could find. Nobody complained about it. The other two units on-site had to endure the heat in the camp outside town.

But Unit B13 hadn't been given the best lodgings because they were unusually skilled, or because they were special. It was because they had Benjamin Flynn, and he was the most powerful precognitive alive.

Benjamin stared at himself in the mirror of the shared bathroom. He had been in there for over an hour, but nobody dared to interrupt. They were all afraid of him.

He couldn't blame them. He didn't like himself, either.

He touched the collar on his neck. To anyone outside his unit, it probably looked like he was just some punk kid with an edgy style, but it was connected to Boyd's computers, and it somehow recorded his visions. The quartz on the left side was Allyson's work, and meant to suppress the small premonitions that peppered his day; the uncut, pebble-sized diamond on the other side was supposed to dampen the big hits. Both of them worked…more or less. He hadn't gone comatose from a big vision in a few months, anyway.

Benjamin thought a bunch of white guys sticking the Black kid in a collar was fucked up, and he told them that. They asked if he would prefer a straitjacket. He said he would rather be treated like a human, and they laughed like he was joking.

Carefully, he wiggled a shard of glass from the broken mirror into the lock. He wanted to fry the Union's electronics. They had built up an archive with thousands of hours of murky video of his prophecies, and written a ton of volumes interpreting them, and he was sick of it. He deserved privacy. The people he saw in his visions deserved privacy. And the collar was stupid.

A spark of electricity flared on the wiring. It leaped to his hand and zapped him.

"Ouch!"

He dropped the glass into the sink.

A fist pounded on the door. When Allyson spoke, it sounded like she had her face pressed against the other side. "What are you doing in there? Did you have a vision? I'm coming in."

"I'm taking a dump," Benjamin replied. "Bad burrito."

"Unlock the door, Flynn."

"Five more minutes."

"You have ten seconds, and then I break the bathroom lock."

She meant it. The Union had done it before. He wasn't really a team member—he was like their pet or something. The dog everyone liked to kick.

Benjamin groaned and swept the shard of glass into the drain of the sink. He flushed the toilet with his foot, ran the faucet for a couple of seconds, and unlocked the door just as Allyson was preparing to shoot it open with her handgun.

She glanced around the bathroom like she expected to find someone inside with him.

"Are you okay?" Her hair was red and shoulder-length, which offset a round face that seemed pudgy even though her body fat was close to zero. She ate and trained with the Union hunters, despite being a witch; she was bulky with muscle and twice as thick as he was.

"My rectum's not okay," Benjamin said.

He was rewarded with a sound of disgust. "Get out of there."

The unit bustled around rooms zero and eleven, discussing summit guests as they registered in the high school gymnasium. The thirty kopides that the Union invited had been trickling in all day. They watched on wireless security cameras that they had set up around town.

"The demons are getting almost as bad as the angels," Boyd said, pointing to one of the monitors. "You see that? Almost all of them are staying in the Warrens. Jesus Christ, the paranoia is contagious."

"Angels," Allyson scoffed as she took position by the surveillance station again. "Rigid bastards with sticks up their asses. We haven't had a single angel check in yet. Probably don't want to lower themselves to talking with mere mortals."

Zettel noticed Benjamin, and stopped filling a magazine with bullets. "What are you doing?" Whenever they spoke, the commander made it pretty clear that he thought Benjamin was a waste of Union resources, not to mention oxygen. And it only got worse since Michele died.

"Nothing."

"Then find something to do," Zettel said.

"Like what?"

"I don't care." He returned his attention to the ammunition. "Make it happen somewhere other than here. You're getting in the way."

Benjamin hadn't been allowed outside on his own in weeks, but he still hesitated by the door. It was dangerous going out. If he had any visions, he could be flattened in public.

But the outcome of that scenario would probably be better than what Zettel did to him if he stuck around.

He put on dark sunglasses and left the room.

Moving through Silver Wells with the glasses on gave everything a dull, gray-brown cast. It only served to make the surrounding buildings look more desolate, as if the desert had sucked the color and life from everything.

The streets were empty. Benjamin was alone as he walked to the convenience store.

Standing on the street corner, by a station with peeling paint and ancient gas pumps, Benjamin contemplated trying to run away again. A year with the Union was a year too long. They had promised to help him; instead, they dragged him around with a bejeweled collar and forced him to rehash his visions in exhausting detail.

But where would he have gone? The Union paid his parents a lot of money to keep him. They would never take him back. And Zettel threatened to break his legs if he tried to leave again. He didn't need his legs to act as a precog. He could have been a floating brain for all the Union cared.

Despair swept over him. He kicked the mailbox on the corner. It didn't do anything—not to the hot metal, and not to his mood.

It was cooler inside the convenience store by about two degrees. He was glad to see the shop was empty, aside from a clerk reading a book by the cash register. No way could an empty convenience store trigger a vision.

Benjamin walked through the aisles of candy and junk food trying to scratch an itch under his collar, and failing. It was too tight to get his fingers around it.

He loaded up with candy and dumped it on the counter. The cashier glanced at him. "That's going to be about fifty bucks. You know that, right?"

"Charge it to the Union."

The cashier paled. "Just take it."

Benjamin snagged a bag from the corner of the counter and filled it. He was grabbing another handful of candy bars when something inside of him shifted—like his brain had just prepared to jump off a cliff.

He grew alert, scanning the shop around him. It was still empty. There was a sign by the bathroom that said it was for use by paying customers

480

only. The TV in the corner was turned off—none of that stuff worked around angels, except the Union's equipment, which was thoroughly buffered with warding magic.

But there was that *shift*. A premonition was coming.

Leaving the rest of the candy on the counter, Benjamin hurried for the exit. The bell over the door jingled. He bumped into someone walking in.

His mind couldn't process the visual information. There wasn't enough time.

His eyes rested on her, and then he was gone.

Benjamin woke up on the floor without his sunglasses some minutes later.

A woman was bending over him. Her auburn hair was a veil of curls hanging at the side of her face. "You okay?" she asked, and Benjamin saw the scar on her eyebrow, the nick on her chin, and the smattering of freckles across her cheekbones.

He already knew Elise Kavanagh's face better than his own. He had seen it in thousands of visions, for years and years, and almost believed she wasn't real—until that moment. He had to stare.

She was so *alive*.

He realized she was waiting for a response.

"I'm fine," Benjamin stuttered.

His head throbbed with a pain unlike any other he had experienced. It was like his skull was packed with shattered glass from the motel mirror, and each shard was new information—things he knew, and wished he didn't. He rolled over and cradled his head.

Elise sat back on her heels. "Here," she said, offering a hand to Benjamin. He stared at it.

Where was her aspis? She shouldn't have been alone.

A pair of legs moved behind her, and he felt an instant of relief before realizing it wasn't James Faulkner at her back. It was some guy with brown hair, a tribal tattoo on his shoulder, and a sullen expression. Benjamin didn't recognize him.

"What do you think you're doing?" Benjamin asked Elise.

"I'm giving you a hand," she said. "Sorry for knocking you over. Come on, get up."

He let her pull him to his feet. She was strong, solid, and very real. He hung onto her for longer than necessary. "You're so young," he blurted out, unable to resist.

"I'm a little older than you are." Elise gave him a thin smile that was more unpracticed than unfriendly. She handed the sunglasses to him. One

481

of the lenses had popped out. "Are you here with somebody? Can I make a phone call for you?"

He shook his head silently. He knew he was still staring at her, but he couldn't stop. Her hair was red—red! And she was so tan. "I must have hit my head," he said faintly.

Her lips pursed. "What are you, epileptic?"

"I don't need a doctor. I'm okay."

"All right." She glanced over his shoulder at the coffee machine. Elise loved her coffee so much. "Try to take it easy, kid."

Benjamin went outside, but he didn't leave. He watched Elise through the window. She grabbed a cup of joe while the other guy—who was he? —went to the counter to ask for directions to the motel. Benjamin stared at their backs. He suddenly wasn't craving candy anymore.

It wasn't every day that Benjamin Flynn met the person who would destroy the world.

Chapter 5

THE MOTEL IN Silver Wells looked like a horror movie waiting to happen: decrepit, wind-battered, and on a lonely edge of town. The welcome sign depicted a cartoon coyote with a broken tooth. Scaling the stairs to the second floor was harrowing—some steps wobbled upon having weight placed upon them, and one near the top was missing entirely. There were no rails on either side.

It was easy to tell which rooms were already occupied by kopides. The motel staff had left the curtains open in the empty rooms, and as soon as someone checked in, the new occupant closed them. If there was one constant between all kopides, it was paranoia.

The curtains for room twenty-nine were parted. Anthony opened the door with their key.

There was no television. The linens on the bed had to be at least thirty years old, and the air smelled like dust. He stepped in to search for the light switch, but Elise reached out to him.

Something was wrong. Her instincts screamed out for him to stop.

"Wait," she said.

Footsteps pounded up the stairways on both sides. Before Elise could turn, hands shoved her into the room and slammed her body into Anthony's.

"On the ground! Now!"

The door banged shut behind them as lights blazed to life. Hands grabbed Elise's arms, forced them behind her back, and shoved her to the floor.

Her cheek was mashed into the carpet. Shiny black shoes passed through her vision.

"I'm Gary Zettel, commander of Union Unit B13. You're under

483

arrest." He turned to address the person holding Anthony. "Take them to the trailers, then separate, strip, and search. Remember protocol. We'll need to defend our actions in court." Zettel immediately left, as though too busy to be concerned about whether or not his orders were followed.

Elise met Anthony's panicked gaze. Then a black hood jerked over his head and cinched at the neck.

Cloth touched her hair, and she threw herself away from her captor with a hard twist of her body. She had an instant to analyze the situation —Gary Zettel, one woman, and three men, all armed—and then she snapped both of her feet into the air. Her heels cracked into the face of the man bent over her. He shouted and fell.

The butt of a rifle smacked into her solar plexus before she could get up. The air rushed out of her lungs.

A blond man's hands clamped on her upper arms and pressed them against her side. Anthony began shouting: "Let me go! I have rights!"

Elise ripped free of the man's grasp and launched herself at the door. She drew her knife with a flash of metal, throwing all her weight into a blow across the face of the man holding her boyfriend.

The instant of freedom was fleeting.

Something struck the back of Elise's knees. She collapsed as they dragged Anthony out of sight.

The hood flipped over Elise's head. The cord tightened around her neck.

Darkness.

Metal bit into her wrists and ankles. She thrashed, but three sets of hands seized her, and she was carried from the room. Unlike Anthony, they didn't even let her feet contact the earth.

The blackness within the hood was absolute. The only way she could tell she had left the room was by the sudden heat of sunlight.

Elise was shoved inside something shaded, and what sounded like the door on a van shut. The vehicle growled to life and began to move. She opened her mouth to call for Anthony, but stopped an instant before giving herself away. "Lucas," she said instead, "are you there?"

No response.

In a void of visual stimulus, James's presence filled her mind. He was walking hand-in-hand with Stephanie along a garden lush with flowers. Elise could smell pollen, hear the buzzing of bees, and feel his girlfriend's long, manicured nails digging into the back of his hand. Stephanie smiled for him, and the red-blond hairs that had escaped her bun drifted around her face in the breeze.

James thought about how beautiful she looked—and then realized he wasn't alone. His attention drew inward.

Elise?

She didn't want him to know what was happening. She shut him out with the practiced efficiency of having to block him several times a day, every day, for weeks.

The garden was gone. She was back in the darkness, and someone whispered beside her.

"Think we'll get to execute them?" It was a man's voice. He had a New England accent, and Elise memorized the sound of it. When she got a chance to fight back, he was going to be the first to go.

"You heard Gary. They're going to court. Eyes forward."

Nobody else spoke as they drove on. Elise wasn't sure how long they traveled. She could hear the mechanisms of guns being moved—removing clips and checking them, sliding them back into the gun, cleaning parts. Nobody else talked.

Time passed.

The van stopped. The door slid open.

Elise was lifted again. Her captors were not gentle. They hauled her by the cuffs at her wrists and ankles and flung her unceremoniously to the ground.

The hood came off, and Elise found herself inside a tent. The floor of the tent was dirt, and blissfully cool in comparison to the heat blowing in from underneath the tarp.

The broad-shouldered woman from the hotel room loomed over her. Elise saw a spark of silver around her fingers that meant she was a witch, and a fairly powerful one. "I'm going to strip-search you. This will go a lot faster if you don't struggle."

Elise responded by slipping her other knife out of her wrist sheath behind her back.

The woman began unbuttoning Elise's shirt. A couple of buttons popped off. The witch reached around to undo the handcuffs and remove the shirt, which freed Elise's left hand.

She swung the knife.

Her arms had numbed from being forced behind her back, and she was fractionally slower than normal. A fraction, nothing more, but it was enough.

The witch dodged the blow and ripped the knife from Elise's hand, taking the glove with her.

"Nice tattoo."

485

"Do you recognize it? Do you know what it means?" Elise spat.

"No."

"It means you shouldn't fuck with me."

The other woman snorted. She stripped off the wrist sheath, then went for the second glove, but Elise clenched her hand into a fist and put it behind her back.

"Open your other hand. You heard me—open your hand!" the witch ordered. Elise threw her body forward, cracking the top of her head into her captor's face. She reeled as blood splattered on her shirt. "I need support!"

A man rushed through the tent flap, took an instant to size up the situation, and swung his rifle.

The room exploded around Elise. She hit the ground a moment later, and the woman pounced on her. She was strong for a human. Her hands patted along Elise's body brusquely, stripped off the other sheaths, and then started to pry her fingers open again.

She couldn't open her hand. She couldn't have both palms bared.

There were far, far worse things than her attackers.

The man slammed his knee down on Elise's arm. "I think she's holding something!"

A badge clipped to the witch's belt momentarily dangled in front of Elise's face, and she had an instant to read it: Allyson Whatley, Union of Kopides and Aspides.

Elise wasn't given the time to wonder why the Union had attacked them. Allyson Whatley's hand squeezed around Elise's just above the knuckles.

For an instant, her hand was hot with the strain of it, and then her bones croaked and groaned and snapped.

She screamed a wordless scream.

Chapter 6

GARY ZETTEL WATCHED on a security monitor as Boyd dropped the McIntyres into the interview room, which was a trailer at the center of the Union camp. It was a sparse box with a single overhead light. The windows had been covered with trash bags and duct tape.

The woman on the left was rigid. She wore a plain gray sports bra and matching underwear, which revealed well-cut abs and arms. Her thighs were thick with muscle. The man at her side wore red plaid boxers, and was likewise well-defined, although he didn't look nearly as fit in comparison to his supposed aspis.

The voices that came through the tinny speakers were whispers. Gary turned the volume all the way up.

"Are you okay? What's going on?" A masculine voice. The man turned his head in the bag, obviously trying to move toward the woman.

"Don't move," she said, and it was quiet enough that he could barely make it out. "Don't speak."

Zettel was still studying them with a hand on his chin when Allyson returned. "What weapons did you find on them?" he asked.

His aspis dropped the captives' belongings on the table. There were wrist sheaths, two knives, and no guns in sight. "All on the woman," Allyson said. "The woman got violent when we removed her gloves to inspect them. It took both Boyd and I to restrain her. We were forced to break one of her hands."

"What was she hiding?"

"Nothing." Allyson seemed insulted by the nerve of it. "She put her hands back into fists after we broke her fingers—she wouldn't even let the medic treat her. She's an animal."

He grunted. "If that's the aspis, how did the kopis react?"

487

"He allowed us to search him, and we found no weapons on his person. He insisted on his innocence at least six or seven times." She showed Zettel her phone. "I took pictures of them."

He took the device. The picture of the woman's face showed obvious anger, frenzied hair, red cheeks. The man had a square jaw and strong shoulders, but a young face. Not exactly the kind of thousand-yard stare Zettel had come to expect from a kopis.

Motion on the camera distracted him. The woman had shifted from her knees to her lay on her side, and she squirmed to maneuver her still-clenched fists under her legs. She didn't show any signs of being in pain. She was absolutely silent.

"This isn't right," Zettel muttered. "There's no way she's an aspis. What's our intel say?"

Allyson swiped through a couple pages on her mobile device. "We don't have any. All we know is what Michele put in her travel request, and that's the name: Lucas McIntyre. There's no identification on these people besides their badges for the summit. I couldn't even find social security numbers for the McIntyres."

"How would Michele have known who they were and how to find them if they're ghosts?" Zettel mused aloud. "Too bad she's not here to ask."

"She's the problem." Allyson jabbed at the woman on the monitor with a finger. "She's not an aspis, and she makes him look like a goddamn fairy."

He glanced down at the photos Allyson had taken. There were pictures of the undersides of their forearms, and the woman had a silvery, near-invisible scar tracing from wrist to the inside of her elbow. The man didn't. It was a telltale sign of having performed a binding ritual, and it almost certainly meant they were not bound—not to each other.

"If they're both kopides, where are the witches?"

Allyson looked a little too eager to find the answer to that. "I don't know. Let me interview them."

"We'll go in together."

Zettel opened the door for Allyson, and she went outside. Surveillance was set up in a trailer beside the interview room, and Boyd leaned against the exterior wall in the shade. A wad of bloody tissues was pressed to his face.

"Bitch broke my nose," he grumbled.

Allyson laughed.

They left Boyd to himself and entered the other trailer. The woman

488

already had her hood off and was crouched beside the man. It looked like they had interrupted her in the middle of trying to free the man.

She froze. Her hazel eyes flashed.

Zettel stalked around the edge of the room, glancing over to make sure Allyson had the door secured, and stood over the woman. "Identify yourself."

"Could I have my hood removed?" the man asked, voice muffled.

"You can, if your partner will behave herself."

She glanced at the hooded man, and Zettel could see the calculations running through her mind. After a moment, she sat back and rested her hands on her knees. Her left hand was bruised, purpling and swelling, and still she had it in a fist.

Allyson jerked the hood off the man's head. He winced and blinked at the bright light.

"Identify yourselves," Zettel repeated.

The man cleared his throat. "I'm Lucas McIntyre. Could I have a drink of water, please?"

"You're Lucas McIntyre? And what is your partner?"

"Leticia McIntyre. My wife."

"I said, *what* is your wife?"

Lucas glanced at Leticia. "She's my aspis. Please—I'm really thirsty."

Zettel nodded, and Allyson left to find a bottle of water. "You swear that you are a kopis and she is your aspis?" When Lucas nodded, he said, "And you *swear* that you are Lucas McIntyre?"

"What's going on? We haven't done anything."

"You're the last person to see Michele Newcomb alive," Zettel said, "and that makes you a person of great interest to the Union. I'm going to ask you to move away from your aspis, Mr. McIntyre. Get over there. On the wall."

He didn't hesitate to obey. Very nervous, like Allyson said. "Who is Michele Newcomb?" asked Lucas.

"She was our recruiter and a witch," Zettel said as Allyson reentered the room with a bottle of water. She gave it to Lucas, who slurped half of it down with a sigh. "She put in a travel request to a private home at an unspecified Clark County address—*your* address. Michele Newcomb was found dead a few miles away. You're the last person she saw."

"I don't know what you're talking about," he said again. "We haven't done anything wrong. Can you let us go?" He was so polite, and he clasped his hands together. "At least return Leticia's gloves. She needs them."

Allyson gestured. "Gary." Zettel went outside to talk with his aspis. "I think she might be a witch after all. There's *something* there. They're also lying. I don't buy that they're married."

"Let's give them a few minutes," he said. "I want to see what's in their bags."

Anthony and Elise sat in silence. The camera in the corner was a clear message—they didn't dare speak where they would be observed. It didn't take long for Allyson to reenter the trailer alone. She threw a pair of gloves at Elise. "This is your territory, isn't it?" the witch asked.

Anthony glanced at Elise, who gave a tiny nod as she gloved her unbroken hand. "Yes," he said.

"The Union apologizes for the rough handling. We'd like to offer medical treatment, Mrs. McIntyre, and we would also like to return your belongings. I hope you understand that the Union must be cautious—for the safety of our staff."

They stood as best as they could with their hands bound, and Allyson removed the plastic ties from their wrists.

When they stepped outside, Anthony was only half-surprised to find himself in the middle of the Union's temporary camp. He caught glimpses of fence topped by barbed wire and passing people who wore all black, like they were commandos. The trip was too short to see much else, for which he was grateful. He didn't want to be paraded around in his boxers.

Allyson led them to a tent with a single table in the center and a very conspicuous camera wired to the corner. Their clothes were laid out on the table, but their possessions—including Elise's daggers—were nowhere in sight.

"I'll be back for you in five minutes," the witch said, and she let the flaps of the tent fall shut behind her. The semblance of privacy it provided was a joke. There was no privacy in the room, not with the cameras watching and people waiting outside.

Anthony pulled on his jeans and t-shirt as Elise dressed in silence. By the time he finished and turned back around, she was struggling to button her shirt. Pain furrowed her brow.

A man clutching a medical kit to his chest entered the tent unannounced. He was a young Latino man, probably younger than Elise, and so thin that a good desert wind could have blown him away.

490

"Afternoon! I'm Francisco—Frank—jack-of-all-trades around the Union camp here. I hear someone's got a broken hand?"

Elise just glared, so Anthony said, "Her right hand."

He tried to spread her fingers. "Ooh, that's a bad one. You must have fought well to earn Allyson's tender loving care! Let's see if we can set these bones."

She didn't speak as the man worked. Frank was surprisingly gentle as he wrapped bandages from forearm to knuckles.

"How's that feel?" he asked, still too cheerfully. Elise didn't respond, and he went on as though he had expected as much. "Fantastic! That should do well enough. Might want to heal yourself up first chance you get, though. Are you a healing witch? Well, find one who is." Frank gave Elise a friendly punch on the shoulder, and she scowled.

The tent flap opened again. Zettel carried a pair of folding chairs under his arm, which he set up in the middle of the tent. "Sit, Mr. McIntyre." Anthony obeyed, but Elise made no move. Zettel folded his arms across his chest. It was a difficult pose; his muscles were so thick that they couldn't have rested flat at his sides, either. "Has your partner's hand been satisfactorily addressed?"

"Yeah. I think so."

"Frank, take Mrs. McIntyre outside. Allyson's waiting to interview her." As soon as Elise and the self-proclaimed everyman had left, Zettel straddled the other chair. "Are you familiar with the Union of Kopides and Aspides?"

"I kind of think I am now, yeah."

The commander ignored his response. "We're an international corporation that trains, organizes, and funds partnerships such as yours. Thanks to private investors, we're in the process of building a worldwide army that stands on the front lines of the war against Heaven and Hell. Are you familiar with the dangers both pose against humans?"

Anthony tried to decide if that was a trick question. He took a little too long to say, "Sure."

"Things are sorely out of balance for the humans. One of the Union's primary missions is to stop in-fighting amongst humans—kopides, aspides, and anyone else with special talents. We have to unite to focus our energies. Take up the sword and shield to defend ourselves." He focused fully on Anthony. "Did you have an old rivalry with Michele Newcomb?"

"Uh, no."

"Then why did you kill her?"

491

"I've never even met her."

Zettel frowned. "You're lying."

"Yeah. Right. I am lying to a man who could shoot me dead on the spot." Anthony rolled his eyes. "That's a smart idea."

"Why don't you have any identification in your luggage?"

"You got in my luggage?"

"How long have you been married?" Zettel asked instead of responding.

Anthony's pulse accelerated. Oh, hell. Allyson was probably asking Elise the same thing. When had they started dating? May? "Just about four months."

"Newlyweds. Congrats. What year were you born?"

"Why the hell do you care?"

Zettel unfolded his arms, cracked his knuckles. Even though he had a schooled, east-coast accent, he still gave the physical impression of being a very smart gorilla with a crew cut. "Belligerence didn't treat your wife very well. There are dozens of Union operatives arrayed throughout this base, and all of them are armed."

"I've never even heard of Michele Newcomb. You can ask all the questions you want and that won't change."

"This can take all day if it needs to," Zettel said. "All week."

"Are you listening to a single thing I say?"

Judging by the commander's expression, Anthony was ninety-nine percent sure that Zettel didn't believe a thing he was saying. "She's aggressive for an aspis," he went on.

Anthony had to laugh at that. "She would be aggressive for a coked-out cage fighter."

"You claim you don't know Michele Newcomb. Would it be possible, then, for you to make any guesses as to why she might have had your name on her travel request?"

"You said she was a recruiter, right? Maybe she wanted to recruit us. How the hell am I supposed to guess at a stranger's motivations?"

Zettel stared at him. Anthony responded in kind.

After a lengthy two minutes, which felt more like two hours, Zettel spoke into his phone. "You done yet? Bring her back in here." Allyson escorted Elise back into the tent. She didn't look like any new bones were broken, but she didn't look happy, either.

"How long have they been married?" Allyson asked.

Zettel smirked. "Four months." They both laughed.

So was that it? Had Elise given the wrong answer? Were they about to

492

get shot and left to bleed out in the desert? Anthony couldn't even find it in himself to panic beyond a slight hiccup of worry. Fear wasn't nearly as heavy as the misery he had been carrying for weeks. It was actually a refreshing change.

But nobody drew a gun. Zettel stood.

"You both understand, this is an important summit. More important than any before. Not only are we dealing with a critical issue, this is the Union's first move to provide some desperately needed organization to the United States. We can't risk this going FUBAR. You got me?"

Elise glowered.

The commander strode to the flap and lifted it open.

"The first meeting is in an hour. I'll expect to see you both there," Zettel said. "We'll be in contact."

"You're letting us go?" Anthony asked, but Elise was already grabbing his arm to haul him outside. The top of his head immediately stung from the sunlight.

"See you around," Allyson said.

Elise shot the Union members a cold look. "Yes. You will."

Chapter 7

THE UNION DROPPED Elise and Anthony off at the edge of town. He waited until the black SUV headed back to camp before speaking.

"Seriously, screw those guys," Anthony said. Elise slowly, carefully, tried to flex the fingers on her broken hand, but it was too painful. Her weekend was not off to a good start. "You know this is a trap, right? They know we're lying. They've only let us go so they can mess with us later."

"Exactly. That's why I'm going back to Las Vegas."

Anthony blinked in surprise. "You can't be running away."

"I'm not. I need answers, and the only person who might have them is McIntyre. And I'm not going to wait to see what the Union will do to us next."

"He's going to be busy with his wife, don't you think?" Anthony asked, frowning.

"They broke my hand," she growled, shaking her bandaged fist at him. "I'm going to break the other one on his face if he knew that we were going to deal with murder charges."

He pushed her wrist down—gently. "Okay, fine. Let's go."

"You're not coming. You have to attend the meetings and do your duty as kopis."

"But I'm not—"

"Shh." She put her unbroken hand over his mouth and glanced around. They were on an empty street corner. The only person she could see was another hot, exhausted kopis dragging himself toward the high school gym. But just because nobody was watching didn't mean they weren't listening.

He whispered into her ear. "I don't know anything about…*anything*."

"You know something about this. Trust me. There's only one issue on the agenda—a violated quarantine on an ethereal dimension," Elise said. Anthony stared at her blankly. "Because someone opened a gate."

Realization dawned. "Oh. *Oh.* That's bad."

"At the meeting today, they will discuss who needs to be responsible for guarding the gates. The Union will make a case for it being their job and insist on stationing a unit or six in Reno. I don't want those assholes anywhere near the gate. You need to insist that the local overlord guard the gate instead."

"But you killed her." He lowered his voice. "The Night Hag is dead."

"That doesn't matter."

"It kind of matters a lot," Anthony said. "I can't face down some crazy organization on my own. Especially not with angels and demons and God only knows—"

She cut him off with a hand on his chest. "Just do it. This is important."

"Then you do it!"

"I'm not going to argue with you. I'm taking care of McIntyre. You take care of the gate. Got it?"

She walked away.

"Elise," he said. When she didn't turn around, he repeated louder, "Elise!"

"Leticia," she shot back over her shoulder.

Elise ducked into the gas station before heading out. She soaked her button-up shirt in the sink and wrapped it around her hair. Then she walked out of town, past the trailers, beyond the "Welcome to Silver Wells, Land of Plenty!" sign, and hiked up the hill to the abandoned the car. Her shirt was soaked with sweat by the time she reached it.

Elise opened the car, grimaced at the blast of hot air, and used the open door to push it onto the road. Only one of her arms was any good, so she leaned her shoulder against the metal. It burned through her shirt.

She pushed it about a quarter mile before getting behind the wheel. Elise turned the key. The engine groaned as the dashboard flickered to life.

The drive to Las Vegas left her plenty of time to stew in anger. After all those years of teaming up with McIntyre—after they had taken down a whole legion together—and he had walked her straight into a trap. Elise didn't trust many people, but she had trusted McIntyre. It was a mistake she wouldn't make again.

Are you okay?

James's voice was tentative in the back of her skull. She tightened her good hand on the steering wheel and tried to focus on the long, flat road in front of her. "I'm fine," she told the horizon.

You're in pain.

"We'll talk about it later."

His presence faded again. *Very well.*

She almost wished he wouldn't go. It was a long drive from Silver Wells to the hospital, and the company would have been nice. But James hadn't been good company lately—they had barely spoken since Betty died.

The sun was high in the sky when she parked in the hospital parking garage. Elise found McIntyre in the third floor hallway. He had taken a chair in the corner and stretched out with his eyes shut. He appeared to be asleep, but she knew he wasn't—kopides weren't wired to sleep in public areas.

"What do you want?" he asked when she approached, voice gravelly with fatigue. He had been unkempt the day before, but after the stress of his morning, he looked downright indigent.

"Who is Michele Newcomb?" she asked. He paled, ducked his head, and scrubbed a hand over his jaw without responding. "As soon as I arrived in Silver Wells, I got arrested by the Union for murder. Apparently, Lucas McIntyre was the last person to see her alive."

"I don't know what you—"

She dropped her voice to a growl. "Give me one good reason to keep up this idiotic charade. One reason. I've dropped everything to help you keep your territory, and I find myself accused of *murder*?"

McIntyre waited for a nurse to shuffle past with a cart before responding. "We can't talk about it here. Listen—they're going to do a c-section tomorrow if this induction doesn't work, and—"

"I don't care if your wife is getting lobotomized tomorrow. Did you kill Michele Newcomb?" Elise leaned forward with her elbows on her knees. She held a hidden blade against her arm, and his gaze dropped to the glint of silver.

McIntyre swallowed hard. "Let's walk. Cafeteria's downstairs. Hungry?"

"No."

"I am."

She tailed him to the cafeteria without putting the knife away. Walking beside another kopis was always a weird dance—two paranoid people trying to keep the other in their sights.

The cafeteria was a gray, unpleasant place built of linoleum and concrete. McIntyre piled a plate high with stale pizza and joined Elise at one of the tables. He dropped a cup of coffee in front of her. She didn't touch it.

"You recognized her name," she said. "You reacted when I said it."

"Michele Newcomb's some Union recruiter. She was the one sending enlistment materials before the summit." McIntyre dug into his food.

"They found her car a few miles away from your trailer."

He slowly chewed his pizza. Elise wished that James were there—he would have been able to read that strange expression on McIntyre's face and know what it meant. Other peoples' body language meant little to her; it was a foreign language she didn't speak. He could have been admitting guilt with that frown, and she would never have been able to tell.

"There are a lot of demons around for the summit," he finally said. "Anyone could have killed her. What happened to your hand?"

Elise held it up. Just acknowledging the break was enough to make it start hurting again. "The arrest wasn't gentle."

He swallowed like the pizza was a rock and grimaced. "I figured the Union would be a pain in the ass. They always are. I didn't think they'd break your hand."

She emptied her coffee in one gulp. "If I find out you knew more than you're letting on, I'm going to come visit you again. And it won't be a little talk over lunch." Elise dropped the cup on the table. "If I find out that you killed Michele Newcomb, I will give you to the Union."

McIntyre wiped his mouth on a napkin. His lips drew into a frown. "Would you? Really?"

Elise really, really wished she could read his facial expression.

She dropped her eyes to the empty cup. "Come on, Lucas. Cut me a break. You are telling me the truth, right?"

His nod was slow. He didn't look at her when he did it.

She shoved her chair back and left the hospital.

Chapter 8

THE FIRST MEETING was held below an abandoned silver mill outside town. It stood on the side of a hill with shattered windows and exposed beams where the cement had crumbled away.

The Union bused kopides from Silver Wells to the site, and it took three large vans to do it. Anthony was assigned to a twelve-seater next to a man with red-brown skin and a big grin. "This is very exciting," said the kopis with a thick accent that Anthony didn't recognize. "All this open space. Isn't it marvelous?"

There was yellow emptiness outside the window as far as Anthony could see. The van's air conditioning wasn't powerful enough to reach the back seats, so he was drenched in sweat. "Marvelous. Yeah."

The other man stuck out a hand. "I'm Ramelan. What's your name?"

They shook hands. "Lucas McIntyre," Anthony said with only a slight stutter. "Where are you from?"

"A village called Gobang in Indonesia. It's nothing like this." Ramelan's teeth were very white against his dark skin. "Our villages are full of rice farms and fishing, and not nearly so vast. I have never seen anything like it."

"Guess you don't get around a lot."

"Oh, I've been many places," he said. "But not on Earth."

Where could a kopis go that wasn't on Earth? The only options that came to mind were Heaven and Hell, and that was subject matter he preferred to avoid. It was a weird enough pronouncement that Anthony decided not to ask about it.

Ramelan turned to another kopis—a young man with brown hair and a big nose—and they talked for the rest of the ride to the silver mill.

The Union lined everyone up outside the building before letting them enter the elevator in groups. Ramelan was in the same group as Anthony. He was extremely bright and outgoing, and Anthony wished he would go away. Elise must have been rubbing off on him.

A Union witch closed the elevator's cage and pressed a button. They descended into the mines.

The mill looked abandoned, but the elevator was well-oiled and smooth. They dropped beyond several shafts that had been encased in solid concrete and kept dropping. Anthony lost count of how many levels they passed around eight or nine. Somewhere beyond that—where the air began to grow hot again, and they had to pump cold air in to keep it breathable—they reached a shaft like every other, and the elevator stopped.

Another Union witch opened the door. The men piled out.

In Reno, the demons inhabited gold mines that had been abandoned in centuries past, so they were filled with exposed wood and crumbling rock. The silver mine was much more recent. The towering machinery was plated with steel, and the offices they passed even had beige computers from the nineties.

There was less cement so deep underground. The walls were raw stone supported with steel I-beams. The kopides were led to a dark, cavernous room with a rock tumbler, where three separate seating areas had been arranged among the machines. Their footsteps echoed off the walls as they moved to take chairs.

Anthony hung back to let the other men select their seats. The front row was marked by "reserved" signs, but he wanted to snag a spot there. If he was going to have to speak up during the meeting—a wholly petrifying idea—then he wanted to be somewhere prominent.

Fortunately, Ramelan saved him from having to pick a spot. "Nervous?" the kopis asked cheerfully. "You can sit with me!" And he took a seat in one of the reserved chairs. It left Anthony next to the Union's desk, which was elevated on a platform. A huge pump whirred behind it, sending water sloshing through overhead pipes.

He leaned around to see who was up there, and a chill rolled down his spine. Zettel and his aspis, Allyson, were already positioned above everybody else. There were a few other people there, too—the red-haired man named Boyd, a petite woman with silver rings on every finger, and a Black boy who couldn't have been older than sixteen.

"I've been excited about this summit for months," Ramelan confessed, drawing his attention away from the Union. "I expect to meet so many interesting people. Demons, I see demons all the time—in fact, I just had lunch with Aquiel last week—but I seldom meet other kopides."

Anthony was too nervous to respond. His hands shook.

After all of the kopides occupied the seats around him, the demons started to file in. They came from the opposite direction as the humans, as though they approached from deeper within the mines. A few passed for human, superficially, but Anthony would never mistake them for anything but demonic. He had run into enough nightmares and incubi to recognize that luminous skin and black hair.

Only a half dozen of them emerged and sat in the front row of their section. Considering the most powerful demons were supposed to be invited to the summit, they looked pretty innocuous. None of them even gave Anthony a headache.

"This is a bad sign," Ramelan murmured.

"Why?"

"The infernal delegation is thirty strong. These are only the servants—not the overlords or masters. And I see no angels yet."

Anthony glanced around. Ramelan was right. The third section was empty.

They weren't the only ones who had noticed the absence. Zettel and his team on the platform were getting antsy.

He checked the clock on the wall. The meeting was supposed to have started five minutes ago. "What's going on?" Anthony wondered aloud. Ramelan didn't have an answer, but he didn't really expect him to.

Another fifteen minutes passed quietly. And then fifteen more.

The angels never arrived.

Elise reached Silver Wells at the same time that the Union returned from the meeting. She lurked across the street from the school to watch as they unloaded the vans—each of which blazed with so much red magic that they were hard to look at.

She squinted into the magical glow. Her ability to see magic was so new that she still had no idea what any of it meant, but James—who was talking to a silver-haired man over a lunch of caprese salad and doing his very best to ignore her—would have known the spells at a glance, if he hadn't been busy. Considering that Leticia's car had died on the approach to town again, she could only assume the magic was to counteract the interference of ethereal energy.

Anthony was completely oblivious to anything strange about his transportation. She waved when he emerged, and he jogged over to join her. "That ended fast," Elise said.

"It never started. The angels didn't show, and the demons only sent their servants."

Her eyebrow quirked. "Really."

"Yeah. What does it mean?"

The Union closed the vans. Most of them headed back to their private compound, while Zettel and his team stuck around to argue in low voices. That strange boy with the dog collar was with them, although he stood a few feet away without joining their conversation. She wouldn't have pegged him for a Union member. He didn't look anything like a kopis.

Zettel was obviously distressed. His face was purple, and spit flung from his mouth as he spoke. Allyson wasn't any happier. They talked over each other like a very old—and very angry—married couple.

A smirk played on Elise's lips. "It means we aren't the only ones pissed that the Union's taken over the summit."

"Good," Anthony said forcefully. He leaned against the rotten boards of the wall beside her, kicked off a shoe, and shook pebbles out. "Did you find McIntyre?" She nodded. He stuffed his foot back into the sneaker. "And?"

"Something is going on. I still don't know what."

Another black SUV approached. It didn't come from the north, where the Union had their compound. It came from Las Vegas instead.

The kid in the collar turned to watch the SUV pass. He looked so worried that Elise had to watch it, too. The windows were tinted black. She couldn't see inside, but she suddenly had a bad feeling.

Why would the Union have been in Vegas?

"What's wrong?" Anthony asked when he saw her expression.

Her gaze fell on the boy across the street, and she realized with a jolt that he was already staring at her. "Hang on," she said.

She met him halfway across the road.

"They have McIntyre," the boy said without preamble. "They've arrested him."

The shock of it was so powerful that, for a moment, she stared at him with her mouth agape.

A hundred questions cascaded through her at once—how he could know that Anthony wasn't McIntyre, how he knew about the arrest, what he was doing with the Union—but she finally settled on, "Who are you?"

"I'm Ben," he said. "Um, Benjamin, actually. Flynn. That doesn't matter right now. The team followed you to Vegas, waited until you left the hospital, and arrested McIntyre. He was in that car."

"What the hell?" Elise asked.

"My thoughts exactly," Allyson interrupted.

Zettel and his aspis had noticed the conversation and joined them in the street. The commander snapped his fingers at Benjamin. "You. Get in the car. Now."

Elise instinctively stepped between them. There was no reason to feel protective of a total stranger like Benjamin—he was with the Union, after all—but she couldn't resist the compulsion.

Allyson reached around Elise and grabbed Benjamin's arm. "You heard Gary. Get in the car." She ushered him to one of the SUVs, and he gave Elise one last desperate look before the door shut on him and the witch.

"What are you going to do with McIntyre?" Elise asked.

"We'll interview him," Zettel said with an unpleasant twist to his lips, which meant that McIntyre was going to get the same strip search they had. "And as soon as we're done with the summit, we'll take him back to Union HQ for prosecution."

"Prosecution? Seriously? What is your problem?"

Zettel gave a cold laugh. "My problem? What's my problem? My problem is that you concealed a killer, lied to me about your identity—"

"You can't arrest McIntyre," she said. "His wife is in the hospital."

"He killed one of my people. The only place he's going is to a Union trial. You should just thank your lucky stars that I'm not dragging you in for interfering with our investigation—whoever the hell you even are. There's no way you're a witch. You're not even married to that guy." He jabbed his thumb at Anthony.

Elise shoved her face into Zettel, gathering all of her five and a half feet to make herself as intimidating as possible. It worked on most people. In fact, it worked on everyone. But Zettel didn't budge. "My name is Elise Kavanagh. I'm a kopis, and I've known McIntyre for years —he's a hell of a man to have at your back. He would never kill someone who didn't deserve it."

The commander stepped forward to crowd her space. His chest bumped against hers. He smelled like aftershave and gun oil. "You saying that Michele deserved to get shot and stabbed and left to bleed out in the desert? You think she deserved to suffer?"

"I'm saying that if he killed her, she earned it. But if you think she didn't earn it, then it wasn't McIntyre. Simple as that." He tried to argue,

502

but she didn't let him. "Let McIntyre go—send men to follow him, use spy drones, I don't care, but let him get back to his family until you know more. I'll find out who killed your recruiter."

"And why is that supposed to impress me?"

"Because," Elise said, "I used to be the greatest kopis."

Zettel laughed again. It was a condescending sound. "Bullshit. That's impossible. The greatest kopis is here in Silver Wells."

That gave her pause. She had realized that going into hiding would mean someone else would inherit the title, but she had only considered it in the most abstract way. She hadn't really given consideration to what it would mean to have another greatest kopis, much less being in the same place as him.

After a beat, she said, "I was the one who came before him. I retired."

"Kopides don't retire. They die."

She opened her mouth to argue, but didn't get a chance. Someone shouted.

Allyson Whatley burst out of the SUV. Elise tensed, but the witch didn't attack. "Flynn's having a seizure!"

"What are the conditions?" Zettel asked.

She shoved a printout in his face. It was gibberish to Elise, but it must have meant something to him. He scanned them, and then stepped back, shielded his eyes, and scanned the sky.

A shadow crossed over the sun, and a lone silver feather drifted in front of Elise's face.

It was followed by another feather, and another. But she didn't wait to see if there would be more. Elise shoved Anthony behind the bar, and Zettel was too busy shouting indistinct orders to his team to notice that they had disappeared.

An angel dropped out of the sky and alighted in the center of the road. His bare feet came to rest on the searing asphalt.

A voice echoed through the air.

"I have come."

It was a powerful noise, booming and resonant, even though the voice itself was barely more than a whisper. Elise still would have heard it if she was miles away, or utterly deaf. It drove through her mind like a spike.

She watched from around the side of the building as the angel stretched his wings to their full capacity, which forced Zettel to step back. Each wing was as long as he was tall, and he scattered downy feathers across the desert like hot snow. He blazed with inner light. She couldn't see his face around the commander's back.

Elise wished that she had brought her falchions.

"If you want to talk to me directly, you're supposed to arrange a meeting," said Zettel, sounding more irritated than fearful. Elise hadn't pegged him for a complete idiot, but she was quickly changing her mind. "You can't just wander around town like this. There are civilians, you know."

The quiet voice roared. "I bear a message."

"So bear it to the meetings. The ethereal delegation missed the first one."

"We will not be attending any of your meetings."

Zettel faltered, stunned to silence. Allyson spoke instead. "The agreement—"

"We made no agreement."

She grew bolder. "So the last three thousand years of summits were… what, a whim?"

"We've fulfilled our promises to the Council of Dis. But the semi-centennial summit has been taken by your human faction, and we have no agreements with you. We won't submit to your rules."

Zettel found his voice again. "It's the same damn summit it's always been!"

The commander's slight movement allowed Elise to glimpse the angel's face. He was a young man with coppery hair that brushed his shoulders, and she was stunned to realize that she recognized him. "We obey the laws of no man," said the angel. He didn't rise to meet Zettel's anger, but there was a flash of annoyance in his pale eyes.

Elise stepped out from behind the tent. "Nukha'il?"

The angel's spotted her over Zettel's shoulder. "Elise?" He completely dropped the Holy Messenger act and sounded normal.

Zettel whirled to gape at her. He composed his features quickly, but Elise ignored him as she strode forward.

It had been weeks since she saw Nukha'il. She assumed that he had taken his friend, Itra'il—who had been enslaved and driven to madness—back to the heavenly planes to restore her sanity. Elise hadn't expected to run into him again. Not two months later, nor twenty years later.

"Where's Itra'il?" Elise asked.

"She rests," Nukha'il said, folding his massive wings behind him. He was no longer gaunt from being fed a constant stream of drugs, and his skin shimmered with a milky white glow. "That is all she does now. I have forced her into hibernation, because when she wakes… Well. It's better if she doesn't wake." He appraised her. "You shouldn't be here."

"You're telling me."

"No. You shouldn't be *here*." His pale hands swept toward the expanse of desert. Elise wasn't sure if he meant that she shouldn't still be in Nevada, where the ethereal city and its dark gates were hidden, or if she shouldn't be on Earth. She never knew, where angels were concerned.

"We have to resolve the issue of the quarantine," Elise said.

Nukha'il's face registered surprise. "There is no issue. They're ethereal, and in our jurisdiction."

"I'm not letting anyone else approach those gates."

"This is why we're having meetings," Zettel interrupted. "It's not an issue for anyone here to decide alone. The Union—"

She rounded on him. "The Union has nothing to do with my territory."

"Your territory? Northern Nevada is owned by demons."

Nukha'il inclined his head. "*Her* territory. Even so—no mortal is capable of maintaining quarantine."

Elise held up the hand that wasn't broken. She didn't have to bare her palm to make the message clear. "I'm not just any mortal."

They shared a long, understanding silence. He knew, as all angels knew, that Elise was different. He had seen it firsthand in the angelic city.

He was the first to speak.

"Very well," Nukha'il said. "The ethereal party will send a representative to negotiate after all. But only if Elise Kavanagh mediates." Zettel opened his mouth, but the angel's glare silenced him. "Those are my terms."

She didn't want to negotiate. She just wanted everyone to leave her, and her city, completely alone. But it was better than nothing. Elise nodded. "Then I'll see you tomorrow."

The angel kneeled and reached his hands toward her.

She hesitated. Elise knew what he wanted, but her palms burned being so close to him. It was a gesture of supplication. He wanted to signify his obedience to her.

A dangerous gesture. She didn't want to have anything to do with it.

But the Union was watching.

After a moment, she rested her good hand in both of his, and he bowed his head to her knuckles. Pain scythed from her palm to her elbow. "She who is above us all," he murmured in that resonant voice, and her skin crawled.

He unfurled his wings and leaped into the air. There was no breeze, but they snapped wide and lifted him as though blown away on a hurricane. For an instant, his body was silhouetted against the sun.

Elise shielded her eyes to search for him, but he was already gone.

Something trickled down her wrist, and her hand suddenly felt like it was being sliced open. With a ragged shout, she ripped a glove off with her teeth and flung it to the dirt.

A gash had opened over her sigil. Her fingers spasmed.

Allyson stared at her as though she had grown horns, and so did Anthony. It was the reaction she had hoped for. But Zettel was no more impressed by the angel's supplication than he was by anything else, and he strode over to shake a fist at her.

"This is our operation! We have control!"

"You have nothing," she spat. "Nothing except my friend."

"A murderer."

"It's a mistake. Take me to the Union compound—I'll talk to him."

Zettel's jaw clenched. A vein bulged on his forehead. "Fine. Get in the SUV."

Chapter 9

RIDING OUT TO the Union compound was a different experience without a black bag over Elise's head, but they were still escorted by men with guns. Zettel took them directly to the trailer they had been confined in before, giving them no opportunity to explore their surroundings. "Five minutes," he said. "Boyd, stay at the door."

The Union locked them inside.

McIntyre was in his underwear—which were boxers covered in the Bat Signal—with his wrists zip-tied and a black bag over his head. Sweat covered his chest. "Let me go," he said when they came in.

"I'm working on it," Elise said.

Surprise registered in his muffled voice. "Kavanagh?" She cut him free and removed the hood. McIntyre had a hell of a shiner and a fat lip, but he looked otherwise unharmed. He must not have fought as hard as Elise had. "What the hell is going on?"

"The Union followed me to the hospital and found you."

"You let them *follow* you? They arrested me outside the maternity ward!"

"I didn't *let*—"

Anthony coughed. "Elise…" He nodded toward the camera in the corner. "They said five minutes. We should make this fast."

"Make what fast?" McIntyre asked.

"I get to interview you before the Union does," she said. "If you want to try being honest, this would be a great time for it."

"I already told you everything I know!"

"Then everything you know isn't good enough. You're about to get dragged across the country and prosecuted for the murder of a recruiter by a Union court. So if you have information that will prove you're

507

innocent before that happens, I would love to hear it."

McIntyre rubbed his wrists. "How am I supposed to prove I *didn't* do something?"

"Do you have an alibi?"

"Not exactly. I was alone at home. Tish and Dana spent the week with her parents."

Elise and Anthony exchanged glances. She raised a questioning eyebrow, and her boyfriend mouthed: *He's hiding something.*

"You met with Michele, didn't you?" Elise asked.

McIntyre's jaw clenched. He lowered his voice and angled himself so that the camera would see nothing but his back. "Okay. I did meet Michele Newcomb. She claimed she wanted to talk about the summit, but when she showed up, all she wanted to talk about was recruitment."

"So you thought you would kill her?"

"She left my place alive. But she was pushy. Michele said the Union would train me, like being in charge of my city since I was sixteen fucking years old wasn't good enough training." He dropped his tone even lower. Elise had to lean in to hear him. "And she said they would give me an aspis."

"You have an aspis," Elise said.

He shook his head. "Look, Tish isn't a witch. Not like James is. She knows what to do with her herbs, but when we tried to do that ritual…" He ran a finger along his underarm. "She's as good as mundane."

She took a closer look at his skin. There was no hint of the telltale scar that resulted from the ritual binding a witch to a kopis. Hers had faded slightly over the years, but she still had a long silver line from wrist to elbow that matched one on James's arm. "So they were going to separate you from your family."

"At first, for training," McIntyre said. "Michele said my family could live with me when I was assigned a team, a new territory…and an aspis."

"That doesn't sound too bad. You could use an actual aspis," Anthony said. He had kneeled beside them so he could listen to their whispered conversation.

McIntyre shot a glare at him, and the room filled with deadly, silent tension.

"Anthony—shut up," Elise said.

"What? It's not like Leticia can protect him like an aspis should."

McIntyre got to his feet. He wasn't usually intimidating, but he was a big guy, and he was mad. Anthony scrambled to his feet. "I'll cut you a break, man. You're new at this. You don't know shit. But a kopis and an

508

aspis is a big deal. There's this saying we have about it: 'More permanent than marriage, more fatal than family, closer than the oldest friends.' It's not like you pick one up on a street corner like a cheap fuck. It's more than that. Tish is…she's *everything*."

"And that's your problem," Elise said. "Nobody should be everything. Not in this business."

McIntyre laughed. "That's really rich, coming from you."

She swung, but he was ready for it. He shielded his face and took the hit on his forearm, then struck back. They exchanged a flurry of blows. She shoved him into a wall with her shoulder, and he kicked her in the gut, hard enough to make her stumble.

"Hey," Anthony said, like he was going to try to stop them.

Elise hooked a leg around his middle, gripped his shirt, and flung them both to the ground. They slammed into the floor of the trailer. The metal walls shook.

She rolled on top of him, and he tried to seize her head, but she twisted from his grip and slammed her good fist into his face. Blood spattered from his nose.

He wrestled her flat and drove his elbow into her ribs twice, hard.

She had to use her broken hand to put him in a headlock. Dull shock rolled up her arm, and he elbowed her again. It was a good, familiar kind of pain, like explosions of white-hot fire in her side. She grunted and flipped him over with her knees.

"Hey, hey! The Union's watching, guys!"

Anthony's reminder of the cameras was enough to stop them—almost. Elise reared over McIntyre, gripping his hair with a fist raised, and hesitated.

He squinted through a trickle of blood from his brow. "You know what, Kavanagh?" he whispered. "I feel sorry for your boyfriend."

She slammed his head into the ground. He groaned.

Elise stood. "Me too," she said, offering her left hand to him. McIntyre took it.

"You're still kicking my ass with a broken hand. I can't believe it."

She jabbed him in the stomach, not too gently. "That's because you're getting soft, and I'm still going to the gym three times a week."

Anthony shook his head. "Come on, guys. Seriously."

"Why did you lie to me? Why not admit that you saw Michele?" Elise asked. She didn't bother hiding that revelation from the camera. The Union was going to find out sooner or later.

"Because I didn't kill her." McIntyre clenched and unclenched his

509

fists. "I don't want to deal with this shit. My wife is probably having a baby right now."

The door opened. The red-haired kopis was silhouetted by the fading evening sun, and he had a submachine gun in his hands. "Five minutes are up," Boyd said, and she recognized that New England accent. He was the one who threatened to kill her when they had been arrested. "Get out."

"I'll be back," she promised McIntyre.

Boyd moved into the trailer and shut the door behind him.

Elise hesitated on the steps outside, staring at the plastic-covered windows behind them. McIntyre had lied to her. It was an unsettling thought. She didn't trust many people, but he was on the shortlist, and she wasn't sure how to proceed if that was no longer a safe bet.

"That's it," Anthony said. "I'm done with this summit."

"What?"

"He lied. He's completely guilty. We should just let him deal with this and get home. I can't believe I'm missing work for this."

She glared at Anthony. "McIntyre is my friend. Maybe the only friend I have left."

"You tried to kick the shit out of him," he said.

"Yeah, but I didn't."

Zettel came around the corner of the path and interrupted their conversation. He was far too cool and composed for the oppressive heat of the desert, which meant he would have been somewhere air conditioned while they talked. Elise would have bet all her money— which was only about fifty bucks, as of late—that he had been watching their conversation.

"Did the 'greatest kopis' learn anything useful?" he asked.

Elise gave him a level look. "You tell me."

Zettel's lips thinned. A vein in his forehead bulged. "You need to get back to the motel."

"Why? So you can watch us sleep on your cameras?"

"So you can rest before the meeting tomorrow. We'll be at the mines bright and early," Zettel said. "If the angels want you to mediate, fine— but you'll do it under Union control. Come on. Move it."

Chapter 10

THERE WERE NO meetings that evening, which left Silver Wells occupied by two dozen bored, overheated kopides with nothing to kill but time. The one place in town that was open and air conditioned was the bar—which Elise was surprised to discover was not abandoned after all—and the kopides flocked to it.

The Pump Lounge was one room with a sticky floor and exposed concrete walls. An elevated step in the corner was meant to be a stage, judging by the dusty speaker and microphone, and the tables looked like they had been in use since the days of cowboys and horses. But the Lounge had liquor, and it was all she needed.

She found an empty spot at the bar, tuned out the raucous laughter of the men surrounding her, and had the bartender bring a shot of tequila. She knocked it back immediately.

Anthony had stayed at their motel room, as he did on most nights since Betty died, and it left Elise alone with her thoughts and the burn of alcohol.

She couldn't stop thinking about McIntyre's lies. It nagged at her worse than the throb of pain in her hand. If he had deceived her about seeing the recruiter, then what else would he lie about? Would he lie about being a murderer, too?

McIntyre, a killer. It was impossible.

And yet...

"Another one," Elise told the bartender, sliding her shot glass across the bar.

"And for me," said a man in a red silk shirt as he slid onto the stool beside her. She squinted at him out of one eye. Definitely a kopis. He had the muscle, and there was no other reason that a man with his foreign features would be in a pit like Silver Wells.

"What do you want?" she asked.

"A drink. I'll have whatever you've ordered."

She rolled the words around in her mind for a moment, considering his accent. "You're from Java."

He brightened. "Have you been there?"

"Once," Elise said. An old man had been possessed by a demon, and she ended up burning a village down. Six humans died. It wasn't one of her favorite memories.

The newcomer stuck his hand out. "My name is Ramelan."

She ignored it and took one of the shot glasses the bartender dropped in front of them. Elise lifted it with a slight bow of her head, then drank it.

He followed suit, emptying his glass.

"Another," she said. Ramelan echoed her. The bartender refilled the shots before moving on, but she didn't immediately drink. She dipped her pinkie finger in the liquor. "Now that you've had that, what do you want?"

"I heard you're a kopis. I'm curious."

Great, someone who wanted to gawk at the sight of a female kopis. Just what she needed. "I'm not in the mood to talk. I just want a few minutes to myself."

"Your father is Isaac. Right?"

Her hand froze halfway to her mouth with the tequila. She set it back on the bar, and turned on her stool to give him her full attention. Ramelan was a handsome man. His dark hair was long enough to cover his ears, and he had broad shoulders and a thin mustache. It was hard to trust someone so handsome with such an easy smile.

"How do you know him?" Elise asked. She didn't bother trying to suppress her suspicious tone.

"He's on the Council of Dis. He's a capstone of one of its statutes."

"Yeah," she said, "but how do you know that I'm his daughter?"

Ramelan took an envelope out of his pocket and removed a picture. "I know because he sent me to Earth with this photograph."

It was a photo of Elise from when she was fourteen years old—just before her parents abandoned her to live with her mother's coven. She was scrawnier then, and less scarred, and her ungloved hands held twin falchions whose blades hadn't been engraved yet. She stared right into the camera like it was a challenge.

Elise drank the shot.

"Why would he have given you that?" she asked, wiping her mouth

512

on the back of her hand. Her eyes burned from the alcohol.

He showed her a second picture. In the photo, Ramelan clasped hands with Isaac—a broad man with the body of a rugby player and Elise's hooked nose—and her mother stood in the background, seemingly unaware she was being photographed. The walls around them were blurred, as if the camera had difficulty capturing the glow of the red clay bricks.

It had been over ten years, but her parents had barely aged since she last saw them.

"Ariane tutored me in English and French," Ramelan said, giving the picture a fond smile. "Isaac and I enjoy sparring."

Her hand tightened on the shot glass. "Oh."

"I've spent five years in Dis," he went on. "That is to say, five years of Earth's time. As you know, it was barely a year in Hell." He returned the photo to the envelope. "Ariane and Isaac told me marvelous stories. They've accomplished very much, but Isaac says his greatest pride is their kopis daughter—one woman out of thousands, and she became the greatest." He heaved a deep sigh. "But news arrived some months back that their daughter died. When we heard rumors that you be alive, they hoped I would meet you at the summit."

She clenched her teeth. Tension radiated through her shoulders, down her spine. "And what did they tell you to do if you found me?"

He looked surprised. "They only want to know how you're doing."

They wanted to know how she was doing. More than a decade since they left her alone "for just a little while," and they wanted to know how she was doing. That was nice. Really nice.

Elise turned her shot glass upside-down, contemplating the amber lights over the bar through the glass's distortion.

"What were you doing in Dis for five years?"

"I went there to study after I became named the greatest kopis," Ramelan said.

Dull shock rolled through her. So he was her successor—this smiling man who called her parents by their first names, like they were close friends.

"What did you do?" she asked.

His smile faded a fraction. Every kopis who became greatest had to do something great to earn the title—something big enough to earn the attention of the Council. It was inevitably something unpleasant. Being the greatest of demon hunters meant blood and pain. "It's a beautiful night," Ramelan said. "I'm enjoying this bar, this alcohol, and your company, and I don't want to talk about such things."

A haggard woman crossed the Pump Lounge and stepped between their barstools. "There you are," she said to Ramelan. *"Finally.* You can't just walk off like that! I'm supposed to be protecting you." Elise watched her waving hands for a hint of magic's glimmer, but there was no sign of it.

"Your aspis?" Elise asked Ramelan.

His smile was gone. "My handler."

"Your bodyguard," she corrected. She faced Elise. "Sorry. I'm Veronika. And you are...?"

Instead of responding, Elise studied the "bodyguard" silently. She had already drunk enough tequila shots that it was hard to focus, but it wasn't hard to read Veronika's signals. Her skin was luminous and she was clad from head to toe in latex. She wasn't beautiful—she was a little too stringy and severe—and there was something subtly disturbing about the unnaturally long lashes that framed her black eyes.

"Nightmare," Elise said. "You have a nightmare bodyguard."

He shrugged. "They sent her to Earth with me. She has no authority outside of Dis." The second part was pointed directly to Veronika.

She huffed. "Zettel wants to see you."

"I'm talking. I'll follow you in a minute."

Veronika took a barstool a few seats away. As soon as the nightmare sat, Ramelan's smile returned. "There are never two greatest kopides at a time. When one dies, the title passes onto the next in line. But you did not die, daughter of Isaac, and that leaves us with a question." He spread his hands wide. "Of the greatest kopides, who is greater?"

She drew a line in the moisture on the bar. "You can be greater. I never wanted the title. It's a pissing contest."

He didn't seem to understand the idiom, but he understood the sentiment. "You competed for the title."

"I was in town. It sounded like fun."

"You didn't think you would win?"

"No, I knew I would win," Elise said. And she knew that meant her parents would hear about it in Hell. It seemed to be the fastest way to tell them she was doing well without them, even if they didn't care. "I just didn't think the Council of Dis would let me be 'greatest.'"

He studied her for a long moment, drumming his fingers on the bar. His eyes were filled with the heat of someone who had come to face their greatest passion—like a painter given a canvas. "Who is greater?" Ramelan mused. "Would you be interested to know?"

514

Some part of her—a large part of her—wanted to refuse on principle. But curiosity itched. Elise had been wondering the same thing. "I'll fight you," she offered.

Ramelan burst into laughter. "You would, wouldn't you? And what would the outcome of that fight be?"

"I would win."

"You're confident, for a dead girl." He clapped his hand on her back. "We'll fight. We'll definitely fight. But not right now! This isn't the time or the place for it."

"No," she agreed. "It's not."

Ramelan finished his drink, set it down, and stood. "Your parents have shown me kindness, so you are a sister to me, sword-woman, for as long as I live and serve the Treaty of Dis. I will be happy to learn if I'm your match. Now, I'm afraid I must deal with my handler...and the Union."

He left the bar without stopping to talk to his bodyguard. Veronika's mouth twisted with annoyance as she followed.

Elise hadn't planned on getting trashed that night. She wanted to investigate the Union's claims, find out what else McIntyre was lying about, and put an end to it all that night. She needed a clear head for it. But she couldn't shake the memory of Ramelan's photos. It unsettled her and left an uncomfortable sickness in the pit of her stomach.

The investigation could wait until morning. She waved down the bartender.

"Another."

Chapter 11

ELISE ARRIVED AT the mine bright and early. It wasn't her choice. Zettel had arrived with a van before sunrise to take her there. She waited for hours in a mine that was silent aside from the thudding of air pumps, but the ethereal delegation didn't show up again. Neither did the demons. In fact, half of the kopides hadn't bothered to show up, either—and those who had were getting antsy.

Her head rang with a hangover, and she had to drape herself over a chair with a hand over her eyes to keep her brain from rupturing. She sat on the Union platform as men bustled around her, arguing and swearing in low voices. It felt like they were rattling a crowbar in the empty trash can of her skull.

"They're screwing with us," Allyson whispered to Zettel at the back of the platform. "First they want that woman to mediate—and she's not even sober!—and then they don't bother to show. They never planned on coming."

Did they have to talk so loudly? Elise massaged her hands over her temples.

Anthony sat below, with a handful of kopides. He caught her attention through the railing and raised his eyebrows. She shrugged weakly.

The Union gave up waiting after a few hours.

"Do you know anything about this?" Zettel asked as he closed the door to the mine's elevator. He had let the other kopides exit first, and then ascended with Elise.

Her head throbbed in time with the squealing of gears. She really needed a drink. "I don't know a goddamn thing," Elise said.

That answer didn't seem to satisfy him. He stood right in front of her,

516

trying to get her to actually look at him. "You know something you're not telling us. Don't you? All this trouble, the murderer, the angels—you're right in the middle of it."

She squinted at him through one eye. "I wasn't even supposed to be here this weekend. I don't want to have anything to do with angels. Trust me."

"That's not what McIntyre told us," he said, and she finally focused on him. The elevator's light felt like a spike directly into her forehead. "He said that angels are your specialty."

She grimaced. "Are we done?"

The elevator rattled to a stop. Anthony and Allyson waited for them on the other side, but Zettel stopped her from opening the door. "Did you find anything about Michele Newcomb's murder yet?"

"I haven't been looking," she said dully. "It's on my to-do list."

"You should know she didn't have her earpiece when we found the body—a Bluetooth device with UKA branding. We need it back. You can borrow one of our cars." He handed keys to her, opened the door, and let Elise get out. "Next meeting is at four. See you in a few hours."

She saluted ironically. "Yes, sir."

By the time Anthony and Elise stepped outside, the last Union vehicle was nothing but a trail of dust vanishing on the horizon. They had left behind a black sedan with an antenna on the hood that was longer than she was tall.

She jingled the keys as she considered the antenna. Taking that car would make them too easy to track. "Okay. You're driving."

Anthony took them out of town at her direction. It was dark and comfortable inside the Union car, which was like a mobile base—the dashboard had three inset monitors, the plush leather seats had buttons on the arm rests, and something beeped every thirty seconds. Elise sank low in the chair and shut her eyes.

"This is so cool," he said, poking the touch screens as he drove.

"Pay attention to the road."

"How could they afford something like this? The car was not cheap, and they have a whole fleet of them."

"They beat up the new kopides and steal their lunch money," she said. "I told you to watch the road."

Anthony left the equipment alone for the drive out of town, though it obviously pained him. Once they reached the hill south of Silver Wells, Elise directed him to stop by Leticia's car, which was still dusty and inoperative on the side of the road.

"We're switching? Are you kidding?" he asked. "The air conditioning doesn't even work."

She ignored him and got into Leticia's car. Anthony reluctantly followed.

The McIntyre's trailer stood empty on their property. The harsh daytime sun revealed all its ugly flaws: the holes chewed by mice, the trash bags piled by the back door, the window that had been replaced by plastic. But the ugliest thing of all wasn't visible to Elise's eyes. It was the residue of powerful magic performed on the premises, with the knowledge that it couldn't have been Leticia who cast it.

Elise closed her eyes and let the sensations wash over her. It was like hearing a foreign language for the first time. She knew the patterns meant something, but she couldn't understand a single word. The magic left a sour taste of iron on the back of her tongue.

Her boyfriend didn't sense any of it. He groaned and wiped sweat from the back of his neck. "It's hot," Anthony said. "I'm going in."

The door wasn't locked. There was no point, that far away from civilization. The marmalade cat that belonged to McIntyre's daughter darted out the door when he opened it.

Leticia had closed all the windows before leaving, and the air inside their tin can of a trailer was utterly unbreathable. Anthony opened the windows and turned on the ceiling fan.

Elise stood just inside the living room and scanned the McIntyre's home, trying to see it anew. Freshly-painted walls. Glass coffee table. Big TV. New couch. The mobile home wasn't very large. If there was evidence, there weren't many places to hide it.

"New furniture," Anthony said.

"What?"

"The couches are new. And they've been moved around recently, judging by the carpet." Without waiting for her input, he dragged the white leather couch away from the wall.

The furniture might have been new, but the carpet wasn't. Moving the couch revealed a burned patch in the floor—too big to be a cigarette burn. Elise crouched and ran her fingers over the paint. Had they been concealing a fire?

Her hand dropped to the carpet. There weren't just burn marks. Something had dried in brown spots underneath the couch, too.

Blood.

She sat back on her heels and tried to ignore the suspicion that crept over her. Kopides bled all the time. Finding a few spots under the furniture was normal—she would have been more surprised to find nothing at all.

But the pattern of burned carpet next to blood bothered her. It bothered her a lot.

"I'm going to search their bedroom," Elise said.

It was even hotter in the McIntyre's room. She took a quick glance around—family portraits on the walls, crib waiting in the corner, sonogram on the dresser—and then tore into their drawers. She wasn't nice or subtle about it. She threw their clothes on the floor as she searched, and found nothing.

The only interesting thing in the closet was a gun safe. It was unlocked and empty.

"Elise," Anthony called.

She found him in Dana's bedroom. Everything was painted a warm, inviting shade of green. Anthony had been riffling through her toy box. "Did you find any demons in the kid's room?"

"No. But I don't think this is a toy." Anthony held up something small and black. "Dana must have found it and thought it was something fun to play with."

Elise took it from him. It was a Bluetooth headset with white letters stamped on the side: UKA.

Her stomach lurched. "Shit."

"UKA—that's the Union logo, right? What does this mean?"

Her fist tightened on the earpiece. "It means McIntyre is a murderer."

That damn earpiece.

Elise rolled it over and over in her hands, trying to wish away the UKA logo, which was a circle crossed by an arrow. It was meant to symbolize the sword and shield of a kopis and his aspis. The Union wasn't the first to use the imagery, but it was the first time that seeing it filled her with dread.

She sat on the step outside McIntyre's trailer until her nose blistered under the sun and her hair was too hot to touch. Anthony stayed inside to enjoy sports on the massive TV. He didn't seem bothered by sitting in a room where a Union recruiter had probably been killed, but then again, not much had been bothering him lately.

Elise knew what she needed to do. She needed to get back in the car, drive to Silver Wells, and give Zettel the earpiece.

It was the right thing. It would be justice.

But she kept turning it over and thinking of the times she fought with McIntyre at her back. She thought of what the Union would do to him when they had proof of their suspicions. And she thought of Dana's little blond head sticking out of the sheets of her parents' bed.

The sounds of a cheering audience and announcers cut off, and Anthony joined her on the step. "Jesus, it's hot out here." He sat at her side. His skin was chilly from sitting next to the swamp cooler. He took the earpiece and ran a finger over the logo. "What are you going to do?"

"I don't know."

"It's weird being here," he said. "At first, I thought that you and this guy were like evil twins. You know, both of you are big, bad demon hunters, but he actually succeeded at having a normal life. He's got a wife, two kids…"

"That doesn't mean he's normal," she said.

"But if some murderer can do it, anyone can do it. Have a family, I mean." Anthony dropped the earpiece on the step and grabbed her hand. "Forget about McIntyre, forget about the Union—let's get married. Right now."

Elise shook his hand off. "Are you kidding?"

"No, I'm completely serious. There are a million chapels in Vegas. We can grab our marriage license in the morning, and…"

She crossed her arms tightly over her chest. "That's how you want to do it? You want to buy rings at a pawnshop, stand in front of some guy dressed like Elvis, and swear that we'll be together until we die? You think that's a good alternative to turning my friend over to the Union?"

He wasn't listening. "Betty would have thought it was romantic. She always wished that she had eloped with her ex-husband at a casino instead of spending so much money on an outdoor wedding with three hundred guests."

"Yeah. But Betty is dead."

Anger clouded his face. "What is wrong with you?"

"I've told you that I don't believe in making that kind of commitment, and I won't keep repeating myself."

"Oh yeah? Well, what about you and James?"

Her eyes narrowed. "What *about* James?"

"I caught what McIntyre said about kopides and aspides. 'More fatal than family, more permanent than marriage.' Those were the words, right?"

"It's just some witch thing," Elise said.

"But that's what it is." The volume of his voice increased with every word. His cheeks were red. "It's permanent. Getting an aspis is the biggest commitment you can make as a kopis. So why is it you don't want to talk about getting married? Is it because you're not ready for it, or because you're not into polygamy?"

"I just found out that my friend murdered someone, lied to me, and let me take the blame with the Union," she said in a measured tone. "At some point, I'm going to have to go tell them what he did. You think this is the time to talk about marriage?"

His mouth worked soundlessly. He stepped off the stairs onto the dirt, fists clenched tight.

"It will always be something. It will always be zombies, or giant spiders, or a murder, or the end of the goddamn *world*. It will never be a good time to talk about marriage. You want to put it off for now? Fine. But you owe me some kind of answer."

"Anthony," Elise said, "I don't owe you anything. Not one goddamn thing."

He stalked off, got in Leticia's car, and slammed the door. It occurred to her, distantly, that it was her only way back to Silver Wells, and that she should probably stop him. But she didn't move except to pick up the UKA earpiece.

The car kicked up dirt on its way out, trailed by a cloud of dust rising over the sagebrush. A hot wind blew it into her face.

But then it was gone, and she was alone.

Elise went inside and searched the kitchen. She had drunk all of McIntyre's beer, but there was a hidden stash of tequila kept on a high shelf where Dana wouldn't be able to reach. She threw the cap in the trash, took the bottle outside, and sat down to get wasted as the sunlight faded.

Anything was better than facing the Union again.

She reclined against the railing and started drinking.

As the sun dropped, the sky turned orange and pink, and then violet. By the time violet faded to navy blue, the tequila was half-empty, and Elise was dozing on the stairs. The security light over the porch turned on. The cat slunk past the stairs, shooting a dirty look at her as it ducked under the trailer.

She hauled herself to a standing position with the help of the railing.

521

Elise was unsteady on her feet, but it was a long walk to the road. She had plenty of time to sober up.

She had just climbed onto the steps when the light bulb over the porch flickered, and then died.

Pain lanced through her hand, and she hissed, jerking it away from the railing.

Blood oozed through her glove, but it wasn't from a splinter driving through her hand. The air buzzed as though swarmed with flies.

She turned around, and came face to face with Nukha'il.

It took her a moment to realize that the tequila and heat hadn't turned her delusional. He was composed, untouched by the heat, but utterly tangible. He wore a black suit with a red vest and black tie, which would have been appropriate for a wedding—or a funeral. His irises were a shade of pale blue that was almost white.

His wings were hidden. He looked like an ordinary man, aside from the way the heat didn't touch him. But she could almost make out the haze of a gray halo behind his head, and it made her queasy.

She didn't realize she was backing up until her back hit the trailer. It took all her willpower not to claw at her palms with her fingernails.

"What do you want?" Elise asked, and she was pleased that her words barely slurred.

"I'm here for the mediation."

"You're in the wrong place. The summit is in Silver Wells."

"The Union is in Silver Wells," he corrected. "The summit is wherever the ethereal and infernal delegations meet with kopis mediation. We're only waiting for the infernal delegation now. And look—here he comes." Nukha'il nodded beyond the trailer.

Elise glanced around the corner and saw nothing but night.

Pressure built in her skull. It was the weight of a thousand eyes on her back, like an entire stadium of men watching her. A sudden wind hissed through the sagebrush and sent rocks skittering across the dry ground. Her braid whipped behind her. She squinted, shielding her face from the dust.

Something heavy thumped against the other side of the mobile home, making the walls rattle. A cat yowled.

As quickly as it started, everything went silent again.

The McIntyres' cat slunk out from under the trailer, sat between Elise and the angel, and curled its tail around its paws. It focused on her. The pupils had devoured the entire eye, making its stare hauntingly black. A halo of dark energy surrounded the cat's head.

522

Dana's cat had been possessed by a demon. Leticia would be pissed.

The infernal delegate is present.

The words slithered up Elise's spine, and a thousand voices whispered in echo of the first. The cat had been taken by one demon, but the entire infernal delegation was in the night surrounding them, giving weight to the shadows.

"And so am I," said the angel. "I am Nukha'il, the ethereal delegate. Elise?"

They were both waiting for her to complete the triad. There were formalities to that kind of thing—a ritual. She had read about previous summits in James's books, but she never expected to be involved.

Adrenaline cleared her head of the alcohol's haze. "The human delegate is here," she said. "We can start."

With that simple statement, the quality of the air changed. The breeze died. The night became silent, almost reverent.

The infernal delegation put forth a dozen issues for consideration at the summit, said the cat. Its voice was silky and masculine. It struck a chord in Elise, like she should have recognized the speaker. *We have so much to discuss.*

Nukha'il turned his cool blue gaze on the cat. "There is only one item worth discussing."

Is that so?

"Don't waste my time. Angels have no interest in the matters of Hell. You want to discuss territory rights? Expansion?" Nukha'il shook his head. "Tell your children to expand as they like. None of it will matter soon. Not if the quarantine has been broken."

If discussions are such a waste of your time, then perhaps I will encourage my children to expand into Heaven. Would that be worthy of your lofty attentions?

"Please. The Council of Dis would crush them by its own rules."

"We don't need to discuss the gates," Elise said. "It's under control. They're in my territory, and I'm going to protect them."

You are human. You are weak.

"I'm not just any human."

"She is the one who is above us all," Nukha'il agreed.

Elise paced. Every step made the fog lift from her mind a little more as her fast metabolism burned away the liquor. "So let me do it."

"The gates are too dangerous—even for you." He gave a deferential nod. "We must watch them. Metaraon has mentioned patrolling them personally."

Metaraon. He was the second most powerful ethereal being in existence. Elise wanted him around about as much as she wanted to break her other hand.

She didn't have to argue. The cat scoffed. *I would be forced to take his presence on Earth as a statement of war. Not that I fear him, of course, but my children are much more sensitive. You understand.*

"Then what do you propose?" Nukha'il asked.

The Reno territory, and all that is above and below, has belonged to demons since humans founded settlements there. Let us attend to the city.

Elise cut them off with a slice of her hand. "Yeah, Reno has been under infernal control for years, but without any supervision. The Night Hag slept on it for decades. Anyone could have opened the angelic city. Demons had their chance—they messed it up."

And you would do better?

"Yes," she said. "Because I'm the person who most wants to keep the gates closed."

Nukha'il rolled his shoulders, like his invisible wings were bothering him. "There's truth to that. What of a compromise?"

Compromising is for the weak-minded, said the demon.

It was barely an insult, as far as Elise was concerned, but Nukha'il went rigid with fury. He strode forward and seized the cat from the ground. "Your choice of forms is a mistake, demon. I could break you." His voice was calm, but his entire body shivered with fury.

The cat hissed and struggled in his grip, lashing its body wildly. It sank its teeth into his wrist and rabbit kicked against his arm. It was a pure feline reaction, but the demon's response was equally poor. The night turned black around Elise. Her skin burned, like magma poured down the neck of her shirt.

She shoved through the thickened air to grab Nukha'il's arm. Laying her hand on him burned through the glove, but she dug her fingers in and didn't let go. "You know the rules of negotiation," she said. "You can't assault him. It's immediate relinquishment of rights."

His muscles quivered. "You heard what he said."

The cat continued to thrash, but a chuckle like melted butter rolled over them. *To be honest, I find this entire subject puerile. Regardless of what decision you two attempt to negotiate, I will supervise the gates. I cannot abide such a thing on Earth without watching them.*

"And neither can we," Nukha'il said.

"I can't stop either of you," she said in a level voice. "But if you're going to be in my territory, I will be the one in charge."

524

The angel and the demon remained locked in deadly anger for a moment before the tension dropped a fraction. Nukha'il's hand opened. The cat landed, walked a few feet away, and began licking its fur vigorously as though it had never been touched.

Nukha'il smoothed his jacket down. "You suggest cooperation."

No. There was no way in hell she would cooperate with anyone over the gates—not angels, not demons, not her own goddamn mother. But if there was one thing Elise had learned from her time dealing with the otherworld, it was that they didn't give two shits what she wanted. Negotiation was a matter of who lied the best. The real issues would be worked out at the end of a blade.

"I know the demons in Reno," Elise said. "They can help me with the gates."

A kopis? Cooperate with demons? It sounded like the idea amused the cat. *What would James think of that?*

She stiffened, quelling her paranoid urge to reach out to her aspis. Everyone knew they were a team. Mentioning him wasn't necessarily a threat.

But, knowing demons, it probably was.

"So you will lead the infernal forces in Reno. We can send an angelic delegate to supervise." Nukha'il bobbed his head. "They won't like it, but it could do."

The cat washed its face with a paw. *Do what you will.* It turned those black eyes on Elise, and there was far too much intelligence in them to look properly feline. *When the summits began long ago, we met out of a desperate need—a need to stop the war between Heaven and Hell, a need to protect humanity from our battles. I sat with Metaraon and Teleklos, king of Sparta, and had the first civil discussion between factions. Much like today, it was brief, but it brought peace to a torn Earth.* The full weight of shadow settled on her shoulders, curling around her throat like the cat's tail, and she couldn't breathe. *This will be the last summit, sword-woman. It's fitting that it should be between us.*

Her skin crawled. "Who *are* you?"

I am the empty space between the stars in the night sky.

"Lucifer?" she guessed.

His laugh curled around her like cool fingers. *No, I am no angel.*

And then he was gone, although there was no way to tell by looking at the cat. It wasn't impressed by its brief possession, or the voluntary exorcism. It looped around Elise's ankles, rubbing its cheek along her calf.

Nukha'il shed his jacket and unfurled his wings. A few downy feathers drifted to the earth. "I hate that guy," he said, throwing the coat over his shoulder hooked on one finger.

"Who was it?"

"He was a man, once. But the centuries do strange things to mortal minds in immortal bodies. I never know if he's going to feel playful or murderous. We're lucky to catch him on a good day." He glanced around the trailer. "I don't see a car. Did you run out here?"

"Something like that," Elise said.

"I'll take you back. Here."

Nukha'il stretched out a pale hand. She stepped back. "I would rather walk."

"A hundred miles?"

Reluctantly, she placed her fingers in his. Nukha'il's wings brightened.

They vanished from the desert.

Chapter 12

BENJAMIN HAD A vision that afternoon. It was the barest of glimpses, for once: he saw Elise and an angel on a long, empty highway with the swollen moon just over the horizon. The image was so brief that didn't even trip the Union sensors. His collar remained silent.

He waited until he was certain Allyson was asleep, and then waited for Elise on the edge of town at midnight.

She was there exactly when he expected, and she didn't seem surprised to see Benjamin sitting on the side of the road. "It's over," Elise said. She pulled a feather out of her hair and grimaced. "If that's what you're wondering."

He wasn't. He had already seen how the summit would unfold. "Can I talk to you?"

She sighed, pulled her braid over her shoulder, and worked her unbroken fingers through the curls to loosen it. She came up with two more feathers. "Sure. Let's go to the motel room."

The shower was running when they reached room twenty-nine. Benjamin swept through the room and removed all the monitoring devices, which were easy for him to find. The Union tried to be sneaky, but their all-encompassing regulations made their practices predictable. He peeled wires off of the bottom of a lamp, crushed a black box he found on top of the dresser, and popped the battery out of a device under the sink.

Elise watched his actions in the mirror as she peeled the glove off her left hand and washed it in the sink. The water swirled pink down the drain. "You're not with the Union willingly. Are you?" He shook his head and dumped the devices in the trash. "Are you a prisoner?"

"Yeah," he said, and then, "but not really. My parents sold me."

She didn't react to that news. She tugged the glove back on. "And you're, what, sixteen?"

"Seventeen."

"Do you want me to break you out?"

The question startled him, but in a good way. Warmth spread through him to the tips of his fingers. It was short-lived—an itch on his neck reminded him of his chains, and he tugged on the collar. "You can't. They always know where I am."

"What if we got that off of you?"

"Then you'd have done something I haven't been able to. I've tried for months," Benjamin said.

Her lips pursed. "I'll give it a shot."

Elise gestured to the floor, and Benjamin sat in front of the bed. He felt the mattress sink behind him as she took position at his back. Her left knee rested against his shoulder.

She tipped his head first to one side, and then the other, with a hand that was firm but gentle. Then she drew a slender-bladed dagger that had the mark of St. Benedict stamped near the handle. "Hold still," she said. He barely breathed as she picked at the lock awkwardly with her left hand. "How did you know my name?"

"I know everything about you."

Elise's eyes flicked to his in the mirror. There was an edge to her that said maybe, just maybe, he wasn't safe sitting between her knees. Her hand stilled for a moment. "Enlighten me."

He gave a shuddering laugh. "Where should I start? Uh... God, I don't know. Elise Kavanagh. You attended the University of Nevada. You worked for an accounting firm for a little while, until that argument with your boss. They still send you angry letters sometimes. You've got a tattoo on your hip—it's this black thing you picked out of the artist's flash because you felt like getting something done, and didn't care what. I think it's supposed to be a thorny flower or something. I never saw it too closely."

She didn't move. It was like she had become frozen.

"I don't like to look at the private stuff," he added, like that would help. "But I can't always help it."

It took her two tries to speak. "Mind witch?"

"Precognitive. Sometimes I have retrocognition, too, and it's hard to tell which is which. The Union says it's like the fourth dimension's all rolled up and stuffed in my head." Benjamin picked at the hole in the knee of his jeans. "I've been seeing you for years."

528

Metal on metal gave a soft *tink* as she went back to picking the lock. "What else have you seen?"

"I know about Malcolm. I know about Anthony now—I've been seeing him all day. I also know about James."

"And?"

She was pushing for a specific answer. Some people wanted to know their future when they found out what Benjamin could do, even though the Union forbade him from doing what they considered "petty fortune-telling."

But he didn't think that was what Elise wanted to know.

Benjamin reached up to touch her hand, hoping that it would soften the blow a little. "I know about the garden."

The blade slipped. It nicked his neck.

He jumped to his feet and clapped a hand to the injury. Elise was frozen on the foot of the bed, and she seemed to have forgotten the knife in her hand.

The shower was the only sound that broke the silence for a long minute. When Elise found her voice, it was hoarse. "*Nobody* knows that."

"I wish I didn't," Benjamin said. "I wish I didn't know so much. Like, how Isaac gave you the swords for your seventh birthday. Falchions aren't meant to be dual-wielded, but he didn't want you to use a shield, so you got two of them. But that's not what he meant, did he? He never wanted you to have an aspis—never wanted you to have *James*—and he'll be angry when he finds out what's happened to you. He will blame James." Benjamin could already see it, as he had seen it a dozen times before. Red sky, red earth, her father so tall.

Elise seemed horrified. That was how they always looked.

He pushed on. "You really liked James's aunt. When they killed her, you felt bad that you never told her that. But not for long. You didn't feel anything for so long. The garden broke you and reformed you, like a cracked china doll. You don't think you've been put together right. James agrees. He would never tell you that, but he agrees, and he fears for you —but sometimes he's afraid of you, too. Anthony…well, he doesn't know enough to fear."

She got to her feet slowly. So slowly.

"That's not true," she said.

"Which part?"

"James isn't afraid of me."

He shouldn't have said that. He changed the subject. "I know everything, so I know you want to know what happened to Michele

529

Newcomb."

"McIntyre did it." Elise's hand tightened on the dagger. "I found the evidence."

"But that's not the whole story. The thing is, Michele... I loved Michele." His voice cracked. Benjamin didn't bother trying to hide it. "She wanted to know the future, so I gave it to her. I told her what's coming."

"What's coming?"

"No," he said. "I can't tell you that. I shouldn't have told her, either. What's coming is bad, it's really bad, and Michele was really good. She wanted to stop it, and...it's hard to explain why, but she thought that killing Lucas would prevent everything." His gaze went distant as he recalled the vision. He had seen it as it happened. "She met him at his home. Dana was playing out back, and Leticia was in the kitchen. As soon as Lucas let her in, she..."

Benjamin shuddered. What details did Elise need? Did she need to know that Michele was a pyrokinetic witch, and that she tried to burn Lucas's house down? Did she need to know that Lucas was so scared for his family that he pissed himself? Did she need to know the way he was pushed through a window, and how certain he was that he would die?

"Michele tried to kill him," he finally said. "She almost did it."

"So he killed her instead," Elise said.

"Leticia shot," Benjamin said, holding out a finger. The wife had come out of the kitchen with Lucas's gun raised, her feet planted, her baby kicking a foot into her ribs. "*Bang*. Michele's face went..." He sucked in a hard breath at the memory. "Michele didn't die—so Lucas drew the knife. He couldn't let her tell the Union what his wife tried to do."

The shower shut off. Anthony would be out soon, so Benjamin hurried to finish.

"You have to understand, Elise—everything you think about your friend is true. Lucas is good. He's *so* good, and the world needs him. But I made a mistake. I told Michele things she didn't need to know, and it made good people have to kill another good person." His hands were shaking. Tears burned hot down his cheeks. "If they took Lucas away, he would die. They would investigate and find the truth of the story, so Leticia would die, too. And their children would have no parents."

Elise's face had gone stony. "Why haven't you told the Union this?"

"Because then they will want to know what I told Michele," Benjamin said. "But I can't tell them. They get pieces of it through this fucking collar, but not the whole story, and they can't have it. Nobody can." He could see the question in her eyes, so he said, "Not even you. And definitely not James."

They stared at each other for a long, long time.

Benjamin wasn't psychic, so he couldn't tell what Elise was thinking. But he knew her well enough to guess. He had seen so much of her life, from the times her mother carried her as a fragile infant into Isaac's battles, to the first time she held a knife, all the way through to the time she would die—not so far from where they stood in time. He had witnessed her first kiss and first heartbreak and first job out of college. He had seen her in the garden and watched her spill blood on the earth again and again and again.

He loved Elise, just as he had loved Michele. She had no secrets from him.

And he saw her considering the story. Trying to decide if he might lie. Hoping it was true, so that she could trust McIntyre again.

The bathroom door opened. Anthony emerged naked, with a towel wrapped low around his hips. When he realized he wasn't alone, he went rigid. "What's going on?"

"You," Benjamin said. His eyelids drooped half-closed, and he took a deep breath in. Anthony had been flitting in and out of his mind for hours.

Anthony set a hand on the lamp, like he was thinking about attacking Benjamin. "Who is this?"

"A precog," Elise said. "He sees the future."

"You do?" A light sparked in Anthony's gaze. "Really?"

"The Cubs will never win the World Series. But I don't need to read the future to know that," Benjamin said solemnly. It was his standard, half-joke response to someone announcing his special abilities.

"If you know that, then what do you see for me?"

Benjamin almost felt bad for him. Almost. "You're not in her future."

Anthony looked like he'd been slapped.

"I'll save McIntyre," Elise told Benjamin, ignoring her boyfriend.

Of course she would. "The night guards switch at four in the morning," Benjamin said. "I shouldn't help you. Gary's already going to be mad at me."

She nodded slowly. "I understand." Elise waved the knife at his collar. "I can't open the lock. But you knew that."

He smiled weakly. "Even when I know the truth, I still have hope." He took a step toward Elise—he wanted to hug her and apologize for everything, especially the things she didn't know yet—but she took a step

531

away from him, shielded Anthony with her body, and raised the knife.

So much for hope.

"Thanks for telling me," she said. Her voice was cold.

Benjamin opened the front door and gave her a small smile that wasn't happy. "I'll see you around, Elise."

Part 3: Hero

Chapter 13

ELISE WAITED OUTSIDE the Union compound and watched the guards patrol the perimeter. Like Flynn promised, they changed shift at four o'clock. When the nearest kopis stopped to speak with his replacement, she used the opportunity to sneak inside.

She stayed low and beelined for the center of the compound. She avoided illuminated tents, ducked around shadows, and found McIntyre's trailer guarded by the kopis named Boyd. He had a gun nestled under one arm, but his hands were occupied with a cup of coffee while he read a magazine. He clearly wasn't expecting trouble. Not so deep in the compound, and not from the outside.

Elise crawled behind him and stood silently.

He hummed to himself, turned the page, and rocked gently back on his heels.

She slammed her fist into the back of his head.

It didn't take much force to bounce the brain against the skull, and it dropped him in an instant. She snatched the gun out of the air before he hit the ground. His cup bounced with a hollow *thunk* and spilled coffee across the dirt.

Boyd didn't get up.

A quick search of his pockets yielded zip ties, and she bound his wrists before dragging him into the shadow underneath the trailer.

Then she slipped inside.

McIntyre hadn't been black-bagged again, but he was still naked and

533

bound, and he slept upright against the wall. He stirred when she opened the door and light fell on his face.

He flinched. His eyes opened. They were puffy, swollen, and bloodshot. Two days of beard growth shadowed his face, and his lips were cracked. "Took you long enough," he said.

Elise cut him free and helped him to his feet. "Let's go. We don't have long."

"Is the Union letting me go?"

"No." She peered around the door. Another kopis was passing, so she held out a hand to keep McIntyre from proceeding. She held her breath until he was gone.

"But you believe me," he said.

Her lips tightened. "I found the Union earpiece in your house." Before he could respond, she moved outside. Boyd groaned and shifted beneath them. "Okay—come on, let's hurry."

McIntyre hurried to keep up with her as she jogged down the path between trailers. His motions were stiff and sluggish. "I wasn't—"

"No more lies," Elise said, keeping her voice low. She crouched behind the corner of a tent. McIntyre followed suit. The kopis who had passed earlier wandered turned the bend, and as soon as his back disappeared, they followed. "It's insulting. I know what you and Leticia did. Why didn't you tell me the truth?"

"What, and let you give my pregnant wife over to the Union? I love her, Kavanagh. I would do anything for her."

Elise swore under her breath. "You can't think that I would turn your aspis over to the Union."

"You've made it clear that you don't think much of me, my wife, or our family. And you've got a sick sense of justice. You would give your boyfriend to the Union if you thought he had done something worth it."

Anger burned hot in her gut, but a light turned on in the tent beside them before she could argue. Voices murmured inside. Dawn was approaching, and the Union was starting to awaken.

One by one, lights turned on in the trailers and tents around them, and the distant noises of activity drifted over the compound. But their path was clear. She hurried away from the tent, and McIntyre followed closely.

She rounded the corner and came face-to-face with a line of kopides.

Each of them was armed with rifles, and each of them was aimed at Elise. Zettel stood in the back with his arms folded and a smug smile.

Elise scanned the guns, and she calculated.

She was fast, but not faster than a bullet. Certainly not faster than six bullets.

Slowly, she lifted her hands over her head.

"Tell me why the Warrens are empty this morning," Zettel said.

Elise had just broken her friend out of custody, and he wanted to know where the demons were hiding? Interesting priorities. "Because the summit is over."

"We've got another sixteen hours. There hasn't been a single goddamn meeting."

"Not that *you've* attended."

Zettel's eyes turned to slits. One of the armed kopides shifted uncomfortably, but he grew still at the commander's hand on his shoulder. "What's that supposed to mean?"

"Everything's worked out, and it's none of your business," Elise said. "McIntyre and I are leaving."

"Hard to leave when you've got more holes in your chest than a wedge of Swiss cheese."

"Then shoot us," McIntyre said.

Nobody moved.

"See, I don't think you can," he went on. "That's not in the Union's directive. We're assets that HQ wants to control. I've got contact information for more than half of the current kopides in active service— that's at least triple what you have."

"Don't flatter yourself. We don't have authority to shoot most humans," Zettel said. "But a murder suspect? His accomplice? We could shoot them. And you can see why trying to escape might make you look very guilty."

Elise's pulse hammered as scenarios whirled through her mind. The commander was closest—she could probably take him down before anyone fired, as long as she moved fast. But if she twitched, bullets would fly. Even if she didn't get shot, McIntyre would drop.

A voice broke through the cool morning air.

"What are you doing?" Ramelan ambled over to study the situation. He was shadowed closely by Veronika, who looked about as interested in the armed men as she was in the dirt beneath her feet. She studied her fingernails. "This doesn't look good."

"We have it under control," Zettel said stiffly.

"Oh?"

"We're about to arrest both of them. Or shoot them. I haven't decided."

"Come now," Ramelan said. "You know who she is. You know *what* she is. You can't kill her. Have them drop their guns." When Zettel didn't speak, he lowered his voice, like he was soothing a rabid dog. "You have no evidence either of them killed the recruiter. There is no justice in this."

"She did *something*," Zettel said. "She drove off the infernal and ethereal delegations. I know she did it."

Ramelan's eyes met Elise's. There was understanding in them. "She did exactly what a greatest kopis is supposed to do."

His words resonated through the encampment. One of the guns dropped, and then another, and another. Zettel didn't try to stop them. Instead, he waved at the others, and they stood down.

"Are we finished?" Veronika asked with a sigh. "I have things to accomplish today."

Ramelan shrugged. "That's up to Gary."

"HQ has given you ultimate authority," Zettel said, like he was admitting something painful and unpleasant. "It's your decision."

"Excellent. Then we'll be going. Elise?"

Ramelan walked them out of camp, and Zettel took one of the other kopis's guns before following them. "You don't need to do that," Ramelan said.

"I'm not letting them out of my sight. Who knows who will show up dead next?" Zettel asked.

McIntyre teeth groaned as he gritted them. He wasn't an angry guy— that was Elise's job—but the Union had obviously earned his animosity. His entire body vibrated with angry tension. But he was too smart, too controlled, to lash out against Zettel.

They were just a few short feet from the perimeter. So close to freedom.

Elise barely breathed until they passed through the fencing, which hummed with electricity. Her shoulders relaxed as soon as they were on the other side.

She faced Zettel. He wasn't following them.

"Let's get out of here," McIntyre said, but she didn't immediately move.

"Wait—that kid. Benjamin Flynn." Elise swallowed, and her throat felt like sandpaper. She didn't ask favors well. "Let him go, Zettel."

He waved the gun. "You're done making demands. Get out of my sight."

"This isn't a demand. Consider it a...strong suggestion," she said. Zettel didn't waver. "Is the Union keeping slaves?"

"He's here by parental consent."

"He's miserable."

"Miserable? *Miserable*? Do you want to know what misery is?" Zettel pointed at his own throat. "Before we collared him, his parents were desperate. Their son was going crazy. He averaged four microseizures an hour, and two grand mal a day. No treatment worked—nothing but Union technology and the best magic our witches have. If he wasn't with us, he might be brain dead by now. Is that misery?"

"So you're keeping him against his will as a humanitarian gesture."

"No," Zettel said. "We're keeping him because we need his prophecies. Nobody else approaches his precision. The things he knows—your selfish, petty mind can't comprehend it. But what's good for us is good for him." He raised the gun again to aim it straight for her. "And like I said. You're not in any place to make demands."

McIntyre stepped in front of the gun, shielding Elise with his body. He didn't have to say a word.

Zettel's finger slipped over the trigger.

Ramelan put a hand on Zettel's arm, but he addressed Elise directly. "He's right. The world needs to know what Flynn knows."

What *did* he know? The question nagged at her. What truth had Michele Newcomb thought to be worth killing a stranger? What would drive good people to murder?

"Let's go," she told McIntyre.

Zettel didn't drop the gun until they were out of sight. Ramelan stayed with them well into the desert.

"Thanks," McIntyre said once they were clear of the perimeter.

Ramelan inclined his head. "You're welcome. I was only a few minutes from staging a release, myself."

"You know each other?" Elise asked.

McIntyre shrugged. "I know everyone."

"Is it true, Elise?" Ramelan asked. "Is the summit over?" She nodded. "What's the conclusion?"

"I've got everything under control."

That wouldn't have been answer enough for the Union, but it was enough for Ramelan. He smiled. "Good."

Ramelan stopped walking. Elise and McIntyre returned to Silver Wells together.

They reached town before the sun got too high, but she was still drenched in sweat by the end of their walk. He followed her to the motel.

She stopped him in the stairwell.

"I'm only going to say this once," Elise said. "I believe what you and Leticia did was necessary. I would have stood with you against anything in defense of that if you'd just told me about it. But you fucked me over. You fucked my boyfriend over. Next time you need help with something? Call a different number in your black book."

She pounded up the stairs, leaving McIntyre alone at the bottom.

Chapter 14

ELISE WATCHED FROM a nearby ridge as the Union prepared to leave. They did it slowly, one or two vehicles at a time. A large convoy would have been too conspicuous, especially passing through a city like Las Vegas. She absorbed as much information about their movements and possessions as she could. A lot of equipment was exposed as they tore down their tents, and even though she didn't know what any of it was used for, she tried to memorize the shapes for later research.

It wouldn't be the last time she saw them. She was certain of it. But next time they showed up, she would be ready.

They were gone before the sun broke over the horizon, leaving nothing behind but flattened dirt. She got up from the hill, dusted off her pants, and realized that she wasn't alone.

Elise turned around slowly. There was a dark form silhouetted against the flaming orange sunrise. His feet were spread wide to distribute his weight, his hands were in a neutral position, and his center of balance was dropped low. Like he was about to explode into a flurry of motion.

Ramelan nodded with a look of admiration. It wasn't sexual—it was purely professional. He had asked who was greatest. She promised they would fight. He was asking her to let him find out.

She nodded as she lifted her fists. Her hand was still broken, but it would have to be good enough.

They approached each other. He moved like a wildcat, with smooth motions that made every one of his well-cut muscles ripple. Ramelan was in his prime, and Elise could see the potential energy in every little movement.

She threw a punch, and he blocked it.

Both of them froze, considering. Did she let him block it, or was he faster than her? Would she have really hit him like that?

He kicked. She stepped out of the way.

Another strike, another dodge.

Gradually, they increased the pace of their blows. Dust kicked up beneath their feet. He swung, she ducked; he blocked her kick.

As they sped, the rhythm of flesh on flesh increased. They danced across the dry earth. Ramelan was fast—much faster than she was. And he had the advantage of weight, too. But she was smaller, and harder to reach, and she made sure to never stand where his blows landed.

He had obviously studied martial arts. Elise recognized the language of the forms. Some of those attacks were ones her father had used. He was probably a better fighter than she was.

But she had avoided dojos and black belts. Her skills were earned from years of killing—and Elise fought dirty.

She scuffed dirt in his face. He cried out. By the time his vision cleared, she had darted around him and mounted his back.

Elise hooked her arm around his throat. He tried to duck his chin to keep her off of him, but it was too late. She tightened her muscles and held firm as he struggled to breathe.

He tried to unbalance her. Shake her off. It didn't work; her hold was too good.

She rode him to the dirt without letting go. Ramelan choked and sputtered, weakening rapidly as she applied pressure to the major veins in his neck.

It took a long time, but he finally tapped her arm.

Elise released him.

She stood back as he gasped for air. Her clothes were covered in dust, her hand was aching, and she thought he might have cracked a rib. Ramelan had hit her much more than she had hit him. But she was the one standing, and he was the one on the ground.

Ramelan gave a choking laugh. "You did that to the last one, too. I read the book. I should have been ready for it."

"My fight against the last greatest kopis is in a book?"

"In detail. It's a matter of public record—anyone in Dis can read about it." He sat up and dusted off his slacks. He seemed perfectly comfortable on the ground.

"What else do they say about me?"

"Very little." He grinned. There was no anger or jealousy in him. "So you are the greatest. Still. After all these years."

Of course she was. Elise didn't think there was a kopis on the planet who could beat her. But it wasn't a fair fight—she was Godslayer, she was legend, and the other kopides were only men. "Don't tell anyone."

"Why?"

"I don't want the title back. I have enough titles." He laughed and reached up a hand. She helped him to his feet. "You're good, Ramelan. You deserve to be the greatest, and everything that comes with that."

"You're very kind, Elise."

"And you're the only one who thinks that."

They walked back to Silver Wells together, enjoying the cool air of early morning in companionable silence. Elise realized about halfway back that they weren't alone—they were shadowed by a figure on a distant hill, so far away that she was nothing but a black speck against brown. Ramelan would never truly be alone. Not with his nightmare bodyguard.

"Veronika will take me back to Dis after this," he said, noticing the same thing Elise did. "The greatest kopis has responsibilities, and I'm beginning to think you were smart for avoiding them."

She chewed questions over in her mind, and settled on asking, "How are my parents? What have they been doing?"

"A lot. Isaac is a prominent and well-regarded figure throughout the city. Your mother handles humans in the great palace, and ensures visitors are comfortable and safe. It's no small feat in Hell. You should be proud of them. They do God's work in a godless land."

"What will you tell them about me?"

He paused mid-step. Folded his arms. Considered the question. "Nothing," Ramelan said. "I didn't see you here. Did I?"

She held out her left hand, and they shook.

"Thank you," Elise said.

They parted ways with no goodbyes.

541

Chapter 15

ANTHONY WAITED IN the hotel room for Elise to return. When someone knocked at the door not long after sunrise, he was surprised to see McIntyre on the other side—especially since he was mostly naked. "Can I borrow clothes?" the kopis asked. He had the decency to look embarrassed.

"What are you doing here? Elise said she got rid of you."

"I don't have any way to get home."

Reluctantly, Anthony let him inside. "Let me grab my spare jeans. I just finished packing."

He was thinner than McIntyre, so the clothes didn't fit well, but it was better than letting him wander around in his boxers. Anthony let him use his electric razor, too. After a short shower, he almost looked human again.

"I want you guys to come to the hospital with me," McIntyre said, helping Anthony repack his toiletries.

"Why?"

"Leticia will want to see you."

"Yeah, but do you think Elise is going to want to see her?" Anthony asked.

"Not a fucking chance. She'll be pissed I'm even here with you right now. But she'll get over it." He scrubbed a hand through his hair. "Well, I *hope* she'll get over it. Otherwise, I won't have a ride back to Vegas."

Anthony frowned. "You've known Elise for a while. Right?"

"A few years, yeah."

"What's her problem?"

McIntyre snorted. "You want the list of her problems alphabetized?"

Before Anthony could respond, the door opened. Elise's clothes were dusty and scuffed. She scowled at McIntyre, but didn't seem surprised to see him with Anthony. "Let's go," she said. "I'm sick of this town."

It was a quiet, uncomfortable drive back to Vegas.

Leticia was no longer in labor and delivery when they arrived at the hospital. It took Anthony almost fifteen minutes to talk Elise into going into the maternity ward.

The nurse at the front desk checked McIntyre's identification when he asked where his wife had gone, and then smiled. "They're in the recovery room."

McIntyre's fists clenched on top of the counter. "Is she okay?"

"She's just fine. They both are."

The nurse gave them the room number, and they went upstairs to find Leticia.

Anthony had only been in hospitals for something bad before. His last visit had been to say goodbye to Betty's body, and even though North Vista Hospital was nothing like St. Mary's in Reno, going up the elevator brought a new swell of grief crashing over him.

He drew in a shuddering breath. Elise shot a look at him. Her expression was blank, as always, but he was certain she was judging him.

The elevator chimed. The doors opened.

Leticia was in the room at the end of the hall. McIntyre made sure they all sanitized their hands before going inside.

The curtains were closed to block out the brutal Las Vegas sun. Leticia's face was puffy and red in the fluorescent lights. Her faded pink hair stuck to her greasy forehead. Dark bags shadowed her eyes. She didn't look like a killer—she looked like she was half-dead. But she smiled to see McIntyre, and when he sank to the bed at her side, his look said that he thought she was beautiful.

His attention was fleeting. Once he saw the bundle of blankets in his wife's arms, he only had eyes for the baby.

It was a private moment, and Anthony didn't know them nearly well enough to be there. Of course, Elise did know them well enough, and she still had the frightened appearance of an animal who wanted to flee. She hadn't even stepped through the doorway.

"Took you long enough to get here," Leticia said, kissing McIntyre.

"Sorry. I got held up." When his wife gave him a Look, he just shook his head. He couldn't stop grinning at the baby. "I'll tell you later."

"We should get going," Anthony said. "Airport and...yeah, you know."

Leticia turned her exhausted stare on them. "Don't you dare. Come meet the new family member." Elise edged toward the door, but the witch wasn't having any of it. "Now, ma'am. Move it."

Anthony had a lot of cousins, and just as many nieces and nephews. Babies were nothing new to him. He thought that they were all the same at birth—like tiny, angry old men. The McIntyre baby was no different. It was much smaller than his cousins had been, and attached to an oxygen machine by a nasal cannula. The fist that stuck out of the blankets could have belonged to a doll. An ugly, wrinkly doll.

"Beautiful," he said, because he had learned that his actual opinion wasn't welcome after Aunt Graciela gave birth to a creature resembling President Roosevelt. "What's with the nose thing? Is she okay?"

"Just fine," Leticia said. "A little early, but they said she can breathe on her own soon."

"Where's Dana?" Elise asked from six feet back.

"She's been with grandma and grandpa all week. Come on, Debora's not going to bite. Not you, anyway."

Elise shuffled a little closer, just near enough that she could peer at the newborn over Anthony's shoulder.

He waited for a reaction. She had never shown any indication of maternal instinct before—in fact, she referred to students of James's preschool dance classes with flattering names like "snot face"—but women *always* melted over babies. It was a girl thing. There was no way she could resist.

Her brow pinched. "Nice," she said emotionlessly.

Leticia gave McIntyre an exasperated glance, and he laughed. He sounded a little giddy. "Don't look at *me*, Tish. I don't know what you expected."

"Here, Elise. Hold her," Leticia said. "I need to use the bathroom."

The shock on Elise's face made the entire trip to Las Vegas and Silver Wells worth it. "No way. I'm not going to—"

But Leticia had already shoved the bundle of blankets into the kopis's arms and struggled to her feet with her husband's help. She hung onto her IV pole as she hobbled toward the bathroom with a groan. "Remind me why I did this?" she muttered.

"Masochism and a broken condom," McIntyre said.

"Yeah, right. That."

They both went in the bathroom and shut the door behind them. Elise held Debora away from her body, as though the baby was a grenade with the pin removed. The cannula wasn't the only thing attached to the tiny infant. A feeding tube led into her mouth, too. It forced Elise to stand awkwardly beside the incubator.

"Take it," Elise said. "Put it in the plastic cage thing."

Anthony grinned. "Why? Scared of a preemie?"

"It feels like a marshmallow. I'm going to break it."

"Aunt Graciela says babies are rubber, not glass," he said. "Trust me, you can't break her. Not even a preemie. I've dropped all of my cousins at least once and they're still running around." He angled himself behind her back so he could shift her arms into a more comfortable position. "Head in your elbow, arm under the butt—"

Elise grimaced at him. "She smells."

"You can handle it. I have faith in you." He circled his arms around her and made adjustments until it almost looked like she was comfortable holding the baby. It was like positioning a mannequin—she was completely rigid. Once they were settled, he hugged Elise's shoulders in one arm as he stroked a finger over the baby's wrinkled fist. Debora's face scrunched tighter in sleep. Her lips smacked.

He expected Elise to soften once they were cozy, but she remained stiff. How could she feel nothing toward such a helpless little creature? Why couldn't she do anything normally?

"Okay. I held it. I'm done," she said.

"Enjoy the moment." Anthony's voice had a slight edge. "You did a good thing. McIntyre is only here to see his daughter because of you. Don't you feel proud?"

"The baby had nothing to do with it."

"They owe you for this. I know that if you were having a baby and I was arrested—"

"Anthony."

"—it would mean a lot—"

"*Anthony.*" She stepped away from him and turned around. Even with the baby settled against her chest, she didn't look like the kind of person who should be allowed to hold an infant. Her expression was pained. "I'm never going to have children. I *can't.*"

It took a moment for her words to sink in.

I'm never going to have children.

Elise had told him that before, but he assumed it was just stubbornness talking. She had never said it was because she couldn't.

"What do you mean, you can't?"

The bathroom door opened. McIntyre helped Leticia into bed again, and then took his baby from a grateful Elise. "Hey, beautiful," he murmured at the wrinkled newborn.

545

Anthony felt numb.

"We need to get to the airport," Elise said, composed once more.

"Thank you. For everything. We'll come visit you and James once I'm back on my feet," Leticia said. "Save some couch space for us. A lot of couch space, actually. Our family's growing."

Elise grimaced. "Yeah. Okay. We'll do that."

She shook hands with McIntyre somewhat stiffly. Leticia insisted on kissing Anthony's cheek. She smelled like witch hazel.

They left the hospital and didn't talk all the way back to Reno.

There were three messages waiting on Elise's answering service when they returned to Reno. The first was a rather optimistic update from James, who was letting her know that his flight would be late—not that she was planning on seeing him when he returned—and the second message was six seconds of silence, followed by a click.

The third message had been left just a few minutes earlier. Elise couldn't understand the first thing the caller whispered, but what she did make out was chilling: "He's back." Neuma's voice was muffled. Judging by the sound of rubbing cloth, the phone must have been in her pocket. "Please, Elise—he's back. He's got the club."

And then it cut off.

Elise considered the phone in her hand. Neuma had known an attack was coming. She had asked for help, and Elise had refused. That choice had left the casino and the gate beneath it exposed to attack.

Guilt wasn't productive. She took a deep breath and went into the bedroom. Anthony dumped the contents of their backpack on the floor before tossing the empty bag in the closet, which was was his idea of organization.

"Feel like beating up some demons?" Elise asked as she donned her spine scabbard and twin falchions.

"You have no idea." His words smoldered with unvoiced anger.

Since their new apartment was so close to Craven's, Elise didn't even bother concealing her weapons before going out. They jogged through an alley, took the back entrance to the casino, and sneaked downstairs.

Eloquent Blood was full for a Sunday night, but not because of partiers. There wasn't a single human on the premises. The floor was packed with demons—every single one an employee of Craven's, which was dark and empty upstairs. They cowered in a cluster on the dance floor.

Elise studied the situation from the spotlight scaffolding. There was an ugly demon on the stage, leather-skinned and clawed, and he wore a crown of iron spikes. It had to be Zohak.

Neuma stood beside him, eyes lowered, legs bloodied, and a tray of drinks in her hands. He had been snacking on her again.

"If I jumped to the next scaffold, I'd be in range for a clear shot," Anthony whispered, pulling the shotgun from his scabbard.

It was tempting. But shooting the leader would leave the employees at the mercy of his minions, who were positioned around the room with blunt swords. Zohak's legion was populated by hunch-backed creatures that would never pass for human. Elise recognized them as a breed of lesser fiend—not quite as strong or sturdy as the ones she had fought in the spring, but a little smarter, which made them a dozen times deadlier.

One of his fiends climbed on stage. It spoke in the demon tongue.

Zohak grabbed Neuma's wrist. "They tell me there is no sign of the Night Hag in the Warrens," he growled in a guttural, thickly-accented voice. He obviously hadn't been on Earth for long.

"I told you, she's out for the week," Neuma said, her voice high and panicked. "She's visiting the San Francisco territory."

"But she has left behind no army. Not a single daimarachnid. I think you are lying to me, succubus." He used her arm to jerk her down to his level. His rubbery lips were already stained with blood. "Lies make me hungry."

Elise hurried across the scaffolds and silently dropped backstage, concealed behind heavy black drapes. Anthony followed.

A fiend was positioned to protect Zohak's back, but it faced the wrong direction. She slipped behind it, slit its throat with a dagger, and dropped it off the back of the stage before anyone could hear the gurgles.

It left nothing between her and Zohak—nothing but the curtain and six feet of stage.

Elise drew one sword with her good hand, and glanced over her shoulder to make sure Anthony was in position. He jacked a round into the shotgun's chamber.

Sometimes, it was important to make an impression.

She stepped from behind the curtains.

"Elise!" Neuma squealed, and the demon-king turned.

Before Zohak had a chance to react, Elise jumped. She knocked him to the stage and kneeled on his throat.

Someone in the crowd screamed with surprise. The fiends lifted their

547

swords and stepped forward, but she pressed the point of one falchion to the demon-king's chest. "Stop," she said, and they froze. "Get out. All of you."

"Or what?" Zohak asked.

She leaned more of her weight on his throat, and he gagged. "Or I will kill you and every one of your followers." His eyes flashed with anger. She pressed harder, and the anger turned into a hint of panic.

He couldn't speak to give orders, but he nodded and wiggled a finger. The fiends scattered.

Zohak kept gesturing. "I think he wants to talk," Anthony said, standing at the edge of the stage with his shotgun aimed at the nearest fiend.

She lifted her weight. Not much—not enough for him to break free—but to the point where he could gasp a breath of air. "Who in the seven hells are you?" Zohak squeezed out.

"I'm Elise," she said. "And this is my city."

DEAR READER,

I hope you've enjoyed the first three books of The Descent Series. The story continues in book 4 (<u>Damnation Marked</u>), which is available now!

If you'd like to know when my next book comes out, visit <u>my website</u> to sign up for my <u>new release email alerts</u>. I hope you'll also leave a review with your thoughts on the site where you bought this book—I can't wait to hear what you think of it!

Happy reading!
Sara (SM Reine)
<u>http://authorsmreine.com/</u>
<u>http://facebook.com/authorsmreine</u>

4618437R00305

Printed in Great Britain
by Amazon.co.uk, Ltd.,
Marston Gate.